Bloodlines

Rafael Canoa

Crystal Lake Publishing
Where Stories Come Alive!

www.crystallakepub.com

WELCOME
TO ANOTHER

CRYSTAL LAKE PUBLISHING
CREATION

For my loving wife, Kristina, without whose unwavering support and encouragement this would not have been possible.

Many thanks to my very good friend John MF for his mentorship and wisdom, and to Rob B, Jodi S, and Joe M, for believing in me and helping to open a door I thought would forever be closed.

A final shout out and my heartfelt gratitude to Derek W, Greg G, Elliott S, Cole A, Ian S, and Greg D, for the countless hours of fun at our gaming table, where the inspiration to share this world with you, the reader, was born.

PROLOGUE

The warm evening air shimmered and rippled, as when a stone is cast into the waters of a still pond. The odd disturbance lasted only a moment, but when it was gone, a lone figure stood in the previously empty alleyway. Had anyone been capable of witnessing the strange arrival, they would have seen a woman of slender build and long dark hair wearing nondescript clothes. Her face was attractive albeit lined by time, her features otherwise unremarkable save for the eyes. Red irises glimmered in the dark, the vertical, reptilian-like black pupils widening slightly when the woman looked beyond the nearby rooftops to take in the star-filled sky and pale reddish light of the enormous globe that hung overhead, the crimson moon rising over the horizon like a lumbering titan. Named Temeros long ago, it was more commonly referred to as the Dragon's Eye. Sighing heavily, the stranger looked away from the largest of Akar's three moons and glanced at her surroundings for the first time.

She disliked coming down here these days, and her presence would not go unnoticed for long by the others, but there was no time to be wasted on wistful thoughts about the past. Pulling the cloak's hood over her head, she headed toward the flickering light coming from a nearby window. A dog barked in the distance, no doubt having detected her approach with its keen senses, but she paid the animal no heed. Should anyone peer into the alley to investigate, they would see no one. A few more steps carried her around the corner and up to her destination and as she did so, another woman's cries of pain could be faintly heard from within the nearby house. It seems she had timed her arrival perfectly, her eyes discerning the outline of another individual standing before a window, its presence shrouded from mortal sight just as hers was. Stopping some distance away, she decided to observe and see if her worst fears would be confirmed.

The window was closed and shuttered, but the figure standing just outside of it had no difficulty peering through a crack in the wooden barrier to watch what was happening. For what was often termed a 'miracle', the scene unfolding inside the house was common enough—a woman sat on a bed, her back propped up by pillows, knees high and legs spread apart while an elderly midwife gently coaxed a new life into the world. The soon-to-be mother's worn face contorted into a grimace while she gripped the hand of a man standing at her side, a pure look of wonderment mixed with concern and alarm in his eyes. A moan rising into a scream escaped the woman's lips once more and she threw her head back, while the man gently used his fingers to brush aside the hair plastered to her forehead and cheeks by sweat. His whispered words of encouragement went unheeded as she strained even harder, grunting from the effort, and then the midwife looked up and announced calmly that the moment was nigh.

Watching intently, the figure outside the window realized that he'd been holding his breath in anticipation. He would not be here if he felt there was another way, but events beyond anyone's control had transpired to force his hand in the matter. So be it, he thought. Let it not be said he'd stood by and failed to act—however his actions here today may ultimately be judged. There would be no turning back beyond this point, and he faced down this final opportunity to change the course of things to come. The decision had been made long ago though, so he resolutely pushed aside any illusion of choice at this point and focused once again on what he'd come to witness. The baby had arrived and was in full view now, the midwife carefully wiping the newborn's face when it began to cry, the tiny lungs taking in air for the first time.

"It's a boy," the old woman said, smiling as she held the wailing infant up to his mother. Tears of pain gave way to those of joy. She took her new son in her arms while the man held her hand fiercely, his face beaming with happiness and pride. The time had come. The man outside the window raised a hand and silently mouthed a single word. A flickering, intricate symbol composed of sparkling motes of multi-coloured light slowly coalesced into existence on his palm, hovered there briefly, and then drifted slowly through wood and glass and across the air of the room beyond. Invisible to the occupants inside, the strange glyph came to rest upon the infant's forehead and then faded into nothingness as if it had never been.

"It is done," the man whispered as he closed his eyes, the relief evident in his words contrasted by the look of resignation and sadness on his face.

"Yes, it is, but you shouldn't have," the quiet and measured woman's voice came from behind him. The man did not react with surprise but simply turned around to face the speaker as if he'd always known she was there. The newcomer stood a few steps away from him, little more than a dark silhouette framed against the night.

"Nice touch," the man replied to the new arrival. "You almost look like your old self again. Pity about the eyes though; they betray your nostalgia for a time long past. Still clinging to those old affections, I see?"

"Perhaps I am, at that—a foolish memento of happier times for us all—but it matters not now," the woman wistfully replied. "They can't see or hear us in these forms anyway, so let's dispense with the small talk. Why are you doing this? You've tried before and failed—what makes you think you'll succeed this time?"

"You know very well why. The imperfection in the first vessel was the result of betrayal and interference, nothing more. We won't make that same mistake a second time. Are you here to try and stop me? Did the others nominate you for this task?" was the terse reply.

"I'm here of my own choice to appeal to you one last time. Despite what you might think, I'm not your enemy. None of us are—not even the one you feel betrayed you the most—though you seem to have forgotten that. What you and your accomplices are doing is committing a grave and monstrous mistake. To place such an unimaginable burden into the hands of a child...not to mention the horror that will come because of all this. To undo so much in a futile quest to return to something we forsook so long ago—it's both unconscionable *and* unforgivable," the shadowy figure accused.

"Don't lecture me on forgiveness," he retorted angrily. "Haven't we done enough for them? Sacrificed enough? We've lived a long and wonderful dream, but now it's time to wake up and face reality," the man growled, pointing at the Dragon's Eye.

The woman shifted slightly, lifting her head and strange eyes to once more regard the giant orb that now covered a full quarter of the night's sky. Turning to look at the man, the woman responded, "You accuse me of living in the past but you're the one willing to sacrifice your soul along with everything else just so you can go back. This has to stop, for all our sakes—yours, mine, and theirs." She gestured with her arms, encompassing everything around them.

The man seemed to consider the words, reflecting inwardly on all the events that had led both to this point in time. Then he shook his head slowly and stared more intently at the woman. Of all his remaining companions, he always felt the one that stood before him now would have been the one on whose support he could count the most. He had been wrong. It wasn't the first time.

"We have a duty to protect them, and we shouldn't give up now. It's what we all swore to do, remember?" the woman pleaded.

The man at the window merely shook his head in defiance. "It's not them you're protecting, it's yourselves and this fantasy we've created. Think on that and do what you must, but in the end, you will fail. They—" he made a sweeping gesture that mimicked hers to indicate the house, the street, and the city all around them, "—don't matter anymore."

The woman nodded slowly, her careworn face shadowed by a sadness-tinged look of acceptance and recognition of the inevitable. "You're starting a war that can have no winners." She sighed in resignation. "How long?"

He shrugged. "A handful of years or so for them—may as well be tomorrow for you and me; do what you must, but you can't stop me. We made a mistake, and it is long past time you accepted that truth." With that, he vanished from sight as if he had never been there.

The woman with the strange eyes stared sadly at the empty air for some time and then walked up to the window and looked through the crack in the shutter, seeing there the child, safe in the care of his parents. She saw the invisible mark as well and knew what it meant. So be it. She already had her own piece on the board, and the game was now in motion. He may be right—she and the others might not be able to stop what was coming—but she wasn't about to sit idly by and let it happen. In the next instant, she too was gone. In the sky above the house, a tiny pinpoint of light flashed briefly but brightly on the distant surface of Temeros. The woman had returned home.

CHEMAR FOREST

NORMARIN

SULMARIN

HOUSE OF HEALING

VANIOR RIVER

KOVEL

ARDENBROOK

FALCON CROSSING

CHEMAR RIVER

HALMARSH

BATTLE PLAIN

QUILLSTON

ROHNE

SEAWALL MOUNTAINS

THE LION'S DEN

INVEROS

ARND RIVER

GLAN

ASPEN

THULWYN FOREST

THUNDERHALL

DELIAN ISLES

JOTUNN'S BAY

ENGIL'S REST

TASARAK OCEAN

EKAT

KRULEA ISLAND

MARKAN

SEAWALL MOUNTAINS

PORT CORAZ

BELAR

STORMP

ROCKYREST

STRACH GVLF
BAY OF ORMAND
MULDAR WILDS
MULDAR WILDS
OAKENSTRAND
ALKAVAR
HALCRYSE
EVERWATERS
DIREHURST
SHAY
VRANIK RANGE
MULDAR FLOW
FLATHORN
VEGROS
ENRIDGE
SALSGLADE
ALDRIK'S FOLLY
FOLGEIR
SWANMEADOW
LAKE HIRLON
DRONIS CASTLE
EVRAS CASTLE
GREYHILL
OR WOOD
IRONSHIELD CASTLE
ALDRIS
FORSAKEN MARSHES
FALDRIS CASTLE
MYSTHAVEN
STONECREEK
UTHIS
ARFELD
JEROTHOS
BRAKIR
STERLINGFELL
SILVERSHEAR
STRAIT OF CORAZ
ARND RIVER
CORVARK
NIGHTSHALE
HARKENFELL
ISLE OF AYELAN
CORAZAN
STORM SEA
0 25 50 75 100
Miles

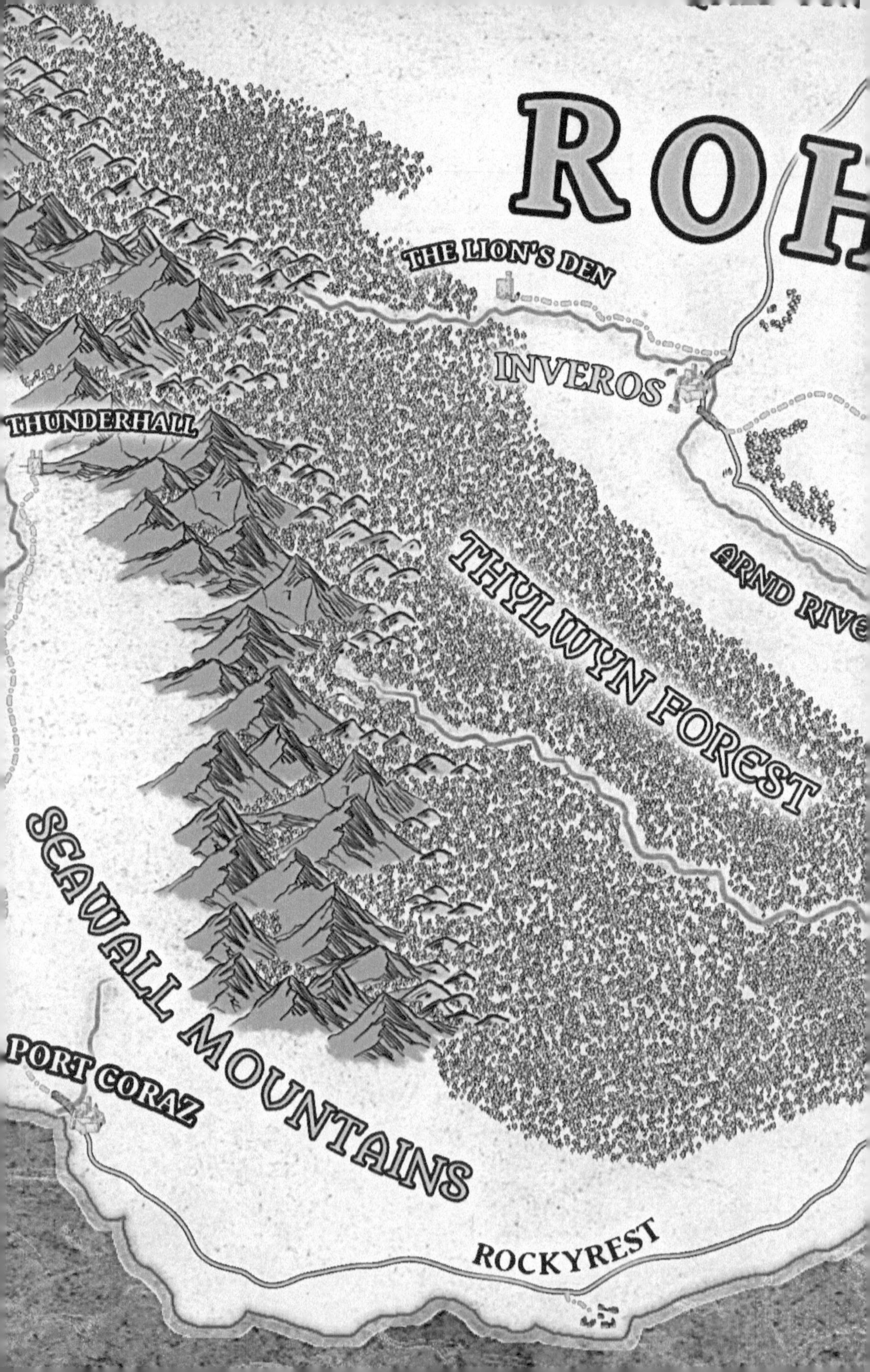

ROH
THE LION'S DEN
INVEROS
THUNDERHALL
ARND RIVE
THYLWYN FOREST
SEAWALL MOUNTAINS
PORT CORAZ
ROCKYREST

SWANMEADOW
LORONIS CASTLE
IRONSHIELD CASTLE
BAENOR WOOD
ALDRIS
NE
FALDRIS CASTLE
MYSTHAVEN
SCARFELD
ANIS
JEROTHOS
ASPENVEIL
SILVERSHEAR
ARND RIVER
HARKENFELL
KNIGHTSHALE
LAR RIVER
CORAZAN
N
W
S
E
TORMPORT
STORM SEA
0   25   5
Miles

CHAPTER 1

It was late spring in Corazan, capital city of the Kingdom of Rohne, and Flynn ran through its streets, heedless of anything and anyone in his path. He was nearly late for supper once again and his father had promised him a thrashing the last time this had happened. The church bell tolled in the distance, and Flynn quickened his pace, the young boy pumping his legs as fast as they would carry him. Three times the bell had pealed since he had started running; four more to go. He could already hear the laughter and teasing of his older brothers as their father removed his belt, and the thought only spurred him to greater speed. His father had never hit him, of course—the belt was just for dramatic emphasis—but he did not relish the thought of getting yelled at again. The shortcut he was taking from the plaza where he'd been playing and back to his house led him through a part of the city that was practically a maze to the unwary, but the boy knew Corazan like the back of his hand. Blue eyes narrowed and head lowered, he ran like the wind.

Four!

A wagon stopped at an awkward angle blocked the narrow alley ahead, the driver of the conveyance gingerly unloading a heavy-looking barrel down a ramp from the back and toward an open doorway in the building behind. A hitched horse was facing his way, and the animal looked at him disinterestedly before returning to thinking about whatever it was that horses thought about. Barely breaking stride, Flynn sped past the animal and dropped low under the wagon, dark hair flying as he ducked even lower at the last second and slid along the ground to avoid bashing his head on the axles. Before the man with the barrel even noticed that someone was there, the boy was already past him and the wagon, turning the corner onto the next street.

Five!

The top of a long stairway appeared before him, broad steps leading down to the promenade below. This was a familiar foe, and one Flynn had dealt with many times before. Without a second thought, he leaped sideways onto the well-worn bronze railing and slid down to the bottom, his feet hitting the ground at a run even as he landed firmly on the smooth cobblestones.

Six!

One more street to go and he would be home. As his house came into view, he barely heard the warning growl and following hiss before a grey tabby dashed out from a shadowed alleyway, startling him out of his wits. As cats often delight in doing, this one ran right across his path, practically getting tangled up in his legs and nearly causing him to trip and fall. Yet even this unprovoked attempt on his life by the feline would-be assassin couldn't deter him from his goal. Jumping at the last moment, Flynn soared over the dashing animal, landing a few mere feet away from the doorway of his home. Grinning triumphantly, he opened the door and dashed in.

Seven!

"I'm home," Flynn shouted in delight.

He was greeted by silence; there was no one around—no sound of the table being set, or his mother's voice calling the family to the evening meal. No sound of his brothers running down the stairs, or his father's impatient reminder for everyone to wash up before dinner. There was nothing.

Flynn could only stare about in puzzlement and then moved past the dining area and kitchen to peer into the bedroom he shared with two of his five siblings. There was no one there either. He was about to look into the second room when he heard the ragged sob from the direction of the stairway to the second floor. Heart pounding in fear, he took the steps two at a time and burst into his parents' bedroom. His brothers stood on one side of the bed, holding one another as they cried, while his father sat on a chair on the other side. Face lowered into one hand, Samuel Castellar's shoulders convulsed, his whole body wracked with sobs. His other hand firmly grasped the still hand of his wife, who lay on the bed, a peaceful look on her kind face. The child entering the room did not need to ask to know in his heart that his mother no longer drew the breath of life.

Flynn felt as if an abyss had suddenly opened up before him, threatening to pull him down to fall for an eternity while simultaneously feeling like a mule had just kicked him in the stomach. The confusion of emotions was so abrupt and powerful that he felt like he would faint. Certainly no one could blame a boy of his age for nearly passing out at the sight of his dead mother, yet somehow, he did not. Instead, he stumbled forward in a daze, the voices of his brothers seeming to come as if from very far away, like he was at the bottom of a very deep well and they were at the top. Approaching the bed, barely conscious of what he was doing, he slowly pried his father's fingers from his mother's and then took her hand in his own. It was still warm to the touch, some distant part of his mind registered, but when he touched her face, the skin was cold and clammy. The warmth must've come from his father's hand then, but why was that detail even important? He didn't know, and he didn't care. Nothing made sense in that moment. He knew only that his mind was a jumble of confused thoughts, disbelief, and a grief so vast that it threatened to engulf the entirety of his being.

"What happened?" Flynn whispered as he sought desperately for something tangible to cling to. He felt as if he was drowning, waves violently closing over his head, and it was only his father's voice that pulled him up from the watery void.

"It was some sort of sickness. She must've caught it some time ago but never said anything about how bad it was. There was only that nagging cough that she had these past few days, but she just kept saying she'd caught a bad draft that gave her a chest cold. Then she climbed into bed this afternoon after saying she felt very tired and never got back up." Samuel's voice sounded dull and dispassionate, as if all emotion had drained from the man. He stared at the body of his wife, but his gaze was vacant, the face expressionless. "She called for you at the end."

Upon hearing those words, the dam broke at last, and Flynn's tears were allowed to flow freely. At twelve years of age, he understood well enough to know that he couldn't have changed anything, but he never forgave himself for not being there during his mother's final moments. Little Flynn had always been Susan's favourite, and he hadn't even been able to say goodbye. Thin shoulders heaving as he wept, the boy tried to touch his father's hand again, but the man flinched at the contact and pulled away abruptly. Rising swiftly, Samuel left the room, leaving his children to grieve for their mother alone.

In the weeks following the tragic event, Samuel fell into a black mood, refusing to eat or even speak a word. So swift was the onset of this dark and debilitating depression that the boys had to fight alone through their own pain and grief of those first few days to have their mother's body taken away and given a proper burial. While they weren't exactly considered wealthy, Samuel Castellar had done well enough for himself as a merchant in the city's cloth trade. Now, his prolonged absence from work began to take a heavy toll, not only on his health but on the family's finances. When the money to buy food began to run low and their father continued to ignore their pleas, the six boys gathered what little coin was left and sent for a priest.

Under circumstances of this nature, a family normally would have called for a cleric devoted to Anval, god of life and health, for none were more skilled in the art of healing any manner of affliction that could befall the physical body than the Anvalites. As misfortune would have it though, this first month of summer was the time when the entire clergy of Anval in Rohne made its annual pilgrimage to the Abbey of Healing on the borders of Chemar Forest, located several days' ride away near the kingdom's northern border. With no members of the sect present in the city, there was only one other option that made sense—the

Janusian Church. As the dedicated envoys of the most eminent and popular of Akar's many faiths, Janusian priests were revered and respected as benevolent, compassionate, and wise. Their devotion to the deity called Janus, the Overgod, was unshakeable, and like the Anvalites and other followers of the true faiths, their spiritual power was so strong that it was said they could perform actual miracles.

On that morning—five weeks since Susan had passed away—the Janusian priest walked out of the bedroom and stood there while lost in thought, then slowly closed the door. One hand absently smoothed the flowing, gold-trimmed white robes, and he motioned for the boys to come closer. They did so, and Joshua, the eldest, screwed up his courage and broke the awkward silence when he approached. "Are we going to lose Pa as well? Does he have the same sickness that Mom did?"

The calm note of resignation and subdued despair in the teenager's voice caused the clergyman to sigh deeply. In and of itself, Joshua's question was normal enough—one commonly heard whenever a priest was called to attend to a house where someone was very ill. But Samuel Castellar did not have any physical ailment—what he was slowly dying from was a broken heart. For all the wisdom and knowledge of the healing arts that clerics normally possessed, no cure could be provided for this sort of thing.

"Your father's chosen to join your departed mother and will not listen to reason. I'm sorry children, there's nothing I can do to help a man that does not want to be helped," the priest said, his words tinged with sadness and compassion. His gaze turned to Flynn, who stood nearby, staring at the floor in silence, and placed one hand gently on the child's head. "You must be the youngest, yes? Your mother loved you most, but love was not the only gift she gave you, was it?" The man's question was strange, and Flynn could not puzzle its meaning through the ache in his heart. Gift? What gift? He looked at Joshua questioningly, but his brother gave no indication that he'd heard what the clergyman had said to him.

"Do you have any other family that can look after you?"

It took a few seconds for the implication of the man's words to filter through Joshua's numbed awareness. The priest spoke as if their father no longer lived, and Joshua was struck by the sudden and dazed realization that he didn't disagree with that unspoken conclusion. "Yes..." his voice trailed off, then came back. "Our aunt's been coming by every day to check in on us."

"She's your father's sister?" the man asked.

"Yes."

"Can you tell me where she lives? I need to speak with her."

Joshua told the priest what he needed to know, and the man left. One by one, the Castellar children walked away from the closed bedroom door. Flynn, however, remained. The child stared at the closed door, eyes brimming with tears.

His hands slowly curled into small fists, and he was startled when he felt a hand upon his shoulder. Flynn looked up at his older brother's grief-stricken face, and when Joshua slowly shook his head, Flynn let out the breath he hadn't realized he was holding. Looking back to the door and biting his lower lip, he turned and walked away as well. The next day, when Joshua came to his father's room in what had become a futile daily exercise in bringing him food, he found the man staring sightlessly at the ceiling, his chest motionless. Samuel Castellar had rejoined his departed Susan at last.

SORUL RIVER
JARKUS
SALAN FOREST
LUKAN
TOROS
THRACH GULF
WESTERN PROVINCE
THE SAURIAN WALL
KRANGOR KEEP
BULL KEEP
SHARP HORN KEEP
THERAGA
URIAN JUNGLES
YISSISSINIA
MOUNTAIN KEEP
WATERS OF SITUR
UR
FIST KEEP
SAURIAN BAY
HIGH KEEP
URIAN JUNGLES
TOL KE
SNAKE KEEP
THE SAURIAN WALL
DORAN KEEP
SOUTH KEEP
LAND'S END KEEP
LERIS
NEW GOL
NAVIS
GAMOS RIVER
AXOS
BALIS
KALAN
IMPERI
STORM SEA
BEROS
REN

SARMARAN
THE BORDER PEAKS
THE BORDER PEAKS
KEROS
VURGAS
ATREUS
NORTHERN PROVINCE
UXAN
TALBAN RIVER
EMPIRE OF GOL
TALBAN
DALIN RIVER
SAMOS
LAKE DAL
EASTERN PROVINCE
CENTRAL PROVINCE
DALIN
PRIAKUS
TURVINIA
JOZRE
GOLANOS
MEZOS
NOXOS
THE HEARTLANDS
EXOS
RAUKAN
TERNAK
THARKAN WO
OS
MURTAUR
EMPEROR'S RETREAT
PALAS
TALBAN RIVER
GOLIAN WOOD
VONIS RIVER
AN
OVINCE
OS
PEL
BOLI
HORAN
XERVOS
SIRILUS
PHE
SOUTHERN PROVINCE
GOLAN
THARKAN RIVER
Miles
0   25   50   75   100

N
W
E
S
SAR
LEGION FORT
KER
VURGAS
LAR
FA
NORTHER
THERAGAS
EMPIRE
DALIN RIVER

AKAN
LEGION FORT
GION FORT
THE BORDER PEAKS
ATREUS
ROVINCE
UXAN
OF GOL
0
25
50
Miles
LAKE DAL

CHAPTER 2

Dawn.

The sky over the eastern horizon looked like a canvas painted in beautiful shades of mauve, orange, and crimson, the colours heralding the imminent arrival of the glorious sun. In the west, the night's fading blanket of deep indigo and black dotted with shining stars slowly retreated to give way to the new day. Above the harsh beauty of the arid steppes of Sarmakan, two of Akar's three moons were no longer visible, with only giant Temeros lingering as it always did at this time of the year, its presence in the sky a near constant through the spring and summer months. The air was still cold at this early hour, but the temperature would soon begin to rise, reaching levels that only the hardiest inhabitants of this desolate yet harshly beautiful land could withstand.

Vurax was not a native to this endless sea of hardy scrublands and reddish soil, but eighteen years as a slave to a Sarmakanite tribe had gradually built up his tolerance to the scorching daytime heat. His large brown eyes glimmered in the darkness of his tent as the first hints of light crept in, and he lay there on top of his blanket on the hard ground, watching the sky slowly change colour through the small hole in the roof of the shelter. He knew it was time to get up, but he closed his eyes and cleared his thoughts, preparing himself mentally for yet another day of back-breaking labour. The previous week had been a particularly difficult one, and he found himself needing to tap into additional reserves of strength to merely summon the willpower to get up and trudge through yet another day of his miserable existence.

Just five days ago, he had watched helplessly while his younger brother got taken into Ikut's fighting pits, and though slaves were not permitted to witness the brutal contests, the fact that his brother had not returned to the holding pen that evening was enough to tell him of his fate. With Aros gone, Vurax was well and truly alone now. There were a multitude of other slaves in the sprawling camp; wretches like him, eking out what could barely be called an existence, but of his family—taken captive in that fateful raid nearly two decades ago—he was the last. His mother had perished from abuse and neglect not long after their capture, while his father had been executed in more recent years for attempting to organize a slave revolt and escape. He vowed that he would never forget their faces, just as he vowed that he would make all his captors pay somehow.

Sighing heavily with resignation, Vurax opened his eyes and rose from his bedding, the effort made awkward by the iron manacles and chains he wore around his wrists and ankles, leaving him just enough slack to take short, shuffling steps. Standing up fully, the small tent was barely tall enough to accommodate his towering frame. He stretched stiff muscles, then bent low and opened the flap to step outside. His only garb was a soiled, greyish cloth, cinched at his waist to cover what little dignity he had left. His nostrils flared reflexively as he took in the scents drifting in the morning air: the smoky aroma of burnt acacia wood from the night's campfires; the musky smell of horse from the corrals on the other side of the camp; and the omnipresent acrid stench of human sweat and urine. His features screwed up in disgust, for try as he might, he could never get used to that last, most offensive odour.

"About time you got up, lazy cow-face!" the mocking voice greeted him as he passed through the slave pen's wooden gate, the tired insult robbed of any sharpness after years of overuse. Turning to the speaker, Vurax gave the man a vicious glare, followed by a toothy grin that made the other take an involuntary step back, visibly unsettled by the facial expression. Vurax was a Golian—or Minotaur, as the humans called them. Taller and more heavily muscled than even the largest of men, Golians physically resembled humans in most ways, with the obvious exception being their heads, which were like that of a bull in every fashion, right up to the sweeping pair of curved horns—a source of pride for the haughty race. Their entire bodies were completely covered in thick, short hair, which could vary in colour from one Golian to another, and they had feet that were a hybrid of a bull's hoof and a human foot, with an additional joint near the calf that gave them a strange gait when they walked. Unlike the bovines they resembled, however, Golians did not have tails.

"Don't be getting any stupid ideas into that hard skull of yours now, Vurax," the human growled, appearing a little less certain of himself. A dusky-skinned hand strayed to the hilt of the wickedly sharp scimitar at his belt, and fingers adorned by several golden rings tapped the weapon's grip meaningfully. The Golian's gaze followed the other's gesture then centered on the jewellery, which extended to gold bracelets around the man's wrist. Several of the thick hoops were inscribed with runes in the language of Gol, and Vurax's eyes narrowed dangerously when he recognized some of the ornaments as having belonged to Aros. Golians were extremely proud of their horns and often adorned them with bands made of precious metals or etched runes into the horns themselves.

"Where did you get those, Bagra?" Vurax asked him, his voice low and tone menacing. He already knew the answer, of course, but waited for it, nonetheless. The special gold bands were traditionally placed around a Golian's horns when they came of age, allowing the soft metal to expand and become firmly embedded in the horns as they slowly grew with time. The only way to remove them was when the owner was dead, though no Golian would ever commit such sacrilege.

"You know damn well where I got them," Bagra said loudly, regaining his confidence when a couple of other guards began to walk over, drawn by the exchange. "Same place where I'll get yours—when you're good and dead like your worthless brother. He died begging for his life like the coward that he was, did you know that?" the human continued taunting.

Vurax's eyes flashed from their natural brown to deep red and he felt the blood rage threatening to take control of him. He knew he had only a few seconds of rational thought remaining—time in which to choose between letting it overtake him, or to step back from the brink. Through the crimson haze that was quickly descending over his vision, he saw the shadows of the two men behind him, hands on their weapons. Any fool could see Bagra was goading him into a fight but fettered as he was by his shackles, the confrontation could only end in one way. Without Aros to protect, Vurax had nothing left to lose and would prove too dangerous of a slave in the long run.

No, he decided. He wouldn't give them the satisfaction. Vurax knew the tribesmen may be barbarians in his eye, but they still followed rudimentary tribal laws, and their chieftain would not condone the wanton murder of a slave. These men needed a convenient excuse to kill him out in the open, and thus Bagra was holding nothing back in his provocation, but Vurax would bide his time and then he would have his revenge, just as he had planned from the day he'd been captured. He only wondered how much more humiliation he could endure before his volatile temper got the better of him.

Letting his breath out slowly and releasing the coiled energy that had been building inside his prodigious muscles, the Golian relaxed his posture as his eyes returned to their normal hue. Baring his teeth again in a frightening smile, Vurax spat his contempt at Bagra's feet, gave the man and his friends a derisive look that let them know this was far from finished and shuffled toward the camp's water well to begin his daily chores.

⸺◆⸺

Months later, sitting down wearily on a large, wind-worn stone, Vurax loosened the buckles and straps of his leather vest, creating enough slack to allow the heavy wooden yoke over his neck and shoulders to slide to the ground. The attached empty gourds followed with a clatter, sending up a small cloud of red dust. Glancing tiredly at the yoke, the irony of the image was not lost on the Golian: back home, identical contraptions were used to harness oxen to plows to till the land before planting. Any comparison made between a Minotaur and a cow was always certain to be a serious mistake for the one uttering it, yet here he was, reduced to little more than a beast of burden himself. Snorting in general disgust at life, Vurax's entire body slumped as he tried to make the most of the short break he was allowed before resuming his work. A handful of other slaves did the same thing nearby but kept their distance, the legendary prickly temperament of Golians enough to discourage any attempt at some form of solidarity between them and him.

As Vurax stared at the ground, unseeing and lost in thought, a shadow came and went in the midday sun, leaving something behind. When he focused his vision on the object before him, his mood grew even darker. What lay inside the small clay bowl could hardly be considered food by anyone's standards, the rancid-smelling gruel and hunk of maggot-infested bread an affront to his remaining shreds of self-respect. Still, as revolting as the meal was, it was the best he could hope to get in his current situation. Truth was, he couldn't really recall the taste of anything else. His hand reflexively began to reach out slowly toward the bowl but then stopped. Fingers curling into a fist, his arm shook with defiance as he withdrew the limb.

Four months had passed now since losing his brother and the last embers of his spirit were dwindling to a very dim glow that was nearly extinguished. With each member of his family that he had lost, the fire within him had burned brighter with thoughts of freedom and revenge, but with Aros now gone, the long years of futile hope and ever-growing despair had taken a terrible toll on the Minotaur. Food was for the living, he mused, and if this was what fate held for him, then he no longer wished to be counted among them. The gloom and misery he felt in the depths of his soul threatened to claim victory at long last, and the defeat festering within him had finally driven the last thoughts of vengeance from his mind.

The camp's well was nearly dry and soon the tribe would begin to dismantle their tent town here in Ikut, moving off in search of another source of water that would support them for a few more months while this one slowly replenished itself. On and on the cycle went, dragging Vurax along with it while they roamed the steppes, each season blurring into the next. When he heard the crack of the guard's whip, Vurax didn't move a muscle. He knew the first strike to the air was only a warning to get back to work; the next would land across his back, likely adding another scar to the dozens of others already there. He didn't care. He had decided the Sarmakanites would be moving on without him, one way or another, so he waited for the whip to fall again... and waited... and waited... but the expected flash of hot pain never came.

After a few more seconds passed without him looking up, a distant yet incongruous sound intruded upon his dulled awareness. He couldn't place what it was at first or where he'd heard it before, but it was not altogether unfamiliar. When it came suddenly to him, he knew that the last time he'd heard it was in a place buried far back in his memories. The sound, pealing again across the dry and empty air, was not the deep boom of the long plains-steer horns the barbarians used, but rather the sharp clarion call of a brass trumpet. Though he'd never experienced one, he'd heard about hallucinations before, such things not being uncommon in hot climates like this, especially when a person was under physical and mental duress. Surely that must be what was happening, he thought, yet when the trumpet rang a third time and was then followed by several Sarmakanite horn calls, he decided to lift his head at last.

The first thing he noticed was the guard's absence. Blinking furiously as he tried to focus his vision in the bright sunlight after staring at the shadowed ground for so long, he noticed the other slaves were not nearby either. Another sound began to distinguish itself then—a kind of dull roar that slowly coalesced into a multitude of raised voices, the crescendo rippling throughout the camp like a gathering desert wind. Coupled with it all was the unmistakable scent of fear, an odour that humans exuded all too often, and one with which his acute sense of smell was intimately familiar. He still had no idea what was happening, but anything was better than the way he had felt only moments ago, and any change in the dismal monotony that his life had become was welcomed. Feeling the embers glow a little brighter, his spirit was rekindled anew and the surge in energy helped him shake the lethargy holding him in its thrall.

Fully undoing the straps of the harness, Vurax shed the restrictive garment like an unwanted second skin and stood. His dark tan hair rippled when he shook off the black flies and dust, and wide nostrils flared while he snorted loudly to clear the last vestiges of fog from his head. As he did so, he became aware of people running past him and around the water well, moving toward the southern edge of the camp. The trumpet had gone silent, but the horns continued to sound over the shouts of alarm, and beneath it all, the distant but rhythmic beat of war drums as hundreds of heavily shod feet thundered against the hard ground in rigid unison. Such well-defined cadence was something the barbarians were incapable of, a detail that was not lost on Vurax. The press of frantic humans around him increased, with frightened Sarmakanite women, crying children, and slaves fleeing away from that ominous sound, while the men continued to run toward it. Vurax didn't need to think twice about his choice and began to walk south as quickly as his chains would allow him, soon arriving at the edge of the camp where the barbarian men were gathering in ever-increasing numbers. His large head looming well above those of the short-statured humans in front of him, Vurax peered past them and beheld what they faced.

Beyond the camp, the air above the sun-baked plain danced and rippled from the heat of the approaching noon sun. The effect distorted one's sight, making it impossible to make out any details other than the obvious: a long, indistinct line, dark at first but brightening as it grew closer, stretching from east to west, its edges lost in the blurry haze. A cloud of dust rose and hung in the sky above, like a light brush stroke of red paint on a canvas of blue. The sound of marching and drums washed over them with stark inevitability while the advancing line seemed to undulate as it moved, like a vast, many-scaled silver serpent with a crested spine. The trumpet, now joined by several others, blasted once more into the still air. Long-buried memories were dredged to the surface as Vurax recalled events from a youth that was forever gone, a time when he'd watched armed columns march down the main street of the city near his parents' farm—columns of his countrymen. As the echo of the trumpets died, so too did the drums grow silent; the marching had ground to a sudden and precisely timed halt.

As the men around him began to form a defensive line in response to this unknown threat, more of them arrived every second, adding to the confusion and chaos. Ferocious warriors in their own right, the Sarmakanites shunned heavy armour in favour of practicality. The climate of their land wasn't suited to wearing metal, nor did the barbarians possess the resources, skill, or training required to craft and wear such things. As such, many fought bare-chested, while others wore hard-boiled leather arm bracers or shoulder pauldrons, and a few even wore reinforced leather breastplates and helms, a sign of individual prestige and wealth among the people of Sarmakan. The true pride of a Sarmakanite warrior, however, was his weapon. The use of shields was universally disdained among the nomadic fighters, and nearly all preferred to wield one of two of their most favoured implements of death: the wickedly curved and razor-sharp scimitar, or the large and brutal battle axe, so massive that it required two hands to swing with deadly efficiency.

Ignoring the humans, Vurax's attention was fixated solely on the horizon, and heedless of their battle preparations, he shoved his way to the front of the line. As he continued shuffling past it in a daze, a shout came from somewhere behind him.

"Slave—go back to your hovel where you belong!"

The Minotaur didn't hear the insult as he took a few more steps and then stopped. He blinked to moisten his eyes against the dry heat of the day and squinted hard to confirm for himself what was out there, and whether it would bring hope or death. Either option would bring an equal measure of relief to him at this point. In the distance, the enormous silver serpent lay perfectly still, menacing and expectant. He took one more step, and the elusive details came into focus. The shimmering scales of the serpent coalesced into a wall of high, rectangular shining steel shields. Above them, the sun reflected brightly off hundreds of polished metal helms, crested with red plumes, while even higher, the spiky crown of the imaginary beast changed now into the shafts and burnished points of a sea of spears. Battle standards hung limply in the heavy air, but he did not need to see them unfurled to know the crests they displayed.

Vurax closed his eyes and tilted his face upward, letting out a long sigh. Slowly, his lips curled back to reveal his teeth in a frightening grin, then he turned and walked back to the line of Sarmakanites. Most of them ignored the hulking figure as it approached, mentally preparing themselves for what was coming and giving their weapons one final check, but a few glared viciously at the Golian. The one that had shouted at him now placed himself in front of Vurax, blocking his way. He barely noticed Bagra's ugly, scowling features.

"What did you see, cow-face? What's out there?" the barbarian growled, gleaming scimitar held tightly at the ready.

Vurax didn't even acknowledge the man's presence when he shouldered past him. The Minotaur's much greater physique caused the smaller human to stagger backward two steps from the shove. Enraged, the cruel Sarmakanite snarled wordlessly and flicked out with his weapon, scoring a shallow but bloody furrow across Vurax's back with the tip of the blade. Feet spread apart and dropping into a defensive crouch, Bagra prepared himself for a reaction that never came. Vurax continued walking away as if nothing had happened.

"What in the...?" Bagra could barely contain his surprise and cursed at the slave's back. "Get back here, you snivelling coward!"

Vurax kept going without so much as a backward glance, the feral grin splitting his face once more. He knew what was about to happen here, and he almost felt sorry for these fools.

Almost.

With singular purpose and determination, Vurax ignored the growing chaos around him and shuffled over to his destination. The tent he sought was in the eastern part of the camp, but with all the barbarians gathering into a battle line behind him, the way there was essentially clear. Under normal circumstances, he wouldn't have been allowed anywhere near where he was going, but these weren't normal circumstances, and as he had predicted, the place had been left unguarded in the confusion of what was happening.

He glanced at the crude but serviceable anvil sitting in a work area outside the large tent, resting on a large, flat stone, and the smith's hammer, hastily discarded nearby. No weapons or armour were fashioned here, but the tribe always needed a farrier and smith to maintain their wagons and shoe their horses. Now he just needed a large metal spike, or something else equally suitable. A short series of trumpet blasts in the distance instilled a further sense of urgency in him. It wouldn't be long now, and he didn't want to miss out. Vurax cast about the farrier's tools and supplies and finally found what he needed: a long, tapered metal pin, commonly used to secure a wagon wheel to its axle. Not optimal, but there was no time or need for finesse. As he set about placing his wrist manacles on top of the anvil's flat surface, Vurax quickly realized his next problem. With his movements restrained by the short length of the chains, he couldn't get his arms far enough apart to properly position the pin and swing the hammer with sufficient force at the same time.

Snarling in frustration after a couple of botched attempts, Vurax tried to quell his growing rage to think clearly. There was a way to do this; he just had to figure it out. It was then that he noticed the solitary figure standing in the tent's opening. His muscles tensed instantly, and he gripped the hammer tightly, but he relaxed almost immediately when he realized that the man—despite being a Sarmakanite—was just another slave. Unlike Vurax however, he was not chained. He knew that all the man had to do was shout once, but he doubted anyone would heed the cries given the noise and confusion occurring just a short distance away.

There was a tense silence, and when the man didn't move a muscle and just stared at him, Vurax snorted in disgust and went back to contemplating his problem. Behind him, the barbarian warriors shouted their rhythmic war chants and stamped the ground with their feet while their chieftain exhorted them to fight with valour and bravery. A shadow fell across the anvil and then a gaunt and soot-covered hand hesitatingly turned over to display a callused, open palm. Vurax looked at the man's leathery, aged face, noting the lines and creases, and saw in his eyes a deep, wordless pain to match his own. The slave opened his mouth as if to say something, but only a harsh and guttural croak came out: his tongue had been removed at some point, no doubt as punishment for some trivial transgression. Nevertheless, Vurax understood and placed the hammer in the man's hand with a grim nod.

With a few quick and precise blows on the anvil, the slave struck the manacles free from Vurax's wrists then did the same for his ankles, using the anvil's stone base as a striking surface for the latter. The Minotaur slowly rubbed the places where the iron had cruelly bitten into his flesh for years, wondering if the deep indentations would ever disappear, but there would be time enough to worry about that later if he survived the battle that was coming, he thought stoically. Stretching his arms, Vurax stood up and loomed over the slave, who stared at him, not with fear, but resignation. The man held out the smith's hammer to him. The Minotaur considered the sturdy tool, knowing what the other meant by the gesture, but then shook his head. Instead, he bent down and picked up one of the lengths of chain, two heavy manacles still attached to either end.

"Get as far away from here as you can," he said to the man, then turned and walked back the way he had come, his movements halting at first as he got used to having a full stride once again but growing surer with each step. He did not look back to thank the man or see if the slave had heeded his advice.

Chief Urkan-Kor, a grizzled warrior and veteran of many internecine wars among the various tribes of the vast steppes of Sarmakan, stood at the centre of the battle line. Try as he might, he could not figure out how such a sizeable force had been able to march up to their camp without being seen or heard much sooner. Sentries regularly patrolled the area beyond the camp, and in this flat and featureless terrain, they should have spotted an approaching army from miles away. It just didn't make any sense.

The Sarmakanite battle line—insofar as it could be called a line—shifted and heaved as the tribesmen awaited the signal to charge. The men shouted curses, clashed weapons against armour, and beat the ground with their feet, causing a cloud of dust to rise into the sweltering air. Impatient and unruly, it was all their leader could do to keep them from rushing forward. Instead, the man ordered what few archers they had to fire. The Sarmakanite bows were short and compact, meant to be used from horseback, and the chieftain was not willing to risk the few horses he had just yet, having lost most of the tribe's precious animals to a devastating drought the year before. Predictably, the arrows fell far short of the enemy line, which stood immobile since it had arrived, an impenetrable wall of shields giving no hint as to what they were up to.

Urkan-Kor suspected there were factors at work here that he had no under-standing of, and the doubts and fears that came with that knowledge were causing him to hesitate overly long in the eyes of his men. In a typical engagement, he would have ordered the charge long ago, but nothing about this situation was normal, least of all the presence of this particular enemy. He knew how to fight against his own countrymen or conduct predatory raids against Minotaur farmers, and his prowess as a warrior had earned him the leadership of his tribe for more than thirty years, but an opponent like this was vastly beyond his experience. The chieftain eyed the gleaming silver line arrayed in the distance before him and made silent peace with his gods. Seeing no further point in delaying the inevitable, and before his men decided to attack without him, Urkan-Kor lifted his scimitar into the air, let it hang there as he savoured the raucous cheers from hundreds of throats, then brought the weapon down sharply. Like a rolling wave, the Sarmakanite warriors surged forward.

The distance between the two forces diminished quickly, and when no deadly hail of arrows came from the enemy force, Urkan-Kor allowed himself a flash of wild hope. Though he was twice the age of most of the warriors around him, the Sarmakanite chieftain kept pace with his men, adrenaline surging through his heart, and the thrill of the imminent clash firing the blood in his veins. He was close enough to see the markings on the large shields now, as well as the heraldry stitched in gold thread upon the red battle standards, and the ornate yet functional design of the plumed helms below them. Mostly though, he saw the curved horns that protruded to either side of each piece of protective headgear, and his suspicions about the true nature of his opponents were confirmed at last.

Golians.

All thoughts on the impossible reality of the presence of an imperial legion here flew from Urkan-Kor's mind when the trilling whistle sounded and several of the standards lowered abruptly in response. Just before the howling horde of Sarmakanites made contact with the Golian front line, the looming shield wall parted suddenly, each individual shield turning with exact precision and timing to reveal a gap in between every pair of curved surfaces. From those openings—and launched with a strength that greatly exceeded that of a normal human—came a storm of javelins, each with a shaft as thick as a man's arm and a triangular steel head ending in a lethal point. At such a short distance, there was no arc to the missiles' trajectories as they flew horizontally at the charging line of barbarians. Urkan-Kor understood at last why no arrows had been used, lulling the Sarmakanites into packing their ranks even more tightly as they advanced, but his surprised realization came too late, the thought cut short along with his life when one of the massive javelins punched clear through his armour and breastbone, the tip of the weapon emerging several inches from his back. The jarring force of the blow lifted him clear off his feet, and launched him into the man running behind him, causing that warrior to stumble and fall. Chief Urkan-Kor was dead before he hit the ground.

Along the entire front line of the Sarmakanite advance, the scene repeated itself with horrible effectiveness as the devastating impact of the javelins brutally impaled scores of the leading barbarians, their death cries and falling bodies affecting the balance of those coming behind, the charge blunted and nearly broken. As chaos and confusion set in, the whistle sounded again, the shrill sound piercing the air above the cacophony of the battlefield. The front rank of the Golian long spears, upright until now, suddenly lowered to a forward angle while the tower shields lifted from the ground. With an ominous rumble and a rhythmic grunt, hundreds of shod feet stamped forward as the entire shield wall moved several steps before the shields lowered again, turning slightly to one side as they did. Into that small gap, the long spears were lowered again, this time into a horizontal position parallel to the ground and then thrust forward in one smooth motion. The razor-sharp, leaf-shaped blades plunged with force into the Sarmakanites who were struggling to advance over the bodies of their fallen comrades, their shorter weapons rendered useless at this distance. With mechanical precision, the pattern repeated itself: The whistle sounded; the shields advanced; the spears thrust. Each time, men screamed and died.

Eventually, the press of bodies was so great that the Sarmakanites finally made it through that spiked wall of death. With savage ferocity born from an intoxicating mixture of fear, desperation, and reckless abandon, the warriors of the steppes somehow managed to create a few gaps in the massive shields through which they could counterattack, many throwing their lives away so that those behind could advance and hack at the enemy behind the wall. Still, anyone could see that the effort, though valiant, was ultimately doomed. Their casualties were mounting with each second that passed, and behind the shield barrier, the Sarmakanites found rank upon rank of heavily muscled and armoured Golian Legionnaires, their discipline unbreakable, their battlefield prowess legendary.

Vurax arrived back at the edge of the camp where the barbarians had begun their charge, the ringing clash of weapons and the screams of the dying filling the air with a horrible din. The amount of red dust being raised by the conflict had the same effect as that of a thick fog covering the battlefield. Indistinct shapes moved about in the cloud, slashing, thrusting, and falling. The Minotaur slave closed his right hand into a fist as he looped the centre of the heavy chain around it a couple of times, testing the weight of the large iron manacles that dangled down to his feet. Satisfied, he snorted once and then closed his eyes. In a flash, his mind relived all the pain and agony that he had endured for the last two decades of his life. All the loss, grief, and indignities suffered came crashing down upon him like a tidal wave of despair that had threatened to drag him down forever several times before. Though he had not succumbed the previous times, he had barely managed to rise back to the surface, waiting in despondent resignation for the next wave. Not this time.

Feeling the fury building within him, Vurax opened himself fully to all the pent-up anger and rage that he had barely managed to suppress throughout these long and excruciating years of captivity. On more than one occasion before he had fought hard and succeeded in controlling the destructive force within him; but today, he threw open wide the cage door and allowed the imprisoned beast to step out so that he could embrace it at last. Like wildfire coursing through his veins, the blood rage took over. His eyes snapped open, no longer clear pools of brown on white, but a deep vermilion shade instead that glowed with frightening intensity. His teeth were bared in a feral snarl, and his nostrils flared wide as he exhaled his anger into the air. Hair rippled and his muscles flexed with tension. His rational consciousness retreated to a place of safety, and a primal instinct that directed him only to kill took over. Vurax lowered his large horned head and took one step, then another, then broke into a run.

The charging juggernaut crashed into the rear of the Sarmakanite ranks with the devastating force of a large boulder rolling down a mountainside during an avalanche. The crushing impact caused two men to go flying into the air, their helpless bodies flipping end over end before landing hard on the ground, while a third man screamed in horrible pain when two sharp horns impaled his back below the shoulder blades. Using his momentum, Vurax swiftly lifted his head and twisted his neck to the side in a single motion, flinging the mortally pierced human up and away from him with a spray of blood that spattered all those around him. His charge slowed, and the Minotaur behemoth—towering above the stunned men beside him—stopped and planted his feet firmly upon the ground in a wide stance. Gripping the chain with both hands, he swung the forged iron links repeatedly until the heavy manacles on the end became a dark blur as they sped through the air. The whirring sound they caused became a herald of death as it was the last thing anyone around him heard before the thick metal bindings crushed their skulls with a sickening crack and explosion of gore, so tremendous was the speed and force of the impact.

On and on Vurax swung the improvised weapon while shouting his rage, his throat raw and hoarse from the strain and dust, the once omnipresent symbol of his enslavement now becoming an instrument of deliverance against his cruel captors. He was stabbed and pierced in a dozen places, the Sarmakanites braving the circle of carnage and death long enough to try and bring down the howling demon in their midst, but Vurax was beyond the ability to feel pain. In the red-filled haze of his limited awareness, there was only vengeance and death to be dealt. Something struck the back of one leg hard enough to cause his knee to buckle. Though he felt nothing, the blow caused him to lose his balance and as his body tilted forward, the swinging manacles hit the ground and stopped, the chain's motion arrested. It was all the time his unseen opponent needed as a wickedly sharp scimitar swung hard at his right arm, slicing through muscle and sinew until it was stopped only by bone. To his side, a second dark shape flew through the air, and he managed to duck his head just in time when the large axe blade whistled by, chipping one horn and drawing sparks as it skipped over his horn rings.

To execute such a heavy swing, the axe-wielding human had overextended his reach and when he attempted to control the weapon on the follow-through, Vurax lunged upward, catching the warrior in the stomach with one of his horns.

The man shouted in agony and dropped his weapon as the Minotaur thrust and shook his head violently, goring the Sarmakanite. When the man staggered back, clutching at the gaping wound in his gut as he died, Vurax dimly felt the scimitar bite again, this time hamstringing the same leg that had been hit earlier. Again, he felt no pain, but when he tried to stand, he found that his leg would not obey and collapsed beneath him. As he fell, he twisted his body and swung his arm out, the chain sweeping low to the ground in a wide arc and catching his opponent's ankle, then wrapping itself around it. Before the man could react, Vurax pulled violently on the chain, lifting the human from his feet, causing him to land hard on his back, and jarring the scimitar loose from his hand.

The raging Minotaur was upon the hapless warrior in seconds. The tremendous weight of the Golian slave effectively pinned the man to the ground, rendering useless the latter's struggles to reach his weapon. When he felt the chain wrap itself around his neck with alarming ferocity and speed, the man desperately fumbled for his dagger, managing to pull the blade out even as he felt the iron links starting to crush his windpipe. He managed one thrust, leaving the dagger deeply imbedded in his killer's side before all strength fled his body, his eyes bulging and staring upward with fear at the bestial face hovering just inches from his own while his opponent watched him die. With one final, vicious pull of the chain, the man's neck was crushed, and the terrified eyes saw no more. A ray of sunlight pierced through a small break in the dusty haze then, reflecting upon metal with a golden flash that sliced through to Vurax's buried consciousness. The red veil that distorted his vision lessened for an instant, and his gaze fell upon the three gold hoops around the dead man's left wrist. The shock of recognition nearly jolted him out of the blood rage, but the implication of their presence here quickly tamped down any return to reason.

Bagra.

With renewed fury fueled by grief, he yanked savagely at the limp arm, nearly ripping it from the dead man's socket as he pulled the rings from the corpse's wrist. Once freed, he gripped the objects tightly in one fist, then picked up a manacle with the other hand. Shouting incoherently, his body shaking with uncontrolled wrath and ire, he brought the iron shackle down over and over again onto his tormentor's face until there was nothing in the shattered mess of blood and bone that could even be called remotely human. When his gore-covered fist finally hit dirt, he stopped, but only to search for a new target for his rage. Some distant part of his awareness told him his body had suffered grievous wounds and that his life's blood was pouring out from many places, but that was no reason to stop; it was only an incentive to kill more while he still could. Dragging his useless leg behind him, Vurax crawled onward.

The battle had moved and shifted away from where he'd fallen, and he searched frantically about for an opponent in the haze. He could still discern fighting somewhere nearby, though the sounds had become more indistinct, and everything was beginning to blend into a dull roar in his ears. He blinked furiously to try and clear his vision but there was nothing there but a darkening blur of red of varying shades and shapes, some of which moved indistinctively, and some which lay still. The world had lost all definition except for the one imperative in his mind that demanded blood. To his left, a cluster of figures seemed to be struggling against one another. He turned ponderously toward them, the chain dragging slowly behind him, its weight seeming to increase with every passing second. He coughed and something thick and cloying seemed to coat his throat and mouth as he did. He spat out the offending fluid and continued on.

After what seemed like an eternity, Vurax reached the fighting once again. He could see nothing now, and the pounding in his ears overrode all other sounds, as if his very heart were beating loudly inside his head. The three golden rings bit into the palm of his hand, their presence the only thing that felt solid and reassuring anymore. Aros was with him; the bastards had to pay; nothing else mattered. Something bumped into him, or he bumped into something. He wasn't sure which, and he didn't care. He lashed out but made contact with nothing but air, and his compromised balance betrayed him, causing him to fall. He tried to rise but was shoved violently from behind and his good leg gave out, forcing him to the ground once more with a grunt. His enormous reserves of strength were nearly exhausted, but not completely.

He struggled to get up as what sounded like a voice coming from an impossible distance tried to overcome the drumming in his ears. The voice was insistent, but he ignored it. He felt pressure land heavily between his shoulders as something attempted to force him back down. The fire within him had nearly gone out, but one last flare of rage heaved his frame upward with such force that he shook off whatever was holding him down, and he tried to lift himself again with an unintelligible snarl of frustration and defiance. Pain exploded in his head then as something smashed into his temple. The red haze in his mind turned briefly into a world of hot, painful white light, and then everything went dark. The incessant drumming stopped at last.

THE INNER SEA
BLADE SHOALS
SUN'S ANVIL PLATEAU
DRUKESHNOR
KRAKEN REEF
LAST HOPE
BREOS
ALDA
VALESIAN PLAINS
THE CITADEL
PALAS
TAN'S
ALLEY
OLD VALESI
HIGH
BARONY OF VALESIA
VALESI
THE DROMKAR
JILDINUR CASTLE
WHITERIM
MAELFORD
CUTTER'S END
TALLTREES
VALES FOREST
ELMSFORD
THE
LAKERUN
STONEGULCH
BLOODWATER
DUNMERE CASTLE
THE STONEGLADE
TREM
MORHAIN CASTLE
REDFORGE
FELGEN RIVER
JASPERHILL
COUNTY OF REDMOOR
BRANCLIFFE
ELDERDUSK CASTLE
MOORTOWN
EAGLE PEAK
FELGEN
GREENSHALE
DAWNHOLLOW
ARLING RIVER
THE
MEADOWLAN
DAGGERVALE
GREAT FOREST
EARLDOM OF FELGENFORD
BRIARGLEN
RAVENSHADE
DALEBU
ARLINGTOWN
RAUVIR'S
STONEBURG
SWAN CA
SCAR
BARONY OF ARLINGFORD
OSPREY CASTLE

CORAL BAY
THE SHINING CRESCENT
PARGERI
OSVEN
GAMARRA
UTELUR
MEZAN
SULARAN
KARASI
KINGFISHER CASTLE
WHITE SANDS
KASTIR
CAMERRA
GREYSTONE
NORHAVEN
TAR KALUR
G RIVER
IA
GRAND DUCHY OF TREMURA
PRINCIPALITY OF MORVIK
SWIFTWATER
THE RE KEEP
ROZIERRA
DOLMAROS
THE SILVERFLOW
GRAN TREMUR
FARFIELDS
FELGEN RIVER
GRAN MORV
THE GREYWATER
CRANE CASTLE
DUCHY OF DOLMAR
VIZO
STARLING KEEP
REMEL
DOLMARIN RIVER
RIVER LOWLANDS
BARONY OF REMELOS
BIRKENFORD
ILLE
THE GRASS SEA
TWINFALLS
RLDOM OF BIRKENFORD
HORIZON'S REACH
BIRKENVILLE
RIVEN-SKY MARCH
AMBERMILL
HILLRUN MARCH
VEROS
MELENN
WINDWALL PEAKS
COUNTY OF GREENDALE
Miles
0   25   50   75   100
MORNWOOD

N
W
E
S
JASPERHILL
MORHAIN CASTLE
REDFORGE
EAGLE PEAK
DAWNHOLLOW
GREAT FOREST
DAGGERVALE
RAUVIR'S SCAR
BRIARGLEN
ARLINGTOWN
BARONY OF ARLINGFORD

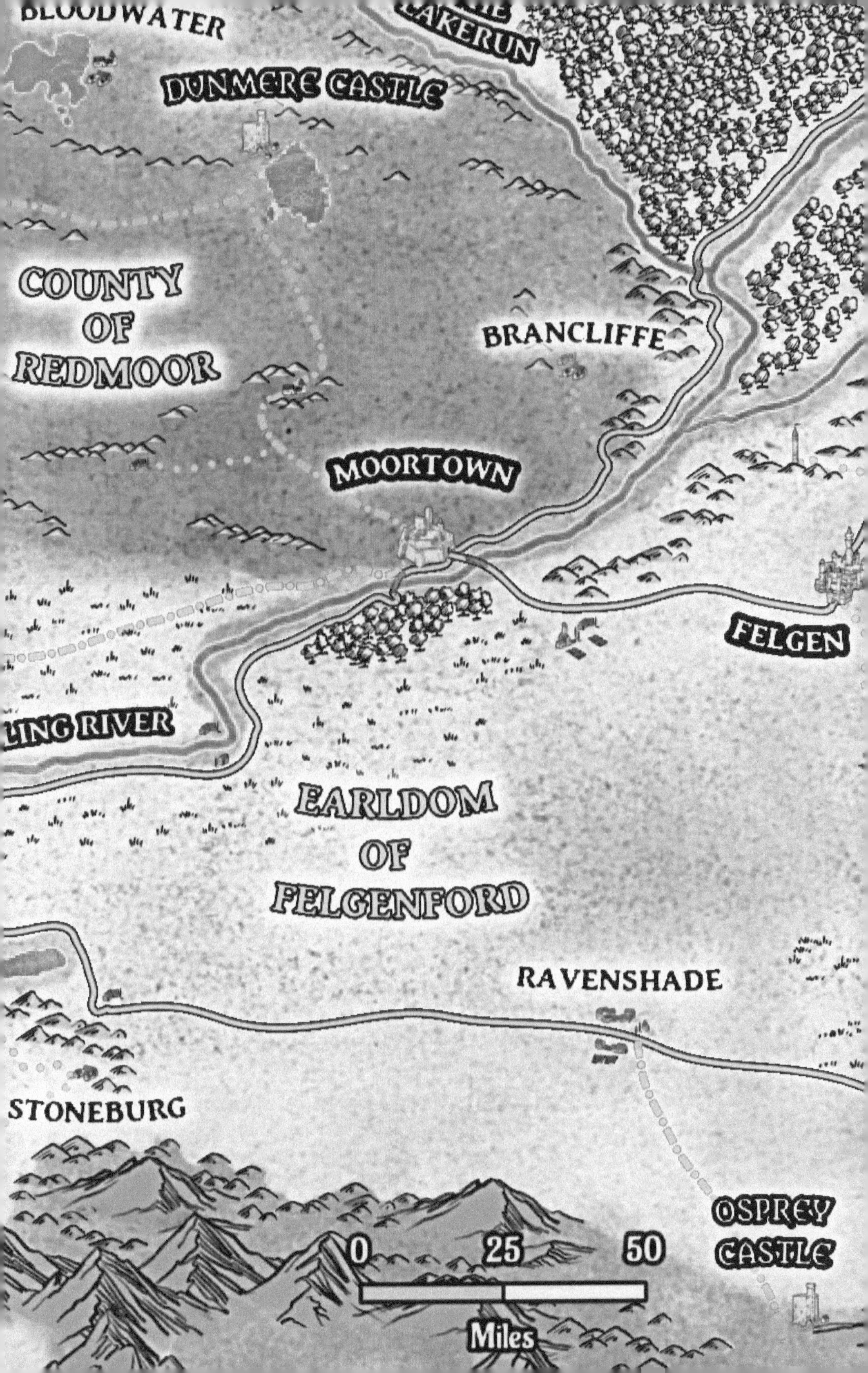

BLOODWATER
DUNMERE CASTLE
THE LAKERUN
COUNTY OF REDMOOR
BRANCLIFFE
MOORTOWN
FELGEN
LING RIVER
EARLDOM OF FELGENFORD
RAVENSHADE
STONEBURG
OSPREY CASTLE
0
25
50
Miles

CHAPTER 3

The dream had always been the same.

The young woman ran naked through a fog-covered forest at night, her skin bathed in the soft and diffuse crimson light of the Dragon Moon. She knew the woman to be herself because she could see her own face. The experience was always disorienting at first—an exceedingly strange sensation that she was somehow outside of her body, observing herself while she ran heedlessly through the trees. There was a feeling of weightlessness and motion each time as she followed the running figure from above, but no matter how much she tried, she could not get any closer. The woman ran with the swiftness and agility of an animal familiar with every root, bush, and branch in the woods, springing nimbly over or around any object in her path. Another figure ran ahead of her, just far enough for its shape to remain teasingly indistinct, frustratingly out of reach as it wove in and out of sight through the mists. Somewhere far within the fog, the sound of a lone horn could be heard periodically, the deep and mournful note dropping sharply at the end each time.

She couldn't recall how many times she'd had this dream, but she knew it was recurring and familiar, and every time she experienced it, she had the distinct impression that whoever or whatever she was chasing was toying with her. Any time she lost sight of her quarry and paused to regain her bearings, the figure always reappeared immediately, standing perfectly still as it waited for her, a dark outline around which the red-tinged fog drifted lazily. Then she would catch sight of it and the chase would begin anew. So, she ran and ran until she could run no more, and the sun had come up at last to lift away the mists, leaving her standing alone in an empty forest. It was always like this—a game that ended the same way without fail.

Except this time, it didn't.

The object of her chase had vanished once more, and she slowed her pace to search for any sign of it, her lithe frame heaving with exertion, the sweat glistening on her bare skin. Observing the scene from a distance, she could feel the exhaustion emanating from her own body, yet she knew that somehow, she would find the strength to continue to run until the dawn came. As it always happened before, the slowly swirling mists parted to reveal the mysterious figure, but when she quickened her stride to give pursuit once more, the figure did not move. For the first time since she could remember having this dream, she saw herself stumble as she stopped in surprise. Seconds passed while she held her breath and stared ahead, then took one hesitant step forward. Again, the figure made no move to flee. Something else was different as well, her awareness barely registering the change. It was only a small thing, but its absence was palpable nonetheless—the horn had gone silent.

She felt an inexplicable and seismic shift in her entire existence, as if her whole life had somehow been leading up to this point in time. She couldn't understand how that would be possible; this was just a dream after all, wasn't it? She would wake up in her bed and go about her day as she had always done. Yet why did she feel like nothing would ever be the same again? She felt the sudden urge to scream at herself, to warn the woman that was her not to approach the figure. In her mind, she heard the desperate cry, but no sound reached her ears. Her mouth hung open, lungs and throat straining, but the silence of the forest was deafening. Unable to do anything but watch, she saw herself walk forward toward the unknown.

The figure was tall, much taller than she was, and appeared to be human in form, though there was definitely something strange about its head. What she took at first to be a cluster of low-hanging branches above where the stranger stood, slowly revealed itself instead to be a large and majestic rack of antlers. Her confusion grew and she paused once again, uncertainty and fear threatening to overcome her curiosity. Had she been chasing a stag this entire time? No, she could clearly see that the being stood upright and that its body resembled that of a person in every other way. She tried to convince herself that maybe the mists were just playing tricks on her but failed miserably. Swallowing her fear and desperate for answers, she resumed walking.

The woman was now only a few paces from the object of her eternal chase, and she could see that, like her, the stranger was naked. Though his lean, muscular, and obviously male body was quite hirsute, what caused her to stop in shock was his face, or rather, the lack thereof. Sitting atop an unusually long neck was a head shrouded in a darkness that obscured any discerning features except for the eyes. It was not the kind of darkness that came from standing in shadows—she could see the rest of the figure clearly enough—but rather an unnatural concealment that befuddled her senses. Confirming what she had gleaned before, a pair of large antlers gracefully crowned the figure's head, and from the darkness below that strange feature, a pair of eyes that lacked pupils glowed softly with a white light that came from within. From some distance away, her disembodied perception could only stare in wondrous disbelief and apprehension as the two of them stood facing each other in silence.

Time seemed to stop while she felt those eyes pierce through her flesh and down to the very essence of her soul. Though 'chaste' was a good word to characterize her as a person, as exposed as she was now—both physically and emotionally—she did not feel self-conscious or uncomfortable under that intense gaze. She couldn't explain how or why, but she knew that she was not in danger and that this being meant her no harm. As if to confirm that acceptance, the stranger wordlessly nodded his head, the antlers dipping down to acknowledge her unspoken trust. Then he turned and began to walk away. Without being prompted, she knew she was supposed to follow, and so she did.

The forest seemed to melt away as they walked, the world losing whatever small grasp on definition it previously had. There was still solid ground somewhere beneath her feet, and the omnipresent fog remained tinged with crimson, letting her know that Temeros still hovered somewhere above, even if unseen. Those two things gave her comfort, providing her with a link to her waking life no matter how far away that reality seemed now, but beyond that, she could see nothing else other than the figure ahead of her. Time—always a tenuous concept in her dreams—became utterly meaningless. She couldn't tell whether they were walking for minutes, hours, or days. There was no point of reference, and even her own thoughts were unreliable—one moment she felt she had been busy contemplating her entire life in minute detail, and in the next, it seemed as if they had merely taken a few steps. Whatever the case, the two of them eventually arrived at their destination.

The forest reappeared again, though something was different. A large dark shape loomed ahead, slowly emerging from the mists like a great beast surfacing from the depths of the ocean. As they got closer, she saw that it was a hill, covered in grass but devoid of trees. Before them, yellow light flickered from somewhere inside a doorway at the base of the mound, beckoning them down into the bowels of the world. The antlered man entered without hesitation, and she noted that despite the increase in illumination, she still couldn't see his features clearly. Strange symbols were carved into the wooden frame of the entrance, and as she passed under the threshold, she thought she caught a fleeting glimpse of a stag's head among them, but then she was through and into the passage beyond.

The short, tunnel-like passage opened into an oval chamber with a low ceiling. The stone blocks that formed the wall of the room seemed ancient and worn, and the air within had an earthy and musty smell to it. A series of small, shadowed alcoves were inset into the curved wall, but the glow from the single candle burning on top of a lone stone pedestal in the centre of the room was insufficient to fully reveal the dimly lit objects that rested within each nook. That fragment of her consciousness that remained strangely apart from her body left her with a nagging sensation of familiarity as if she'd seen this place before. However, the more she tried to recall, the more she got the distinct impression that she had repressed that memory for some reason. The realization flooded her with unease and doubt once again, but she'd come too far to turn back now.

The stranger walked to stand in front of the rough, altar-like stone in the centre of the hollow, then stopped and remained motionless, his back to her. Leaving the tunnel, she took a step into the chamber. Gathering her courage, she found her voice and uttered the first words to be spoken ever since she'd begun to have this dream.

"Who are you?"

Her voice sounded odd to her ears, as if it was coming from somewhere nearby and not quite from where she stood. She glanced about, uncertain, but saw no one else there. When she looked at the man once more however, she saw that he had somehow turned to face her without her noticing the motion at all. More startlingly, his hands now rested on the shoulders of a child who stood in front of him. The boy was no more than twelve or thirteen years of age, his perfectly shaped features and blue eyes framed by thick, dark hair. He was barefoot but wore a simple shirt and pair of slacks made of homespun cloth, and stared intensely at her, betraying no emotion on his expressionless face. She looked at the young man uncomprehendingly. Where had he come from? Who was he, and why was he here in her dream? Whatever sense she had felt she could try and glean from this dream had been completely undone by this new development, which admittedly was no stranger than the ones that had preceded it. She felt arrested by the boy's stare, and it took a great deal of effort to wrest her eyes away from his.

"Who are you?" she repeated her question to the strange being standing before her.

"Look within yourself if you wish to find me, for I have always been there." She heard the voice which—like her own—seemed to come from somewhere else. It sounded deep and authoritative as it resonated throughout the chamber, yet somehow gentle and nurturing at the same time.

"And the child?" she continued.

"He too you must find, and help," came the reply.

"Help? Help with what?"

"To make the choice when the time is upon him."

"Choice?" she felt like her head was spinning. "What choice? Could you please speak plainly?" she begged, her frustration beginning to build up.

"The choice that will either destroy or preserve all of existence as we know it," he said, his voice equally level and devoid of emotion, as if what he'd just said was as inconsequential a matter as commenting on the weather.

The words stunned her into silence, and she struggled to process what she'd just heard. The feeling of dizziness grew worse, and she felt her balance begin to falter. Her stomach twisted into knots, and nausea nearly overcame her when bile rose suddenly in her throat. Speaking became an effort. "This is a dream... none of it is real..."

"Yes, this is a dream, but here the line between your world and mine is thin. Here, I can set you on the path you have always been meant to walk," he soothed.

She felt like she was suffocating and fell to her knees, one hand clutching at her throat while the other lifted toward the stranger in mute supplication. The boy continued to look at her dispassionately, his blue eyes glittering in the candlelight.

"When?" was the only word she could manage.

"When all three watchers veil their faces, look for the boy where the druid's golden blade pierces the blue mantle of the world."

Her sight began to blur and dim. Some part of her became aware that all the alcoves had begun to glow brightly, as if a miniature sun was contained within each of the stone enclosures. The light was so painful that she had to squint to see, but the chamber became washed in white radiance, and all that she could make out was the outline of the stranger, his eyes glowing with an intensity that outshone the rest.

"...please..."

"I'm sorry, that is all I am permitted to reveal," he said, his voice growing even more distant than before. She thought she could detect a note of regret in his voice, but she couldn't be sure of anything at this point; only that her head felt like it was going to explode, while her insides threatened to spill themselves out onto the stone floor. The woman felt rather than saw the stranger and the child dissolve slowly and soundlessly in the light, leaving nothing behind but an afterimage in the flare of brilliance that washed over her with a blast of painful, searing heat.

She screamed as she sat up in bed, her eyes flying open, the disturbing dream over at last.

CHAPTER 4

The priest stood outside the house and waited patiently. Flynn's brothers had already departed earlier that morning after an emotional, tear-filled farewell, and were gone now, off to live with their Aunt Marissa. Joshua, Esmer, and Torbin were old enough already to work and earn their keep, while Cay and Lenn—recently apprenticed to their late father's trade—would be well taken care of. Flynn would not be joining them.

Inside his bedroom, the place where Susan had delivered him unto this world, the boy stared at the floor as he stood there motionless. A swirl of conflicting emotions raged inside his lithe frame, most of them having to do with loss, grief, and melancholy. Saying goodbye to his brothers was the most difficult thing he had ever done. His vision blurred briefly, and he swayed unsteadily on his feet, his small body shuddering while he tried and failed to stifle a trembling sob. The remembered sound of distant laughter in the house echoed in his ears; voices belonging to his brothers as they boisterously played in that very room; the enticing sounds coming from the kitchen when his mom prepared a delicious breakfast; the gruff tone of his father's voice warning them to get dressed and wash up for school. All sensations of a life that was fading before his very eyes—the memories and happiness of an innocent childhood cut short by tragedy. Unable to stop himself, and not really caring to, Flynn sat slowly on the floor and began to cry.

He wasn't sure how much time had passed, and he didn't care. He knew the man was waiting outside, but he wasn't quite ready to leave yet. Looking around the room for the hundredth time, he rubbed at his red eyes and finally willed himself to get up. A small bundle lay on the bed, the modest amount of clothes that he would be allowed to bring. Forcing one foot in front of the other, he walked to the bed and carefully placed the clothes inside a cloth shoulder bag, but before he picked it up, he turned to the small wooden trunk in a corner of the room. His heart threatening to overcome him with sadness once more, Flynn opened the container's lid and felt his eyes watering again as he looked at the contents. His brothers hadn't taken much, too old now to play with the children's toys their father had carved for them. Flynn had been told to leave such things behind, but he reached in on an impulse and slowly drew out his favourite: an armoured knight with raised sword and holding a shield, meticulously and lovingly whittled out of aspen wood from the trees that grew outside the city.

When his fingers touched the wood, his blue-eyed gaze slowly took in the details of the figurine, and Flynn saw himself as a tiny child running through the forest, his brothers behind him, searching for pieces of wood of the right size and shape for their father to carve. In a clearing not far from them, their parents busily laid out the picnic fare they had brought for the afternoon. The memory was so vivid that Flynn could feel the sunshine on his face, the rich smell of the trees, meadow grass, and blooming flowers in the air, along with the melodious birdsong that trilled in the breeze. Without realizing he had shut his eyes, he opened them with a start, his grip on the knight so tight and fierce that he was in danger of snapping the fragile arms and sword. For a moment, he'd imagined that the figure represented his father, and he had wanted the wood to break. Relaxing his hand, he resolutely closed the trunk, walked back to the bag, and carefully placed the figurine inside. Picking up his meagre belongings, Flynn left the room at last. As he passed the stairway leading up to Susan and Samuel's bedroom, the boy paused briefly and glanced upward, fighting the urge to go upstairs one final time. No, he resisted, knowing it was time to go, and then walked outside.

Flynn closed the door to the house where he'd lived his entire short life, took a step back, and mouthed a silent farewell to the place that had been the centre of his small universe. A slight motion to his left drew his attention and he saw the grey tabby from the alleyway staring curiously at him. Flynn nodded solemnly to his old foe, and in response, the cat licked the back of one paw several times before retreating into the shadows behind the house. That last ritual performed, the boy turned to look at the man standing nearby, his young face betraying no emotion.

This was not the same priest that had come before. In the faraway land of his birth, the man's features would have been considered completely unremarkable and commonplace, the sort of individual one forgot almost immediately after meeting them. His height was average, his build stout but not overly so, and a trimmed fringe of curly, greying black hair that circled a balding pate. Dark brown eyes looked down at the boy from a round and gentle face, a smile tinged with sadness turning the corners of his broad lips upward. Yet it was the colour of his skin—a rich, nutty brown—that left Flynn speechless. He'd never seen anyone of that colour before, and he marvelled at how beautifully it gleamed when it caught the rays of the sun just so. Past the sixth decade of his life now, the man was clad in the white robes of his faith, the blue trim on the sleeves and collar denoting his middling rank, a common colour within the church hierarchy. Around his neck, a silver medallion on a chain bore a pair of grey eyes inside of a blue starburst—the symbol of the Overgod, Janus.

"Hello, child," the man spoke, his voice deep, clear, and as mild as his demeanour. "My name is Brother Owen. I've come to take you to the new place where you will be living from now on." When the boy did not move, the priest added, "When you're ready, of course."

Flynn regarded the man silently. He was too young to have an opinion on the church of the Overgod, or any other faith for that matter. Like the majority of the citizens of Corazan, his parents had not regularly attended mass or surrounded themselves with the trappings of religion. They had nevertheless observed the holy days, especially at Yule time, and performed the perfunctory everyday rituals, such as invoking the blessings of Janus before the partaking of a meal or asking for his watchful protection before going to sleep. What little education Samuel and Susan Castellar had been able to afford to give to their children was imparted by the Loremasters, a sect devoted to yet another faith. The patron of arts and knowledge, Canamur was one of a collection of lesser deities venerated by human civilization on Akar, nearly all of which were subservient to the church of the Overgod. Flynn had paid little attention to such theological nuances and hierarchies, more interested in the tales of ancient battles fought by great heroes in far-off lands.

Still, he did know that the Janusians tended to an orphanage in Corazan as part of their diverse duties in the city, and he correctly suspected that's where the priest was going to take him. It had always been a strange thought to Flynn—the concept of children without parents to look after them—and now he found himself to be just one such. While he mused on what life in such a place would be like, Brother Owen held out his hand, his smile welcoming. Flynn was not generally shy around strangers, but that didn't mean he wasn't cautious, just as his mother had taught him to be, yet something about this man's demeanour and presence immediately put him at ease. He couldn't quite put his finger on why, but the boy somehow instinctively knew he could trust this priest. Taking a few steps forward, he reached out his own small hand and accepted the man's gentle grip. Without further word or delay, the two began to walk, leaving the Castellar home behind them, silent and empty.

The cleric set a leisurely pace so as to allow his young charge some time to process all that was happening before they reached their destination. As an orphan himself, Brother Owen knew what Flynn must be feeling, and so he kept to himself, knowing the child would speak when he was ready to and no sooner. Whenever they passed others on the streets, the citizenry of Corazan never failed to show their deference to the priest with a slight nod of the head, even if most did not meet his gaze or return his smile. He could only sigh in resignation at this for he well knew the source of their barely concealed resentment. Nevertheless, determined to not let his frustration rise to the surface, he maintained his outward appearance of pleasantness and pressed on.

"Why are people looking at us in a funny way?" Flynn couldn't help asking, observant and blunt in a way that only a child could be.

"They are?" Brother Owen arched his eyebrows in mock surprise as he looked down at the boy. "I hadn't noticed."

Sensing the older man was playing with him, Flynn tried another topic. "Why can't I stay with my brothers?"

"Your brothers are all of an age where they can already take care of themselves with very little supervision. As such, they will not prove to be an undue burden on your widowed aunt, who has children of her own to mind. In your case, it was decided that the church would look after you until such time as you reach that same age," the priest explained patiently.

Flynn had heard this before, on the night that other priest and his Aunt Marissa had come to his house. "Yes, but who decided this?" he continued, still uncomprehending of how and why grownups did things a certain way.

"My superiors," Brother Owen replied, raising one arm to point ahead.

Flynn's eyes lingered briefly on the man, then turned to look in the direction the other was indicating. The street that they were on was situated on a small hill, affording them a great view of the sprawling city below. As the capital city of the Kingdom of Rohne, Corazan was the largest urban centre in the realm, home to thousands of souls dwelling within its tall walls. Criss-crossed by a host of stone bridges like the one they were now approaching, the Arnd River wound its way through the metropolis like a languid snake. In the hazy distance beyond, above the streets and tightly packed buildings, rose another, much taller hill, the heights topped by the imposing battlements and soaring white towers of King Aldrik's castle, the third of his name. There, he could just barely make out a multitude of many-coloured pennants that fluttered in the breeze, with the noon sun shining dazzlingly off burnished gold roofs. Near the bottom of the hill, no less magnificent in size and construction than the royal dwelling above, stood the beautiful cathedral of the Overgod, its curving arches, flying buttresses, and narrow spires a marvellous feat of ingenious architecture. Flynn knew that it was the church the priest was pointing at, not the castle above.

Crossing the bridge over to the eastern side of the city, Flynn indulged his curiosity by peering over the railing at the river passing below on its way south to the not-too distant sea. Docks and wharves of different sizes dotted both shores beyond the bridge and away from the city, as vessels ranging from tiny fishing boats to medium-sized caravels and even larger, three-mast galleons, plied the wide river in pursuit of their various trades. Seagulls and other aquatic fowl drifted lazily in the air above or bobbed in the calm waters below, their calls mingling with the sounds of daily life all around. The strong breeze blowing from the south carried with it the distinctive tang of salt and Flynn fondly recalled how he had always wanted his father to take him to look upon the ocean one day. The thought of Samuel struck him hard, and he struggled to push the painful memory and feelings of angry betrayal aside. He had decided that he would not let the priest see any weakness, for the sooner he acted like a grownup, the faster they would let him go back to his brothers. Sighing heavily, Flynn composed himself, squared his shoulders and turned from the railing to walk back to the waiting priest. Together, they walked on.

"Brother Owen?" Flynn spoke up after walking in silence for a long time.

"Yes?" the priest smiled, gratified to hear the boy use his name for the first time. The pair was nearing their destination, and Flynn's burning curiosity finally overcame his reticence to talk.

"Why is your skin so dark? I've never seen a person of your colour before and I've been to every part of the city." It was a reasonable enough question, one that might easily be expected from a child of this age. It didn't surprise or offend the cleric at all, but it did bring with it a sad reminder of how fleeting the innocence of youth really was. Alas, children couldn't be protected forever, and soon they would have to make their own judgments in life, free of the adult influences that helped shape the person they would one day become. In the teachings of Janus, it was written that individuals were not the mere product of their upbringing, but ultimately reflections of their own choices as well, and this was a lesson that Brother Owen took to heart. The face he saw when he looked in a mirror was not the total sum of his being.

"The world is much bigger than just this city, you know," he jested in response to the boy's question.

"Oh, I know that," Flynn said quickly, not wanting the man to think he was some kind of ignorant bumpkin. "My dad once took me and my brothers to visit some relatives in Jerothos, and I've learned about other faraway lands to the north, like Lundia, Firien, and even Avamor," he said proudly. Jerothos was a large Rohnian town, just less than fifty miles north of Corazan, but to a young boy of twelve, it may as well be half a world away. Brother Owen arched his eyebrows and nodded sagely to show how impressed he was by Flynn's geographical knowledge, which made the boy feel thoroughly pleased with himself. "Are you from one of those places? There's lots of Lundians here in Corazan, and they look just like us, and my dad said that we are all part Avamori here in Rohne—whatever that means—so I think they look the same too, which means that you aren't one—Lundian or Avamori—I mean, so... that is..." he stopped, half confused. "Will you just tell me, please?"

For someone that had been so quiet for the majority of their journey to the church, the boy had suddenly become very talkative. Brother Owen could only assume that this was a hopeful glimpse of the boy's normal self, and he took it as an encouraging sign that Flynn was making an attempt to distract himself from dark thoughts about the recent tragedy that had upended his young life. Children could be resilient in ways that often surprised adults, and though Brother Owen knew from personal experience that the process would be long and difficult, he knew he should do what he could to nurture and support the boy's self-defence mechanism. The priest laughed as they turned one last corner and walked up the wide street toward the ornate bronze gates at the far end, beyond which lay the grounds of the Janusian church.

"Alright, young man, no need to get upset," Brother Owen held up his hands in mock defense. "I come from a land very far from here called Laenis," he said, solemnly placing one hand over his heart and dipping his head slightly forward while they continued walking.

'Laenis'—Flynn silently mouthed the unfamiliar word a couple of times, then looked askance at the priest. "Is that even a real place? How come I've never heard of it?" he stated, clearly skeptical of this outlandish claim. He was well acquainted with the annoying habit that adults had of sometimes telling harmless lies as a way to amuse themselves at the expense of gullible children. Well, he decided he was going to have none of it. "I thought Janusians were supposed to be nice and never lie," he accused with a slight pout, convinced the man was making fun of him. Steps away from the gates, Brother Owen came to a stop, bunched the lower half of his long robes in one hand, bent his knees slightly, and lowered himself carefully so that his dark eyes could be level with Flynn's. The boy crossed his arms and looked away, annoyed and defiant, but when the priest did not budge and continued to stare at him patiently, Flynn reluctantly turned his head to look into those clear brown orbs.

"Flynn, some Janusians are nicer than others, and this one does not lie—not to a child," the priest said with a calm, kind sincerity that Flynn found impossible to ignore. "The name given to me by my parents is E'on Abdalla, and the land of my birth is far to the south of here, a few weeks' journey by ship beyond what you call the Storm Sea. There, everyone looks just like me," he said with a wink, but the warm gesture was a deliberate way for him to keep the full weight of a personally painful memory from his expression. "When I was just a little bit older than you, explorers on great ships appeared on our shores one day. They were strange beings that we'd never seen before, men with the heads of bulls—those you know as 'Golians'. At first, they seemed friendly, wanting only to draw maps of our coasts and rivers, all the while looking for things that they could bring back to their faraway home, like fruit, spices, and the yellow metal called gold that was found in abundance in our hills and mountain streams. But things soon changed. More and more of the bull-men began to arrive, and this time they brought captive humans with them to do their work, men whose skin was lighter than ours—skin like yours. Before long, even these men were not enough, so the Golians turned to us. Friendship and trade ceased, and warfare, bloody and violent, took their place. Only they did not kill; they stole us away instead—some to labour there by force, but mostly to bring back to their land," Brother Owen told the story, fighting hard to maintain a neutral tone in his voice despite the emotions he was feeling.

The priest was keenly aware of how unfair it was to burden the poor, recently orphaned boy with this heavy account of his own tragic tale, but what he saw when he looked into Flynn's blue eyes as he went on was not confusion, revulsion, or even fear, but compassion and a deep sense of empathy. Brother Owen didn't know if his own parents were alive or not after all these years, but he'd felt himself an orphan immediately upon being ripped away from them and brought across the sea in iron chains. The clergyman was temporarily overcome with shame, a sensation that he thought he'd long ago rid himself of. He was proud of his heritage, and of having had the courage and mettle needed to survive a long sequence of difficult events before he could be who he was today, but he would always be surrounded by subtle reminders that he was different, such as the way some of the citizens of this very city he'd called home for many years still looked at him. Yet it was what he saw in this young man's eyes that gave him hope and faith in the promise that people could be better than that.

"My work here at the orphanage is the least I can do to give lost and abandoned children a sense of family and belonging, something that was taken from me, just as it was from you," the priest finished, fighting hard to hold back the tears that threatened to spill forth. Flynn looked at him in awkward silence, unsure of what to say. He decided he liked this man and wanted to know more of his story, even if it was scary, but he sensed that perhaps further questions should wait. Well, maybe just one more couldn't hurt.

"Why did you change your name? I like E'on."

Brother Owen grinned from ear to ear and let out a heartfelt laugh, feeling all the pent-up emotion slowly ebb from him. Leave it to a child to find the simplest way to defuse a charged moment. "The Golians never really bothered to use my name, but when I eventually came to Rohne, the folks here had trouble pronouncing it. After a time, I simply changed it to something simpler and easier for them to use, and so now I am Owen."

"Doesn't sound like they tried very hard," Flynn said, frowning in disapproval.

The priest chuckled at that. "No, I don't think they did. Now, would you help an old man straighten up? My back isn't what it used to be," he asked, holding one arm out. Flynn promptly took it and placed the man's hand on one of his shoulders, providing support as Brother Owen straightened his knees and stood up. Then he took the priest's hand in his own, and together they walked through the open gates.

CHAPTER 5

Vᴜʀᴀx ᴏᴘᴇɴᴇᴅ ʜɪs ᴇʏᴇs slowly, blinking a few times to adjust to the light intruding upon the soothing darkness. It took a few seconds for the bright glow in front of him to come into focus, but the first thing that he saw as he stared straight up caused his heart to sink with dismay. The venting hole in the tent's roof was all too familiar, a sight that had greeted him every morning for as far back as he cared to remember. He closed his eyes again and heaved a deep sigh as he lay there on his old blanket. It had all been a dream then, he thought to himself, a foolish dream of sweet but momentary freedom and satisfying vengeance. The sun was already high, and he had missed his time to get up for another day of work, but he didn't care. Let them come for him. The feeling of loss and bitterness inside were so great that he did not want to face another waking day in this world, and thus he tried to force himself to go back to sleep again to try and recapture that wonderful dream. He hoped to never wake up again.

As he shifted slightly, he felt something gripped tightly in one hand. The objects were unfamiliar, and he did not understand at first what it was that he held. Without opening his eyes, he moved the items slightly between his palm and fingers, feeling three distinct metallic bands—Aros' horn rings. The sudden realization fell upon him like a bucket of ice-cold water, and his eyes flew open when he sat up suddenly. Several things become apparent all at once: it was not his tent that he was lying in; his body was covered with bandages and ointments; and the abruptness of his movement caused no small amount of pain to explode in his head, which he only noticed now, was bandaged as well. More importantly however, was the fact that the three hoops in his hand were indeed real.

The Minotaur took some time to collect his thoughts and adjust his brain to this strange new reality. The events that he remembered had been real then, something that was very solidly confirmed by the fact that he was no longer manacled. Not only had all those things happened then, but he had survived somehow, though he remembered nothing past the instant he'd allowed the blood rage to overtake him. Only once before in his life had he discovered that he could do such a thing—the fires of rage and fury consuming him and ripping apart every last shred of self-control the day he and his family had been taken into captivity. When he had regained his senses the next day, his father had told him that some few Golian warriors possessed the ability to lose themselves in a deep battle frenzy, where nothing else mattered but the need to slake their thirst for their enemy's blood. For the damage he had caused that day, his captors had punished him severely. So appalled was he when shown the men he had killed and the horrible manner of their deaths that he swore to himself to never let it happen again. It was a foolish promise, made by a foolish young bull many years ago, one who had little to no experience of this world and the horrors that were to come. That promise was broken now, but the only regret Vurax felt was that he had not done it sooner.

Glancing at his dressings, he wondered why he did not feel more pain than the one pounding in his head, which was thankfully already subsiding. He gingerly tried to get up and found that he could do so without problem, his arms and legs supporting his great weight without much effort. There was some stiffness, to be sure, but the Minotaur felt surprisingly good considering what he had gone through. Whatever explanation there was for what was going on, he concluded he wasn't going to get any answers by staying in the tent. Stepping outside into the heat of the day, Vurax brought one arm up to shade his eyes from the glaring light of the sun before looking around.

"Finally up, are you?" came the voice to his left. Turning toward its source, Vurax saw the other Golian standing next to the tent flap, one hand resting on the rim of a large rectangular shield that rested upright on the ground, the other holding a tall spear at attention. The Minotaur wore banded mail armour over a red tunic, the sturdy steel bands polished to such a mirror-like finish that Vurax had to squint to look at him, so brightly did the sun reflect off the metal. On his horned head, the Golian Legionnaire wore a steel helm with a lion's head crest, ornamented cheek guards, and red plume that ran transversely from one side to the other, marking him as a centurion. A pair of sturdy, hard-soled leather sandals laced halfway up his calves completed the ensemble.

When Vurax did not respond right away, the soldier continued, "If you're feeling well enough to take a walk, the tribune would like to have a word with you."

It took Vurax several moments to realize the soldier had been speaking to him in the native tongue of the Minotaurs. He understood it of course, but it had been a very long time since he'd heard it spoken or uttered it himself, for that matter. The Sarmakanites discouraged all slaves from speaking in anything other than the common tongue of men, and reminders of that rule often came at the end of a whip. While the barbarians spoke their own dialect amongst themselves, they communicated with foreign slaves by using their own bastardized rudiments of the common tongue spoken universally through all the lands that had once been under the sway of the Avamori Imperium in ages past. To hear the Minotaur language spoken so naturally again felt alien and unsettling, and even the sight of one of his countrymen was strange to him. He despised humans, but having spent so long among them, he suddenly felt uneasy and self-conscious in the presence of his own people. Shoving his apprehension aside, he nodded his assent to the centurion.

As they walked through the camp of his former masters, Vurax dispassionately took in the brutal and swift efficiency with which the Golian soldiers went about their duty. Many of the tents and other temporary structures of the nomadic camp of Ikut had been completely razed, and the remainder were even now being taken apart. The materials were then piled into evenly spaced areas and set ablaze, joining the dozens of other columns of thick and heavy black smoke already rising into the sky. In the large, corralled area where the Sarmakanites normally kept their horses, the Minotaur saw a crowd of human women and children; all those who had failed to flee or had been caught while trying to do so. Golian soldiers moved among them, binding their wrists and ankles with iron manacles, and organizing them into orderly lines for marching. Other than a few men that were already slaves, Vurax saw no able-bodied Sarmakanite males among them, but a glance toward the southern end of the camp and the multitude of carrion-feeding birds circling the area quickly confirmed their fate for him.

The irony he witnessed in the reversal of fortune of the people that had enslaved him for years was not lost on him. Yet for some reason that he could not discern, the thought gave him no comfort or sense of satisfaction. The practice of slavery was very much alive and well in the Golian Empire, and though he had never spared it a thought when he lived there, the knowledge and first-hand experience of the kind of life that awaited these people turned his stomach. Certainly, he knew that—at least in most cases—his people treated their slaves with more care and dignity than the Sarmakanites did, but a life of bondage and labour was something he could not now contemplate or wish upon anyone else, regardless of race. As they passed the line of dirty, weeping human faces, most cast their eyes down at the ground, avoiding his stare. There was one among them that did not do so, and Vurax did not fail to notice the slave who had helped him break his bonds at the forge. The Minotaur felt an unfamiliar pang of sorrow for the fate of the man, wishing that the slave had heeded his advice to escape. Perhaps the human had tried and failed. It didn't matter now. The man's expression was unreadable but when he saw the regret in Vurax's eyes, he smiled faintly and nodded his head once. The Minotaur returned the gesture by lifting the golden bands he held and touching them to his heart. Perhaps some humans were worthy of respect after all, he considered. He kept walking and never saw the man again, though he would never forget him.

The pair of Minotaurs passed a few more blazing bonfires, their heat adding to the already barely tolerable high temperature of the day. Not for the first time, Vurax could not hide his admiration for the soldier marching beside him and all others he saw, stoically carrying out their orders in their heavy armour. The training regimen and conditioning of the Imperial Golian Legions was legendary, but to see it on full display like this was something else. After a while, they arrived before a large square tent, the Golian design and craftsmanship starkly distinguishing it from everything else around. Two legionnaires stood guard before the closed flap; their spears crossed over the opening. When Vurax's companion approached however, the guards saluted and moved the weapons out of the way.

"Wait here," the centurion said before entering the tent. Vurax complied, realizing he had involuntarily flinched when he'd heard the command. The embarrassment he felt at the reaction led him to glance furtively at the two guards to see if they had noticed, but the two continued to stare ahead, seemingly oblivious to his presence. Weakness and submissiveness were not traits to be encouraged in Golian society, and while he did not consider himself to be either, he had learned some harsh lessons on how one's survival was more important than foolish pride. As he ruminated on that knowledge and how it might impact his life to come, he also recognized that nothing was a given. He had no idea why these soldiers were here or what they would do with him. That he was still alive was a good first step, however.

"The tribune will see you now," the centurion that had accompanied him returned and nodded toward the tent. Vurax stepped into the spacious interior, glancing briefly about as he did so. The contents of the tent were sparse and functional, comfort being a luxury that all officers and soldiers alike learned to live without during a campaign. Lit by oil lamps hanging from the tent's supporting poles, the centre of the space was dominated by a large rectangular table that sat on a rug covering the dirt floor. Three Golian officers spoke in low tones while they pored over a map on the table, with several metal figures cast to resemble miniature soldiers resting in different areas of its surface. Vurax marvelled at the exquisite detail of the map, deducing that it was a representation of the steppes of Sarmakan, judging by the prevalence of red and brown terrain features. At one edge of the map, a dark line of mountain peaks separated the red from swaths of green beyond. That way lay the homeland he barely remembered.

The three officers continued to ignore him as they discussed troop movements and supply lines. He couldn't make out all that they said, but enough to understand that out of the ten cohorts that normally made up a Golian Legion of five thousand soldiers in war time, only two were present here at camp. That would make sense, he thought, as a thousand legionnaires had been more than sufficient to wipe out nearly the entire barbarian tribe in one engagement. To think there were eight other cohorts represented on the map and where they might be piqued his curiosity to no end, but he wisely decided to remain silent as the three bulls continued for what seemed like an eternity. At his side, his escort remained unperturbed and at attention. Finally, two of the officers saluted the third and filed out of the tent without sparing the Golian standing there a mere glance. Vurax watched them go then looked back to the one whom he assumed was the tribune.

Typical for his position, the Golian Tribune was still fairly young, likely not more than a decade or two at most past Vurax's own age of forty years. A long-lived race, most Minotaurs did not begin military service until their third decade, the time at which they entered adulthood. Had he not been captured by the Sarmakanites when he was but twenty-two, he would likely be serving out his compulsory draft right now, perhaps even in this very legion cohort itself. Tribunes often came from wealthy and privileged families, aspiring to become Legion Legates one day, or perhaps even attain the lofty position of senator. Whatever the case was with this one, Golians placed a high importance on observing formalities, and thus Vurax raised one fist to his bandaged chest and thumped it once in the proper salute. The tribune regarded him coolly, then acknowledged the gesture with a nod as he sat down in a field chair behind him. His armour, resplendent and spotless, practically glowed in the light of the lamps, the golden breastplate with its carved lion's head mirroring those he'd seen on the legionnaires' helms and battle standards.

"I am Herem Jalx, commander of the third and fourth cohorts of the Eighth Legion. What is your name?" the officer spoke at last, his rumbling voice sounding like one who was accustomed to shouting orders.

"I am Vurax," he replied, offering nothing else. The tribune leaned back in his seat, rested his elbows on the arms of the chair and slowly stroked the dark hair of his chin with one hand.

"Just Vurax?" he remarked, arching one brow. "What is your family name?"

Vurax hesitated and looked down and away. While he did so, Jalx shifted his gaze to focus more intently on the former slave's horn rings. Whatever it was that the tribune saw there, it was enough for him to cast a furtive glance over his own shoulder at something unseen behind him. When he looked at Vurax once more, the other was still staring uncomfortably at the floor of the tent.

"My family name was dishonoured the day we were taken captive. It is no longer worthy of being uttered," Vurax responded at last. While his voice did not waver, his closed fist tightened ever so slightly. The tribune again nodded his approval at the statement, but his keen eyes did not miss the almost imperceptible shift in the other's body and the glint of gold in that fist. He looked pointedly at Vurax's hand.

"Those horn rings you carry—someone close to you, I presume?" Vurax nodded his head in agreement once, but the look in his eyes convinced Jalx not to press the issue further. "You fought well yesterday—undisciplined, wild, dangerous, but effective and deadly, nonetheless. Where did you learn to fight like that, and how long have you felt the blood rage?"

Yesterday? Vurax was convinced he'd been unconscious for several days at least, judging by the severity of his wounds compared to how little they bothered him now. He was so distracted by this realization that he forgot to answer the tribune's question. When Jalx cleared his throat to prompt him, he stammered a reply. "I...at a very young age, sir," he managed. "I don't recall exactly when." That was a lie, but he moved quickly past it. "I've only lost myself to it once before...before yesterday, that is. As for my skill in battle—" he paused, grimacing at the unpleasant memories, "—well, there are only two ways out of the fighting pits."

"I see," the tribune mused. "The blood rage is a rare gift, or even a curse, some would say. Something that is best suited to fighting alone, as I've heard tell it can be difficult to distinguish friend from foe, no?"

Vurax understood what Jalx was driving at. He felt a warm flush come over his skin and prepared himself for the worse. "Sir, if I've—"

"Relax, my friend," the tribune smiled for the first time, "you did not cause harm to any of my soldiers, though there were some tense and dangerous moments as they attempted to subdue you before you bled out on the battlefield. In fact, the centurion here affirms your head is nearly as hard as his shield. Luckily for everyone involved, the shield proved harder." Vurax turned to regard the Golian at his side. The other met his gaze, then glanced meaningfully at the upper rim of his rectangular shield, the dented metal reminding Vurax of the pain he still felt in his head. "I know you have questions, so go ahead and ask," Jalx continued.

Knowing he likely wouldn't get another opportunity to address the tribune, Vurax plunged in. "How am I still alive?" he asked bluntly.

"A good question," Jalx paused as if to consider his next words. "You suffered wounds fatal enough to down five of my best fighters combined. I've heard the blood rage can make someone fight on far beyond the limits of mortal endurance, feeling no pain or fatigue. When it leaves you, however..." he paused again. "Well, it seems we got to you just in time. We brought you to the Horn of Zarvon, who tended to your wounds and brought you back from the brink."

Vurax swallowed dryly. A Horn of Zarvon. He shouldn't be surprised a tribune would have the services of a priest at his disposal, but to call on the divine favour of Zarvon, the god of the Golians, was no small task. Such rare privilege would normally be reserved for the tribune and his highest-ranking officers, not wasted on a mere commoner such as himself. That puzzle aside though, he felt more than a little conflicted about what he'd just been told. All Golians were taught to revere the mighty and terrible Zarvon, the stern and unforgiving father of the Minotaur race. As with all things, some were more fervent and devout in this belief than others, and Vurax did not entirely trust in the existence of this almighty being. After years of captivity, hardship, and tragic loss, those harsh trials had soured him on the concept of faith and hope that some remote and uncaring celestial force would take notice of his whispered pleas for deliverance. After a time, he had simply stopped wasting his time and breath pleading.

"The confusion in your face is impossible to ignore," the tribune noted. "I can guess what you are thinking, and my response to you is this: you are the reason we are here, to put it in simple terms." When Vurax couldn't help himself and his jaw dropped open in disbelief, Jalx laughed. "Oh, not *you* specifically, but rather what you represent—Golian citizens that have been forcefully taken from our lands and enslaved by these vermin." Vurax recovered from his surprise and composed himself as Jalx went on. "This affront has gone on long enough and though there has been little appetite in the senate to act in the past, things have changed of late. You see, when you only show weakness and indecision, your enemies grow bolder and contemptuous as a result, and when the northern province begins to withhold food shipments to the capital in protest against unanswered raids, those in power begin to feel uncomfortable pressure to take action. There are few things in this world more frightening than an angry mob; fewer still that are more 'persuasive' than when said mob is also hungry."

Jalx paused and poured himself a cup of wine from a brass decanter. He poured a second cup and held it up in Vurax's direction. "Here, take it." Vurax didn't have a taste for wine, having tried it only once or twice in his youth, but did not feel it would be wise to refuse the offering. He walked around the map table and took the cup from the tribune. "To your freedom, your health, and that of our dear emperor, by whose direct command we choke daily on the damned dust of this forsaken land." He intoned with a smirk and raised his cup, downing the contents of the cup in one motion. Vurax did the same. "You are the ultimate prize of our campaign here, living proof that an effort is being made to free the suffering citizens of Gol, taken unjustly against their will. And you wonder why a Horn of Zarvon would deign to heal you? Well, just think how the masses will cheer with joy when you are paraded down the streets of the capital for all to see." Jalx poured himself another cup of wine while Vurax allowed the words to sink in.

Eighteen years. A father, a mother, a brother, and who knows how many other Golian lives and families destroyed before and after that of his own. Yet, only when their grip on power had been threatened had the bureaucrats been moved to action. It wasn't because they cared about the lives of those who had been taken; it was because they were in danger of being overthrown. Vurax didn't know who was worse: Sarmakanite slavers or Golian senators. Outwardly, he betrayed no hint of emotion, but inwardly he seethed with anger. He didn't blame the tribune—these military types were bred and trained to be unswervingly loyal and to follow orders unquestioningly. Still, personal opinions were every Golian's right, and the disdain in Jalx's tone was self-evident. He didn't know if Jalx had designs on a senate seat, but if his first impressions were right, he had a feeling it wouldn't hurt to have more Golians like this tribune making decisions. The emperor might be the supreme leader of Gol, but when unified with one voice, the senate wielded just as much power.

While Jalx appeared lost in thought, Vurax took the opportunity to glance at the map again, noticing for the first time that six of the cast metal figurines representing the Golian cohorts were arrayed in a semi-circle before a singular feature in the centre of the map—a broad plateau that rose above the surrounding plains, crowned by a lone peak at the back. Fed by a stream from above, a large lake rested at the foot of the plateau and a single word below it read 'Bantar.' When the remaining four cohorts arrived, the entire area south of the plateau and lake would be effectively surrounded. He knew of Bantar, of course, the only permanent settlement to be found in all of Sarmakan.

The city—if such a label could be loosely applied to the sprawling collection of thousands of adobe huts and tents squatting around the southern base of the highland—was equal parts holy site and trading hub. It was the single place in this vast land where the various tribes could gather to conduct commerce, celebrate festivals, and observe religious rituals without fear of violence. In Bantar, all rivalries were set aside by strict and ancient laws. Vurax had been there several times, as Urkan-Kor brought his tribe there annually. Aside from his own family, it was the only other time he had caught a glimpse of other Golians before the events of the last two days. Of course, those other Minotaurs had been slaves like him, and he had not been permitted to approach them, but the significance of their presence there helped explain why the entirety of the Eighth Legion was converging on the area.

Jalx watched Vurax in silence while the other studied the map with interest. "Does the emperor mean to conquer Sarmakan?" the former slave asked, not understanding why such a thing would even be considered or whether it was even possible.

"Conquer?" Jalx sounded amused. "No, there's nothing much here beyond dirt and goat dung, and the emperor has no interest in either. We'll be outside Bantar in three weeks' time, and then we can finish this once and for all. I'm looking forward to leaving this blasted wasteland and returning home. With most of the wandering tribes already eradicated, that rat's nest of theirs won't have many bodies left with which to defend itself. The legate is going to make sure they never come south again."

Three weeks. Vurax thought about that for a second, judging the distance from their current position in Ikut and back to Gol to be twice as long at the rate an army could march. He feared he might be overstepping his bounds, but his curiosity got the better of him and he decided to test the tribune's unusual willingness to share information with someone of his insignificant standing. "But this damned heat, and the water needed for so many soldiers. How is this—?"

"Possible?" Jalx finished the question. By way of an answer, the officer turned his head to one side and glanced at something behind him. At the back of the tent, the shadows that danced in the flickering light of the oil lamps shifted as a figure stepped forward. Vurax was startled and with good cause, as he could have sworn there had been no one else present in the tent this entire time. Unlike the weak eyes of humans, a Minotaur's vision was like that of a cat's, able to see well enough even in the gloomiest of nights. Other than himself, the tribune, and the centurion behind him, they had been alone. Or had they? The presence stopped behind Jalx, taller than the tallest Golian Vurax had ever seen. It wore a voluminous black robe made of the finest silk; the face hidden within the dark depths of a large hood. Horns swept out to either side of the garment, curved gracefully downward, and inscribed with strange symbols and runes in a language he did not recognize. The figure's hands were clasped together in front of it, and the white hair—that rarest of colours among Minotaurs—confirmed to him that he stood in the presence of a Kal-dkar, one of the feared and mysterious War-mages.

The Kal-dkar was one of a small handful of ancient, magical sects existing throughout Akar. Its creation lost in the dim recesses of time and memory, the presence of the Kal-dkar to this day in the Golian Empire was both an anachronism and an anomaly. A practical people, the Golians did not particularly care for magic, nor did they encourage its use in their society, although they certainly acknowledged its existence. Ignoring it was not difficult however, since for some reason that even the wisest scholars among them could not explain, only those rare few born with completely white hair were somehow gifted with the ability to master the arcane energies that permeated the world, and able to use that talent to bend such forces to their will. Over the centuries, the number of white-haired Golian children being born continued to decline inexplicably, and the event was so infrequent now that whenever such a birth occurred, the Kal-dkar immediately appeared out of nowhere and took the infant with them to be brought up under their guidance and teachings. While the practice appeared strange and cruel on the surface, the parents of such individuals learned to accept that their child had been born to a greater destiny and surrendered the newborn peacefully.

So few were their numbers rumoured to be today, that the emperor and the senate used the Kal-dkar only sparingly and reluctantly. As a nation with a fiercely proud and exceptional martial tradition, the Golians did not need to depend on War-mages to win their battles for them as some other cultures might, but sometimes there were obstacles that could give even the most valorous legions reason for pause. Vurax understood now how the two cohorts of the Eighth had not only managed to approach the camp undetected until such time as it was too late for the entire tribe to flee, but also how its legionnaires were seemingly unhampered by the extreme temperatures of this land. The situation in the capital must be dire indeed if members of the Kal-dkar had been sent to render their aid to the Eighth Legion. Recalling the tribune's words earlier, he realized what the other had meant by claiming the Sarmakanites would never come south again—once the dread power of the Kal-dkar was brought to bear against Bantar, there wouldn't be a single living thing left behind.

Vurax felt the War-mage's unseen eyes upon him, the sensation not unlike that of thousands of insects crawling all over his hair and burrowing their way down into his skin. The urge to scratch was nearly unbearable but he told himself that it was all in his mind and squeezed down hard on the golden bands in his hand to concentrate on not moving. Then he felt it—another consciousness within his own. The experience was brief and over before he could react, but while it was there, he had felt a probing presence; cold and unemotional, searching, and relentless.

"He approves," the voice that came from within the hood was distinctly female, though it sounded distorted—hollow, and metallic-like. Was the Kal-dkar wearing some kind of mask under that cowl?

"Don't do that again," Vurax growled dangerously. The violation of his thoughts felt worse than any physical humiliation he had been subjected to during his life as a slave. The onset of the blood rage was so violent and sudden that it took every ounce of his control to hold the primal impulse in check. The War-mage didn't move a muscle and continued to stand there impassively, seemingly unconcerned by the threat, but the tribune didn't miss the flash of red in Vurax's eyes. The officer rose from his seat in one fluid motion, muscles tense and alert, one hand on the hilt of his sword.

"Do not forget yourself, citizen!" Jalx warned, locking his stern glare on Vurax's, and forcing the other's attention from the Kal-dkar. Nervous seconds passed while the two bulls stared at each other, a tense confrontation needing only one wrong word or movement to be ignited and turned deadly. When neither came, the tribune was inwardly relieved to see the anger fade slowly as Vurax calmed down at last and relaxed his aggressive posture. "I won't make apologies. We had to be sure," Jalx exhaled as he spoke, unaware that he'd been holding his breath. Though Vurax could not know it, the officer's intervention had been for his sake, not the Kal-dkar's. Jalx knew with chilling certainty that the other would be dead before he'd taken more than one step toward the War-mage.

"Be sure of what?" Vurax asked curtly, unable to hide his irritation.

"That there were no misguided feelings of empathy for the fate of the Sarmakanites despite what they've done to you and your family. I can't stress enough how deeply unpopular—even dangerous—such an opinion would be upon your return home. Remember that." Vurax considered what the other was saying and recognized the wisdom in the words, even if a part of him still seethed at what the War-mage had done to him. His thoughts were interrupted when he heard the centurion snap to attention behind him and he knew the meeting was at an end.

"You needn't worry. These filthy humans are getting exactly what they deserve. I am eternally grateful for my freedom, Tribune Jalx, and I shall never forget that. Glory to the Empire!" he thumped his chest in salute, surprising himself at his sudden revulsion when he spoke such hateful words. His painfully acquired perspective on what it meant to be a slave was something that transcended racial boundaries, and his own people were no strangers to oppressing others, but this was not the time or place for such dangerous notions. For now, he was content to not question his luck, or how he'd been able to deflect the Kal-dkar's mental probe and have those deeper thoughts exposed.

Seemingly mollified, Jalx returned the salute. "Safe journey home, Vurax."

⊷◊⊶

Standing outside the command tent, Vurax closed his eyes and inhaled deeply. In the air, the familiar camp smells that he remembered lingered still, but were tainted now by the addition of the sharp tang of metal, burnt wood and leather, and the faint yet distinct malodour of bodies left to rot in the sun. Try as he might, he couldn't feel any elation at the prospect of returning to Gol. In fact, the more he thought about it, the more he came to the conclusion that he didn't feel anything at all. The idea of returning home one day—the very thing that had kept him going all these years—now seemed empty and devoid of meaning, and feeling his brother's horn rings in his hand, it wasn't difficult to understand why. Additionally, his uncertain future was also being forcefully complicated by having to go to the capital, a place he'd never been to before, to be paraded around like some kind of trophy. He couldn't shake the nagging impression that he was trading one form of bondage for another, more subtle one.

Before he'd walked into that tent, he'd had every intention of asking the tribune for permission to accompany the cohorts wherever they were going. When he'd learned their destination was Bantar, that feeling was further reinforced, his need for revenge a long way from being appeased, but the unsettling experience with the Kal-dkar had somehow changed all that. The defilement he'd felt lingered still, as if the War-mage had left some insidious remnant of itself within his mind, and the recollection of the sensation filled him with disgust. He now wanted nothing more than to be as far away from that creature as possible. Not only that, but it was also easy enough to predict that the battle for Bantar wouldn't be so much a battle as it would be a wholesale slaughter, and he had no interest in being a part of that. Not because he felt pity for the humans—that much about what the Kal-dkar had gleaned was true—but because there was simply no honour or challenge to be had for him. No, he decided. There was nothing left for him in Sarmakan except bad memories and the scars they had left on his body and soul.

He looked at the unassuming centurion that stood patiently next to him. "Do you have a name?"

"Turanis Kael, centurion of the Eighth Northern Legion, third cohort, twelfth maniple, first centuria," the Golian officer rattled off his rank.

Vurax stared at the bull. "Can I just call you Kael?"

"As you wish."

"So, what now, Kael? Where do we go from here?"

"I have orders to command a small detachment and escort you to the capital, Golan. We are to depart as soon as you feel well enough to travel." Kael paused, looking at Vurax up and down. "I presume you don't need much time to pack your belongings?" he added. Humour being an emotion that Vurax could not recall feeling in such a long time, he did not detect the unfamiliar nuance in the centurion's speech right away. He glanced down at his simple loincloth and tightened his grip on the rings reassuringly.

"I think I have everything I need, but if you could find me something to wear that would improve my dignity just a notch or two, I would appreciate it," Vurax replied.

Kael smiled. "It would be my pleasure. This way."

—◦—

A while later, Vurax stepped out from the quartermaster's tent and looked down at the new gear he'd been given to wear. All the equipment was standard military issue: a comfortable and practical short-sleeved red tunic that stopped just above the knees; a leather belt with long strips down the front and decorated with brass studs; and lace-up, sturdy leather sandals. Knowing they would be travelling without the benefit of the Kal-dkar's protective magic, Kael had counselled Vurax to avoid wearing armour. Having never received any formal combat training, this didn't bother him in the slightest, but he did ask for a pair of polished, steel vambraces that protected his forearms from wrist to elbow. Completing the ensemble was a leather harness from waist to shoulder for the heavy, double-bladed battle axe on his back. Lastly, secured around his neck by a sturdy strip of rawhide, his brother's horn rings rested over his chest.

The centurion looked at him critically and nodded his approval. "Sparse, but serviceable. It wouldn't do to go through all this effort to free you just to have you die on the road home."

"Are you expecting danger?"

"Not really. The Eighth has pretty much cleared everything in its path, but that isn't to say this land is safe by any means. Caution and constant readiness will do wonders to keep you alive. The army is moving on tomorrow morning, and I intend to begin our journey then. Be ready by sunrise."

"Wouldn't it be wiser to travel at night while it's cooler?"

"Normally, yes, but we will be taking back some of the empty supply wagons with us, and the horses don't do so well in the dark, even with the pale light of Temeros when the skies are clear."

Vurax nodded, then took his leave of the centurion. As he walked through the camp, he did not feel entirely at ease, but the additional weight and unfamiliar sensation of wearing proper garments after so long was something he knew he'd have to get over eventually. Worse, the bandages all over his body were beginning to itch horribly and he longed to be rid of them. Aside from a bit of nagging stiffness, he felt no pain or discomfort and thus opted to remove the bandages once he was back in the privacy of the tent that had been assigned to him. Given how severe he'd been told his wounds had been, he marvelled at the fact that his hair and skin were unmarred wherever he removed the wrappings. Except for his old scars, there wasn't a single mark on him to indicate he had fought and nearly died in battle the day before. The power of the Horn of Zarvon was miraculous indeed, but his general distrust of gods and their obsequious servants was not lessened by that discovery. Snorting his contempt into the air of the tent, he lay down and felt overcome with weariness. Clearly the effects of the healing magic were not fully over. Before long, he fell into a dreamless sleep.

Vurax woke up to his second day as a free Minotaur, waiting a bit before rising to allow the sensation to fully sink in. It still did not seem real in many ways, and he kept waiting to come out from what surely must be some form of cruel dream. But he was already awake. This was reality. He got dressed and picked up his new axe, feeling its reassuring heft before strapping it in place on his back. He stepped outside and saw Kael standing in the same place where he'd found him the previous day.

"New shield?" Vurax remarked with a smirk.

"Nah, same one; had the smith hammer out the dent last night. I figured I'd keep it as a memento of our first meeting," Kael chortled. Vurax laughed as well, surprised at how good it felt upon hearing the unfamiliar sound. He found himself growing fond of the centurion despite only having known the Golian for less than two days. He reminded him of Aros in some ways, with his quiet dutifulness, and steadfast presence.

"I'm ready," Vurax stated confidently, eager to leave the camp and start his life anew. The two Golians walked to the southern edge of the camp where several open wagons were being made ready to depart. A small group of ten legionnaires busied themselves loading the few supplies needed for the journey home, and each one turned to salute Kael as the centurion paused to inspect each vehicle. Not too far away, what was left of Urkan-Kor's tribe sat huddled on the ground, chained and dejected as they awaited their fate.

"These men will be coming with us," he indicated toward the soldiers. "We don't have enough horses to spare for riding so the wagons will provide transportation. It's a very long way to have to walk back," Kael explained as he placed his pack inside one of the wagons. When he didn't hear Vurax say anything, he turned and found the other staring at the group of newly enslaved humans. "You're wondering about them, aren't you? They will be held here for a time, then taken back to Gol once the campaign is over. After that, who can say?"

Again, Vurax didn't say anything. He didn't need the centurion's explanation to know the slaves wouldn't be riding in wagons when they began their own trek. He also knew most weren't likely to survive the arduous three-week journey through the inhospitable terrain between here and the border with Gol. Though these were a hardy people, and this was their land, it was an altogether different experience to traverse it while wearing shackles and having your food and water rationed every day. No one knew that better than him. Their plight was not his concern, yet though he told himself the Sarmakanites had earned their fate, somehow the justification felt hollow and left him feeling empty. He shoved the bothersome sensation aside and turned to Kael. "Let's go," was all he said.

The five wagons, drawn by large sturdy horses bred for that purpose, wheeled slowly away from the camp. When they skirted the area where the battle had been fought, Vurax saw the bodies of the barbarian warriors arranged into several piles. There their flesh would continue to be picked clean by scavengers; their bones eventually left to bleach in the sun to decorate the red soil of the steppe. The tribune had given strict orders not to burn their corpses so that a stark warning would be left behind for any other Sarmakanites who might pass this way. As they circumvented the gruesome spectacle, Vurax turned away and instead fixed his gaze on the entrance to a narrow gorge coming up on their right. There, the ground angled downward where cliffs rose to either side, leaving the passage heavily cloaked in shadows this early in the morning. Sitting beside him in the lead wagon, Kael followed the direction of the other's gaze, noting the faraway look in his expression.

"What's down there?" the centurion asked, interrupting Vurax's reverie.

"A fighting pit," the other answered after a short pause, his voice catching slightly as he did so. "Slaves were taken there and forced to fight for the sport of their masters against each other or dangerous beasts captured out in the wastes."

"Is that where your brother...?" Kael didn't finish the question. There was no need to. Vurax simply nodded and turned away to stare at the horizon straight ahead. He lifted one hand to his chest and gripped the golden bands hanging there. Silently, he bid farewell to his family and vowed never to return to Sarmakan so long as he drew breath.

CHAPTER 6

Ellianna Delaris walked among the vendor stalls in Arlingtown's crowded market square, absentmindedly picking up various wares, then placing them back. Uncertain as to what she was doing, she had forgotten several times already what she'd come to buy. One of those objects she put back was a mirror, the metal surface polished so finely that the reflection of her face was nearly perfect: eyes of emerald-green on a face that could best be described as delicately beautiful, her sun-bronzed skin framed by fine, silky auburn hair, tied in a long braid worn over one shoulder. She was tall but not overly so, her lithe figure caught in that awkward transition phase between gangly teenager and the fuller curves of womanhood. She wore a long green skirt and white linen tunic with a black lace-up bodice and low black shoes with brass buckles. Yet today, she saw a stranger in that mirror staring back at her and the effect was unsettling.

The early morning sun was warm this midsummer's day, its light beaming down upon the wide square as it cleared the eastern ramparts of the city wall, but when that light fell upon her face and eyes, she felt suddenly faint. The market was already crowded at this hour, and feeling irrationally embarrassed by this strange weakness, she did her best to try to walk steadily to one of the benches that surrounded the fountain at the centre of the square. She just needed to sit down for a bit, but before she made it halfway to the fountain, someone accidentally jostled her shoulder when they passed by, causing her to stumble and fall as one foot caught on the hem of her skirt.

She didn't know how long she'd been sitting there on the ground, dazed and disoriented. All she knew was that each time she tried to rise, the world seemed to spin all around her, and the ensuing vertigo brought her right back down to the worn flagstones of the plaza. Various passersby gave her odd looks, disapproving and judgmental expressions plain on their faces. No one stopped to offer her help and when she felt tears of frustration welling in her eyes, she closed them in a vain effort to stop from crying. She found no relief in that action when she saw the afterimage of the stag-headed man and the boy, as if they had been seared permanently into her mind. She bit her lip, resisting the urge to scream and banish the awful dream of the past night from her mind, when a loud voice broke through her anguish.

"Out of the way, you bloody idiots!" someone cursed gruffly. "Pray the day never comes you need help with something, because when it does, I'll be there to spit in all of your ugly faces." Strong, callused hands took hold of one of her arms and helped her steady herself enough to rise from the ground.

"Thank you, Grandpa," she smiled weakly at her saviour.

Considered tall for one of his kind, the top of the Dwarf's head nevertheless only just barely stood level with her shoulder. What he lacked in height, however, Thurgod Splintershield made up for it in girth. He wore a sleeveless black leather vest over his barrel chest, and each of his heavily tanned, thickly muscled arms was as large around as one of her thighs. A wide belt held up a pair of utilitarian breeches fashioned of brown linen, which in turn were tucked into heavy leather boots that came up to just below his knees. In a poor attempt to mask the concern evident in his blue eyes, the newcomer grinned frightfully at her through his bushy and greying yellow beard and then took a step back to look at her, making sure she could stand on her own. Ellianna straightened her frame and took several deep breaths. When the dizziness threatened to come back, she quickly placed a hand on Thurgod's shoulder to keep from falling again.

"Whoa, girl," he exclaimed in surprise, supporting her once again. "What's come over you? Never took you for an early-morning drinker. That's more my thing, truth be told," he chortled.

"I don't know, but can you help me over to the bench? I need a minute to collect myself," she asked, ignoring the joke, which she knew was just a poor attempt to hide his apprehension. The Dwarf nodded, lending her his arm and shoulder as they slowly walked to take a seat by the fountain. Once there, Ellianna picked absently at the end of her long hair braid while the Dwarf shifted uncomfortably on the bench, the soles of his boots dangling just a fraction of space above the ground.

"Confounded things," he grumbled, "no respect for short folks." As the awkward silence that followed wore on, the Dwarf glanced furtively at Ellianna, wanting to give her some time while he struggled to temper his curiosity with patience. The young woman was clearly lost in thought, and so he hummed to himself and glared at anyone who walked by and looked in their direction. It wasn't so much that Dwarves were an uncommon sight in the predominantly human settlement of Arlingtown; it was the fact that Thurgod was well known to have an infamously bad temper—one all too often fueled by the consumption of unwise amounts of ale. In a town of just a little over ten thousand people, it didn't take long to earn a less-than-sterling reputation. If the Dwarf did have a weakness in his rough exterior though, it was Ellianna. He'd known the girl since she'd been little more than a tiny, unwashed waif dressed in filthy rags, emaciated, and walking alone out of the woods one day and up to the door of his farmhouse to beg for a scrap of bread. He'd forgotten much in the ten years since that day, but he remembered that event as if it had just happened yesterday.

The child wasn't very talkative at first, telling him her name and saying only that her home was far away, deep within the forest, and that her parents and everyone else in the village got sick and died. Thurgod didn't know if she was making the story up and had simply run away, but he quickly decided that it didn't matter. Wherever the truth lay, he felt certain he couldn't take her back and so he tried to think of what to do with her. He'd lived alone nearly all his life, unmarried and childless. A generally bad disposition and foul mouth may have played a part in that, but no one would ever have the courage to point that out to him. His own family was long gone, and he preferred not having anyone around to irritate him anyway. Which is why as soon as he'd given the girl some soup and a warm bed to sleep in for the night, he determined to be rid of her the next day. Let her be someone else's burden. It would be best for both of them that way.

The task proved more difficult than facing down a pack of vicious wolves. None of the townsfolk appeared willing to help him, and more than one door was slammed in his face as he attempted to find someone to take care of the girl. It didn't help his case that at some point in the past, the irascible Dwarf had likely insulted every single one of them. Even the one person in the whole blasted town that he could ever call a friend—a farrier and smith who looked after his farm tools—already had five children of his own to care for, so he couldn't work up his courage to ask the man for help. He briefly considered taking the girl to Arlingtown's small orphanage, but he didn't like the aspect of the man that looked after the place, and the rumours he'd heard filled him with unease. Exhausted and frustrated, he walked back to his farmstead outside the city walls that evening, the child meekly walking along behind him, blissfully oblivious to the fact that no one wanted her. The following morning, everything changed.

The little girl sat at the table, beaming with an innocent smile of pure wonder as she watched him break some pieces of freshly baked almond sweetbread into a bowl filled with warm milk from one of his dairy cows. He then sprinkled a couple of spoonfuls of sugar—a rare commodity in these parts—over the whole thing and placed the bowl in front of her. After she devoured the breakfast treat with sheer pleasure, she looked up at him in gratitude.

"That was delicious, Grandpa!" she said. "Can I have some more tomorrow? Can I call you Grandpa? You look like a grandpa with that big fluffy beard." The words took him aback. He stared speechlessly at the child, utterly confused and unprepared for the emotions that he was feeling inside. His mouth felt suddenly dry, and he longed for a drink, but surely not in front of the girl. Swallowing hard, he smiled at last and then began to laugh, a sound that he'd not heard himself make in many years.

"Yes, you can call me Grandpa. I've been called worse," the Dwarf replied between guffaws, "And yes, you can have more tomorrow, and the day after that too." He had no clue what he was getting himself into, and he decided then that he didn't care. He had no idea how to raise a human child—or any kind of child for that matter—but he felt he was off to a good start, and that made him happy in a way that he hadn't felt in a very long time.

Thurgod smiled wistfully and leaned back on the bench, lost in the memory. That little girl had grown up to be a fine young woman, with a quiet and introspective personality that proved a good counterweight to his bluster and outspokenness. Having a different perspective on things could be useful occasionally, and Elliana's presence in his life had helped him understand humans a little better—a skill that was particularly useful when living among a culture so different than the one he'd been born into. Conversely, she often spoke up on his behalf, helping him navigate some of the more delicate social interactions. Thurgod Splintershield could boast having some of the best vegetables, grain, and dairy products one could buy in Arlingtown, but you could hardly attract customers if you constantly cursed at them for squeezing the produce too hard.

"Hrrrmmm," the Dwarf cleared his throat. When that failed to elicit any kind of response, he just plunged in. "So, are you going to tell me what's going on?"

Ellianna didn't look at him but just stared straight ahead. She wanted to tell him about the dream— after all, he was the person she most trusted in this world—yet she felt a real fear that he simply wouldn't understand, and it didn't help things knowing that she didn't understand any of it either. Mostly she just didn't want him to be worried for her. "Just a dizzy spell, I guess. Not sure what brought it on, I've never experienced anything like that before. I felt faint and nauseous, and every time I tried to get up, it got worse," she attempted to explain. "I'm sure it's nothing, though. I feel fine now," she added quickly, seeing the frown already forming on his craggy forehead. Thurgod briefly pondered what he was hearing, and then had a sudden, horrifying thought that made him look at her with a wide-eyed expression of dread.

"You're not...?" he spluttered, barely managing to blurt the words out and unable to complete the question out of fear that voicing what he was thinking would somehow make it reality. It took her only a couple of seconds to clue in as to what he was asking, and when she did, her expression went from confusion, to shock, and finally to amusement.

"Gods, no!" she laughed out loud. "It's not that," she protested, feeling the heat rise to her cheeks and letting the awkward moment between them pass quickly.

The Dwarf let out the breath he hadn't realized he was holding with a loud whoosh, making no attempt to hide his relief. He wasn't sure his racing heart could take another fright of that magnitude. As he composed himself, Ellianna smiled as she gently caressed his head as she often did, making a futile attempt to straighten some of that shaggy, unruly mess that he called hair. There was genuine fondness and love in that touch. If not for his kindness in taking her in when he had, she couldn't imagine where she'd be today. She owed him more than she could ever repay, but it did concern her more than a little that his overprotectiveness was only growing worse as she'd gotten older. On occasions like this one, she dreaded the day when she would inevitably decide to claim a life for herself, separate from his.

"Why don't you take a rest for the remainder of the day, Lil," he suggested, using the affectionate diminutive he'd taken to calling her since they had first met. "I'll finish picking up the things we need. Your chores can wait until you feel better."

Ellianna couldn't help but laugh again. "Grandpa, have you forgotten already?" she chided with mock hurt in her tone. "Today is my birthday. You've already given me the day off from my duties at the farm," she reminded him. Seeing the look of chagrin on his face, she added, "Though I'm very grateful, nonetheless. I know the harvest is done so tomorrow I'll start helping you get the fields ready for the next season, as I promised."

"Oh, I'm not upset about the fields," he grumbled, "they won't be going anywhere. It's just that I can't believe I didn't remember that your birthday is today. Well, I did but clearly forgot again. My old head isn't what it used to be. Eighteen, is it? Hells, after all this time, I'm still not used to how fast humans grow up. When I was that age, I was still playing children's games with my brothers..." he trailed off, his brow furrowing as he stopped talking, and stared hard at the ground in silence. Ellianna didn't say anything and gave him some time. It wasn't often that Thurgod spoke of his past, and when he did, it came only in broken, very brief fragments, like this one. She'd given up long ago trying to get him to reveal more when it became abundantly clear that something very tragic had occurred that haunted him to this day. She had a strong suspicion that his heavy drinking was a result of that, but she couldn't be sure, and he wouldn't share more with her.

Thurgod got up and straightened his vest with both hands. "Alright then, if you feel okay now, I'll stop embarrassing you and leave you be. This is your day. See you at home for dinner?"

"I'm fine, and yes, I'll see you later," Ellianna smiled reassuringly as he walked off into the crowd. Eighteen, she thought to herself. It was an approximation, really. She knew she'd been eight years old when she arrived at Thurgod's door ten years ago, but she didn't recall the exact day she'd been born. She remembered only when her parents would tell her the day had come, and that it was in the middle of summer like it was now. When her adopted grandpa—always organized and methodical—insisted that they pick a day, she'd settled upon this one, the day that marked the beginning of a weeklong summer celebration known as The Great Hunt. Hunting had been a particularly important activity in the village where she'd grown up, and her father had participated in the event every year, even winning the ritual contest on more than one occasion. Many of her childhood memories had faded with time, but every year on this day, she always recalled vividly when he had returned home, proudly carrying the majestic stag he'd caught.

A stag.

She'd been about to get up from the bench when the memory struck her with the force of a charging horse, so she was glad she was still sitting when her muscles froze again. The being that she had been chasing forever in her dream, she recalled with undeniable clarity, had the head of a stag. And what was a chase but a form of hunting, she thought further. This had to be more than mere coincidence. She felt some of the panic that she had experienced when waking up this morning returning. Remembering to breathe, she tried to calm herself and made an attempt to sort her thoughts. Try as she might, she couldn't dispel the notion that her personal connection to this day—the timing of the dream, and its strange contents—were related in an obvious yet confusing way. She felt as if someone was watching her, and the feeling was unsettling in its intensity. When she looked around, however, she didn't notice anyone paying undue attention to her; merely the various townsfolk going about their day. Thankfully, the feeling passed almost as quickly as it had come, though it left her feeling perturbed. Getting up at last and leaving the market area, she came to the sad conclusion that the enjoyment that she had planned to derive from this day was utterly and irrevocably lost. She needed answers, and she could think of only one place where someone might have them.

⚊⚊⚊ ◆ ⚊⚊⚊

The boy peered out from the alley as he watched the young woman get up from the bench and walk across the market square. If truth be told, he wasn't exactly a boy anymore, being scarcely a year younger than the person he was observing, but so thin and slight was he of build and stature that everyone often made the mistake of thinking him to be just a child. This lent him an air of unassuming innocence that made most dismiss him without more than a casual glance. These qualities, coupled with his light step, nimble fingers, and ability to squeeze into small spaces with ease, made him extremely proficient at what he liked to do—steal things.

The market was particularly busy that day, and he had his pick from dozens of unsuspecting targets, but once he had selected his mark, he focused on it with singular purpose and determination. It was a game he greatly enjoyed playing, and he liked to think he was quite good at it. He'd seen the young woman before, just one of many farmhands that came into town regularly, and for that reason, he hadn't paid her any heed on those previous occasions. Farm workers didn't typically have much to their name, yet today he'd been watching her the entire morning, or more specifically, the coin purse that she carried, pulled out on several occasions, and then placed back without ever spending a single copper. If he thought her behaviour to be a little on the odd side, it didn't show. What mattered to him was that her purse remained full by the time he got his hands on it. It was when the woman fell to the ground that he began to have second thoughts.

He wasn't a malicious person by nature, and though he often didn't consider the impact of his actions upon those he was stealing from, he knew that what he did was wrong. It's just that he simply couldn't help himself. He was easily bored, and the thrill and challenge of what he did gave him a release and escape from the drudgery of working in his father's shop or having to look after his two small brothers when his parents were out of town on business. He certainly didn't do it because he needed the coins for anything. Instead of spending them, he just stashed them in a space under the floorboards of his bedroom, hardly caring that he had them even while already anticipating the excitement of chasing down his next acquisition.

As he watched other people walk by the young woman without offering a hand in help, he began walking toward her before he even realized what he was doing. He was only a few paces away when he caught himself and stopped. What was his plan? Was he going to help her or simply take advantage of her vulnerability to relieve her of her coin purse? He never got to find out the answer because his momentary hesitation had cost him the opportunity to act either way. Always mindful of what was always going on around him, he heard the Dwarf cursing and shoving his way through the people behind him and so he resumed walking so as to not rouse suspicion. Certain no one had noticed him, he walked casually back to his place of observation near the alley's entrance and continued to watch.

The Dwarf and the woman conversed at length, but he wasn't interested in whatever they were discussing. He didn't know the Dwarf personally but was well aware of the farmer's legendary temper and didn't want to risk life and limb by drawing his attention. If there was one thing he'd learned as part of his hobby, it was to have patience, and lots of it. So, he waited, and when the Dwarf finally left and the woman got up shortly thereafter, he followed her. Heading east from the market square, the main street she was walking down led to a central plaza where a large stone statue on horseback of the hero Arling Taffen served to commemorate the founding of the Barony of Arlingford centuries ago. The statue was a favourite place of his, standing as it did at the end of the thoroughfare that began further south at the main city gates. From the statue's long shadow, he liked to observe newcomers coming into the town and pass away the time while deciding which ones would be worthy of his helpful efforts to lighten their load after a long journey.

He half expected the woman to turn right toward the gates since most of the farms outside the town were in that direction, but when she kept walking east, his curiosity was piqued. Keeping a discreet distance, he continued to follow her. Arriving at another intersection, she paused and seemed to hesitate as if unsure of which way to proceed. At one point she turned around to look for someone, possibly to ask for directions, but he quickly withdrew into a shadowed alleyway before she could spot him. Seeing no one else around, she started walking again, taking the southernmost of three possible routes. The choice both puzzled and concerned him at the same time. She was clearly lost, and on the slight chance that she wasn't, he wondered what business she could possibly have in the most dangerous section of Arlingtown, the slums.

The streets were narrow in this old part of the town, allowing less daylight to shine through and lending to the dingy feel of the area. Most of the buildings were grimy and dilapidated and in sore need of repair, while the refuse and garbage lying on the streets in the warm summer air gave off an aroma that was eye-watering. The few people that she passed gave her sullen, suspicious looks while completely ignoring whatever she asked of them before walking away. It wasn't long before she got completely and unsurprisingly turned around in the maze of streets, alleys, and dead ends, and had to pause to try and get her bearings. Remaining unseen, he watched as she drew the attention of a small group of street urchins, dirty faces looking up at her, hands held up for a handout. He knew what was about to happen, and he didn't like it one bit.

The tactic was one of the oldest in the book, and while the smaller children provided a distraction, he saw the pair of older boys in another alley across from him preparing to move in on their prey. He knew these two well—uncouth ruffians that weren't afraid to depend on violence to supplement their criminal way of life. He despised people like them, who relied on bullying and force to get what they wanted, unapologetic about the pain and humiliation they caused in the process. He had little use for rules, but there were two of his own making that he always tried to follow: to never be seen doing what he did, and to never physically harm anyone that didn't have it coming. He may be a thief, but he wasn't human trash like these two. This wasn't going to end well for someone, he decided then, and it wasn't going to be the girl.

Shaking his head in exasperation at her naiveté when he saw her pull out her purse and give the children a few coppers, he stepped out into the open at the same time as the other two boys. The urchins had boxed the girl in while they pressed against her, cornering her at the junction of two houses, and making it difficult for her to get out without pushing them out of the way. Leaving no uncertainty as to their intentions, the two street thugs leered at the young woman as they approached but pulled up short and paused when they saw him walk up.

"Hullo Gregor, hullo Will," he greeted nonchalantly. "Nice day for a walk. Out enjoying the air? The two of you could do with a little more sunshine."

Their expressions at seeing him looked sour enough to curdle milk. "Nice day for a beatin', more like it. Run along and fuck off now, this ain't your territory," the tall, thin one growled, one hand moving behind his back.

Their job done, the urchins scattered and disappeared into an alleyway, but the red-haired girl remained, unmoving while she stared at the three of them in silence. She had no idea what the newcomer's intentions were, and his poised air of confidence indicated to her that he could possibly be an even bigger threat than these other two. She briefly considered calling out for help but knew deep down it would be a futile gesture. None of the inhabitants within earshot would be likely to interfere, and she hadn't seen anyone even remotely resembling one of the town guards ever since entering this part of town.

"□Nice day for a beating'," the newcomer slowly repeated. "That's a winner, Gregor. Congratulations, been working on that one long?" he taunted, shifting his eyes from the other boy's face and down to his arm. "What have you got back there? That little cheese cutter you call a knife?"

"Why don't you come closer and find out, Darken?" Gregor snapped at him, his face growing flushed as he spat the words, lacing the other boy's name with a heavy dose of venom. He glanced meaningfully at his stout companion, who began to circle to one side. The one who'd been called Darken smiled, keeping a wary eye on Will while continuing to focus his attention on Gregor.

"Before I make you regret getting up this morning from that flea-ridden dog blanket you call a bed, here's what I'm suggesting," Darken said, his tone remaining casual but with an undercurrent of menace that gave the other two boys pause. "The two of you are going to stop bothering the lady here, turn around, and go back to whatever shithole you call a home."

"Or what?" Gregor was nearly beside himself with rage, flecks of spittle flying with every word.

Darken sighed. "You seem to have a short memory. Unsurprising, considering how many times your lowlife mongrel of a dad beats you about your hollow head every day. Tell me, how attached are you to your remaining ear? Remember when I took the other one?" Darken stopped smiling and reinforced his point, or rather both, when two sharp and wicked-looking daggers appeared in his hands in a movement faster than the other two boys could follow. At the sight of the deadly weapons, Will held his hands out in front of him and slowly began to back away, clearly wanting no part of this. The look of disgust on Gregor's face as he watched his ally's cowardly retreat was the only thing that prevented his fear from showing even more. For all his anger though, like every other bully when confronted by someone who wasn't afraid of him, his nerve and confidence were quickly evaporating.

Slowly releasing the grip on the handle of his undrawn knife, Gregor deliberately held his hand forward to show that it was empty. Humiliation battled with hatred as he too began to back away. "This isn't over," he pointed one finger at him, making a last attempt to salvage some dignity in front of his companion.

"Funny, isn't that what you said last time? Maybe I should take your tongue instead just so you stop embarrassing yourself," Darken quipped, feigning boredom by stifling a yawn. Gregor would have said something further, his need to get in a last word nearly overriding the little common sense he had, but self-preservation won the day. That, and the fact that he knew with cold certainly that Darken only appeared to be jesting—the ugly scar where his right ear had once been proved just how serious the other boy's threat really was. Wisely keeping his mouth shut, he fled down the same alley Will had run into just seconds before.

Ellianna stared at her unlikely saviour, carefully noting the undisguised look of naked contempt he shot the other two boys as they ran off. There was no doubt in her mind that had he not intervened, she would have been robbed, or worse. Yet, it was clear from the exchange she had just witnessed that this was not an individual to be underestimated and that perhaps her well-being wasn't the sole reason he was here. He may have saved her, but it didn't take much to see that he was clearly disappointed he hadn't been given further cause to teach those two a harsher lesson than the one they had just learned. At first glance, he looked harmless enough; the youthful face almost childish in a way, but unremarkable enough otherwise that you would be likely to forget it shortly after having met him. His black hair was short and cropped very close on the sides and back, and only his penetrating dark brown eyes indicated that he might be slightly older than he appeared. His clothing was likewise unexceptional in style, though she did note that the plain but well-kept tunic and trousers were of a quality that told her he did not live around here. The soft-soled leather shoes he wore made no sound as he walked over to her.

Standing before Ellianna, Darken looked at her with a carefully neutral expression, trying to gauge her emotional level after what she'd just experienced.

When he saw her giving him the same calculating look, he decided that she was made of sterner stuff than he had judged at first and that knowledge pleased him immensely. Flashing a crooked smile, he made the daggers disappear somewhere into the back of his trousers, then bowed without taking his eyes off hers.

"Darken Valhik, at your service, milady," he greeted politely.

"Ellianna Delaris, at yours, and you can drop the 'milady' please, I'm not noble-born," she corrected him, though she was fairly certain he already knew that. "I'm grateful for your assistance, Darken. It was kind of you to intercede on a stranger's behalf like that—most people around here don't seem willing to give me the time of day."

"Lucky for you, I'm not from around here," he grinned. "Besides, any chance to make those two idiots crap their pants is not something I can pass up."

"Then I'm glad I was able to assist in providing you with that opportunity," she smiled back. Darken took an instant liking to her. He often found most people dull and uncomplicated, which was a big part of the reason he often found himself to be his own best company, but he sensed a sharp wit and intelligence in her that was a match for his own. It was mostly a gut feeling for now, but his gut had yet to steer him wrong. They both shared a laugh, which slowly died down into awkward silence.

"Odd name, Darken..." she mused out loud, hoping to find a way out of the uneasy quiet.

"It's short for Darkenpos, but I've never liked it. Sounds too pretentious, for some reason," he shrugged. "So, are you lost or something? Because I can't understand what a girl like you is doing wandering around this part of town," he asked, wanting to change the subject.

"Possibly," she conceded. "I was on my way to the Anvalite church, but I think I took a wrong turn somewhere."

"Just one? I think you took several," he laughed, being careful not to let on that he'd seen her take every one of those wrong turns he'd just alluded to. "At any rate, the church is up near the River Gate, at the north end of town. These are the slums, and there's nothing godly about them."

"That might be helpful if I even knew which way north is at this point. I don't suppose I can trouble you further by asking you to show me the way out of this place? I've been inside the walls many times but only to go to the market with my grandpa."

"It's no trouble at all," he exclaimed, surprising himself at his own enthusiasm, which no doubt was derived from the prospect of spending more time in her company, though he wouldn't have admitted it. "In fact, I was just thinking you shouldn't take another step alone in these streets. Gregor and Will aren't the only dangers around here."

"You seem to know them well," she observed.

"As well as you can know a rabid and irritating dog that barks itself silly every time you walk by," he dismissed, motioning for her to follow. "They won't bother you again while you're with me," he confidently stated.

They retraced her steps out of the slums, Darken making each turn without hesitation, which confirmed to Ellianna that he was well acquainted with these streets. As they neared the plaza with the statue, she recalled something he had said. "What did you mean earlier when you said, 'a girl like you?'"

It was rare that Darken didn't have a reply ready for anything that came his way, but the question surprised him into silent hesitation. It wasn't surprise at the fact that she had caught that, but rather that he suddenly had to ask himself why he'd said it. He could feel her looking at him as they walked, awaiting a response.

"Your dress is pretty," he stammered, cursing inwardly at how stupid he knew he sounded, but forging ahead anyway, "and your face is clean, and your hair is washed and smells nice."

Beyond the River Gate, there was a large bridge spanning the Arling River, and the sensation he'd felt in his stomach one warm summer day when he'd jumped off that bridge and into the cooling water below for the first time was not unlike what he felt right now. The difference then was the refreshing relief he'd felt after, whereas right now there was nothing but the flush of rising heat and growing discomfort that he thought would never end. When he heard her laughter, his humiliation and shame were complete. He stopped and gave her a stony stare. Seeing the look on his face, Ellianna was suddenly mortified and quickly tried to make amends.

"Forgive me," she pleaded. "I'm not laughing at you. That's the sweetest thing anyone's ever said to me, believe me. I was just laughing at the irony. I work on my grandpa's farm, so on any given day I'm sure I look and smell just like any other girl back there," she nodded in the direction they'd just come from, "but today is my eighteenth birthday, so I thought I'd make myself a little more presentable before coming into town. Thank our Lady of Fortune that I did or I'm not sure you would have noticed me."

He appeared mollified by what she said. "Sorry for overreacting," he offered sheepishly, trying to hide his relief and eager to move past his embarrassing confession. "Just so you know though, it wouldn't have made any difference that you're clean and pretty. I still would have helped you—even if you're a year older than me," he added with a mischievous smile.

She smiled warmly at him. "You're sweet, you know that?" Her comment prompted him to blush even more furiously, and he looked away, hoping she wouldn't notice. "Have you ever thought of becoming a Justicer? They could use one in those slums."

This time it was his turn to laugh. "A Justicer? No, thank you. I don't envy the prospect of walking around with a stick up my ass all day. Besides, I enjoy doing what I do far more."

"And what is it that you do, Darken?" Ellianna asked, bemused.

"Oh, all sorts of things. Today, I shall add rescuing nice girls to my list," he winked.

Again, she laughed but did not miss the fact that he had wiggled out of answering her question. Fair enough, she thought. Her grandpa had often told her to stay out of other people's business. It was just safer that way, but she couldn't help but wonder what he was hiding.

Arriving at last at the horseman's statue, Darken bowed again and took his leave. "Here you are, as promised. Now, to get to the church, follow this street to the River Gate," he pointed out the correct direction, "you'll see the baron's keep up on the hill to your left, and the church is on the opposite side, to the right of the gate. Can't miss it."

"Apparently you can," she joked. "I should have just asked for directions as soon I walked away from the market."

"If you had, we wouldn't have met," he observed.

"That's true. It's been a strange and eventful day, Darken, but you've been the best part of it thus far. Thank you one more time. Will I see you again?"

"Only if you promise to come into town more often," he smiled, his heart soaring at the prospect. "I don't much like farms."

"Ha!" Ellianna teased. "Well, I don't much like towns. Farewell, Darken," she waved with a smile, then walked up the street he'd indicated moments ago.

"Farewell, Ellianna, and happy birthday," he called after her, cursing inwardly for forgetting to say that while they had stood face to face.

"Call me Lil," she shouted back.

Watching her go, he was seized by the impulse to follow her again. It wasn't just that he wasn't prepared to see her go so soon, but that throughout their conversation, he'd been puzzled at how someone could live so near the town and yet not know where the church was. He supposed it was possible, but what made him more curious was why she hadn't simply asked that Dwarf for directions if that were the case. Or was it because she didn't want him knowing where she was going? There was only one way to resolve this mystery, he told himself, so he took two steps forward to go after her only to walk squarely into the chest of someone who appeared suddenly in his path.

"Hey!" Darken yelped, jumping back. "What the hell?"

The man stood in front of him in a wide stance, feet firmly planted apart and hands on his hips as he scowled silently down at the boy. Rubbing his nose, Darken looked up into the other's face and groaned, rolling his eyes. "Oh hello,

Uncle Garick," he greeted with a resigned tone. Though he stood a full head taller than the youngster, the older man's family resemblance to Darken was undeniable in every detail down to the same eyes and hair, with the addition of a short black beard that Darken always envisioned himself growing one day.

"Impressive bit of work back there, lad," Uncle Garick offered by way of a greeting. "Turning over a new leaf?"

"What 'bit of work?'" Darken asked, confused.

"Don't play stupid with me; you know it never works—I'm talking about that whole business with the girl and those two boys."

"You... you've been following me this whole time?" Darken sputtered, incredulous.

"Keep your voice down, you're drawing attention to yourself." Garick smiled charmingly at a couple walking by, waited until they had passed, then grabbed his nephew by the shoulder and pulled him out of the open and under the shadow of the statue. "Yes, ever since the market, and you never even saw me, did you? Do you know why that is? You were so focused on that girl that you forgot half the things I've taught you, that's why. That kind of stupid inattention will land you in a heap of trouble one day," his uncle berated him, his voice barely above a whisper, but harsh enough that there was no mistaking his anger.

Darken looked sullenly to the side, avoiding the other's accusing eyes. His uncle was right, of course, but going from feeling so good to having his mood swiftly and thoroughly spoiled like this left him feeling angry. He couldn't help himself and glanced wistfully in the direction Ellianna had gone, just in time to catch a last glimpse of her green skirt before she disappeared down the busy street. Feeling suddenly deflated, his irritation ebbed slowly out of him, and he stared down at his shoes with a sigh, looking very much like the child that he appeared to be. He felt his uncle's hand on his shoulder again, but this time there was compassion in the touch, not exasperation.

"Look, lad, you did a good thing. I'm not here to take that away from you. But you need to pay attention, you hear?"

Darken nodded.

"Alright then. Forget the girl for now; I'm sure you'll see her again. Since you didn't ask, your mother sent me to find you. Your parents need help packing the wagon for their trip to Aldamor tomorrow at first light, or did you forget about that?"

He hadn't forgotten, but he'd been avoiding going home just the same. He dearly loved his kind and gentle mother, Phymira, but Felnan Valhik was another matter. Nothing he did was ever good enough for his overly stern and rigorous father, and when he'd shown no interest in the family's generations-old toy making business, Felnan had never forgiven his eldest son for his lack of devotion to what was traditionally a duty that every Valhik had carried on. Their relationship had been strained ever since, and matters hadn't improved when a young Darken took a shine to his uncle Garick, Felnan's estranged brother. Garick and Felnan had been partners since inheriting the shop from their own parents, but the relationship soured when Garick's gambling debts nearly drove the business into bankruptcy. It was only Felnan's perseverance and personal sacrifice that had managed to save what was left of the family trade, but the acrimonious process had forced him to break ties with his irresponsible brother. Now that brother was back after an absence of many years, and while Felnan quietly tolerated Garick's return to maintain harmony within the family, he simmered inwardly at the knowledge that Darken was beginning to display a few of his uncle's bad traits.

"Why can't you help them?" Darken asked, feeling petulant again.

"Your father didn't ask for my help; he asked for yours. Besides, I have business to attend to in preparation for tomorrow night, or did you forget that too?" these last words were barely audible as Garick scanned their surroundings, ensuring no one was within earshot even as he said them.

Darken swallowed, his throat suddenly very dry. He hadn't forgotten that either, but he'd pushed it from his mind because every time he thought of it, he was filled with anxiety and self-doubt, and he didn't like how that made him feel. For the first time since his uncle had begun to teach him skills that ordinary folks would consider unsavory, he was going to be trusted enough to come along on something that Garick had promised would be very big. He still didn't know what it was, but that his uncle felt him ready for this was a huge point of pride for him, so it shouldn't come as a surprise that the man had been upset at Darken for his lack of attention earlier. A part of him had briefly hoped his mistake today would have excused him from participating in whatever Garick had planned for tomorrow, but he quickly silenced that voice of caution. He'd been waiting for this for a long time, and he wasn't about to let some childish fear stop him from showing his uncle that he was ready for anything.

"Go on home now. We'll talk tomorrow after they've gone," Garick said, ruffling Darken's hair. The teenager gave him his crooked smile, nodded, and then ran off. Pensively, Garick watched the boy go—there was a lot riding on tomorrow, and he prayed fervently that he wasn't making a big mistake.

CHAPTER 7

Flynn stared at the vast and imposing bulk of the Cathedral of Janus, casting its shadow over the surrounding outbuildings like a monarch reminding subjects of their place. The sound of many voices raised in song floated in the air from within, the cadence of the religious hymn having an almost hypnotic quality in the steady heat of the early afternoon. The grounds of the church, lovingly tended by a small army of priestly gardeners every day, consisted of a multitude of colourful flower beds, carefully manicured bushes, and pristine lawns, all criss-crossed by stone paths that led to and from the various outbuildings. Here and there, benches fashioned from white granite rested beneath the canopies of various trees, where robed priests sat enjoying the shade as they conversed with one another or simply indulged in a quick nap away from their stern superiors.

On the western side of the church grounds and huddled near one of the high stone walls separating the church from the streets beyond, the Janusian orphanage was comprised of a small collection of sturdy and practical buildings that performed various functions and had been added over the years. The original orphanage house itself—still in use today and serving as the children's main dormitory—was a squat and unlovely structure that predated much of the current construction in the city. During Corazan's centuries-long rise from a backwater frontier outpost to the capital of a powerful kingdom, the old edifice had withstood the test of time through war and famine, fire and storm. Originally built to house the first missionaries from the Avamor Imperium to travel to this part of the world, it had subsequently been relegated to serving as a shelter for the homeless after the new cathedral was built many years later, and then as an orphanage in more recent times.

Standing just inside another set of bronze gates that led into the secluded courtyard and private area of the church where the orphanage stood, Flynn looked at the building with a mixture of apprehension and curiosity. Several children of various ages were playing outside, either in small groups or alone, supervised by a pair of clergymen who stood nearby. Flynn noticed immediately that they were all boys, something that struck him as being very strange. He had several schoolmates who were girls, even if they were kept separate in different rooms when classes were in session, so he wondered if they observed the same rules here. The unbidden memory of his former school forced him to face another new reality of his life—that he likely would never see his friends again. Not until he was much older anyway.

"Come," Brother Owen said, taking his hand once again and walking toward the building's main doors, "I will show you where you will be sleeping." Eyeing the stone-cool interior of the orphanage with visible relief, the effort of the long walk across the city under the sweltering summer heat was noticeably apparent on the priest as he wiped the sweat from his brow. Accustomed to spending many hours outdoors throughout the year, Flynn wasn't the least bothered by the temperature, but he hurried his pace for the man's benefit as he concluded that the other likely didn't get out much. Once inside, Brother Owen led his young companion through a door and into an office where another priest in identical white and blue robes sat at a desk, his attention absorbed by a large book he was reading. When the two of them walked in, the man looked up and Brother Owen cleared his throat to speak.

"Greetings, Brother Melton. This is Flynn Castellar, our newest charge here at the orphanage," Brother Owen said cheerfully after the other man nodded for him to proceed. A thin, bald man of middling years with a hawkish nose and small eyes, Brother Melton muttered a barely audible greeting in return, put away his book with obvious annoyance, and opened a heavy ledger resting on the desk. Dipping a feathered quill into an ink well, he wrote down the answers but did not look at the boy while he asked a series of questions in a monotone voice, including Flynn's birthdate, the name of his parents, and the circumstances surrounding their deaths. When Flynn hesitated on this last question, Brother Owen helpfully answered for him, silently cursing his fellow priest's lack of tact. Surely the information was necessary for the records, but there was no reason it could not have waited. Not for the first time, Owen wondered what Melton had done to get this dull assignment. It was surely punishment for some minor transgression, Owen had often mused, for it was a poorly kept secret that the dour and humourless man did not like children, thus being forced to record every detail about each new arrival was certain to irritate the cheerless cleric.

While the pair waited, Brother Owen's impatience with his fellow priest grew as the other made a show of leafing through several pages of yet another ledger, rhythmically tapping his fingers on the desk. He knew Melton was clearly enjoying making him wait and was taking full advantage of his position as assistant to the orphanage's headmaster to purposefully aggravate Owen at every opportunity. Knowing that even the divine source of his vast capacity for patience had its limits, Owen cleared his throat meaningfully once more, walked over to a clay jug sitting on another table nearby, and poured himself and the child a couple of cups of cold water. As both noisily gulped the refreshment down, Owen put his cup back on the table and stepped toward one of the comfortable chairs in the office. This had the desired effect as Brother Melton's eyebrows shot up in consternation while he slammed the ledger shut with a loud sound.

"Cell twenty-four," Melton snapped, dropping his intentional delaying. His beady eyes narrowed even further, and he glanced at the door meaningfully. Sighing in mock disappointment as he gave the chair one last, longing look, Brother Owen left the office with Flynn in tow.

"The Light of Janus be with you, Brother," he called out with a smile. There was no response as he closed the door. Looking down at Flynn, he gave the boy a mischievous wink and was rewarded with a broad grin in return. Together, they walked down the long corridor of the orphanage to find cell twenty-four.

◆◇◆

Flynn lay in his small cot with hands crossed behind his head and stared at the featureless ceiling while he thought back on this eventful first day. His room—or cell, as the monks that once lived here had called it—was little more than a tiny cubicle with three windowless walls and a curtain separating it from the hallway to afford him a bit of privacy. Having shared a room with two of his brothers all his life, this was more space than he had ever had to himself, and the experience was not a little strange. In the long days ahead, however, he would come to appreciate that having his own cell was a privilege. Many of the other children in the orphanage had to share sleeping accommodations in large communal rooms, where dozens of cots like his were lined up from wall to wall or stacked on top of one another in bunks. When he inquired as to why he was being put here, Brother Owen had told him that the most recent arrivals were always given a private cell at first, until they grew more accustomed to their new life at the orphanage.

After he'd arrived, he was left alone for part of the afternoon, so he busied himself by depositing his clothes into the footlocker and placing his wooden figurine on the small nightstand, the only two other pieces of furniture in the cell besides the cot. When evening neared, a teenager named Carlo, wearing black robes trimmed with white of an Initiate of the Faith, came by to take him to the bathhouse where he had to scrub himself clean in a wooden tub full of hot water. When he was finished, the Initiate returned to trim short his long dark hair and then handed him his uniform. It consisted of a simple, long-sleeved, and just past the waist-length white linen tunic, with two pockets low in the front, and made to be worn over his own shirt. A pair of plain, loose-fitting trousers completed the functional ensemble. Washed and properly attired, Flynn had barely returned to his cell when another Initiate came and gathered all the children in this wing and led them all, single file and procession-like, to one of two refectories on the main floor of the orphanage for supper.

After lining up to receive his food from the few Initiates dispensing the evening meal, Flynn walked to a bench set before the longest table he had ever seen, feeling very self-conscious as all the other boys near him fell silent when he approached. After a few uncomfortable seconds, the chatter around him resumed after sitting down and he was pointedly ignored for the rest of the meal, which came as something of a relief. The fare, prepared and cooked by the orphanage's kitchen staff, was a stew consisting mainly of vegetables and potatoes, but containing the rare hint of herb-spiced beef here and there. A chunk of dark bread and a tin mug of water rounded out the simple meal. As he ate, Flynn took the opportunity to furtively observe the other children. They were all boys, no girls, he noted once again. As for age, he couldn't be certain of course, but they seemed to range from as young as six-years-old to just a little older than he was—fourteen, fifteen perhaps? He had heard Brother Owen refer to another refectory within the orphanage, so he assumed any older boys must be there. If there were children here at the church younger than the ones in this room, they must be elsewhere as well. All the boys wore the same uniform he did, though a few of the older ones wore dark blue armbands over their left arm. Every head of hair was shorn close; every face lively and scrubbed clean.

When the meal was finished and the plates cleared, each table's occupants got up in turn and the children filed off to their cells and shared rooms for the night. The Initiates then ensured each boy was bedded down before dousing all but a few of the lamps that provided illumination every few paces along the long halls of the orphanage. Alone with his thoughts in his cell, Flynn couldn't fall asleep. The windowless walls seemed too oppressive, and the bed felt strange. He could not hear the familiar soft breathing of his brothers as they slept, and worst of all, he missed his mother terribly. He felt a sudden, almost irresistible urge to jump out of his cot and run back home, but he fought down the impulse, knowing what he would find if he went back: darkness and silence. Same as what he had right now, he realized, but at least here he'd made a friend in Brother Owen. He hoped fervently he would see the priest tomorrow. Thinking about the day when he would be old enough to leave this place, he finally fell into a deep and dreamless sleep.

He would have gone on sleeping well into the morning hours, but that was not the way things were done here at the orphanage, as Flynn quickly found out. Just as the Initiates made sure every boy was in his bed at night, so too did they ensure that they all got up at the same time each morning. Carlo's clear voice rang out down the row of cells where Flynn slept; rousing all the children from their slumber and bidding them to get dressed, use the lavatory, then assemble in the refectory for breakfast. If any thought to try and sneak a few extra winks of sleep, a Monitor—the title given to those wearing the blue armbands—would swiftly put an end to that endeavour. When one of them prodded him in the side with a wooden rod that first morning, Flynn muttered something unintelligible and turned over to face the wall, pulling his blanket over his head. He felt the rod jab a second time into the small of his back, this time more insistently.

"Time to get up, buttercup!"

Flynn heard the Monitor's shrill voice, the other boy clearly relishing his role as tormentor. He slid the blanket down and sat up on his bed, rubbed the sleep from his eyes, and stared blearily at the Monitor.

"What's the matter?" the other boy mocked. "Couldn't sleep last night? Are the accommodations not to your liking? Poor baby."

Flynn scowled at him and shivered when he put his bare feet on the cold stone floor. The Monitor, a stocky youth with wavy red hair and pale skin covered in freckles, merely smirked back.

"I only just arrived yesterday, leave me alone," Flynn replied sullenly, pulling his shirt over his head.

"Aw, the poor princess," the Monitor teased in his irritatingly high-pitched voice. "First morning in the House of the Unwanted, is it? I thought your face looked new around here. Sure thing then, I'll give you one extra minute to-day—and only today—to get yourself ready. Tomorrow, when you hear Carlo, you'd best be up before I look in on you, you hear?"

"Sure, whatever," Flynn muttered under his breath, rubbing his eyes while the other boy departed to go find another victim to harass.

A short time later, he was washed, dressed, and sitting down with the other children for their early morning meal, which consisted of a hard-boiled egg, a strip of fried ham, and a single slice of honeyed toast with a cup of fresh milk to wash it all down with. Famished, he quickly devoured the contents of his plate, staring mournfully at it once it was empty. At home, he would have asked for seconds. Looking around hopefully, he didn't think that would be a likely option here, a fact that was confirmed when he locked eyes with the Monitor from earlier. Sitting one table over from his, the red-haired boy made an exaggerated face as if he was crying, then grinned and made a rude gesture at him with one upraised finger. A few other boys around him snickered and Flynn made a mental note to pace himself at the next meal. One day in this place, and he already hated it.

When a small bell near the doors rang three times to signal that mealtime was over, the Initiates separated the boys by age groups and walked them outside to a long rectangular building across the courtyard from the dormitory. Inside, and throughout both floors, a series of large, windowed chambers functioned as classrooms, complete with dark wooden desks and chairs for each boy, much like in Flynn's old school. The Initiate leading Flynn's group took them up a staircase to the second floor and then stopped in front of one of the classroom doors. Being new, he waited in the hallway until the other children filed past him to take their places, and then sat at an empty desk near the back. The desk's surface was slightly angled and lifted on a hinge, revealing a small compartment below which held a small stack of blank parchment sheets, a stoppered inkwell, and a quill. While everyone settled in, he observed what the other boys did and mimicked their every move by pulling out one sheet, setting it on the desk, and placing the inkwell in a carved round receptacle made to keep it steady while in use.

"Summer's barely begun," Flynn whispered to the boy to his left, a sandy-haired lad with a pleasant face, sharp nose, and bright green eyes, "why are we in class?"

The other looked at him and shrugged. "The Brothers teach that an idle mind is a wasteful thing."

Flynn made an ugly face that he hoped no one noticed. He was willing to tolerate a lot given he'd really had no choice in coming here, but classes in the summer? That was a crime of the most heinous nature, as far as a boy of his age was concerned. Still, no help for it, he supposed. "How long have you been here?" he asked the other out of curiosity.

"Since I was two, or so I've been told," he shrugged. "I don't remember being anywhere else."

That had to explain why the boy was being so casual about this clear violation of childhood rules. If he'd been here all his life, he clearly had no idea how things were supposed to work beyond the orphanage walls, such as the fact that summer was reserved for nothing but playtime and fun. He really, really hated this place now and wondered yet again how long before he became old enough so that he could walk out of here and never come back.

"Name's Elias, what's yours?" the boy asked.

"Flynn," he replied, reaching across the aisle to shake Elias' proffered hand.

One of the many questions Flynn had since arriving here popped into his head, and now that he'd made a new friend that he could ask, he did not hesitate. "Elias, why are there no girls here?"

"Girls?" Elias snickered. "Girls are dumb, and their games are silly and tiresome, with too many rules. Thank Janus they're housed with the Sisters at the convent on the other side of Castle Hill. They keep all the little ones there as well, even boys. When they grow old enough, about six years or so, they send them over here. We only get to see the girls during the Yule Festival, but they're such a bore anyway."

Flynn thought to object—a couple of his best friends at his old school had been girls and he thought they were pretty great—but was rudely interrupted before he could say anything.

"Shhhhhhhhhhh!" someone hissed from a couple of rows in front of them. Flynn looked up and stared at the now familiar face of the Monitor from earlier that morning. The other boy had turned in his seat and was glaring at him with an expression that promised further unwanted attention in his future. A hooded priest entered the classroom just then and the Monitor turned to face the front once more. Flynn looked at Elias and lowered his voice to a whisper, hoping only the other boy could still hear him.

"Who *is* that asshole? It's like he's everywhere."

"Peter," Elias muttered in disgust. "He got promoted to Monitor last month, and now he runs around not letting anyone forget it."

At the front of the class, the priest—a tall, thin reed of a man with long white hair, wispy beard, and in his late years—cleared his throat and sat down at the desk next to a large blackboard that was mounted on an easel. At first, Flynn thought the cough had been intentional to get the children's attention, but as it went on, the sound of hacking and phlegm became disturbingly familiar to him. The old priest sounded just like his mother did before she had died. Flynn winced and hoped that he was wrong about what he was hearing, but none of the other children seemed concerned so he figured this must not be unusual. After several uncomfortable moments while the man struggled visibly to get some air into his wheezing lungs, he finally composed himself, smiled at the children, and then picked up a note on his desk to read it.

"Good morning, class," the priest said, the raspy voice fitting for his frail appearance.

"Good morning, Brother Edward," the boys greeted him in unison.

Brother Edward squinted at the note again before putting it down. "Today we have a new student with us, so let us welcome Flynn Castellar to our class, shall we?"

"Welcome, Flynn," the children's voices rang out together.

Flynn squirmed in his seat, feeling himself blush. He'd never liked attention drawn to himself, especially not of the sort that Peter was sure to continue giving him, and as if to confirm and emphasize that fear, Peter turned around once again and sneered meaningfully at him.

"Good," Brother Edward continued, "let us resume our studies then. Today we will learn about the southward expansion of the Avamor Imperium in more detail, including their first contact with the original inhabitants of our Rohnian peninsula. Flynn, we've only just begun this particular subject two days ago, so you should have no trouble catching up."

So, the lesson began, followed by several other classes as the day wore on toward the afternoon, interspersed with regimented breaks for recess and lunch. There were five learning periods per day, though Flynn soon learned that there were more subjects mixed in throughout the week. These ranged from things he rather enjoyed, like Brother Edward's history class and the one on geography, to other classes he absolutely hated, like arithmetic, and having to learn the language of Gol, which he found particularly difficult to grasp owing to its strange alphabet and harsh-sounding pronunciation. This last was not something he had been learning at his old school, and when he asked why they had to, he was told that it was because the empire of the Minotaurs across the wide gulf to the east was Rohne's second-most important economic partner. As such, the bull-men regularly sailed to Rohne in ships laden with trade goods, and not all of them spoke the Avamori common tongue of the western kingdoms. He remembered one day when his father had taken him and his brothers down to the mouth of the river Arnd. There, he had marvelled in awe when he caught his first and only glimpse of the hulking Golians from afar while they busily worked to unload crates from one of their ships and into a warehouse within their merchant enclave in Corazan's bustling harbour.

After some time, he realized he didn't mind being back in school so much, but like any normal child, it was the small breaks between classes that he most enjoyed. They had three in total each day—a short reading period in the morning where each child was given a selection of books to choose from to read; a long break of one hour beginning at noon for lunch in the refectory; and a half-hour of play time in the courtyard during mid-afternoon, just before the final two classes of the day. Right now, it was lunchtime during the final school day of the week, and Flynn walked out of the kitchen serving area holding a small wooden tray containing his lunch. He stopped near the same table he'd sat at every day since his arrival here and was looking about for a place to sit when he caught the eye of the boy he'd met in class that first morning—Elias. The other kid waved at him and then made some room on the bench for Flynn to sit down. Grateful for the invitation, Flynn took a seat next to Elias.

"Hi Flynn," Elias smiled.

"Hey Elias," he greeted his new acquaintance and then leaned forward to sniff the steaming contents of the bowl on his tray. It was an aroma he was quite familiar with, but one that always made his nose wrinkle a bit in distaste—vegetable and potato soup. It was one of the things his mother had cooked most often, mainly because it was affordable and could be easily made into a portion large enough to feed a family of eight like his had been, but that didn't mean that he was fond of it. With a sigh, he grabbed the chunk of dark bread on the tray and dunked it into the soup, blowing on it to cool it down before taking a bite. They had also given him a generous slice of smoked cheese and a pear, but he decided to save those treats for the end of the meal.

"Stripes and I are going to starve to death like this—soup for lunch three days in a row? What's Umberto thinking?" a boy sitting on the far side of Elias muttered despairingly.

While he chewed, Flynn glanced at the speaker, taking in the other kid's astonishingly large size. Even though he was seated, Flynn could tell the boy was very tall for his age, which he guessed couldn't be much beyond his own, if at all. Along with the height though, the lad was quite heavyset—even portly, one could safely say. His dark brown, wavy hair was long and down to his shoulders, and his equally dark brown eyes appeared small, sunken as they were in a pudgy face with chubby cheeks and full red lips that formed a pout around his small mouth. His chin flowed into his neck with almost no visible separation between the two, and his rotund belly pushed up against the edge of the table, smooth pink skin showing where the tight shirt he wore had come free from the top of his trousers.

"Flynn, this is Eric. We call him Big Eric for obvious reasons," Elias giggled, nudging Eric playfully in the side with one elbow.

Eric stuck his tongue out at Elias. "I'm not big, it's the whole lot of you that are small, even the new kid," he grumbled. "Hi Flynn, nice to meet you," he added politely.

"Hi Eric," Flynn waved between two spoonfuls of soup. "So, who's Stripes?" he asked out of curiosity. "That the kid next to you?"

"Nah, this is Georgie," Eric said leaning back a bit so Flynn could see past Elias and him to get a better look at the kid sitting on Eric's far side. It would be no exaggeration to say that Georgie's physical appearance was the complete opposite of Eric's in every way. The lad was small, his frame spare and lean, almost too much so. His black hair was close-cropped, and he had large and expressive pale blue eyes on a face that was thin and mousy. His lips were little more than a narrow line, but he smiled shyly at Flynn before his timid gaze darted back to the food in front of him. "He doesn't talk much, but don't let that throw you off. He's the smartest kid around here—even smarter than I am."

This elicited an eye roll from Elias. "That's not hard to do," he laughed. "Where is Stripes anyway?"

At this, Eric shifted his considerable weight around with some effort so that he could peer under the bench. "Bugger! I thought he was right here. Probably left when he smelled the soup," he said, looking around the refectory. "Ah, there he is."

Flynn followed the direction of Eric's gaze to the doorway that led to the kitchen and saw a striped orange cat come sauntering out, tail in the air. The animal was like a feline version of Eric—big, round, and heavy-looking. Having recently found something more to its liking than soup to eat in the kitchen, Stripes promptly sat down by the door and began to wash its face by contentedly licking one paw and running it over its head. Flynn smiled. He'd always had a fondness for cats, remembering the grey tabby that lived in the alley next to his house. "Big cat," he remarked.

"That's because he's not really a cat, you see. Stripes followed old Bartholomew down here from the castle three years ago and he's been here ever since. I took him in and now he's mine, though he lives down here in the kitchen because the headmaster won't let us take pets to our cells. Umberto the cook said he's a good mouser, so he's allowed to stick around," Eric stated proudly.

"What makes you say he's not really a cat, and who's old Bartholomew?" Flynn asked.

Before Eric could answer, Elias jumped in. "This big dummy thinks Stripes is actually a tiger that Bartholomew shrunk during one of his experiments. Old Bartholomew is the court Magen-dkar, you see...or was, actually—he passed away this spring. Anyway, everyone knows that's a load of poppycock. There're no tigers in Rohne, Eric," he rolled his eyes again in exasperation. "You wouldn't even know what one looks like if Brother Owen hadn't described them to us in class one day." He turned to Flynn with a smug look. "There're tigers in Laenis, where Brother Owen came from, but not here."

Eric crossed his arms and glowered at Elias. "He is a tiger, I tell you. Bartholomew was a wizard, so he could conjure up anything he wanted, no matter from how far away. Besides, how do you think Stripes got so big since he's been here? The magic is wearing off and one day he'll be back to his full size, you'll see. Then, when he's looking at you like a snack and I'm the only one that he'll listen to, you'll be saying 'Sorry Eric, you were right, now please call off your big tiger before he eats me.'"

"He's big because not only does he catch and eat all the mice around here, you're also constantly feeding him scraps off the table at every meal. No wonder he's huge. You two are perfect for each other." Elias waved one hand at him in a dismissive gesture and returned to his soup.

"Georgie, you like to read books about magic. Tell this fool I'm right." Unwilling to concede defeat, Eric turned to his right looking for backup. Flynn was so entertained by the exchange that he didn't even notice that he'd finished his soup. He started on the cheese while listening in on what Georgie had to say. He was quite enjoying the company of his new friends.

The small kid looked up at Eric, clearly uncomfortable with having to speak, but his big friend wasn't having any of it. "Well? Tell him!"

Georgie looked back down at his soup, pushed the spoon around a bit then spoke in a voice so low that Flynn had to strain to hear what he said over the din in the refectory. "Bartholomew wouldn't have let a wild animal that could be a threat to children wander around the orphanage, Eric. I'm pretty sure Stripes is just a cat."

"Hmmmph," Eric didn't look pleased or convinced by the answer but didn't say anything further. Instead, he pushed his bowl of soup away in disgust, ate the slice of cheese in one bite, and stuffed the piece of bread and pear into his pockets.

"So, how old is everyone?" Flynn asked.

"Same as you, or we wouldn't be in the same class," Elias replied. "Twelve."

"Eric's only twelve? He's so tall! And how come he gets to have long hair?"

"I don't know, but he just keeps growing, upwards and sideways," Elias laughed at his own joke. "As for the hair—Eric, why don't you tell him?"

Eric was in the process of trying to convince another boy sitting across from him as to why he should give him his cheese. The other lad only frowned and moved his meal protectively out of Eric's reach. "Thanks for nothing, Robbie. I hope you feel guilty when they find me dead from hunger by tomorrow," Eric said crossly. "What's that? Oh yes, my hair," he said brushing one long strand from his face. "Well, I've got the voice of an angel, Archbishop Marcos himself once said, and because all the angel statues in the cathedral have long hair, those of us that sing in the choir are allowed to wear our hair long." He sounded inordinately proud of this, eliciting a scoff from Elias.

"Yeah, except your voice changed this year and now you can't sing worth a damn," Elias teased the big kid. "Eric hasn't sung in the choir for months," he told Flynn before turning back to Eric. "You're just lucky Brother Melton hasn't remembered to cut that greasy mop off your head. Besides, you know that stuff about the angels is just a bunch of nonsense. Georgie's in the choir too and his hair is short like the rest of us because he's not a pretentious ass like you."

"My angelic voice will come back, you just wait. This is just a phase," Eric argued back.

"Whatever," Elias snickered. Then the bell rang three times, and it was time to go back to school.

⚬

What quickly became Flynn's favourite class didn't come until three days later, at the beginning of the next week. The subject was theology, and the instructor was none other than Brother Owen. He wasn't sure why, but he felt a pang of indescribable relief when he saw the kind priest's smiling face for the first time since the day he'd arrived at the orphanage. When the dark-skinned cleric greeted him personally after class and asked him to stay for a moment, Flynn was glad to finally have someone to talk to. All the boys from that very first class with Brother Edward were the same ones as for all the other classes, and though he'd begun a growing friendship with Elias and some of the others during recess, he still kept largely to himself. Mainly, he spent most of his time avoiding Peter.

"How are you getting on, lad?" Brother Owen asked him after everyone else had filed out.

"Alright, I guess," Flynn shrugged his shoulders noncommittally. "Most of the other boys seem nice, and I've even made some new friends. I miss my brothers though. I wish I could see them," he answered, looking up with a hopeful smile.

Brother Owen placed a hand on the boy's head in sympathy. "I have no doubt you will someday, just need to be patient for now. How are your studies so far?"

Flynn thought about this carefully before answering. "Mostly good, I think, but it's really not fair that we have to be in school all year-round," he pouted in clear annoyance. "I really like your class though. Learning more about the gods is interesting and fun." He turned his frown into a smile, hoping the priest would be pleased with his declaration.

Brother Owen laughed with genuine amusement at hearing that. "Fun, you say? I've heard people say many things about the gods all my life, but characterizing them as 'fun'? I must admit that's a first for me."

"I guess maybe I just don't know enough about them," Flynn reflected, wondering if he'd said something stupid. "But I'll learn more in your class, right?" he beamed up at the man.

"Of course you will," Brother Owen grinned. "Oh, and don't fret about the prospect of being cooped up in a classroom for the rest of your childhood. Classes are reduced in the winter, and we have a nice long break around Yule time, with lots of exciting games and activities for everyone. Then, when spring comes, you'll get a break from lectures and a chance to learn useful and practical things like manual trades, as well as devote some time to whatever arts you like, such as illustrating, painting, and even sculpting. Now, doesn't that sound a little better?" the priest said with a wink.

It did indeed, Flynn mused, and the thought gave him renewed hope that his time here might not be quite as miserable as he had allowed himself to envision during these last few days. Of course, he'd still much prefer to be able to just go back home to his family, but he reminded himself with a sigh that such a thing would never be possible. It was hard to let go of the notion, but at some point, he would have to try and make a serious effort to do it. "Well, I suppose I should go. I'm almost late for Brother Paul's calligraphy class down the hall and he hates it when he has to wait for anyone."

"Run along then, young Flynn. I'm glad you're enjoying my class, and I'll see you here again tomorrow," the priest waved farewell to him. "We'll be studying a different god tomorrow, so I know it will be exciting."

Already halfway to the door, Flynn stopped midstride and looked at Brother Owen in surprise and wonderment. "Oh! Which one? Which one?"

"Mighty Zarvon, the fearsome Minotaur god," the cleric said in a low, serious voice for dramatic emphasis while making a scary face.

"Yes!" Flynn nearly squealed with delight. On an impulse, he ran back and placed his arms around the priest, hugging him tight. Owen was taken by surprise at first but did not hesitate to return the sudden display of affection. Feeling the man's comforting embrace, Flynn felt some of his loneliness ease. Then he detached himself from the cleric and ran out of the classroom.

⸺◆⸺

The long days of summer wore on and Flynn slowly began to adjust to his new life at the orphanage. His friendship with Elias continued to blossom until the two became nearly inseparable, always playing together at recess, and sitting next to each other at mealtime. Being accepted into Elias' small group certainly made things easier in discouraging Peter's attention, but the bully still found a way to corner him when alone, the stronger boy always watching from afar and waiting for the right opportunity. These encounters invariably ended with some form of verbal threat, of which Peter seemed to be overly fond, but occasionally, particularly when Flynn dared to talk back, there would be a shove and a kick added in for good measure to ensure that Flynn never forgot who was in charge. He would climb into his cot on those nights, holding his aching side, and plotted his revenge a dozen times over before falling asleep. One day he even decided to bring Elias in on teaching Peter a lesson he wouldn't soon forget, but the other boy quickly dissuaded him from the notion.

"Just do your best to ignore him, please. He'll eventually get bored and find someone else to pick on," Elias said with some concern.

"But why should I? I hate his ugly face so much," Flynn was shaking with anger, still smarting from his last encounter with the Monitor. "I'll kick him in the stones when he least expects it, then spit on him while he's on the ground, like he does to me," he said, picturing it all in his mind as he threw his leg out in a practice kick, imagining how good it would feel.

"Aye, and it would serve him right, but do you think you'd be the first to try something like that? Listen, Peter enjoys Carlo's protection. You must've noticed by now—Carlo's one of the top Initiates, and it was he who promoted Peter to Monitor. You try and stand up to Peter and you'll have to deal with Carlo. I've seen it happen, and it doesn't end well," Elias warned, a look of remembered pain and fear flashing fleetingly across his face.

It was a late afternoon and the two of them sat side by side on a courtyard stone bench long after classes had ended for the day. Other children played nearby, chasing each other loudly through the gardens, but Flynn remained focused and gave Elias his full attention. He didn't miss the brief visual cue and looked at his friend with mingled surprise and alarm. Elias was a gentle soul, a calm and complacent counter to Flynn's fiery and energetic spirit. He wondered now if the other boy had always been that way, and if not, what had happened to change that? Sure, he liked to tease Big Eric mercilessly at every chance, but it was all good-natured ribbing, and Flynn knew the two boys shared a closer bond than most. On impulse, he put his arm around Elias's shoulder, trying to work up his courage to ask. The other boy stared at the ground with a melancholic look, and Flynn decided he simply had to know. After all, if the same fate was in store for him, he wanted to be prepared for it.

"What happened?" he asked nervously.

Elias didn't reply but the question brought the awful memory back in vivid detail and he looked up involuntarily to stare at something across the courtyard. Flynn followed the direction of his friend's gaze but saw no one there. The refectory bell had just sounded to signal supper time would be soon and the other children had run inside to wash up, leaving the two of them alone in the courtyard. Flynn looked on in puzzlement, trying to figure out this mystery. There was the ivy-covered outer wall of the orphanage; the main entrance that led to the streets of Corazan; and next to that closed gate, the old and crumbling stone tower that they were always told not to play near because it was dangerous.

The tower, Brother Edward had taught one day in history class, had been an observatory in ancient times, built by the Avamori monks to study the stars. It was one of the few original structures still left standing from those bygone days, and some of the early priests with an interest in astronomy had constructed a device called a telescope and placed it at the top of the tower to watch the night sky. Over the years, as Corazan grew in size and population, the amount of light given off by the increasing number of streetlamps at night began to interfere with these observations, and the tower was used only occasionally. Still, many interesting books and recorded studies on scrolls were stored there and the tower found a new life as a place for quiet contemplation and reading. That all ended about a century ago when one of the most violent storms to ever pass over the city unleashed a mighty bolt of lightning that struck the top of the tower. The observatory, along with nearly the entire domed roof, was destroyed, and the heavy telescope crashed through the lower floors, broken beyond repair. In the time that followed, the tower was deemed structurally unsound and not worth repairing beyond some stabilizing work, so it was closed forever, with the children being told to stay away. Then there were the creepy stories whispered at night among the children in the dormitory—stories about the tower being haunted, owing to a priest who was inside at the time the lightning came down. It was also said that his body had never been found.

"The haunted tower?" Flynn's mouth fell slack, feeling a cold shiver pass through his body.

"They put me in there, Flynn," Elias said at last. His voice sounded strange, and Flynn looked at him to see tears rolling down his cheeks. He sobbed and his body shuddered. "There were two of them—Peter and this other kid called Dario—they picked on me practically every day. I was only eight at the time, but I'd had enough. I complained to Brother Melton, but he didn't do anything, said I was probably exaggerating and that boys were just being boys. It didn't seem like there was a point telling anyone else after that. Then one night, I really had to pee, so I got up and went to the lavatory, but Peter and Dario were in there. I don't know what they were doing, and I didn't care, but they were upset and furious to see me. The pair of them grabbed me and kicked me, and said that if I ever told anyone, that it would get a lot worse, and just to give me a taste of that, they put one hand over my mouth so I couldn't scream and dragged me outside." He recounted the horrifying event and pointed at the tower with one shaking finger. "They took me there."

Flynn struggled to comprehend the magnitude of sheer terror Elias must've felt. Like all children, his imagination was quite fertile, and to him the old tower was one of those dark and creepy places where bad things happened to careless boys like him. The thought of being taken there against your own will was simply horrifying. He was scared to learn more, but curiosity overcame fear. He looked around in concern—assembly must be taking place by now, and they would quickly be missed during the head count before supper, but no Initiate had come looking for them yet. There was still time.

"What... what happened?"

Elias sniffled, wiped the tears with the back of one hand, and summoned his courage to tell the rest of his story. "They threw me to the ground in front of the door. I thought they were just trying to give me a good scare by taking me out there, and I said if they didn't let me go, that I would tell Carlo and they'd be in big trouble. That's when Peter pulled a key out of his trouser pocket and said 'Go right ahead. Who do you think gave me this?'"

"No way," Flynn exclaimed.

"It's true," Elias said earnestly. "Then they unlocked the door and threw me inside, but that wasn't even the worst part."

"You must tell me! Was there a creepy ghost waiting inside?" Flynn's curiosity and excitement had overcome his horror and empathy for Elias at this point. If his friend was here, safe and sound and telling him the story, how bad could it have been?

The other boy frowned and gave him an unhappy look before continuing. "Flynn, I'm being serious—I was terrified. It was dark, dusty, and it stank of mildew and old rot. I could barely see anything, but they'd obviously been in there before because they knew exactly where they were going. I heard what sounded like a creaky old trapdoor of some kind being lifted, and they forced me through the opening and down a decrepit ladder that I thought was going to break for sure. Then they laughed and slammed the lid shut. I heard them drag something heavy over the trapdoor, footsteps moving away, then nothing...just silence. Only it didn't stay that way for very long."

Flynn stared at his friend, speechless. He almost didn't dare breathe, imagining the anxiety and fear that Elias must've felt in those moments and feeling it in himself. Elias stopped sobbing and his eyes took on a distant, faraway look as he stared at the ground. "It was pitch-black down there, and there were puddles on the floor of old, putrid rainwater that must've leaked in from above. I felt my way to a wall somehow and sat down to wait. I was so scared, but thought they couldn't possibly leave me down there forever, or could they? Once they'd had their fun, they would have to come and get me. There were bugs crawling about, and other dark, slimy things. I heard skittering and other noises that had to be mice or rats. I don't know how much time passed, but it felt like forever. I cried and imagined how someone would just find my bones down there some day, picked clean by the rats. But then something changed. The noises in the dark stopped suddenly, and I felt like I was truly alone. I listened and listened, but there was nothing; just the sound of my own breathing. Flynn... it got cold all of a sudden... really cold. There was a draft of chill air on my face, and I swear I heard a voice whispering something. I thought I was going to die of fright, and that's when I felt the hand on my shoulder."

Flynn's eyes nearly bulged out of his head as he heard this. He looked again at the tower across the courtyard, fully expecting to see something horrible come through the door. "And then...?" he asked slowly, not taking his eyes off the ominous structure.

"I screamed and jumped up. I ran until I crashed into the ladder, and then I climbed up as fast as I could. When I got to the top, I banged on it as hard as I could and screamed for help. I didn't want to look behind me—didn't dare to—but I felt that cold air again, and that horrible whispering coming closer. I thought I was going to die, Flynn, or worse. I pissed my trousers I was so scared," Elias tried and failed to choke back another round of sobbing. "But then the trapdoor opened, and I felt a pair of hands reach down and pull me out. It was Peter and Dario, and they had a lamp this time. I scrabbled away from the opening as fast as I could while they closed it, but they looked at me like I was crazy. Then Peter laughed when I told them there was something down there and he said there was nothing but rats, and that I was the biggest one of them all, and that if I ever said anything about that night, that they would bring me back. They even said that this time, they wouldn't return for me. They let me go, and I ran outside and saw that it was almost dawn. I ran to my bed and missed all my meals and classes that day."

"What do you think it was?" Flynn managed, so enraptured by the story he completely forgot someone would be looking for them by now.

In response, Elias slowly and hesitatingly reached up to pull the collar of his shirt away from his shoulder, exposing his pale skin. There, faint but impossible to miss, was a bluish discolouration in the shape of a person's hand. Flynn gasped and sat up with a start, taking a step back and away from Elias. He swore— something they weren't allowed to do—uttering a bad word he'd often heard his father use, but he didn't care. His friend's reaction was pained as if he'd instantly regretted his decision to show him the strange mark, and Flynn felt ashamed. Before he could say anything though, he heard footsteps approaching on the gravel path behind them and turned around abruptly to see Carlo standing there in his black robe, a glare of disapproval on his lean face.

"What are you two up to? Didn't you hear the supper bell?" the Initiate demanded, peering past Flynn to look intently at Elias. Flynn risked a glance behind him and was relieved to see that his friend had covered up his shoulder. He must've seen Carlo approaching at the last second.

"We're sorry, Initiate Carlo. Elias wasn't feeling well after our last class and we were just waiting until it passed before we went back inside," Flynn offered by way of an apology and explanation, his eyes downcast in what he hoped was a contrite gesture. He didn't really have an opinion about Carlo. Due to being older—and by reason of their supervisory duties—the Initiates were generally regarded as being nearly the same as adults in terms of how serious they were. As a result, there was a tangible separation between them and the children they were tasked with keeping in line on a daily basis. In the case of this particular Initiate, all of that had changed when Elias had told Flynn of his frightening experience and the Initiate's connection to it. Standing in the shadow of Carlo's tall figure and suspicious stare, Flynn felt an undercurrent of menace emanating from the older boy that left him feeling frightened. Carlo didn't say anything, and Flynn continued to avoid the Initiate's gaze in deference, hoping that by doing so, he wouldn't give off any hint of the lie he'd just told. At length, Carlo stepped around Flynn and looked at Elias more closely. The other boy shifted uncomfortably on the bench, placed one hand on his stomach, and winced for effect.

"Initiate, may I please be excused from supper? My stomach really hurts, and I just want to lie down for a bit if I could," Elias asked in a pleading tone.

Carlo considered the request, his expression pensive but no less dubious than before. He drew his lips into a thin line, his dark eyes narrowing. "Very well," he said finally, "you are excused. Go see Brother Paul at the infirmary if this—whatever it is—persists. As for you," he turned to address Flynn, "I expect you to wash up and be seated at the table in no more than five minutes from the second this conversation ends, understood?"

"Yes, Initiate Carlo," both boys replied promptly, walking back at a brisk pace toward the dormitory building. Carlo watched them go, then turned his head and glanced at the tower, his face unreadable. When he looked back in the other direction, both children were already gone from sight.

CHAPTER 8

THE TALL LINE OF the Border Peaks loomed before the small wagon train, a natural barrier separating the barren and sun-baked expanse of Sarmakan to the north from the lush, verdant valleys of the Golian Empire to the south. The summer would soon be at an end and the long rains would follow, but the prevailing weather patterns in this part of the world would ensure that the life-giving moisture fell only on one side of those mountains; the side that mattered, as far as the Golians were concerned. As he looked on at the impressive barrier that shielded the land of his birth, Vurax couldn't help but think that whatever explorer had named the geographical feature so literally had definitely been lacking in imagination.

After so many monotonous and largely silent days of traversing the featureless steppes on their way south, the legionnaires broke into an old song celebrating a soldier's homecoming when the wagons began to make the ascent into the foothills. Listening to the words, Vurax struggled to hide his envy. These men truly were returning home—beyond those mountains, there was a life, a house, a family waiting for them. Yet for him, none of those things were true. What did Gol hold after all these years? He would be a stranger there, having lived the entire latter half of his life outside of it, forcefully immersed into a culture and people that were not his own. The conflicting emotions that had begun to war within him since he'd been freed had dominated his thoughts for the majority of the ride. Fear of the unknown; fear of what lay on the other side of those mountains; fear of whether he would be able to fit in and resume a life of normalcy as a citizen. These were all thoughts that left him feeling like he was suffocating on his own anxiety. Only at night, when he slipped into a dreamless sleep under the stars did he find peace, but the struggle always began anew each day when he opened his eyes and remembered he was no longer in his familiar tent.

"Just a few more days and we'll be through to the other side," Kael smiled beside him, his spirits buoyed by the song. "I know I'm probably just imagining it, but it feels cooler already, doesn't it?"

Vurax didn't reply at first. He'd grown more and more taciturn as the days wore on, and the centurion's attempts to engage him in conversation were often met with uncomfortable silence. He genuinely liked the other Minotaur, and he appreciated the sincerity of his efforts to try and make him feel at ease, but he felt like he was retreating farther and farther behind an emotional wall as dark and inscrutable as the mountains that towered before them. He managed a smile for the other's benefit.

"No, I think you're right; the air is becoming less warm. Do you know that, in eighteen years, I've only seen rainfall twice?" he mused, hoping some idle chatter would chase the melancholic thoughts away.

Kael couldn't contain his surprise. "Are you being serious?"

"I wish I wasn't, but yes, it's true. Water is more precious to the Sarmakanites than all the riches in Gol. Their ability to find just enough in the ground to survive each year was something that never ceased to amaze me."

"You admire them, don't you?" the centurion observed, looking at him pensively.

Vurax looked sharply at the other. "I admire their ability to endure in such a harsh land, nothing more," he snapped back defensively. It wasn't an unfair question for the other Golian to make, given the circumstances, but he felt irritated by it, nonetheless.

"I can understand that," Kael continued. "You're a survivor too."

Vurax thought about that for a minute. Yes, he was a survivor; he just wished he could shake the suspicion that he would need every one of those survival instincts once he crossed over into Gol.

It was painfully obvious to Kael that Vurax didn't wish to talk any further, but he decided it would be best to try and get him to confront whatever it was that he was struggling with, and sooner rather than later. He'd seen the former slave in the unshakable grip of the blood rage, and he shuddered to think of what the other might do if he continued to avoid talking about what was bothering him. That Vurax possessed a volatile temper was plain to see. However, maintaining control of it now that his life no longer depended on that carefully exercised discipline was something Kael felt critically important that Vurax understood for his own sake. He pressed on. "You never told me why they took your brother to the fighting pits and not you."

"Who said they didn't?" Vurax replied, staring fixedly ahead at the mountains. "Aros was not a fighter. Whenever the humans wanted to entertain themselves with something a little more challenging, they'd come for us, but always I asked to take his place, and they allowed it. It was my duty as the eldest to protect him—he was all I had left. But he'd grown sick in the last few months of his life and thus his usefulness as a slave was at an end. Some form of wasting illness had taken hold of his lungs and he was prone to long fits of coughing that left him weak and listless for days at a time. When they came for him again, they ignored my pleas. I could not fight for him as I always had before…" he meant to say something more but couldn't. His shoulders heaved with a sob, and he closed his eyes at the memory of that day when Aros was taken away, never to return.

Kael wanted to offer words of sympathy, but anything he could think of felt hollow and unnecessary. He allowed Vurax to release some of his pent-up grief and shifted the conversation back to the earlier topic. "You know, I never thought I'd miss rain, but after a few weeks in Sarmakan, I do. In fact, there was a time in my career as a soldier when I swore by Zarvon's stones that if I never saw another day of rain, I could die a happy Golian," he chuckled softly in a bid to alleviate the mood, then said no more. The wagon wheels creaked as the horses continued the climb, and the soldiers' song was winding down to the final refrain. He was gratified when Vurax finally took the bait.

"What do you mean by that?"

Kael adjusted his grip on the reins and then shifted in his seat before continuing. "I was born in the south, in a small fishing village on the coast whose name would mean nothing to you. Hells, it's so unimportant that most maps seem to forget it's even there," he laughed again. "Anyway, what matters is that when I was old enough to be drafted, I was assigned to the Fourth Legion. Have you ever heard of the exploits of the Fourth?" When the other shook his head, he snorted loudly. "Huh! The senate's propaganda minister is not doing his job then. The Fourth is stationed in New Gol," he paused to give the other a mocking look in jest. "You do know where that is, right?" Vurax gave his own snort in response, the good-natured sarcasm pushing down thoughts of his brother.

"Alright, good—had to be sure, you know?" Kael winked at Vurax, then resumed. "Well, for the last four hundred years of its illustrious military record, the Fourth has been tasked with not only protecting New Gol but also making the occasional foray across the Saurian Wall into Ur. Now when I say 'occasional', I mean several years' worth of campaigning that typically last as long as whomever is sitting on the imperial throne at the time. You may think that Sarmakan is about as bad as it gets, but let me tell you, I'd take those clear skies and firm ground under my feet any day over the stifling, steamy inferno of the Urian jungles," Kael spat and cursed.

Vurax gave the centurion a sidelong glance and shrugged, unconvinced. "Heat is heat."

"Oh no, my friend," Kael remarked earnestly. "In Ur, it's not so much the heat that gets you, but rather the humidity that comes with it. The jungle is so dense that you can't see more than ten feet in front of you at any given time. It's full of viny Trebur trees, taller than you can possibly imagine. There are insects the size of your fist buzzing about, a swampy, mist-covered mushy ground that pulls constantly at your every step, and the rain...the never-ending rain. You can walk for weeks and never see the sky, the air so thick with moisture that you can scarcely breathe at times. It's a lush but dark and soggy world in there, teeming with strange and exotic life."

The former slave tried to picture what Kael was describing but failed. He remembered trees, of course, and rain as well, but everything else was not even remotely within his realm of experience. "Sounds like a charming place," he quipped. "Why in blazes would an entire legion go in there?" he asked, genuinely curious.

"Why indeed..." Kael became lost in the memory of those early years of his service. "Trebur wood, that's why," he said as he leaned closer and used one finger to tap the long haft of the battle axe Vurax wore strapped to his back. "Rare and highly prized, it grows only in Ur. Harder than iron, it can only be worked with adamantine tools, and it takes a work crew of a dozen bulls two weeks to fell a single Trebur tree, but the wood harvested from it can be fashioned into enough weapons to outfit nearly an entire cohort. I think it speaks volumes about how impressed the tribune was with you that he gave you that axe. Unfortunately, the Trebur trees are sacred to the Urians, so as you can imagine, they don't take kindly to us cutting them down."

Born in the remote borderlands of the northernmost province of Gol, Vurax was unfamiliar with the political machinations of the empire as a whole but being that far removed from the great cities of the south didn't mean he was completely oblivious to Gol's blood-soaked history. New Gol was a sizeable stretch of land in the far southwestern corner of the Minotaur realm, sandwiched between the Saurian Wall and the Storm Sea. Only it hadn't always belonged to Gol. Over the course of several decades and costly campaigns, the region had been conquered over five hundred years ago and permanently occupied by the Golians, with the native Urians driven back beyond the mountains that protect the heart of their realm. That much he remembered being taught by his father, and he recited the lesson back to Kael.

The centurion nodded, impressed by the other's knowledge, but noted there were important gaps in it. "In the years since, over two-thirds of New Gol has been deforested of Trebur trees. During that time, this ample supply was enough to sate the empire's hunger for this priceless resource, but when the remaining trees recently began to inexplicably sicken and die, the Fourth Legion was ordered across the Wall; again, and again, and again. We may be the most feared fighting force in the world, but in there—where the mist in the air makes visibility non-existent and the swamp can swallow an armoured Golian whole in seconds—not even the best training and tactics the legion can offer will prepare you to survive against an enemy that you can't see. Have you ever seen an Urian, Vurax?" The question was clearly rhetorical and so Kael didn't wait for the negative reply.

"Neither have I, and I was in Ur three times—three very long incursions during which we lost several hundred brave legionnaires, and all just to get a few of those damn trees. Not once did I or anyone else in my maniple catch more than a glimpse of those cursed devils. You only hear a sibilant whispering all around you before they strike, like a constant hissing sound that insinuates itself in your mind. Just when you think you are about to be driven mad, there is the barest flash of blue-green scales, followed by a blur of venomous fangs and wickedly curved blades before soldiers are cut down and dragged off screaming into the jungle, never to be seen again." Kael stared at the road before them, but his gaze was unfocused as he recalled those horrible experiences. The soldiers had stopped singing now but he didn't notice. "It takes incredible courage not to panic, and not a few lose control when the enemy is upon us. Even when we manage to fend them off, our extensive knowledge of warfare is woefully unsuited for that nightmarish land, but do you think the senate cares?" he laughed bitterly. "When I got promoted to centurion, it was all I could do to request a transfer north to the Eighth. Most of the bulls I served alongside weren't as lucky. Give me solid, dry ground to sleep on, and a charging horde of enemies that I can see, and I haven't got much else to ask for as a soldier."

While Ur certainly sounded like a place that Vurax never wanted to visit, something about Kael's story didn't make sense to him. "What about the Kal-dkar?" he asked, recalling his very recent experience with a member of that shadowy order. "If these trees are so important, why not send one of them along with the cohorts of the Fourth?"

Kael nodded, acknowledging the tactical astuteness of the question. "They did, back in the early days, and it was a tremendous boon to have one of them alongside the legions. But that was when the empire established New Gol. When you cross the Saurian Wall into the darkest heart of Ur, something changes." His voice had nearly lowered to a whisper and Vurax wondered if the centurion was afraid of something or just being overly dramatic for emphasis.

"Such as?" he asked, frowning.

"Once you cross those mountains to the other side, the magic of the Kal-dkar simply fades away. We had one of them with us during our first campaign, so I witnessed it myself. The strangest part is that he seemed unaware that anything was different until it was too late, of course. He died just as easily as any soldier; easier in fact, because when you strip away their power, they are as defenseless as a newborn calf. The second time, the senate sent two of them. It made no difference. Much as they tried, something about that land prevented them from accessing and using their magic."

"What happened to them?" Vurax asked, curious about the fate of the mages despite himself.

"One fell during the first ambush that hit us. When it became obvious that they were powerless to protect themselves and the legion, the legate ordered the other one back to Gol immediately, lest she suffer the same fate. From that day onward, the soldiers began to whisper about the Tale of Sstur," Kael related, a haunted look in his eyes.

Vurax was finding this story increasingly tough to swallow and began to wonder if the other was having some fun at his expense. "The Tale of Sstur?" he asked with an incredulous snort. "The children's story about the Living God of Ur?"

When Kael looked at him, there was no hint of amusement in his expression. "Yes, the very same. Before she left us, the Kal-dkar said she felt the ominous presence of the Living God, He Who Walks Unseen Among the Trees. She said that is why the War-mages were powerless. I've never heard such terror and fear in someone's voice."

"Nonsense!" Vurax snorted. "Come on, Kael, you can't possibly believe that tripe, can you? They're just stories to frighten little ones when they're misbehaving. Hells, some even claim the gods aren't real."

"Who healed your wounds when you were dying then?" Kael snapped back, then went silent and turned to look at the road once more, keenly aware of Vurax's disbelieving stare upon him but refusing to meet his eyes. When the former slave gave an exasperated snort of disgust and turned away as well, the centurion muttered under his breath, too low for his companion to hear.

"You weren't there. I was."

⎯⎯⎯⎯ ◆◇◆ ⎯⎯⎯⎯

The road climbed higher into the mountain pass, the shadows cast by the towering peaks and cliffs completely engulfing the slow-moving wagons for long stretches at a time. Though the highest summits were perennially covered in snow and autumn was fast approaching, the tree-covered slopes and valleys still boasted a vibrant mantle of green, the last vestiges of the arid steppes left far behind. The crisp air was filled with birdsong, accompanied occasionally by the sounds of mountain stream water rushing over well-worn stones as it made its way down into the lowlands of Gol on the far side. A few wisps of white clouds drifted lazily westward in an otherwise perfectly blue sky. The scenery was breathtakingly gorgeous, highlighting sights and sounds that Vurax had given up hope of ever experiencing again. For all its beauty, however, the awesome display of nature failed miserably to lift his mood.

He had been brooding ever since his last conversation with Kael yesterday, and for his part, the centurion hadn't spoken a word to him either. Vurax was used to being alone with his thoughts, but whereas in the past they had been mostly filled with resignation, he now felt only unease and irritation. He searched constantly for answers within himself as to why he felt this way and always came up with the same reason: he was alone and without purpose, and the future frightened him. When he'd been a slave, he knew what his role was, but now? He was no longer sure of anything.

The clatter of distant hooves snapped him to attention; all his senses alert now, muscles tensing in readiness. He glanced at Kael, ready to take his cue from the other's reaction, but saw that the centurion appeared relaxed as he scanned the trail ahead with interest. "What is it?" he asked.

"Just a patrol," Kael responded. "We've probably been spotted some time ago. Now they're making sure we know that they've seen us."

Vurax's unease returned. He didn't like the knowledge that he'd been watched without being aware of it. The sensation vaguely reminded him of when the Kal-dkar had violated the privacy of his mind. He realized Kael was staring at him and when he lifted his chin questioningly, the centurion merely shook his head as he shifted his gaze to Vurax's hand. It was only then that he realized he'd been tightly gripping the haft of his axe for some time now. With a grunt, he reluctantly let go of the weapon.

"You're going to have to learn how to trust people again, you know?" Kael's concern for him was evident in his tone.

"I thought you told me to always be cautious and ready," Vurax retorted.

Kael sighed. "Yes, I did. But you are in Gol now. You're home."

As the mounted patrol came into view around a bend in the trail ahead, Vurax considered those words. So, this is it, he thought to himself. He'd returned at last—crossed that invisible line from the world he knew and back into the world he had once known. No, he decided. Being cautious and ready was critical now more than ever. The approaching Golian soldiers trotted their horses up to the lead wagon and pulled up to a halt a few paces away. Though they wore legionnaire armour, the reinforced leather and chainmail was much lighter than the type worn by the infantry troops Vurax had seen back in Sarmakan, and the shields slung over the saddles were small and round, rather than large and rectangular. There were very few horse breeds capable of bearing Minotaurs as riders and even so, it was paramount to not burden them needlessly. A blue pennon bearing a golden gryphon on the lead rider's spear identified the patrol as being attached to the Tenth Mountain Legion, and the front to back orientation of the blue plume on his helm denoted a rank lower than centurion.

"Hail, centurion," the mounted officer thumped his fist to his chest.

"Hail, optio," Kael returned the salute.

"What is your business on this road and your destination?" the optio queried, observing the formalities of his role as a border patrol commander.

"We're transporting a liberated slave to the capital from the Eighth in Sarmakan. As for being on your road, optio, there isn't exactly much of a choice around these parts," Kael smiled.

The Golian officer gave Vurax an appraising look, then turned back to Kael and grinned. "No, I suppose there isn't. Welcome back, centurion, and you as well, citizen. We're searching for two scouts that have gone missing in this area. They were due to report back two days ago, but we've had no luck and were about to return. We'll escort you to the nearest mountain fort of the Tenth where you and your unit can rest before continuing your journey, if you'd like."

Kael inclined his head. "We've not seen any sign of your scouts, but then they probably wouldn't be doing their job if we had. We are grateful for your company and look forward to the hospitality of your fort." As the patrol took up position alongside the wagons, the centurion flicked the reins and resumed their progress.

"How fares the Eighth?" the optio asked conversationally after some time as he rode alongside their wagon.

"As well as can be expected. The Sarmakanites fight well—for humans—but they are no match for us. All cohorts should be nearing Bantar now, by my estimate," Kael mused.

"Ah," the other nodded, "it's most likely over then. They'll be marching back this way in no—" the optio's words were cut short in mid-sentence when his body broke apart abruptly in a shower of bloody gore. Beneath what was left of the unfortunate Minotaur, the horse buckled and fell onto the road, neighing in terror. The enormous flying boulder that ended the Golian's life with shocking suddenness crashed into their wagon with earth-shattering force, sending shards of wood flying in every direction as the vehicle blew apart, scattering its occupants and contents violently through the air. Thrown clear of the vehicle, Vurax managed to tuck his limbs and roll as the ground came up suddenly, thus avoiding any damage worse than a few nasty scrapes and bruises. Chaos unfolding all around, he caught a glimpse of Kael, the centurion's body having slammed hard into the trunk of a large nearby tree and then fallen to the leaf-covered ground to lie there unmoving. All around him, he heard the shouts and startled cries of legionnaires, whinnying horses, and the loud, crushing sound of more boulders landing among them. Jumping to his feet, he surveyed the situation at a quick glance.

Three of the five wagons were completely destroyed, what little was left of them buried beneath boulders as large around as four Golians with linked arms. Of the horses that pulled them, those few that had survived either pulled fiercely on their harnesses to escape or had already done so, galloping away from the carnage around them. Too much was happening all at once for Vurax to take an accurate head count, but he could see the bodies of several soldiers of the Eighth, some crushed beneath the massive hunks of granite, others scattered about; a few of them moved, most did not. Down the road, behind the last wagon, he saw what was left of the Tenth's mounted patrol fighting to regain control of their panicked mounts. As they did so, one of the soldiers raised an arm to point up high and to the left to shout a single word.

"Giants!"

Vurax looked in that direction. Above the tall oaks that covered the rising slope to the east, a rocky ridge loomed a good distance away, giving anyone who stood upon its edge a perfectly clear view of the stretch of road they stood upon. Impossibly large figures moved there, their great arms lifting as they prepared to rain another deadly barrage of rocks upon the surprised Golians. The fate of the missing scouts seemed all too obvious now.

"Into the woods, quickly!" Vurax yelled. "We're completely exposed here!"

He had no military rank but was gratified to see the surviving legionnaires immediately respond with discipline and efficiency to follow the sensible command. Their reaction came not a moment too soon when more boulders began to fall from the sky, sending great clumps of dirt and showers of gravel into the air wherever they fell. The remaining unfortunate animals still tethered to the wagons perished in that second volley, as did two wounded legionnaires who were struggling to rise from the first attack. The rest of them managed to escape the killing field that the road had become and fled into the protection offered by the thick forest trees. Those few that were still on horseback abandoned their mounts to improve their chances of not being seen, knowing the horses would have had difficulty among the close confines of the forest.

Running behind the wide trunk of the nearest oak, Vurax stopped and pressed his back against the bark-covered surface, pausing to catch his breath while trying to not present a target to their attackers. Now that their prey was out of sight, it wouldn't take long for the giants to come looking for survivors. Before this day, he'd never seen one of the reclusive, powerful creatures, but he'd heard enough stories to know that their chances of survival were slim at best. Looking to either side, Vurax made a quick head count. He saw two legionnaires of the Eighth, and four of the Tenth. Out of twenty-two soldiers, only six were left, and all in a matter of seconds. He was no coward, but he recognized the looks of fear and apprehension on the faces of those around him, and that convinced him that fleeing might be the only viable option. There was no surviving officer left among them and the soldiers looked to him as if awaiting direction. He closed his eyes and gritted his teeth, trying to decide what to do. A groan from behind and to the right of him paused his thoughts.

Peering out carefully from behind his tree, Vurax tried to locate the source of the sound. Someone was still alive out there. A small movement by a nearby tree caught his eye. It was Kael. The downed centurion shook his head dazedly and tried slowly to rise but cried out in pain and collapsed back down again, clutching at one leg. Vurax winced when he saw the bloody shard of bone protruding from flesh just below the left knee. He cursed—things had just gotten way more complicated.

"How much farther to the fort? Can we make it?" he asked one of the patrol survivors.

"Half a day's ride," the soldier replied, grimly shaking his head.

Vurax struggled with indecision and doubt, his instinct for survival threatening to override all other considerations. He was nothing more than an ordinary Golian, an unassuming and insignificant farmer turned slave who had somehow managed to make it this far in a life filled with nothing but tragedy. He was not responsible for the lives of these soldiers, nor did he want to be. Yet Kael was still out there. The Golian centurion had saved his life back in Sarmakan and in the short time that he'd known the other Minotaur, he'd become the only person that he could remotely call a friend in a world where he had nothing else. A life without honour and loyalty was not one he felt worth living.

The air was still, except for the sounds of anxious breathing from the hiding Golians, but the reprieve was brief. Soon, the crashing of heavy footsteps could be heard as the ground trembled slightly in response and the very trees protested, shoved aside to make way for what was coming. Vurax removed the battle axe from the harness on his back and readied himself. The others took their cue from him and drew their weapons as well. The giants would be upon the road very shortly so there wasn't much time to discuss any form of strategy, but as he spotted the pair of horses through the trees several yards from their position, he made the attempt anyway. He turned to the nearest soldier of the Tenth Legion, a strong and able-looking fellow, and spoke just barely above a whisper.

"Legionnaire, what's your name?"

"Dalos," the other replied.

"Dalos, when I give the signal to attack, run for the centurion back there and use your dagger to cut him loose from his armour. Get him on one of those horses somehow, then ride for the fort, and don't look back. We'll try to hold them off as long as we can. Once you're clear, we'll disengage and follow. Understood?"

The soldier nodded grimly, already calculating the distance to the wounded officer and back to the animals. Vurax tightened his grip on the axe and listened to the approach of the giants as they drew closer. He could hear their guttural grunts now and briefly wondered if it was some form of primitive language. It didn't matter in the end, as he felt certain there was only one goal on their minds—destroy anything that still moved. As the thought passed through his head, he dared one more look at Kael. The centurion was lying motionless at the base of the tree once again. He hoped fervently that the officer had heard the giants coming and was merely remaining as still as possible rather than the alternative. Stilling his breath, he prepared himself. He did not feel the blood rage stirring within him and questioned whether he should attempt to summon the destructive force. While it would definitely help him in the coming fight, he was wary of its inability to allow him to distinguish friend from foe. During the battle of Ikut, he'd been a slave, uncaring of whether he lived or died. Things had changed now, however. He had his newfound freedom to live for, but not at the cost of having his countrymen's blood on his hands. If Kael and these others were going to have a chance, he was going to have to keep all his wits about him.

A loud snarl heralding the arrival of the giants interrupted Vurax's deliberations. There were four of them, enormous humanoid brutes as tall as a full-grown oak, their boulder-sized shaggy heads covered in coarse black hair. Each held a massive wooden club in its gnarled hands and wore a crude garment sewn together from various animal pelts over one shoulder, tied at the waist by a thick length of rope. While one scanned both ends of the road, the others busied themselves poking through the devastation they had caused, making huffing sounds as they searched. As a child, Vurax's parents had told him stories about the ancestral enemies of the Minotaurs—terrible, gigantic creatures that lived in the mountains—and how they ate anything that they caught, including small Golian children who didn't finish their supper. Yet, peering out from behind his tree, he noted that the creatures showed no interest in the dead horses or Minotaurs, other than to make sure they were no longer breathing. He concluded that this was no ordinary hunting party out foraging for food, though what that meant, he hadn't the faintest notion. Whatever they were doing here, the search didn't take long. The one giant that had stood back watching the road grunted once and lifted its club to point at the edge of the woods in the direction the Golians had fled and where Kael had fallen. This was it—they were nearly out of time.

Vurax briefly considered charging out to meet them but realized that fighting out in the open gave the giants the advantage. Here, nearer to the trees, the brutes would be hindered by their great size. He glanced to either side and caught the nervous looks in the eyes of the others. He shook his head slowly, signalling them to wait just a bit longer. The giants needed but two large strides of their muscled, trunk-like legs to take them to the edge of the woods, and then one bent down to prod roughly at Kael's prone form with its weapon. Wood scraped against bone and the centurion could not stifle a moan of agony, causing the giant to grunt in surprise and call out to his fellows. Now they were out of time. Heart pounding fast in his chest and filling his veins with adrenaline, he closed his eyes for a split second and inhaled sharply. Then he let his breath out in a rush.

"*Now!*" Vurax yelled.

As one, the Golians sprang from their places of hiding, weapons held before them to rush the gigantic humanoids. The mountain giants were momentarily caught off-guard, clearly startled by the fact that the puny creatures before them were attacking rather than having fled, but the surprise was all-too brief. Vurax and Dalos ran toward where Kael lay. While the legionnaire made quick work of Kael's armour straps and struggled to hastily pick up the officer, Vurax charged the giant that loomed above them in an attempt to buy Dalos some time, even as it raised its club to strike at the impudent Minotaur. The massive hunk of wood came down with a tremendous crash that sent a spray of dirt upward, but he deftly dodged the blow without losing speed. Swinging the two-handed battle axe with all his might, he was rewarded with a bellow of pain as the sharp steel bit deep through the tough flesh of one oversized calf, then used his momentum to rip the weapon free and run between the giant's legs to stop behind the creature. The battle, chaotic and brutal, was joined.

The creature swung around ponderously and levelled another attack at the Golian. Sidestepping another of the club's devastating blows, Vurax saw Dalos finally lift a limping Kael to his feet and help support the centurion's weight, the pair moving back under the cover of the trees as fast as they could. A short distance to Vurax's right, a giant caught one of the soldiers of the Eighth in one huge hand and lifted the struggling Minotaur bodily from the ground. With his one free arm, the desperate soldier slashed repeatedly with his sword, scoring bloody gashes along the giant's hand, but the brute seemed oblivious to the pain. With a horrible sound of snapping bones, the giant squeezed the legionnaire's frame until the bull's agonized scream ended in a wet gurgle, dark blood gushing from his mouth. Like a bored child discarding a broken doll, the giant released his grip, and the limp body crashed to the ground.

Squaring off against his opponent, Vurax stared grimly at the horrible visage leering down at him from a great height. The mountain giant's facial features resembled those of a human, but whereas he'd always considered humans to be ugly, unlovely things, this face was positively horrendous by comparison. With its bulging, uneven eyes, misshapen bulbous nose, bushy mane of a beard, and crooked mouth filled with cracked, rotting teeth, the giant's face was the stuff of nightmares. The club came down again, and again Vurax jumped to the side, narrowly avoiding being smashed to a pulp. Before the giant could lift the weapon once more, he lashed out with his axe again and landed another solid blow, this time on the creature's wrist. Yet, while his skill and luck had carried him this far, he knew he would begin to tire soon. At his own considerable full height, he only came up to the giant's knee, and he was beginning to despair that he would be able to hit a vital area before that club eventually found him.

More critically, he saw that the other Minotaurs were faring no better. While two of the soldiers fighting in concert had managed to bring one of the giants to its hands and knees using their long spears, the one that had crushed its victim moments earlier turned to aid its downed fellow. Wheeling about to face the new threat too late, one of the legionnaires was lifted clear off his feet and catapulted through the air to crash lifelessly to the ground a good distance away, his ribs smashed by the devastating sweep of a club. Ignoring his companion's ghastly fate and knowing that it meant leaving his back turned to the second giant, the second soldier bravely thrust his spear at the exposed throat of the first downed hulk with a cry. The heavy, broad-bladed weapon penetrated deep, hot blood spraying with force as a vital artery was severed. The giant clutched uselessly at its neck while its life spilled out, its struggles growing weaker until it finally lay still, but its killer did not have a chance to enjoy his victory. Even as the soldier freed his weapon from the giant's neck, a shadow fell over the Golian, followed a second later by an enormous foot crudely wrapped in leather hides. The tremendous weight and force bore the unfortunate legionnaire to the ground. Pinned with no chance of escape, the Minotaur was pulverized as the giant cruelly and gleefully ground his foot down.

Vurax tried to look beyond his own opponent and into the woods behind it. He could no longer see Dalos and Kael and could only hope that they had managed to reach the horses, assuming of course that the already frightened animals hadn't been spooked further by the noise of the battle. The brief distraction nearly cost him his life, and he cursed out loud when the club clipped one shoulder and arm. It was only a glancing blow, the full force of which he'd barely managed to avoid, but he felt the bones shatter from the impact. Grimacing in pain as he switched to a one-handed grip on the axe, he considered his options. One giant was down and the other three were bloodied but not fatally wounded, including the one he was facing, but the last of the legionnaires had just gone down fighting bravely but hopelessly against two opponents. The fight, such as it had been, was nearly over and he was overwhelmingly outmatched, and now outnumbered as well. He'd done his part. With a burst of energy and speed, he dashed past his adversary before its friends could arrive to help and ran back into the tree line. Ignoring the pain that flared horribly in his arm with every movement, he weaved past several trees as he ran toward the area where he'd last seen the horses. When he arrived, there was no one there, horse or Minotaur.

He leaned against an oak, his chest heaving from exertion while he tried to catch his breath. Behind him, the crashing sounds of the pursuing giants were impossible to ignore. Of all the ways he'd imagined his death during those countless nights while he fell asleep in his tent, he never imagined this as its eventual shape. In the final moments that were left to him, he couldn't decide which would have been the harsher form of fate: to die ignominiously as a slave or to have briefly felt the sweet taste of freedom, only to have it end cruelly on a remote mountainside, alone. Rather than despair, he began to chuckle mirthlessly.

"Zarvon, if you're listening, I hope you've enjoyed your poor joke," he spat. Then he turned inward and channeled his bitterness into rage. Let it come, he resigned himself; there was nothing left to lose now but his own worthless life. His vision began to dim as the green of the forest quickly became tinged with crimson. The pain in his arm dulled and faded into the background until he no longer felt it. Muscles bulging as he loudly snorted his anger into the air, Vurax stepped out from behind the tree and planted his legs apart, axe in his good hand, ready to face his doom. The approaching lead giant grinned grotesquely when it saw the Golian walk out before him and onto the open forest floor. The other two cunningly circled to either side, cutting off any avenue of escape and watching warily as their leader prepared to finish off their prey. The giant slowly raised its club in preparation to smash the motionless Minotaur, its limited powers of reasoning having deduced that the Golian had simply chosen to accept his inevitable fate. In a manner of speaking, the giant wasn't wrong, but he didn't know that the Minotaur planned to drag them all down to death with him.

CHAPTER 9

The walk to Arlingtown's church was not very long, but it gave Ellianna sufficient time to think about the boy she had just met. Darken was an odd one, to be sure, but then her social experience with boys of her age did not extend much beyond the small handful that worked seasonally alongside her at Thurgod's farm. Under the constant threat of the Dwarf's watchful glower, however, they generally focused on their work rather than interact with her in any meaningful way. The encounter with Darken had helped lighten her mood and push the episode at the market to the back of her mind and she liked how that made her feel. She wasn't sure yet how she would keep her promise of seeing him again though, or even how to go about doing that, but she had a feeling that Darken would find her first.

Once the fields were prepared for this year's coming winter, there wasn't much to do on the farm except tend to the animals and wait for planting season to come again. Under Thurgod's guidance, her natural affinity for plants had blossomed and flourished until her skills nearly rivalled his, but it was the farm animals that held a special place in her heart. She always felt happiest when she visited the barn to milk the dairy cows and goats or stopped by the chicken coop to collect the eggs. Without other children around to play with, these had been her only true friends and companions since she'd begun living at the farm, so the prospect of a friendship with Darken was both exciting and frightening at the same time. Then there was the challenge of telling her grandfather. Her ingenuous nature wouldn't allow her to even consider keeping this from him, but it would require all her tact and every gentle word that she could muster to try and sway him to accept her new friend.

As she pondered the monumental task before her, she nevertheless kept some of her attention on the street, diligently following the directions Darken had given her. The baron's ancestral home of Arling Keep was impossible to miss, sitting as it did atop a low hill at the northern end of the town, the tall, dark grey stone walls and battlements commanding an impressive view above the rooftops of

Arlingtown. At each corner of the ancient fortification, a banner hung over the wall, the gold-trimmed blue fabric emblazoned with the baron's coat-of-arms—a charging boar over a pair of crossed hunting spears. Since the time of its founding generations ago by Arling Taffen, the Barony of Arlingford had been ruled over by the Taffen family, though the whispers in some circles these days were that Baron Edmund Taffen II would be the last to bear that storied family name.

Ellianna didn't rightly understand all the complexities of noble titles and succession, but as her grandpa had recounted the sad tale one time, the current baron's wife had died some years ago in a tragic boating accident. Though Edmund was still relatively young and presumably perfectly capable of taking another wife and siring a child, he'd been so devastated by grief and guilt at holding himself responsible for the loss of his love that he vowed to never take another woman into his heart or bed again. Thus, it was widely expected that his sister's son would one day assume the title of Baron of Arlingford. Thinking about the baron and his family, she remembered with clarity the first time she'd seen the keep from afar upon her arrival in Arlingtown as a little girl, and thinking how wondrous it would be to live in such a fantastical place. Today, as she walked past the forbidding structure, she felt it looked grim, uninviting, and cold even in this warm summer air.

The twin guard towers flanking the gatehouse of the River Gate loomed ahead and she knew that she was nearing her destination. The large ironbound gates stood open as they always did during daylight hours, and beyond them she could see the long span of the stone bridge over the Arling River. Guards wearing the baron's blue livery stood nearby, casually looking over anyone entering the town, but they barely spared her a glance as she veered eastward before reaching the gate to walk along a street that ran parallel to the town wall. A few more steps brought her to another plaza, this one much smaller than the one that hosted the town's marketplace but impressive in its own right, mainly owing to how pristine and well-kept it looked, with its white stone benches, marble fountains, and carefully manicured garden spaces. After her recent sojourn through the slums, the homes in this area—and the plaza in particular—stood out in stark contrast from the poverty and trash-ridden streets at the other end of town. Yet the large building at the far end of the square unequivocally commanded one's attention when entering this beautifully serene place.

Broad steps led up to a tall marble colonnade that encircled the domed and circular central part of the building, the pillars spreading to either side of the elegant rose-coloured stone edifice and along two identical, rectangular wings to either side. Within the shade of the graceful arcade, large twin doors wrought of intricately carved dark wood stood closed, though a smaller door inset within one of these was open and led to the shadowed interior beyond. During morning mass, the big doors were thrown wide open, inviting the townspeople to come to worship in the house devoted to Anval the Healer, the benevolent god of life, health, and the medicinal arts. For the remainder of the day however, only the smaller door stayed open, allowing the faithful to freely enter this holy domain if they felt in need of personal guidance, or simply wished to enjoy some quiet time of reflection in the calming presence of Anval.

The pantheon of divinities worshipped by the peoples of the land was large and varied, and despite her grandfather's open skepticism at the notion and existence of such godly beings, Ellianna had nevertheless grown up with a private and quiet belief in something greater than herself that watched over her life and destiny. She couldn't explain the source of her faith, nor was it focused on any particular deity—all of which she wasn't afraid to confess she had very little knowledge of—but it was a feeling she'd had ever since she had walked out of that forest ten years ago. Something—or someone—had watched over her when everyone in her village had perished, delivered her safely to the door of a kind Dwarf who took her in to raise as his own, and she was almost certain now that the stranger in her dream was connected to all of that, and perhaps even responsible in some way. If higher powers were at work in her life, then she needed to know for sure and she could think of no other place to begin her search for answers than a church.

She walked slowly across the courtyard, marvelling at the aesthetically complex yet simultaneously functional architecture of the temple building in front of her. She had no understanding of how such things could be conceived of and constructed, but the undeniable effect of awe that they imparted upon an observer such as herself was clearly successful proof of the intent behind the design. Looking at the stunning church, nestled perfectly within its carefully ordered setting, she was filled with peace and an appreciation for life and all it had to offer. As she approached, she thought she could hear the faint sound of beatific voices raised in song coming from within, but she couldn't be certain if the enchanting hymn was real or a product of her fertile imagination. Climbing the steps up to the tall doors, she felt suddenly very self-conscious about her appearance and peasant's attire, but the fleeting doubt passed when she reminded herself that she'd always heard that the church was supposed to be a place that welcomed people from every station of life as equals. Without further hesitation, she crossed the threshold of the small door.

The interior of the church felt cool and invigorating, an instant and welcome respite from the sun outside, but it took a few moments for her eyes to adjust to the dimness within. She stood in a large square-shaped foyer, bare except for a couple of benches along the walls, with a closed door on either side and another set of closed double doors in front of her. In the centre of the room was a carved marble plinth supporting a basin, and what little light there was that didn't come from the exterior door was provided by a few burning candles mounted on wall sconces. The singing seemed to be coming from the area beyond the double doors, the haunting melody echoing throughout the building, low and soothing. Walking to the basin, she peered inside and saw what appeared to be rose petals floating in clear water, noticing for the first time that there was a subtle floral scent that permeated the air in here. Uncertain as to what to do, she waited a few minutes, but no one appeared. On an impulse, she placed her hands gently within the basin and submerged them in the cool water. When nothing happened out of the ordinary, she was left feeling sheepish for thinking that something might.

She looked around as she tried to work up her nerve to open the double doors leading further into the temple but felt apprehensive about doing so for some reason. Staring at the ornate brass handles, she searched her feelings and the only conclusion she kept reaching was the eerie premonition that her life would be forever altered if she stepped beyond that threshold. She couldn't explain why she felt this way, but there was a sense of impending inevitability that shook her to the core. Anval was said to be a compassionate, nurturing god, but fear of the unknown and an answer to the truths she sought suddenly made this place feel ominous and foreboding. Her determination wavered and broke at last, and she took one step to leave. This had all been a mistake. She was a timid little girl again, and the overwhelming desire to be back in her grandpa's cottage, listening to the old Dwarf's fantastical stories as he tucked her in at night was too strong to overcome. She cursed her foolish impulse to upset any part of that life, but just then—smoothly and soundlessly—the inner doors of the temple opened as if pulled by invisible hands.

Ellianna froze, watching wide-eyed as the doors slowly came to a stop. She wasn't just imagining it— there was no one there, yet the doors had opened somehow. Her urge to flee began to quickly lose ground to a new and stubborn resolve, as well as a burning curiosity. Before she could change her mind again, she walked up to the threshold and then stepped through it. The temple's inner sanctum was a large, round chamber, beautifully fashioned from marble, just like the outside of the building. She stood on the uppermost level of a semi-circular row of seats, like an amphitheatre, that tapered down in successive steps to a raised dais in the centre of the domed hall. The far wall of the gracefully curving chamber was covered in magnificently crafted stained glass, each long and narrow pane carefully placed between a row of tall columns covered in alabaster carvings and expertly arranged to bathe the tall marble statue that stood over the altar in a dazzling array of multi-coloured sunlight. Though the ethereal singing she'd heard previously still echoed through the air, she could detect no obvious source for it. In fact, the large nave of the temple seemed to be completely unoccupied.

As she focused on the dais below, she soon saw that she'd been wrong in her initial observation. Motionless like the statue that loomed above, a solitary figure knelt before the altar, clad in flowing robes as white as the purest snow, head covered by a hood. Ellianna's gaze lifted to take in the details of the statue itself, which depicted an older man garbed in a simple cassock tied at the waist, arms lifted above his shoulders, hands open, and palms held upward. The kind and gentle face, framed by wavy hair and a long beard, had been perfectly sculpted to capture an expression that conveyed both tranquility and sorrow at the same time. The entire setting was so peacefully transcendent that Ellianna realized with a start that she'd been holding her breath. When she let it out with an audible gasp that disturbed the serenity of the scene, the hymn slowly dwindled in intensity, and the kneeling figure rose to its feet as the last notes of the chant faded into complete silence.

Though the church was open to one and all, Ellianna couldn't help but feel that she was intruding upon something private. Again, she fought down the urge to leave and simply waited in silence to see what would happen next. After a while, the figure turned, and Ellianna inhaled sharply once more. The woman was incredibly tall and slender, with lustrous raven locks of long hair spilling out of a hood that framed an achingly beautiful face. Her skin was as pale as the marble stone of the temple itself, and her eyes were a piercing blue that shone with an inner light. On her breast, a medallion hung from a silver chain, the round disc showing three crossed staves within a circle of cerulean and sapphire. Yet it wasn't the woman's striking appearance that had shocked her, but rather the fact that the woman wasn't alone, as she had initially surmised. As she turned to face Ellianna, the young woman saw that the other's hands rested on the shoulders of a small boy who turned to face her as well. The similarity to the imagery in her dream was impossible to ignore. She stumbled backward a step and had to steady herself against a nearby pillar when she felt her heart racing impossibly fast.

Neither the woman nor the child spoke, and when both regarded her impassively, she took a second to compose herself. The light she had seen in the woman's eyes was no longer there, and she wondered if it hadn't been merely a trick of her imagination. More importantly, and with the initial surprise now past, she noted that the boy did not look like the one from her dream. This child was younger by some years, and his hair was sandy blonde and trimmed short. Still, she couldn't shake the uncanny resemblance between this scene and what she had witnessed in the vision. Was it a coincidence? She had to believe so because nothing else made sense.

"Go find your father, Mika. Tell him I'll be a little while longer," the woman said, bending down to kiss the child gently upon the back of his head. The boy looked up at her and smiled before running off the dais with the boundless energy of youth, up one set of steps along the seating area, and finally disappearing through a side door to another part of the temple.

Mika. That was the name of the baron's nephew, Ellianna recalled overhearing at the market once, which meant this woman must be his mother, the Lady Jana Morhain. She felt suddenly embarrassed by her utter lack of knowledge of protocol and etiquette, and while she was certain her attempt at a curtsey was laughably clumsy, she attempted anyway. Lady Morhain responded graciously by smiling warmly with a nod and beckoned for her to come down. Mindful of her step while pulling the hem of her skirt slightly up, Ellianna walked down the central stairs toward the altar.

"Welcome to Anval's house, my child," Lady Morhain greeted Ellianna with a warm smile, motioning for her to take a seat on one of the pews in the front row. "What can I do for you?"

Ellianna took the seat and marvelled at the woman before her, in awe of such unearthly beauty and feeling extremely plain and self-conscious by comparison. When she realized that she was staring, she blushed furiously with embarrassment and looked away, pretending to admire the statue behind Lady Morhain. When she dared to look back, the woman had removed her hood and merely stood there, smiling patiently at her.

Ellianna was feeling decidedly lost, unsure how to even properly address the woman before her. As a member of the clergy, 'your grace' would be an appropriate honorific, but Jana Morhain was also a highborn noblewoman, so she hoped that 'my lady'—as Ellianna had commonly heard Jana referred to—would suffice. "I'm sorry, my lady, but I didn't mean to disturb you. That was a lovely hymn I just heard, but I don't see the choir anywhere. Are they in another chamber nearby?"

"Something like that," Lady Jana replied with a mischievous wink and merriment in her dulcet voice that instantly made Ellianna feel more at ease. She smiled in return, uncertain what the answer meant, but it didn't matter. What mattered was that she suddenly remembered she was forgetting her most basic manners.

"Forgive me. My name is Ellianna," she introduced herself. "I... uh... I am in need of some personal guidance and advice and wasn't sure where to turn. I wouldn't presume to take up your valuable time with such unimportant things, so if there's someone else you can suggest...?" She hadn't really meant to rush into her reason for being here like that, but she was mortified at the thought of importuning this clearly important individual with her personal problems, so she decided to get straight to the point.

"Nonsense," Lady Jana exclaimed. "My time is freely given to those in need. The grace of Anval blesses his children with the miracles needed to heal not only what ails the body, but also our spiritual essence. So, Ellianna, please tell me how I can be of service to you?"

'Of service to you'—this great and noble lady? It took Ellianna some time to absorb that statement, and to understand that Jana Morhain was being completely sincere with her. Her demeanour certainly didn't match her grandfather's less-than-flattering views on the nobility in general, and the upper class of Arlingford in particular. Of course, Jana was the first and only personage of such status that she'd ever met, so perhaps she was an exception? Whatever the case, she was pleasantly surprised.

"I'm honoured that you'd consider me worthy of your attention," she stammered with gratitude, lowering her eyes, and bowing her head in reverence and awe. She felt a light touch on her chin where Lady Jana placed two fingers and gently lifted her head to look into her pale green eyes.

"Would you please stop that? We are all equal in the eyes of Anval. An individual's worth should not be measured by an accident of birth, even if the artificial construct of class brings society a measure of necessary order."

Ellianna merely nodded, accepting that Jana's views on such complicated topics were far wiser and more informed than her own, though the irony that the lady's own son would one day rule the barony did not escape her. Perhaps it had to do with that necessity she spoke of? At any rate, she hadn't come here to engage in a philosophical debate with a stranger, and despite the lady's thoughtful words of reassurance, she didn't want to overstay her welcome.

"You're very kind, my lady. Alright then—I've come here because I'm troubled by a recurring dream. I know this sounds silly—everyone has dreams, even ones that repeat once in a while, or so my grandpa tells me—but this one is" she paused, struggling to find the right word, "important somehow." She shifted uncomfortably in her seat and averted her eyes once again; fearful she'd sounded stupid.

"Dreams can be complicated, even mysterious at times, but most can be dismissed as the tired musings of our subconscious minds while we sleep. That isn't to say they are all meaningless, however," Jana added when Ellianna looked quickly up at her in disappointment. "Tell me more about this dream. How long have you been having it?"

"Several years now, ever since I came to Arlingtown from my former home. It's always the same, but it doesn't come every night. Or maybe it does, but you know how sometimes we are sure that we dreamt of something but can't remember it in the morning? Maybe it's like that, only last night it was different. It's always—always—the same, but not last night. Today is my birthday, and I think there must be some significance to all this, and even if there isn't, I just want someone to help me understand what's happening." She hadn't meant to sound like she was pleading, but she had to admit to herself that she desperately needed some reassurance that she wasn't going crazy and that there was a reason for all this.

Jana sat attentively next to Ellianna, eyes observing the girl's mannerisms and gestures as she spoke; ears listening carefully to every word. Yet her mind was elsewhere, the part of her consciousness that formed the spiritual conduit to Anval travelling along that invisible pathway to answer the summons she had felt there. The contact was brief—less than the time required to blink—but that single instant was all it took for her to understand that Ellianna was not here by mere chance. And there was more, so much more.

"Describe your dream to me, please. Leave nothing out. First, retell it to me how you've always remembered it, and then tell me what was different this last time."

There was a slight shift in Jana's tone from friendly to serious, and Ellianna did not fail to perceive the change. Encouraged once again that she wasn't being dismissed outright for bringing a trivial matter before the priestess, she did as she was asked, leaving no detail out. It wasn't difficult after all—she'd had the dream so many times that it had become an indelible part of her memory. In fact, she could recall it more vividly than many things about her early childhood that she wished she could remember. When she thought of the dream in that light, she realized she wanted nothing more than to be rid of it. It had dominated her thoughts for so long that she ached for a life when it no longer plagued her sleep with its unwelcome presence. When she finished, she felt a great sense of relief. Being able to finally share this with someone was liberating in and of itself, let alone someone that might actually understand what it all meant. She dearly loved her grandpa, but something inside of her had always prevented her from sharing this intimate part of her with him. With a stranger, it was somehow easier.

She waited patiently for Lady Jana to say something, but the other woman appeared lost in thought, a faraway look on her face that made Ellianna feel as if the cleric was staring straight through her. Unsure as to what the prolonged silence meant, she began to fidget a bit, unable to keep her nerves from showing. She wasn't sure what she'd expected would happen and was about to politely clear her throat when Jana's eyes suddenly focused on her own with an intensity that took her by surprise.

"Where did you say you were born?" Jana asked.

"I... I'm not sure," she confessed with some measure of embarrassment. "It's strange, I know, but all the memories of my life before coming to Arlingtown are very fragmented and vague, almost as if they're hidden behind a veil of fog, like in my dream."

"What do you remember?"

"Not much. There was a forest and a small village where people lived... my parents... my father was a hunter, and every year he took part in something called The Great Hunt. It always took place in the summer, and one year I remember that he won and brought home a stag. It was my birthday—just like today. That's the last memory I have of him...of them. Wait, that's not true," she stopped then, feeling a lump in her throat and pang in her heart when a painful image surfaced briefly through the mist that clouded her memory of the past.

"What is it?" Jana asked with concern, placing a comforting hand on her shoulder.

"I'm sorry. This was a mistake. I think I should go," Ellianna brushed a tear that had appeared unbidden in one eye, but when it became clear that she was about to get up, Jana leaned in to put her second hand on the girl's other shoulder.

"Please, don't leave. I'm sorry if this is difficult for you, but I think it's very important that we figure this out together. I think I can help you, but you need to tell me one last thing, alright?"

Ellianna sniffled and nodded, instinctively guessing what the question would be.

"What is the last thing that you remember of your home and your parents, Ellianna?"

She had only talked about this on one other occasion years ago—when Thurgod had asked her what she could remember—and then she had buried it deep inside whatever dusty lockbox her mind had placed all the other lost memories of her prior life in. Now she had to open that box again, peer deep within, and confront her pain once more. "They were dead, just like everyone else. A sickness came to the village and took everyone—everyone except me. I didn't know what to do, but I knew I couldn't stay. They were all rotting, even before they died. It was awful..." she couldn't go any further and began to cry, sobbing into Jana's shoulder, heedless of dampening the cleric's immaculate robe.

"There, there, child... it's alright," Jana murmured, running one hand gently through Ellianna's silken red hair. She waited quietly until the young woman's tears were spent, giving her time to compose herself. "Wait here and I'll be right back. Promise me you won't leave?" she asked and waited for the girl's nod of acquiescence before getting up and exiting the chapel through one of the side doors, leaving Ellianna alone in the utter stillness of the large space.

She looked around for a bit, unsure of what to do or think. Lady Jana had certainly seemed to take her tale very seriously, but she still couldn't shake the feeling of being an idiotic little girl who had placed herself in a situation way out of her depth. It was her own fault—no one had forced her to come here—but now that she'd done it, she kept second-guessing herself. She tried to return to the sense of relief she had experienced earlier after relating her dream by focusing on the peaceful expression carved into Anval's marble face but failed miserably. All she really wanted right now was to go home and forget this entire day. She was looking over her shoulder at the main exit doors to the chapel and pondering doing exactly that when Jana finally returned, sparing her the shame of being caught trying to leave after she'd promised to stay.

The woman walked back to sit beside her once more, a thick book with a midnight blue cover held between her hands. There was a title written in gold leaf, but she did not recognize the symbols as being part of the language commonly used in northern Dravin. From that moment, all thoughts of fleeing evaporated from Ellianna's mind as she peered curiously at the book while Jana flipped through the pages in search of something. She arrived at a section of the tome that contained several beautiful illustrations, each page depicting a single individual of some kind, but they passed by too quickly for her to glean any further details. Jana's fingers eventually came to a stop on one of those pages, and she turned the book slightly so that Ellianna could see the illustration a little better. There, within a painted frame of colourful leaf-covered branches and against a forested backdrop, stood a naked man, his body covered in a considerable amount of hair that nevertheless did little to hide the well-defined contours of his lean musculature and form. In one hand he held a wondrously carved longbow; in the other, a single, green-fletched arrow. Yet the main detail on the illustration that drew her eyes irresistibly toward it was the unmistakable fact that where the man's face should be, there was that of a proud stag's instead, a magnificent rack of antlers towering above his head and entwining themselves at the points with the branches that framed the image.

"Is that the being from your dream?" Jana asked Ellianna, carefully observing her expression as the girl gaped at the illustration.

"Yes," she replied after a small pause, "that's him." It was only then that she noticed what she assumed was a word carved into the thick branches at the bottom of the page, beneath the strange man's feet. The lettering used resembled the symbols on the book's cover. "What does that say? Who is this?"

"Ilfandor—also called the Guardian or the Forest Master, but more commonly known as the Lord of the Hunt. The gods can take any form they please, but this is the one that Ilfandor most prefers. Are you absolutely sure this is what you saw?"

'Ilfandor', Ellianna silently mouthed the word, slowly yet apprehensively, as if the very act of doing so would cause the god to manifest himself before her. "Yes, I'm very sure. What does it mean, Lady Jana?"

"Many, many years ago, there was a village deep within the wilds of the Great Forest that covers most of northern Arlingford. Its name was Dawnhollow, and it was a small community of hunters, trappers, and woodsmen. Though a part of our barony even back then, they lived a life of relative isolation, having little contact with anyone else outside of that wooded realm. Because of that, when word finally reached some of the settlements outside the forest that a terrible plague had struck down the inhabitants of Dawnhollow, it was already too late. This was strange because such things typically only happen in larger towns and cities, where there's lots of people and disease is not uncommon. The baron in those times, my ancestor, wanted to send help, but was counseled against it, for the risk and danger of bringing that sickness back here was simply too great. So, it fell to him as the ruler of these lands to make a very difficult decision—Dawnhollow was declared off-limits to all citizens of the barony, and anyone caught disobeying that decree would face severe punishment. The village and the tragic event that doomed it were slowly forgotten, and no one was thought to have survived. Few living today that do not study the history of these lands would even remember anything about Dawnhollow, including its location." Jana finished her tale, carefully studying Ellianna's expression for any sign of recognition.

"I've never heard of Dawnhollow—though to be fair, I've never been anywhere outside of Arlingtown since coming here—but what little I do remember makes what you're saying feel like a very strange coincidence. That couldn't possibly be where I came from if it's a place that's long gone, but where then? Why can't I remember more, and what does the dream have to do with any of it?" Rather than finding the answers she craved, there were only more questions.

"I don't know. I think I would have heard of something like what you're describing happening in more recent times, but I haven't. Perhaps you were lost longer than you think? The sights you witnessed—family and friends, all dead—clearly had a traumatic effect on you. I think perhaps your mind tried to block most of that out as a way of protecting yourself from something so horrible. As for the dream—as a woodland community, it would be natural for the people of your village to devote themselves to the worship of Ilfandor. He is the protector of nature and the forests of the world, as well as the beasts that dwell therein, but he also honours the cycle of life and provides the hunter with the bounty of his gifts, teaching them the ways of nature and the skill needed to feed their families. This Great Hunt that your father took part in is an ancient, ritual contest, meant to bring Ilfandor's blessing upon the whole community."

"I think I understand all that, but it still doesn't explain why I'm having this dream. Why is Ilfandor appearing to me? Who is that boy, and what did those strange words at the end about '*the three watchers veiling their faces*' mean?"

Jana closed the book and pondered these questions. The brief glimpse into Anval's mind had shown her some of the answers, but not everything. She needed to be certain of it all before she could reveal any of it to this girl, and even then, she wondered if that would be the right thing to do. Sometimes ignorance was the best form of protection. The gods delighted in testing mortals, but before she could understand the cryptic challenge before her, she must know more. The priestess looked at the looming statue's face, never ceasing to marvel at how the sculptor's hand had so perfectly captured that gentle expression of compassion and peace. More so than any other depiction that she had ever seen of the Healer, she always thought this was the one that best represented his essence, and being in its presence always filled her with quiet reassurance. She nodded imperceptibly at it, accepting the task with humility and devotion. So be it.

"Ellianna," the cleric began, choosing her words with care, "I'm going to have to ask you to be patient while I try to learn more about the things you've told me. It will require a considerable amount of thinking, reading, and meditation, and these are activities that require time, but if you can give me that, I promise that I will do everything that I can to help you. I do have other duties to tend to, not the least of which is being mother to an oftentimes unruly boy," she smiled as she spoke this last, prompting Ellianna to blush in embarrassment. She'd been so wrapped up in her own problems that she'd neglected to think of anyone else's needs.

"I'm so sorry, I've been incredibly selfish. Yes, of course, please don't mind me and go about your life. Oh, that didn't come out right. You don't need my permission for that! I just meant—", she tried to stop herself before she could utter anything else that was stupid, but her mouth had seemed to have taken control. Thankfully Lady Jana interrupted her with a laugh. At first Ellianna was upset and ashamed of the fact that this great lady would be amused by the fumbling manner of a simple farm girl like her but seeing the look of consternation and humiliation on her face, Jana moved quickly to reassure her that was not the case whatsoever.

"My dear girl, how much you remind me of myself at your age," she smiled tenderly, thinking back to an innocent, less complicated time of her life. "Never apologize for wanting to tend to your own needs. You want to find your voice and sense of purpose, and before you can do that and truly claim your place among those destined for great things—and yes, I do sense that about you—this mystery of yours needs unravelling and unravel it we shall. Together. Alright?" She looked expectantly into Ellianna's clear green eyes, silently willing the teenager to trust her, and hoping to forge the bond of trust between them that would be necessary to see this through. It was a fragile moment, she knew, and the final decision must come from the young woman without any further words from her.

Ellianna smiled back timidly at first, and then slowly regained her confidence while she searched deep within Lady Jana's blue eyes, plumbing those limpid depths for a hint of anything that might give her pause in accepting the offer. She was no expert at reading people, especially given how isolated her upbringing had been, but her instinct had never steered her wrong before, and she saw nothing in Jana Morhain but a firm promise of genuine friendship and support. This was what she'd come here for after all, and there was nothing more she could ask that wasn't already being freely given.

"I accept," she said, unable to hide her surprise when Lady Jana pulled her close and gave her a firm hug.

"Wonderful, that's settled then." The priestess stood up and Ellianna did as well. "Why don't you come back tomorrow at this same time? Would that be possible?"

"Oh," Ellianna exclaimed, surprised yet again, but very pleased that she would be seeing the Lady Jana again so soon. "Yes, of course. I'll be here." In her mind, she was already working out how to best get all her chores done at the farm nice and early so that she could return here by midday. Of course, that would involve having to give her grandpa some kind of excuse that wouldn't raise his suspicions, but she would figure something out. "Thank you again," she smiled and made an attempt at a curtsy, then waited politely.

"You're most welcome, and you may go," Lady Jana granted her leave, smiling as she watched Ellianna walk up the stairs, turn around once to wave excitedly, and then exit through the great doors at the top of the chamber. The woman continued to stare at the doors for a while longer. Her smile faded, replaced by a look of sadness. She wondered if she would ever have the courage to tell that sweet girl what she'd been shown about what awaited her, for innocence, once lost, could never be regained.

CHAPTER 10

Autumn came and went over the city of Corazan—a brief, transitory season before the coming of winter, and one which signalled but a mild change in the weather—an event punctuated mainly by the trees throughout the orphanage shedding a few red and yellow leaves. By comparison with many of the realms much further north, winter in Rohne was relatively mild, bringing with it a period of dry, cool air that brought welcome relief from the sweltering heat and rainfall of the summer months. The change in the amount of daylight was barely noticeable this far south, and Flynn wondered what it was like to live in places where snowfall was a common thing, and the land was covered by the darkness of night for months at a time. In school, he'd learned the names of such faraway lands where these things happened—names like Culsak, Norlan, and the remotest stretches of northern Avamor—and fantasized about seeing them one day. He was thirteen now, he reminded himself while staring dreamily at the overcast sky outside the classroom window, and another year closer to getting out of this place and going somewhere—anywhere—that wasn't here. He'd told no one about his birthday except for Elias, not wanting to make a fuss of it or give certain other individuals further opportunity to pick on him. Brother Owen knew as well, of course, but the priest respected Flynn's wish to remain quiet about it. His mind was brought back to the present when he heard the door open and the priest walked in. The murmur of the other boys quieted down, but he didn't look up, instead reaching under his desk for a sheet of paper and preparing his quill for use.

"Good morning, boys. I bring you some sad news on this day." Upon hearing the voice, Flynn looked up in sudden confusion to see Brother Owen standing at the front of the class, hands clasped together before him, his expression a grim picture of sadness. Disoriented, Flynn thought he'd sat down in the wrong class, but a glance at the old tapestry map of Rohne and the paintings of past kings and queens that hung from the wall behind the desk was enough to tell him that this was indeed Brother Edward's history class. He glanced at Elias seated next to him, but the other boy merely shrugged his shoulders. No one said anything; everyone stared at Brother Owen.

"It is with a heavy heart that I tell you that Brother Edward passed away some time last night, may Janus bless and keep his gentle soul," he said. He closed his eyes and bowed his head, silently mouthing a prayer in remembrance of the kind old priest. The children did the same, some of them visibly upset and unsuccessfully holding back tears. Brother Edward had become increasingly absent-minded and more forgetful in the short months since Flynn's arrival, sometimes repeating a particular lesson more than once. Yet he'd never failed to show care and affection for his students and often brought a basket of freshly baked sweetcakes from the kitchen to share with the children after class. As shocking and upsetting as this news was, Flynn couldn't help but feel that it wasn't unexpected. Ever since that first day when he'd heard the old priest's troubling cough, he'd suspected the cleric wasn't long for this world, but that didn't make the occasion any less sad. Brother Owen finished his prayer, gave the boys a little bit of extra time to compose themselves, then announced that tomorrow, he would be temporarily taking over the class until the start of the Yule break, which was in just two weeks. For the rest of the day, though, classes were dismissed.

Fitting to the nearness of the Yule holiday that was fast approaching, the next day's lesson centered on its origins over three thousand years ago as a ritualistic festival celebrated by the ancestor peoples of what was today the Avamor Imperium. During those early times, before the worship of Janus became commonplace and dominant, many of the clans living in the pine forest-covered valleys of northern Avamor had followed primal, nature deities like Ilfandor of the Hunt, Olmara of the Earth, and Dalial of the Sky. So prevalent and deep-rooted were these ancient traditions, that even after the miraculous event that historians and scholars referred to as Starfall brought with it a new era of religious awakening and enlightenment, the Avamori continued to honour their past traditions. Thus, for the period of four weeks that marked the passage of one calendar year to the next, a series of rituals and feasts were held to remember the old gods and their ways. As the Avamori began to expand southward, conquering and absorbing other peoples and cultures that they encountered, the northerners found that many of these ancient rituals were shared as part of a common human ancestry. When the last indigenous tribes of Rohne were defeated seven centuries ago and the peninsula became an imperial province for the following four hundred years, the Avamori soldiers and settlers brought the holiday of Yule with them. Today, Rohne stood as an independent kingdom, but many customs from those times still remained, especially those of religious significance.

As usual, Flynn was fascinated by all this information, his young mind eager to absorb all knowledge, especially when it related to history, which he found to be a fascinating subject. Today though, his attention found itself divided over the still fresh news of Brother Edward's death. He wasn't sure why he was feeling this way or what the exact reasoning for his belief was, but he couldn't shake the thought that the elder priest had somehow caught the same affliction that had robbed him of his mother. In Susan's case, however, and unless his mother had managed to hide her condition for a long time from his father, she had passed away rather quickly. Yet even supposing the two illnesses were the same, Brother Edward had managed to hang on for months despite his advanced age and obvious frailty. Flynn had no idea what the significance of this might be, or if there was even any, but it continued to bother him enough that once the class was over, he walked up to Brother Owen and asked the cleric if he could speak to him later. When the priest nodded and said to come find him in his classroom after study period was over, Flynn nodded and headed out to his next lesson.

A few hours later, Flynn sat at a desk in the front row in Brother Owen's now vacant classroom and waited patiently while the dark-skinned man finished correcting some assignments. When the priest placed the last paper on a small pile, he rubbed his eyes tiredly, then looked at Flynn and smiled. "So, what can I do for you, young man?"

"Do you know how my mom died?" Flynn asked bluntly, cutting straight to the heart of what was bothering him.

Brother Owen appeared unfazed by the question. "Yes, I read the account that was written down at the time. Whenever possible, we keep a record of every child's family history before they are brought here, including the circumstances around how one or both parents passed away."

"One parent? You mean some of the kids here have a mom or dad that is still alive?" Flynn asked, not understanding how that could be possible. He'd always just assumed that everyone else had come to the orphanage under circumstances similar to his own. Because he didn't like to talk about the sad events that led to him being brought here, he'd decided that that wasn't something that he should ask the other kids. The only exception had been his friend Elias, who'd been at the orphanage since he was barely one year of age and didn't mind sharing with Flynn what little he knew. The other boy said he didn't remember his parents, only that someone had brought him here one day. He'd always just assumed that something bad had happened to his mom and dad, and with no one to care for him, the orphanage had been the only option.

"Flynn," Brother Owen began, searching for the best words that would allow a child to understand a difficult subject like this, particularly one so sensitive to an orphan. "Sometimes bad things happen in the life of an adult that makes it impossible for them to properly look after a child. Yes, it is true that most of you are here because death sadly took your parents away, but in some cases, a child is given unto our care because it is better for them to be here rather than with someone who cannot give them a good life and future," the priest explained gently. "I know this may sound strange to you, but bringing them here for that reason is, more often than not, an act of love."

Flynn thought about this for a minute. He was having trouble imagining how it could be love for a parent to abandon their child. It felt more like cowardice and betrayal, but his harsh judgment was tempered by the realization that in the relatively short time he'd known Brother Owen, the man was always full of wisdom and good advice and had never steered him wrong. So, he gave the priest the benefit of the doubt. He still couldn't entirely grasp what the man was saying, but perhaps he simply needed to be an adult in order to understand such complex concepts. In his straightforward and uncomplicated view of the world, giving up your own child was just something that wouldn't happen.

"When I grow up and Janus blesses me with children of my own, I'll never abandon them," the boy vowed earnestly.

Brother Owen arched his eyebrows and smiled. "I'm glad to hear it. Now, is there anything else you'd like to talk about?" he asked, knowing from experience how easily a child's mind could go down a multitude of side paths, and so he tried to nudge Flynn gently back onto the main road.

"Yes, I wanted to talk about my mom." Thinking about Susan always made him sad. He'd loved his mother dearly and the day that she left him forever was like crossing over into a completely different life from the one he'd had before—a new existence in which nothing was recognizable, not even himself at times. Her passing was the triggering event that caused all of the remaining pillars of his life to be knocked down in quick succession—his father, brothers, and the house he was born in. But Flynn had always been strong and wilful from a very young age, possessed of a quiet determination that had saved him from giving into the melancholy and despair that his father had succumbed to. He thought about his mother every single day, but since hearing about Brother Edward's passing, he felt her loss even more keenly today. "Do you think Brother Edward had the same sickness as she did?"

"Are you sure you want to talk about such grim things?" the priest asked, growing uncertain of where Flynn was going with this.

"It's just that..." he mused, trying to put his finger on what was bothering him. Suddenly, it was there. "It was the day after I arrived here when I first met Brother Edward in class and heard him cough. There was something about the sound—as if I could hear my mother coughing in the exact same way. He was so out of breath after, and weak, just like she was in those few days before she was gone. If he died of the same sickness that my mom had, wouldn't that mean that someone else brought it in here from the outside?"

"It's possible, I suppose," the priest said, considering the matter carefully. He was intrigued by Flynn's reasoning, but something about it didn't quite line up. "But not very likely. Brother Edward had been sick for quite some time—I would go so far as to say his health had been in steady decline for at least a year before your mother passed away. Also, there's a variety of ailments and conditions that can make a person cough like that. He was simply old, Flynn—old and frail."

The boy recognized the wisdom of those words, nodding to himself, but remained unconvinced. He wasn't ready to give up. "But what if he got worse because of it? A few days ago, I heard some boys talking about how a coughing illness took the life of Umberto's father recently, and Brother Edward came to see Umberto every morning in the kitchens to get his fresh sweetcakes. Brother Edward never left the orphanage—he was here all the time, every single day. Some of the other Brothers go out into the city—like you—but not him. Umberto often goes out to the market to buy things and visit his family, so what if he brought back something his father caught and passed it to Brother Edward?"

"I'll admit there's a similarity in the two events, but that doesn't necessarily mean there's a meaningful connection," Brother Owen pondered. "We don't live in isolation here, as you pointed out—many of us do indeed go to the city every day to perform our duties as priests in our community, and citizens come to the cathedral to worship daily. Merchants from the market deliver the many goods that we need to keep everyone here fed and clothed, and some that work and live here, such as Umberto the cook, go out often as well. I know what you're thinking, but no one else here is showing any symptoms of being sick. Also, your mother apparently was sick for only a very short time before she passed, so if Brother Edward had the same fatal illness, how is it that he lived with it for months at his age? Unfortunately, there's no way for us to know if Brother Edward's death was due to something that he caught around the time you noticed the familiar sound of his cough, or as a result of a condition that had been ailing him for a long time and just gradually worsened until it caused his death."

Flynn nodded again, acknowledging this was a flaw in his theory that he'd run up against already and couldn't explain—yet. It was really all too complicated for his young mind to grasp, yet he continued to feel there was more at work here than mere coincidence. Three people with similar symptoms followed by three deaths—was there a link between them? Or was he just desperately trying to bring some sense of purpose and understanding to the passing of two people he cared about? Instead of letting it go, he thought about it some more, delving deeper into what the priest was saying. One of his favourite pastimes when he was alone was to put together puzzles. He'd had several at home that his mother had given him and that he'd put together over and over. When he arrived here, he'd been delighted to find several puzzles in a box in the activities hall where the boys played on days when the rain forced them to stay indoors. He loved to work on them alone, but if other kids were watching him, he took pleasure in showing them how fast he could solve them. This was a puzzle too, and Flynn just needed to see all the pieces laid out before him so that he could solve it.

"Brother Owen, do you think this thing began...when my mom died?" he asked at last.

The priest swallowed dryly. "Flynn, there is no 'thing' here, whatever you think this 'thing' might be. I can guess what you're thinking, and we can't know for certain that your mother was the first," he cautioned. People lived, and people died, and that was the way of the world. This was, in all likelihood, just a coincidence, and he needed to be careful about this boy talking himself into taking on some misguided burden of guilt for something that he couldn't possibly have had control over.

"But you teach in your class that all things have a beginning, middle, and end. Only the gods are eternal. What if my mom *was* the first?" Flynn emphasized the word 'was', trying to make sense of what it could possibly mean, if true. "What if other children that have arrived here after me, did so for the same reason that I did? Wouldn't that prove that maybe what I'm saying is really possible?"

Brother Owen was impressed by the boy's rationale even if he continued to feel this wasn't a constructive use of Flynn's time and energy. "As I said, we can't know that for sure, but I can see that this is going to bother you very much until you have an answer. Just remember, whatever conclusion you come to, it changes nothing about what happened. We can't bring her back, Flynn, and punishing yourself for thinking that she is somehow responsible for all this is only going to make you feel even worse about her death than you already do." Brother Owen tried once more to gently dissuade the boy from this line of thought, but Flynn was having none of it. The boy was certain he'd uncovered a central piece of this puzzle, and he was determined to discover how to build outward from it. Unlike how one tackled a traditional puzzle, he didn't think this one could be solved by forming the edges first.

"Alright," the priest conceded finally, knowing there was only one answer he could give that would satisfy the boy for now. "I'll speak to Father Lorimer and ask to examine the records." It was a harmless and easy enough concession to make, and after nothing turned up from this effort, maybe Flynn would be convinced to let this go.

Flynn was pleased with this. Father Lorimer was the headmaster of the orphanage, and someone that he'd only glimpsed from afar during weekly mass and on a handful of other occasions since his first few months here. Brother Melton guarded the records like a hawk, but if anyone could order a review, it would be Father Lorimer, and if Brother Owen could convince the latter to help, they would be off to a good start. He wondered what—if anything—would come of this. He was convinced there was a connection here, and that it was important, but he simply didn't know how or why. Either way, he was thrilled to have something exciting to do and was about to say goodbye and run out to play when he remembered one more thing he'd wanted to ask about.

"Brother Owen?" Flynn asked, halfway out of his chair, his voice tentative as if he felt he might be testing the adult's patience by this point with all these questions.

The priest arched one eyebrow, sensing yet another difficult query coming from the boy's infinitely inquisitive mind. "Yes?"

"Who died in the old tower?" There, he'd asked it and there was no turning back now. It had been bothering him ever since Elias had told him his story, and though the tale of the ghost in the tower was known to all the boys in the orphanage, no one, not even the older ones, knew much more beyond the tale of the stormy night and the lone priest inside when the lightning struck. Flynn had always been skeptical of the whole thing, recognizing a story told to frighten children when he heard one, but his mind had quickly changed when Elias had shown him that strange bruise. The other boy, ashamed of what had happened and afraid of more punishment if he spoke up, had never shown the mark on his skin to anyone until now. Flynn had sworn to keep Elias' secret to himself, but he said nothing about trying to know more about the chilling history of the tower and its mysterious, otherworldly occupant.

"Flynn," Brother Owen leaned forward to stare intently at the boy, "you know you're not supposed to play near that place. It's dangerous."

"I haven't, I swear!" he said defensively. "It's just that... well, we've all heard the story, and—"

"—you decided that you simply had to know whether it's true or not?" the priest finished the sentence for him.

Flynn averted his eyes. He sat back down, looked at the desk and began meticulously tracing a pattern in the wood surface with one fingernail. "Well, kind of... I mean, if it's dangerous because it could fall, then why is it still there? Someone could get hurt."

"Not if you children do as you're told and stay away from it," Brother Owen admonished. "Look, the priests back in those days had the city undertake some shoring up of the structure so that it wouldn't just collapse over a loud sneeze, but that's as far as things got. When the orphanage opened, Archbishop Anton did put in a personal request to the king to have something done about the tower out of concern for his new charges. Unfortunately, it's gone on ignored for decades, and with the city buildings on the other side of the wall so close, some now fear there is as much of a risk in taking it down as there is in leaving it up," the cleric explained. "And it has remained thusly ever since—*undisturbed*." The priest emphasized this last with a meaningful look at Flynn.

"Alright, makes sense I guess," the boy said begrudgingly. He'd been really hoping there was another, more interesting and secret reason for it, and he decided this logical—yet boring—explanation wasn't the full truth, so he tried again. "So, is it true then that someone died in there?"

Brother Owen sighed, exasperated. Flynn was a very determined young man, and he knew him well enough by now to know he wouldn't rest until he got some form of answer that appeased his curiosity. The priest also had a dangerous character flaw when it came to these kinds of questions: he didn't like lying at all, especially to children, even if the truth wasn't always the best thing for them. He would just have to be careful about what he said.

"Yes, it is true. His name was Father Mateo, and he was the chief librarian here in his time, as well as the last priest that still devoted himself to the study of astronomy and other celestial phenomena. There were more like him in the days the tower was built, but as the practice gradually fell out of use throughout the years, Father Mateo became the only one here who liked to spend time alone in the tower, poring over all the books he'd lovingly stored in there for reference, and frequently using the telescope at the top to watch the stars on a clear night. Some of the stories I've heard passed down through some of the Brothers that have been here longer than me say that he was a lonely man who kept largely to himself and seemed more comfortable in the company of his books and dusty instruments than other people. Some even say that when the tower fell into disuse, it was a blessing for him, because he now had a place where he could study, isolated and unperturbed by worldly distractions," Brother Owen related, recalling the old tales he'd heard about the peculiar cleric.

"He would spend uncounted hours in there, sometimes days, emerging only occasionally to get something to eat. No one really knew what he was working on, if anything, but on the rare occasion that someone would cross his path during one of his rare outings from the tower, he could supposedly be heard muttering about being close to a breakthrough discovery of some sort. Unfortunately, no one ever got to find out what that was—Father Mateo died tragically when the worst storm in Rohne's recorded history passed over the city. It was thought that he'd been using the telescope at the time and was crushed beneath the huge instrument when it fell through the floor of the tower after being struck by lightning, but even when the worst of the debris was finally cleared, his body couldn't be found. They tried searching for him elsewhere in the tower, of course, but it was difficult and dangerous, so eventually they gave up. The tower was too unsafe, so the decision was made to lock it up and never use it again. Other than the stabilizing work that was done immediately after, no one's been inside for nearly a hundred years except for birds and rats, I'd imagine," Brother Owen concluded his story with a shrug.

He didn't know about birds, but rats of a sort had most definitely been in there, Flynn thought to himself—rats of the two-legged variety. He wondered about Father Mateo and his work. Unlike the heroes in the tales that he enjoyed reading so much, the senior cleric's accidental demise didn't sound very heroic at all, but there was something inspiring about the notion of dying while doing the one thing that you loved most. The irony that Father Mateo was killed by something that came down from the very skies he'd spent his entire life studying was not lost on him. "Are ghosts real, Brother Owen?"

The priest did not answer and instead made a show of gathering his things from his desk, hoping to send a clear message to the boy that the conversation was nearing its end. Either Flynn didn't pick up on the hint, or he didn't care. When the boy didn't get up and simply continued staring innocently at him, Brother Owen closed the leather satchel into which he'd placed the assignments he had been working on, got up from his chair, and slung the bag's strap over his shoulder. He walked three steps to stand before the desk where Flynn sat, smoothed his robes with his hands, and sighed. "Flynn, you're full of questions today, more than I have time for. If it were possible to learn all that there is to learn in one single day, life would quickly lose all of its flavour and excitement. I commend and encourage your thirst for knowledge, but learn to pace yourself in its pursuit, or you will quickly find yourself overwhelmed. As to your question, all I'll say is that everything in this world has an explanation, and more often than not, that explanation is far more mundane and far less fantastical than our imaginations would have us believe. Think on that, my good lad, and I will now leave you to your day." The priest gave him his familiar wink and left the classroom.

Flynn watched the priest go and sat there a few minutes longer, lost in thought while he mulled everything he'd heard. '*More often than not*,' the man had said. Hah! So, the ghost *was* real. The boy smiled mischievously and left the room, feeling rather smug. He already knew he wanted to have a peek inside that old tower—he just needed to figure out how to get a hold of the key.

⸺◆⸺

The hour was late, but sleep couldn't find Flynn, likely owing to the fact that his mind kept going over and over all the things he and Brother Owen had talked about earlier that day. He felt restless, as if there were things that he should be doing, but when he tried to figure out what those things should be, he kept drawing a blank. He stared upward in the darkness that swathed his cell, and though he couldn't see them now, he had memorized every hairline crack, seam, and imperfection in the grey stone ceiling. Tossing and turning restlessly from side to side for a few minutes, he flipped onto his back again with a sigh of exasperation and tried to focus on what was bothering him the most in an attempt to brush the preoccupations aside, one at a time. He was excited for the coming of Yule, of course, but that wasn't it. He thought about the tower and the key to its door, but that was going to require time, careful planning, and a clearer mind than he had right now. Then there was the sickness that took his mother and the persistent, nagging feeling that something about it was somehow important. He'd done all he could, and now he had to wait for Brother Owen to do as promised, which was frustrating because of how adults moved at their own pace and couldn't be hurried no matter how much you tried.

'Brother Edward'—the name jumped into his mind suddenly.

The sad news of the old priest's passing hadn't fully sunk in yet, and the fact that another person that he'd gotten to care about and seen nearly every day for the past few months was now gone was a frightening thought for him. He'd really enjoyed Brother Edward's class and company, and the man had been game for any question about history, of which Flynn always had plenty. The priest's willingness to talk was rivalled only by his vast knowledge, and the two had become kindred spirits in a way, even if the old man often meandered off into one of his stories, most of which he'd clearly forgotten he had already related to Flynn just the day before. Death—it was beginning to feel like an old, unwanted companion, following him wherever he went. It shouldn't be a topic that featured prominently in a young boy's life, but there it was again, lurking around the corner with dogged persistence and eternal patience. Mostly, it was the suddenness of it all that bothered him the most—his inability to say goodbye. Susan had been taken from him when he wasn't there, and now the same had happened with Brother Edward. He decided that he'd like to say his farewell to the old man. Though reaching his resting place was no small task, Flynn knew in his heart that the priest would have liked that.

Since slumber continued to elude him, he was relieved to have found a way to channel his energy. By the very faint and distant glow of the lamp in the hallway bleeding through the edges of the curtain, Flynn got up, dressed himself, and then stuffed some spare clothes under the blanket to make it look like someone was asleep in the cot. Shoes on, he drew back the heavy fabric and peeked both ways before stepping out—all clear. He timed his exit since he'd last heard the footsteps of the Initiate that patrolled the halls of the dormitory at night, and so he knew it would be several minutes before the older boy would pass that way again. Stepping out, he headed right, swiftly took the stairs down to the main floor, and looked again to see if anyone was about. When he saw no one, he carefully advanced toward the building's main door, which he knew to be locked at night. Undeterred, he slipped into a musty cloak room across from Brother Melton's office and sleeping cell. It was completely dark in the confined space, but he knew the exact location of the bench under the window, having studied the room before while pretending to stand casually outside one time.

He climbed onto the bench as quietly as he could, swung open the glass pane first, and then felt for the latch that secured the window's shutters. A common feature throughout the compound, each one of these had a small lock to prevent children from doing exactly what he was attempting, except he'd found out from Elias that this particular latch was loose, and the whole thing could be slipped off with little effort. He sent a silent prayer to Janus hoping that the latch hadn't somehow been fixed recently and was rewarded when the slack wood screws fell into his hand, allowing him to pull the latch gingerly from the shutter and overcome the obstacle of the lock without ever having to open it. That done, it was a simple matter to push one of the wooden panels open and climb through to the outside. Soft grass cushioned the short drop to a small space concealed behind some bushes, and he peered out from under the window, seeing no one in the courtyard ahead. Perfect.

From there, it wasn't far to the main cathedral, but Flynn took care to stick to the shadows wherever he found them. Thankfully the night was overcast, the cloud cover diminishing Temeros' ever-present crimson luminescence down to almost nothing. He made it all the way to the vine-covered stone wall that divided the orphanage compound from the main grounds of the church, stopping before the Ivy Gate under the archway that formed a short passageway through the tall barrier. This one should be unlocked; he thought and smiled when he pushed on it to find that he'd been right. He slipped through and closed the gate behind him before proceeding down the tunnel and across to the other side. Just ahead, the massive shape of the cathedral loomed in the darkness, its tall spires rising sharply into the night sky. Though he'd seen it close up many times before, the sight of the magnificent structure never failed to fill him with awe, even at night. The children weren't usually allowed on this side of the wall, and Father Lorimer's weekly sermons and spiritual services for the orphans were always delivered from the confines of the orphanage's own dedicated prayer hall. Still, once a week the boys had to practice choir, and there was no other building on the entire grounds that could even come close to matching the magnificent acoustics inside the cathedral's nave.

As he planned his next move, Flynn noted the flickering candlelight that shone faintly through a couple of the beautiful stained-glass windows on one of the building's twin bell towers—no doubt some cleric up late perusing an old tome or performing some other late-night task. Eyeing the door that was his target, he again thanked Janus for his good fortune that no other insomniac soul like him had picked this evening to come out for a breath of fresh air. Not wanting to test the Overgod's patience by waiting too long, he strode quickly from his hiding place near the wall and made for one of the side doors near the back of the cathedral. Up the broad steps he climbed, then a brief pause to listen before he carefully turned the handle on the postern door in front of him. The small entrance, normally reserved for priests, was inset within a pair of enormously tall doors, easily three times the height of a man. Identical to the pair on the other side of the building, as well as the main ones at the front, these huge and ornate doors were only open once a week during holy mass. On that day, the devout citizens of Corazan filled the spacious nave with the loud murmur of prayer, and the entire structure soared with the sound of song and worshipful praise. Tonight though, the small door dutifully swung open, and Flynn stepped silently and alone into the house of Janus.

Mindful of his trespass and hoping it would be forgiven, Flynn hastily made the sign of the Overgod over his chest while peering across the open space to the opposite end of the cavernous side chamber he was in. There, a tall archway led into the nave itself, and beyond, he could just make out the dark outline of the pulpit from where the current head of Corazan's church, Archbishop Marcos, always delivered his mass. The main altar could not be glimpsed from where he stood, however, and Flynn was inwardly relieved at that. Though he was certain that Janus knew he was here tonight, he was nevertheless grateful for the fact that he did not have to pass in front of the enormous statue of the Overgod, with its stern visage and piercing, all-seeing eyes. Again, he listened carefully for any sign of the sexton that would surely be about, doing his rounds and tending to the few lit candles inside. When he heard nothing, he crept across the patterned tile floor and over to the elegantly carved white granite balustrade that encircled the stone steps leading downward into the subterranean bowels of the cathedral's lower level. At the top of the spiral staircase, Flynn paused in hesitation, giving a moment of consideration for what he was about to do. He'd never been below the main floor of the cathedral, but he knew from overheard conversations that that's where the crypts of the clergy were located. He couldn't think of anywhere else that Brother Edward would have been taken, and he'd already come too far to turn back now, so before he could change his mind, he drew a deep breath and took the stairs down, carefully navigating the steps in the dark.

The staircase turned upon itself twice before Flynn reached the bottom, and he was thankful to discover that the passage he found himself in was lit by a softly glowing crystalline globe mounted high up on one wall. He marvelled at the light source, seeing no flame or smoke, and wondered how it worked. In

Brother Owen's theology class, he'd been taught that the gods rewarded their most faithful servants with the ability to perform feats of divine magic—more commonly referred to as miracles—by opening a spiritual conduit between their soul and that of their chosen patron. Infused by this holy energy—known as the *etherus*—the priest could shape it into a practical form to be used in several ways, such as imbuing a small object with light. That must be what made this crystal glow, he thought. He'd never seen one of the Brothers perform a miracle because, not only was it supposedly taxing for the individual, but the prayers that invoked such blessings were to be used only sparingly and privately whenever possible, and never in a frivolous or wasteful manner. Given such stringent restrictions, it was no surprise that most common folk would never see a miracle performed in their lifetime and simply took the existence of such things upon faith. Flynn extended his arm and fingers upward but couldn't quite reach the globe to touch its surface, yet he came near enough to it to notice that he felt no heat from the golden light. Grinning from ear to ear, he decided he'd quite like to be able to do something like that someday. Pleased with the thought and without further delay, he proceeded down the corridor.

The featureless passageways beneath the cathedral proved labyrinthine, most of them ending in closed and locked ironbound doors, with the few that he did find open leading only into dark and dusty storerooms, often filled with old things that probably hadn't been disturbed in years. Each corridor was lit at regular intervals by the glowing globes, and every time Flynn came to a dead end in his exploration, he carefully retraced his steps back to the last place where the corridors intersected and tried a new passage, always choosing his left to avoid getting lost. He reasoned that the area that housed the crypts should be obvious—he just had to find it. He was, however, very conscious of how much time was passing and began to worry that he might have to turn back or risk not being in his cell when dawn came. He very nearly gave up when one of the last passages he had yet to try eventually led to an intersection that—if his sense of direction hadn't failed him—was located directly beneath the Overgod's altar in the nave. There, he found something unexpected—another staircase. He stopped in puzzlement. He hadn't known or expected that there would be another floor beneath this one, and he nearly turned away and down one of the other side passages because he reasoned that it didn't make sense that the priests would labour so hard to take a body down all these staircases. Following that line of thought as he stared at the dark opening on the floor, he was about to leave when he nearly jumped out of his skin at hearing what sounded like someone whispering his name right in his ear.

'*Flynn...*'

The boy gasped in fright and wheeled around abruptly, thinking he would find the sexton standing there, though he had no idea how the man could have snuck up on him so silently. Only there was no one behind him, just an empty passageway. He pressed his back against the stone wall, his heart racing and pounding in his chest. Either his imagination was playing tricks on him, or someone else was—another one of the boys, perhaps? Did someone follow him without him noticing? No, impossible. The voice had been right behind him, and there was no way anyone could hide from sight that quickly.

"Hello?" he called out tentatively, his voice tinged with fear. There was no reply, no sound except for his own anxious breathing. Then a thought struck him: if he believed there could be a ghost in the old tower, why couldn't there be one down here, where dead priests were laid to rest? For all his confidence, daring, and determination in coming here tonight, he was just an impressionable and defenseless boy—the perfect prey for the hungry, restless spirits of the netherworld.

'Stop it, Flynn. You're being an idiot!' He repeated that admonition several times in his head, fighting to convince himself of what he was saying. Even if such things were real, what would they want with someone so small and innocent and who meant them no harm? I'm only here to say goodbye to one of you, he pleaded silently but earnestly, hoping that any invisible presence would listen and believe that he was telling the truth. He realized he'd closed his eyes and did not want to open them for fear of what he might see. He was absolutely certain he'd heard a voice speak his name, and whether it was his imagination running away on him or not, he swore he could hear more whispers now, growing more agitated and insistent with every second that passed. He almost couldn't take it any longer, fearing he would be driven mad by fear.

'Flyyyynn...'

"*Aaaaaahhhh,*" he yelled as he opened his eyes, not caring if anyone heard him. In fact, he hoped someone would—someone living. His shout echoed down the corridors, instantly banishing the whispers as if they'd never been. He looked frantically in every direction, but again no one was around. When the last echo of his voice had faded, he took several breaths to calm himself and then looked at the stairs again. This is a test, isn't it, he asked silently. He didn't get a response, nor did he expect one. Drawing himself up, he walked to stand over the top step. Like the previous staircase, this one too spiraled down into darkness, but this time he detected a faint scent in the air coming from below...something that seemed somehow familiar. He searched his mind for the source of the vague memory and then it came to him—the smell in his parents' bedroom after his father had been dead for some time and they'd had to wait through two days of summer heat before someone came to take the body away. It was a sweet yet vaguely off-putting aroma of decay, mixed with the incense someone had burned to mask it. It was barely there, just the smallest hint in fact, but Flynn knew he wasn't mistaken. He would never forget that awful time or any detail associated with it, no matter how minuscule. That was all the confirmation he needed—the crypt had to be down there. He puffed his cheeks out and then expelled his breath in one long and loud gush before resolutely climbing down.

The air in the lower subterranean passage was decidedly colder, and there was a stale and musty quality to it that fought against that other odour, making for a combination that left Flynn's nose wrinkled with distaste. Like the floor above, this one too was lit by the glowing globes, though there were far fewer down here. Thankfully, there was only one direction to follow at first, but the single passageway soon split into a multitude of long corridors radiating outward from a central hub like the spokes of a wheel. Choosing one at random, he discovered that the passage eventually ended before a solid stone door, heavily adorned with religious carvings and iconography. On the lintel of this imposing barrier, the Eyes of Janus stared down the passage, and below that omnipresent symbol was affixed a rectangular bronze plaque, the metal surface covered with a green patina of age. Aided by the glow of a nearby globe, he squinted up to read the faded writing on the plaque and realized that it was composed of two groups of numbers, not letters. Years, he quickly deduced, the sign clearly denoting a time period of exactly one century. Behind that door must be the crypt housing all members of the clergy that had passed on from this world during those years, Flynn reasoned. All he had to do then was find the doorway that corresponded to the current date.

It only took a few minutes of careful exploration to see that the crypts had been laid out chronologically, with the leftmost passage and door being dated the earliest, and the numbers on the plaque above dating back over eleven hundred years. These must've been the very first monks to arrive in these lands, Flynn thought as he placed one hand with reverence and awe on the cold surface of that first door. Since the cathedral above had been built much later, this section of the catacombs must predate everything else, he figured, his keen eyes noting the subtle yet gradual transition in the age and detail in the craftsmanship of the stone and bas-reliefs from one corridor to the next. He ran his fingers over the ancient carvings and thought about the brave men and women of those long-ago days, so far from their homes and families. They had come to spread the word of their faith to those who knew nothing of it—often risking their lives in the process, for not all were welcomed with open arms. Sometimes he daydreamed about what it would've been like to live back then, when so much was still new and unknown, but then he would remind himself that there was still so much for him to learn, and that even several lifetimes might not be enough to know all that there was to know. He smiled and moved on back to the centre of the wheel, counting passages.

There were twenty in total, but after the twelfth one, the remaining passages did not yet have plaques over their doors. Clearly these were meant to house future generations of priests, so in theory, the last eight corresponding chambers beyond should be empty. He therefore ignored them and chose the corridor that led to the twelfth crypt, the one matching the current century. As he approached the threshold, he noticed that the cloying scent he'd detected earlier was growing stronger with each step. There was no doubt in his mind now that he'd finally arrived at his goal, for there it was, on the plaque above the lintel:

3301-3400 Ano Imperius

Gathering his courage before attempting to enter the crypt, he performed the sign of the Overgod once more, bringing his hands to his chest, the tips of his index fingers and thumbs touching together to form the all-seeing eyes, and with the remaining fingers in a steeple above them to represent the apex of humanity's faith. Hopeful this would be a sufficient sign of respect and that Janus would forgive him for yet another trespass this night, Flynn placed his hands tentatively on the stone door and pushed, unsure whether the imposing barrier would yield at all. To his surprise, the door opened without effort, feeling much lighter than it had any right to be. The flickering light of candles beckoned to him from beyond the threshold, and without further hesitation, he entered the crypt.

The octagonal-shaped sepulchre was larger inside than he thought it would be, but when he considered the possible number of departed clerics the chamber was meant to hold, it made sense. Each one of the eight walls—including the wall surface to either side of the doorway—was lined with evenly spaced, rectangular cavities, each opening stacked above the next so that they formed neatly ordered rows and columns. These rose from the polished tiled floor to where the vaulted ceiling began, which in turn was supported by eight carved black pillars, each inset wherever two walls met. At a glance, he could see that the wall cavities were approximately the width of a person at the shoulder and half that in height, a clear indication that the bodies of the deceased were put in feet or headfirst to maximize space. Roughly half of these spaces were sealed with a white marble slab that sat flush with the wall, while the remainder lay open, revealing only empty darkness and dust beyond. Though his curiosity compelled him to take everything in at once, it was to the centre of the crypt that his attention was irresistibly drawn.

A black marble bier rested on the floor, its sides intricately carved with beautiful depictions of the angelic and saintly servants of Janus, and lying-in-state upon the smooth surface surrounded by rose petals was the body of Brother Edward. The old priest was clad in funereal silver robes trimmed with black, his hooded head resting on a purple velvet cushion. The lined face was peaceful in death, and his hands were joined together over his breast as if he were merely sleeping. At the four corners of the stone table were tall candelabra fashioned from twisted brass, each one holding a black candle that burned steadily without melting the wax, and hanging by a chain from the centre of the ceiling above was a wrought iron censer from which emanated thin wisps of white smoke. This was clearly the source of the incense he had smelled earlier, and though the aroma was much stronger in here, the light haze in the air was not nearly thick enough to hinder breathing, owing to the small vent holes no doubt cleverly concealed somewhere in the stone above.

Flynn's eyes were wide as saucers as he stared at the corpse of his former instructor. Sadly, he was no stranger to the sight of a dead body, but it was not something that he felt he could ever grow used to. The boy stepped up to the stone block, wanting to take a closer look. Brother Edward looked indeed like he was merely asleep, but the boy knew that the old priest's slumber was eternal. He reflected on the teachings of the church, which said that the body was merely a vessel for the soul—a temporary waypoint on a much greater journey to what lay beyond. Once the body expired, the person's soul—their *etherus*—returned to the divine Wellspring, there to dwell in peace and harmony before the glory of the gods. As he thought about this, Flynn hoped fervently that it was all true. His parents hadn't been particularly devout, and he admitted he hadn't given such things much thought in the past, for what child would? Yet the drastic upheavals his life had undergone in less than a year had caused him to become much more introspective and faithful in this belief that there simply had to be something better that awaited everyone beyond life. The alternative was simply too frightening to contemplate, but just as he often did nowadays, he thought about it again at that moment. What if there was simply nothing after life but empty darkness—the complete and utter absence of consciousness? Everlasting oblivion.

His stare went from Brother Edward's face to the multitude of open receptacles on the walls of the tomb. Each one seemed to stare back at him, invoking an eerie image reminiscent of the empty and dark eye sockets of a skull, like yawning gateways into impenetrable shadow surrounded by cold, unfeeling stone. Would one of these be his final resting place one day? What was the purpose of life if your ultimate and unavoidable fate was to end up in a place like this, doomed to fade slowly from memory and into obscurity, forever forgotten? Not true, he reminded himself, pushing back the dark anxiety he felt rising within himself. What about those great heroes he'd learned about, the ones that inspired him to be something greater than a simple orphan boy? Their names and deeds were still talked about today, long after the times in which they had lived had come and gone. Perhaps life's meaning was about what you did with it in the years given to you. He wanted to be remembered, but a place in history had to be earned.

Looking at the old priest again, he recollected what little he knew of the man in the short time he had known him and was saddened to realize that there wasn't really much to go on. What had he been like as a child? Had he loved someone special? What had brought him into the service of Janus? Would anyone but his students and fellow clerics remember him, and what about when they were gone? The old man's body would remain on the bier, likely another day or two at most, while his fellow priests came to pay their final respects and say goodbye, and then what? The inscriptions on each marble slab that sealed the occupied tombs in the chamber revealed the final answer—a few brief words that attempted, often inadequately, to summarize the essence of an individual's lifetime. Other than the person who had carved them, who would ever really read them? Not many, Flynn thought somberly; perhaps no one. This was a place for the dead, not the living, and the longer he remained, the more he felt like an unwelcome intruder. He cleared his mind of all these depressing thoughts, having lost track of time and worrying suddenly about how long he'd been standing there in deep thought. Without realizing that he had done so, he looked down to notice that he'd placed one small hand over those of Brother Edward's. The pale flesh was cold, of course, and the telltale odour of the beginnings of decay defied the best efforts of the incense to mask the inexorable advance of time. It made him think of his parents and his brief clarity of thought and calm crumbled once more. He began to cry at last, releasing his pent-up grief of the past few months, and all the deep sorrow and misery he'd fought hard not to show so that the other boys wouldn't think him weak and make fun of him.

Shoulders heaving as he wept, he knelt before the bier and rested his forehead against the uncaring stone. His hand still gripped the dead priest's own, but he drew comfort from the touch regardless. Other than Brother Owen and Elias, he felt very much alone and wondered what would become of him. He missed his brothers; he missed his mom and dad; he missed the life he could never have again. He was trying hard to like being at the orphanage, but he could never forget why it was that he'd been brought here, and that meant he could never really be happy so long as he remained in this place. It was not somewhere anyone could truly feel they belonged anyway—each and every one of the orphans someone that had been tragically discarded by life in one fashion or another. From here, only two choices seemed possible—acceptance or change. He knew which of the two paths he wanted to follow.

'Flynn'

He almost didn't hear the whisper at first, so wrapped was he in the sounds of his own misery. He quickly dismissed it as a product of his troubled thoughts and continued to sob.

'Flynn'

This time he opened his tear-filled eyes and slowly unclasped his fingers from Brother Edward's, dislodging the corpse's hand in the process and leaving it to dangle at the side of the table. He felt a draft of cold air at his back, something that shouldn't be possible in the confines of these underground passages and chambers. He felt the hair at the base of his neck stand up on end, not so much from the drop in temperature, but from the sensation of fear and dread in his throat. Someone—or something—was in the tomb with him, and he was sure it was the same presence he'd felt earlier. He stifled back any last remaining tears, took one last sniffle, and wiped at his face with a sleeve. Then he listened, eyes staring wide at the figures chiseled into the black marble block in front of him, too afraid to turn around. The sepulchre remained as utterly enveloped in silence as when he'd walked in, but Flynn couldn't shake the certainty that he was no longer alone. A sliver of motion out of the corner of his eye drew his attention, and he shifted his gaze sideways without moving his head to see the flame of one of the nearby candles flicker and bend as if caught in a breeze. That was more than he could take. Summoning every ounce of courage he could muster, he slowly rose back to his feet and turned around to look behind him.

Flynn's back had been to the open doorway of the tomb, so that was the direction he turned to face. There, standing just to one side of the opening, was a tall figure completely shrouded in black, its features obscured within the impenetrable shadows of a deep hood. The edges of the dark apparition seem frayed and ragged, its tattered edges blowing in a wind that came from no apparent source. If there was any lingering doubt in Flynn's mind that what he was seeing was not otherworldly in origin but a living human being instead, that notion was irrevocably dispelled when he realized that he could see the outline of the wall and individual tombs behind the figure. It was translucent, he realized with a shudder. He was well past the point where he could find his voice and scream like he'd done before. Numb with horror, he stumbled backward into the table behind him and had to throw one arm out across Brother Edward's body to prevent a fall to the ground when both of his heels came up against the hard, unyielding stone. Then he pivoted around in the same motion and ran to the other side of the pedestal to crouch there, seeking to put a barrier between himself and the silent figure.

It didn't come any closer, a fact for which Flynn was eternally grateful, but as he peered fearfully at it from just over the prone form of Brother Edward, his eyes widened with fright when the spectre slowly raised one arm. This is it, the boy thought. He'd been dwelling so much on the finality of death that it had manifested itself at his calling, come to take him away and sate his curiosity as to what awaited on the other side. 'Janus, forgive me for doubting you,' he pleaded frantically and silently to the Overgod. 'I don't want to die...please.' He felt tears welling up in his eyes again. Janus was supposed to be a loving and caring parent to all his children, not a cold and cruel spirit of vengeance that sent a herald of death to punish a wayward boy. Swathed in a fluttering, ghostly sleeve, the arm continued to rise, and Flynn could almost imagine a giant scythe forming there, gripped in the skeletal hand he imagined to be under the ethereal fabric. It was just like the fanciful illustration he'd once seen in an old book in Brother Owen's class.

But no reaping tool of death appeared. Instead, a long thin finger surrounded by a nimbus of pale bluish light slid out from the garment and the phantom turned slowly to point at one of the walls. It hovered there for a moment, and then the presence disappeared altogether as if it had never been. Flynn had to blink several times to assure himself that it was truly gone, and not for the first time, he wondered if his mind was playing tricks on him, and he'd imagined the whole thing. He looked around slowly, but the sepulchre chamber was as it had always been—quiet and forlorn, empty of anyone but him. He looked at the flame on the candles and the incense smoke, but nothing disturbed them now. Nevertheless, he stayed hidden and crouched behind the table a while longer, afraid that as soon as he got up, the spirit—or whatever it was—would come back. He didn't want to move, and the thought of the long walk back through all those gloomy and silent passages was daunting, but he reminded himself that he couldn't stay here. It would be dawn very soon, and if he wasn't in his cell when Peter did his morning check, he might find himself wishing that he was back down here and taking his chances with a ghost.

He screwed up his courage one more time and got up, every muscle and nerve in his body taut with tension and fear, ready to bolt for the door if anything else happened. Nothing did. Tentatively, he walked to the doorway and stood near the spot where the figure had manifested itself. He tried to imagine that he could feel something, some kind of lingering connection to that briefly glimpsed *other side*, but there was nothing. Then he remembered the gesture it had made just before it disappeared—not to summon some horrible way to dispatch him into the afterlife, but to point toward the wall. At what, exactly? Near to that side of the door were the first few rows of wall tombs, the resting places of the first priests who had died shortly after the turn of the current century. Had the spirit been trying to show him something? Overcome by curiosity and awakened interest in this new mystery, he quickly forgot about his urgent need to leave. He stared at the rows of marble plaques and inscriptions a while longer, then walked back to where he'd been hiding by the table to again visualize the figure pointing, the image etched in his memory—there, second column, right from the door; third row up from the floor. That's where it had been pointing. He rushed over to that spot and examined the inscription on the indicated plaque:

Father Mateo Veros
3239 – 3302 A.I.
May the stars you so loved in life welcome you home into
their heavenly embrace

Flynn's mouth fell open with astonishment. This couldn't be a coincidence, he thought. But why him, and what did any of it mean? His mind raced with excitement mingled with apprehension. Exploring the tower where Father Mateo had died had just gone from an adventurous distraction to something far more meaningful and foreboding than he could comprehend. Was he frightened at the prospect of what he would find? Most assuredly. Was that enough of a deterrent against his earlier plan? Not by all the gods in their celestial abodes. Filled with renewed determination to somehow get that key from Peter, Flynn decided it was time to go, but not before doing one last thing. He walked up to the bier where Brother Edward lay and reverently returned the priest's arm to its former position, gently entwining the fingers of both hands together once more in a tender gesture of respect for the old man. He smiled in a silent farewell, looking upon the kind old face one last time, and it was then that he noticed that when he'd reached backward to stop himself from falling, he'd managed to somehow pull at the cleric's hood, leaving the old man's head exposed and slightly askance on the cushion. Carefully, he adjusted the pillow and then brushed back the white hair over the priest's ear so that he could draw the hood back. He stopped and stared. It was subtle but unmistakable—the tip of Brother Edward's ear came to a point.

It was a shock of an altogether different nature from the one he'd just had earlier. He continued to stare, not quite understanding what he was seeing. Tentatively, he ran the tip of one finger over the odd deformity and then walked around the table to look at the other ear. It was the same, telling him immediately that this was no random abnormality—not whatsoever. Well, this night certainly hadn't been short on surprises, and he would be in for a nasty one if he didn't leave right then. For now, all he could think of was that he might have somehow unwittingly stumbled upon the answer as to why his old teacher had managed to live with the sickness for so long when someone half his age had succumbed within days.

Brother Edward hadn't been human—or at least not fully so.

"Goodbye, Brother Edward. I won't forget you, and I'm going to find out who you were...who you really were. I know it's important." And with that, he ran from the crypt as fast as his legs could carry him, making it all the long way back to his cell just before the light of dawn broke over the city walls.

During class that morning, Flynn was distracted and absent-minded, owing to the disturbing experience he'd had the night before. His mind went through every detail over and over again, committing as much to memory as he could, so certain was he that it was all significant somehow. More than once he wondered if he hadn't simply dreamt it all up, but he dismissed the notion as quickly as it came—it had been real, he was sure of it. He was also eager to share everything that had happened with someone else, but he was both unsure of with whom, or whether he even should at all. He naturally thought of Elias first, but despite his strong bond of trust with the other boy, he didn't think Elias would be so keen to hear about Flynn's ghost story in light of the horrifying encounter he himself had had with a supernatural phenomenon. There was a sense of fragility about Elias that made Flynn feel very protective of his friend and thus he decided that for now, it wouldn't be a good idea to upset him with this.

The next option was Brother Owen, of course. He trusted the adult implicitly, but he also expected that he'd be in for an earful—and possibly worse—if the priest found out what he'd been up to. Brother Owen was an expert theologian—Flynn couldn't think of anyone more suited for him to ask about spirits, souls, and the afterlife—but beyond the tantalizing morsels the cleric doled out during his lessons, Flynn knew that much of what he wanted to know would only be gleaned by asking some very direct questions, which would in turn entail revealing where he'd been. He wasn't sure he was prepared to test the priest's tolerance for any young-boy shenanigans that much just yet. Of the remaining children and priests who he was relatively comfortable around, there were none he felt nearly confident enough to share what he'd seen with. With a sigh, he decided that he would just have to keep it all to himself for now. It was frustrating, but he saw no other choice. When he finally returned his attention to his surroundings, he realized that Peter was staring back at him, an inscrutable look on his freckled face. Flynn felt a sudden cold fear in his stomach—had the Monitor found out somehow? No, impossible. He'd been back in his cot and pretending to be asleep for at least half an hour before the other boy had done his walkthrough to ensure everyone got up. He was just being paranoid. On impulse, he stuck his tongue out at Peter and crossed his eyes. It was a childish gesture, but he felt a deep satisfaction when the Monitor seemed clearly taken aback by his defiant impudence. The red-haired bully narrowed his eyes and turned back around in a huff, leaving Flynn's thoughts to drift back to the eventful past night.

CHAPTER 11

"Come on you bastards, let's get this over with," Vurax growled. He was in no hurry to die, but he knew there was only one way this could end. Badly outmatched by the three towering humanoids before him, ready to fall over from exhaustion, and with one arm broken, even the blood rage would not be enough to see him through this. As the fury rapidly took over his last shreds of rational thought, he was thankful that it would at least rob him of his capacity to care. The leader of the giants gave the Minotaur a horrible leering grin, the disgusting mess of broken, rotted teeth being the last thing it knew the brazen creature before him would see. When it saw the Golian's eyes flash a full crimson, its satisfaction only deepened; this one had fire, and it liked a good fight. The giant raised its massive weapon and took one step forward, eager to pulverize its quarry. It was the last thought that it would ever have.

There was only a slight blur of motion, accompanied by a sharp whirring sound, both coming a split second before the green-feathered end of an arrow shaft appeared in one of the giant's eyes. Though the creature's head was enormous, the projectile must've been long enough to penetrate all the way through to its brain as there was only a brief instant of confusion in the remaining eye before it rolled back in its socket and the giant toppled forward, dead. Before its body hit the ground, a series of similar hums cut the air as more deadly missiles flew, striking the other two giants with deadly accuracy and effect. The quick staccato of thuds left both fatally pierced through the heart and throat. It all happened so fast and abruptly that the surprise was jarring enough to cut through Vurax's final vestiges of unclouded perception, allowing him to witness what had just happened. Summoning every last ounce of strength that he had left, he wrestled down the blood rage, matching his formidable willpower against the raw and unbridled energy that desperately sought to claim control of his body. The Golian leapt to one side to avoid the toppling giant, then fell to his knees and threw his head back with an angry cry as he fought the battle inside himself. In the end, he won.

His shoulders heaving with exertion, he stared at the ground and blinked furiously to clear the fog from his vision. He didn't hear a single footstep, but he could see well enough already to notice the slender shadow fall across the forest ground before him. He knew better than to dare believe that these silent killers were imperial archers, but he also knew that if they were enemies, he would already be as dead as those three giants. He shook the last lingering traces of the rage from his mind and then lifted his head to look at his saviour. The figure was as tall as a Golian, but any other resemblance ended there. Clad in a leather cuirass and green-dyed deerskin pants, the ensemble was complemented by tall buckskin boots and a long cloak that so perfectly matched the hues of the surrounding forest that the wearer would be virtually invisible when standing still among the trees. A longbow made of supple yew was held in one hand, a partially nocked arrow in the other, while the hilt of a blade protruded above one shoulder. The hood on the cloak was down, giving Vurax a clear look at the stranger's face. At a glance, he appeared human, but a closer look revealed the immaculate tanned skin and delicately sharp facial features, with high cheekbones and almond-shaped green eyes. The alien face was framed by closely cropped brown hair, emphasizing the pointed, leaf-shaped ears.

"Syldar," Vurax muttered while snorting in disgust. He'd never seen one of the reclusive Elves before, but he'd heard enough stories in his youth to recognize the individual that stood before him as one of those legendary and ancient people.

"Golian," the Elf acknowledged simply in return, the mellifluous voice betraying no hint of emotion or intent. When he saw the Minotaur's gaze fall meaningfully across his bow, the Elf shrugged then lowered the weapon, pointing the arrow at the ground between them. "A precaution, as I'm sure you understand," he offered by way of explanation, then decided to elaborate. "You seemed like you were lost in the midst of some form of battle trance, so we couldn't be sure of your reaction." The Elf's command of the Golian language was nearly flawless, even if his accent was awkward and stilted. The use of the word 'we' reminded Vurax that this Elf was not alone. He couldn't see any others, but he was sure that was exactly the point. Grunting at the effort, he picked up his axe and rose to his feet, being careful not to jostle the arm that dangled uselessly at his side yet wincing with pain at the movement, nevertheless. Holding the bow and arrow in one hand, the Elf proffered his other hand to the Minotaur in a helping gesture. Vurax ignored it and drew himself up to his full height.

Unfazed, the Elf spoke again. "I am called Treeweaver, of the Moon Lake clan."

"Well, Treeweaver of the Moon Lake clan," Vurax responded acidly, "for someone that looks like they know their way around the wild, I'm not sure if you realize that you're inside the borders of Gol. I'm not entirely up to date on current events but for as long as I've known, our two peoples aren't exactly on good terms with each other, so... what are you doing here?"

The Syldar Elves lived in a vast, forest-covered valley to the east of Gol, the Elven realm geographically shielded from the Golian Empire by two mountain ranges that came together to form a point known collectively as the Wedge. Six decades ago, after centuries of relative peace—and during the most recent of Gol's more aggressive bouts of imperial expansion—the Minotaurs had crossed the Wedge and invaded the lands of the Syldar. What followed was a series of intermittent battles that saw neither side claim conclusive victory over the other. However, since the Syldar were only concerned with defending their homes and had no interest in Gol, the opinion of any non-Golian historian was that the Syldar had won, though no Golian would ever admit that. Faced with mounting losses and little to show for their efforts against the tenacity of the Elves, the Golians eventually withdrew and abandoned their plans for conquest altogether. As no formal peace treaty was ever signed, the two nations remained technically enemies, even if the last major engagement was recorded more than fifty years ago, and both sides seemed content enough to stay in their own territory for now.

"Saving your hide, apparently," the Syldar Elf remarked, thin eyebrows arched.

"Yeah, it's becoming a habit of mine," Vurax snorted bitterly.

"What is?"

"Getting myself into situations where my hide needs saving," the Golian answered as he took a step toward the felled giant and nudged its head with one foot. "Ugly bastard," he spat and cursed. "That was a nice shot. Thank you," he added almost grudgingly. "You still haven't answered my question, though."

The Elf acknowledged the Minotaur's gratitude with a slight incline of his head, then placed the arrow back in its quiver and slung the bow across his back. When he was done, he raised one hand and made a quick, complex gesture with long, delicate fingers. Vurax looked around, expecting something to happen, but the surrounding forest remained quiet and inscrutable. "My companions will remain out of sight and warn us if there are any more of these creatures in the area. In the meantime, I suggest we move away from here as soon as you feel ready. All this death is sure to bring scavengers before long," Treeweaver stated as if he'd read the Minotaurs' thoughts.

With a grunt and a nod of assent at the wisdom in the Elf's words, Vurax began to walk back to the area of the road where the initial ambush had taken place. The Golian was no stranger to carnage but the sight of the torn bodies of his countrymen left him filled with unfamiliar nausea and revulsion. In his mind, he was looking at his dead brother and parents and he had to shut his eyes to banish away the stark and ghastly vision. After several deep breaths, he steadied himself then moved to the remains of the wagon he'd been riding in to see what he could salvage in the way of supplies. The two wagons in the rear had escaped unscathed, but unfortunately, they weren't the ones carrying the provisions for their journey. The contents of the vehicle he was searching now had been smashed apart, and the task was made especially difficult by the fact that he only had the use of one arm. After several unproductive minutes, he gave up in frustration and smashed his fist into what was left of a water barrel.

"This is pointless," the Minotaur sounded exasperated. "The water's gone and the food's ruined, my arm hurts like a son-of-a-bitch, and I've no idea where the fort is."

Treeweaver watched him impassively, giving the Golian an opportunity to vent before speaking. "If you'll allow me, I can help set the break in your arm and build a splint for it. When we rest this evening, I can brew a tea that will help ease the pain until we can find a healer. Do not concern yourself with the supplies; these woods are abundant with sustenance and water, and I can provide for the both of us with ease. As for the fort, I can only surmise it lies further up this road you were following. Shouldn't be hard to find if that's the case—I assume that's where the two Minotaurs that escaped are heading?"

Vurax had only been half-listening, too wrapped up in his own misery to pay much heed to the Elf's droning words. When the other mentioned his missing companions though, he looked up sharply. "Two Golians? On horseback?"

"Yes," Treeweaver nodded. "One was injured, but both were riding southward, further up the mountain and parallel to the road."

Then Kael and Dalos had escaped and were alive, Vurax thought, and the knowledge brought with it much-needed relief and a renewed sense of purpose. "Alright, I accept your offer of help, but not before you tell me what Syldar Elves are doing in Gol." For all he knew, the Elves could be on a scouting mission to probe the defenses in the area, although once he thought it through a little more, why would they have bothered to save his life if that was the case, or offer to walk him right up to the gates of an enemy fort? None of this made sense, and that's why he was determined to get some answers out of this Elf before taking another step.

"We can speak as we walk, but let's move off the road. We're too exposed here. There's nothing more you can do for them—let them return to nature, as is the way of all things," Treeweaver said while walking back to the forest's edge. Vurax watched him go, then turned to look back at the battle scene one last time. The senseless loss of life made him feel angry and helpless. He knew he hadn't been responsible for the death of these bulls—they were professional soldiers after all and had given a good account of themselves, or at least those that survived the initial onslaught of flying boulders had. Somehow, he couldn't shake the feeling that this hadn't been a random attack, though. He knew next to nothing about giants, but the reactions of the others and the complete shock of the attack told him that what had just happened here was highly unusual and unexpected. Not only that but there was also the matter of the missing imperial scouts. This was beginning to feel more and more like a deliberately planned ambush, but he couldn't fathom what the giants had to gain from it. Surely, they knew this wouldn't go unanswered? Too many questions swirled in his mind, but there was at least one that he hoped would be answered soon. He struggled for some meaningful words to say but came to the sad realization that he knew none for an occasion like this. No words that mattered anyway. Turning his back, he followed the Elf and left the bodies for the waiting crows.

The Syldar and the Golian walked together in silence for some time, with neither one speaking at first. In every other respect, in contrast to his companion, the Elf moved with a flowing grace and natural expertise that made his passage utterly soundless, leaving no trace of his presence behind as he went. By comparison, the Minotaur practically stomped along, displaying an uncanny skill in finding every dry branch on the forest floor to step on, causing the snapping and crackling sounds to echo throughout the still air of the woods. For all that, Vurax noted the Elf seemed unperturbed by his lumbering about, most likely safe in the knowledge that his unseen companions were out there and would alert them to any danger. The Golian had needed to be alone with his thoughts for a while, but he hadn't forgotten the Elf had volunteered to talk, so he decided it was time to remind him.

"Well?" Vurax's rough voice broke the relative silence.

"Well, what?" Treeweaver queried back without looking at him.

"Don't play games with me," the Minotaur snarled, struggling to contain his impatience. "Tell me who you really are and why I'm leading you to a military fortification of my people."

Treeweaver did turn to him this time, a bemused look on his angular features. "First, I already told you—I am Treeweaver of the Moon Lake clan. Second, I'm the one leading *you* since you stated earlier you had no idea where this fort is. And thirdly, your people don't make any attempt to conceal their presence wherever they settle, so your 'military fortification' is hardly a secret. We've known of its existence—and that of several others in this region—for as long as they've been there."

Vurax snorted in irritation at the response, not so much because the Elf was probably right, but because he was sure he detected a hint of smugness in his tone. "Ok, fine, whatever. What are you doing here then?" he tried again.

"Events have transpired in my homeland that I am not at liberty to reveal to you at this time. However, I can say that they are grave enough to necessitate my journey to the capital of your realm in order to discuss said matters with your emperor. As such, my companions and I have crossed the border into Gol and that explains why I am here," Treeweaver explained very matter-of-factly, sounding as if the simple explanation was more than sufficient and nothing more needed to be said on the subject.

Vurax stopped walking and stared at the Elf, incredulous. "You're going to Golan?" he stammered despite himself. "You?"

"Yes."

The Golian's response was to throw his head back and laugh. Treeweaver stopped walking and regarded the Minotaur with an expressionless face. "Something amuses you?"

Still chuckling, Vurax looked at the Elf and wondered if the other was either incapable of humour or was so masterful at it that he betrayed no hint that he was actually joking. "Okay, I'll play along. Assuming you even get within a hundred miles of that city, what makes you think they will let you in? Have you met any other Golians other than me? We have an unfortunate tendency to either kill or enslave anything that doesn't look like one of us."

"No, you are the first one of your kind that I've ever spoken to, and yes, we Syldar are painfully aware of your people's regrettable propensity toward racial intolerance. It does not alter the urgency of my mission, nor the fact that I must try. If your ruler chooses to ignore me, he does so at his own peril," Treeweaver stated flatly. All traces of amusement left Vurax. So, the Elf was being serious, after all, the Golian mused. "Besides, I have two things to my advantage: I am the grandson of Queen Baliela of Syldar, and I've saved the life of a Golian," Treeweaver continued. Vurax let those words sink in, and then he began to laugh again.

"I've been saved by an Elven princeling? Well, this day has certainly been full of surprises. As for using my rescue as leverage, I hate to tell you this, but I'm nobody. I've been a slave for half my life, so do you actually think they will care about me, or the fact that you saved my worthless hide?" Vurax's laughter grew bitter.

"So, you were a slave. Who freed you, then?" Treeweaver asked.

"They did," the Golian snapped, gesturing back to the road and the dead they'd left behind.

"Then someone does care about your 'worthless hide,' don't they?" the Elf replied, no hint of mockery in the echoed words, which somehow infuriated the Minotaur even more. When the Syldar resumed his pace, the Golian bit back a retort and followed in silence.

The pair walked for a few hours until the sun began to set, with Treeweaver checking the ground every so often for signs of passage of the two horses. Progress was slow through the unforgiving terrain and while the road remained tantalizingly close, their decision to remain off it was justified more than once. What sounded to Vurax's ears like innocuous birdcalls turned out instead to be warnings from the Syldar scouts that told Treeweaver there was danger nearby, and which direction to travel in order to avoid it. The Golian didn't know what was out there, but he could guess—more giants. He slowly concluded that even if he had survived the ambush, he never would have made it to the fort alone. As the climb took a steady toll on his flagging energy, he marvelled at Treeweaver's seemingly limitless endurance. When he began to lag behind at last, the Elf called for a stop. Though there'd been no warnings for some time now, Treeweaver called out with a warbling whistle, then paused for a response. When it came, he nodded in satisfaction.

"The area is clear for now, so we'll make camp here. I think we can risk a small fire. It's high time we took care of that arm."

Too tired to care, Vurax removed his axe from its harness, placed his back against the trunk of a large oak, and slowly slid down into a sitting position. His feet and calves ached in protest, and he closed his eyes with a sigh, one hand moving up to absently rub the golden horn rings dangling from his chest. Moments later, he fell into a dreamless sleep. When the scent of sizzling meat touched his nostrils, he finally opened his eyes blearily. The soft reddish light of Temeros filtered down through the tree canopy, telling him that he'd been out for several hours, and across from him, a small fire shed a ruddy glow over Treeweaver's face as the Elf sat cross-legged on a flat stone while turning what looked for all the world like some animal's leg on an improvised spit. As droplets of fat hit the flames, delicious bursts of aroma were released, making his mouth water involuntarily.

"Won't they smell that?" Vurax wondered.

The reflection of the flames danced in the Elf's green eyes when he looked up at him. "Unlike you and me, giants cannot see well at night, even with the Dragon's Eye fully unveiled as it is tonight. While out hunting for this small mountain goat, I confirmed with the others that the creatures are far enough from us as to not be a concern. They can't see our fire from this distance, and we are downwind from them, so the smell of our meal won't carry."

Vurax nodded, accepting that the Elf was in his element and clearly knew what he was doing. He watched as Treeweaver turned the meat a few more times and then removed it from the fire. After it cooled off a bit, he produced a small hunting knife and carved a small portion for himself, then handed the Minotaur the remaining juicy haunch of goat. The two ate in companionable silence, the Syldar taking his time with small, deliberate bites, while the Golian ravenously devoured the meal, gnawing every last morsel from the bone.

"Good?" Treeweaver asked, smiling. Vurax grunted in agreement, licking his fingers and looking despondently about for more.

"In a while," the Elf replied to the unspoken question. "We need to set your arm before the bones begin to heal incorrectly. I've gathered some wood that will serve perfectly as a splint, but I'll have to brew something for the pain first." He reached into his pack and pulled out a small tin cup which he filled with water from a canteen. Then he nestled the cup into the glowing embers at the edge of the fire and waited a few minutes, adding a pinch of herbs from a leather pouch when the water warmed up. Vurax, watching the Elf's graceful yet precise movements, tried for the hundredth time to puzzle through what he'd been told. He didn't seriously believe that Treeweaver could simply walk into Golan and gain an audience with the emperor himself, but the Elf certainly seemed convinced of that, and he was curious to find out what was so important that these Elves would risk their lives by crossing into Gol. His life of newfound freedom certainly wasn't turning out anything like he'd imagined.

"Here, drink this," Treeweaver passed him the cup. Vurax sniffed the steaming contents suspiciously, wrinkling his nose at the bitter odour. If this was supposed to numb the pain in his arm, it was likely that it would dull his senses as well. The Minotaur hesitated before bringing the cup to his lips; this was clearly dangerous territory, and he was placing a lot of trust in this stranger. If he was drugged, he would be unable to defend himself. On the other hand, this same stranger could have already left him to die once, and with a broken arm, his ability to fight was severely compromised. Shrugging, he drank the hot herbal concoction in one gulp. The taste was unpleasant, to say the least, and he looked at Treeweaver with undisguised skepticism as he passed the cup back to the Elf.

"Give it a few seconds," Treeweaver said, rinsing the cup with a bit of water and placing it back into his pack. Vurax snorted and settled back against the tree, watching the fire pensively while he waited. The dancing flames took on a hypnotic quality as he slowly felt a thick fog enveloping his thoughts. His head felt surprisingly heavy, and he tried several times to keep himself from nodding off, but the effort became too much, and his eyelids drooped. A tingling sensation that began at his stomach slowly spread throughout the rest of his body, and when it reached his broken arm, he felt a pleasant numbing that gradually eased away the throbbing pain into nothingness. He was vaguely aware of Treeweaver's approach, followed by a sudden jerk and twist on his arm, though the limb felt so heavy and dense that it was almost as if it was not attached to his body. He must've fallen asleep then because he didn't even remember the Elf wrapping his arm and putting the splint into place.

The sun had already crested the mountain peaks, telling Vurax that it was late morning by the time he finally woke up. His head felt full of cobwebs, and he had to rub his eyes with one hand before his vision finally came into focus. He noticed two things almost immediately: his left arm was immobilized from the shoulder down to just past the elbow, and there was no sign of Treeweaver. He couldn't do much about the latter, so he took the time to inspect his arm. The splint was sturdy, and while it prevented him from using his arm in any way other than to stiffly hold something in his hand, he was surprised to feel no pain. In fact, the limb felt strangely cold under the bandage, and he could smell a faint, pungent odour like mint coming from under the wrapping. Satisfied with what he saw, he took stock of his surroundings.

His axe lay beside him right where he had laid it the night before, and the campfire had been put out, although he couldn't help but notice that the Elf had left him breakfast in the form of a second haunch of goat meat on the now cold spit. Feeling famished, he reached for the food and pondered the situation between bites. He briefly considered leaving before Treeweaver returned, but dismissed the notion almost as quickly as it came. The Elf had proven trustworthy for now, and as self-sufficient as he liked to be, he had to be realistic about his chances of traversing these mountains on his own, much less finding Kael. No, he concluded—he needed the Syldar's wilderness expertise, for better or worse. Before he could finish the thought, the Elf appeared suddenly, his approach clearly undetected despite the Golian's best efforts to be alert and watchful. The way Treeweaver simply seemed to step out of the forest background only reinforced his conviction that he was making the right decision in travelling with the Elves.

"How do you feel?" Treeweaver asked.

"Well enough," Vurax responded, placing his weight on his right arm as he rose stiffly from the ground. Picking up his axe and sliding the weapon into its harness, he looked at the Elf questioningly, sensing the other had something else to say.

"We've scouted the trail left by the two horses and the good news is that there's no sign of the giants nearby. Their obvious trail still leads south however, which is puzzling," Treeweaver reported.

"And the bad news...?" Vurax could tell something wasn't right.

"We've found one of the horses and its rider, or rather what's left of them. Both have been torn to pieces but there are clear signs of what happened to them. We were able to determine that the other horse managed to escape and continued south further up the mountain."

Vurax swallowed dryly and felt his heart sink. He sensed that familiar feeling of despair and hopelessness begin to tug at him, but he dismissed the negative emotions with a snarl of defiance. "I thought you said the giants had moved off," he said almost accusingly, though he knew the Elves weren't responsible in any way.

"They have. This was done by a gryphon. One of the horses must have been wounded and the scent of its blood would have carried for a great distance, becoming impossible to ignore. There is nothing a gryphon craves more than the taste of horse flesh. The unfortunate rider was probably little more than an afterthought to it—an obstacle to be overcome as it sought its true meal. We saw one of the creatures circling above the area before flying off when we approached, so there is no question in our minds as to what happened. I'm sorry."

The Minotaur waved off the Elf's expression of regret with a dismissive gesture. It's not that he didn't appreciate the words, but rather that despite their sincerity, they still rang hollow to his ears. Another comrade fallen—possibly the one person in this entire world he could call a friend—and he'd been helpless to do anything about it. Unable to help himself, Vurax began to run through all the possible scenarios in his mind that he could have come up with that might have resulted in a different outcome during that battle. In every single one, the end was the same: death. He tried hard to accept that he'd done the only thing that he could have done, but now either Kael or Dalos was dead, and quite possibly both.

"Take me there," was all he could manage.

The hike further up the mountain took just over an hour before the Minotaur and Elf arrived at the grisly site. Treeweaver hadn't exaggerated when he said there wasn't much left. Gryphons were large and powerful creatures, magical beasts that combined the physical characteristics of a lion and an eagle, and with a voracious appetite and hunting instincts to match that of both apex predators. They struck from the air with blinding speed, overpowering their prey with the sheer strength of razor-sharp claws and beaks. Vurax was no stranger to scenes of slaughter—the results of yesterday's bloody battle alone would have been enough to shock even the most seasoned warrior—but the horrific butchery he saw before him now caused him to stagger to one knee and visibly struggle to avoid spewing forth the contents of his churning stomach. Steeling himself for a second look, the Golian fought through the sharp tang of blood in the air and the drone of buzzing flies to answer the burning question in his mind. Thankfully, he didn't need long. A shred of blue cloth that wasn't covered in gore identified the dead rider as a member of the Tenth Mountain Legion. It was Dalos then, Vurax concluded. He felt a wave of relief and hope because this meant Kael was possibly still alive, but the feeling was tempered by the grief and sorrow at the loss of the brave soldier who had valiantly borne the wounded centurion away from certain death.

A sharp whistle cut through the air, bringing Vurax's thoughts back to their current predicament. He looked up at Treeweaver, the Elf having waited in silence since they had arrived at the scene of the slaughter. "What now?"

"More trouble. Come," was all the Syldar said before moving off in the direction of the road at a brisk pace. A short time later, the two stepped out onto the mountain trail and Treeweaver pointed up toward where the sky was visible through a gap in the trees created by the road. In the distance, a column of dark smoke billowed upward, drifting steadily eastward with the breeze.

"The fort!" Vurax shouted, following it up with a series of colourful expletives that made Treeweaver raise both eyebrows. "We have to find out what's going on, and hope we run into Kael between here and there."

"Agreed, though if the continued search for your companion places us in unreasonable danger, we may have to give up," the Elf warned. Vurax gave him a sharp look but said nothing as they both resumed walking. He didn't want to consider what the Syldar was suggesting, though he knew Treeweaver was right. The prospect of abandoning Kael to his fate haunted his conscience, so he avoided thinking about it for now and tried to focus on something else. He had no idea what they would find once they reached the fort, but the more he thought about the events of the past two days, the more something he couldn't define continued to nag him. That Treeweaver hadn't told him everything about his mission was evident; the Elf had admitted as much, and that, coupled with Vurax's lack of concern over the political relations between the Elves and Minotaurs, had satisfied his curiosity for the time being. However, the more he thought about the Syldar's words, the more it bothered him that he felt he had missed something. When he finally hit upon the answer, he cursed himself for being so stupid as to not see the obvious, but he could be forgiven for the error given the stress of what he'd just been through.

"You said you're going to Golan?"

"Yes," Treeweaver answered, pausing to examine the ground for something.

"Then why did you travel so far to the northwest of your realm? I may have been a slave but I'm not a complete idiot, even if it took me a day to figure out what was off about your story. The kingdom of the Syldar lies to the southeast and is much closer to Golan than where we are currently. You're weeks away from where you should be and in the wrong direction. It just doesn't make sense."

The Elf gave no indication he'd heard the Minotaur, his attention absorbed by something else. He ran his fingers lightly over a small stone, turned it over, and then brought the tip of one finger to his tongue. Vurax watched him with growing irritation but decided to wait.

"The giants came this way," Treeweaver concluded. "Now we know what's happened to the fort."

"That fort is the base for an entire cohort of Golian Legionnaires. That's five hundred soldiers. I think they can handle a few marauding giants, and if those brutes were stupid enough to attack a fortified position, then they're all dead by now," Vurax scoffed after he recovered from the surprise of what he'd just heard.

Treeweaver got up and gave Vurax a solemn look. "Your five hundred soldiers are no match for what's up there. Most likely, they're the ones who are all dead already."

Vurax wanted to laugh at the utterly ridiculous statement, but when he looked hard into the Elf's pale eyes, he saw no humour or deception there, only conviction. It was time to end this charade. Slowly, deliberately, he reached behind his back with his one good arm and pulled the battle axe free. He did not raise the weapon, but there was no mistaking the threat his action was meant to convey. "I owe you my life, and that is not a debt I take lightly, but continue to make a fool out of me, and I will end your existence, my honour be damned," he growled.

Treeweaver stared at him with that infuriatingly calm expression of his. "There's no need for pointless violence. I will tell you why I've come to these mountains since you'll find out very shortly anyway. I'm following the trail of a god."

It wasn't often that Vurax was struck speechless, but Treeweaver had nearly managed to do it twice in the space of as many minutes.

"A...a god?" the Golian stammered at last, the axe nearly falling from fingers that felt suddenly numb.

"Yes, a god," Treeweaver confirmed as if it was the most natural thing in the world to say.

CHAPTER 12

The following day, Ellianna and Lady Morhain sat across a desk from each other inside the priestess' private chamber within the temple. The lady had greeted Ellianna warmly upon her arrival and bid her sit down while she finished perusing a book lying open in front of her. That gave Ellianna a bit of time to look around and take in her surroundings, as well as ease her nerves about being in Jana's presence again. The room was an interesting mix of personal and religious décor, a portrait of the Morhain family directly across the wall from shelves replete with ecclesiastical tomes and religious paraphernalia. A large painting of Anval—depicted here as a much younger man than the statue in the hall of worship—hung on the wall behind Jana's chair, dominating the view of anyone entering the room to sit before the high priestess of Arlingtown, but it was to the family portrait that her eyes were drawn, and she studied it intently.

The setting was that of the tall front doors of Arling Keep, and Lady Jana stood in the centre at the top of the steps, looking radiant in a white and gold dress, her long, raven hair standing out in stark contrast to the pale garments she wore. The noblewoman beamed with pride and happiness as she held her newborn child in her arms, and the painter had done a remarkable, if somewhat fanciful job in capturing Mika's resemblance to his mother, even as a tiny infant. Next to Jana stood her husband, Sir Friedan Morhain, looking resplendent in the ceremonial silvered steel armour he'd worn on the day of his marriage to Lady Jana. Friedan was a tall and handsome man; with a chiseled jaw proudly set in a square face that gave him an air of dependable strength and courage. The very image of the quintessential knight in the tales of old, Friedan's union to Jana was a much-welcome reaffirmation of the long-standing alliance between the Taffens of Arlingford and the Morhains of Redmoor. Looking at the people in the painting, Ellianna searched her memory for what little she knew of Arlingford's not-always-peaceful history.

Kinsmen to the ruling Giantcutter clan of the neighbouring County of Redmoor, Sir Friedan was descended from a long line of Morhain lords and ladies dating back three centuries to a time when his valiant ancestors answered a plea for aid from the people of Arlingford. For their service and bravery in helping turn back the tide of a Goblin incursion from the lands of Kor-Zalan, many of the Morhains were given land and title in the barony and remained one of its most distinguished and powerful families today. Next to Sir Friedan stood two older men, also dressed in armour that bore the crest of their ancestral lands of Redmoor—a pair of crossed battle axes under a crimson sunrise. The similarity of their features to those of Sir Friedan left no doubt in Ellianna's mind that they were very close relations indeed, perhaps a father or much older brother? There were three other individuals in the portrait, and the first of these stood on the other side of Lady Jana. There was no mistaking the careworn face of her brother, Baron Edmund Taffen, his hair long and dark like his sister's, but touched with grey at the temples, just as with the salt and pepper beard that gave him his distinctive look. The ruler of Arlingford wore his robes of office, the dark blue garment trimmed with white ermine, while from a broad leather belt at his waist hung a large broadsword with a two-handed hilt and jewelled scabbard. Next to the baron stood a smiling young couple holding hands and dressed in noble attire.

"Do you like it?" Jana asked Ellianna. Her attention had left the book some time ago, and she'd merely sat there quietly observing the girl while Ellianna admired the painting.

"Yes, very much," Ellianna replied, continuing to look at the portrait and the individuals therein. Everyone looked so beautiful and regal—wealth and importance clearly on display, but not in a manner that made her feel inferior by comparison. It was hard to pinpoint why she thought that, but after her admittedly brief experience with Lady Jana so far, she was certain that beneath all the trappings of nobility, these were just normal people like her. "I recognize your brother and Sir Friedan, of course. They attend the harvest festival every year, and I remember seeing them from afar many times. Who are the two older knights? They look so much like him."

"This was painted by the renowned artist Tal Geroz of Pargeri and commissioned as a gift by the Duchess Konstanze Sanovun of Tremura herself to celebrate my son Mika's birth. It is one of my most treasured possessions. Those two gentlemen are Lord Alfred Morhain, my dear Friedan's grandfather, and Sir Robert Morhain, his uncle. I could not have been blessed with two kinder and more generous men in my life than they were. We miss them deeply," Jana said sadly.

Curiosity winning out by a slight edge over her fear of being indelicate, Ellianna ventured to ask. "I'm sorry. What happened to them?"

"Do you remember that terrible drought five years ago? The heat was so horrible that no rain fell for nearly the entire year, most crops withered away, and far too many livestock perished?"

She'd only been thirteen at the time, but as someone who lived and worked on a farm, she recalled well how difficult that year had been for everyone in the small rural communities that dotted the countryside outside of Arlingtown's walls. Thankfully, she and her grandpa had managed to persevere—the always-conservative Dwarf having the foresight of prudently maintaining additional stores of provisions on hand in the case of such inclement weather events. If nothing bad came to pass, he would just sell off the surplus grain at the end of the season before it could spoil. That year, his preparedness had served them well, but only just barely. Many of their neighbours had not been so lucky.

"Yes, I remember it all too well. So many of our poor animals died," Ellianna said, her voice choking with emotion. Her natural affinity and empathy for animals had made that experience all that much more difficult to bear.

"Well, as hard as things were here in Arlingford, it was much worse in Redmoor. It is a realm filled with ruggedly beautiful highlands, but it is also a much harsher and unforgiving land in some ways. The soil does not easily yield sustenance in Redmoor, and what little they do have must be supplemented by what more bountiful neighbours like Arlingford, Felgenford, and Birkenford can supply through trade. Alas, if we can barely feed our own people in times of dire need, there is simply not enough to share with others. The effects of the drought were particularly grim for Redmoor, and it wasn't long before a terrible famine began to take its toll. Unable to feed their families, the farmers and peasants of the county rose up in rebellion, demanding that the nobles living in Moortown not only share their food stores but use their wealth to purchase and send for food from the distant cities on the coast of the Shining Crescent. There was arguing, of course, and much anger fuelled by desperation and inactivity on both sides. Meanwhile, people continued to die, so it was inevitable that things would end in violence. With Moortown and other towns under threat of attack by the famished rebels, Count Brin Giantcutter sent a call for help to his kinsmen in Arlingford. With my brother's blessing, Lord Alfred answered the call, taking Sir Robert with him and a small handful of men-at-arms to help quell the rebellion," Jana related the story while Ellianna listened attentively.

"While the Count and his men were busy suppressing the rebels in Moortown and the surrounding lands, the Morhains and the fighters of their household rode further north to their ancestral holds near the Dromkar range to lend their aid there. Tragedy struck when the well-armed but small party was waylaid in the moors during a foggy evening by a large group of peasant folk turned to desperate brigandage, that had heard of their coming. Badly outnumbered, Lord Alfred

Morhain, his son, and their men fought bravely but were slaughtered to the last. It was a terrible tragedy for our family, but I never cease to give thanks to Anval that my dear Friedan did not go with them because Mika was barely one year old at the time and Friedan could not bear to leave our side. If he'd gone, he would have suffered the same fate."

"That's awful, I'm so sorry," Ellianna whispered. In the face of such heartbreak, the loss of a few cows and pigs seemed very inconsequential. "I hope those people were eventually brought to justice."

"They were. After receiving news of the ambush, Count Brin invoked the articles of the Alliance Treaty that the realms and cities of the Shining Crescent signed three centuries ago, and which provides all members with the right to request official aid from one another during emergencies. With that done, it was not long before a punitive force of Azure Knights rode from Tremura to Redmoor and put a bloody end to the brief rebellion." There was no hint of righteousness or even satisfaction in Jana's demeanour as she related this, and Ellianna wanted to ask why but didn't feel comfortable enough to do so. She didn't have to.

"I can tell what you're thinking," the priestess said, her eyes moving from Ellianna to look at the painting, "and no, it was not what I wanted. Revenge is a hollow, empty thing. A Valorian Justicer may tell you that a life taken must be paid for in equal measure, but Anval teaches us that all life is sacred and to be preserved. Those farmers were not 'evil' men and women bent on murder and destruction, but simple people like you and me, trying to live their lives and finding themselves unable to do so because they had nothing to feed their children with. Fear and desperation are powerful motivators, ones which can drive even the best of us to commit the most regrettable of acts, but when we fail to show understanding for the underlying reasons, that's when we prove ourselves no better. Had Count Brin not been so stubborn and swallowed his pride sooner in invoking the Alliance articles for food rather than military subdual, both my family members and those farmers would still be alive today."

Ellianna pondered these words carefully. She'd never had cause to think about ideals like these, but what Lady Jana was saying sounded both sensible and wise. Like most people of low social status like hers, she spent a fair amount of time daydreaming of how wonderful it would be to be a powerful and respected member of the upper class, where untold wealth and dominion over the lives of others left you wanting for nothing. Yet when Jana Morhain turned to regard her once more, she saw herself in a new light. A window of understanding had opened in her self-awareness, and through it, she saw a noblewoman sitting across from her and looking back, not with arrogance and conceit, but wistful envy. She got the distinct impression that Jana wanted to learn as much from her as Ellianna hoped to gain insight into herself from the cleric's stores of knowledge and wisdom. It was a frightening thought, that someone as uncomplicated as she viewed herself to be could provide someone like Lady Jana with a different perspective and something new. She felt even more intimidated and self-conscious than before, so she tried to move the conversation onto something else.

"Who is the lovely young couple standing next to the baron?"

"Ah," Jana smiled with obvious pleasure. "That's Braydon Aukren and his wife, Brianna Khelen. Braydon is Sir Robert's son, making him Friedan's cousin."

"Aukren?" Ellianna spoke the unfamiliar name. She knew of the Taffens, Morhains, and even the Khelens, but Aukren was not a name she'd heard before—not that she was all that knowledgeable about the names of the noble families of Arlingtown, she had to admit. "Why isn't he a Morhain like his father?"

"That's another long story, the details of which I won't bore you with right now, but let's just say that Robert was a...difficult youth—idealistic and brave, to be sure, but also brash and irresponsible in the balance. Exasperated with his antics, Lord Alfred arranged for Robert to be wed to a quiet but strong young woman from a distinguished family in Briarglen."

"That's a small village to the west, right? I'm sorry, but I've never been there. In fact, I hardly ever step out of Greenbury," Ellianna admitted, blushing. "But please continue, I'm not bored at all."

"It's alright," Jana laughed. "I know you didn't come here today for a lesson in my family history—or geography for that matter—but you did ask. I promise we will get to you very shortly." The lady's jovial manner immediately put Ellianna at ease, so she continued. "It was Lord Alfred's hope that sending Robert off to a distant, quiet corner of the barony to live in a sleepy village where nothing exciting ever happened would settle him down. And it worked. Nalia Aukren was the best thing that ever happened to him, and after Braydon was born, he thought he'd put his sword and armour away for good. That is until his father summoned him back many years later and... well, the rest you already know." Jana paused with a reflective sigh and then continued. "But to answer your question, old naming traditions in the Crescent are such that a newborn takes on the family name of a parent that was born in the same town as the child. In the event both parents are from the same locale, the family name typically defaults to that of the father's. Therefore, Braydon took on the name of Aukren from being born in Briarglen. Had he been born in Arlingtown, he would have been a Morhain, but what's in a name anyway?" Jana winked as she said this. "Do you have a last name?"

"Yes, it's Delaris."

Jana's smile froze upon hearing this but Ellianna, proud as she was in remembering at least this one small thing from her past, did not notice the subtle difference in the woman's expression.

"Is that a name that your grandpa gave you?" Jana asked carefully, the stare of her pale blue eyes reminiscent of a very cold winter day.

"No. I mean, it's not even a real last name, I don't think—at least not in the way you were describing them just now. It's what I recall other folks calling my father, and because I can't remember if that's what my family name was or if I even had one, I simply took his name as my own."

"I see," was all Jana said. This last came out as barely more than a whisper, causing Ellianna to finally become aware that the priestess was looking at her strangely.

"What's wrong?" Ellianna asked, dismayed that she might have said something so stupid that she had offended this wonderful and gracious woman.

Even as the question still hung in the air, the Lady Jana blinked and warmth returned to her eyes, the thaw spreading to bring a hint of colour to the pale skin of her cheeks and calm reassurance back to her smile. Perhaps the priestess had been distracted by a stray thought, something that could happen to anyone, but if so, the strange moment had come and gone. Without answering, Jana closed the book that she'd been reading earlier and turned it so that Ellianna could see the cover. It was not the same tome from yesterday—this one had a deep burgundy colour to it, with the shape of the words in the title pressed into the leather and then painted with black ink.

"The Primals," Ellianna enunciated slowly, peering at the words. Most, including herself, might consider her a simple peasant girl that didn't know much about anything, but Thurgod had gone to great lengths to teach her how to read, and for the second time today, she allowed herself a small measure of pride and satisfaction when Lady Jana showed how impressed she was by the slight arching of her eyebrows and the slow nod of approval.

"Very good," Jana said, letting the girl bask in the well-earned compliment. "Now, do you know who—or what—the Primals are?"

"Uhm... I know that they are gods, but..." Ellianna's proud grin turned to a sigh of frustration and shame. She bit her lower lip and avoided meeting Jana's eyes by staring at the book instead.

"But...?" Jana prodded gently.

"Well, it's embarrassing to admit, especially to someone of your station and obvious devotion, but my grandpa is not very fond of the gods. He calls them 'a waste of time' and 'foolish nonsense', and that people should spend more time looking to the ground where they step and live, rather than the sky and mooning over uncaring deities floating in the clouds." She cringed inwardly as she said these things, but she felt it best to be upfront about the Dwarf's disdain of religion, and how he had tried his best to instill that in her and failed, much to his eternal chagrin. Having said that, while she didn't consider herself a particularly devout person, she was nevertheless accepting and even curious about the various faiths that folks espoused with conviction—even enthusiasm, in many cases.

"Floating in the clouds, eh? Well, I must confess that's a new one, even for me, because trust me, I've heard more than a few curious notions about how the gods spend their time," Jana laughed. Her mirth had the desired effect and Ellianna smiled shyly back, looking at her once more. "This grandpa that you've mentioned many times now—who is he?"

"He's not my real grandpa, but if 'real' means someone who loves me and took care of me when no one else would, then he's the only family I have that matters to me. Oh, there's also Uncle Caeden and Aunt Reyna, of course. My cousins too; can't forget them." She recalled all their faces with fondness but focused back on the question when she sensed that Jana was waiting for her. "Thurgod Splintershield," she said proudly. When the name failed to elicit any form of reaction, she tried to elaborate a bit more. "He's a Dwarf farmer. We live out by Greenbury village, not far from the Field Gate."

"Yes, I'm familiar with Greenbury—sturdy, dependable folk. Unusual profession for a Dwarf though, that of a farmer, but there's nothing wrong with that."

Ellianna wasn't sure what Jana might be implying by that, but she nevertheless felt the urge to defend her grandpa. "He's one of the best around for miles and miles. The merchants in town pay good prices for our grain and dairy," she said defiantly, feeling very protective of the old Dwarf.

"Of that I have no doubt," Jana replied, holding her hands up in a placating gesture. "Without such hard-working folk, even the richest lord's table would be empty of sustenance. We all depend on one another. I simply meant that Dwarves are an uncommon sight this far south of the Dromkar, and what few do pass through Arlingford are typically either mercenaries looking for work, or traders in iron, precious metals, and gemstones."

Ellianna reflected on this, realizing that she knew less about Thurgod's past than she could recollect about her own. He always changed the subject whenever she brought it up, and she'd learned that if he was ever going to open up to her about his family and where he'd come from, it would have to be in his own good time. After ten years of living with him, she was still holding out hope for that day to come. "He doesn't like to talk about his people, so I really don't know anything about them or what they're supposed to be like. I've seen other Dwarves in town on occasion, but my grandpa never seems interested in talking to them and I don't question why."

"You're very sensible for your age, you know that?" Jana said with a fond smile. "Some people carry heavy burdens through life, ones which can be difficult to talk about, even with loved ones. I'm certain that if he feels it's important for you to know about it, then he will share that knowledge with you when he's ready. Anyway, we digress. Your grandpa's attitude toward the gods isn't so surprising—many folks share the same view, and some don't even believe in the gods at all. It's not my place to convince anyone that doesn't want to be convinced, but I most certainly welcome those who wish to learn more, and I think you are one such person, am I correct?"

"Yes, I confess I am curious, and if it helps me understand more about this dream, then I'd like to learn more about Ilfandor, and Anval too!" she added quickly, hoping the priestess wouldn't feel slighted that the patron of the healing arts wasn't the foremost thing on her mind. Perhaps once she had this all sorted out, then she could speak to Lady Jana more about her religion. The thought of spending more time in this lady's comforting presence pleased her immensely.

"Very well, let's get back to this then," Jana said, placing her hand on top of the book's cover. "There are three groups of gods, and this one is known as the Primals. Do you know what that distinction means?" When the girl shook her head, the cleric continued her lesson. "Primals is the ancient name given to the group of deities that shaped our world out of the chaos of the void. Each one represents an important and core facet of Akar, and it was only once the work of the Primals was done that the Creators arrived, followed last by Universals, but we will speak of those other groups of gods another time. The Primals—and that which they hold dominion over—are Anval, life—Kalut, death—Dalial, air—Valsemar, water—Olmara, earth—Ederos, fire—Kronus, time—Galion, etherus—and Ilfandor, nature. Some of these names are familiar to you, I'm sure, but we will focus only on Ilfandor for today. With the help and blessing of Anval, Ilfandor gave being to all the natural life of Akar, be it plant or animal, and he stands as their guardian and protector. His role is important for he has tasked himself with maintaining the delicate balance between what is needed for the peoples of Akar to survive, and the wasteful and wanton destruction of nature without purpose. For those foolish enough to engage in the latter, their crime does not long escape the keen senses of the Lord of the Hunt, and his punishment is as swift as it is brutal—the haunting sound of a wailing horn on a fog-filled night has heralded the doom of many who once were the hunter, only to suddenly find themselves now the prey."

Ellianna felt a shiver run down her spine as the words invoked vivid images of her dream. "The fog and the horn," she whispered. "But in my dream, I'm the one chasing the stranger like prey—the one you say is Ilfandor. What is he trying to tell me, if anything?"

"Did you have the dream again last night?" Jana asked.

The question was innocent enough, and she almost answered without thinking before she paused, a puzzled look on her face. "No," she said, frowning.

"Are you certain? Could it be one of those few times you mentioned as perhaps simply not remembering having had the dream after waking?"

The girl thought about that. "No; somehow, I'm certain of it. More certain than I've ever been of anything in my life. There was no dream. Isn't that odd?"

Jana pondered the question for a few moments, pensively tapping the nail of one slender finger on the cover of the book. "Some may call it coincidence, but for those in my vocation, the lines that connect everything around us can become visible, if only very briefly. When someone tugs on one of those lines from one end, there is a palpable reaction on the other end. Because of this, I'm convinced you will never have the dream again."

"Why?" Ellianna could scarcely comprehend what she was hearing. No more dream? It was almost too extraordinary a notion to contemplate. It had become such an integral part of her existence that, despite wanting to be rid of it for so long, she now faced the prospect of its absence with a strange and profound sense of loss.

"Ellianna..." Jana paused, carefully searching for the right words to explain, "I think your dream was a way to send a message. That message has been given and acknowledged now, therefore the dream itself is no longer necessary."

"A message? You mean those words at the end? But if you're right, then why did it take years for me to finally hear them?"

Lady Jana had expected the question and was prepared for it. "The answer to that lies locked inside the meaning of the message itself. The gods do not perceive time the same way that mortals do, so from Ilfandor's perspective, only a brief instant may have passed for you to either grow old enough to act upon the content of the message and thus be able to hear it, or that the event itself that the message speaks of will soon come to pass."

Ellianna was trying very hard to follow what Jana was saying, but her head was beginning to swim with the complexity of it all. "Alright," she said, holding up one hand for Jana to pause so that she could collect her thoughts, "so you're saying that whatever those words mean, it's going to happen soon, and that I'm somehow supposed to do something about it because... why?"

This too Jana had considered and was ready for. "Knowing the mind of a god is not something that is within our capacity as frail and transient souls of this world to comprehend. Even someone like me, who has devoted nearly all her life to Anval, has been granted but a few rare and brief glimpses of his will and design. The Primals—and indeed all the gods—have at times chosen an earthly vessel to be the bearer of that will, and to perform a task whose end only they can truly know. There is a significant and deep connection between you and Ilfandor that has manifested itself in the form of this dream, and its culmination two nights ago has set your life down a path of great importance."

Ellianna looked at the priestess with naked fear in her eyes. She didn't even know what this task was supposed to be, and it already felt impossible. What could a god possibly want with a mere farm girl who barely knew anything about the world, much less do something important on his behalf? She couldn't help but think that this had to be a mistake somehow. And what if she refused? Surely a being as powerful as Ilfandor could find someone more suited to do his bidding? She had only wanted to understand what the dream meant; she'd never imagined that the answer could be this terrifying.

"Lady Jana..." she struggled to find the words, "I don't think I can do this. I don't even know what 'this' is. Is it possible that Ilfandor could be wrong? I'm a simple peasant who works the fields, not someone who does big and important things like you." She tried to hold back tears but couldn't. Much to her embarrassment, she turned her face away and began to weep openly, feeling more lost than the day she'd walked out of the woods as a child.

Jana pushed the book to one side and reached across the desk with one hand to place it gently on Ellianna's shoulder, just as she'd done yesterday. As one dedicated to the well-being of others, her capacity for compassion and empathy was vastly beyond that of the average person, and thus it pained her deeply to see this girl so distraught. The revelation was no small thing, and this initial reaction of denial and self-pity was to be expected, but if what Anval had shown her was indeed the truth—and she knew of no reason why it shouldn't be—then she was truly sorry for what Ellianna would have to endure before it was over.

"My dear, don't underestimate yourself. You've already shown a great deal of courage and initiative in coming here to seek a greater understanding of all this, and it's my firm belief that there are greater reserves of strength and determination within you than you believe possible. The gods do not make their choices lightly, and your innocence and humility will be your most valuable assets in the days ahead."

Ellianna looked at Jana, her vision clouded by tears. "You say that as if you already know what I need to do. Can you please tell me what that is?"

Jana sighed deeply and considered how much she could—or should—reveal. Foreknowledge was powerful yet dangerous, but what Anval had shown her was meant to merely guide Jana in helping to prepare this girl, not so that Ellianna's choices could be influenced, and thus the outcome of her task imperiled as a result. The girl's freedom of choice must be preserved, even if she wouldn't understand why such a thing was crucial. Jana had revealed about as much as she was going to and would have to choose her words carefully from now onwards.

"Before one can step forward, one must know what lies behind. To understand what you have to do, you must first understand yourself, and that means returning to your beginning."

"Please don't speak in riddles," Ellianna pleaded, the emotion in her voice wrenching at Jana's heart.

"I'm speaking as plainly as I am permitted—you have to go home." The priestess began to feel a pounding at her temples and tried rubbing at them to ease the sudden discomfort.

"Home? To Greenbury?" Ellianna's confusion only grew. Was the Lady Jana done with her for the day?

"No, Ellianna...*home*." The pressure became a lancing pain behind her eyes, causing Jana to wince visibly and shrink from the looming presence in her consciousness. The conduit to Anval thrummed in warning, but she pushed back defiantly—she would pray for forgiveness later. For now, this poor girl deserved a little more from her. "Dawnhollow." The word had barely escaped her lips when the priestess collapsed with a low moan, slumping forward onto the desk. Ellianna let out a cry of shock and rose from her seat, the fear and confusion she'd felt rising to a panic that made it hard to breathe and think. What just happened?

"Lady Jana?" Ellianna reached out hesitatingly to the woman, uncertain what to do. Relief flooded her being when the cleric stirred in response to her touch, Jana's eyes fluttering open to focus slowly on her.

"Are you alright? Should I get help?" In her concern, she completely forgot to ask the priestess why she'd brought up Dawnhollow again.

Jana's throat had gone dry from the ordeal, so she worked to create some saliva in her mouth before she was able to form words. The pain in her head had subsided, but its source was not far. "No, I'll be fine." Noting Ellianna's expression of mingled doubt and concern, she managed what she hoped was a reassuring smile while she steadied herself and leaned back in her chair. "Really, I am," she said, raising one hand to forestall any argument or questions. Her gaze focused steadily on Ellianna. "Come back tomorrow at the same time. There is one last thing I wish to do, but I need some time to prepare for it. Today is my brother's birthday celebration and I have preparations to make for the festivities to be held this evening, so that's going to keep me quite busy for the rest of the afternoon."

"Of course! Baron Taffen's birthday—how stupid of me to forget. It's a big day for the town, and I always remember it because it's the day right after my own, but with all that's happened—"

"It's fine," Jana interrupted. "Given the circumstance, that's certainly understandable, wouldn't you say?" Jana winked at her, and Ellianna was grateful for the flash of humour, taking that as a hopeful sign that the woman wasn't upset with her over what had just happened. "Now go, and don't speak of this to anyone for now, alright?"

Ellianna nodded and stood up to take her leave. She was reluctant to do so because not only did she feel safe in the priestess' presence, but because taking a step outside that door meant stepping out onto a world where her role in it felt fundamentally altered in a way she could not yet describe. No help for it now. She performed what she hoped was a better curtsy than the one she gave yesterday and left without further word. Jana watched her go and sat there motionless for several minutes staring at the closed door, organizing her thoughts before focusing on the presence that waited with patience—or was it restraint?

'Please forgive me,' she began with the proper deference.

'You know that I do.'

'Does it really have to be this way?'

'You know that it does.'

She bowed her head in defeat.

'Do not despair. Had I truly wanted to stop you, I would have, but she must remain free to make her choice when the appointed time comes. Matters between my brothers and sisters are coming to a head, and the Fated have been set in motion one final time.'

'The Fated...' she whispered in awe.

'Do not envy them, for no mortal soul can long endure the burden. One by one, the tasks they have been appointed will consume each in turn. For some, that destiny has already claimed their life.'

'And for her?'

'Only time will tell if she is as strong as you think she is.'

'Do you think Ilfandor chose well?'

'For all your sakes... I hope so.'

There was nothing more she could say, so she waited for the god to grow silent and the conduit to close.

'Jana.'

'Yes?'

'I sense the unmistakable presence of two others of the Fated in Arlingford, but I do not yet know if they are friend or foe. Their paths are converging—you must warn her. This night, with Temeros fully veiled, one of them shall be revealed,' and with that, he was gone.

CHAPTER 13

The next two weeks went by quickly and after the last class for the year had ended, the children were assembled in the refectory where the headmaster officially declared the beginning of Yule. The boys cheered loudly at the long-anticipated break from their studies, and the excitement for all the fun that the festive season would bring was palpable throughout the large hall. Caught up in the enthusiasm, Flynn was eager to see what would be in store for them, finally emerging from the quiet and melancholic mood that had gripped him since his clandestine sojourn to the crypt. At his old school, when Yule came around, the children were simply dismissed for the one-month period and left to observe the festivities in whichever manner their families saw fit. In the case of the Castellar family, Samuel would skilfully make new carvings each year, each one a careful and detailed representation of the Universals—the group of gods that represented the many facets of day-to-day life on Akar. Flynn and his brothers would then take the little statues and set them in their places of honour throughout the house, putting up other decorations while Susan made a list of all the things she would need in preparation for the traditional feast meals, and then took her boys to the market to help her carry everything back. It was a time of joy and warmth that Flynn remembered fondly, and he dearly hoped to recapture some of that magic here, even though he knew it would never be the same.

"...and so, with the celebration underway as of this moment, we shall begin with the traditional token draw, which I will now explain for the benefit of our newest charges," Father Lorimer was saying.

The headmaster was a handsome man of middle years, tall and well-built, with a full head of prematurely grey hair that looked incongruous on his unlined face. The red-trimmed robes denoted his position as a senior cleric within the church, and he smiled benevolently as he looked out over the gathered children from the podium that had been set up along one wall of the refectory. Traditionally, higher positions within the Janusian clergy were accorded through a seniority system based on an individual's age and experience, so Flynn had never quite understood how Father Lorimer had risen to his office before dedicated, older men like Brother Owen or Brother Edward. When he had asked, the answer alluded to the fact that Father Lorimer's family was rather wealthy and influential in the realm and had donated considerably to the church in the past. Flynn didn't understand what that had to do with anything—his belief was that if such responsibility was to be equated with a man's strength of virtue and good nature, then Brother Owen should be no less than archbishop of the entire realm. True to his unassuming self, Brother Owen had laughed at this, expressing that he was quite content with his humble role and had no such aspirations. Perhaps Flynn would feel more inclined to believe the headmaster was more deserving of his post than his friend if the man would just allow Brother Owen access to the orphanage's records, but thus far there had been no word, and every time he asked—which was often—the latter simply counselled the boy to be patient.

"Based on your performance throughout the school year thus far, the Brothers have selected one student from each class to represent their age group. These boys will be the leaders of their team during Yule, each of which will be tasked with using their creative talents to decorate the orphanage and church grounds with their best work representing one of the Universals. For fairness and balance, each group will contain a few boys of other ages, some older, some younger. After the first week, I will personally judge their work and declare the winning team, who will then be accorded the privilege of putting up the final decorations in the cathedral to honour the Overgod, our Lord Janus. We will now reveal the group leaders, so when you hear your name called, step forward and take your turn drawing a token," Father Lorimer declared, holding up a small leather bag for all to see. "When you have your token, step back and do not reveal it until all leaders have taken their turn. When the last one has gone, each class will find out which of the Universals has chosen them for the Yule celebration. Let us begin with our youngest," the headmaster said, looking down at the list that had been submitted to him and reading off the first name. "Savio Mezar."

A small chorus of cheers erupted and a small boy of six years of age shyly stepped up and tentatively placed his small hand into the bag. Withdrawing a closed fist, he walked to stand to one side of the podium where several of the Brothers stood looking on. While the second name was being called, Flynn sidled up to Elias and whispered. "I wonder who our leader will be. I bet it's Eric; I think he's pretty clever and our best chance."

"Big Eric? That doofus? No way! It's gotta be Georgie for sure. He stays after class all the time to study even more after we've gone out to play. He may be a suck-up, but he's got smarts like no one else." Elias snickered. Seven boys had been called up now, the oldest of them being twelve. It was their turn next, and both Flynn and Elias perked up to hear who would be called, each one eager to be correct in their guess.

"Flynn Castellar," Father Lorimer read the name aloud.

Flynn's mouth hung open in confusion and surprise at hearing his name—surely someone had made a mistake. A few of the boys around him cheered to congratulate him and Elias beamed with pride, clapping him on the shoulder. Flynn gave his friend a look of consternation, feeling trapped—he didn't like attention, and he still considered himself a newcomer here in many respects. He certainly didn't feel comfortable with the sudden prospect of leading an entire group of boys, most of which had been here much longer than he had. How could this have happened? He didn't have to wonder long for when he glanced wildly around, he saw Brother Owen smiling at him from across the hall. When he met the priest's eyes, the man gave him one of his customary winks. Flynn did not return the smile, feeling betrayed, and his worst fear was realized when someone shoved him roughly from behind, causing him to stagger several steps forward through the crowd.

"Go on, smartass—don't make the headmaster wait," Flynn heard Peter's hateful voice mocking him.

He gave the Monitor a sullen look, and the red-haired boy responded by subtly making one of his usual obscene gestures. Gritting his teeth, Flynn walked to the front, put on a forced smile as he approached Father Lorimer, and reached into the open bag. Inside, he felt the remaining four disc-shaped wooden objects about the size of a large coin, their worn and smooth surfaces giving no indication of what was on them. He passed the tokens through his fingers for several seconds, eventually settling on one. Before he could pull his hand out though, he felt a strange sensation, like a premonition in his mind that he'd somehow made the wrong choice. On pure instinct, he heeded that inner voice and picked a different token, pulling his hand out before he could change his mind again. The object concealed firmly in his fist, Flynn joined the other boys to the side, glaring as he did so at Brother Owen who stood behind them.

When it came time for the last and oldest group to be called upon, Flynn wasn't really surprised to hear Carlo's name being called out. Many of those now in their mid-teens were elevated to the rank of Initiate, the first formal step in entering a lifetime of service in the clergy of Janus, and Carlo was prominent among them. There was no particular requirement in doing so other than a willingness to pursue a devotion to observing and spreading the faith and living your life out as a priest. He didn't really know anything about Carlo's past, but the usually taciturn and sinister teenager gave him deep misgivings about the wisdom of letting someone like him assume a position of even greater authority here. Whether Carlo was a good enough student to have earned the position of leader of his team appeared irrelevant, if one took note of Father Lorimer's smile of approval and pride as the older boy stepped up with confidence and drew the final token. That done, the Initiate took his place alongside the other ten boys and waited for the signal to reveal which god had chosen them.

"Reveal!" Father Lorimer called out, and all the murmuring in the room died to a hush as everyone waited expectantly. As one, the class leaders held out their closed hands and opened their fingers to reveal the token resting on their palms. Flynn couldn't hide his disappointment at what he saw in his own hand. The symbol, carved and painted in vivid colours on the dark wooden disk, was that of a horrible face, bits of rotting and putrefied flesh clinging to the pale bone showing beneath, and a pair of eerie eyes that stared out from sunken eye sockets—Gaurkur, the lord of diseases and plagues, and the natural decay of all living things. As a blunt and unwelcome reminder of how he'd lost his mother, the rictus grin on that ghastly visage felt like it was openly mocking him. Seriously? Out of the eleven hallowed Universals, this was the one that he drew, he thought to himself in astonishment and anger. He'd been fervently hoping for one of his favourites—exciting deities like Unamos, the Warbringer, or mysterious ones, such as Sillion, the patron of trickery and deceit. But no, instead he'd gotten Gaurkur. Even Beria, the sappy Lady of Love and Joy would have been preferable to moldering Gaurkur.

He remembered the odd compulsion that had made him drop his initial choice and select this one instead. Seeing the result now, he deeply regretted giving in to it. He cast a surreptitious look at the token in Carlo's hand and glimpsed the crossed swords of Unamos. It just figured, he groaned inwardly, and to add insult to injury, the look on the Initiate's face as he caught Flynn stealing a glance could only be described as exceedingly smug. His knowledge of what was done to honour and celebrate Gaurkur was rudimentary at best, and his earlier misgivings about being thrust into this unwanted role were turning into full-blown panic now. He recalled that when he'd lived at home, his brother Joshua had always placed Gaurkur's figurine among their mother's small collection of jars and pots containing various salves and balms, dried herbs, and other medicinal household sundries. As the tradition went, any home thus warded from Gaurkur's unwanted attention would be safe from serious illness through the coming year. Nothing but superstitious nonsense, he thought angrily, given Susan's tragic fate. Flynn closed his hand over the token and squeezed hard, wishing he could make the hated object disappear. He had no time to react when he felt the wooden disc grow impossibly hot in his hand and a wave of debilitating nausea washed over him with shocking suddenness, causing him to retch once, then collapse to the floor, unconscious.

"Hello Flynn, how are you feeling?"

The voice was familiar, but Flynn's mind felt so adrift in a thick fog that he couldn't put a name to the speaker. He opened his eyes and saw Brother Owen's kindly face hovering over him. The man was smiling but couldn't hide the concern in his dark eyes. Flynn realized he was lying on a bed that definitely wasn't his own as he took in the details of the walls and ceiling behind the priest. Shaking off the fuzziness in his head, he lifted himself gingerly on his elbows to look about. It was a large space, and the sun shone brightly through a series of narrow windows set high up on a nearby wall and angled so that the light coming in beamed down upon the floor between two rows of neatly ordered beds on opposite ends of the high-ceilinged chamber. There was a distinct scent in the air—sterile, clean, and medicinal. Doors led out from the room at either end, but other than Brother Owen, there was no one else about.

"Easy, lad," Brother Owen cautioned, reaching out and placing the palm of one hand on Flynn's forehead. The priest's touch felt cool and soothing, and as he focused more on that sensation, Flynn gradually became aware that something wasn't right. His stomach burned like fire and a chill ripped through his body, causing him to shiver uncontrollably. He lay back down, feeling nausea and rising bile in his throat while a strange lassitude crept over his limbs, bringing a strange numbness with it.

"Where am I? What is this place?" Flynn managed to croak out, his voice sounding harsh and strange to his own ears.

"Your fever is still quite high," the priest remarked, taking his hand from the boy's head. "Try not to move around too much and conserve your strength." He reached for a pitcher resting on a side table next to the bed and poured a cup of water which he carefully held up to Flynn's lips to drink, holding the boy's head up carefully so he could imbibe the liquid. Then he poured more of the cool water onto a cloth and placed the damp fabric on Flynn's forehead. "This is the church hospital," he explained. "We brought you here after you collapsed in the refectory."

The refectory? Of course. The Yule celebration and token draw—the memory came rushing back to him in a flood of images and sounds, a disorienting sensation made worse by the physical discomfort he was experiencing. He remembered everything clearly now, right up until the second he had looked at the token in his hand, and then...nothing. Something scratched at the back of his mind, and he mustered enough energy to pull his right arm out from under the bed covers.

When he looked at his hand, he saw that it was heavily wrapped in bandages right down to the wrist, leaving his fingers free to move, albeit with some difficulty. He stared uncomprehendingly at it and then looked at the cleric in wide-eyed dismay.

Brother Owen sighed. He knew well how resilient children could be, both physically and emotionally. He also knew that such inner fortitude wasn't necessarily immediate, and the preceding reaction tended to be far worse than the situation actually warranted. When a five-year-old accidentally fell during play and scraped a knee, the resulting cries of pain and dramatic display of anguish were well beyond the severity of what the child was really feeling. Nevertheless, all one could do was allow the child sufficient time to let them work that out on their own. As one grew older, this behaviour gradually lessened until it was eventually gone, but he'd seen many an older boy involuntarily revert to that infantile instinct when faced with a sudden and traumatic event like this. When he'd first met Flynn that day outside of his house, he sensed an inner core of resilience and strength in the boy that impressed him greatly. He was therefore not surprised to see Flynn's face go from shock to acceptance, and finally calm determination, all within the space of a few heartbeats.

"Your hand was badly burned, but we've tended to it, and it should heal well with time. I myself prayed for the miracle while you slept," the priest explained. Flynn's eyes widened again at this—someone had used divine magic on him, and he'd missed it? Well, that absolutely just wasn't fair. It was then that he noticed another detail. Where the skin of his fingers disappeared under the wrappings, the flesh was blackened and cracked. The appendages glistened with some kind of ointment, and though he was relieved to see that he could wiggle them, he otherwise couldn't feel anything past his wrist.

"How long have I been here? I really should get back to my group; they'll be expecting me to begin the decorations—somehow." He had no idea what to do, and an injured hand was sure to prove a serious and unwelcome hindrance. Still, even though he had never wanted the role of leader, he wasn't about to shirk his responsibility. He paused briefly, remembering something else, and his expression changed to one of naked resentment. "Why did you put my name forward?"

Brother Owen met the boy's accusatory look and tone with silence before forming a careful reply. "It was my judgement that you needed a distraction. I know some things have been weighing heavily on you of late and giving you a task that would require your energy and attention would be a good way to take your mind off those things. I'm sorry, Flynn; it appears my presumption was a mistake."

"You should have asked me," Flynn retorted sullenly, finding it difficult to remain angry at the man. He averted his eyes, his hurt and resolve wavering under the priest's apologetic words and sincere gaze. Deep down he knew the cleric was right in his assessment, and that the decision had come from a place of care and concern, but he didn't want to admit it just yet or give the man the satisfaction of that knowledge. "You don't understand—grownups never do," he moaned. "I don't know what to do. Now a bunch of my classmates are looking to me to lead them and I'm not sure I can. It's too much pressure. Oh, and this isn't going to help," he complained, holding up his bandaged hand.

"Flynn—" Brother Owen began but the boy cut him off abruptly.

"Why did I have to draw Gaurkur anyway? I don't really know anything about him. We haven't even gotten around to learning about him in your class," Flynn continued to vent.

"Flynn, I—" the priest tried once more, only to be interrupted a second time.

"And what exactly happened? The last thing I remember was that stupid token getting really hot in my hand and now I feel sick, and my hand is like this. Why did—"

"*Flynn!*" Brother Owen sternly raised his voice, causing the boy to stop talking abruptly and stare at him. "Listen to me—forget about your group for now. I've asked Eric Murklen to take your place because you've been sleeping for five straight days. The healing miracles have this effect sometimes, depending on the severity of what's ailing the patient. As I said, your hand should heal just fine, but you are still suffering some strange ill effects from your ordeal, and that's going to require that you stay here a little longer." He held up a finger when Flynn seemed about to argue with that last point. "This is not a negotiation, young man. You need to stay put until we're sure you're over this. Just so you don't get any ideas, those doors will be locked day and night," he warned.

"Five days?" Flynn blinked several times in disbelief. He couldn't fathom anyone sleeping that long but apparently he had, all the while managing to miss nearly a quarter of Yule in the process. "Big Eric is the leader now?" he surprised himself at how irritated he was at hearing that. He hadn't wanted to be the leader of their team, but being told that he'd been summarily replaced somehow filled him with disappointment and...jealousy? He didn't know why that bothered him so much, and the emotion nearly made him forget the far more important event that had landed him in the hospital to begin with. "Am I going to be okay? My stomach feels funny, sure, but I don't want to spend the rest of the Yule celebration in here. It's not fair."

Brother Owen's customary smile and wink helped to ease some of his worry, and the priest's next words helped instill a sense of hope in him. "The worst is over, and the best part is that you slept through it all. As soon as your fever breaks—and I feel that will be very soon—you'll be free to go and enjoy Yule with your friends. How does that sound?"

It did sound great indeed, and Flynn was confident that he'd be up and running around by tomorrow morning. There was no way he was going to miss the rest of the festivities, and so he lay his head back on the pillow, determined to will himself into feeling better so that he could prove to the priest that he could go when the next morning arrived. Satisfied, Brother Owen sat up and bid Flynn a good rest, but not before pulling a book from the folds of his robes and placing it on the nightstand next to the pitcher. Flynn looked at it curiously. "What's that?"

"*The Legend of Starfall*," the priest read out the title. "Brother Edward once told me of your particular fondness for this tale, so I took this book from his cell when we stored away his belongings. I think he would have liked for you to have it, so I had meant for it to be your Yule gift on Gods' Day, but now seems like a more appropriate time, wouldn't you say?"

Flynn nodded eagerly, grinning from ear to ear. This was indeed his favourite story, one which recounted the heroic adventures and deeds of Avakan, the clan leader of the brave Avamori tribe, and how during his people's darkest battle and most desperate hour, he raised his sword to the heavens to plead for a saviour, and a star fell from the sky in answer to his call—the event that heralded the arrival of Janus, the Lifegiver. All of this was recorded in the Holy Scriptures that they read and studied every week during mass, of course, but Flynn had always thought those particular writings lacked a sense of wonder and imagination. What he held in his hands was a much richer and satisfying account, told in the tradition of a warm fireside tale, and lacking all the preaching and moralistic lessons that took all the fun out of this fantastic saga. While the book he held wasn't exactly considered heretical, many priests didn't even try to hide their disdain for it, owing to its fanciful and sometimes irreverent tone. He was glad Brothers Edward and Owen weren't those type of clergymen, and he liked the book because it made Avakan feel like a real person—complete with flaws and an actual personality—and not the saint on a pedestal that he was regarded as today. Flynn only knew of the book's existence because Brother Edward had shown it to him a few times after class, reading him several passages to entertain the boy's fertile imagination.

"Thank you," he said, feeling truly overwhelmed. Flynn was grateful to have someone like Brother Owen step into his life at such a difficult time, and it wasn't just because the man genuinely cared about his young friend; it was because they understood each other as kindred souls. It was true that most of the other priests here were orphans themselves, but only a rare few—like E'on Abdalla—still remembered what it was like to be a child and remember the world as it was before the filter of adulthood took away that innocence forever.

"You're welcome," the man smiled, placing the book in Flynn's uninjured hand. "Now remember—stay in bed, someone will be bringing you something to eat in an hour or so, and I'll stop by again before nightfall. The chamber pot is under the bed when you need to relieve yourself." The boy gave him an earnest nod, and with that the priest left the hospital room, leaving Flynn alone with his thoughts. He lifted his bandaged hand and examined it several times by turning it from side to side slowly. While he did so, a faint sensation, like an itch, tickled the palm of his hand. He took that as a good sign that feeling was slowly returning, shrugged, and settled in comfortably to read his new book.

———◆———

'Are you certain?'

'Yes, Father Lorimer. We looked everywhere for the disc but could not find it. Whatever caused it to burn the child's hand must've resulted in its destruction.'

'Very strange. How are the other children?'

'Shaken by what they saw, but otherwise everyone's fine. We've postponed the beginning of the celebration until tomorrow, as you requested.'

'Very good. Owen... what do you make of all this?'

'I honestly have no explanation, Father. We've used those same tokens year after year; there's nothing special about them and no particular reason for something like this to happen.'

'And the boy?'

'A good student with few friends; quiet yet headstrong at times, but otherwise unremarkable. I know what you're thinking, and it's simply not possible—he's too young.'

'You're probably right, but I want you to be absolutely sure. If there's something I need to hear, I hope it reaches my ears first before Archbishop Marcos', am I understood?'

'Perfectly, Father.'

Brother Owen sat alone in a small room located on the basement floor of the classroom building. Cluttered with reams of loose papers, piles of rolled-up scrolls, and several unsteady-looking stacks of heavy tomes, the windowless chamber's official designation was that of instructor's office for the unassuming cleric. In reality, it was more of a personal refuge and place where he often spent time engaged in his personal research and scholarly pursuits. He much preferred the isolation and quiet here to the bustle and distractions of the church's main library. Thinking of the library, he glanced bemusedly at several of the books lying about, including the one he was reading now, and wondered when he would make the effort to return them. Knowing how crazy it drove Brother Melton to see those empty gaps in the stacks, he decided with a wry smile that that day could wait a while longer.

The priest took a sip of his hot tea, leaned back in his chair, rubbed his tired eyes, and once more went over the conversation he'd had with Father Lorimer five days ago—the day Flynn had collapsed in the refectory. The headmaster, like everyone else, was justifiably unsettled by the event. Where the two men disagreed, however, was on the potential cause behind what had occurred. He couldn't dispute that Flynn's *etherus* had somehow manifested itself in that moment. There could be no other explanation for what they'd witnessed. The token itself, despite seemingly being a commonplace, inert object, must've been the catalyst for the reaction. What he needed to figure out was why, and how someone of Flynn's young age could have done that. According to everything he already knew—and had read repeatedly just to reaffirm that knowledge to himself—only when an individual was on the cusp of adulthood did the *etherus* have a chance to appear in an outwardly physical fashion.

He passed his hand over the glowing orb that provided light in the room and the globe shone just a little brighter. His eyes were hurting from the strain of reading for hours in here, his vision growing tired and blurry, but he pressed on, convinced the answer was buried somewhere in one of these old books. This particular one was aptly titled *The Mysteries of the Etherus*, and he returned to the passage he'd been studying:

> *When understanding the etherus and how it behaves, it is important to remember that there are some facts which appear immutable, first and foremost of these being the form each and every one of us takes when coming into this world. What we are shapes and determines what we can do with the etherus, as well as when. Its presence is all-encompassing—meaning the etherus is present within every individual—yet Elves and Dragons are born in perfect harmony with it; Dwarves and giants are blocked from accessing it; Minotaurs, Goblins, and Saurians require specific hereditary traits to access and manipulate it; and we Humans seemingly can only do so when our bodies transition into adulthood, and even then only in a very few individuals that are randomly sensitive to it. Why it happens thusly is cause for much debate, and if it is to be believed that we are but the creations of the gods, then perhaps this is a question best posed to them. What we do agree upon though is that the etherus—that which is often colloquially referred to as 'magic'—is synonymous with the idea of a soul.*

These were all things he already knew and not what he was looking for. He scanned quickly down the page, then through several more. Nothing. Closing the tome in frustration, he set it aside and paused to consider his method. Maybe he was simply looking in the wrong place? When one looked at a problem too closely, there was a risk of not seeing the greater picture from a distance. With that in mind, he decided to try a different angle. What was the commonly held view on the source of the *etherus*? Some scholars argued that it simply *was*—meaning a part of everything, yet also apart from everything—while others theorized that it was merely another natural aspect of Akar, like wind, rain, or even life itself. The prevalent theory however, one espoused by his own church, was that the source of the *etherus* was divine—the spark of godly creation that separated the intelligent races from unthinking beasts and monsters, hence the idea of likening it to having a soul.

'Source'—for some reason, the term stuck in the priest's mind. Where had he seen that word before within these books? Ah yes, of course! He lifted his gaze to a row of books neatly arranged on a shelf above his desk. These tomes of knowledge were his own possessions, not ones he had borrowed from the library. As an instructor in theology, he often prepared his daily lessons from these cherished works, and he was intimately familiar with their contents. Still, it never hurt to refresh one's memory on a particular topic, and tired like he was, his recollection of detail was growing a little fuzzy. There were thirty volumes in all, one for each of the Gods of Akar, arranged alphabetically from Ahrkmakul to Zarvon. The cleric's hand stopped roughly in the middle of the row and pulled out the one titled *Galion the Magus*. Carefully placing the aged book on his reading stand, he opened it to the first page and began to read:

> *Galion the Magus is the acknowledged patron of magic in all its forms. Known by his followers as the 'Source', he is the ultimate font of all magical energy in the world, that which is manipulated by the mages of Akar. He is also responsible for teaching the most important spells and magical rituals to arcane practitioners. Galion is a scholarly and relatively peaceful deity, but his wrath can be terrible to behold when magic is used irresponsibly and is able to forever withhold magic from a mage who has displeased him. Only mages of great power have the ability to commune directly with Galion, although he is fond of sending dreams and portents to his lesser disciples.*

Gods were very fond of titles, and Galion was no exception. That he was called the 'Source', however, was a topic of contention among the various religions, and the Janusians were no exception to that age-old schism between the faiths. In reconciling the notion that magic and the *etherus* were one and the same, many took issue with the assertion that Galion had a claim of dominion over a gift that the other gods bestowed upon their own followers. As expected, this implied form of control did not sit well with the church of Janus in particular. For them, it was unfathomable and unacceptable that a divine being that reigned over his siblings by the title of 'Overgod' could in any way be dependent on a lesser god for anything. As a student and scholar of all the faiths, Brother Owen had a mind that was more open and tolerant than that of the vast majority of his Janusian brethren; therefore, he accepted that several things could be true at the same time, including the idea that no one god's power was absolute and that each deity was but a small part of a much greater whole. Recalling various discussions he'd had on the subject with other theologians, he realized that he was getting sidetracked in his thoughts. Making an effort to focus once more, he took another sip of his tea, and then skipped ahead to a section of the book that explored the idea of a 'Source' in relation to inanimate objects:

The manipulation and expenditure of magic demands practiced skill and effort, and can be a very taxing process for practitioners of the Art. When the magic is depleted, it is only through carefully regimented periods of rest and meditation that a mage can recharge and renew their stores of energy anew. Because the ability to draw upon the ambient magic of Akar quickly diminishes with every spell that is cast, a mage can—at great risk to his or herself—call upon their own inner reserve of etherus to extend and expend that power temporarily. This sacrifice of personal energy should be reserved for only the direst emergencies, however, for the toll upon the user can be terrible and irreversible. Debilitating weakness that leads to lengthy unconsciousness is not uncommon, and in some extreme cases, some have never risen again.

For this reason, strict rules on the use of magic are taught to all practitioners from the start of their studies, which unfortunately did not prevent one unscrupulous group of mages from finding a way to circumvent these rules. That abominable act—the violation of siphoning the etherus from another living being to power one's own magic—was the unforgivable perversion that led to the devastating

Great Sorcerous War and the unintended creation of Husks, but we will discuss that at greater length in the next chapter. What will be examined now is the much safer and accepted practice of storing a portion of one's own etherus in an inanimate object for use at a later time.

These objects—or foci—must be carefully prepared beforehand, and the attempt can often result in failure, but if done successfully, the mage can gain a valuable reserve of power that can be drawn upon when needed without exhausting the user. Like the mage that created it, the foci can be replenished over time, but only as long as they are not fully drained of the etherus within them. If that happens, the foci become inert forever and the process must be performed again on a new object. In many ways, a mage's focus is another form of what priests use to channel their divine magic—their symbols of faith. These ornamental tokens—carrying symbolic depictions of the gods and often worn as medallions—enable members of the various priesthoods to channel the etherus from their divine connection rather than themselves, empowering the use of what they term 'miracles'.

Brother Owen took his eyes off the page to ponder the implication of this information as it applied to what he was seeking. Was it possible that the token Flynn had pulled out of the bag had been a holy symbol at some point? His fingers moved involuntarily to touch the silver medallion hanging from a chain at his breast. He felt the familiar response gently tickling his skin and nerves, not unlike the sensation one experienced when a dormant limb slowly regained feeling. One of the final rites of investiture when being ordained as a priest involved receiving the symbol of faith and accepting confirmation in the eyes of Janus by experiencing the medallion's response as a sign of approval. He remembered his own ceremony like it was just yesterday. He also remembered he'd been at least five years older than Flynn during that event, as were nearly all Initiates chosen to become priests. Something very odd was going on here, but before he could investigate any further, he would need to consult with Father Lorimer again. Putting his empty teacup down, the cleric closed the book and dimmed the light. He meant to take only a brief rest before heading out to seek his superior, but exhaustion claimed him before he even finished forming the thought, and he slumped forward into a deep and dreamless sleep almost immediately.

Brother Owen woke with a start, becoming instantly aware of the pain in his lower back from having fallen asleep doubled over his desk. He looked about in confusion at not finding himself in his bed, then straightened with a wince and got up from the chair to work some circulation back into arms gone stiff. He had no idea how long he'd slept but figured it must've been an hour or two at most, so he was shocked when he left his office and walked outside to discover it was late morning of the following day. Luckily it was Yule, otherwise, he would have missed his own class, he thought sheepishly. Two priests deep in conversation walked by him and nodded politely before moving on. As he smiled in response, he was reminded that he needed to speak to Father Lorimer after he got some breakfast, but first, he really ought to check in on Flynn before doing anything else. He turned his steps toward the hospital, entered the structure through the main door, and frowned upon noticing that the Initiate—normally posted there to immediately notify one of the priests if a child came in feeling ill or with an injury—was absent. The cleric pulled at the ring of keys looped around his belt, found the right one, and placed it into the keyhole on the inner door that led to the infirmary where Flynn was, but his misgivings deepened when the key met no resistance from the mechanism. The door was already unlocked. He opened the door in a rush, his eyes going immediately to Flynn's bed—but no one was there.

Owen froze temporarily in confusion and then walked swiftly to the bed. It was unkempt—unlike the others in the room—the blanket was missing, and resting upon the ruffled sheets was the book he'd given the boy the day before. He picked up the copy of *The Legend of Starfall* and stared at it with growing apprehension. He could believe that Flynn would disobey him and had somehow found a way out of the hospital, but he never would have left the book behind. And where was the Initiate that was supposed to be on duty? Something near his feet caught his attention and he bent down to see what it was. There, partially under the bed, he found a small pile of discarded linen wrappings—the dressing from Flynn's injured hand. What had taken place here? He looked about the room once more just to confirm that no one else was about, picked up the book to hide it in the folds of his robes, and then walked out to begin his search. Breakfast was going to have to wait.

CHAPTER 14

"THE GODS AREN'T REAL," Vurax affirmed for the third time as they continued their climb higher up, openly walking upon the mountain road. The need for concealment was over—only speed mattered now. Not because Treeweaver felt anything could be done to aid the Golians at the fort—in his estimation, their fate was already sealed—but because there remained perhaps a slim chance that they could still find Kael before getting too close.

"Your personal belief—or lack thereof in this case—does not preclude their existence. They are real; never more so than now," the Elf shot back, setting a blistering pace that was taking a toll even on the hardy Minotaur.

"By the sun and stars, Treeweaver, do you actually believe all that nonsense that the priests spout all the time? Almighty beings that control our fortune and destiny, and upon whose fickle whims the fate of our world rests? It's nothing but a bunch of sanctimonious drivel meant to control the weak of mind. I thought you had more common sense than this," the Golian continued, astounded at the other's stubbornness. He hated discussing this topic because while there were some that shared his view, he'd encountered far more that felt the exact opposite, and he couldn't comprehend why. Not that slaves were particularly preoccupied with philosophizing on the finer aspects of theology, but that was precisely the point to him. As far as he was concerned, no entity capable of the power attributed to the gods that claimed to care about its worshippers could possibly exist and simultaneously permit some of the horrors and injustices he had witnessed while living a life of squalor, misery, and servitude. He simply could not accept that. To him, the gods were an artificial construct that conveniently absolved people from responsibility for their own despicable behaviour and for committing atrocities in the name of 'faith'.

The Syldar stopped and turned to look at the Minotaur and then advanced on him. For the first time since he'd encountered the Elf, Vurax saw the impassive veneer the other always wore like a mask fall away to reveal genuine anger. So, the

Elf was capable of emotion after all. Taken aback by Treeweaver's strong reaction, Vurax braced himself for whatever was to come.

"I have seen what one of them can do firsthand," Treeweaver spat, the words flying like daggers and full of vitriol. "Perhaps if you witness it with your own eyes, you will understand," the Elf stepped back, having come within mere inches of Vurax's face as he delivered his invective. Realizing how close he'd come to losing control, Treeweaver composed himself and forced every trace of ire from his body. "Keep following and do not fall behind. I wish I could say that all will be made clear, but I have no idea where this is all leading. All I know is that if there is any chance to stop it, you had better begin opening your mind to certain things. If I am right, you will have a part to play in all this before it is over."

Mechanically, almost without thinking, Vurax did as Treeweaver asked and followed. He was stunned into silence by the Elf's words, and while he was unable to understand outright what the other was on about, he nevertheless felt a nameless dread inside of him, as if the things he'd just heard had stirred something that had long lain dormant. Or had it? He certainly didn't feel as if there was anything special about him. He was nobody and wished to remain that way, with no ambitions beyond living a quiet life where he was free to determine his own path. The notion that perhaps he had some greater destiny, one that involved make-believe deities no less, was a thought too frightening to contemplate. Rather than open his mind as Treeweaver had asked, his self-defence was denial and the raising of higher walls around that rejection of belief. Nothing and no one was in control of his fate but himself, and he was going to prove it.

It took some time, but the labour of their search finally bore fruit, and not a moment too soon as Vurax felt his endurance flagging from the arduous trek. With the air growing noticeably chillier, the Golian found himself pausing every so often to catch his breath while Treeweaver continued to show no signs of fatigue. When a whistle cut the air, the Elf gave his companion a meaningful look and quickened his pace even more. Vurax didn't need words to know they had found Kael. Filled with a sudden boost of energy, he surged forward, desperately hoping that the centurion was still alive.

Before long they saw the horse through the trees, its head down as it drank from a cold mountain stream; a red-uniformed figure slumped forward in the saddle. Before Vurax could get any closer, Treeweaver raised a fist, signalling him to stop, followed by a gesture indicating silence. "Stay here and don't move," the Elf whispered, and the Minotaur acquiesced with a nod, fighting down his impatience. The Syldar moved forward soundlessly, angling his approach so the horse could have a clear view of him. Now that they had found Kael, it wouldn't do to blunder in, spook the animal, and cost them more time chasing it down once again. The horse took note of Treeweaver, lifting its gaze and eyeing the elf with caution. When one hoof stamped the ground and the animal shook its head with a snort, Treeweaver stopped and reached out with one hand, speaking soft words. From his hiding place behind a tree, Vurax held his breath in anticipation. The horse's tail swished back and forth, but after its initial alarm, the steed seemed calm now, allowing the elf to approach. Treeweaver did so, using one hand to take hold of the dangling reins while the other soothingly stroked the chestnut hair just above the nose. Throughout it all, there was no movement from the rider.

When Treeweaver finally motioned Vurax forward, the Minotaur did not hesitate, although he still tried to move cautiously when he came closer. Thankfully, the horse was well trained and quite comfortable with the scent of Minotaurs, giving him a calm look that gave Vurax enough confidence to walk up and help him ease Kael from the saddle and onto the ground. The centurion moaned weakly from the effort and Vurax breathed a sigh of relief but winced in the next breath when he got a close look at Kael's wounded leg. White bone glared at him sharply as it stuck through the rent flesh at an angle, the whole festering and bloody mess causing even Treeweaver to grimace and shake his head.

"This is beyond my skill to repair—if he's to ever walk again, we'll need to find a priest or a skilled healer, and soon," the Elf advised. "Hold him while I clean the wound. We'll have to immobilize the leg, and if we can keep the infection at bay, he might have a chance. He also appears feverish, so I'll have to give him something for that." Treeweaver took off his pack and began laying out what he needed. Vurax nodded gratefully and looked at Kael with concern. The centurion's eyes were closed, and he appeared unaware that they were even there. While he was elated that Kael was still alive, he began to wonder if a swift death in battle might not have been a more merciful fate for the veteran soldier. He couldn't fathom a bull like Kael living out his days as a one-legged cripple. Pushing the grim thoughts from his mind, he focused on the present and on helping Treeweaver do everything they could for now. He still didn't know what to make of the Elf and his incredible story, but his willingness to help two complete strangers could not be easily dismissed. That both he and Kael were Golians—effectively enemies of the Syldar people—made Treeweaver's actions appear even more extraordinary.

Sometime later, Treeweaver made Kael imbibe one of his herbal concoctions with practiced ease and then inspected the bandage and splint one last time. After easing the centurion's head to rest comfortably on a rolled blanket taken from the horse's saddlebags, he looked up at an anxious Vurax. "This will ease his pain while keeping him unconscious for some time, and the splint should stop that broken bone from tearing up more of his leg. How far are we from your people's nearest town?"

Vurax tried to think. During their journey south, Kael had often pored over a map, showing him their planned route from Sarmakan and all the way south to the coast where Golan was situated. After crossing the Border Peaks, the road they were on would take them directly to the northern city of Vurgas, which itself was not far from the rural community where he was born. "It's at least a week away, and we only have one horse," he glanced down at Kael. "He won't last that long. Surely we can still make for the fort; they will have healers there."

The Elf sighed. "Vurax, you've seen the smoke. What do you think that means? I did not jest earlier—even if any of your people are still alive up there, they won't be in any position to help us."

"But we're so close now. What have we got to lose at this point by trying? Suppose you're wrong?"

"You don't understand—" Treeweaver began.

"Then help me understand, damn it!" Vurax snapped back. "You said earlier I needed to see with my own eyes. Fine, so show me then—show me what you're so afraid of," he challenged.

Treeweaver stared at the ground in silence, then shook his head before looking back at the Golian. "I spoke in anger. Going up there will be folly and quite likely to place us in needless danger. Are you sure you want to do this?" He asked the question, but he could already see the answer in the other's eyes. The Minotaur didn't just want to go; he was prepared to do so alone if need be. The Syldar made his decision. He put two fingers to his lips and called out into the forest with a loud, trilling sound. Several seconds passed then two figures entered the small clearing from opposite directions. The Elves were garbed in similar fashion to Treeweaver, except their hoods were drawn up over their heads and a black cloth masked their faces, leaving only their eyes visible. The telling curve of their hips and chest cuirasses revealed them to be female. Vurax was again amazed at the Syldar's ability to vanish so seamlessly into their surroundings and waited while the three of them exchanged a few words in their strange, musical language.

"This is Alis and Seren," Treeweaver motioned to the new arrivals. "They will watch over Kael while we are gone. If we do not return before the sun sets, they have instructions to depart. There is nothing else they can do for him. Do you understand and accept this?"

The offer was unambiguous but fair. "Very well," he replied.

⚊⚊◆⚊⚊

Minotaur and Elf both lay prone atop the small ridge, concealed by low-lying brush as they surveyed the chaos unfolding below.

Built on a plateau overlooking the road that continued south into the Golian lowlands, the Tenth Mountain Legion's fort—one of three in this region built in the last decade as an effective deterrent against increasingly bolder Sarmakanite raids—was strategically located where it could effectively guard the high pass and valley beyond. The tall, wooden palisade walls were erected over a raised earthen embankment for additional height and surrounded by an exterior moat lined with sharpened stakes. A wide battlement platform along the inner perimeter provided the legionnaires with a vantage point from which to defend the fort from any assailants, with heavy ballistae positioned at regular intervals for support, and a heavily fortified watchtower at each of the four corners of the camp's square layout. A drawbridge and bulky gatehouse with two large ironbound gates completed the impressive defenses. Inside the protection of those walls and towers, the camp itself sprawled: a collection of low, utilitarian wood-framed buildings, organized into precisely ordered groups and straight rows, forming an efficient grid of avenues between them. The size of a small town, the fort housed an entire cohort—five hundred Golian soldiers and officers, and half that amount more in support personnel.

Or rather, it would have looked that way only a day ago.

Multiple fires still raged, and rising from the shattered hulks of dozens of buildings, myriad columns of black smoke drifted upward to coalesce into a single, ominous column of darkness that cast a pall over the whole scene and obscured much of the far end of the fort. Even through the hazy air they could see that three of the watchtowers had collapsed entirely, their remnants poking upward like scorched skeletal claws, while a raging inferno currently consumed the fourth tower. Here and there, the crushed and mangled pieces of Golian siege engines could be seen. The walls themselves had been breached inward in several places; their wreckage mixed with that of the battlements beyond. The two gates lay on the ground, blown inward, the wood and metal a mass so twisted that they were barely recognizable. As for the fort's stalwart defenders, their fate was plain to see, even from this distance, with hundreds of Golian bodies lying strewn haphazardly over the devastation of the dying fort. Vurax and Treeweaver didn't need to get any closer to see that many of them had been violently torn apart.

Vurax could only stare uncomprehendingly. "I just don't understand... what could have done such a thing? What were they fighting? I see no bodies belonging to any sort of enemy," he whispered, his normally gruff voice humbled by confusion mingled with dread and awe.

"Giants," Treeweaver replied solemnly. "More giants than anyone has ever seen gathered in one place before, at least not within living memory. Normally disorganized and highly tribal by nature, they've been brought together for a singular purpose by the one who leads them."

But despite asking the question, Vurax was only half listening to the answer. "We need to get down there. Some of those bulls might still be alive and need our help." He began to rise, but Treeweaver grasped one of his wrists firmly in an iron grip that belied his slender build.

"No," he warned with a shake of his head. "You'll only be joining them in death."

"What do you mean? There's nothing moving down there. If giants did this, they've clearly left," the Golian asserted. Since arriving at their vantage point near sunset, he had surveyed the remnants of the fort for several minutes and had seen no movement, no sign of the enemy.

"Keep watching," was all the Elf said, and something in his eyes made Vurax pause. Reluctantly, the Golian lowered himself back down and continued to observe. More time passed while nothing happened, then his body suddenly convulsed as he felt a needle of white-hot pain lance through his heart. Though mercifully brief, the sensation was so agonizing that he gasped aloud while clutching at his chest, a tortured moan escaping from his throat. Treeweaver looked at him sharply, his mouth going slack with disbelief. Then it happened again, and again, and yet again. As the Minotaur writhed on the ground in clear distress, the Elf gave him some space, his gaze flying back and forth between his companion and the scene below. Confirming his suspicions, he saw a dim flash of blue light pulse briefly through the smoky haze concealing the part of the fort beyond the largest fires. Occurring at short intervals, every time that ghostly light appeared, Vurax groaned in pain.

"What...is...happening...to me?" the Golian managed to gasp between two sharp stings of agony. In response, he felt two hands take hold of his large head with some effort and direct his eyes in the direction of the fort.

"You wanted to see with your own eyes—so look," the Syldar told him.

Summoning every ounce of strength and self-control that he could muster, Vurax tried to steady his thrashing, fight through the horrible pain, and attempt to see what the damnable Elf was trying to show him. Drawing upon reserves of endurance built up over a life of forced labour, sadistic masters, and humiliating deprivation, Vurax gritted his teeth, grasped his brother's golden horn rings for strength, and found the calm centre in the eye of the storm. Regulating his breathing and bracing himself for the next inevitable jab, he looked.

With the sun now almost completely vanished below the line of mountain peaks in the west, long shadows and deepening gloom advanced steadily over the devastation that had once been a formidable fort housing a sizeable contingent of one of Gol's vaunted legions. The pulses of blue light continued unabated, the eerie glow they cast lending the cloud of smoke a surreal aspect to the scene. Vurax could see that there was movement to those lights, appearing near the ground at first, and flying swiftly upward before disappearing some distance above and near the air around the thickest column of smoke. Then something within that smoke moved.

Despite the considerable distance between them, Vurax could see that the figure below dwarfed anything he had ever seen before, even the giants he had recently battled. It was just a vague outline at first, hidden by the smoke, its humanlike shape periodically lit by the lurid glow of the blue lights, but then it took one enormous step forward, revealing itself more clearly to him. Standing as tall as the massive watchtower still burning not too far away, the juggernaut resembled a human in every way except for its immense height and size, and the pale, turquoise blue tone of its skin. Its muscular body was clad only in a simple, loose tunic of white fabric of some kind cinched at the waist, and it wore huge sandals upon its feet. Its facial features—unlike the misshapen mockery typical of a giant's face—were perfectly chiseled as if from pure marble, lending it the look of an ancient, classical statue. The head was crowned by long and thick black hair, and a short beard framed the imposingly square jaw. Eyes closed, the colossus held one arm out slowly over the ground before it, fingers spread wide apart.

Nothing happened at first, but then Vurax's eyes widened in horror when the scattered, broken bodies of several Golians shook as if manipulated by invisible strings, then collapsed and lay motionless again seconds later. When they did, a glowing nimbus of blue light rose from the lifeless forms and hovered briefly, seemingly struggling against something, before being drawn upward to flow into the waiting hand of the gargantuan figure and vanishing from sight. When the macabre spectacle was over, the behemoth opened its eyes at last, and Vurax saw the white light that shone intensely from them. Despite his best efforts to fight it, the pain had simply become too intense and excruciating to ignore. It felt like his heart would burst, and he clutched at his head as if in a final plea for it all to stop. The tortured Minotaur managed one last glimpse of the huge being and saw its head turn slowly, the brilliant stare from its eyes seeming to focus sharply on the direction where he lay hidden. The light was so intense that it forced him to close his own eyes, but in that brief instant when their gazes locked and he saw beyond those strange, blazing orbs, he felt himself teetering on the edge of a vast abyss of unknowable depths, a chasm filled with a swirling maelstrom of azure lights, and a pure wave of raw fear that blasted him backward with violent force. He tried to stop himself from falling but the ground simply wasn't there. His body felt oddly weightless as he spun out of control into a void of utter darkness and his consciousness mercifully shut down at last.

CHAPTER 15

Darken sat by the window of his upstairs bedroom, staring through the glass while night's shadowy mantle slowly covered the town outside. He'd lost track of how long he'd been sitting there, watching while the streetlamps were lit one by one and the citizens of Arlingtown gradually retreated into their homes for the evening. Huge Temeros was in a new moon phase tonight, thus the usual dim red glow that gently illuminated everything at night was completely absent—which of course was the reason his uncle had chosen this particular evening to do what they were about to do. The house was completely silent and had been so for most of the day, with his parents gone that morning on a trip, and the twins staying with friends of the family in town. Normally, he would watch over his brothers Valpos and Raspos while his parents were away, but only when one of their frequent trips took them to one of the nearby communities of the barony. This time, however, their journey would take them far away from Arlingtown and all the way to Aldamor, one of the great cities of the Shining Crescent. It was a trip that Felnan and Phymira made every year to visit her parents, and though the children had accompanied them in past years, his father had decided that the shop could not afford to remain closed for an entire month this year.

Under normal circumstances, Darken would have been quite upset over this development—he was bored to death with the sleepy life in Arlingtown, and the prospect of the annual trip to a vibrant place like Aldamor was something he looked forward to all year. But the last few days had been anything but normal for him, and the anticipation that gripped him now was both thrilling and scary at the same time. First, his uncle Garick had told him that he would be needed for something very important tonight and Darken couldn't wait to put his skills to use on anything more exciting than stealing coins from hapless merchants in the market. Second, he couldn't get his meeting with that girl, Ellianna, out of his thoughts. To say that he was equally exhilarated and terrified at the prospect of seeing her again would be an understatement, but the thought had consumed his mind so much over the past day that he'd barely been able to focus on preparing for tonight—which was admittedly hard to do since his uncle hadn't deigned to give him any details yet. After their conversation by the statue yesterday, he knew better than to underestimate Garick's perceptiveness, but he felt he'd done a good enough job of giving off the appearance that he was prepared for this. Now that the time was almost upon him though, he wasn't so sure if he was.

The soft knock on the door brought him back to the here and now and Darken marvelled at how he'd not heard—even as distracted as he was—a single footstep on the house's creaky wooden stairway. He heaved a sigh and gave the street outside one last glance. Nothing had moved out there for the last hour or so, not even a stray dog. As he'd surmised, it must be time.

"Come in." The door opened and Garick Valhik took a step inside the room.

"Step over into the light and let me get a good look at you," his uncle said without preamble. Darken got up from the stool he'd been sitting on next to the window and walked to stand close to the small oil lamp he kept by his bed, then spread his arms out to his sides and turned slowly around.

"Not bad. Looks like a good fit. How does it feel?" his uncle said while running one hand appraisingly over his bearded chin.

In response, Darken pulled uncomfortably here and there at the sleek material covering his body, the black leather outfit hugging his slender figure like a second skin. Other than its glossy newness, it was virtually identical to the one his uncle now wore. "A bit tight in a couple of places, but I like it," he answered.

"Good, and don't worry, it will wear in. The important thing is that it'll allow you to blend well with the shadows and give you a better chance to turn aside a blade that gets past your own."

"A blade? You didn't say anything about blades. What is it exactly that we're doing? I think now would be a good time to tell me," Darken asked, using a tone he would never dare use with his father. Felnan and Garick could not be more different as brothers, and while Felnan's typical answer to his son's question would likely have amounted to little more than a cold and silent glare, Garick's response was to walk up to Darken, put his hands on the boy's shoulders, and smile warmly at him.

"The armour is just a precaution, nephew. Better to have and not need, than to... well, you know the rest. I've drilled the lesson into you enough times, have I not? As for carrying your blades with you, the same rule applies. If all goes well, then none of these things will be needed, but I couldn't forgive myself if something happened to you because I neglected to give you the tools to protect yourself."

Darken smiled up at Garick, but then his shoulders slumped, and he shifted his gaze to the floor.

"What's the matter?"

Darken shrugged without answering but Garick kept hold of him and gave his arms a reassuring squeeze. "Tell me—best that you let it out and clear your mind so that whatever is bothering you now doesn't cloud your ability to react quickly later. I need you to be sharp tonight, Darken."

"It's just that..." Darken began, uncomfortable to delve into the subject, but knowing that if anyone had intimate knowledge of this, it was his uncle. "... I just wish that my father cared about me half as much as you do. Of course, he wouldn't approve of any of this, but even when I do the things that he asks—and I know that I do them well—he does nothing but glower at me and never shows any pride or gratitude. It's almost as if he resents my very existence. I don't know what else to do, and I'm almost at the point where I don't care anymore. I'm never going to be what he wants me to be, so I may as well stop trying. Was he always this way?"

"No, he wasn't," Garick replied, reflecting on his own youth and growing up with his brother. Letting go of the boy, he walked over to the window and glanced outside, nodded once to himself, then sat down on the stool previously occupied by his nephew. "We still have a bit of time, so have a seat," he said, motioning to the bed. Darken complied and sat down, sensing that his uncle was about to share something personal, which made him naturally curious and instantly attentive. For Garick's part, he'd been avoiding having this conversation with the boy for a long time, but he already had more regrets in life than he could count. The burden of guilt he carried could perhaps be alleviated just a small bit if he could muster the courage to talk about it. After all, wasn't that the same advice he'd just given Darken?

"Though you wouldn't think it now, your father and I were very, very close once—any closer and we'd have been twins, like your brothers," he grinned. "He and I often travelled out of town on our father's business, always looking for opportunities, new clients, and ways to expand his passion for toy-making. It's what the Valhiks have done for generations, and we were just the newest members to carry on that long family tradition. Believe it or not, Felnan was far more of a dreamer than I ever was. He had an ambition in him that fuelled an insatiable drive to succeed and prove himself worthy in our dad's eyes. For my part, I was content to let him take the lead and just be there to help him with whatever I could. He was the eldest, after all, so I accepted my role without any resentment or bitterness, because truth be told, I couldn't be sure that a life devoted to making and selling toys was what I wanted to do until the end of my days. In that way, my brother's singular devotion to our family business took the pressure off me." Garick paused, lost in thought, his gaze focused inward as he recalled the past with a bittersweet smile. Then he resumed his tale.

"Felnan always dreamed of expanding the business to the large cities of the Shining Crescent. Along the coastal waters of Coral Bay is where all the important trade in Dravin takes place, and that's where we needed to be, not mucking about here in this backwater barony on the edge of civilization. So, we started by going to Aldamor since our father already had some acquaintances there. This part you already know, but it was during that trip that we met the Rasgrims, your mother's family, but also very influential members of a powerful trading consortium. It took several trips after that and a long courtship that I often teased your father about, but Felnan and Phymira did fall in love, and the rascal somehow managed the nigh-impossible task of convincing her conservative parents to let him bring your mother back to Arlingtown after they were wed. The day he carried her into this house in his arms... I don't think I'd ever seen your father any happier than he was at that moment."

Darken sat and listened in silence with a wide-eyed stare. He was having a great deal of trouble imagining his father as the adventurous and romantic person that was being described to him. Throughout his life, he only had memories of his sire being a cynical and humourless man, consumed by bitterness and anger, and he'd just assumed he'd always been that way. He often found himself wondering how his mother, so gentle and caring, was ever attracted to someone with his temper, but now he was beginning to understand that Felnan had been a very different man once. Hoping that this tale would answer why, he eagerly waited for Garick to continue. Across from him, the man's smile faded, replaced by an expression tinged with sadness and...regret?

"Things were going very well for a while after that, and we were close to finally opening our first shop in Aldamor, but then our mom and dad both fell sick at the same time. They hadn't been well for some time but got progressively worse to the point that it took every ounce of time and energy that your parents had to care for them. Felnan became unable to run the business properly as a result and took it upon himself to remain here with them and his new wife, so it fell to me to handle things in Aldamor. Your father put all of our family's money and trust in my hands and gave me the responsibility of carrying on with our dream—his dream—when he could not. Your mother came with me a few times to help set things up with her family but..." Here Garick paused again and avoided Darken's eyes by turning his head to look out the window again. As before, the street was dark and quiet.

"I was weak, Darken—young, irresponsible, and weak. The strong will and resolve that I possess today and have tried to instill in you are not qualities that I had back in those days. You've been there before, so you know that Aldamor is nothing like Arlingtown, and beyond sheer size and number of people, there are opportunities there that can make a man rich beyond his wildest dreams.

But if you are a naïve fool like I was, then those opportunities very quickly turn into a trap for the unwary." Garick could see his nephew's imperfect reflection in the window, a face so much like his own back in the time he was describing now—youthful and full of promise.

It was obvious that his uncle was working up his courage to share a particularly painful or humiliating detail of his life with him and Darken wasn't sure he wanted to know anything that would sully the perfect image he had of this man. Yet he had to know. Nothing Garick could ever say or do would make him think any less of his uncle, and if there was a vital clue as to how he could still salvage his relationship with his own father, then so be it.

"What did you do?"

Garick didn't answer right away. Just like Darken, he too was fearful of anything that could damage his bond with this boy, so he briefly considered ending the conversation here. He'd been called quite a few things in his life, most of them not nice, but only one insult—the one uttered by his own brother—had ever cut him so deep that his heart still ached from it to this day. He wouldn't allow his nephew to call him a bloody coward as well.

"I couldn't stand the thought of putting all the money we had into another shop, not when we had no guarantee that it would ever succeed. Not while we had suppliers to pay. Not when it could have been put toward getting better care from the priests for our ailing parents. Not when I knew it was needed to support the family that your father wanted to have someday. But it was Felnan's dream, and I didn't want to disappoint him, so I thought of a way to do all those things—I took every last coin he'd given me and gambled it away hoping to double it. Gambled...and lost." The silence in the room took on an oppressive weight, cut only by the tense breathing of the two individuals who sat without facing each other. Garick looked at Darken in the glass, but his nephew had lowered his head and shifted his gaze to the floor.

"The thing about vice, you see, is that it constantly feeds upon itself. The more desperate your situation becomes, the more you are doomed to repeat the mistakes that landed you there in the first place, so down you go, spiralling ever deeper until you hit rock bottom. Yet just when you think there is no further that you can fall—ah, Darken..." Garick shook his head ruefully as if to emphasize his point, "...there is always an even darker hole waiting for you. You see, I didn't just ruin our family; I ruined your mother's as well—kind and trusting Phymira, to whom I turned in my despair, and who could not bring herself to tell her husband what I had done. She secretly gave me more and more of her family's fortune so that I could repair the damage that I had caused, but I managed to squander and lose that, too. By then I was too ensnared in a web of lies and crime, trying to evade the dangerous people whom I owed money, while still stupidly gambling away everything that she gave me. Then, when her parents found out and there was no more, I did the only thing I could do—I ran away. I was too ashamed to even be present when my mother and father passed away, and your parents were left with almost nothing."

"Where did you go?" Darken's voice was barely above a whisper.

"It doesn't matter. Far away and long enough for the trail to grow cold, I suppose. I couldn't stay away forever, though, not when I found out that I was an uncle three times over. I'd managed to earn a little bit of that money back by then, and I knew your father needed it desperately. Even so, his pride and anger wouldn't allow me to buy back his forgiveness. If it hadn't been for your mother staying his hand and convincing him to accept the help, I wouldn't be standing here today."

Darken wondered what his uncle meant by that last comment, but he was too stunned by everything else that he'd just heard to ask. Perhaps he was beginning to understand his father now. He wanted desperately to feel anger—something, anything—against this man who had carelessly nearly destroyed his family, but in the end, he couldn't bring himself to. Instead, he felt only pity and love for someone who had always given him nothing but kindness and unreserved, unconditional affection. How could he do anything less?

"So, I've been here ever since," Garick continued, "my presence tolerated by my brother only for so long as I work to repay my debt to him. When that's done... well, we'll see what happens then, but here is an even harder truth, nephew: an honest day's work is all an honest man needs to go to bed every night and sleep peacefully—to feel good about himself. Me? I've stopped sleeping like that a long, long time ago. The past may be behind you, but the consequences of what you've done never cease to affect the present—or the future." As if on cue, a slight movement on the street outside caught his eye just then, so barely perceptible that had he not been devoting part of his attention to waiting for it, he would have missed it entirely. She was here. Garick swallowed dryly and heaved a loud sigh—time to end this.

"No matter how far or how long you run, the past catches up to you, always. Tonight, I have a chance to erase the mistakes I've made, and I want you to come with me so that..." his voice briefly shuddered and faltered, "...so that you learn that in all the many things that you'll do in your life, it's not the intention behind them that matters, but the result. The two aren't always the same—one is the thing you want; the other is the thing you end up with. Consequences—remember that."

In response, Darken sat up and walked to a spot near the wall opposite the foot of the bed. He knelt stiffly; his movements somewhat awkward in the unfamiliar leather garment he wore. With practiced ease, he lifted the loose nails from both ends of a floorboard and then wedged the tips of his fingernails in the cracks between boards to lift the one plank he'd just freed. Reaching into the space below, he pulled out a leather pouch with some obvious heft, stood up, and walked over to his uncle.

"Here, take it," he said, holding the object out in front of him.

Garick had watched his nephew in puzzlement at first, but the jingle of the pouch's contents left no doubt as to what this was. "No, that's yours. You've earned it."

"I don't need it. Take it and pay my father back the rest of what you owe him. That way we won't have to go out there tonight and do whatever it is that you are on about," the boy said earnestly.

Garick smiled with a mixture of pride and sadness in his eyes. "Oh, my dear lad... you're already a far better person than I was at your age—far better. Sadly, what you have there wouldn't even make a dent in the fortune I wasted with my idiocy. No, you keep that. This is the only way."

"But it doesn't have to be," Darken was beginning to feel anxious. He wasn't superstitious, but something in the manner his uncle had been speaking these last few minutes had left him filled with foreboding about this night. He still didn't know what they were about to do, but now that he was beginning to understand the stakes, he was frightened. Not for himself, but for Garick. "Please, uncle, let's just forget about this. The shop is not doing so badly lately, and I know you've been working hard. Now that I know what's going on, I'll help out more, I swear. Together we can work to pay this back."

Garick stood up, feeling a lump in his throat. He ran the fingers of one hand gently through his nephew's dark hair. "Darken, haven't you been paying attention? It's not just your father that I owe. You and I could work two entire lifetimes, and it still wouldn't be enough. Trust me, I've had a lot of time to try and think of another way, and there isn't one. Do you understand?"

A silent nod was the only answer he got. It would have to do.

"Let's go then."

⸺◆⸺

Garick and Darken crossed the street in front of the Valhik residence and stepped into an alley on the other side. With Temeros absent and its smaller siblings veiled by clouds, the narrow gap between buildings shielded them from the bright illumination of the street lamps beyond, making the shadows there almost impenetrable—exactly the conditions preferred by the one who waited for them. The figure detached itself from the wall almost as if it had been a part of it and took two steps to stand in front of uncle and nephew in the middle of the narrow passage. Darken peered through the gloom but couldn't make out much beyond the fact that someone was standing there, their features and identity hidden. He hadn't expected to be meeting anyone else tonight, but the lack of reaction from Garick told him that his uncle knew this person would be here.

"Took your time, Garick." The voice was distinctly feminine, the tone one of unmistakable annoyance. It also sounded slightly muffled and Darken wondered if the woman was wearing a mask of some kind.

"Nice to see you too, Melios," Garick replied. "Apologies for the delay but it was unavoidable. Fear not, we still have plenty of time." Despite the familiar manner of his words, there was an edge in his voice that told Darken that while these two obviously knew each other, they weren't exactly friends. He wondered why his uncle hadn't mentioned anything about someone else coming along, but he trusted the man implicitly and had learned long ago to accept his judgment and to go along with it. Though Garick had only minutes ago revealed to Darken how flawed that judgment had been in the past, he was confident that his uncle was a much different person now and knew exactly what he was doing. Based on that private assertion, he decided to keep his many questions for a more opportune time. Melios' only response was to step aside and gesture with one arm, indicating for Garick to take the lead.

The trio of figures proceeded to glide silently and expertly through the backstreets and alleyways of Arlingtown, angling their way toward the affluent neighbourhood located on the north side near the River Gate. Though the streets were deserted at this hour, there could still be the odd person about, or worse, a guard patrol. With Garick scouting ahead at every turn, however, they avoided any lit areas and being seen by anyone. During one of these brief stops when Darken and Melios paused to wait for Garick to signal moving ahead, Darken risked a glance at the mysterious figure accompanying them. His vision had adjusted somewhat to being in the dark since leaving his house, so he could see well enough to find his way and perhaps even catch a detail or two about Melios as the woman crouched in the shadows just a few feet away from where he was.

As he had surmised earlier, she was garbed in a fashion similar to his, the black leather outfit allowing her to blend in perfectly with the dark surroundings. Her head was hidden within the confines of a black hood, but she must've sensed the boy's stare and turned slightly to look back at him. The lower half of her face was indeed hidden behind a dark mask, but her golden eyes were visible beneath pencil-thin eyebrows, and they were startling not just in colour, but in appearance as well. They must've caught a small bit of ambient light from the street beyond because they glimmered in the darkness with a glow of their own that made him blink in astonishment. The nearest thing he could equate the effect to was that of cat's eyes in the dark.

"What?" Melios whispered harshly.

"Uh…" Darken stammered, aware that he'd been staring. "Sorry, nothing. I'm Darken, by the—"

"I don't care," she cut him off, moving forward at Garick's sudden signal and bringing the awkward exchange to an end.

Darken cursed inwardly for making a fool out of himself. What the hell was wrong with him? This was hardly his first night out of the house, so why was he being so easily distracted? It did seem ironic that in his effort to keep himself from thinking about Ellianna, his uncle had only given him an even bigger distraction to dwell on with the story of his past. He didn't begrudge Garick his opportunity to get that off his chest, though. It was clear this had been bothering the man for quite a long time, and he was determined to talk some more about it later because he'd decided that he was going to do everything that he could to help his uncle lay those demons to rest. He rose from his crouch and followed the other two before he lost sight of them.

Before long, they arrived at their destination in the North Hill district of Arlingtown. The neighbourhood was one that Darken rarely ever set foot in, owing mainly to the fact that there were no shops here or anything else of interest to him. What North Hill had plenty of however, was a small collection of mansions and estates belonging to the few rich and noble-born families that called the Barony of Arlingford home. Unlike the cramped, smaller, and often adjoined houses in town where most common folk lived, these large and spacious dwellings were dotted around the green hill that gave the district its name. Each house was surrounded by its own bronze-work fence or stone wall that enclosed a collection of expansive, carefully tended gardens, small ponds, gazebos, and shaded benches for one to sit on. After carefully checking that no one was about, the three figures dashed from the alley and across the main street that encircled the hill and crouched behind a dark hedge near the tall fence belonging to one of the mansions.

"This is the place then?" Melios asked.

"Yes. The object your master seeks is inside," Garick replied.

"You're certain of that?"

"I'm certain, Melios. I'd stake my life on it," he said confidently.

Listening to the exchange, Darken noted the barest hint of narrowing around the corners of Melios' eyes. Was she grinning under that mask? The thought made him uneasy for some reason. "Who lives here?" he decided to ask.

"Lord Khelen and his family," answered Garick.

"Khelen?" the name sounded vaguely familiar which was unsurprising, considering the relatively modest size of Arlingtown. "Aren't they—?"

"—related to the baron? Yes, which is the reason we are here on this particular night. This past day was Edmund's birthday, and the celebration at the Keep is sure to last well into the small hours. These nobles do love their social events, and with Giordy and Anika Khelen out enjoying themselves for the night, we should have more than sufficient time to get what we've come for."

"And what is that?"

"Nothing that need concern you—you're not going inside."

"What? Uncle!" Darken was stunned by this. "Why did you bring me then?" Upset and confused, his voice had risen considerably in volume, prompting a hostile glare from Melios.

"Keep your voice down!" Garick admonished him with a harsh whisper. "Your part in this is just as important as ours. I need you to keep a lookout. Every job like this needs an attentive set of eyes as a form of insurance against something going wrong. This is too important to mess up, which is why it's going to take all three of us to pull off. Do you understand me?"

"Yes, uncle," the whispered reply was equal parts resigned conformity and undisguised sullenness.

"Darken, remember what I told you about focus. I need you at your sharpest right now, so if you're going to be resentful—and I get why—you need to save it for later, got it? We can't afford for you to be distracted," Garick said, placing a hand on his nephew's shoulder as he often did when talking to him. Darken avoided Garick's eyes but nodded, nonetheless.

"This is all very sweet but the night's not getting any younger," Melios hissed in disdain. "Can we get this over with?"

Garick didn't look at her but instead reached into a pocket and pulled out two identical pieces of black fabric with straps attached. He held one out to Darken, and when the boy took it, he placed the other one over the lower half of his face, tying the straps into a knot to secure the mask in place. "Put that on." Only when Darken had done so did he turn to Melios. "Alright, we're ready."

The woman left their leafy concealment and slunk to one of the nearby stone posts that anchored the bronze-wrought fence every few paces. The barrier was nearly twice her height, but she made short work of it by climbing up with quick, fluid, and agile movements. Not pausing to linger at the top, she vaulted over the post to land softly and soundlessly on the grass beyond.

"Go," Garick prompted, making sure the street remained deserted. Darken did not hesitate, moving from his place to approach the post. Fingers and toes expertly finding the shallow lines in the masonry that provided the best support for his slight frame, he climbed the height with relative ease though the stiffness of his new armour slowed him down somewhat. Jumping down on the other side, he joined the waiting Melios. A moment later, Garick was beside them, the three wasting no time in quickly making their way across the grounds, moving from cover to cover to approach the house from the west side. The looming, two-storey structure was dark except for a pair of lamps on the front porch. All the windows were shuttered, and no sound disturbed the warm night air but for the nearby trill of crickets. Huddled under the shadow of one wall, the three figures paused to review their plan one last time, or in Darken's case, the first time.

"Our objective is in the main bedroom on the second floor. We'll climb to the balcony from here and slip in through one of the exterior doors," Garick explained, while Melios only half-listened as she kept an eye on the street and main path leading up to the house from the gate. "The Khelens have two small children who will be asleep in their own rooms upstairs. There should be no one else in the house other than the governess that cares for the children, and she too should be asleep in her quarters on the ground floor. The rest of the staff goes home at night. This will be a quick and uncomplicated job, but one can never be too cautious. Darken, you stay here where you can see the front gate. If anyone approaches, you are to warn us immediately, understood?"

"How am I supposed to do that? I won't exactly be able to call out," Darken asked, trying to contain his chagrin once more at being relegated to performing the least exciting task of this heist.

"With this," Garick replied, holding out a slim band of silver. Darken took the ring from him, staring at it in confusion. "Put it on—I'm wearing one just like it. At the first sign of trouble, focus your thoughts on me and on the act of warning me of danger. As soon as you do that, your ring and mine will quickly grow warm to the touch in response. I'll feel it, of course, and be able to react accordingly. Got it?"

"I think so," Darken nodded, quickly slipping off the leather glove from his right hand to slip the ring onto one finger. He'd never owned anything magical before—such objects being quite uncommon—and he became even more curious than before about his uncle's colourful and intriguing past. Garick put both hands on Darken's shoulders and the boy steeled himself for yet another speech about responsibility, but when he looked at his uncle's face, there was a strange sadness in the man's eyes above the mask that gave him pause. It was the same look he'd given him before they'd left the house.

"Your task is simple but important, and I know you're eager to do more. I recall well the excitement that you're feeling right now, but just remember one thing: after tonight, you'll only need to keep doing this if you want to, not because you have to, like me. Make the right choice while you can," Garick said, solemnly.

Darken nodded in silence, unsure of what to say. Garick had been behaving oddly ever since he'd walked into Darken's bedroom earlier, but he was sure his uncle would be back to his old self by morning when this was over. Garick drew him close and hugged him tightly, and Darken returned the gesture somewhat awkwardly, once more taken aback by this uncharacteristic behaviour. What was going on? Before he could think to ask the question aloud, Garick let him go, turned to the wall, and began to climb up a vine-covered trellis that went all the way to the distant roof, but not before it passed next to the edge of the balcony above them. Once he was level with his target, the man leapt nimbly from the trellis to the railing, crouching down inside the balcony and out of sight to those below. Melios passed Darken on her way up, giving him an inscrutable glance as she walked by, and then she was up the wall and gone as well.

Trying to keep his misgivings about this whole thing under a tight grip, Darken looked around for a good spot where he could hide and see both the street and gate, just as he'd been instructed. He spied a large bush not far from the corner of the house where he stood and decided it would be perfect. Making himself as comfortable as possible in the shadows behind the plant, he settled in to watch and wait, the leather-covered fingers of one hand absently rubbing the shape of the ring he wore on the other.

CHAPTER 16

His mind felt like it was slipping in and out of a thick fog, making it difficult to focus his thoughts, but Brother Owen was determined to get to the bottom of whatever had happened, so he pushed on. The first place he searched after leaving the hospital was in Flynn's cell, but the boy was not there, and nothing looked disturbed recently. Fear mixing with anger, Brother Owen walked over to the main orphanage courtyard, enclosed on each side by the dormitory, the refectory, the schoolhouse, and the old tower in the distance. Anxiously, he looked around the large open-air space with its stone paths, green lawns, graceful statuary and fountains. Children loudly chased each other around in play, and priests walked by while going about their business, but he found what he was looking for when his searching gaze settled upon the black-robed Initiate leaning under an archway while keeping a bored eye on the boys under his watch. The teenager glanced up when he saw the cleric walking toward him, immediately straightened up, and took an uncertain step back upon seeing the look of anger on the man's face.

"You there," Brother Owen said without preamble.

The Initiate looked nervously around as if searching for an escape route, wondering what he'd done wrong. The priests of the orphanage were expressly forbidden from disciplining any of their charges by physical means, but a strongly wrung ear had been known to happen on occasion when patience ran thin with the more disobedient ones.

"Yes, Brother Owen?" the young man replied timidly.

The priest wasn't surprised the Initiate recognized him—after all, he was the only black priest in the entire clergy of Janus in Corazan. Likely due to his own increasing irritation, however, he was having trouble putting a name to the boy's nervous face.

"Thomas, is it?"

"No, Brother, my name's Alfonso."

"Sure. Hand me your daily curriculum," the priest held his hand out, his tone brooking no argument.

"My cu—curriculum...?" the teenager stuttered. Several of the nearby younger kids had stopped playing and were staring at the uncomfortable exchange. Alfonso heard a couple of them stifle a giggle, which made him lose his composure even further.

"Yes, your duty list! Let me see it," the priest repeated the request for what the Initiate was sure would be the last time. Without further delay, the boy fumbled about in his robes to find the inner pocket containing the daily assignment list for every Initiate at the orphanage. He pulled the paper out with a shaking hand but before he could place it in the cleric's own, the adult snatched it abruptly to look at its contents. The list was prepared every day before the sun was up by Brother Melton and then multiple copies were left on a small table outside his office for the Initiates to pick up. Owen had no desire at this point to ask his fellow priest for a copy, or the patience to answer any of the questions the overbearing man was sure to pepper him with. Finding an Initiate was just more efficient, and now he had what he wanted. He scanned the list quickly until he found the line item he was looking for and then looked at the name beside it.

Hospital station – dawn to noon hour: Initiate Carlo

Satisfied, he thrust the paper back into Alfonso's hand and walked away without further word. The Initiate watched him go with a mixture of relief and puzzlement and silently thanked Janus that he wasn't the final target of Brother Owen's fury. Armed with a name, the priest began to walk about the entire orphanage to inquire of child and fellow priest alike as to the whereabouts of Initiate Carlo, though it soon became apparent that no one had seen the teenager that morning. Something felt very wrong about all this, and his frustration and anxiety were mounting to a nearly unmanageable level. Taking a pause to sit down on a bench under the shade of a large olive tree, Owen did his best to calm down and reason through what his next course of action would be by collecting his breath and thoughts. It was becoming clear that he couldn't do this alone, and he decided that he would have to report everything to Father Lorimer and then see what the headmaster proposed they should do. He'd meant to speak to the senior cleric anyway, but before he got up, he felt that strange cloud of torpor and confusion settle over his mind once more. Whatever this strange sensation was, it was an additional concern he didn't want to deal with right now, so he did what he could to push it aside, closed his eyes, and took several deep breaths to centre himself.

"Brother Owen, are you feeling alright?"

The child's voice sounded like it was coming from a great distance, but when he opened his eyes, he saw Elias standing in front of him within arm's reach. He managed a weak smile while he rubbed at one temple.

"I'm fine, Elias, thank you. Missing breakfast doesn't agree with me. Sit here for a while, will you?" The boy acquiesced and sat next to the priest, concerned. Despite his words of reassurance to the contrary, the cleric was perspiring and looked decidedly unwell. "Tell me, have you seen your friend Flynn today?"

"Flynn? No. I thought he was still in the hospital," Elias replied, his attempt at sounding confused compromised by an undertone of fear in his voice. Having been around children for the entire latter half of his life, Owen could easily glean more information from how they said things, rather than from what they actually said. He knew the two boys were very close, so if Flynn had gotten out of confinement on his own, the first person he would have sought would have been Elias. As always, he felt extremely uncomfortable with the prospect of lying to anyone, even when it might be in Elias' best interest to not know the truth, therefore it was an easy decision not to do so now.

"Listen to me carefully, Elias. Flynn is not where he's supposed to be, and I've been searching for him all morning. Have you seen anything strange going on? Heard anything? This morning, or perhaps even last night before you turned in? It's important that you tell me the truth."

Elias' concern for the priest congealed into fear for his friend Flynn. An adult never asked you this sort of thing unless it was deadly serious, and Elias knew a thing or two about keeping his mouth shut when it came to self-preservation. Yet this wasn't about his safety but his friend's, so he impulsively blurted the word out before he could change his mind. "Yes."

Brother Owen looked sharply at the boy, but kept his voice calm so as to not frighten Elias. "Tell me everything you know."

Elias avoided the priest's eyes and picked up a fallen olive from the ground in front of his feet. He turned the small black fruit in his fingers several times, taking the time to gather his courage before speaking. Owen kept his impatience in check, understanding that whatever the boy was about to reveal could be critical.

"Please don't tell anyone else, okay? I don't want to get in trouble with the other boys for telling on them," Elias pleaded at last, laying out the conditions of his cooperation. Brother Owen had fully expected something like this, and thus it was an easy promise to make since he had every intention of honouring it.

"You have my sincere word that this will be our secret," he assured the boy while looking discreetly around to make sure no one else was within earshot.

Having no reason to doubt the man, Elias launched into his story. "I often wake up in the middle of the night because I have to pee really badly. If I don't, I'll wet my bed and then get in trouble with the Initiates. The last time it happened, the rest of the kids found out and I couldn't live it down for months." His voice caught, and he paused, avoiding the priest's eyes. Brother Owen placed his hand on Elias' shoulder reassuringly, appreciating how embarrassing this revelation was for the boy, and how much bravery it took to speak about it. Children could be very cruel to one another, and Owen felt nothing but empathy for the teasing Elias must've endured over this. Collecting himself, the boy continued. "There's a lavatory just down the hall from our room, so I go there and back real quick without disturbing anyone, but last night, before I was done, I heard low voices coming so I quickly hid in the shadows behind the door and tried not to make a sound so I wouldn't be discovered." Elias had to choose his words carefully, not wishing to reveal to the priest that this wasn't the first time a situation similar to this one had occurred. The last time he'd had the misfortune of running into someone in the lavatory at night, things had not ended well for him. He pushed the painful memory down and focused on the more recent encounter. "There were three of them. They were there for a while and it was hard to hear because they were whispering, but I know I overheard them say something about paying someone a visit that night."

Brother Owen's hand involuntarily tensed on Elias' shoulder. "Did you get a look at these boys?"

"I got more than just a look—I followed them," Elias replied as he absent-mindedly tossed the olive back down onto the ground.

"Who were they?"

Elias knew he would be doomed if they ever found out he'd tattled on them. In fact, since his late-night toilet visits were not exactly a secret among the other children, it was likely that they would piece together how they'd been found out, but Elias didn't care. If they'd done something to Flynn, he wanted them to pay. "It was Peter, Dario, and Carlo."

Carlo again, Brother Owen remarked to himself. It couldn't be a coincidence that the Initiate had been assigned to the hospital the following morning after this excursion then. He was going to have to have a meaningful conversation with that boy, but first, he needed to know more. "Tell me everything, Elias. This is very important."

The boy nodded and continued. "I waited until I heard them leave and then slipped out to follow them. I stayed back just at the edge of sight, and I was barefoot so I knew I wouldn't make any noise. They went downstairs to the main entrance and Carlo used his key to leave the dormitory, but I heard him lock the door after they stepped out."

This puzzled Brother Owen, and he frowned. "And you followed them outside?" The boy nodded in response. "How did you get out?"

"There's a window in the vestibule across from Brother Melton's office that has a bad lock on the shutter—that's how I got out." There, he'd revealed the secret exit to an adult. Now he was really in for it, but to his surprise, the priest didn't react in any way except to prompt him to continue. "It was pretty dark, and they'd gotten far ahead of me, but I managed to spot them at the edge of the courtyard, so I ran along behind the bushes to see where they were going."

"And...?"

"The hospital. There's a dark stairwell on the side of the school building that faces the hospital, so I hid there and watched what they were doing."

Brother Owen knew the location all too well—it was the very same stairwell that led down to the subfloor of the school where his office was located. It frustrated him to realize that he'd been sleeping just a short distance away when all this was taking place. "Go on."

"They went inside, and then nothing happened for a long time. I started to shiver—it was cold out last night—and I nearly gave up and went back to the dormitory, but I was too curious and worried, so I waited as long as I could. Then suddenly the door opened again, and they came out, only something was very wrong," Elias looked up at the cleric with a worried expression that deeply concerned the priest. Owen was anxious to get to the end of this story, but he knew the importance of allowing the boy the time he needed to relate the events of the previous evening. If he rushed him, an important detail could be missed.

"What did you see, Elias? Think hard, and don't leave anything out."

"Carlo came out first, and he had someone over his shoulder, but I couldn't see who it was because they were covered in a blanket and not moving. Then Peter came out after, and he was dragging someone by the ankles. I think it was Dario, but I couldn't be sure. He wasn't moving either. Brother Owen...?" he paused.

"Yes?"

"I think Peter was crying. Carlo said something to him, but I couldn't hear what, but it sounded harsh, like he was cussing, and then he cuffed him. Then they split up, going in different directions. Peter was slower because he's not strong enough to carry another person very fast, so I decided to wait a bit until I could be sure I wouldn't be seen and then followed Carlo. I lost track of him though—he'd gone towards the cathedral but when I got near the gate, I couldn't see anyone about. There was something that caught my eye, though."

"And what was that?"

"Well... Father Lorimer's house is near the gate, and I saw a light on inside."

The strange lack of focus and difficulty in gathering his thoughts came back again with sudden force and Brother Owen had to struggle to speak. "Are you sure?" he managed. The priest wiped at his brow with the back of one hand, feeling the excessive dampness there, and his mouth felt dry and fuzzy.

"Yes. I wasn't sure what to do so I ran back to where I'd last seen Peter, but he was gone too. I looked in the courtyard but there was no one there either, so I went through the dormitory window again and back to my room. That's it."

Brother Owen fought back a wave of nausea and vertigo. He felt an urge to vomit but managed to keep the impulse in check. He was beginning to suspect someone had done something to him, and that the timing of these seemingly disconnected events was not mere random chance. There was also another possibility, he thought suddenly, one that horrified him with its implications, and so he dismissed it immediately. The list of people he needed to talk to was growing longer by the minute, but everything seemed to point to one person that would have all the answers, and he was certain now that's where he would find Flynn as well—Father Lorimer. He tried to look at Elias but saw only a vague shape where the boy should be, blurred and washed out of all colour. What was wrong with him? Thinking became a struggle, and there was a bitter taste in his mouth now that reminded him of...tea leaves? It was the last thought the priest was able to form before he pitched forward from the bench where he sat and crashed heavily to the ground.

———◦———

"Children, stop crowding around and give me room to work, please," Brother Paul admonished sternly, and the small group of children that had gathered around Brother Owen's prone form stepped back reluctantly. Only Elias remained close, certain that the request wouldn't apply to him—after all, he was the one that had run to fetch help, and he simply needed to know if Owen would be alright. The shock at seeing the priest suddenly fall to the ground had lasted only a moment, and the boy had wasted no time in running to the nearby building where the Janusian priests had their living quarters and the young priest, Paul, just happened to be the first adult he'd laid eyes on. By the time they got back, a small group of curious onlookers had already gathered, staring wide-eyed and frightened at the unmoving cleric.

Brother Paul worked quickly, not liking what he saw. Owen's dark brown skin had an unnatural ashen tone to it, his lips were nearly white, and the older priest was bathed in sweat. Paul pulled his long blonde hair back and into a knot so that it would not be in the way, knelt next to the other man, and then placed his ear on Owen's chest, listening for a heartbeat. He couldn't hear anything over the children's voices. Before he could say anything, Elias yelled at them to be quiet, startling them into silence. There it was—Brother Paul exhaled the breath he'd been holding in relief—but it was faint and barely audible. He placed two fingers on Owen's neck under the jaw and felt the pulse just to be sure. He found it, but only just. Placing a hand on Owen's forehead quickly told him how elevated the man's temperature was, so he hurriedly tore a long strip of fabric from his robe, then handed it to Elias. "Run to the nearest fountain and soak this in water—hurry!"

The boy did as he was told, pushing through the other kids as he ran. Racing past the school and down the lane between that building and the refectory hall, Elias made for one of several fountains that adorned the orphanage's main courtyard. He was just coming back around the final corner, soaking wet cloth held before him when something tripped him and he fell hard to the ground, scraping his knees and elbows bloody on the unforgiving stone pavers of the pathway. Somehow, he managed to hold the cloth aloft, preventing it from touching the ground. The boy grunted in pain but rose quickly to his feet, knowing his mission was urgent. As he did so, someone stepped out onto the path in front of him, and Elias couldn't hide his dismay when he saw Peter's hateful, sneering face.

"Where you goin' in such a rush, you little shit-breath?" the Monitor demanded, moving swiftly to one side to block Elias' way when the other boy tried to go around him.

"Let me go, Peter, this is important!" Elias pleaded, knowing it was futile trying to reason with this bully but seeing no choice in the matter.

"'*Let me go, Peter*,'" the red-haired boy mocked, mimicking Elias' high-pitched voice and purposefully making it sound extra whiny. "Why should I? And why do you care what happens to that ape, Owen? He's not one of us—not a proper Rohnian. Hells, he's barely even human," Peter spat, balling his hands into fists.

"He's more of a human being than you could ever be, even in your dreams, you pasty, freckle-faced asshole!" Elias shot back, staring hard and defiantly at Peter, his eyes full of hatred for the other boy. Peter clearly had not expected that reaction and his passing shock and confusion at his prey's audacity was all the distraction Elias had hoped to generate. Peter saw the shadow come into his field of view a split second too late before he was shoved violently from behind. As Peter stumbled past him, Elias quickly side-stepped the other boy and stuck his leg out in the same motion, returning the favour from earlier. Unable to avoid the trip, Peter tried to put one arm out to break his fall but failed and landed awkwardly, the arm folding under him and his face smashing into a paver. The Monitor cried out in pain and looked up dazedly, wiping blood that streamed from a broken nose. A large silhouette stood over him, blocking out the sunlight, and Peter had to blink several times to focus his gaze. When he could finally see properly, it was Big Eric's face that he saw glaring silently down at him.

"You'll pay for that, you fucking fatso!" Peter sputtered in rage, nearly choking before a bloody tooth flew out of his mouth. "You and that stupid cat of yours—you're both fucking dead!"

Eric's dark brown eyes narrowed at this, and Peter saw a very dangerous glint in those orbs. The Monitor sensed he'd made a mistake and tried to scramble backwards on the ground to escape while fighting through the sharp pain in his arm, but Eric was already moving, his big hands wrapping around the ankle of one of Peter's flailing legs.

"You really shouldn't threaten Stripes," the stout lad said in a disturbingly calm tone as he roughly pulled the helpless Peter closer, then bent down to twist one hand around his shirt's collar to lift the Monitor bodily from the ground in one motion. "You think you're tough, but you're just a scared little mouse. Do you know what a cat does with a mouse?"

Speechless with fear, Peter looked around wildly, his eyes frantically darting around for anyone that would help him, but the two boys were alone in the narrow path between buildings. Even Elias was long gone. He tore at Eric's arm to try and loosen the solid grip he was in, but the other boy held him fast and was simply too strong. He gave up and whimpered, closing his eyes just before the first fist blow fell across his face.

⚬

Elias sped back as fast as he could and thanked his lucky stars that Big Eric had shown up when he had. He owed his friend a huge favour, but he couldn't think about that right now. As for Peter, he doubted the Monitor would be bothering him again anytime soon. He gave the two boys no more thought as he shoved his way past the other kids, all of whom stood in rapt silence. When Elias reached the bench where Brother Owen had collapsed, he saw the reason for their awe. Brother Paul was still kneeling next to Owen, but his eyes were closed, and his forehead was heavily furrowed with intense concentration. One of the young cleric's hands was closed over his Janusian medallion, while the other was held flat over Brother Owen's chest. Elias' mouth fell agape in wonder when he saw the golden glow of light under Brother Paul's hand, pulsating softly while its radiance and divine energy flowed from one man to the other. Entranced by what he was witnessing, he nearly forgot what he'd been asked to do, but managed to take the last few steps forward to carefully place the cold wet cloth across Brother Owen's feverish brow.

"What's going on here?" Another figure pushed its way through the crowd of children, who quickly stepped aside to let the new arrival through. Elias looked up to see Father Lorimer standing there, flanked by two black-robed Initiates. One of these latter was Carlo, and Elias paled when his eyes met the teenager's intense stare. He was positive the older boy hadn't spotted him last night, but the way Carlo was looking at him made him doubt himself. He quickly averted his gaze to look at Brother Paul instead. The young cleric opened his eyes and locked stares with Father Lorimer, and something in Paul's expression made the headmaster stop before he could utter anything else. It was bad form, even dangerous, to interrupt a miracle in progress, and so the senior cleric reluctantly crossed his arms while he waited impatiently for Brother Paul to finish. Several tense moments passed before the glow finally faded from beneath Paul's hand. The priest's shoulders slumped, the toll from performing the feat clearly visible to the onlookers, but he smiled triumphantly as Brother Owen's breathing deepened, and a semblance of colour began to slowly return to his face.

"What happened?" Father Lorimer demanded when Brother Paul rose somewhat shakily to his feet. He smiled at Elias, who had rushed to his side and helpfully provided a shoulder for him to steady himself.

"I'm not certain, Father," Paul replied after a moment. "This boy came running up and told me Brother Owen had collapsed. I rushed here and found him like this, barely breathing and burning up. I don't know what's wrong with him, but Janus granted me his blessing to save this man's life."

"Praise be to Janus," Father Lorimer intoned the ritual thanks, and all the gathered boys uttered the same words in unison. "You two," he turned to the two Initiates with authority, "help me get Brother Owen to the hospital. Brother Paul, I am grateful for your assistance, but perhaps you should get some rest now. We'll see to Brother Owen's well-being. The rest of you, go back to what you were doing. Remember that you only have until midday tomorrow to finish the Yule decorations before I declare the winner."

Now that the excitement was over, the children scattered, chattering excitedly about what they'd just seen—only Elias lingered about uncertainly. He watched Carlo and Hugo help Father Lorimer carefully lift Brother Owen from the ground and then carry him toward the hospital. Brother Paul walked slowly in another direction; no doubt headed back to his sleeping quarters. Torn with indecision, he thought briefly of checking to see if Big Eric was ok, but his concern for Flynn and Brother Owen overrode that thought. Eric could handle Peter, he was quite confident, so Elias decided to follow Father Lorimer at a distance. It wasn't far to the hospital once they rounded the corner of the library, and before they reached the structure, another priest had come to assist, relieving Father Lorimer of his burden. When the group neared the doorway, the headmaster finally noticed the boy trailing them a few steps back. While the others went inside, Father Lorimer stopped in front of the door, blocking the way.

"Where do you think you're going, young lad?" the senior priest asked him.

Elias stopped and looked down at his feet. "I... I just wanted to be sure Brother Owen is going to be okay," he offered timidly. Like most children at the orphanage, he felt intimidated and uneasy in the headmaster's presence. Whether it was because he was such a figure of authority in their lives, or because the man generally lacked a level of warmth towards the children that was evident in most of the other priests, Father Lorimer was someone they always just gave a wide berth. For his part, Elias had always gotten the distinct impression that the priest didn't mind the distance. "We were just talking and—"

"He was speaking with you?" Father Lorimer was suddenly more attentive, and Elias cursed himself inwardly for his slip. "What were you two talking about? Did he seem sick?"

"Nothing important. I was just telling him how my team was doing, and he said he'd missed breakfast and was feeling faint, then he tried to get up but just fell and didn't move. I went to find one of the Brothers straight away, and then you showed up...Father," he was so flustered that he just barely remembered to add the title at the end, hoping his lie was innocent and believable enough that the man wouldn't ask him anything else. The priest merely stared at him impassively, noting the boy's uncomfortable fidgeting and refusal to meet his gaze.

"What happened to your knees, Elias?"

"Oh, that. Well... uh, Brother Paul asked me to get some water from a fountain, so I ran really fast and didn't watch where I was going. I tripped and fell on the way back, that's all," he explained. He really wanted to go inside the hospital. He didn't trust Carlo or Father Lorimer around Brother Owen—not after what he saw the night before—but he wasn't sure how to get around this obstacle.

Again, there was an uncomfortable pause. "Perhaps you should come inside after all and have that looked at," Father Lorimer said at last. The headmaster stood to one side, leaving the path clear through to the doorway. This was exactly the excuse and opportunity Elias had been hoping for, and yet as soon as the offer was made, every instinct in his body screamed at him to not go in there. He looked at Father Lorimer and saw the man smile reassuringly as he beckoned, but the gesture had the exact opposite effect on him. He desperately wanted to make sure nothing bad happened to Brother Owen, but after Flynn's unexplained disappearance and everything that had followed, he simply couldn't trust Father Lorimer's intentions—especially not with Carlo in there as well, and he was terrified of the Initiate. He made up his mind immediately and replied quickly so as to not appear too hesitant.

"Uh, I'm fine, it's nothing—just a scrape, really. I'll run to the lavatory and wash up," and before the priest could say anything more, he turned around and walked away, trying hard not to run. Father Lorimer's smile faded, and he watched the boy intently until he was out of sight before he stepped inside and closed the door.

⟞⟶◆⟵⟝

Brother Owen's eyes fluttered open and the world came slowly into focus. Someone was standing over him, and when his vision finally cleared, he first recognized Father Lorimer's familiar grey hair, followed by the headmaster's stern face watching him in silence. He took stock of his surroundings, and when he realized where he was, he experienced a sharp sensation of déjà vu of when it'd been himself standing there, and Flynn lying on the hospital bed. As he thought of Flynn, the memory of the details of his entire conversation with Elias came back to him in a rush, and when he saw Carlo standing nearby, he felt a deep and uncomfortable level of uncertainty as to how things were going to unfold from here. Since no one was saying anything, he tried to speak but his reward for the attempt was a fit of coughing that lasted for some time. The effort brought on a wave of dizziness, and he rested his head back on the pillow, but he didn't miss the fact that Father Lorimer had taken a cautious step back, only approaching again when the coughing had stopped.

There was that strange sensation again of events repeating themselves when Father Lorimer poured some water from a jug into a cup and offered it to him, just as he had done with Flynn. Owen accepted the cup but paused just before the vessel touched his lips. He stared intently at Father Lorimer's face before tipping the cup slightly so he could peer into it and then passed it under his nose.

"It's water, E'on, nothing more. Do you have reason to suspect it might be something else?" Father Lorimer asked, raising one eyebrow to accentuate his question. He rarely used the priest's birth name, but he felt that in this instance, it might help set the other's mind at ease.

Owen didn't answer, but instead focused his gaze and faith on the symbol of Janus hanging on a silver chain from the headmaster's neck and took a deep sip of the liquid. It was cool and refreshing and soothed his aching throat enough that he could speak. "Well, at least it isn't tea," he said pointedly, watching his superior carefully for a reaction.

"Tea? I'm afraid I don't follow," Father Lorimer said.

Brother Owen searched the man's face again, looking for any hint of deception hiding there, trying to decide whether he should be direct with the headmaster or hide his suspicions. Father Lorimer had always been something of an enigma to him. It didn't take extraordinary powers of perception to see that the headmaster was not overly fond of children, which made him believe that the senior cleric's posting here wasn't borne out of a desire to improve the lives of their charges, but rather for personal advancement. If Lorimer had designs on becoming the head of the church in Corazan and all of Rohne one day, then this was certainly one of the paths of least resistance. His family had generously made much-needed monetary contributions to the religious institution, including funding for an expensive restoration of the cathedral itself—the approval of which had unsurprisingly coincided with Father Lorimer's rise to the position of headmaster. He had the confidence and ear of Archbishop Marcos, and the elder man had already revealed that he planned to step down in the coming year, citing a desire to spend his remaining years in solitude and reflection at his estate by the sea. With Marcos' likely endorsement of the headmaster to the Holy Patriarch in Avamor when the time came, Father Lorimer was all but guaranteed to be wearing the mitre and ring of Rohne's archdiocese in the near future. All these things Owen had to weigh before his next words.

"The tea I drank last night while I did the research you asked—I believe it was poisoned," Brother Owen replied. The path of directness had been chosen, and there was no turning back now.

Father Lorimer frowned at this and then turned to the two Initiates who stood a short distance away. "Leave us." The black-robed young men bowed and departed, and once the door to the patient care area had closed behind them, the headmaster pulled a chair closer to the bed before sitting down upon it. "Brother Owen," he began, "we've worked closely together for some years now, and though it's no secret we've had our share of small disagreements over that time, the time has come to be frank with one another. Your love and care for our wards is plain for all to see—a commendable quality that makes you an invaluable asset to this orphanage. However, I fear it can also cloud your judgment at times, this being one of them."

"What does my care for these boys have to do with any of this?" Owen challenged, unsure of the headmaster's point.

"I'm saying it prevents you from seeing what's right in front of you."

"And just what would that be, Father?"

"That perhaps the cause of what happened to you today has nothing to do with some bad tea, but rather something else far more concerning," Lorimer replied.

A sliver of doubt crept into Owen's mind. He had a feeling he knew what his superior was implying, but he had dismissed that very same notion earlier today as something too frightening to contemplate. Confronted with it once more, he was being forced to face that fear again. "You can't possibly be suggesting that—"

"How much time have you spent in the company of that boy, E'on?"

There was no need for a name—Owen knew precisely of whom Father Lorimer spoke. He refused to consider the idea, so he brushed the question and its implications aside, focusing instead on finding out where Flynn was. "What have you done with him? I know you had him taken away last night. Why?" he made an effort to sit up, his consternation giving him the energy to attempt, but another coughing fit quickly forced him to reconsider and he leaned back on the pillow, feeling exhausted.

Father Lorimer poured a second cup of water and offered it to the priest, who feebly managed to accept it. While Owen sipped the water, the headmaster reflected on what the priest had just said. So, Owen knew—at least in part—about the events of the previous evening. Remembering his awkward conversation with Elias outside, Lorimer didn't need to dwell further on where that knowledge might have come from. "I felt it best that he be isolated after what happened last week when he drew the token. In hindsight, I should have done it immediately rather than bring him here, and it took me until yesterday before I decided to correct my error."

"Your error? What are you talking about? What is it you know? Give me a straight answer, damn it!" Owen grew agitated, feeling his patience and self-control slipping away.

Father Lorimer covered his medallion with one hand and lifted his eyes to the rafters in the ceiling of the room as if seeking guidance and patience there. At length, he sighed and looked down at Brother Owen again. The headmaster's shell of calm demeanour lowered for a moment, and what the priest saw beneath the usual confidence was fear and doubt to mirror his own.

"He killed another boy, E'on," the headmaster said, his voice lowered to a whisper, though there was no one else around that could hear them. "Carlo brought him to me because he didn't know what else to do."

Brother Owen stared, stunned into silence. Flynn had killed someone? Impossible. There had to be some mistake. He didn't trust Carlo, and he was having trouble accepting the things that Father Lorimer was telling him, but beyond that, how could an innocent, good-natured, thirteen-year-old child recuperating from a grievous injury manage such a thing? If somehow true, however, it would line up with Elias' account of having witnessed Peter's distress as he dragged someone away. Something bad had happened in this very room last night—he just refused to accept that Flynn was somehow the one responsible.

"Dario?" he managed to ask, already knowing the answer. Father Lorimer nodded, not asking how Owen would know that. "How can that be? And why were they here? Did you send them?"

"Don't be absurd," the headmaster exclaimed, visibly offended by the accusation.

"You said it yourself that you decided to correct your 'error' yesterday, and then this happens. Is that a coincidence, Father?"

"Do you honestly believe that I would be irresponsible enough to send three boys to fetch him in the middle of the night? What do you take me for, Brother? I'll forgive your tone considering your current condition and your understandable concern for the lad, but your continued insinuations that I have anything but these children's best interests at heart are beginning to wear thin," the headmaster said through gritted teeth. This was the most emotion Owen had ever seen the always-collected headmaster display, and the vehemence of his manner was sufficient to give him pause. Something was still very off about all of this, but if he continued to press Lorimer in this fashion, he would be in danger of closing a critical door. He decided he needed to try a different approach.

"Forgive me, Father. You are right, of course. I'm having difficulty thinking straight, and yes, my concern for that boy—or any child here—is affecting my judgment." The apology must have had the right amount of obsequiousness in it because its effect on Father Lorimer was plain to see. The headmaster took a deep breath to calm himself and composed his face back into the passive expression he always wore. The senior priest gave Brother Owen a thin smile, but somehow, he didn't feel reassured. He nevertheless tried to smile back. He was about to speak again when Father Lorimer held up one finger pre-emptively.

"Flynn is fine, if in shock over what happened. Boys have natural rivalries, and we can only do so much to curb their nature and penchant for such behaviour at this rebellious stage of their lives," Father Lorimer explained. "Their decision to come here last night was stupid and impulsive, yes, and one of them has paid the ultimate price for giving in to baser instincts that we must all strive to control. Whatever their petty reasons or intentions were, that's not important here; what is important is that Flynn is far more dangerous than they—or you and I—could have imagined. According to what Carlo told me, there was a struggle, and Flynn's dressings came undone from his injured hand. Something happened when Flynn touched Dario with that hand. The description was vague, made by a sixteen-year-old clearly perturbed by what he saw, but as near as I can gather from what Carlo said, Dario's skin oozed and bubbled from the contact. They tried to pry him away, but Flynn wouldn't loosen his grip, so Carlo had to knock him out by striking him over the head with the chamber pot. When they checked on Dario, he..." the headmaster's voice trailed away, and he swallowed before continuing. "E'on, the boy's flesh—his entire body—had completely withered away. He was barely recognizable as anything previously human."

Owen's mind struggled to accept what he was hearing. It was all too fantastical to accept. There had to be some explanation for all of this, he tried to reason. How could Father Lorimer trust the word of an Initiate who had clearly proven himself unworthy of that trust? "Have you seen the body?"

"Not yet, but I intend to. For all his remarkable lack of wisdom in all of this, Carlo had the presence of mind to get Peter to hide it. I don't need to tell you what kind of panic will result if someone were to catch a glimpse of something as grisly as what was described to me. I can barely countenance the thought, never mind a large group of impressionable children."

"Where is Flynn now?"

"I have him locked up in a room at my house. He hadn't regained consciousness yet when I left to come and find you this morning, and find you I did."

"Locked up? Father, this is a child we're talking about, not some common criminal. What about Archbishop Marcos?"

"What of him?"

"Does he know about any of this?"

Father Lorimer's face twisted into an anger-filled expression that took Brother Owen aback with its intensity. "Of course not! And he must never know, am I clear? This is not the sort of news one brings to a man at the end of a long and quiet life of service to his church and community. No, this would be the absolute end of him, not to mention the fact that the king will be making his annual visit to the orphanage on the last week of Yule, or have you forgotten that? Just imagine the scandal if this gets to His Majesty's ears. I simply won't have it." His face was flushed, and the headmaster took a pause to collect himself before continuing. "So, can I count on your help and your silence in resolving this matter?"

Owen was reluctant to agree before understanding what exactly 'resolving' this matter would entail. He suspected Lorimer's consternation had more to do with how this unexpected tragedy might affect his ambitions to become Archbishop Marcos' successor than out of any concern for the old man's health, but he had to concede the point that it would not benefit anyone if word of this began to spread. Especially not with the king's visit looming—something that had indeed slipped his mind with all that was happening. He tried to think of other options, but none presented themselves, leaving him with little choice. He could see there was only one answer that Father Lorimer would accept from him. "Alright, what is it you wish me to do?"

"I'm going to send you away, E'on."

Speechless, Owen blinked uncomprehendingly. He wasn't quite sure he'd heard right, but when he tried to ask the headmaster to repeat himself, he found that the air had fled his lungs once again, replaced by disgusting phlegm. He wheezed and coughed violently to clear his throat, his entire body convulsing with spasms that left him feeling drained again once the fit finally passed. "Why?" he croaked, voice hoarse from a burning throat.

"Why?" Father Lorimer leaned closer in after having pulled back apprehensively and drawn his sleeve across his mouth and nose when Owen had begun to cough. "Listen to yourself, E'on. You're sick—very sick—and I cannot risk you remaining here to risk the health of others. I believe there's a connection between what's happened with Flynn and your current condition, and you must seek help for yourself before it's too late. Therefore, I'm going to make arrangements for you to journey to the House of Healing in Chemar Forest. You will carry a letter from me to the Grand Abbess of Anval explaining what's happened—if anyone can help you, it will be the Anvalites."

"Then Flynn must come with me as well. It's too dangerous for him to remain here, by your reasoning, and perhaps they can help him as well with whatever this is," Owen replied, his mind still reeling at the prospect of what Lorimer was proposing. Leave the orphanage? He could scarcely countenance the idea of leaving the place he'd called home for nearly forty years, not to mention the children. Yet, it was undeniable that he was indeed very sick, and suddenly his conversations with Flynn about the nature and origin of this illness became critically relevant.

"*My* reasoning? You still refuse to admit that boy may be responsible for this? If he's not, why have you requested to examine the children's family records? What are you looking for?" the headmaster asked, his dark eyes narrowing.

"I'm looking for evidence of what you already seem so certain. Don't you think it's important to have more proof before we rush to conclusions? You had me reading book after book searching for clues about this and suddenly none of it matters anymore?" Owen retorted.

"That was before a boy lost his life and you ended up on the ground fighting for your own. I'd say the time for looking for answers is past, and action is what's needed now. Having said that, I will pass your research onto Brother Paul, but anything you can learn from the Abbess will surely be invaluable to us."

"And what about Flynn?"

"No, absolutely not—he will not be going with you. You need to be as far away from him as possible before you get any worse. He does not appear to be a danger to himself, only to others, so I will keep him isolated until we can figure out how he did what he did. That's why you'll be taking Dario's body with you—if anyone can solve this mystery, it will be Abbess Talia. I know the Anvalites have a temple here in Corazan, but no one has the wisdom and knowledge that she does in matters of the body. Being alive for over two centuries has its benefits, and experience is one of them. Besides, remaining in the city is too risky as the archbishop would find out in no time and that would lead to questions."

Isolated? A thirteen-year-old boy? The headmaster may as well have sentenced Flynn to death. What Father Lorimer was saying made sense, but there had to be another way. Try as he might though, he couldn't see one, and he was near to acknowledging defeat. Perhaps the best that he could hope for now was that he could get better and return as quickly as he could to help Flynn. He was going to concede and make one final request of the headmaster when the door to the infirmary opened abruptly and Carlo and Hugo came in, carrying an unconscious Peter between them. Blood dripped onto the floor from a broken nose and split lip, and both of the boy's eyes were swollen shut by ugly, purple swellings. Worse, one of the Monitor's arms also had a worrisome-looking bruise quickly forming from wrist to elbow.

"Oh Janus, grant me infinite patience," Father Lorimer sighed in exasperation. "What now?" The headmaster stood up and walked over to them and pulled a handkerchief from his robe, covering one hand with it, then carefully lifting Peter's chin to peer at the boy's puffy face. "What happened?" he asked, searching through the boy's thick red hair to his scalp for signs of a more serious injury and thankfully finding none.

"He was found like this on the path between the kitchens and the school. The boys that found him and came to get us said that he was alone. No one saw anything," Carlo reported.

"Of course not," Father Lorimer grumbled, feeling his level of irritation rising again. He let Peter's head droop back down, unwound the bloody handkerchief from his hand, and handed it to Carlo like an afterthought. "Put him over there and then go get Brother Rodrigo to come tend to him," he said, gesturing to a small row of beds on the opposite side of the room and as far away from where Brother Owen lay. As the two Initiates moved away to comply, the headmaster returned to the priest's bedside.

"His arm," Owen remarked, "it looks broken."

"What?" Father Lorimer appeared distracted, his mind elsewhere. "Oh, that. Yes, well, Rodrigo knows what he's doing. He can set the break and put the arm in a splint, and he'll be fine in no time," he said, dismissing the matter.

"A splint? Why not just heal the boy with a simple miracle?"

"Simple? Let me tell you what's simple—the fact that these children need to understand that for every action, there's a consequence. If we go around calling upon Janus to fix every scraped knee or elbow around here, these boys will never learn to be responsible or appreciate the value and sacrifices that our faith demands of us. When they go out into the world one day, we won't be there to hold their hand," Father Lorimer replied with a vehemence that made Owen frown.

"Father, this isn't a scraped knee," he protested. I have the utmost confidence in Brother Rodrigo's skill as a physician, but if there's even a small chance that break doesn't heal correctly, that boy could be crippled for life. Why take that chance when it costs us nothing?" If he already had his misgivings about the headmaster's capacity for compassion, this exchange was all the proof he needed that there was very little, if any, to be had. He truly feared Flynn's fate if he had to leave the orphanage, but he was powerless to change that for now. First, he had to get better.

Father Lorimer stared Owen down, his eyes hardening like cold iron. "This isn't about what it costs us—it's about what it will cost them if we coddle them.

My word is final, and my mind will not be changed on this matter. Now, if there's nothing else?"

Brother Owen sighed in defeat and let it go. There was nothing to be gained from arguing this further and expending whatever good will he had left with his superior. Not when he still needed something from him. "May I see the boy before I leave, Father? He listens to me, and it might help alleviate what he's going through right now if I can talk to him. He must be frightened and confused. Please, I beg of you, this one small thing."

Father Lorimer considered the request, seeming almost distracted as he watched the two Initiates leave the room to go fetch Brother Rodrigo. He was inclined to refuse due to feeling irritated and that he'd already indulged the subordinate priest's impertinence more than he should have. Still, there was some merit to what he was saying, and knowing how close the two had grown, he knew Flynn was going to be a lot less cooperative than he needed him to be if he allowed Owen to depart without at least saying farewell to the boy.

"Very well. Get some rest for now and regain your strength, you have a long journey ahead of you as soon as Yule is over. I'll have Brother Paul check in on you later this evening, and help you pack your things when you are ready. We don't know how much worse you can get, or how quickly, so time is of the essence. You can see the boy before you depart, but keep your distance." With that, the headmaster rose from his chair and left without further word. Owen watched him go, still trying to make sense of everything. It had all happened so fast—in the space of a few scant hours, his entire life had been turned upside down and he was being told to leave the orphanage. Whatever was wrong with his health felt secondary—he wasn't afraid to die, but he didn't want it to happen while separated from the children he loved. All that remained now was to ensure that he made it to where he was supposed to go, recover from this illness, and return to help Flynn. With those thoughts swirling in his head, he fell into a deep and dreamless sleep.

CHAPTER 17

Vurax couldn't recall when the falling sensation changed into one of floating weightlessly, but he decided that he liked the feeling. In time he became aware of motion—a wind that passed through the hair covering his face and body and brought with it a soothing coolness. Dreams of flying were one of the most common for everyone, and when he lay down to sleep each night, he hoped that he would dream of leaving the oppressive shell of his life behind on the ground and take to the air to bask in the glorious feeling of freedom. He couldn't see anything, but he didn't mind. If this was indeed a dream, then opening his eyes would surely end the wonderful retreat into the depths of his subconscious and signal a return to the waking world, along with all the burdens and demands that came with it. No, he decided—he wasn't ready to go back. Not yet. Thus, he allowed his thoughts to slowly drift back into that reassuring and hazy twilight realm where no cares existed, and no chains could bind him. Time became irrelevant.

The Golian gradually became aware of the solid ground beneath him. He knew what that meant and his mind rebelled, trying to chase down those last fading wisps of blessed sleep and pull them over himself like a comfortable blanket. Yet try as he might, they eluded his grasp, trailing off and dissipating into nothingness. He sighed in resignation, following that up with a groan of displeasure. The smell of grass and the cloying scent of many flowers came to his nostrils, and he felt the soft growth beneath him, cushioning his weight. The air felt warm—much warmer than before, and he could sense the brightness of the sun through his closed eyelids. Was he dead, he wondered? Is this what the afterlife had in store for him—flowery fields and sunny skies? It could be worse, he supposed, but there was only one way to find out, so he finally opened his eyes.

The Minotaur had to blink several times to give his eyes a chance to adjust to the light, and then he attempted to prop himself up on one elbow to take stock of his surroundings. He did so awkwardly due to one arm being wrapped in a splint for some reason, and he looked at it in confusion. It was then that the memories of the past few days came rushing back all at once. No idyllic realm beyond death could possibly be so miserable as to bring his injuries along with him, so that cynical observation dispelled the fantasy once and for all. Then he remembered the gigantic being with the glowing eyes and sat up swiftly, clutching at his chest. He felt panic and his breathing became so fast that he found himself gasping for air.

"Welcome back," he heard the familiar voice, turning his head to find its source, eyes wide and chest heaving.

Treeweaver stood a few paces away, his back to the Golian but with his face turned to look over one shoulder in his direction. The first obvious thing Vurax noticed was that they were not on the tree and brush-covered bluff overlooking the legion fort, but rather on a wide stretch of rolling plains, covered in green grass and a profusion of small white and yellow flowers. Beyond the Syldar Elf, Vurax could see the distant wall of the Border Peaks. With great effort, he calmed his breathing down and swallowed dryly.

"Where are we?" he managed after a while. His voice sounded hoarse, and his throat felt like the dusty steppes of Sarmakan. "Got any water?"

"Canteen is on the ground to your left," the Elf replied, turning to look back at the mountains. "We are about half a day's travel by foot north of that city you mentioned—Vurgas, I think you called it?"

"Vurgas?" the Minotaur blinked in confusion. "How did we... how long have I been out?" He opened the water container and tipped his head back to drink, gulping the cool liquid down thirstily.

"Three days."

"Three—what?" he sputtered, scarcely believing what he'd just heard. "That's impossible!" Another memory fell into place. "Kael—what's happened to him? Where is he?"

"Down there," Treeweaver pointed somewhere to their right.

Vurax glanced in that direction but a small rise in the terrain prevented him from seeing anything but grass and sky, so he rose to his feet to get a better look. What he saw caused his eyes to widen again. The Golian centurion's prone figure lay motionless on a gentle grassy slope near the bank of a small, meandering stream. Nearby, another Elf stood watch. Was it Alis? Seren? One of the other Syldar he hadn't seen? It didn't matter—a few paces away from the clearly un-concerned Elf, two large creatures drank deeply from the flowing stream, dipping their heads downward first, then raising them high and tipping them back to allow the water to flow down their throats. If the motion reminded him of a bird, the impression was starkly reinforced by the fact that the beast's heads resembled those of majestic eagles, complete with long white feathers, and yellow raptor beaks that curved down sharply to black tips designed to rend flesh with ease.

Each one had a pair of enormous brown and white-feathered wings that lay folded down against their bodies, but that's where any similarity to an eagle ceased, for those same bodies were four-legged, with sinuous, yet powerful muscles rippling beneath tawny coats of lustrous fur. Strong legs ended in large paws armed with fierce claws, and long tails that tapered to a black tuft of fur swished lazily in the air.

"Gryphons," Vurax mouthed the word in amazement, his voice subconsciously lowered to a whisper lest any sound alert the beasts to the fact that he was watching them. Each of the creatures was easily the size of two horses combined, if not larger, and if their half-closed black and yellow eyes had taken note of his presence nearby, they seemed thoroughly undisturbed by him as they continued to drink. Images of Dalos' torn body flashed before his eyes, and any moment now, the monsters could turn around and do the same thing to the helpless Kael. His hand instinctively moved to grasp the haft of an axe that wasn't there.

"It's alright, Vurax," Treeweaver said as he approached. "I know what you're thinking, but you have nothing to fear from these creatures. Unlike the one that killed your other friend, these are tamed gryphons and well under Windstrider's control."

"Tamed?" he repeated the word, unable to contain his skepticism. "And where is my axe?"

"Yes, tamed. Windstrider is a Beastmaster, a rare talent even among my people. This pair was bonded to him from the time they were hatchlings, and they will not attack any Syldar. Your weapon is down there with the centurion. I felt it best to bring you up here without it and away from the gryphons after we landed precisely because of your predicted reaction."

Vurax's nostrils flared as he snorted his irritation and dismissed the explanation, which he grudgingly but privately admitted had been right on point. He thought more about the Elf's words, allowing them to fully sink in. "Landed? You mean to tell me we got here on the backs of those things?" The flying sensation he had felt while dreaming came back to him, and he wondered how much of it had been intermingled with reality. The thought of being carried through the sky, so far from the safety of solid ground was terrifying enough, but to do so on the back of a dangerous and unpredictable creature like a gryphon went well beyond the boundaries of what his practical mind could fathom. He struggled to make sense of how the Elf had managed this feat, but a part of him understood that there could be no other explanation for how they'd travelled so far in such a short time span. The Minotaur felt suddenly lightheaded, and a wave of dizziness caused him to sit down heavily upon the grass.

"Are you alright?" Treeweaver asked, squatting next to him.

"Yeah, it's nothing," Vurax managed after a time. The vertigo had passed but left a queasy feeling behind in his stomach. He took another sip of water and then tried to collect his thoughts. When he was ready, he looked up at the Syldar Elf with a haunted look in his large brown eyes. "What happened up there? What was that thing we saw?"

Treeweaver sighed and looked away, then turned to look back at Vurax with a pained expression that matched the Golian's. "That was a Titan, one of the few that remain of a very ancient and noble race that walked this world long ago. Or rather, that's what it once was. Now, I firmly believe it is a vessel for the divine essence that lives within it and commands its actions. It is Jokunkivaard, the god of all giantkind."

Vurax stared at the Elf. His first impulse was to repeat his old mantra—the gods weren't real. Yet, after what he'd seen in those mountains, and in the face of Treeweaver's unshakeable conviction and continued sincerity, he began to doubt himself. The world was filled with many strange and inexplicable things. Men and women of all races devoted their entire lives to the pursuit of knowledge in a never-ending quest to seek answers to those questions. Sometimes they succeeded; more often than not, they failed. A life of slavery at the hands of the Sarmakanites had not afforded him the luxury of scholarly pursuits, to say the least, but in the face of recent events, he had to concede that perhaps his narrow view of the world—one brought on by the practical necessities of day-to-day survival—was overly simplistic and naïve. To him, a simple world was easy to understand and navigate, when just making it from sunrise to sunset was all that mattered. Complexity meant difficulty, and the confines of his servile existence had not permitted his mind to expand in the ways necessary to freely accept Treeweaver at his word. But that life was behind him now, a past that he desperately wanted to move on from, and to do so clearly required that he modify his way of thinking. He would never stop being the grounded individual that he was, but if Treeweaver—and even Kael—told him that he needed to believe certain things, then he owed it to the two men who had saved his life to at least listen.

"What does it want?" he asked. Part of him was genuinely curious. The other part wanted nothing to do with whatever the answer might be. Still, if they expected him to believe that gods not only existed but now walked the world as well, he wanted to know why.

"I wish I knew," Treeweaver responded.

Vurax gave him a suffering look. "Come on, you're going to have to give me something more than that. You've been holding back ever since I first encountered you, but I think it's high time you tell me everything you know."

"I've held back because I can't be certain of what little I do know," Treeweaver tried to explain.

"No, I can't accept that as an answer. You seem to know enough to have made some very startling conclusions. Just start at the beginning and help me understand what you think is going on. That thing slaughtered hundreds of my people and I have a feeling it won't stop there, and you wouldn't be risking going to Golan if you didn't think you could achieve something significant by it, so out with it. Please."

Again, the Elf looked away to stare at some distant point on the horizon as if searching for courage or resolve there. His unwillingness to talk until now wasn't out of some misguided selfish desire to not share important information, but because some of the things the Golian wanted to know were intimately painful details that he himself was still struggling to understand and accept. Sharing them with a relative stranger—especially a skeptic like Vurax— hadn't felt like a particularly constructive course of action at first, but after what he'd witnessed happening to the Minotaur at the legion fort, he could no longer deny that Vurax had earned his right to know. If he was correct, his companion needed to be prepared for what was coming.

"Alright then," he said at last, and began to tell his story.

⸺◈⸺

The still surface of Moon Lake was smooth as glass and covered with mist. The dark blue dome of night above was filled with thousands of glittering stars, and huge Temeros floated in their midst like a brilliant crown jewel hung among lesser stones. Shedding its crimson light down upon the vast body of water, the large moon caused the low-lying fog to take on a ruby-red hue. Arrayed along the northern shore of the lake stood the ragged remnants of the Syldar army, their battle lines drawn for what they knew would be their last stand. Giving their weapons one final check, hundreds of archers stuck their remaining arrows point down in the sand at the water's edge, ready to make every last one count. In front of them, some two thousand grim-faced warriors tightly gripped shields and drew blades, knowing there would be no further retreat. In the air above, less than a score of gryphon riders—all those that were left—circled the area while watching for the inevitable arrival of the enemy, their anticipated warning the signal that would begin the final battle. Yet it was not the stars or moonlight that lit the faces of the assembled Syldar host of *ëler* and *nëler*—Elven men and women—as if it were daytime; it was the bright glow of the raging fire that consumed their home while they watched in anguish and resignation.

Much of the forested slopes that surrounded the lakeshore were ablaze with fires, but the orange-yellow flaming inferno that ravaged the immense and ancient oak upon whose magnificent branches the wondrous Elven city was cradled was the horrifying image that pierced their hearts with unbearable grief. The legends told that the majestic tree had stood in this place since the beginning of time, the first of its kind, with its primordial trunk the full width of a human town. The wide green canopy, stretching hundreds of feet into the air, was so high that it could be seen for dozens of miles, and as clearly as a distant mountain. From the gigantic roots below to the highest branches above, the Syldar had lovingly and organically crafted their living metropolis by carefully shaping and weaving the wood to suit their needs, but always in a fashion that respected the tree and never caused it harm. Here had Syld, the first queen of the Syldar Elves, brought her people to make their home when the world was still new, and they had named it mighty K'orontïrthon, the Oakhearth. So strong and enduring was the home of the Syldar that no flame made by Elf, Dwarf, Golian, or Man could harm or even so much as singe the bark of K'orontïrthon, but the conflagration that now consumed and destroyed the capital of the Syldar kingdom did not come from any mundane source. Even through the blazing glow and wall of smoke that raged before them, the Elves could see the blue pulses of light that flashed with intensity at brief intervals somewhere within the fire.

Queen Baliela of Syldar stood regal and proud on the front line, her stance undefeated by exhaustion, her exquisite beauty unaffected by the soot and grime that covered her cheeks and forehead, or the sweat that made her long brown tresses cling stubbornly to her face. On her perspiring brow she wore the delicate yet simple wooden circlet that symbolized her rule over the Syldar people and custodianship of the realm, and she was clad in the oaken breastplate and greaves given to her long ago by her grandmother, Syld herself. In one hand she held a longsword whose blade was fashioned from a sharp splinter of K'orontïrthon, and in the other was a wooden shield shaped like an oak leaf. The reflection of the flames danced in her pale green eyes, but it was not to her former home or what lurked beyond that she directed her gaze, but to the Syldar nëler at her side who even now clutched at her heart in pain while she knelt upon the sand.

"Be strong, my daughter," the queen said, the obvious tenderness and compassion in her voice betraying the stern expression on her face. "He is nearly here. We will do what we can to distract him and give you time, but you are the only one who has any hope of stopping him."

"Mother... I don't think I can," Caralia looked up with pleading eyes. "I can feel my strength faltering. This pain—it's too much."

"You must. It very well may be that we cannot end this here and now, but we will at least have given our people the time they need to escape."

"Why are our cousins not here?" Caralia continued through gritted teeth. "You said they would come. The power inside me feels fractured...incomplete. It won't be enough."

Queen Baliela did not know the answer, but she could guess. The Syldar monarch had dispatched messengers to the other Elven realms but had received no response. They were too far away, and there was not enough time—there never had been. She suspected they were facing similar crises of their own, and even if help was on the way, it would arrive too late. The best she could hope for was that the bulk of her people who had fled already would find refuge among their distant kin, but hope was in short supply now.

"Caralia, listen to me," Baliela tried to reach her once more, shifting her attention between her daughter and the vague shape within the flames. The flashes of blue were growing more sporadic, the intervals between them becoming lengthier. Not much longer now. "Erliandol chose you for a reason—not me, not your son, not your daughter—he chose you. All the long years of your life have come down to this instant in time, where you must accept and fulfill your destiny. I know you feel it's a burden, but whatever happens here this night, your name will be sung and honoured in Elven memory until the end of time."

Caralia stared in the direction of the fire, but her gaze was unfocused, unseeing. The pulses of light had nearly ceased altogether, and with them, the horrible pain that they brought. She could hear her mother speaking, but the words were indistinct over the dull roar in her ears. A tingling sensation spread over her body, beginning at her extremities, and leaving her flesh numb as it passed through her. She was tired; so very tired. The Syldar had been fighting this implacable foe for days now, and to no avail. Thousands of its minions had been slain, and still they had been unable to slow its inexorable advance to the very foot of K'orontïrthon. Too late did she guess at the significance of what lay within her, and her fumbling and unlearned attempts to use that power had been ineffective at best. She simply didn't know what to do with it, her normal confidence and poise shattered by self-doubt and guilt. The more of her people that died, the more she grew weaker, which in turn led to more despair and loss of control over something she barely understood. In the end, she just gave up and shut it away altogether. Why had this happened to her? Why was any of it happening?

A gryphon's screeching call from high above pierced the chaos and fog of Caralia's thoughts. She knew what it meant—it was coming for her at last. She felt a rising panic in her throat and fought down the urge to run and escape this duty she had not asked for. Looking about wildly, unsure what to do, she saw her mother lift her sword high, followed by the sound of multiple bows being drawn back in preparation to fire. Her eyes turned up the hill to the wall of flames and she saw the line of giant figures rolling menacingly forward, somehow protected from the intense heat by the one who led them. So many, she thought. Wild mountain giants, grotesque two-headed ettins, vicious cyclopes, lumbering ogres, massive trolls—all manner, shape, and size of brutish giantkind, come down from their high villages, caves, and lairs in the hillsides and mountains of the Wedge and beyond to wage unprovoked war against the Syldar. Had it just been these creatures, the Syldar could have dealt with the threat, even unified in this fashion as the giants had never been before. But the presence of the Titan had changed everything, his unstoppable might scattering the Elven defenders like so many leaves in the wind, slaughtering and burning his way to the Oakhearth. Tonight, caught between the advancing fire and the water's edge, the few remaining protectors of the Syldar kingdom could retreat no further.

The giants hollered and snarled as they formed the barest semblance of a battle line. Alternatively bashing massive fists against burly chests, thumping enormous clubs upon the ground, or waving rudimentary iron-forged blades in the air, the cruel hulks vociferously demonstrated their unabashed hatred for their Syldar opponents, who endured the raucous display in stoic silence. Above the incredible din of shouted taunts and crude profanities, the very ground shook as the Titan revealed himself at last, emerging from the flames unscathed, with slow and deliberate strides, to stand looming over the violent throng of his army. The white light shining from its eyes passed over the ranks of the Elves like a malevolent searchlight, causing not a few to flinch under that awful gaze. Then those glowing orbs fell upon the kneeling Caralia and paused. A sudden, eerie hush came over all the giants as they looked up at their leader expectantly. A moment later, the colossus raised one long arm and pointed silently at the Syldar nëler. With a thunderous shout, the bloodthirsty horde surged forward.

Locking stares with the Titan, the Syldar princess felt her mind retreat and hide behind an impenetrable wall of fear and repudiation. Time stopped while she lay there, huddled and shivering in the dark recesses of her consciousness, but she knew she was not alone. A gentle and warm hand took hers, and she lifted her frightened face to look upon a luminous being so radiant that she could barely see any details other than the vague, Elf-like outline of someone standing there. In that touch, the fear clouding her thoughts dissipated like night retreating before the coming of the sun. A calming presence enveloped her entire being, causing her heart to swell with peace and recognition.

"Are you...?"

"Yes."

She nodded. It wasn't so much a voice that she heard, but rather what sounded like a series of crystal chimes jingling softly against one another in a gentle summer's breeze. Finding her courage, she asked the one question that had terrified her all along.

"Am I going to die?"

"Yes."

She braced herself for a wave of self-despair and denial but was surprised to feel only serene acceptance, mingled with sorrow for the family and friends she would never see again. Ever since she had felt the presence, she had known—she'd simply refused to accept that inevitability.

"But you will *see them again. This is not the end. Your sacrifice will make certain of that."*

She nodded again and closed her eyes. "I understand now what I must do."

The wall of darkness she had erected around herself became riddled with cracks, the fissures widening quickly and crumbling away to reveal the light behind. The radiance spilled over her until her form and that of the luminous being before her became one.

Caralia es-Syldarë opened her eyes, golden light blazing forth from them, and rose to her feet.

"Loose!" the queen gave the command.

Behind her, hundreds of bows thrummed their song, the sound a harbinger of doom that hung in the air just before the deadly rain of arrows pierced the flesh of giants with merciless accuracy. Score upon score of the behemoths fell as they charged, never to rise again, ruthlessly ground into the dirt beneath the uncaring feet of those that came running behind them. Gryphons screeched and dove from above with dizzying speed and shattering force, lethal beaks and claws ripping and tearing into the enemy with savage ferocity. Queen Baliela's sword was still raised in the air, her warriors waiting for the weapon to lower in what would be the signal to charge, but her arm froze in place when she glanced at her daughter. A look of understanding passed between the two nëler, and Baliela's eyes welled with tears of love. She kept her sword held high and waited.

Her form awash in golden light, Caralia turned swiftly to the waters of the lake behind the ranks of the waiting Syldar. She raised her arms, causing a sudden wind to rise from the south to blow with increasing speed across the lakeshore and up the slope toward the advancing giants. Behind them, the Titan watched her impassively as he casually and effortlessly snatched a gryphon out of the air that had dared to fly too close. With contemptuous ease, the colossus closed his humungous hand into a fist, crushing the unfortunate creature and rider in its pitiless grip. Before the gruesome remnants had even hit the ground, a flash of blue light flew upward from the slain Syldar's body and into the Titan's bloody hand. Caralia shouted her rage into the sky and the wind increased in intensity, becoming so strong that the giants' charge slowed and nearly halted altogether. All around her, the Elves flattened themselves on the ground to avoid being blown over, and the few remaining gryphons still in the air barely managed to climb higher and away or risk being driven into the wall of flames that was itself being pushed back. Only Queen Baliela stood, resolute and unbowed, her rigid body somehow defying the storm that was raging all around her. She looked proudly at her daughter one last time, smiled sadly, and then lowered her sword sharply.

Caralia's figure lost all definition and became a pillar of blazing light, a beam of glowing energy lancing out from where she stood. Far out on the lake, the beam struck the surface, and something began to stir the placid waters. A whirlpool formed there, small at first, then growing in ever-increasing spirals shaped by the twisting winds above. The water spun faster and faster around the centre of the disturbance, beginning to rise into an ominous waterspout of frightening proportions. Higher and higher the pillar of furiously twisting fluid climbed, growing taller and thicker than any of the trees surrounding Moon Lake, except for K'orontïrthon. On the shore, the waters receded swiftly back to feed the maelstrom, while the windstorm had become so intense that nothing withstood its force now with the exception of the Titan and Caralia. Unaffected by the hurricane that was pushing back his minions as if they had all the weight of mere feathers, the Titan charged forward suddenly, reaching the Syldar princess in the span of a few long strides. Interlacing his fingers, he joined both his hands into one colossal, hammer-like fist and raised his arms high, preparing to unleash a devastating attack upon his opponent.

Before the deadly blow fell, however, another beam of light shot out from the Elf, enveloping and binding both of the Titan's wrists and effectively arresting their descent. For the first time since he had appeared on the battlefield, his face registered emotion, and it was an expression of surprise. Massive muscles strained mightily against the restraints while veins stood out on his neck from the herculean effort, but it was all for naught. Slowly, relentlessly, the Titan was forced to his knees, glowing eyes widening in apprehension at first, then outright fear as Baliela's sword emerged from Caralia's glowing form. The wooden blade hung in midair, suspended by an invisible power, its needle-like point slowly turning toward the immobilized Titan. A gift from the Oakhearth to Syld, the splinter of the First Tree was stronger than any metal and said to be blessed by the one who had nurtured the mighty oak from a tiny sapling to the majestic height that it was today—Erliandol, the wandering god of the Elves. Vibrating with pent-up eldritch power, the sword became a blur of motion and arrowed abruptly toward the Titan's heart with blinding speed.

As fast and sudden as Caralia's attack came, and despite his enormous size and ponderous appearance, the Titan was somehow impossibly faster. Though he remained bound by the coil of energy around his wrists, he managed to twist his body just enough so that the lethal missile buried itself in flesh mere inches from his large heart. The white-hot pain was excruciating nevertheless, and the

Titan threw his head back from the impact, mouth open in a soundless scream. Pulsating blue light seeped outward from the wound like blood, mingling with the coruscating golden glow of Caralia's essence. Enraged beyond reason, the Titan pulled with all his incredible strength and his hands slowly began to draw apart as the Elf faltered from the continued effort of containing him. The brute's victory would be short-lived, however. Forgotten but by no means gone, the towering funnel of water at the centre of the lake came crashing down with overwhelming force, creating a massive tidal wave that rolled toward the shore, gaining speed and height as it came. Nearly spent from the incredible exertion of constraining the Titan while she controlled the wind and water, Caralia collapsed at last.

"Come, my child, you have done all that you could," said the chime-like voice.

The world melted around her—fire, wind, lake, Elves and giants, even the Titan; all absorbed by the golden radiance that enveloped her. She felt warmth and contentment flowing through her, and so she let go.

"I'm ready."

The shackles gone in a flash of light, the Titan grasped with fumbling fingers at the small weapon embedded in his flesh, digging frantically and somehow pulling out the odious needle to howl in thunderous agony when he did so. He flung the sword aside as the azure radiance continued to flow from the wound and placed one hand over the puncture, trying to staunch the energy that fled from his body. He directed his hate-filled gaze at the pitiful, motionless figure on the ground before him and lifted one large fist again to finish her off, but the Syldar princess no longer held the breath of life in her ravaged body.

Time—it was all Queen Baliela had said they needed a little of. Time enough for what happened next.

The wall of water slammed into the distracted Titan, the tremendous impact lifting him bodily and flinging him backward like a ragdoll in a tidal wave that washed indiscriminately over everything that lay in its path, Elf and giant alike, and carrying them inland to slam into the wall of fire still burning angrily. Flames battled briefly against rushing water but inevitably lost, sending a gigantic cloud of steam into the air. The great trees of the Syldar forest snapped like twigs when the brunt of the water hit them, ravaged and weakened as they had been by the devastating conflagration consuming them. Onward and upward the fury of the Moon Lake continued, the body of water emptying itself to erase all traces of the conflict that had unfolded upon its shores. Amidst all the destruction, tall and ancient Oakhearth towered still, and for a fleeting breath, it looked as if the mighty First Tree might survive even though the water could not reach the branches that still burned higher up. Alas, mortally wounded by the unnatural fire, the gigantic trunk shook when the Titan's large body smashed directly against it, the force of the crash resounding with a loud crack and a shudder that reverberated all the way to the top. At the point of impact, what began as a small fissure slowly widened into a series of large gaps that shot upward, splitting the wood apart while they travelled quickly up the doomed tree.

Tall K'orontïrthon could take no more—with a low groan of protest, the First Tree began to slowly lean forward when more and more sections of its trunk came apart like dry, brittle tinder. When it finally came down, it wasn't the tremendous sound of its fall that brought low the hearts of the thousands of Syldar refugees fleeing on their long march far beyond the southern shore of the lake, but the mournful ache in their souls that would forever define them as a people from that day forth. Omnipresent on the horizon wherever they went, they watched in silent horror as their home of past millennia vanished from sight forever. What lay ahead for them now, none could predict—all that they knew for certain was that they could never go back.

⁕

Sometime later, a lone gryphon set down among the debris, a vast field of splintered wood and broken bodies stretching for as far as one could see. The rider's boots splashed onto a muddy morass as he climbed down from his mount to silently survey the devastation that lay all around him. Once one of the most naturally pristine and beautiful vistas to be witnessed anywhere on Akar, there was almost no trace left now of the former capital of the Syldar kingdom. The waters of the lake had retreated at last, leaving behind a desolate landscape filled with the wreckage of hundreds of smashed trees, many of which still smouldered with isolated pockets of flames at the very edges of where the water had climbed. The formerly immaculate surface of Moon Lake itself was covered in the same flotsam as the land, a multitude of water-logged giant and Elf corpses floating alongside one another, unseeing eyes open and staring either at the gloomy depths below or at the uncaring moon above shedding its pale light upon them.

Looking around, Treeweaver felt completely numb inside, unable to process what he was seeing. He had participated in the defense against the charging giants from the vantage of his flying mount, but when the winds had forced him higher, he'd been unable to do anything more than helplessly witness the events unfolding below and watch in grief and dismay as both his mother and grandmother perished while they fought the monstrosity that led the attack. His thoughts turned to the last time he had seen their enemy and he looked at the shattered remains of the Oakhearth. The tree that had served as the home to hundreds of Syldar families had toppled forward after being hit by the wave, collapsing on top of the Titan when it did so. It gave Treeweaver some satisfaction that at least the sacrifice of so many of his people had not been in vain, but it was a hollow feeling that brought him no joy whatsoever. The price paid had been too high by any measure.

He walked aimlessly along the devastated shoreline for a time, searching for some elusive meaning or purpose in all the death that surrounded him. Something on the ground near his foot drew his attention and he bent down to uncover the circular object partially covered by mud in a shallow puddle. It was a wooden circlet, the crown of the Syldar that his grandmother had worn on this night for the last time. A forlorn symbol of a broken house, he thought grimly, clutching the crown tightly to his chest. He was at a loss as to what to do. It didn't help matters that none of them knew why they had been attacked in the first place, who or what the Titan was, and what it had sought to gain by destroying the kingdom of the Syldar. With their homes and forests ruined, what hope was there for any of them out there in a world they had long ago turned their backs upon? K'orontïrthon was gone and could never be brought back. Their only chance at survival now was to forsake thousands of years of isolation and seek help from the outside world. Perhaps their Nuamekar kin would take them in—if they could reach them.

His contemplations were interrupted when the body of a Syldar ëler suddenly twitched on the ground just a short distance away from him. He thought he was seeing things at first, but while he watched, he saw it happen again. He ran toward the fallen Syldar, elation filling his heart. If one had survived, surely there would be more. Yet when he got closer, it was impossible to miss the unnatural angle of the Elf's neck and limbs. Something was very wrong, and he stopped, but continued to observe the ghoulish twitching with fascination. The corpse continued to move spasmodically for a few more seconds before a translucent form, ringed by a corona of soft blue light, began to rise from the slain ëler. The ghostly shape's face was the same as that of the Syldar lying on the ground, but its expression was one of anguish and terror. The apparition caught sight of Treeweaver and turned its haunted eyes to him, dark mouth open in a mute plea, arms reaching forward in a gesture of pitiful supplication.

Treeweaver recoiled in fear, unsure of what he was seeing, but before he could try to overcome his dread and communicate with the spirit somehow, the ethereal form abruptly jerked once then flew past him in a blur of speed. The sudden movement seemed involuntary, almost as if something had violently pulled the phantom away against its will. He turned swiftly to look at where it went and felt his heart sink when he saw the glowing form just before it disappeared into the grip of an enormous grime-covered hand that slowly emerged from beneath a massive piece of the fallen Oakhearth. The Elf couldn't believe his eyes. How could that thing still be alive? The answer came in the form of more bodies nearby that began to shudder and contort like the one he had just witnessed. He didn't need to see any more. Putting fingers to his lips, he ran toward his waiting mount and whistled loudly to the surviving gryphons that kept watch above. Shortly after, all six beasts and their riders had landed near Treeweaver's own gryphon. The Elf didn't need to look at his companions' distraught faces to know that nothing good was happening behind him.

"Nerinë!" he shouted the name as he approached one of the waiting Syldar, the wooden circlet held forward in one hand. The other Elf looked at him and waited for his instructions. "Find my sister and give her this. Tell her she is queen now, and to continue to lead our people south and away from here—all the way to the sea if she must. Do not turn back; there is nothing left for us here but sorrow and death. I will try and find help and return when I can." The nëler took the crown from his hand with clear apprehension, but nodded to indicate she understood what he was asking. Placing the circlet into a saddlebag, she urged her mount into the air and was gone. Treeweaver climbed onto his own gryphon's back and caught a glimpse of the gigantic form of the Titan, rising from the dark muck like a dark leviathan out of one's worst nightmares. A multitude of blue lights swirled toward it from the bodies strewn over the battlefield, seemingly giving it the strength necessary to heave the tremendous weight of the First Tree off its body. Treeweaver ordered everyone up without further delay, putting as much distance as they could between themselves and their revived enemy lest they join the rest of their people in death. He looked down one last time, trying to memorize every last detail of a home he would never see again, but gave up when he realized that place existed only in his memory now. Winging westward, the flight of gryphons chased the fleeing night until they were specks in the distance, while the sun crested the horizon behind them.

CHAPTER 18

Crouching together on the balcony floor, Melios watched Garick intently as the latter took off his gloves for a better tactile feel and made short work of undoing the inner latch that held the door's wooden shutters closed. With that minor obstacle out of the way, he carefully and very slowly swung one of the shutters open just in case the hinges had not been oiled recently. A set of windowed doors waited past the shutter, the room beyond shrouded in complete darkness. Garick peered at the lock on the doors, not needing to try the handle to know that they wouldn't open. It had been a warm and sultry summer thus far, but people like the Khelens didn't just leave their windows open at night like poorer folk. Putting away the slim metal tool he'd used on the latch into a hidden fold on his left sleeve, he pulled out a pair of different ones and began to work on the lock. All the while, he could feel the woman's strange eyes on him. She wasn't watching what he was doing; she was watching him.

"Well? What is it?" he whispered, growing annoyed with her scrutiny.

"Why haven't you told him?"

"Told him what?"

"That you're his father."

Garick's hand twitched involuntarily, nearly causing him to snap the lockpick. As it was, the sound that it made, though barely audible, was loud enough to his ears to cause him to cringe and curse inwardly at her successful attempt to get under his skin. He didn't look at her and resumed what he was doing. "What makes you think that?" he asked, trying to sound unperturbed. Under that mask, he knew Melios well enough to know that she must be grinning from ear to ear.

"You really thought your indiscretion with his mother during that time back in Aldamor wouldn't be noticed? You're even stupider than I thought," Melios sneered, her voice dripping with contempt.

"Valerios had you follow me even then?"

"Every single day. You don't just let a debt as large as the one you owe walk around without keeping a constant eye on it," she remarked even though she knew full well that he knew why.

"Can't be that important seeing as I still managed to give you the slip," he bit back, not holding back on the smugness that permeated every word. "Besides, it only happened once. You can't be sure that he's mine."

It was Melios' turn to be irritated. It was a very sore point to her that Garick had managed to disappear right from under her nose one day, and she'd paid a heavy price when she delivered that news to her employer. She didn't blame Garick for that, only herself, but it didn't make her hate him any less. "It doesn't matter how you were able to get away. You're a sentimental fool and your family is your weakness. I knew if I watched them long enough, you'd eventually surface here. The way you look and talk to that boy—try again, Garick. You're not fooling anyone, and you wouldn't have dared show your face to your brother again if you didn't want so desperately to be near your precious whelp. Felnan knows, doesn't he? That's why he treats his 'son' like shit. Ha! Some father you are."

Continuing to concentrate on what he was doing, Garick took the barb and then shot back a retort of his own. "More than you'll ever know. It must really eat you up inside to not have someone care about you whatsoever. I guess it comes with the territory when you're a cold, miserable, and lonely creature, doesn't it?"

Before Melios could reply with anything more than a scathing glare, he was rewarded by the feel of the last tumbler falling into place. With a small click, the lock was finally defeated. His companion did not wait and shoved abruptly past him, knocking him off balance while she opened the door and proceeded inside at a low crouch. Garick kept his temper in check, putting his tools away and hastily donning his gloves. Not for the first time in recent days, he cursed his luck in having to work with Melios once again. With Darken's help, he knew he was perfectly capable of handling this job on his own, but the letter from Valerios Glimmerdawn that she'd sneeringly delivered to him spelled out the terms—this was his last chance to square his debt, and she was to come along as insurance. Given their history, he really couldn't fault the sly old man for his decision, but the added punishment of having to work alongside her was not lost on him. Memories of a regrettable past swirling before him, he followed Melios silently into the gloom.

Though he could barely see anything, he was sure the bedchamber was large and richly appointed, attesting to the great wealth of the house's owners. Besides being one of the oldest and most well-established families in Arlingford, the Khelens' blood connections to the Taffens and Morhains made them a name that was known as far away as the cities of the Shining Crescent. That Giordy Khelen was master of the Goldsmith's Guild and controlled the export of some of the finest examples of exquisitely crafted jewellery in northern Dravin only furthered that recognition. But whatever fabulous wealth the Khelens were sure to possess and keep in this house was not the purpose of their presence here. What they were after was somewhere in this room, and while he waited for Melios to scan the near-impenetrable darkness with her uncanny eyes for their goal, Garick pondered why he was here. Born and raised in Arlingtown, he knew the settlement better than most, but if Melios had already been here for some time observing him, then this was all information that she was more than capable of acquiring on her own. Not only that, he knew with certainty that for all his expert skill in getting inside a place like this, it was also something she could accomplish alone and with ease. So why had Valerios insisted that they do this together? If this was so important to him, why risk involving Garick—someone who had already broken his trust once?

Ever since he'd finished reading the letter from his former master, he'd been fully convinced of the fact that it didn't paint a complete picture. There was far more to this heist than met the eye, which is why he'd insisted on Darken coming along. He'd trained the boy as well as he could, and though he was used to working alone, his deep suspicion of Melios and Valerios prompted him to bring someone along that he knew he could trust and rely on without question. That Melios had so easily agreed to this one condition only filled him with more misgivings. Had he made a mistake in involving the lad? He couldn't afford to second-guess himself now, and besides, it was too late to do anything about it. All he could do was remain as alert as possible and watch Melios very carefully for any sign of treachery. There had to be a reason Valerios wanted him here beyond mere repayment of his debt.

"Clear. We're alone," he heard Melios' whisper.

"Should we risk a bit of light? I can't see a damned thing," he whispered back into the darkness where he could just barely discern Melios moving slowly about.

"Yes but close the balcony door first—don't want anyone seeing the glow from a distance," she replied. "I think I've found it."

Garick turned and carefully closed the shutters and door before reaching inside a small flap on his belt to remove a small, round object. Bringing the smooth river stone to his face, he lowered his mask briefly to blow on it gently and was rewarded by a soft glow of pale light emanating from the white rock. It did not illuminate more than a dim candle would, but it would allow him to at least see what he was doing. He paused for his eyes to adjust, blinking several times to help the process. Details of the bedroom came into definition while he turned slowly around, including the large four-poster bed with its fine silk covers and pillows, several artfully painted wardrobes, a large desk and chair, and a closed door that led out of the room. Melios herself stood near the desk, and when the light passed over her form, her golden eyes shined back at him, the strange pupils narrowing quickly from round orbs to thin slits. She blinked in annoyance and turned her masked face away, motioning to the desk with one gloved hand. The piece of furniture was large and beautifully crafted out of dark-stained wood, replete with multiple drawers, cubbyholes, and an angled desktop so that someone seated at the chair could write comfortably. Several loose papers, ledgers, and rolled-up scrolls covered nearly every available surface, but it was not to these that Garick's eyes were drawn.

On the wall above the desk hung a large, framed portrait of three middle-aged men within a forested backdrop, each one dressed in fine hunting attire, well-groomed, and smiling as they stood over the carcass of a freshly slain and very large boar. Garick identified the pleasant-faced man in the middle as the owner of this very house, Giordy Khelen. The one on the left he knew to be Lord Friedan Morhain, the baron's brother-in-law, but he wasn't sure who the man on the right was. It didn't matter though; the painting already forgotten when he saw the object that sat on the wall-mounted shelf between the portrait and desk. From black tip to yellowed base, the massive curved and tapered object was easily the full length of his outstretched arm. At first, he took it to be a horn of some kind, but the shape, thickness, and curvature were all wrong. A claw then, but if so, what colossal beast had it come from?

"What in blazes is this thing?" he whispered in awe despite himself. He'd seen his fair share of strange objects that people treasured, but this was unlike anything he'd ever experienced.

Melios looked at him curiously. "How could you know that this was here yet not know what it is?"

"The letter said to uncover the whereabouts of Ahrkmakul's Legacy, so I thought it must be a dragon statuette or some sort of draconic-themed gold jewellery, not...this. What is it?"

"Precisely what we came for—Rauvir's claw," she answered, turning to look more closely at the shelf and mount that supported the object.

'Rauvir's claw,' Garick mouthed. Where had he heard that name before? Then it dawned on him. "Rauvir," he exclaimed. "*The* Rauvir?"

"Yes, *that* Rauvir. How many Rauvirs do you know of?"

"Only one, but—"

"But what? You thought he was just a legend?"

"Well, yes!" he blurted.

Everyone was familiar with the stories of how, many thousands of years ago, dragons filled the skies of Akar and battled one another to the death for supremacy over their kind. Yet when the gods brought the races into existence to populate the world, the chaos and destruction wrought by the dragons was too much for them to allow continuing on unchecked. United against Ahrkmakul—the one who had given life to the powerful and massive beasts—the other gods banished the dragons from Akar, exiling them to the great moon of Temeros. From that remote and barren prison in the heavens, they could only watch in impotent rage as the world they once dominated lay forever out of reach. Ever since that fabled time, Temeros had been called the Dragon's Eye, and there the winged behemoths remained for what should have been an eternity—until one day the greatest and largest of their kind defied the ban and returned to exact his revenge. The subsequent tales of the wake of destruction left by Rauvir and the many battles fought before finally putting an end to his wrathful rampage were many and varied, each one as different as the person who told them. What was generally agreed upon, however, is that they were just that—nothing but fanciful tales sung by the fireside by imaginative minstrels deep into their cups.

"If this is just one claw, then Rauvir must've been—"

"—enormous? Yes. Stand back and let me work, you're crowding me," Melios grumbled while pulling out a small pouch from a pocket on her vest. Standing close to where the claw was, she loosened the strings holding the pouch shut, then slowly and carefully shook out the contents into the palm of one hand. Garick took a cautious step back behind her when he saw the glittering silver dust forming a small conical pile in her cupped hand. After the last few specks had fallen out, and much like he'd done earlier with the light stone, Melios brought her face close to the hand holding the dust, pulled her mask down to her chin, and blew out a quick but strong puff of breath. The silver dust billowed out in a large cloud that hung in the air in front of her for a single heartbeat before descending slowly to settle down upon the claw—or it would have had it not been stopped by the shimmering and intricate network of red glowing filaments and strange symbols made of light that flared brightly to life everywhere the dust particles fell. In no time, the entire length of the claw lay under a now visible dome of energy that enveloped it like a protective shell.

"A magical ward," Garick needlessly voiced the obvious. "That's just fucking great."

⸺◆⸺

The muscles in his legs starting to ache a bit from crouching, Darken decided to sit down on the ground instead. Several minutes had passed since the others had gone on into the house without him and he was growing bored and impatient, always a dangerous combination for someone his age. He kept an eye on the gates as he'd been told, but his thoughts were consumed with imagining what was going on inside without him. He knew his task as a lookout was vital, but on the excitement scale, the activity couldn't come in much lower than what he felt right now. Though he tried several times to think of a way to figure out what his uncle and that strange woman were up to while he kept watch at the same time, he quickly grew frustrated of playing a mental game that had no solution. The sad conclusion that he arrived at instead was that he had no choice but to stay put, and so he did exactly that. There was no way he was going to disappoint Garick.

Before long, his thoughts turned to Ellianna. There had been much that had happened tonight to distract him from the memory of her face and their encounter, but he wasn't surprised to discover that she was still very much on his mind. When he wondered about what tomorrow would bring, he didn't think about the results of what he was doing now, but rather whether he would spot her at the market again. It didn't take long for him to become distracted, and so he nearly missed seeing movement on the street in front of the house. Luckily, whoever was coming was making no effort to mask their approach, and the sound of laughter and conversation shook him out of his daydreaming. Peering through the broad leaves of the hydrangea bush, he tried to make out what was going on under the distant glow of the streetlamps. Before long, in the distance through the bars of the fence, he spotted two or three small clusters of individuals walking down the street. They were well-dressed and some were clearly inebriated—if their erratic movements and loud voices were anything to judge by. Overall, nothing too unexpected to be witnessing at this time of night on a city street except for one thing: they were all coming from the direction of the Keep, and that was definite cause for alarm.

He didn't know what the hour was, but he'd assumed his uncle had timed their task to give them the best chance at completing it without interruptions, but the presence of these revelers could only mean one thing—the festivities had ended earlier. The whys weren't important; what mattered was that whatever time they thought they originally had was now about to be cut short. His hand moved involuntarily to touch the ring Garick had given him, but he stopped short of activating its magic as he'd been instructed. What if none of these people were the owners of this house? If he gave the warning prematurely, he could be ensuring that the job would be botched. If he waited too long, on the other hand, he could be risking much worse. What to do? He hadn't actually expected that anyone would come home this soon and that he'd been asked to sit out here in the dark just for something to do. As it had happened numerous times before, he'd been wrong, and his uncle's foresight was right. Making his decision, he decided to continue watching a while longer to see what happened.

The first small group passed by and continued down the street without stopping. He expected that most of Arlingtown's nobility had been present at the baron's birthday celebration, so it followed that this was the path that many of them would take to reach their homes in North Hill. Perhaps he would get lucky and the Khelens—being related to the Taffens—would stay longer at the party. The next group of people was nearing the gate to the house now, and he held his breath when one of them broke off from the others and ran right up to the closed bronze barrier. He had a clear view of the young man—who looked to be right about the same age that he was—as he playfully and quite drunkenly made a clumsy attempt to climb the gate in an unwise effort to impress his friends. He breathed a sigh of relief knowing that these folks couldn't possibly be the Khelens and even chuckled to himself in the dark when the poor fool fell victim to his alcohol-induced lack of coordination and promptly fell back down to the ground, much to the amusement of his two companions. Before long, his friends had picked up the nearly senseless young noble and the three wandered off happily into the night, singing loudly and out of tune.

In their wake, the third and final group approached, and seeing that it was a couple walking hand-in-hand, Darken paid extra attention. When they stopped to talk a short distance from the gate, he began to experience a sinking feeling in the pit of his stomach. Could this be them, or had the two simply picked that spot by coincidence to have a conversation? Again, he decided to watch and wait while readying himself for the worst. A minute passed, then two. He glanced nervously up at the balcony but there was no sign of the others. When he looked back at the gate, his heart nearly leapt out of his throat when he saw that while he'd briefly looked away, the man had stepped up to the entrance to unlock it, holding it open for the woman to pass through. Giordy and Anika Khelen were home, and they were definitely early.

"Shit, shit, shit!" he whispered harshly while trying not to panic. He grasped the ring immediately, focused on his uncle's face, and pictured himself screaming at the top of his lungs to warn him of danger. He was rewarded by a sensation of warmth as the magic began to function exactly as Garick had described it. If it worked, Garick's own ring should be reacting in response at the exact same moment. He watched anxiously when the couple began to walk up the path, but he could only wait helplessly and see what would happen next.

"What's the plan, Melios?" Garick calmly asked his companion. Though he had not expected to encounter this formidable challenge, Melios seemed to have known exactly what to look for and had come prepared with a way of detecting it. That, coupled with the fact that she clearly knew more about what they were after than he did, made him suspect that she would also have a method on hand for dealing with this. What else hadn't she told him? "Last I checked, neither one of us is a Kal-Dkar, so how do we get past this?"

"This is not the work of a Kal-Dkar; this was put here by Jana Morhain," she replied, carefully examining the intricate gossamer threads of magic that shielded the claw from them and now bathed the entire room in a soft, red light. "You can put your stone away; you don't need it anymore."

"The baron's sister? How can you be sure of that?" he asked, blowing on the stone again to douse its light before placing it back on his belt.

"Valerios taught me more than just how to sneak into a house. He would have taught you as well, had you had the courage to stay with us. There's a very subtle difference between a spell woven by an *etherus*-wielding mage, and one that is channeled directly from a divine source. The energy is the same, yes, but the origin and conduit through which it flows are very different. Pull out your dagger," she said without even deigning to look at him.

Once again, he had to suppress his irritation at her arrogance and superior attitude, and he was about to ask her what she wanted with his dagger when his keen hearing picked up a brief sound that seemed to have come from outside. He had closed the shutters, but the windowed doors remained open, and he could have sworn he'd heard what sounded like distant voices. He turned to look toward the balcony, ears straining to detect anything more. "Did you hear something?" he whispered.

"No."

She was about to say something else, but he held one hand up to silence her. He listened attentively for a while longer but heard nothing. Had his imagination been playing tricks on him? Darken was keeping watch outside, after all, and he was confident the boy was alert, so he shook off the momentary distraction and focused back on the job at hand. "What do you need with my dagger?"

"*Your* dagger—which you stole, I might add—is imbued with the same kind of power that this ward is made of. It was fashioned precisely for this sort of thing. Only an idiot like you would not realize the truth of what he's holding and use it for such mundane tasks as cutting purse strings."

He didn't even care about the insults this time, only the implication of what she was saying. "You brought me here tonight because you knew all along that I held the key to this whole thing, didn't you? Did Valerios foresee this?"

Valerios Glimmerdawn wasn't just the most powerful crime boss in the Shining Crescent cities of Aldamor, Breos, and Pargeri; he was also a seer—an individual possessed of a rare gift known as the 'Sight'. Able to catch glimpses of the future, as well as predict the outcome of certain choices with a remarkably high degree of accuracy, it was easy to understand how one man had been able to achieve such success and power. Garick didn't know what Valerios wanted with Rauvir's claw, and it didn't matter. What bothered him was to learn that he'd been a pawn in a long game that his former employer had been playing, and Garick didn't like being used.

"So, he let me steal the dagger because he saw that this moment would come?"

"Congratulations on figuring it out," she said, not bothering to hide her condescension.

"But why not just give it to you and let you do it?"

Melios sighed in exasperation. "Because at the time, he did not yet know that he would one day want Rauvir's claw, but when he saw you and the dagger together, he decided that he should allow you to take it, thus ensuring that this event would come to pass. Not only that, but the visions are also often nebulous, and he couldn't see where this was to take place, so he had me find you after all these years because the time for this to happen was near and that meant your location and that of the claw's would be the same. Seeing the claw in his vision made him research it extensively, and now that he knows what it can do, he wants it very much indeed."

Garick's head was beginning to spin while he tried to follow the convoluted path that had seemingly led him here tonight. "That's all good and well, I think... but it still doesn't explain why he couldn't just get you to do it."

"Haven't you been listening?" she hissed impatiently. "He saw you do this! You. Not me. To alter the vision in any way endangers the outcome in unpredictable ways. Besides, your cooperation was guaranteed because of your debt to Valerios, and lastly, that blade is bonded to you now. There's no way for me to use it."

"Well, you might have started with that last bit," he remarked in annoyance.

"It wouldn't change anything. You honestly think Valerios wouldn't have collected on your debt by now if he didn't need to make sure he could make you be here tonight? Well, this is your chance to be free of his influence and manipulation once and for all. Now get your dagger out."

"Fine," Garick snapped at her, drawing forth the weapon from a cleverly concealed sheath under one forearm with a simple flick of his wrist. It was a fairly non-descript dagger in its design, with a slightly curved guard, and a round pommel inset with a glittering black opal gemstone. What was most unusual about it was the rare ebon steel of the blade itself, which perfectly caught the reflection of the ward's glowing energy on its mirror-polished surface. When he glanced at it, he was astonished to see that the symbols now looked like normal letters, though whatever words they formed, they were not in a language that he could read. Yet when he looked back directly at the dome over the claw, those same symbols remained as cryptic and indecipherable as before. "Are you seeing this? What does it say?" he remarked to Melios.

"You wouldn't understand if I told you. Now, see this small nexus point here where the different strings of symbols converge?" Being careful not to touch the filaments, she pointed to a specific area where the strange cryptograms all spiralled to one central point. "Push there with the tip of the dagger, and then turn slowly to the left, as if you were unlocking a door with a key."

He was about to ask her if she was sure about this, but it seemed pointless. They'd come too far to stop now, so he stepped forward, dagger raised.

CHAPTER 19

The last week of Yule had come, much to the collective disappointment of the orphanage's children. Only a few more days of fun and festivities left before a return to the drudgery and routine of school as life eventually settled back into its normal routine. Before that though, there was one big event that everyone was eagerly anticipating, and it would be happening today—the royal visit. This yearly tradition, established by King Caldor long ago, was something that every boy always looked forward to. Every one of them had grown up on tales of King Aldrik's brave exploits and most dreamed of becoming one of his knights, wearing resplendent armour and riding off to battle. Not every one of the orphanage's wards was destined or expected to become a member of the church, so the king's visit and his speech helped to give them all a glimpse of the varied and important roles they would one day perform as productive citizens of the realm.

Sitting on his bed that morning, Elias pondered back on the events of the past two weeks. It was a long list, and he had the distinct impression—if not certainty—that aside from Carlo and Peter, he was the only one among all the other boys who knew there was far more going on than what they'd been told. If he had any doubts about that, he had only to remind himself of how Carlo looked at him every day when the two crossed paths, his silent stare making it plain that Elias was being carefully watched. As a result, he'd grown even more fearful than before whenever he caught a glimpse of anyone wearing black robes, and he kept to himself for the most part, hoping to not draw any unwanted attention. In the end, his life hadn't really changed all that much as a result, he reflected sadly. He had only a few more minutes before going down for breakfast, so he went over everything in his head again, just as he did every day when he got up.

First, there was Flynn, of course. His friend had not been seen since the night he'd been taken from the hospital, and the explanation given was that his grave condition had required him to be transferred to the temple of Anval. He couldn't be certain whether this was true or not, and what he'd seen with his own eyes that night told him there were a lot of missing parts to this story. Ever since then, every time he passed near the headmaster's house, he glanced at it furtively, always wondering whether Flynn was inside, and always coming to the same conclusion that he must be. Getting in there to confirm that however, was impossible. Next was Brother Owen. After his shocking collapse, the priest was still in the hospital recovering from an undisclosed illness, and none of the children were permitted to visit him. Elias desperately wanted to talk to Owen, but with Carlo scrutinizing his every move, he didn't feel brave enough to try that, either.

Then there was Peter. The Monitor had spent a few days in the infirmary after his painful encounter with Big Eric, before coming out with a splint and bandages over his broken arm and a number of dark bruises that were taking their time to fade away, much to Peter's humiliation. The rumour going around was that Peter had taken a rather nasty fall when he didn't look where he was going, but Elias definitely knew this one story wasn't true. He was certain there would be a reprisal coming for his part in what had happened, but he'd kept his mouth shut in the hope that his silence might spare him Peter's wrath. For his part, the Monitor had become withdrawn and taciturn and generally avoided being anywhere near him—or Big Eric, most especially. Elias wasn't even sure if Carlo knew what had transpired that morning to result in Peter's injuries, but he guessed the Initiate must have his suspicions. Was Peter too embarrassed to tell him? Whatever the case, and however much Elias was enjoying not having Peter constantly harassing him anymore, he wished he could somehow find out from him what they'd been doing on that fateful evening, and more importantly, what had happened to Dario.

Dario. The more he thought about the vanished boy, the more he realized that no one had really known much about him. He'd been a quiet loner for the most part, not unlike Elias. At some point he'd fallen in with Carlo and his group and the other children began to avoid him, which wasn't hard to do as Dario had never really associated with many of them anyway. Now that he was gone, Elias wondered about his fate. Screwing up his courage a few days ago, he'd walked into Brother Melton's office—the one priest whose business it was to know of everyone's comings and goings from the orphanage—and asked about Dario. The cantankerous man had put down the book he'd been reading, peered at him in irritation over the edge of his spectacles, then simply told him a previously unknown relative of the boy had come to visit and had taken Dario away to live with his distant family outside of the capital. The priest said nothing more and Elias left, knowing an obvious lie when he heard one, but seeing no point in drawing any more attention to himself with questions. It's not that it didn't happen from time to time—children being adopted or retrieved by relatives and taken from the orphanage—but he was convinced that hadn't been Dario's fate.

Elias sighed. His mental review of things ended at the same point where it always did since he'd begun to do this every day—the dejected conclusion that he was helpless to do anything about any of it. Today was a special day though, he reasoned. Perhaps something would finally be different. Squaring his shoulders with newfound resolve and hope, he hopped down from the bed, slipped his shoes on, and walked to the lavatory to wash his face and make ready. Out in the hallway, a steady stream of children was already on the way to the refectory where the king would make his appearance later in the day. The chatter and excitement were palpable and infectious, and Elias felt himself buoyed by the feeling. Not wanting to be late, he ran into the bathroom but stopped abruptly when he saw Peter walking from the urinal to the sink, struggling as he fumbled with his one good hand to cinch his pants. While Elias understood the concept of coincidence, he was beginning to wonder why it was that he always ran into the Monitor in this particular setting.

Peter froze when he saw him, blue eyes narrowing with suspicion, but Elias did not miss the look of apprehension that flashed across the boy's still bruised freckled face before it was quickly hidden by the customary scowl. "What're you looking at, shit-breath?"

For his part, Elias ignored the routine insult, said nothing, and walked over to the sink and began to wash his face, using his fingers and water to tamp down a few unruly strands of sandy blonde hair. He could feel Peter glaring at his back but pointedly ignored the Monitor until he heard him curse in frustration under his breath.

"Do you want some help?" Elias asked on impulse. While most would rightly say that Peter was undeserving of any compassion and had more than earned the beating he'd received for his reprehensible behaviour, it just wasn't in Elias' nature to be vindictive. He couldn't stand Peter and would never forgive him for the torment that the Monitor had foisted upon him over the years, but that didn't mean he wasn't bothered by feelings of guilt at what Eric had done to Peter on his behalf.

"You just stay away from me, you hear?"

Elias shrugged without turning. "Fine with me—if you want your pants to fall down while you stand before the king, that's your choice." The boys' modest lavatory didn't have the luxury of a mirror, but Elias could imagine Peter's face contorting with rage at the suggestion of the scenario he'd just described, and the ensuing hilarity and humiliation that would be sure to follow. For all of his genuine willingness to do as he'd offered, Elias couldn't help but experience a brief and surprising sensation of perverse pleasure at the thought of seeing Peter shamed publicly like that. The feeling passed, and when Elias heard a sob, he turned around to look at the Monitor in surprise. Tears streamed down the other boy's face, and the look of pain that he gave Elias dispelled any last lingering thoughts of revenge.

"Hey, I was only kidding," Elias said awkwardly, taking a step toward him.

"Why? Why did you let him do this to me?" Peter cried, lifting his bandaged arm with obvious effort. "You could have called him off, but you didn't. I fucking hate you, Elias. I hope you die. You and all your asshole friends!" this last statement was made with such venomous intensity that Elias stopped in the middle of reaching out to the other boy. He let his arm fall to his side and felt his heart harden. He'd allowed himself to think that perhaps there could yet be some redemption for Peter, but he could see that he was only fooling himself.

"What he did to you?" Elias was beside himself with disbelief and indignation. "You mean the same you would have done to me had he not shown up when he did? Fuck you, Peter. Good luck with your pants," he said, and then turned around and left, leaving the other boy to sputter impotently at his back and cry by himself. Standing outside in the hall, the renewed hope and optimism he'd felt before leaving the dormitory just minutes ago had been dimmed by his encounter with Peter, but he did his best to brush that aside and found that he succeeded with remarkable ease. Having found the courage to stand up to his most relentless enemy had given him an unfamiliar sense of confidence that left him feeling invigorated and like a new person. More importantly to his conscience, he'd done it while offering Peter the opportunity to understand that empathy and consideration could still provide a path forward for them. The Monitor had made his choice clear, however, and Elias wouldn't let his guard down a second time.

Falling in behind a couple of late stragglers and the Initiate that was ushering them along, Elias joined the small group and hurriedly made his way down to the large refectory hall where they always ate their meals. He took his usual seat next to Georgie and Big Eric and began to quickly eat the already cold breakfast on his plate. He didn't miss the mournful look that Eric gave him while Georgie snickered.

"What's so funny, and why are you looking at me like that, Eric?" Elias asked between mouthfuls of fried potatoes and egg mixed with a bit of pork sausage.

"He's sad that you showed up because he was getting ready to eat your breakfast," Georgie mumbled, trying to keep his mirth under control.

Elias tore up a chunk of bread and used it to mop up some of the tasty sausage fat that was on the plate. Watching his friend bring the morsel of food to his mouth and chew it with gusto, Eric sighed dejectedly at Elias. The latter had been famished, but he could never eat as much as Big Eric. Taking one final bite, he pushed his half-filled plate over to Eric who smiled beatifically at him before proceeding to devour the rest of the food. "I swear, one of these days you're going to explode," Elias joked. He drank some cold fruit juice, wiped his mouth, and then looked around the hall.

The Yule decorations had been completed, lending the refectory—and indeed the entire orphanage—a festive look that the children enjoyed tremendously. Here, in the hall where the contest had begun, the red banners bearing the crossed swords of Unamos, the Warbringer, hung from every wall like a sour reminder to him that Carlo's team had—unsurprisingly—won the competition. It wasn't that Eric hadn't made a valiant effort after he'd replaced Flynn as leader of their group but drawing Gaurkur's token had made the whole endeavour a losing proposition from the start. In every past Yule celebration that he could remember, no team had ever won the contest after getting stuck with the grim and disgusting God of Decay. He honestly couldn't understand how anyone could worship such a vile deity, but Gaurkur was one of the Universals, and tradition demanded that the eleven members of that group of divinities be honoured equally during Yule.

The plates were being cleared now, the Initiates moving among the tables to get everyone ready for what was to come next. Elias could feel the anticipation in the room as the children enthusiastically waited to be called by age group to assemble by the far doors that led to the central garden. When their turn came, he and his friends got up and formed a line behind the group in front of them. Despite his gloomy thoughts earlier, Elias couldn't help but grin from ear to ear as he looked from Big Eric, still busily licking his greasy fingers, to Georgie, normally so quiet and thoughtful, and now practically bursting with excitement. He dearly wished Flynn could be here—it was his friend's first Yule at the orphanage, yet fate had somehow conspired to make him miss nearly the entire event and it just didn't seem fair.

When everyone was ready and the outer doors were finally opened, the children eagerly filed out in orderly fashion under the supervision of the Initiates and Monitors. Elias caught himself involuntarily looking for Peter, but the red-haired boy was nowhere to be seen. Outside, the slight chill of the morning air was easily ignored in the face of the perfectly clear blue sky and glorious sunshine. Standing before the central fountain and flanked by Fathers Anthony and Oliver, was Father Lorimer. The headmaster smiled as his wards approached, greeted them with his daily blessing, then turned to lead the entire procession toward the cathedral. As they passed the infirmary, Elias whispered a silent prayer for Brother Owen's health, but when they drew near the headmaster's house just before passing through the Ivy Gate, Elias couldn't help but wonder for the hundredth time if Flynn was inside or not.

Once past the gate and tunnel, the children walked toward the open western doors of the cathedral's majestic and imposing edifice. The boys all filed in, forming carefully organized groups to sit down upon the pews along the left-hand side of the grand nave. To their right, the eastern doors were open as well and a steady stream of girls—led by Mother Sandreia and the Sisters of Janus—flowed in to take their seats on the pews on the other side. This was the only time of the year the boys and girls of the orphanage saw each other, and there were a lot of furtive looks, giggling, and ugly faces made, though the Monitors and Initiates on both sides did their best to quickly quash any unseemly behaviour. A few of the children from each side split off from their respective groups to stand on raised platforms on opposite ends of the main altar. These were the choir singers, and Elias grinned proudly at Georgie as his friend took his place among the back row of altos.

At the front, Father Lorimer and Mother Sandreia bowed to each other in ritual greeting, then turned to kneel before the altar and empty pulpit, above which towered the gigantic white marble statue of Janus. Depicted as a youthful man of perfect physical appearance, the Overgod had exquisitely chiseled and beautiful facial features, and was dressed in flowing robes, with both arms raised to the sky as if to support the vault of the cathedral itself. A benevolent smile graced the statue's frozen lips as the All-Seeing Eyes of the god looked down upon the assemblage of his faithful. At a subtle signal from an Initiate near the pulpit, the murmurs died to a hush, and everyone present rose to their feet when a small but ornate door built into the statue's massive pedestal opened and Archbishop Marcos Andaril walked out to take his place in front of the altar. Despite being in the eighth decade of his life, the Bishop of Corazan and Archbishop of all Rohne walked steadily and unbent by age, holding his gilded crozier with authority as he moved to the pulpit. He was dressed in his finest, grey-trimmed liturgical robes of office—with the pallium draped over his cassock and mitre worn on his head—all superbly woven in rich fabric of vibrant gold, white, and blue hues, and elegantly decorated with the symbols of the church.

The venerable cleric's brown eyes peered out from below bushy white eyebrows and the many lines on his aged face crinkled as he smiled gently upon the gathered children and lifted one hand to give his benediction. Everyone's heads bowed in silent prayer as they remained standing, and the archbishop turned slowly to face the altar, raising his arms in supplication and purposeful imitation of the god's statue. After a short period of time during which not even a whisper could be heard inside the nave, Marcos faced forward once again and tapped the crozier's metal-shod end down once upon the polished marble floor, the sound echoing throughout the great space. At this, the crowd turned as one toward the far southern end of the cathedral where two Brothers stood by. The priests then took hold of the large pull handles and swung open the ponderous southern doors. There, standing on the landing over the broad steps at the front of the church, was King Aldrik of Rohne.

Aldrik Ormandos III was the fifteenth monarch of the Kingdom of Rohne, and sixth scion of his House to hold that title since his great-great-grandfather Caldor Ormandos had wrested back the crown from Engil the Usurper during the Krulean Uprising, one hundred and seventy-eight years ago. At sixty-five, Aldrik remained just as physically imposing as the day he'd taken the throne at twenty-one years of age after his father, Melinor Ormandos, was treacherously slain during an ambush while campaigning in the Seawall Mountains. The king wore his father's heavy suit of armour, consisting of overlapping polished steel plates over gleaming chainmail and a padded gambeson, topped by a surcoat depicting the kingdom's crest—the Gold Lion of Coraz and Red Eagle of Ormand. Together, these symbols represented the alliance of the two Houses that had unified under Rohne Corazi and Vania Ormandos and founded the kingdom over four centuries ago. He did not, however, wear his great sword—the fabled Jötunnslayer—at his side today, for even the lord of all the land was forbidden from bearing arms inside the church.

The king's golden crown rested upon an unruly mane of light brown hair, and his craggy but still handsome face was dominated by a pair of steely grey eyes famous for their penetrating stare. Aldrik's nose was bent and crooked, a combination of having been broken several times and the ruler's stubborn disdain for magical healing. A long scar ran from just under his left eye and all the way down to his square jaw line where a giant's spear had come close to ending his life on more than one occasion. Squaring his broad shoulders, the king stepped inside the holy house of Janus and strode toward the main altar with the confident poise and practiced gait of one who is accustomed to wearing armour like a second skin. As he passed row after row of wide-eyed and silent children, red cape flowing in his wake, a crack finally appeared in his stern face and his lips curled upward to grin at all those small faces. He had few duties these days that still brought him any joy, but the yearly visit with the orphans never failed to lift his spirits.

Three other people followed Aldrik, walking in single file behind him, and Elias strained to see around some of the taller boys around him to catch a better glimpse of the king's entourage. He was understandably curious as this was his eighth Yule royal visit since being old enough to be permitted to attend, and on every previous occasion, the king had only brought two others with him. The first was the familiar face of old Beran Wyl, Aldrik's steadfast and dependable chamberlain. Wearing his customary blue robe and golden sash, the aged man was not just the overseer of the castle's daily operations, but also the administrator of the kingdom's affairs. More importantly, he'd been a father figure to Aldrik after King Melinor's untimely death. After Aldrik's young wife, Queen Marigold, became gravely ill during the birth of their second child and both her and the newborn passed away, the king had fallen into a dark depression for several years, and had it not been for Beran Wyl's wise and capable hand, the kingdom would have descended into chaos. If Aldrik could be considered to be the beating heart of Rohne, Beran Wyl was surely its sharp mind and eloquent tongue.

Following patiently behind the slow shuffling steps of the chamberlain was a woman of middle years in a hooded black tunic with short sleeves that left her arms bare, black trousers, and knee-high black leather boots. Her long and shiny dark hair was pulled back into a utilitarian bun which did little to soften the sharp angles of her face and her narrow black eyes. This was none other than Alyssa Dumar, the court's new Kal-dkar, and whenever her gaze met that of a child's, they quickly averted their eyes, feeling as if their souls were laid bare to her intense scrutiny in that one brief instant. Every boy and girl in the orphanage knew why the mage was here, and that knowledge came with a strange mixture of fear and excitement. Though he was still too young for the Test, Elias was confident that he would be chosen when the time came. It was his dream, and one that he had shared with no one—not even Flynn—for fear of ridicule. But it was the third and last figure that everyone focused on now as the small procession made its way to the front row of pews before the altar.

The young woman was only in her late teens, but there was a decided solemnity about her demeanour that belied her tender age. Thick and wavy dark brown hair cascaded down past her shoulders, framing a face that could only be described as breathtaking in its regal beauty. Her eyes were limpid blue pools of expressiveness, yet there was a poignant sadness behind them that caught one's breath when looking at her. Her nose and mouth were perfectly shaped, lips full and red like a rose in bloom. She wore a simple but elegant light blue dress that hugged her tall and slender figure and complemented both the silver tiara at her brow and the sapphire pendant that hung around the pale skin of her shapely neck. Eyes fixed forward, she didn't even so much as glance at any of the children—boys and girls alike—that watched raptly as she glided silently past them.

"Who is that?" Elias whispered to Eric, unable to shake his awe or the strange stirring of confused feelings that seeing this girl stirred within him.

"Who else could it be? That's Princess Gabriela, you dork," Eric scoffed as if it should be an obvious thing. In fact, though it was no secret that the king had a daughter; it was also true that she was seldom ever seen in public. That she was here today was nothing short of momentous, but living sheltered lives of their own at the orphanage, the children had no real way of appreciating how rare her presence was.

"Oh...okay. Well, she's really—"

"Tall? Yeah, for a girl, I agree. Gangly even, I'd say," Eric snickered.

"I was going to say beautiful..." Elias trailed off, barely hearing what his friend had said as he continued to stare at the princess, who was even now taking her seat next to the Kal-dkar at the front of the girl's section. Across the aisle from her, the king and his chamberlain sat down on the boy's side of the nave. Eric made a disgusted face as he looked at his friend, but his reply was cut short when a Monitor sitting at the end of their row leaned forward and shushed them.

With the royal party seated, the rest of the assemblage took their seats once more and Archbishop Marcos began the Yule mass, his voice—still powerful despite being raspy with age—echoing throughout the vast space of the cathedral's interior. Elias faithfully recited the passages from the scriptures of Janus on cue along with the rest of those present but found himself daydreaming throughout the entire service. When the choir began to sing near the end—a part Elias always enjoyed—he closed his eyes to fantasize that the voices belonged to angels floating high up near the frescoes that decorated the nave's vaulted ceiling. In his mind's eye, all of the heavenly beings had Princess Gabriela's face.

<hr>

Brother Owen stood outside Father Lorimer's house and pulled on the thin chain beside the door that rang the small bell inside. While he waited, he listened to the sound of children's voices raised in song drifting on the air from the nearby cathedral, the sweet hymn a bittersweet reminder of all that he would soon be leaving behind. By all rights, he should be at the Yule mass with everyone else, just as he had every year since coming into the service of Janus. Yet the headmaster had decreed that the priest would not only be departing the orphanage today, but he would be doing so during the service so that none of the children would be unduly upset by the event. That he couldn't say goodbye to his beloved wards was something that both confused and rankled him at the same time, but having won this small concession of being allowed to see Flynn before leaving had been enough for him to not push the issue with his superior any further.

He took a deep breath of the crisp morning air, feeling better today than he had for the past two weeks. The illness that was ravaging him inside seemed to have periods when it was quiescent and Brother Paul had instructed him on the brewing of an herbal concoction that, despite tasting awful, helped tremendously in calming his coughing fits. He still wasn't convinced that undertaking such a long journey would be the best idea in his condition, but again, there was no further debate to be had with Father Lorimer on the matter. He would do as he'd been ordered and hope for the best outcome when he reached the House of Healing. He pulled on the bell chain once more, taking the time to review his travel attire for the tenth time since donning it. The priestly robes he'd worn like a second skin for nearly as long as he could remember were gone, replaced by a black doublet and tan slacks worn under a simple dark blue travel coat. Sturdy riding boots completed the ensemble, and the rest of the few belongings he'd chosen to bring along were already waiting for him in the wagon he would be riding in. He pulled at the unfamiliar garments in a futile attempt to adjust them so that they didn't feel so strange, but it was useless.

His hand was reaching for the chain for the third time when the door finally opened and Initiate Carlo stood in the doorway, looking at the priest with that inscrutable expression he always wore. "Good morning, Initiate. The Light of Janus be with you. I believe I am expected?" Owen greeted. The teenager gave a perfunctory response to his salutation and waved him inside. Brother Owen stepped into the house and then paused, waiting. When Carlo didn't move, the priest gave him an odd look. "Well? Aren't you going to take me to him?"

The Initiate stared inscrutably at him in silence then nodded and moved off abruptly. "This way." Owen watched Carlo walk down the hall into the next room and shook his head with a frown before following. He'd been to the headmaster's home several times before, but there had never been any reason to go beyond the nicely appointed living room where Father Lorimer sometimes entertained visitors or other members of the clergy. Following Carlo, he walked through an archway at the back of the room and into the kitchen area. There, beyond a doorway near the back wall, was a stone stairway that led downward. When he reached the bottom of the short flight of steps, Brother Owen looked around curiously, noting the much older stonework in the passage below and the various archways, as well as the distinct aroma of wooden casks and wine in the air. He knew from history that the old missionaries had made their own wine and kept it stored in a warren of old cellars beneath the original mission, but he had no idea that one of those entrances was right here under the headmaster's house. It was strange that the smell was so potent after all these years, but the areas beyond the lit passageway were dark and he could not see what lay there.

He followed Carlo to a reinforced wooden door at the end of the passage, growing steadily more apprehensive the further they went. Father Lorimer had said Flynn was secure in a room for his own safety, but this wasn't at all what he'd imagined. This was more like a dungeon. He watched while the Initiate pulled an iron key from his robes and turned it in the lock, the hinges groaning in protest from disuse when the door swung open. Carlo stood to one side, allowing the priest to pass in front of him. The room beyond was not overly large but not small either, and must've been used as a storage room originally, but it was clear that it had been recently converted into a living space for its current occupant, who looked up from the table where he sat reading a book.

"Brother Owen!" Flynn Castellar shouted. There was naked elation and delight on the boy's face as he rose from his seat and dashed across the length of the room toward his friend, but he caught a glimpse of Carlo's face as he did so and stopped short a couple of paces from the priest. He stood there awkwardly, wanting to throw his arms around the man, but just stammered an apology instead. "I'm sorry—Father Lorimer said I shouldn't get too close to any adults."

Owen pushed past his relief and happiness at seeing the boy and reminded himself of the conversation he and the headmaster had had. He wasn't convinced that his superior's theory was correct, but if it was, it was already too late for him. Still, best not to tempt fate and make matters worse, if such a thing were even possible at this point. He grinned and nodded silently in understanding, unable to find words that could adequately express the joy he was feeling. He looked about the room, noting the comfortable bed, small table with two chairs, wash-basin and chamber pot, and even the remains of a recently consumed breakfast. The room was brightly lit by magic globes; the temperature was just right; the air fresh despite being underground; and several books lay on the table. Every effort had been made to ensure Flynn had everything he needed, but Owen saw the windowless space for what it truly was—a cage.

"May I?" Owen asked, gesturing at one of the chairs.

Flynn looked at him in confusion, not used to having an adult ask him permission for anything. "Uh...sure," he said, walking back to sit in the same chair he'd been in while the priest took the one across from him. He brought up his right hand and closed the book he'd been reading, pushing it to one side before quickly putting his arm back at his side as if embarrassed, but not before Owen noticed that the hand was completely hidden by a black leather glove.

"*Precepts of the Universals,* uh? Not exactly light reading," the priest quipped.

"No," Flynn admitted sheepishly.

"Not *Legend of Starfall*?" Owen winked.

The boy looked distinctly crestfallen at the mention of his favourite book. "No," he replied sullenly. "I asked for it, but Father Lorimer said I shouldn't fill my head with such nonsense. Still, it's interesting to learn what makes the Universals different from the other gods."

Brother Owen was about to speak again when he remembered something. He looked at the doorway where Carlo stood unmoving and silent since they'd arrived, staring intently at the priest and the boy, his mouth a grim line. "You may go now, Initiate. I'll call for you when I'm ready to leave." When the teenager failed to react in any way, the cleric raised his voice just enough to be sure that he couldn't be misheard and repeated his request. Again, the dark-haired, black-robed Initiate did not move. Owen didn't miss the fearful look in Flynn's eyes when the boy glanced up at him, or how he avoided looking at Carlo the entire time. The priest decided he'd had enough, and got up from his seat to face the Initiate. "Are you having trouble hearing me? I said leave." His tone brooked no argument, but the spark of defiance that flared suddenly to life in Carlo's blue eyes promised otherwise.

"No," the Initiate said with surprising firmness and confidence.

Brother Owen wasn't sure he'd heard right, so he gave the Initiate the benefit of the doubt even as he felt the last shreds of patience evaporate. "What did you just say?"

"Father Lorimer left me very specific instructions. I am not to leave your side," was the even reply. It was the sort of thing a boy of his age would say with smugness when they thought they had the upper hand in speaking with an adult, but Owen detected none of that arrogance in Carlo's flat voice. He'd always felt the Initiate to be cold and oddly emotionless at the best of times, but he was beginning to feel downright unsettled by the way the lad was looking at him.

"You have been ordained as an Initiate in our Order, which makes me your superior. That means you must do as I say without question. Now leave." Unsettled or not, his patience was most definitely at an end. The Yule mass would be over soon, and he was expected to be gone from the orphanage by then. He needed to speak privately with Flynn before he left but he could see now that the headmaster had never intended to allow him to do that.

"Father Lorimer outranks you and I'm doing what he asked. You can't order me away."

Born to a fierce warrior tribe, E'on Abdalla had been scarcely younger than Carlo when he was taken by Golian slavers, and though the years had been long and hard since the last day he'd seen his father's face, he'd never forgotten the things his sire had taught him. He credited those instincts and skills as the things that had allowed him to survive when he'd seen so many others die in captivity around him—right down to the day he'd taken the life of his overseer and made his escape. A little over four decades had passed since that angry and desperate young man had fought to overpower a Golian twice his size and strength, and he'd dedicated his life to peace and compassion for others after committing that act, vowing never to kill again. Yet he could not—and would not—ever forget his past and that part of himself, or the fire within him that had never been fully extinguished. His dark hands curled into fists so tightly that the skin under his fingernails turned white from the pressure and he took a step toward the Initiate before he even realized what he was doing. "Angolé. N'ota. *Leave. Now.*"

Brother Owen had lapsed into his native Laenisian tongue, but Carlo did not need to understand the growled words to interpret their meaning, or the danger implied by the priest's body language. The Initiate's mask of impassivity cracked at last, and the teenager shrank back, stepping away from the doorway and out into the hallway. Fear and astonishment were quickly replaced by a defiant glare, however, as if to say that Father Lorimer would soon be hearing about this.

Owen didn't care. He took another threatening step toward the door before Carlo slammed it shut, and he could hear the Initiate's running footsteps receding quickly down the hall. He knew that Carlo wouldn't dare interrupt the mass, not with the archbishop and the king in attendance, so he still had some time, but not much. Owen remembered himself and took several quick breaths to calm down before turning to Flynn, who was staring at him with huge eyes.

"That was incredible," the boy said, unable to contain his excitement and admiration for the man. "I thought you were going to give him a thrashing for sure."

The priest was about to deliver a standard platitude about violence never solving anything when he silently admitted to himself that if that were really the case then he wouldn't be standing here today. He'd ask Janus for forgiveness for his sinful trespass later, but for now, he merely smiled and sat back down. "No, I just needed to scare him a little to remind him of his place, and it worked," he said, winking.

"Well, he still has the key so it's a good thing he was probably so worried about not crapping himself that he forgot to lock us in," Flynn laughed heartily.

"Oh, I'm not worried about that. They want me gone from here as soon as possible, so locking me in with you would not be conducive to accomplishing that."

At hearing this, Flynn's expression changed immediately, his grin melting into a frown. "Gone? What do you mean?"

"I'll explain in a moment, but first tell me how you've been. Have they mistreated you in any way? Done or said anything that you should tell me about?"

Flynn looked silently down at the table, tracing the outline of the wood grain with one fingernail of his left hand. Brother Owen was not surprised by the hesitation—the boy had surely been through a lot in the last three weeks—but he couldn't tell if the reluctance was borne out of shame or fear. "It's ok, Flynn. You know that I'm your friend and that you can tell me anything. Why don't you start with the hospital? What really happened that night?"

Flynn looked up apprehensively. "You know about that?"

"Yes, Father Lorimer told me everything."

At the mention of the headmaster's name, the boy paled visibly. "What did he tell you?"

"It doesn't matter. I want to hear the truth from you because I know that's what you'll give me." The cleric did consider Father Lorimer might have instructed Flynn to recount the same version of events that he'd given him a few days ago, but he weighed that against his firm belief that the boy wouldn't lie to him. It wasn't Flynn he was suspicious of; it was the headmaster.

For his part, Flynn became morose and upset at the request. "Do I really have to?"

"Yes, you do. This is very important, and we don't have much time, so please tell me," Brother Owen pleaded with sincerity, hoping that his growing urgency didn't alarm the boy and cause him to retreat further into his shell. He wasn't sure if Father Lorimer would risk appearing improper by excusing himself from the Yule celebration to come here, especially with the king present, but he didn't want to push his luck by overstaying the concession he'd been given. He had promised he'd be gone from the orphanage before mass was over and he intended to honour his word, thus he breathed an inner sigh of relief when Flynn began to speak.

"Oh, all right then," Flynn agreed. The boy took a deep breath and began his tale. "I don't really remember much, it was all so strange and happened so fast. It was late and I was in bed reading my book when the door opened—it was Carlo, Peter, and Dario. I told them to go away or I'd yell and get them in trouble, but they didn't care and said no one would hear me. They surrounded me on the bed and started to taunt me and call me names like 'cripple' and worse, said the gods had punished me for being a know-it-all and your pet. They said some awful things about you too," he hesitated, hoping the priest wouldn't ask him to repeat those slurs.

"It's alright, Flynn," he reassured him. "I've had to endure that sort of thing for most of my life. It's hurtful, yes, but I've learned to disregard it and silently forgive people for their ignorance and hatred of anything different than themselves. Go on, please."

"Well, I guess Peter was mad that I'd drawn the token of Gaurkur—he was in my group and blamed me for that because it meant we wouldn't be able to win. Why this would bother Carlo, I don't know, but I think it was just an excuse that he threw out for why they were there. He said he was going to teach me a lesson and break every bone in my hand, and that nobody would know because it was damaged already, and no one would believe me if I said it was them. Then Carlo told Peter and Dario to hold me down and he pulled out a hammer from under his robes. They grabbed both my arms, and I yelled for help but no one came. I kicked and struggled but their grip was too strong, and then Carlo put my book under my right hand and lifted the hammer up in the air. I panicked and yanked so hard that my wrist slipped out from Dario's grip. I guess his fingers got caught in the bandages and they came loose, and everyone paused in surprise, even me, because..." he stopped, staring at the table, lost in the memory he was recalling so vividly.

"Because what, Flynn?"

"Well, I thought my hand had been horribly burned and would be disfigured. I still remember that awful searing heat when I held the token in my hand, yet when I looked at it, my hand was whole. The skin was completely normal."

"Yes, that was to be expected," the priest explained. "I prayed to Janus for the miracle to heal the damage while you were still unconscious, and he granted my request," he smiled. He'd anticipated this, so he wasn't surprised by Flynn's revelation. It was what supposedly had happened next that he was most interested in hearing about.

Flynn mulled over Brother Owen's words. "Oh. Yes, you did tell me that, it's just... well, I thought you were only trying to make me feel better. I could see some of the burns when you came to see me and..." he paused again, unable to hide his embarrassment.

"And...?"

"I guess I didn't have faith." He looked downcast, his voice lowered to almost a whisper as he made the confession.

"Flynn, don't feel bad or blame yourself, you hear? You're just a child—a very intelligent and perceptive one—but still only a child. You know I would never lie to you, but faith is something that cannot be taught; it must be experienced. I think perhaps now you understand the truth of that, yes?" Flynn nodded and looked up shyly, but with a smile of clear relief. "Tell me what happened next."

The smile faded almost immediately, and Flynn's face became grim while he continued. "Peter recovered first and was enraged. He started hitting me in the face, but it only made me angrier and struggle even more. Carlo yelled at Dario to grab my right arm again but when he lunged for it, I swung at him and took hold of his wrist before he could grab mine. He, uh, he screamed in pain when I touched him. It was a horrible, agonizing sound like nothing I've heard before and we all froze again—except him. He thrashed around and tried to shake his arm loose but—it was so strange—I couldn't let go of him, even though I tried. It was like my hand was not my own anymore and was locked like a vise or something around his wrist. Then we all saw the skin on his hand and arm start to bubble and ooze with pus and turning grey and then black and I..." he stopped then, unable to continue. He closed his eyes to try and block out the horrible vision, but the memory had been indelibly imprinted in his mind and he knew he would relive the horror of that event for the rest of his days.

Brother Owen didn't say anything. He wanted to comfort the boy, but there was nothing he could say just then that would relieve Flynn of the guilt and fear he was feeling. Sometimes all that was needed was the silent presence of a sympathetic ear, and that he could do for him. Flynn's thin shoulders shook as he sobbed, and the priest reached out across the table to steady him with a comforting touch. While he did so, he tried to puzzle out in his mind what all of this could mean. The story matched what Father Lorimer had told him, but he still had his suspicions about the true extent of the headmaster's involvement in the actions of those boys that night. He didn't know why he felt that way, but he did, and his instincts had never led him astray before. That Lorimer was so intent on ridding himself of him only cemented his belief that the senior priest was up to something.

"Flynn," he said gently, "let me see your hand."

The sobbing stopped at once and the boy shrank back in fear from his touch, sliding the chair backward across the floor until it hit the wall behind him. His right arm was pressed to his side; the gloved hand tucked firmly under one leg. There was plain fear in his face now, and his lips were pressed into a grim line as he shook his head vehemently. "Father Lorimer told me to never take the glove off."

"Did he also tell you what became of Dario?" The response came in the form of a quick nod. "Then you know how important it is that you let me help you. Please, show me your hand."

"Brother Owen, please—I'm scared. What if the same thing happens to you?" Flynn pleaded, the tears returning to his eyes. "Father Lorimer said what I did was very bad, and I should be kept away from others for their safety. Is he right?"

Brother Owen sighed. "He's right to be concerned, yes, but he's wrong to punish you like this. Flynn, I want to help you, and I'm going to do everything I can to find out why this happened, but I must leave very soon, and I can't go without seeing your hand...please."

Flynn swallowed, his implicit trust in the priest warring with his fear of accidentally hurting him—or worse. The struggle was brief and, in the end, hope and belief in his friend won out. Not daring to come any closer, he carefully pulled his hand out from under him, slowly removed the black leather glove, and then held the appendage out in front of him so that Brother Owen could see. The hand and fingers looked perfectly normal, the skin whole and smooth, unmarred by any traces of scarring.

"Turn it and show me your palm."

Flynn felt the dismay coursing through him. He naively thought he'd outsmarted the priest, but he really ought to have known better. Slowly and with obvious reluctance, he turned his wrist so that the palm of his hand was facing Brother Owen. There, where he had grasped the token, was the circular outline of the disc, along with every clear detail of Gaurkur's skull-like visage seared into the soft flesh of the boy's hand like a gruesome tattoo. Other than the skin being slightly more pinkish in tone in that area, the mark looked as if it had always been there. Plain consternation creased Brother Owen's brows, and he involuntarily leaned slightly forward across the table to get a better look, prompting Flynn to withdraw his hand in fear. The priest remembered himself and drew back, lifting both of his own hands before him in silent apology.

"Thank you, Flynn. You can put your glove back on." He tried to smile reassuringly, though he wasn't sure which of the two of them he was trying to convince. "Do you remember anything else from that night? Anything you're leaving out?"

"No. After I grabbed Dario, something hit me in the head and the next thing I remember was waking up in this room and that's it, nothing else."

Owen nodded. "As I said, I'm going to try to get to the bottom of this if it's the last thing I do. I don't have an explanation for it right now, only a theory, but I'm going to a place where someone might know, which brings me to the other reason why I am leaving the orphanage." He took a deep breath in anticipation of the boy's reaction. "Flynn, I'm very sick, and I need help that I can't receive if I remain here."

Flynn had been listening as he put the glove back on his hand, but looked up in alarm the second his friend's words sunk in. "Sick?"

"Yes. I wasn't aware of it until I collapsed outside on the morning after you were brought here. I fell asleep while reading after I'd spoken to you at the hospital the day before, and when I woke up and found out you were gone the next day, I tried to look for you. I began to feel ill while searching and... well, no need for all the details, but Father Lorimer is convinced that I need to seek out the Anvalites for help with what is ailing me. As much as I've tried to tell myself otherwise, I think he's right and—"

"It's my fault, isn't it?" Flynn interrupted. "You have the same sickness as my mother and Brother Edward, don't you? *Don't you?*"

"Flynn, I—" before the priest could say anything further, the boy burst into tears and began to weep uncontrollably. Owen's own eyes teared up with pity for the child and he tried once more to find words that could comfort him, but anything he thought of immediately rang false to his own ears. All signs were pointing to Flynn's original theory being correct, however improbable it had all sounded at first, and anything he could try and say to the contrary now would never convince Flynn. Yet he had to try to at least instill some hope in the boy. "I can't be certain. None of us can—not even you. What you have to remember is that responsible or not, it is not a conscious act on your part and that makes all the difference in the eyes of Janus."

"What does that even mean?" Flynn asked between sobs.

"It means that these deaths are a consequence of something that is happening to you rather than something that you're doing on purpose to others. Don't you see? I know it seems like it's your fault, but it's not."

"Okay, but then what about Dario?" Flynn wailed, holding up his right hand. "I touched him, and he died! That's my fault and you can't say it's not."

"Did you know that was going to happen? Did you intend for him to die when all you tried to do was to stop him from hurting you? Of course not. Flynn, I'm not trying to minimize what happened—Dario is gone and that's a tragic thing for anyone to witness, let alone know that they were the cause of—but it was an accident; nothing more." He searched Flynn's eyes for any sign that he was getting through to him and what he saw there was a frightened boy that was desperately trying to find some reason and meaning to any of this. He was not alone. "We can't bring him back, but we can try to make sure it doesn't happen again. Listen to Father Lorimer, and do as he asks, but only if it seems right to you. I know you have good instincts and intuition—trust in them. I must go now, Flynn. I wish I didn't, but I must."

This caused another fresh wave of sobbing from the boy. As alone as he'd felt in the days since he'd been confined to this room, at least he'd been able to draw some comfort from the fact that Brother Owen was somewhere near at hand and would eventually come for him. To know now that his friend was leaving the orphanage, leaving him well and truly alone, nearly overwhelmed him with fear and despair. "Please don't leave..." Flynn's voice sounded as small and lost as he felt right then. "You don't look sick. Are you sure you have to go?"

Owen's heart was shattering inside his chest. He wanted nothing more than to clasp this unfortunate child close to him and stay here to protect him from whatever the future held, but he couldn't do so in his current condition. Before he could help Flynn, he needed to help himself. "I'm sorry. If there were any other way, you know I would find it. I may seem alright for now, but it will get worse—just like Brother Edward. Just like your mother. I will be back as soon as I can, and that's a vow I make to you, alright?"

Flynn sniffled and wiped his wet cheeks with his left hand, nodding forlornly in resigned acceptance. Maybe the priest wouldn't be gone so long. The Anvalites would fix him up and he would be back in no time, and maybe that hideous mark on his own hand would heal up and fade away completely and everything would go back to the way it was before. Yes, that's how it would be, he told himself. It had to, and his mind refused to consider any other outcome. He watched the priest get up, dreading the final goodbye that was to come. He got up as well but waited there, not knowing what to do. When Brother Owen stepped around the table and held his arms out, Flynn threw caution to the wind and ran into the man's warm embrace. He sobbed again while the priest ran one hand through his dark hair and whispered words of encouragement to him. Then the priest lowered himself so that his eyes were level with Flynn's while holding his shoulders at arm's length.

"Be brave, my boy, and never give in to despair. You're a lot tougher than you think." He looked intently into Flynn's blue eyes and this time he was rewarded by the glint of strength and determination that he saw there. "That's more like it," he said smiling. Then, he let go of him and reached into his robes to pull out Flynn's lost book, placing it on the table while Flynn stared at it with speechless joy. "To keep you company while I'm gone. Don't let Father Lorimer see it," he added with a wink. With that, he walked to the door and opened it to leave, but before he stepped out, he took one last look at the boy. "Goodbye for now, Flynn. We'll see each other again soon, I promise," and then he was gone.

"Goodbye," the whispered reply came, long after the door had shut, and the footsteps had echoed away.

CHAPTER 20

Vurax stared at the ground, trying to comprehend the enormity of what he'd just heard. Treeweaver had stopped the retelling of his tale a while ago, but the two of them simply sat in silence for some time afterward, both lost in private contemplation. The Golian was no stranger to personal tragedy and loss, but what the Elf had gone through—witnessing the destruction of his homeland and people—was beyond anything his mind could conceive of. Even seeing firsthand the aftermath of the legion fort's destruction three days ago paled in comparison with what it must've been like to watch the obliteration of Syldar unfold from inexplicable beginning to tragic end. As if that weren't bad enough, Treeweaver had had to watch the death of his own family, a painful experience that Vurax was intimately familiar with. It was a realization that made him feel a strong bond of kinship form between the two of them.

"I'm sorry for what happened," Vurax offered quietly, knowing how lame he sounded and that there were no words that could minimize the other's pain, but he felt a duty to try anyway. "Thank you for telling me your story. I know I pushed you into it, but if I'd had any idea—" he stopped speaking when Treeweaver put up a hand and shook his head.

"No," the Elf said, "do not apologize. You needed to know what happened, even if I felt that it was too personal of a thing to share with a stranger at first. We Syldar do not easily share our grief, but I think we are both past that. Hopefully now you can begin to understand that something is happening that transcends you and me, or Gol and Syldar. I never did tell you precisely how I came to be where I was when we first met, did I?"

The Minotaur remained silent and waited expectantly. He had indeed asked Treeweaver that question more than once in the past, but the Elf had never given him a more detailed explanation other than to say he was on the trail of a god.

"The day after the battle, I decided to fly back to our former home to try and ascertain what the Titan's purpose was following the destruction of the Oakhearth and the deaths of my mother and grandmother. We knew it would be a dangerous prospect, but I simply had to know whether the giants would turn south and pursue our people. Thankfully—and puzzlingly—they did not. In fact, by the time we spotted him, the Titan had already turned northwest in the direction of Gol. All the giants with him dispersed while traversing the Wedge, but he continued toward the Barrier Peaks with singular determination. Knowing that the refugees were safe, at least for now, I decided to investigate what purpose drove this creature. For all the destruction and grief he had wrought, I was desperate to at least find some meaning in what had happened. I don't believe it was coincidence that brought us both to that mountain path," he paused, allowing the words to sink in. "After what I witnessed at the legion fort, perhaps it's becoming clearer why I've drawn some of those startling conclusions you alluded to earlier."

Vurax nodded his assent but decided to change the subject a little, not willing yet to tackle the complex implications of the Elf's statement. "So, your sister leads what's left of your people now?" the Minotaur asked. "Why are *you* not king?"

Treeweaver smiled wistfully at the question. "Since the days of the Sundering and Syld's discovery of the land we would one day call home, the Syldar have always been a matriarchal society. We've never had a 'king', and we never will, for no one is better suited to the role of leadership than those with the ability to bring life forth into this world. Ultimately, it is often only nëler—those you call 'women'—that possess and display the wisdom necessary to nurture and guide their children in peace and love. We ëler are too quick to turn to anger and war to resolve our differences, sadly."

The Golian stared at the Elf wide-eyed, wondering if perhaps the Syldar had received a head injury recently. He held back a snort of derision out of newfound respect for Treeweaver, but the Elf was more than perceptive enough to see the Minotaur was struggling with the concept of what he'd just said.

"I understand your reaction and I'm not offended," Treeweaver continued, still smiling. "This is a hard notion for a Golian—and many other cultures for that matter—to accept, but it's been our way for thousands of years. Among the Syldar, ëler and nëler are considered equals in all other aspects of life except when it comes to who governs them."

"A female emperor..." Vurax mused. "Now there's a thought sure to drive the entire senate into a state of apoplexy. Speaking of which, if you expect any help from them, I suggest you keep your revolutionary philosophies to yourself."

Treeweaver couldn't help but chuckle a little at the well-intentioned advice. "Revolutionary? You do know the Syldar have walked this world long before the first Minotaur ever learned how to speak, right? I think we've had sufficient time to have figured a few things out," he offered with a mischievous wink.

"Yes," Vurax conceded, "but you must admit our skulls are much thicker than yours. Different ways of doing things come slowly, if ever, to my people."

Treeweaver laughed again. The levity felt good after the grim events of the past few weeks, and for a brief time he felt the shadow lift from his heart. It was a fleeting moment that helped to elevate his battered spirit, but like all else, it passed and then it was gone, leaving a bittersweet aftertaste in him. His expression became sad and introspective for a minute but then he shook himself out of it and looked up at the sky with a frown. "The sun will set in another two hours or so. We've only flown at night to avoid being easily spotted from the ground, and when it gets dark, we'll go up again. We'll look for a dense stretch of woods not too far away from Vurgas and conceal the gryphons there. Windstrider and I will remain with them while you get help from one of the nearby farmsteads and take your friend into the city before it's too late. You did say there are lots of farms around these parts where you were born?"

The Minotaur nodded. "What's your plan after that?" he asked, not wanting to think about the prospect of flying again just yet.

"I need to reach the capital and gain an audience with your emperor. I've sent the others to check on our people's progress and tell them of my intention, but if all is well, my sister will soon be leaving Syldar lands with the refugees. I'm sure you can appreciate that the sight of thousands of Elves suddenly massing on your border will not be a welcome sight for Gol. I need to not only warn your leader of what has led us to this desperate act but also ask permission for passage."

"Passage?" the Golian wondered aloud. "Passage to where?"

"To the sea, of course. Where else can we go?" Treeweaver shrugged as if the answer should be obvious. "North are the steppes of Sarmakan and beyond that, the Demorran badlands. To the east lies nothing but the empty and trackless wastes of the Avanar desert, and west is your empire. Therefore, our only hope is to go south to the sea. We've long known of lush, uninhabited islands in Malka Bay, and we hope to reach them with the aid of our sea-dwelling kin, the Nuamekar. Perhaps there we will have a chance to rest, regroup, and think on what to do next, but first we must cross part of your country without starting a war."

Even as a Golian growing up in relative isolation, Vurax was still somewhat aware that diplomacy was not his people's strongest suit. Throughout Gol's violent past, many had tried to sue for peace with the aggressive Minotaurs. Today, nothing remained of the Tharkan, Dal, and Salanite peoples except for a handful of windswept ruins and geographical features that still bore their ancient names. Only the Urians and Syldar had been able to check the Golian advance to where it was today. "You still want me to come with you?" the Minotaur asked, going back to an earlier discussion. He was circling around to asking some questions he didn't want to but could no longer ignore.

"Yes," Treeweaver affirmed. "I think you realize by now that there's something different about you."

"You mean like...?" Vurax didn't want to finish the question.

"My mother? Yes, I think so."

Vurax felt the world spin again and was grateful for the fact that he was sitting down. It took him a second to shake off the vertigo before he looked at the Elf again. "How is this possible? Why me?"

"I don't know, Vurax." Treeweaver sounded genuinely regretful. "Who can fathom the mind of a god? Just as Erliandol chose Princess Caralia, and Jokunki-vaard chose that Titan, it seems that Zarvon has chosen you."

There it was.

The Elf watched the Golian carefully. When his mother had come to this same conclusion months ago, it had nearly destroyed her then, and not even the wisest among the Syldar elders could understand what this portended. How could a mere mortal possibly comprehend what this incredible burden of responsibility meant, or what was required of her? Once past the inevitable denial, Caralia's attempts to make sense of the power within her had come close to driving her mad. It was only her own mother's calming presence and loving guidance that had brought her back from the brink—that, and the arrival of the Titan. With a clear purpose before her, she had found the strength to do what was needed, even if it cost her life in the end. Was it Vurax's destiny to die as she had, defending her people from a seemingly unstoppable threat? Treeweaver didn't know of course, but he was certain that after telling Vurax his story, that very same thought would be going through the Golian's head right about now—which is why his eyes widened in surprise when the Minotaur suddenly threw his head back and laughed wildly.

"You think I'm going to end up a martyr, don't you?" Vurax said between chuckles.

Treeweaver's face deepened into a frown. "I don't know what to think, and I'd like to say that it's ultimately up to you, but that would probably be a lie as my mother didn't seem to have much of a choice when it came down to it."

"Right," was all the Minotaur could say as he continued to laugh.

The Elf's expression grew darker. "I'm glad you think this is funny while thousands of my people are dead and many thousands more are homeless. We are facing a dire crisis here that affects more than just the Syldar, but perhaps you don't see that. Perhaps Zarvon made a mistake in choosing you."

Vurax stopped laughing with a snort and gave the Elf a sharp look. "Oh, you can be most certain he did, considering I don't even believe he's real," he said, getting up and walking off. "I'm sorry this happened to your folk, but it's not my problem."

Treeweaver bit back an angry retort and watched him go. He tried to temper his irritation by telling himself that he likely wouldn't feel much differently had their positions been reversed. Unlike the Golian, he was a firm believer in the existence of the gods, but he also believed in one's own ability to chart their own fate. To him, Erliandol, the Father of all Elves, was a pillar of spiritual strength and faith, not the master of his destiny. After witnessing what happened to his mother, however, he could no longer be sure where the truth lay. He had a sneaking suspicion that sooner or later, Zarvon would make his will known. What Vurax decided to do with that knowledge when it came, he couldn't say, but he hoped the stubborn Minotaur would survive the choice he would inevitably have to make.

<hr>

Vurax shifted his position on the gryphon's broad back for the hundredth time. Each time he did so, he elicited a glare from Treeweaver, to whose waist he clung with his one good arm and visible apprehension. The movements had little to do with physical discomfort and everything with unabashed fear. The Golian could accept that he'd travelled in this fashion once already—being unconscious then had definitely been a good thing. However, flying for the second time—and now fully aware of the great distance between himself and the ground—Vurax couldn't quite believe he'd allowed himself to be talked into this. People just weren't meant to fly, he kept repeating under his breath, and he now had a new experience to add to the very short list of things that truly terrified him.

"Will you stop that already?" the Syldar Elf sounded exasperated as he yelled back so that he could be heard over the dual sounds of rushing air and powerful wings that rose and fell steadily. "The more you move, the more you increase your chances of falling. Just breathe and close your eyes if you must. We're almost there."

The Minotaur had been told the same thing a few times now, but true to form, he was too stubborn to listen. If he was to meet death tonight, he was determined to do it with his eyes open. A flash of movement off to their right caught his attention and he risked a glance. His neck and shoulders screamed with pain and stiffness due to being locked rigidly in the same position, the tension and anxiety having gripped his body when he'd climbed onto the beast's back an hour ago. The dubious wisdom of the entire endeavour was made worse as soon as he realized that there was no saddle or harness of any kind. When Treeweaver had explained that the gryphons did not tolerate such restraints, Vurax had asserted that was all the more reason to not fly on the back of one. Unsurprisingly, the argument had fallen on unsympathetic ears. Straining to see across the darkness and distance, he could barely make out Windstrider mounted on the second gryphon. The Elf sat behind Kael's unconscious form, keeping hold of the Minotaur with his arms while his knees and heels maintained an expert grip on the gryphon's flanks. Despite the centurion's critical condition, Vurax couldn't help but feel envy that his friend was completely oblivious as to how he was being transported.

"How can you be sure where we're going? I can't see a thing down there," Vurax inquired dubiously, eyes tearing up from the wind as he looked forward again, trying to see past Treeweaver's head.

"Very simple," the Elf responded, pointing somewhere ahead.

It took several moments to discern what Treeweaver was referring to, but then he spotted the large number of pinpoints of light revealing the location of the city hiding among the blanket of darkness that was the ground below. On most nights, the landscape would be dimly lit by Temeros' ruddy glow, but tonight the large moon was hidden from sight by a thick cover of clouds, which was exactly what Treeweaver had counted on.

"There, that looks good," he said, giving the gryphon the signal to bank left and downward. Vurax's eyes couldn't compete with the Elf's far sharper vision so he couldn't see the forest that must be coming up below, but he did manage to catch a glimpse of the other gryphon descending as well. All he could think about was that the feeling of the ground beneath his feet again couldn't come soon enough. The landing was surprisingly smooth, the gryphons gliding silently down to alight upon the grassy field with only a slight jolt when their large leonine paws contacted the solid surface. Despite his earlier assertion to not do so, Vurax had closed his eyes on the way down and only opened them when he finally felt Treeweaver climb down from the gryphon's back.

From ground level, the lights of Vurgas were less obvious as most were hidden behind the high city walls, but its presence a good distance away to their right was still unmistakable. To their left, the dark presence of a forest loomed silently, and between the city and the woods, there lay a long stretch of farm fields, crisscrossed with fences and hedgerows, and dotted with farmhouses and barns. Vurax jumped down and promptly dropped to his hands and knees in an overly dramatic show of gratitude for having survived this ordeal. Treeweaver shook his head at the display, then walked over to help Windstrider carefully lower Kael to the ground. The two Elves checked on the centurion's condition and exchanged a grim look.

"When you're done cutting such a ridiculous figure, you need to start thinking about getting your friend inside those walls. I'm afraid he's nearly done for," Treeweaver warned.

Ignoring the slight, Vurax stood up immediately and hurried over to where the two Elves stood over the other Golian's prone form, grim concern evident on his face. "Can't you give him more of those herbs or whatever they are?"

"The more we give him, the less effective they become, and he's already been given more than we should have. Despite our efforts, the infection has taken root, and he will soon wake up. When that happens..." Treeweaver didn't elaborate further, but Vurax took his meaning well enough. "We'll wait for you out of sight beyond the treeline while you do what needs to be done."

The Minotaur urgently scanned his surroundings and spotted the nearest cottage, already calculating the time it would take him to walk there. It was still fairly early in the evening, and he could see a light flickering in one of the house's windows. Good, he thought; this would be much easier if the farmer was still awake and not startled out of his sleep by a sudden stranger at the door in the dark.

"You'd best get yourselves and those things out of here then," he dipped one of his horns in the direction of the two gryphons. "How long are you going to stay in those woods? What if I don't come back?"

"We'll wait two days, no longer. As I told you when we first met, I think your words can lend great weight to my plea. I grant it is unlikely your leaders will listen to me, but it might be different if one of their own tells them the truth of what we've seen," Treeweaver responded. "I can't force you to come to Golan, but I'm asking you to please consider it. More than we know may depend on this".

Vurax mulled over the Elf's words, feeling uncomfortable with the sudden pressure of making such an important decision. Saving Kael's life was weighing heavily on his mind now, and he didn't want to think about things he could barely understand, much less entertain the thought of himself, a former slave, standing before the emperor and relating a fantastic story that felt more like a dream than reality at times. His survival instinct screamed at him to bid farewell to this Elf and be on his way; his stubbornness and honour demanded otherwise. He knew he was going to regret this somehow, but he owed Treeweaver a life debt, and he would never renege on that.

"Alright, damnit!" he swore. "I think we're both fools, but I won't turn my back on you now." He was about to depart when he suddenly remembered something. Years of living away from civilization took a toll on one's memory of things once taken for granted. "I'm going to need some coin, and I doubt my people will accept whatever it is you Elves use for currency."

Without hesitation, Treeweaver reached into a pouch at his belt and pulled out several coins, passing them over to the Minotaur. Vurax looked at the silver and gold pieces, noting their octagonal shape and the bull's head stamped on one side of every coin. His brows arched in surprise.

"These are Golian coins," he noted, giving the other a dubious look. "Corpse looting, Treeweaver? And here I thought you Elves were above such things."

The Syldar laughed. "I really don't know where you get your notions about us, but if you'd prefer that I hadn't taken those from the dead legionnaires we came across and didn't have them to give to you now..." he shrugged.

Vurax had to admit that the practicality of what the Elf was saying made complete sense. His fingers closed over the coins, and he put them away with a snort and a smirk. "Two days, then."

The Elf nodded and proffered his hand to the Golian. The two of them clasped each other's forearms firmly and shook once. Without any further words, Vurax turned into the night and began walking at a brisk pace toward the farmhouse in the distance.

—◆—

The grizzled Golian looked up from his bowl of warm chicken, carrot, potato, and pea stew to stare at the door of his cottage. He thought he'd only imagined the first knock, but when the second, more insistent thud made itself heard, he sighed in exasperation at this unwanted interruption of his quiet dinner. Larios lived alone in his home—his wife had passed some years ago, and his three sons were all grown and had moved away. He had neighbours, of course, but none would ever be out at this hour unless something was very wrong. The farmer considered not answering the door, solitude and quiet being two things he treasured highly at this stage of his venerable life. He quite liked that his farmstead was as far away from the city as possible while remaining close enough that he could still make the trek to the market once a week to sell some of his vegetables and buy what he needed.

Maybe if he doused the lamp they would go away, he pondered briefly, but when the knock came for the third time, Larios resolved to get up. Even bent with advanced age, the old Minotaur still cut an imposing figure, broad frame and muscles hardened from years of toiling in the fields. He straightened his stiff back with a wince caused by ever-bothersome arthritis, sighed once more, and walked over to the door to open it, but not before grabbing hold of the stout wooden cane that leaned against one wall. The Minotaur that stood outside on his doorstep had one fist raised to knock again but stopped himself just in time when he saw grey-haired Larios suddenly standing there with a sour look of annoyance on his face.

"I'm sorry to disturb you at this hour, old one, but I urgently need your help," the stranger said, getting straight to the point.

Larios gave the other Minotaur an appraising look, noting the style and design of his breastplate and the haft of the axe protruding over one shoulder. His eyes moved to the splinted arm and the multiple scars that crisscrossed the younger Golian's brown hair. "You're in the service?"

Vurax hadn't had much time to come up with a story, and lying was not something he was comfortable with, but the truth being an overly complicated matter just then, he decided it would be best to stretch the facts a little.

"Yes, I serve in the Eighth Legion. My centurion is not far from here, but he's gravely wounded. I need to get him inside the city walls before it's too late, but as you can see for yourself, I'm unable to carry him there," he explained, holding up his immobilized arm and hoping the old bull wouldn't ask too many questions.

Larios puffed his chest out slightly with pride and closed one fist over his heart in a soldier's salute. "Queren Larios, principales of the Tenth Legion—retired of course. My two youngest are in the Tenth as well."

Vurax returned the gesture and inclined his head forward, dipping his horns in deference to the old veteran while simultaneously fighting to hide the dismay that flashed in his eyes. The shocking fate of one of the Tenth's cohorts stationed at the mountain fort was still very fresh in his memory, and he hoped fervently for this old-timer's sake that his two sons had not been posted there when the massacre happened. When the farmer didn't say anything further, Vurax surmised that news of the attack must not have reached the city yet, which made sense given how recent it was.

"Vurax, munifex legionnaire," he said by way of introduction and giving himself the lowest rank possible within the legion.

"You said you're with the Eighth? They passed through here three months ago out of Talban and headed up north on some campaign or other. Took them an entire day to march through, damn impressive sight they were. But of course, you know all that since you were with them," Larios smiled longingly with a faraway look, visibly relaxing his grip on the cane he was holding. "So, what happened?"

"Our cohorts are still up in Sarmakan, but my small detachment was returning to Gol with some wounded when we were ambushed in the mountains by giants. Only the centurion and I survived, though he was badly hurt, and our horses finally collapsed of exhaustion just short of the city." It was a gross oversimplification of what had truly occurred, but it would have to do. He only hoped it would be sufficient as he would have to repeat the lie several more times once he entered Vurgas. "Do you have a cart and animal I can use to transport him with? You have my word I will return them both before the sun sets again."

"I do, but it's very late and I've already put the oxen in the barn for the night. I suppose I'll have to go and wake up Tobus, but I just know he's going to be cranky and difficult at this hour. Come to think of it, he's like that all the time," Larios rolled his eyes.

Vurax cringed inwardly but asked the question anyway. "Is Tobus a slave?" Just the act of speaking that very word left a bad taste in his mouth.

Larios' expression instantly turned sour again. "I don't keep slaves. Never have and never will. Everything I have has come from the work of these two hands, and that's just how it should be, you hear me?" he snarled in challenge, holding up two heavily callused hands. With those words, Vurax's estimation of Larios as an individual went up immeasurably. Still, he knew it wasn't exactly a popular view to hold in Gol, so he suppressed a grin and merely held up his own hand in a placating gesture and nodded in acknowledgment. Turning with a satisfied grunt, Larios grabbed a cloak from a hook near the door to ward off the night's chill and gave one last wistful glance at his bowl of stew before closing the door.

Tobus, as it turned out, was a rather decrepit-looking mule that eyed the two Golians approaching its pen with a suspicious eye. When Vurax saw the old animal, he gave Larios a questioning look, prompting the old Golian to grumble something about needing his oxen to be well-rested for the coming morning's work. Larios managed to coax the reluctant mule through the small gate with a few soft words of encouragement and the three of them walked toward the large barn. Once inside, the farmer harnessed Tobus to a two-wheeled cart, climbed aboard, and let Vurax lead them out onto the field where Kael lay. Vurax looked around furtively, relieved to see that there were no signs that less than an hour ago, two Elves and two gryphons had stood in that same spot. Having witnessed how invisible Treeweaver and his people could become when necessary, it really didn't come as a surprise. Kael's condition appeared unchanged, thankfully; he was alive but unconscious, and with some effort, the two of them managed to lift the centurion from the ground, placed him in the back of the cart, and began the trek to the city gates.

"Where did you say you were from again?" Larios asked casually, walking alongside Vurax while Tobus and the cart followed behind.

"I didn't," was the only reply. Several minutes passed as they continued on their way, and though Vurax kept his attention on the ground ahead, he could feel the other's eyes on him, waiting. "Talban," he said eventually. It seemed like as good a place as any.

"Is that right?" Larios mused. Vurax was lost in his own thoughts, so he didn't immediately notice that the steady sound of the mule's steps and the creaking of the cart's wheels had stopped. He turned to look back, staring at Larios in puzzlement.

"Something wrong?"

"You tell me." The farmer narrowed his eyes as he stared at the younger Minotaur.

"I don't understand. What—"

"You've been lying to me ever since I opened my door," Larios stated. "Oh, not about your friend—I can see well enough that he's dying—but about who you are. So, this is your one chance to retain my goodwill. What's really going on here?"

Vurax fought to suppress his irritation at this delay. "I told you. My name is Vurax, and I'm a legionnaire in the Eighth—"

"Horseshit!" Larios unceremoniously cut him off and took two steps to close the gap between them to stand in front of Vurax. "I may be old, but my eyes are still sharp. I recognize the rune markings on your horn rings. They're identical to the ones worn by my sons, and they were made by a well-known goldsmith in Vurgas—same as my own, in fact. You're not from Talban; you're from around here, and you can't be in the Eighth because they only recruit from the river lands between Lake Dal and the Northwood. So, are you even a soldier, or is that a lie too?"

Vurax cursed inwardly. In his haste to concoct a story, he'd somehow forgotten that Golian horn rings contained not only family markings but also denoted one's birthplace. He'd been away from Gol too long to have such details be fresh in his memory, and the concern over saving Kael's life was making him careless. "I was transferred to Talban after my draft," he tried to deflect, remembering Kael mentioning his own transfer from the Fourth to the Eighth.

"Another lie, so try again. You said you are a munifex, but you can't get a transfer until you attain the rank of hastaii. For someone who claims to be a legionnaire, you seem to lack even the most basic knowledge about how the legion functions," Larios accused, crossing his arms. "This is your final chance to tell me the truth."

Vurax bristled visibly at the other's tone of voice. He'd been patient so far, but precious time was being wasted because of this stubborn old farmer. "Or what?" he growled menacingly, taking a step forward.

Unimpressed, Larios stood his ground and shook his head in disappointment. "That's your answer? To threaten an elder with violence and bring dishonour down on your father's house in this shameful fashion? I thought he'd raised a better son than the lying, impetuous fool I see before me now."

Vurax stopped cold in his tracks, his body quivering with mounting rage at the insult. "What are you insinuating, old one? What do you know of my father or my house?"

"I told you I recognized the runes on your rings. Those scars you bear are whip marks, and you don't get those serving in the legion." Larios narrowed his eyes while he pressed. "There was a small village on the north side of the forest east of here that was destroyed by raiders almost twenty years ago. Just far enough away from the city that help couldn't arrive in time. Some were killed, but most were taken. The village blacksmith—Zerik Baurus, his wife, and two boys—were among the missing. One of them was named Vurax, as I recall; headstrong, but a hardworking lad. You see, Baurus was not just an honourable, honest bull—he was also my good friend."

Vurax felt the anger drain instantly from him when he heard the name of Zerik. The family name he'd not uttered or allowed himself to think of since the day they'd been captured and forced to endure that violation of basic dignity that was the institution of slavery. Shame overwhelmed him then—shame and self-loathing. His stare had never left Larios, and for a split second he saw himself through the other's eyes and felt nothing but disgust at himself for his failure on that fateful day. He closed his eyes, and the memories came flooding back, repressed for years, but never buried down far enough that they didn't continue to haunt him forever.

The world was a distorted reality, crimson-filled with overwhelming wrath, soaked in blood, and choked with primal rage. Bodies and severed limbs lay strewn everywhere, separated by the wickedly sharp blade of the long scythe gripped tightly in his hands, the farming tool designed to harvest wheat now become a lethal, reaping instrument of death.

'Accept me,' the strange voice had said, not so much a request as it had been a demand. Watching his family get dragged away in bonds, blades at their throats, the choice had been no choice at all. Without a second thought, he dove headlong into the bottomless well of fury inside of him and surrendered himself completely to the unstoppable force he found there waiting with open arms.

He stepped over the brutalized body of the human raider he'd just killed, murder plain in his red eyes, teeth bared in a savage grin. Ahead of him, the main group of slavers was even now attempting to load the last of the villagers into their fast but sturdy chariots, ready to disappear into the wilderness and flee north before the Golians could mount a response to the raid. The faraway part of his awareness that was still Vurax recognized the faces of Zerik Baurus, Varina, and Aros among the prisoners. His father caught sight of him then, but the look that he gave his son was not one of hope and relief, but naked horror instead. Vurax stopped his advance, puzzlement and doubt wrestling with his desperate need to slake his unending bloodthirst. Baurus was looking past him now, and Vurax looked around momentarily, his red-tinged vision focusing long enough to allow him to see the Golian bodies grotesquely mingled with those of the Sarmakanites in some gruesome orgy of slaughter and carnage. Had he done that? Impossible. It had been the Sarmakanites. Yes, it had to have been them. He had only killed to save his people—his family! Yet, the doubt took hold and froze him in place now.

'It was necessary,' he heard the voice again. 'Sacrifices must be made. Now, kill them. Kill them all.'

This wasn't right. It couldn't be. He fought against the compulsion until the strain of this internal battle of wills became too painful to bear. He threw his head back and howled his rage at the heavens. Someone was shouting at him. Through the blood pounding in his ears, he could just barely make out the frantic, fearful words.

"Drop the weapon! Take another step and we'll slit their throats!"

Eyes flashing with vermilion fury, the threat had the exact opposite intended effect, almost causing him to lose the small shred of control he had managed to attain. How dare they? He did drop the scythe, but only to curl his fingers into claws in the same motion. He lowered his horned head in preparation for a devastating charge against his family's tormentors, ready to tear them apart with his bare hands. The last thing he saw was his brother Aros' look of pride and acceptance as he prepared himself to die, the blade tip under his neck drawing a bead of blood from the pressure against his skin.

He wants this, Vurax realized belatedly, seeing that same look mirrored in the eyes of his parents. His family would rather die than be taken away in chains. And for himself? A life lived with the crushing guilt of knowing he had been responsible for the deaths of those he loved. Would he have the courage to end his own life and spare himself eternal misery and despair? No. He knew the thing inside of him wouldn't let him take that path. This was what it wanted, therefore defying its design here and now was the only way that he saw forward. The rage ebbed from his body like a tide receding to the sea. Muscles lost their unnaturally fueled strength, and he slumped forward, collapsing to the ground in sudden exhaustion. He felt hands take hold of him, cold iron manacles snapping around his wrists and ankles. He closed his eyes and heard the scornful laugh of derision echoing in the dark recesses of his mind, but it didn't come from his captors. It came from inside of him.

'Coward.'

"Vurax, wake up!" the faraway-sounding voice called. There was an odd ringing in his ears and a feeling of nausea in the pit of his stomach. He opened his eyes and found himself staring at the night sky, only realizing then that he was lying on the ground. Larios' face focused into view after he blinked several times, the older Golian looking visibly concerned.

"Wha... what happened?" Vurax managed to stammer.

Larios bent down slowly, mindful of his back, and helped Vurax sit up. "One moment you were standing in front of me, and the next your eyes rolled up in your head and you collapsed to the ground, senseless. Are you alright?"

"Yes," he lied, allowing Larios to steady him as he rose to his feet. Physically, he felt fine, the last vestiges of disorientation and dizziness fading quickly. His pride, however, had suffered a tremendous blow. Golians—males in particular—generally took a dim view of any form of weakness in an individual, be it real or perceived, and their measure of one another was typically based on the strength, toughness, and confidence projected by said individual. When he'd passed out in Treeweaver's presence while they were scouting the fort, Vurax hadn't been proud of his weakness then either, but the other being an Elf and not a Minotaur, he felt some relief that he wouldn't be judged by his own people's harsh standards. But here he was now, not only fainting in front of another Golian, but one that apparently knew his family and who he was.

Vurax paused to allow that thought to sink in. The odds that the first Minotaur that he encountered upon returning to his people after an eighteen-year absence would be someone who would recognize him was something that defied his ability to dismiss as mere coincidence. When viewed in that light, it was becoming increasingly difficult to ignore Treeweaver's belief that some greater purpose was at work here. All he could do was add that to the growing list of things that he was having trouble accepting. For now, he had more pressing concerns, such as getting his dying friend inside the city before all of his efforts came to naught.

"Listen," he said, trying a new approach, "I understand I'm asking much and giving little in return. I'm sorry for not being straight with you from the beginning and for losing my temper, but I can't afford the time or distraction of explaining everything to you right now." He swallowed hard, overcoming his reluctance to depend on others any more than necessary, but he realized with no small amount of shame that that's all he'd been doing since he'd regained his freedom. "If you were indeed my father's friend, then I ask you to please honour my request."

Larios listened to the plea in silence, his eyes narrowing shrewdly while he eyed the younger Golian. "Do you know who your father *really* is?"

Vurax gave the older bull a puzzled look, clearly taken aback by the odd question. "Was—he's been dead for a decade—but in life he was a smith, as you said, and a respected member of our village; nothing more, nothing less. Why do you ask?"

"I think we need to have a long conversation after we've seen to your friend. You asked for my trust, now I ask you for yours—if you want to avoid unnecessary questions in the city, I'd recommend shrouding your horn rings," Larios said pointedly.

Vurax waited for a further explanation, but the other's demeanour told him the subject would have to wait for now. He considered the horn rings, realizing he'd forgotten about them again, and Larios' reminder was forcing him to appreciate just how valuable the other's aid had become. In Golian society, it was customary for an individual to shroud his or her horn rings under two specific sets of circumstances: black for mourning, or red for dishonour. As each member of his family had perished in captivity one by one, Vurax had never bothered to observe the custom. He hadn't been in Gol then, and traditions had become irrelevant in the face of reality; but he was most certainly in Gol now, and so he had to adjust his way of thinking accordingly. Directing a meaningful gaze to the black fabric of Larios' cloak, Vurax shrugged apologetically. The old veteran snorted in resignation, then proceeded to tear off two lengths of cloth from the garment's inner lining and handed them to Vurax. He looked on while the other tied the black strips around his horn rings, effectively covering them up.

"That was my favourite cloak," Larios muttered despondently before they set off again.

"Your suggestion, old-timer," Vurax retorted.

<hr>

As Golian cities were measured, Vurgas was not as sprawling or as affluent as those nearer to the imperial capital in the far south, but in its role of administrative seat for Gol's northernmost province, it did enjoy the distinction of serving as the empire's most populous centre in the north. It also served as the headquarters of the seasoned Tenth Legion and was responsible for nearly half of the realm's entire agricultural output, second only to the Heartlands. Its beginnings shrouded in the distant past, the strongly fortified Golian walls and buildings were erected over the ruins of a much older human settlement—just one of several in this remote region that had been inevitably ground beneath the relentless heel of Minotaur expansion centuries ago. Over the subsequent years, however, the conquered site and surrounding countryside had quickly risen in prominence and size from a small frontier town to what its residents today proudly called the 'Jewel of the North', a label that elicited no small amount of condescension and amusement from the more cultured southerners.

Looking up at the impressive main city gates, with its gatehouse towers constructed in the traditional Golian fashion to look like a pair of curving horns, Vurax felt a strange mix of emotions. Between the small farming community where he'd been born and this city, it was the closest to anything that he'd ever called home. During his long years in Sarmakan, there were many nights when he'd lain awake, staring at the stars, and trying to never let the memory of these places fade permanently. Yet, after longing hard for this moment for so many years, he found nothing but a peculiar feeling of emptiness inside of him. The experience certainly felt surreal, but it couldn't be further from the homecoming he'd always envisioned. He didn't know what to make of this unexpected disappointment, but there was little time to dwell on a past life that would never return. Nodding once to Larios to signal that he was ready, the two of them proceeded to guide the cart toward the wicket door that stood open within one of the large gates.

"Let me do the talking," Larios had said, and Vurax was only too happy to comply.

Fortune smiled upon them that night when one of the two guards recognized Larios and quickly assented to opening the main gate so that the cart could pass through. After performing a cursory inspection of the cart's contents, they barely spared Vurax a glance as they saluted and waved the pair of them through. From there, the two continued for a time down the main street that led to the heart of the city's commercial district, thankfully empty at this late hour. Veering left after reaching the large central plaza, they found themselves on another street, this one ending after a short distance at a massive, squat building with several horn-like towers like the ones at the city gates, over which stood an immense golden statue of a Minotaur with one fist raised to the sky—the temple of Zarvon. Approaching the church's carved wooden doors, Vurax eyed the opulent depiction of the Golian god looming overhead with a mixture of apprehension and disdain. On the way to the city, he had argued vehemently for taking Kael to the legion headquarters for help, but Larios had advised against that course of action and convinced him to bring the wounded centurion to the temple instead. The legion's healers would almost certainly be located within their fortified encampment a considerable distance to the south of the city, and help could be gained much faster by going to the priests of Zarvon in the city proper. Vurax didn't like this one bit, as every second he delayed brought his friend one step closer to death, but he bit his tongue and accepted the older bull's advice.

While Vurax waited with Tobus and the cart some distance away, Larios climbed the broad stone steps and pounded on the thick doors, setting off a small chorus of barking dogs from a nearby darkened alleyway. There was a brief pause before one of the doors opened slowly to reveal a thin-looking, balding man of advanced years, wearing a red-coloured toga and holding an oil lamp in one hand. Raising the flickering light to peer suspiciously at the Golian before him, the human and Minotaur greeted one another, speaking in low tones. From this distance, he couldn't hear what was being said, but Vurax began to grow impatient when the exchange seemed to drag on forever, with Larios growing more animated even as the old man remained cool and impassive throughout. Finally, the slave disappeared back inside and Larios rejoined Vurax at the bottom of the steps. As they began to gingerly unload Kael from the cart, Vurax supported his friend with his uninjured shoulder while Larios took the other side.

"What was that about?" he asked, unable to contain his curiosity any longer.

"Just a stubborn old fool who's grown a little too comfortable and self-important in his role as the temple's door warden," Larios snorted. "He wasn't inclined to disturb any of the priests at this hour, but I changed his mind when I reminded him that he'd be the one explaining to them why there's a Golian soldier's corpse on their doorstep come morning."

Vurax wanted to chuckle at that, but a glance at Kael's condition served to remind him that Larios wasn't joking. He was no healer, but he'd seen plenty of death in his time. The centurion would not live to see another sunrise. Carrying the unconscious soldier through the doorway, they were met by the door warden once more. Following the man's shuffling steps and the bobbing light of his lamp, they were guided down a long hall and past several closed doors, turning into a side chamber just before the open doors to the temple's shadowed central nave. A thick smell of incense lingered in the air throughout the building's interior, and a light haze of smoke hovered near the ceiling, making Vurax feel light-headed and drowsy. He didn't recall Kael being this heavy, and he was relieved when the old man directed them to place the centurion on a long stone table in the centre of the room. In the well-lit surroundings, the door warden gave them one last disapproving look, wrinkled his nose as if he'd smelled something unpleasant, and left without a word.

Larios ignored the departing human and glanced about the chamber's sparse furnishings, noting the braziers in each corner that were filled not with burning coals, but stones that glowed brightly with a yellow light of indeterminate origin. Another long table stood against one wall, its surface covered with a profusion of metallic instruments and pans, alchemical apparatuses, and several rows of leather-bound tomes, all neatly organized and precisely arranged on shelf units made of dark wood. On the wall behind the table hung a long, red silk banner, with a pair of upswept golden horns embroidered into the fabric—the symbol of the Horned One. Opposite to the door through which they had come, another door stood closed. While the former legionnaire looked around, Vurax took two steps over to the single bench in the room and sat down heavily upon it. His body felt lethargic and his thoughts increasingly unfocused.

"Are you alright?" Larios asked.

"I don't know," Vurax replied, though his mouth felt full of cotton. "Why do they have to burn so much damn incense? Don't you find it hard to breathe in here?"

Larios gave him a puzzled look, "Incense?" Inhaling deeply, the grizzled bull took in a couple of long breaths before he shook his head in confusion. "Are you sure? I don't smell anything."

"Well, it's there, damn it, and it's making it hard to think or do anything..." he muttered, rubbing his tired eyes with the heels of both palms.

"Maybe you should go outside and clear your head then. I'll take care of this but come back inside when you feel better so you can have that arm looked at."

Vurax nodded and tried to rise from the bench, stumbling forward and almost falling if not for Larios just barely catching him. The surge of energy brought on by shame at the momentary display of weakness gave him the brief clarity of mind to remember his coin pouch. He fumbled to release it from his belt and then dropped it into Larios' hand, mumbling something about the other needing that before he left the room. As he passed through the door, he nearly careened into someone else coming in at the same time, the red-robed priest stepping out of the way just in time to avoid a collision. The black-haired Golian cleric gave Vurax a stern glare as the latter sped by and left the room, then turned to look at Larios questioningly. An apologetic shrug was the only answer he received.

Vurax's breath came in short, ragged gasps. He felt like he was suffocating and the need for air became an all-consuming thought. His eyes stung from the acrid smoke in the air, and the resulting blurred vision, coupled with deep disorientation, caused him to stagger down the hall to where he could just make out the heavy double doors that he knew would lead him back outside. Taking hold of one of the brass handles after he passed through, he slammed the door shut behind him. With considerable effort, he took a long, deep breath to clear his lungs, but managed only to choke and cough even more than before. Blinking furiously to see better, he was dismayed to realize that he'd completely gotten turned around and had somehow walked into the temple's main hall of worship.

The inner sanctum was cavernous in size, with multiple rows of tall stone pillars and arches supporting the ceiling far above, all leading from the door to the raised altar at the far end, over which towered yet another imposing statue of the god Zarvon. Dim, reddish lights flickered and glowed somewhere within the large space, lending the entire area a hazy, dark atmosphere, where shadows danced and played tricks on the senses. In the condition that Vurax was in, the effect of confusion only became more amplified. Cursing, he turned to pull hard on the handle again to leave but try as he might, the door would not budge. He tried again, shaking the door violently, but felt himself growing weaker and was wracked by another fit of coughing. He tried to shout for Larios, but a hoarse-sounding croak was all that issued forth from his throat. There had to be another way out, he thought to himself, feeling panic set in.

He took one step away from the doors, then another, but collapsed to his knees. It felt as if he was swimming against a raging current and his muscles no longer had the strength to continue. He raised his head in one last futile attempt to find a means of escape, but what he saw then convinced him that he could no longer trust his perception of reality—the statue above the altar had just moved! He could swear its head had turned slightly to regard him impassively with carved golden eyes—or had it? He could no longer be certain of what he was seeing, shapes blurring and becoming indistinct from one another. He tried to take another breath but found that he couldn't, so he lay weakly on the floor, one hand clutching at his throat as he gasped for air that wouldn't come. His tongue lolled out and his eyes bulged, gaping upward at the indistinct ceiling in terror of the end he felt coming...and found himself staring down at his own body.

CHAPTER 21

From his hiding place, Darken watched in growing alarm as the couple unlocked the front door of the house, walked inside, and then closed it behind them. The entire time he sat there, he continued to channel all of his panic into a mental cry of warning through the ring that his uncle had given him. He had to assume Garick was aware of his distress by now, but his confidence in that quickly eroded every time he looked up at the balcony and didn't see his two companions leaving the house in response. He wrestled briefly with what to do, his eyes darting from the door to the bedroom balcony while his indecision froze every other muscle in his body. Something must be wrong. Either the ring wasn't working, or Garick was ignoring it for some reason. Whatever the case, he had to act fast, or they would be caught for sure. Door or window, he considered. Which way?

The door was the closest and most accessible, so he seized on that to make his decision and spring into action. Staying low to the ground in case more people passed in front of the house, he dashed quickly but carefully to the front porch to crouch before the door. Fighting down the anxiety he was feeling inside, he tried to turn the handle, doing it slowly so as not to make undue noise. It was locked, of course. He should have known they wouldn't just leave the door open and cursed at the time wasted. His next choice was whether to attempt to pick the lock. He had brought his tools with him, not because his uncle had asked him to, but out of habit. He wasn't as proficient at it as Garick though, and because it was not a task that worked well when rushed, he abandoned the idea almost as soon as he'd thought of it. That left only the balcony. Not wasting another second, he moved to the side of the house and stopped before the trellis that covered the wall. The wooden latticework provided plenty of hand and footholds, but was thin and delicate enough that if he didn't distribute his weight properly while climbing, the attempted ascent would be cut short in disastrous fashion. His uncle and Melios had made it seem easy, but he knew it wasn't. The fence was one thing; this was another.

His quick assessment of the obstacle was barely finished when he heard a woman's scream from somewhere above. Without any further hesitation and spurred on by panic now, he put his hands on the trellis and began to climb. Again, the stiffness of the armour worked against him, hampering his movements considerably while he adjusted to compensate for the unfamiliar feeling and burden. He was definitely moving slower than his companions had, even if to a casual observer he was climbing with astonishing speed. In Darken's mind, however, he was taking an agonizingly long time. Speed was essential, yes, but he couldn't afford to make a mistake. After what felt like an eternity, he reached the top and vaulted onto the balcony. The shutters were closed, but all other considerations flew from his mind when he heard more raised voices, followed by a grunt of pain. There was no time for anything else. Throwing caution to the wind, he drew his blades and kicked the doors in.

———◦———

Garick's arm tingled all over, the sensation not unlike what one feels when blood rushes back to a dormant limb, except in this case the process was happening in reverse. Though all he saw was air and light, there was a palpable and definite resistance to the dagger, as if there was actually a physical barrier before him. He cautiously pushed the tip of the blade into the exact spot Melios had pointed to, watching as the steel slowly moved a distance roughly equal to the length of his thumb, and then no more. His arm was practically numb now, and the dagger—wielded with ease like an extension of his own limb for so many years—felt like an unfamiliar object, alien and heavy.

"That's good, now turn it," Melios prompted him, the excitement in her voice mirrored by the eager stare of her strange eyes.

Garick didn't hesitate, fearful that he would lose all feeling in his arm if he delayed any longer. He turned the dagger to the left and watched as one by one, in a pattern that radiated outward from the dagger's tip, the symbols flared once and then winked out altogether. The reflection they cast on the black surface of the blade, however, did not. It was almost as if the weapon was absorbing the magic of the ward unto itself. The dagger felt incredibly heavy now, and he had to place his other hand under his elbow to support the unfeeling limb that held the weapon.

"Melios... I don't think I can... hold it much longer," he said through gritted teeth while fighting the strain of holding the dagger aloft. More than half of the ward had been dispelled, but he wasn't sure he could complete the task if the blade—itself now covered in glowing runes along its ebon surface—became any heavier. No sooner had he finished speaking when the door to the bedroom swung open. His task demanded so much effort and concentration that he would have missed what was happening had he not caught a glimpse of Melios moving out of the corner of one eye a split second before.

"What is the meaning of this? Who are you, and why are you in my house?"

Garick turned his head toward the door to see the finely dressed man and woman standing in the lamp-lit hallway beyond, shock and indignation flashing across their faces. He tried to say something but after barely managing to move his neck, he found that nearly every muscle in his body refused to respond. His mouth formed slow words, but no sound reached his ears as a result. All the while, he could see Melios crouched in the shadows next to the door, just out of sight of Giordy Khelen. The nobleman took a step forward into the room to stand protectively in front of his wife. The father of two was clearly unarmed, but his body language promised violence at seeing the sanctity of his home violated thusly—then more of the runes on the ward suddenly winked out and Giordy noticed for the first time what Garick was attempting to do.

"What are you doing? Get away from that!" Blue eyes wide and face contorting with rage, the man broke into a run, charging directly at Garick.

The thief tried to react and defend himself, but no part of his body would answer now, only the hand that held the dagger, still turning the impossibly heavy weapon with inexorable purpose. But he did not have to. Giordy Khelen was barely halfway to where Garick stood in front of the desk when he saw Melios spring from behind the door like a cat pouncing upon a mouse. She was behind the man in a flash, the glint of steel in one hand barely glimpsed before something plunged into the man's back with expert and lethal efficiency. Garick tried to yell the word 'no' but could not, watching helplessly at the stunned look of surprise on Giordy's face as the man's body stiffened visibly from the blow before pitching forward onto the floor, one hand flailing futilely at his back to clutch at the dagger buried there. His feeble efforts were for naught. With cold and deliberate cruelty, Melios pulled the blade out, placed her other hand on the man's shoulder to flip him onto his back, then swiftly drew the dagger's keen edge across his throat, his struggles ended forever with a horrible, wet gurgling sound.

An ear-piercing shriek cut the air, issuing from the throat of Anika Khelen. At the sight of her husband shuddering his life's blood onto the floor and the menacing, black leather-clad figure standing over him, the woman lost all fear and reason and launched herself at the assailant. Melios sidestepped the clumsy attack with contemptuous ease, causing Anika to fly past her and trip over Giordy's still form. The noblewoman lay on the floor, her body convulsing with sobs and wailing grief as the brief will to fight fled from her. Covered in her husband's blood that was soaking into the expensive rug beneath them, Anika crawled protectively over the corpse to raise one red-stained hand to the assassin standing there, watching her impassively.

"Why...?" she implored, tears streaming down her cheeks.

In response, Melios raised one hand to remove the mask from her face. A short distance away, had Garick been able to make a sound, he would have gasped in surprised confusion, for the visage that was revealed in the dwindling light of the room was none other than Darken's.

Paralyzed by his own dagger's magic, Garick had watched in utter dismay while Melios had taken Giordy Khelen's life with brutal determination. As he'd explained to Darken in the past, their trade could be a dangerous one at times, and that necessitated expertise with weapons and self-defence as a means to get out of a difficult situation, but what he'd just witnessed went well beyond what any reasonable person would consider justified. Now it seemed that Anika Khelen was about to suffer the same fate as her husband, and he was powerless to stop it. He couldn't help but wonder how the couple had made it into the house without a warning from Darken. What had gone wrong? Had something happened to the boy? Concern for his son's safety nearly numbed him to everything that was happening before him until he found himself staring dumbfoundedly at Darken's face. The eyes that stared back at him were not those of his son. The face across the room curled its lips up in a horrible mockery of that disarming smile he'd seen countless times before, and the hand that held the dagger lifted in the air along with them. On the floor, Anika whimpered in fear and helplessness while she waited for the blow to fall.

The final group of symbols on the ward flashed brightly once and then faded away, leaving the claw of Rauvir unprotected at last. If not for the reflection of the light off the runes still captured on the blade's black surface, the room would have been plunged into darkness once more. With the spell undone, Garick collapsed under the impossible weight of the dagger, man and weapon falling to the floor with a crash. Whether by chance or fate, he landed facing Melios and was therefore able to continue to observe what followed. Unsurprisingly, all the noise had awakened the children sleeping in their room somewhere nearby, and he could hear their frightened voices calling out for their parents. He half expected Anika to respond to their plaintive cries, but the woman—after staring uncomprehendingly at the killer's face—had prostrated herself with anguish over Giordy's body and did not move. The brief interruption caused by Garick's fall now over, Melios shifted the grip on her dagger and brought the pommel end down with just enough force against the back of Anika's head to render her instantly unconscious.

So that was her plan then, Garick concluded, fighting to regain control of his body as the tingling sensation began to wash over the tips of his fingers and toes first, then spread slowly up his arms and legs. Melios had never intended to kill Anika but rather had allowed the noblewoman to see the face that would eventually take the blame for everything that had happened here this night. What he couldn't understand was how she'd manage to accomplish this. He'd seen some good disguises in his time, but this went beyond any trick or skill that he'd ever heard of—magic then, or something else? He wondered fleetingly if this was even Melios at all and if he'd been deceived from the start but decided that it had to be—she'd known too much about him to be anyone else but the person whose love he'd betrayed all those years ago. Now he was about to pay the price for his disloyalty. He watched while Melios walked to the door and swung it closed, throwing the lock from the inside. Then she looked at him with Darken's face, menace in those feline-like eyes that were still her own.

"You got old, Garick. Old, slow, and careless," she taunted. The voice was a perfect imitation of Darken's, but there was no mistaking the source of its venomous contempt. Reaching under the cuff of one of her leather bracers, she pulled out the silver ring he'd been wearing and held it out for him to see. "So easy to distract...tsk, tsk," she clicked with her tongue in mock disappointment. "And to think I once admired you so."

She wasn't wrong, he admitted inwardly with chagrin. She'd jabbed him enough with personal insults and insinuations to disturb his focus sufficiently that when she'd bumped past him while his gloves were off, she'd taken the ring from him—which could only mean she'd somehow known the Khelens would be returning early and had set this whole thing up. How could he have been so careless and foolish? He knew now his life could be measured in seconds—Melios was merely giving herself the satisfaction of gloating before she finished things—but it was not for himself that he was afraid, but rather what would befall Darken. He'd squandered the last chance he had to tell the boy the truth, but perhaps it was for the best. He would have to die with one last regret.

"Valerios...?" he managed to sound the name.

Melios grinned from ear to ear. "Quite dead, I assure you. For all his precious 'Sight', the one thing he so desperately sought to prevent was the one thing he never saw coming—his own death. Another score settled, just one left to go." She flicked the ring away into a corner of the room and readied her dagger.

"Wait," he grunted. Since she liked to gloat, he was going to give her another opportunity. "Why Darken?"

Melios seemed genuinely taken aback by the question. "You really have to ask? That boy is the only thing you've ever loved—not I, not your sister-in-law, not even your brother. Before I send you to the next world, I want you to die with the knowledge that the choices you made in your life will forever ruin his," she grinned maliciously.

He'd stalled long enough. With control of his muscles mostly returned and his weapon's strange heaviness gone, he tightened the grip on the hilt of the black blade and prepared to strike. Before he could swing his arm up though, the weight of Melios' boot came crashing down suddenly on his wrist, pinning his hand to the floor, and forcing him to release his hold on the weapon.

"Old, slow, and careless," she repeated. Still prone, Garick twisted and swung with his other hand in a closed fist to punch hard at her knee. She grimaced as her leg buckled and nearly lost her balance, but recovered almost immediately, her speed and agility more than a match for his. She was on him before he could twist away in time and Garick grunted once, staring in astonishment at the dagger plunged deep into his heart. The pain was indescribable but strangely passing. He felt nothing but a curious lassitude creeping over him again, and the edges of his vision began to grow dim. Two hands cupped his face, lips touching his own in a gentle farewell. Her face was her own again, just as youthful and as beautiful as he remembered.

"You did this to yourself, Garick," were the last words he heard.

"Uncle!" the balcony shutter doors blew inward with a loud crash and Darken took two quick steps into the room, stopping to shout in dismay when he saw the horrific scene before him. He barely registered the fallen figures of the Khelens or the glowing dagger on the floor—his attention was solely focused on Melios. The woman looked up at him as she gently lowered Garick's head to the floor. Were those tears in her eyes? He couldn't be sure, and it didn't matter, for the next thing she did was to pull her bloodied dagger from his uncle's chest and rise slowly to her feet, clearly favouring one leg. He didn't need to ask what had happened here—he could draw his own conclusions, and he made his grim intent plain by raising one arm to point the tip of one of his blades meaningfully at her, his face contorting with silent rage behind the mask he still wore.

"Don't be stupid," Melios warned. "Put those toys away before you hurt yourself."

"Step away from him," he growled.

"I don't suppose you'd believe me if I told you he did this?" she gestured carelessly at Giordy's body. This was the first time he could see her face, but the way she didn't even attempt to hide a smile as she made the ridiculous suggestion was more than enough to confirm everything in his mind.

Darken's response was swift and explosive. He closed the distance to Melios in a blur, one dagger held low before him, the second one high and back. If you were going to fight with two weapons, keep them wide apart and divide your opponent's attention, his uncle had always told him. Darken had trained extensively with these daggers—a gift from Garick that he'd never dared to show to his parents. So diligent and expert was his training that he'd managed to impress his tutor with his fighting skills, and he knew from personal experience that was no easy feat. He'd also been taught about the dangers of overconfidence and hubris. Though he was nearly blind with rage and grief, the part of him that was all about self-preservation didn't lose sight of the fact that his opponent was most assuredly a hundred times deadlier than the street toughs he normally tussled with. The look of exasperated annoyance that Melios gave him as he attacked should have been an indication of how this might turn out, but he didn't care.

His uncle's former associate dodged his lunge with practiced ease, avoiding the attack from the low blade in the process, while her bloodied dagger parried the high blade with a ringing sound when he twisted his body to follow her movement, flying past her and striking at where she would be rather than where she'd been. He'd anticipated that his charge would leave him off-balance, so he used his momentum to turn his dive into a tumble, coming up on his feet near the far wall and facing her in one motion, daggers held at the ready.

"Not bad," Melios admitted, impressed in spite of herself, "but final warning—walk away."

Darken made no effort to hide his contempt for her offer. He circled his target slowly, calculating his next attack to take advantage of her leg injury. He needed to end this quickly if there was any hope of still saving his uncle. The thought caused him to involuntarily shift his eyes quickly to Garick's body, lying there in a growing pool of blood.

"How touching," he heard Melios mock, guessing what he was thinking. The brief distraction nearly cost him everything, the throwing knife that jutted suddenly from his left shoulder the price he paid for taking his eyes off his opponent for a split second. He could hear Garick's voice in his mind scolding him for the mistake, but he ignored both it and the pain, going on the offensive once more. The daggers flashed in a flurry of expert thrusts and slices that would have left a lesser opponent mortally wounded several times over. But Melios was no ordinary foe. Even with her injured knee, her movements were an impossibly fast blur he could barely follow. With only one weapon in hand, she somehow still managed to block and avoid every single one of his attacks. Undeterred, he pressed on. If he couldn't kill her, perhaps he could at least delay her long enough for the Justicers to arrive.

"You're an open book, Darken. You really ought to have listened to Garick better," she taunted.

She'd again somehow guessed what he was thinking, or perhaps it wasn't really all that hard to figure out, given the circumstances. Whatever the case, the goading worked because he stopped giving any thought to defending himself and unleashed an all-out assault with the aim of pushing her into a corner of the room. For the third time, she anticipated his tactics, slipping away nimbly and easily just when it seemed he had maneuvered her into an advantageous position. It was painfully clear now that she was toying with him—like a cat and its hapless prey. He realized that other than the hit she'd scored with the throwing knife, she had only defended herself thus far, but that ended abruptly when she danced out of the path of a brutal lunging attack from him that would have pinned her to the wall behind her.

Darken—tiring, wounded, enraged, and frustrated—overextended himself in that last thrust, one dagger driving deep into the plaster surface of the wall and becoming wedged solidly into the wooden stud within. He didn't even attempt to pry the weapon loose, but his back was to her long enough that he knew this mistake would be his last. Yet the blow never landed. He dropped to the ground and turned at the same time, coming up in a crouch with his remaining dagger held defensively before him. Melios stood a short distance away from him, grinning in a way that only infuriated him further. It was an odd thought to have just then, but it struck him how exotically beautiful she was, with olive skin and perfectly shaped lips and a nose that flawlessly complimented those strange, mesmerizing eyes. The effect was intoxicating, he admitted reluctantly, but his momentary fascination with her striking features turned to horror and confusion almost immediately.

The skin on Melios' face, so smooth and flawless, began to ripple and heave like something twisting and moving restlessly under a piece of silk fabric. So disturbed and confused was he by the strange display that he was witnessing that he could only stand slowly and gape in shock and fascination, all thoughts of attacking driven from his mind. It was over very quickly, but when it ended, and just when he thought he couldn't be surprised anymore, he found himself staring at Garick's face. Every detail was perfect, right down to the old scar above the left eyebrow, the slight crook of the nose, and the light hint of grey coming through in the beard. Only the eyes were still those of the woman that had stood before him. Even her body had altered itself, eschewing her feminine figure and slight frame for that of Garick's greater height and slightly heavier build. He had to look at his uncle's body lying on the ground nearby to reassure himself that his mind wasn't playing tricks on him.

"What in the name of all the gods is this?" he managed to stammer.

"I thought you'd be happy to see me, Darken," his uncle's voice mocked back at him. "Here, let me fix that for you."

Had he not been so completely stunned by this strange development, he might have detected the threat before it was too late. His eyes dimly registered the dagger coming, but his brain was too sluggish to react accordingly and defend himself from the sudden attack. Less than a second later, pain exploded in his head when the weapon's razor-sharp edge scored a deep and bloody furrow on his forehead and through his right eye, continuing down to his cheek while slicing his mask open in the process. The agony was more than he could bear. He screamed and dropped to one knee, blood spilling through his closed fingers as he pressed his hand tightly to his face and ruined eye. He held his remaining dagger weakly before him in a defensive posture, but Melios didn't press the advantage. She didn't need to. The assassin walked to the desk and produced a black silk cloth from somewhere on her vest, then carefully lifted Rauvir's claw from its stand to envelop it in the dark fabric. She paused briefly to glance at father and son, one lying still and staring sightlessly upward, the other moaning in pain, his good eye warily following her movements with undisguised hatred. The face that stared back at him was hers again.

"You have a choice now. That throwing knife in your shoulder is coated with a lethal poison, so you can stay here and join him in death or try and save yourself and flee while you still can. If you choose the latter, don't look for me. If you do, your swift reunion with Garick will be all that you'll gain for your effort. Goodbye, Darken." After delivering her ominous pronouncement, she walked past him with a slight limp toward the window. He swung feebly at her, but Melios easily avoided the clumsy attempt and before he could do anything more, she was gone into the night.

Darken stared at the open balcony door, the vision in his good eye beginning to blur. Had she said something about poison? The slash to his face hurt horribly, and there was a burning sensation in the wound on his shoulder that was slowly spreading throughout his body. He didn't know how much time he had, but he suspected that it wouldn't be very long. He crawled over to his uncle's body, already knowing what he would find, but wanting to be sure, nonetheless. Garick's chest and heart were still, the blood no longer pumping through the gash in his chest. Darken's eye stung with tears, and he took off his glove to run one hand slowly and affectionately down one bearded cheek. The grief he felt was indescribable and, in his despair, he considered simply laying there next to his uncle and waiting for his own end to come. This ill-fated night had taken too much from him already. For all the things Garick had revealed to him earlier, he had the distinct impression the man had been trying to tell him something more. Now, he would never know what it might have been.

He wasn't sure how long he lay there, sobbing in misery while draped over Garick's body, but he was abruptly brought back to the concerns of the world of the living when the banging on the door began.

"In the name of Valoria, open this door!" came the muffled shout from the other side as the knocks grew louder and more insistent.

Justicers. The governess must've summoned them, but then he'd expected that. Melios' final words came echoing back to him—stay or run. He decided he owed it to his uncle—and himself—to seek out the answers to everything that had happened here. More importantly, and despite Melios' warning, she had a heavy debt to repay him, and it was one that he intended to collect on. The only clue he had to follow was the letter his uncle had received, and a quick search thankfully turned up the bloodied and crumpled paper stashed in Garick's belt, which he quickly tucked away into his own. Now he just had to figure out how to stay alive long enough to make good on that promise, and it had to begin with not getting captured by Arlingford's keepers of the peace. Bidding Garick a silent farewell, he struggled to lift himself, shaking off the torpor that had steadily been creeping over him. For the second time this evening, he had to think fast despite the cobwebs in his mind—that door wouldn't hold for much longer.

He stepped to Anika's still form—unaware that the noblewoman still drew breath—and quickly ripped two strips of fabric from the hem of her skirt, tying one around his head and right side of his face to make a crude bandage. Next, gritting his teeth in anticipation, he pulled the knife from his shoulder with a groan and dropped it on the floor, doing his best to quickly stuff the second piece of cloth through the gash in the leather and over the burning wound. Lastly, he turned to his dagger still embedded in the far wall, but before he could race over to retrieve the blade, the unnatural light in the room—dwindling ever so slowly while everything had unfolded—finally went out altogether. His uncle's dagger, he remembered with a start—it would be fitting to end Melios' treacherous life with it. Buoyed by that sudden and poetic notion, he picked up the weapon where it lay near his feet and then dashed for the balcony.

Darken had barely reached the railing when the door to the room crashed open but he didn't waste time looking behind him. The teenager didn't doubt the fate that awaited him if he got caught, and he quickly but cautiously glanced down at the ground first before he began his climb. His foresight proved fortunate, giving him just enough time to lean back sharply as the glowing bolt of white energy shot by, narrowly missing him. 'Shit, an Enforcer,' he cursed inwardly. When you were as wealthy as the Khelens, no effort was spared in swiftly bringing justice to bear, it seemed. Climbing down or going back inside would be suicide, which left only one option—with no time to spare, he climbed the railing and grabbed hold of the trellis to ascend to the roof. He knew the Enforcer's rod would only take a few seconds to recharge, but the brief pause should be all the time he needed to make his escape. He hoped. Blind in one eye, face throbbing with pain, and fighting against the debilitating poison from the wound in his shoulder, he gave it his best try.

The bedroom was on the second floor of the house, and thus the lip of the roof's overhang was not far, but he may as well have been attempting to scale an interminably tall cliff for all the effort it took him. Fear and determination drove him on, and he ignored every painful protest that his body screamed at him while he climbed. Two Justicers ran onto the balcony he'd just vacated, the one in the lead lunging up to grab at his trailing ankle but missing just as he lifted his leg out of reach. By the time the armoured men had drawn their swords, he was already hoisting himself up onto the roof, and not a moment too soon when he heard the Enforcer's rod discharging again only a split second later. The air sizzled and crackled when the missile of raw *etherus* clipped the edge of the roof, shattering the tiles on impact, and causing a shower of clay fragments to rain down upon Darken. He pressed his body flat against the sloped surface so as to not present a target and began to drag himself as fast as he could to the other side of the house. When he felt he was far enough away from the edge, he stood up and ran up one side of the roof and down the other.

"East side—go!" he heard one of the men on the balcony shout to his partner on the ground.

That did it. He'd seen firsthand what happened to a person when struck by the magic force of an Enforcer's rod, and he didn't relish the thought of experiencing it. Standing at his customary spot by the marketplace one day and observing from afar, Darken had scoffed at the thief's amateurish work and its inevitable result. What struck him as incredibly stupid was that the man then stuck around to argue with the merchant who caught him in the act. While most of the people nearby gave the scene a wide berth, he quickly spotted the one diligent citizen hurrying away, clearly intent on finding a member of the city watch to deal with the miscreant. When he predictably returned a couple of minutes later, it was not with some mere guardsman in tow, however, but two Justicers, one of them bearing the insignia of a dreaded Enforcer. The stern-looking man and woman in their telltale black and white plate mail armour were devout followers of Valoria, the strict and unyielding goddess of law and justice. It was not a very large sect, even within the bigger cities of the Crescent, but wherever the local ruler was able to afford their steep fees and efficient services, crime tended to be a much riskier activity than usual. If this fool didn't run now, he was about to find out why, Darken thought to himself.

And run he did when he saw them, though it was already too late. The crowd dispersed quickly just then, anticipating what would happen. He watched as the female Enforcer swiftly drew the steel rod from her belt and pointed the baton-like object at the running thief's back. The blast of energy crossed the intervening distance in the wink of an eye, slamming into the man squarely between the shoulders. Paralyzed instantly by the magic, the unfortunate criminal pitched forward to crash unceremoniously to the ground, his nerveless legs suddenly unable to bear his weight and carry him forward. Worse, every muscle in his body relaxed involuntarily, causing the poor man to suffer the indignity of voiding himself publicly in every manner humanly possible. When the two Justicers moved in to apprehend their helpless prey, Darken turned away in disgust, not so much at the sorry spectacle, but for the needlessly harsh and draconian measures they were so quick to use, especially the rod-wielding ones called Enforcers. They claimed that they were but the mere earthly agents of Valoria, dispensing her judgment with impartiality, but privately, Darken was certain that they perhaps enjoyed their duty a little more than they would admit.

The memory and image of that unlucky thief firmly in his mind, Darken ran to the roof's edge, uncertain of what his next move would be when he got there. Seeing the wide boughs of a tall tree growing above the house over by one corner, he aimed for that direction. He came to a stop at the brink, knowing that he had mere seconds before his pursuers would figure out where he was. The base of the tree was surrounded by thick bushes, but the trunk was too far, and the branches didn't look like they could hold his weight. There was no more time to think, so he doubled back for a short running start and jumped. Fresh pain lanced through his wounded shoulder, but he caught the branch he'd aimed for and was grateful to be wearing gloves as he did so. The tree limb bent first, then snapped just as he'd expected, but the split second it took to do so was enough to reduce some of the height and inertia from his initial jump off the roof. Thus, when he fell to the bushes below, the fall's distance had been cut by a third. It was still rather high though, and while the bushes cushioned the impact somewhat, and the leathers he wore protected him from the sharp branches, it was a rough landing, nevertheless. He felt more than one of his ribs give but didn't let the growing list of injuries lessen his fear of capture by Justicers.

Darken got to his feet, a little more slowly than he would have liked, and took off at a run, taking the shortest and most direct route to the fence that surrounded the Khelen residence. Just in time too, he thought, hearing the shouts of the Justicers when they came around the side of the house and found him already gone. Again, he didn't waste time looking back, knowing that every second mattered. He tackled the fence at a run, foregoing any finesse or stealth, intent only on surmounting the barrier in the quickest way possible. Speed over his pursuers was his only ally now, and whatever was coursing through his body from that knife wound was working quickly to deny him that last advantage. He made it over to the other side, letting go of the fence to fall the last few feet to the ground just before another crackling bolt smashed into the bronze bars with a loud ringing sound, sending a shower of bright sparks into the air. Keeping his head low, he took a brief second to orient himself. He was not far from the point where they'd entered the grounds of the mansion, so all he had to do was cross the road and lose himself in the maze of streets and buildings beyond. He would be exposed while he did so, but there was no other choice.

He felt winded and his strength was flagging, but he made it to the first alley between buildings before the Justicers had even crossed the gate of the house. There, in the welcoming shadows away from the streetlamps, he leaned against a wall and took two seconds to catch his ragged breath. He'd lost all sensation in his left arm, and his sides throbbed with dull pain from his fall. While the agony in his ruined eye had dulled somewhat, he knew once the rush of adrenaline from his escape subsided, that he would be in serious trouble. He needed to find help fast, but who? His uncle was gone, his parents were out of town, and the gentle, kind folks who were caring for his two brothers would be horrified to find him bloody at their doorstep. He thought of Ellianna, but there were dozens of farmsteads outside the town walls, and he had no idea which one she called home. Besides, even if he knew, he doubted he would be able to make it that far. What he needed most right now was a little bit of rest—rest and time to think. He needed to get home. He had to hope the Justicers would take some time to discover his uncle's identity before they came around to the Valhik house seeking answers. He needed to be long gone by then. But what if the poison killed him before morning?

The clear sound of pursuit approaching rendered Darken's inner monologue moot, and he forced himself to move. If he got caught, none of it would matter. Before he headed home, he had to lose his would-be captors, and since his best chance of doing that would be in the slums, he ran in that direction. Panting while he held one side with his good arm, he briefly considered giving up and letting himself get caught. He knew the thought was borne out of his growing anxiety, fear, and doubt over his ability to survive until tomorrow, so he had to consider every angle possible. That he was guilty of a crime this night was not something he would dispute, but he was no murderer. What if he could somehow convince the Justicers of the truth? That someone else had killed the Khelens and Garick while leaving him for dead? The followers of Valoria valued truth and justice above all else, so would they not at least listen? Perhaps they would at that, he thought, but then what? Regardless of who had wielded the fatal blade, he'd been an accomplice to a botched heist that had cost three people their lives. Even if they believed him, he was likely to spend the rest of his days rotting in a dark dungeon cell. If that was the fate that awaited him, then he'd rather die in his bed tonight.

Despite being the capital of the Barony of Arlingford and its most populous settlement, when measured by the standard of those who lived in the cities of the Crescent, Arlingtown was a small, backwater town. Still, with its six distinct districts, it was more than large enough for Darken to successfully evade his hunters. Once he'd reached the slums, his intimate knowledge of the labyrinthine network of narrow streets, twisting stairways, back alleys, and dead ends proved to be the Justicers' undoing, and it didn't hurt that they were weighed down by their bulky armour. While he'd stopped hearing them quite some time ago, he had nevertheless made sure that he'd led them sufficiently far in the wrong direction to leave them hopelessly lost for now, before beginning to double back toward the marketplace and the neighbourhood where he lived. It had been a successful, sound strategy. Unfortunately for the young thief, it had also cost him every ounce of what little remained of his fading stamina.

Still within the slums and huddled in the shadows next to a broad staircase that led to a street above, Darken sat on the ground with his back to the wall, covered in sweat, sides heaving for air. He was desperate to rid himself of the leathers he wore, and he felt the armour was slowly constricting the life out of him. Nothing hurt anymore—or at least the parts of his body that he could still feel. The fact that he was no longer in pain was a blessing, but he feared what that might mean. Worse, when he finally attempted to get up and move on, his legs wouldn't respond. He chuckled to himself in bitterness, thinking perhaps it would be for the best if it all just ended here and now. He didn't think he could bear disappointing his father one more time anyway, or to see his dear mother cry over the mess he'd made of everything with his choices.

"Consequences," Darken muttered. The very word Garick had used earlier that evening and the one that summed up everything between that moment in time and this one. He couldn't be angry with the man. He'd wanted to be there, and now he would die with that choice. He wished he'd been able to see Ellianna one more time, and this was the last thought he had before he closed his eyes, and his head slumped down onto his chest.

CHAPTER 22

Brother Owen stood outside Father Lorimer's house and took a couple of deep breaths to steady his emotions. Not since the day he'd leapt from the deck of a Golian ship and into the sea to swim for freedom or die in the attempt, had he felt such a strong combination of fear and uncertainty. Yet here he was, about to plunge into the unknown once more. Flynn would be alright, he told himself—the boy's welfare would never be far from his mind, but he needed to focus on what he had to do. The priest looked up and saw that the sun was now almost directly overhead. He could no longer hear the choir in the air, which confirmed to him that the Yule mass was nearing its end, and that Archbishop Marcos would soon finish delivering the final words of his sermon. It was time to go.

When he rounded the corner of the building that housed the hospital and came within sight of the orphanage's main gate, he saw the wagon waiting there for him under the shadow of the old tower, along with two horses. One of the animals was hitched to the four-wheeled conveyance, and the other was saddled and ready for its rider. While he walked up, two figures emerged from the tower's open doorway carrying something hidden from view by the thick fabric it was wrapped in. The back of the wagon was already open, and the two men lifted their burden in one motion to place it inside the vehicle, latching the small gate shut for the journey. One of the men then stepped over to the tower door and locked it shut. So that's where they'd hidden the body, Brother Owen mused. It made sense, he figured, as that was the last place an errant child or priest would be likely to wander into and accidentally stumble upon Dario's remains. It was not until he drew closer to the wagon that he realized that one of the individuals was not a man at all—or at least not an adult one. It was Carlo. The teenage boy finished securing the key to the tower on the ring at his belt and gave him a sullen look that spoke volumes.

The priest briefly returned the cold, hard stare, but otherwise ignored the Initiate, walking past him to approach the other figure who was in the process of giving the wagon one last inspection. The man paid Owen no heed as he moved to check the draft horse's harness, only turning to face the waiting cleric after he was satisfied that everything was ready. Brother Owen did not know the plain-garbed man—middle-aged, stubble-covered face, unremarkable features—but that didn't mean anything. He never expected that it would be another member of the clergy or even one of the orphanage's non-ordained staff that would accompany him. In fact, he'd fully expected to be travelling alone, but that didn't seem like it was going to be the case. The man removed his floppy brown hat, brushed back a strand of greasy-looking dark hair, and nodded as he introduced himself.

"Name's Emilio, yer grace," he said with a yellow, gap-toothed smile. "At yer service."

Though he stood a few feet away, Owen caught the unpleasant sour scent of stale wine on the man's breath. In the orphanage, and indeed throughout the city at large, the priest had a reputation for being one of the most congenial and tolerant members of the Janusian clergy, yet he couldn't help but feel an instant dislike for Emilio. The man's clothes were not of poor quality, but there was a general unkemptness about him that hinted at slovenly and unwholesome habits. What a man did in his private life was his own business, but Owen always felt that one should always at least take a small measure of pride in their own appearance, at least while out in public. He tried hard not to wrinkle his nose in disapproval and nodded politely in return.

"Brother Owen will suffice, thank you. I take it you are to accompany me?"

"That'd be what I was paid for, yes. Would yer grace care to ride the horse or drive the wagon?" Emilio asked with that foul smile again.

"Don't call me that, please. I'll take the horse." Truthfully, the wagon's cushioned seat would make for a far more comfortable journey, but the thought of becoming trapped downwind from Emilio was beginning to turn his stomach. The smell of the horse beneath him would be far more tolerable, and riding would afford him far more mobility should he need it.

"Suit yerself, Brother." With that, the man climbed aboard the wagon and took the reins in his hands, giving him a bored look and a shrug while he waited. Owen walked up to the white and chestnut spotted mare, patted the animal gently on the neck, then put one foot on the stirrup and climbed onto the saddle. It'd been many years since he'd last ridden a horse—mostly during a time when he used to visit the small farming communities between Corazan and Jerothos—but the sensation of being on the horse felt comfortable and familiar almost immediately. As part of their duties to the faithful citizens of the realm, members of the clergy often travelled to villages and even homesteads where there was no church nearby. It was a part of his life that Owen looked back on fondly, but as he'd gotten older, he'd come to appreciate and enjoy the comforts of a less physically demanding life at the orphanage far more than being on the road.

"Father Lorimer bids you a safe journey and speedy return."

The voice pulled him out of his reverie, and Owen glanced down to see Carlo standing next to his horse. He'd completely forgotten about the Initiate, and it was just as well as the sight of the teenager filled him with sudden and irrational annoyance. Surely the words as delivered by the headmaster had been sincere, but Carlo's delivery of them was decidedly lacking in anything that remotely resembled any genuine regard for his well-being. Man and teenager exchanged stares, and there was something sinister and knowing about the way Carlo's cold, blue eyes looked at him that gave him pause. The priest suspected there was a darkness festering in the lad's soul, and the thought of leaving Flynn behind in the company of this quiet and menacing youth filled him with a wave of fresh uneasiness. He would curse himself later for letting the boy get under his skin and perturb him so much that he would forget his vows, but for now he couldn't help himself, so he leaned down in the saddle, looked hard into the Initiate's unblinking eyes, and spoke in a low voice so that only Carlo could hear him.

"If anything happens to Flynn while I'm gone, I'll make you sorry. Very, very sorry." With that, he straightened up, tapped the mare's flanks with his heels, and spurred the animal forward through the open gates, staring straight ahead. He never saw the contemptuous sneer that contorted Carlo's lips as he watched him go or heard the ugly-sounding chuckle of private amusement that Emilio gave when he drove the wagon past the motionless Initiate. Once the vehicle had rolled through the gate, Carlo stood there a while longer, staring in silence as the horses and wagon clattered down the cobbled street, then closed and locked the gate.

⸻⊙⸻

Now that mass was over, the children stood lined up outside the cathedral, the various Initiates scrambling about to organize everyone before the walk back to the orphanage grounds. Everyone was supposed to be on their best behaviour on this day of all days, but even so, the temptation for mischief and play was too great for some to resist, especially among the youngest. Two such little scamps were chasing each other past where Elias waited, a clearly flustered Initiate in tow behind them as he struggled to catch them while trying not to trip over his own long robes at the same time. On impulse, Elias stepped out in front of the two small boys—both barely six years of age—causing them to stop to avoid a collision and delaying their escape just long enough for the pursuing teenager to catch up.

"Whoa! Boys, slow down!" he grinned, extending his arms out to both sides. The two lads looked up at him with wide eyes and sized up their new opponent, incorporating him into their game with the speed and spontaneity that only children were capable of. No stranger to this sort of thing, Elias anticipated their move a split second before the two small lads broke left and right to try and slip around him. He swept them both up into his arms, holding them fast while they giggled at being outsmarted. The Initiate caught up to them and relieved Elias of his burden by taking the two rascals and ushering them back into line with some stern words of admonition. Smiling as he watched, Elias caught the Initiate's eye, and the older boy winked back at him.

"Thanks, Elias. I owe you one," the other said.

"It was nothing, Alfonso," Elias called back, feeling immensely pleased with himself. He couldn't exactly figure out what had changed inside of him, but ever since his encounter with Peter that morning, his feeling of newfound confidence had only continued to strengthen as the day wore on, rather than fade once the initial euphoria had passed. His blissful enjoyment of the sensation was interrupted by a playful shove from behind and he turned around to give Big Eric a look of annoyance.

"'It was nothing, Alfonso,'" his heavy-set friend teased, imitating Elias' soft voice. "Would you look at this suck-up?" Eric said to Georgie standing at his side. The other kid clearly wanted to laugh, but was too afraid to offend his friend Elias, so he just smiled nervously and looked away as if embarrassed by his own reaction. Eric rolled his eyes and scoffed at his unreliable ally before turning to Elias again. "You trying to skip Monitor and go straight for wearing the black robes or something?" he continued to badger his friend.

"No, ya big lump," he stuck his tongue out. "Just trying to help and get this thing going a little faster."

"Riiiiiight..." Eric drew out the word, sounding dubious. "More like you're in a hurry to get back inside so you can catch another glimpse of your 'beautiful princess', huh?" Elias blushed visibly when the jest hit the bullseye, prompting a guffaw from Eric. "Yeah, I thought so. See, Georgie? He's turning as red as a ripe tomato. I told you—this fool's head's been in the clouds all day." Unable to contain himself, Georgie sputtered with mirth and his shoulders shook as he covered his mouth with one hand. His pale blue eyes pleaded for forgiveness as he looked at Elias.

"Don't be an ass," Elias tried to deflect, knowing it was too late. "Besides, I thought you'd be eager to get back to the refectory, too."

"Oh, why's that?"

"One word—lunch."

Eric's expression went from one of amusement to that of stunned apprehension as his mouth formed a perfect 'o'. Right on cue, his stomach gave off an audible rumble, and he looked anxiously about, suddenly impatient that the line wasn't moving yet. Grinning from ear to ear, Elias shook his head at his friend's predictable reaction and turned to the front again, waiting patiently for the priest at the head of his group to call for them to start walking. When the signal finally came, the boys began their march back to the orphanage.

As in previous years, the king and his chamberlain would move on from the cathedral with the archbishop and visit with the girls at the Sisters' convent first. In the meantime, the Kal-dkar would follow with the boys over to their side and administer the Test before lunch. After the meal, the mage and monarch would exchange places, the latter making his visit to the boy's orphanage in the afternoon before the royal party returned to the castle and Yule was declared officially over. The Test was always a strange and mysterious ritual, one that generally filled the children with a nervous mixture of excitement and unease. Candidates were always few and far between, but even so, the Janusian priests still felt resentment that the Kal-dkar could arbitrarily take any one of their charges away so suddenly. However, because the gift of the *etherus* was so rare, the royal decree that gave the Kal-dkar power to remove someone from the orphanage could not be countered, not even by the archbishop himself.

Seated back at their tables in the refectory, the children waited with anticipation for the court wizard to make her entrance through the main doors. Elias tried to look nonchalant as he looked about, feigning disinterest and trying to make a show of appearing calm before Eric and Georgie. Truthfully though, he was anxious to see Princess Gabriela again. He wasn't sure if she would be accompanying the mage now or only appear later in the company of her father, but Elias didn't want to wait that long. As these thoughts raced through his mind, he stopped to mentally scold himself. What was wrong with him? Until this very morning, he'd always thought girls to be bothersome and useless creatures. So, what was different about this one? He really ought to stop being so silly, he continued in his imagined conversation with himself. Not only was Gabriela older than he was, but she was also a princess while he was nothing more than a stupid orphan boy of no name or importance in her eyes. Stop, stop, stop! Why did any of those things even matter? He was acting as if she was somehow going to notice him out of a couple of hundred other boys, any of whom she couldn't possibly care less about. He wasn't special, he told himself; he was just being an idiot.

That old and familiar sense of futility began to take hold of Elias, but the new part of him that refused to be downcast forced him to look up with renewed hope when the doors to the refectory opened and Alyssa Dumar walked through.

Alone. It seems he would have to wait a while longer then; he mused with a longing sigh. He could hear Eric snickering beside him, but he ignored the other boy and watched as the Kal-dkar approached the head table, bowed perfunctorily to Father Lorimer, then took a seat at his side.

"She looks scary," Eric commented. The large boy found all of this terribly unexciting but knowing that the only thing that interested him—lunch—wouldn't be happening until after the Test, he decided to make the best of it. "I much preferred old Bartholomew, but he was ancient—older than Brother Edward, I think. Do you think he died or something?"

Elias shrugged. "I don't know...probably? She looks serious, but I wouldn't say scary. Unless you're afraid, of course," he looked at Eric, feeling anxious again, but for a different reason.

Eric gave him a strange look and then tried to sound casual. "Afraid? Nah. We've got nothing to be afraid of, not for another couple of years at least. Even so, how bad can it be to finally get plucked out of this place and trained to be a mage? I think it's kind of exciting, actually—more than the thought of becoming a priest, that's for sure. What a bore that's going to be."

"Shhhhhhh!" Elias frowned, worried an Initiate might overhear. He didn't necessarily disagree with Eric, but he didn't want to be disrespectful to the men who spent their lives caring for them, either.

The other boy looked unconcerned as he continued. "Besides, in the last five years, they've taken what? One kid? Yeah, one. What was his name?"

"Martino," Georgie said quietly. The normally shy lad had been staring intently at the mage ever since she'd entered the hall, though neither of his friends had noticed his uncharacteristic behaviour. Georgie was a master at making himself unnoticed, and part of that skill lay in his refusal to look anyone in the eye for more than a second.

"Martino. Sure, I knew that. Look—it'll never happen—but maybe with some luck, she'll take that idiot, Carlo. He's old enough now. Where is he anyway? I haven't seen him all day," Eric remarked, looking around for the brooding Initiate.

"Who cares," Elias replied, growing steadily weary of Eric's incessant prattle. While their absence was odd, he was glad that neither Carlo nor Peter were around today, and that Dario—whatever his fate—was gone from the orphanage altogether. He didn't wish them any harm of course—even after all the things they'd done to him—but life certainly felt more enjoyable without their constant, menacing presence. He watched the mage quietly conversing with the headmaster and was suddenly struck by an odd thought. "Weird. They sort of look like each other, don't you think?"

"Who does?" Eric asked, feeling another hunger pang coming on.

"Father Lorimer and the king's new Kal-dkar."

"Huh? Oh yeah, they really kind of do. It is weird," Eric commented as he peered more carefully at the pair seated a few tables away.

"They're brother and sister," Georgie spoke up again. Both Elias and Eric looked sharply at their friend, finally noticing his strange, faraway look.

"How do you know that?" Elias asked after he'd recovered from his surprise.

The small boy didn't respond at first but then blinked several times and shook his head slightly as if coming out of a trance. He looked at Elias with wide eyes. "She just told me."

Elias gaped at his friend, dumbstruck. Before he could organize his scrambled thoughts and say something, he felt a hand firmly grasp his forearm and he tore his eyes with effort from Georgie's confused face to look at Eric. The big youth had evidently noticed something else occur at the same precise time that their friend had made his startling revelation. Elias followed Eric's wordless stare to look at the refectory doors and the two figures that had walked in just now and his jaw went slack for the second time in as many seconds.

It was Carlo and Flynn.

❖

Brother Owen approached the city gates leading north out of Corazan and stopped his horse before passing through. He turned in the saddle and looked over his shoulder, his gaze slowly taking in the wide panorama of the city he'd called home for most of his life. It was a view he'd seen numerous times before, but one he never got tired of. Far in the distance now, Castle Hill loomed over the centre of the capital, but from here he could no longer see the spires of the Janusian cathedral below, located as it was on the southern face of the tall rise. Dividing the city into roughly equal-sized halves, the Arnd River cut a ribbon of blue across the centre of Corazan before finding the sea a couple of miles to the south. It was midday now and normally the largest urban centre on the entire Rohnian peninsula would be bustling with activity, but not so on this day, the last of Yule. The typical steady stream of wagon, cart, and foot traffic that normally passed through the gate—merchants, farmers, and other travellers, all going about their business—was notably absent. It was just as well, he thought, lest he run into one too many familiar faces and the inevitable questions they would ask about his imminent journey.

He loved this city dearly, and Corazan was his adopted home, but it was strange that he still thought of it that way, considering he'd spent over two-thirds of his life here. At the core of his essence, he would always remain a Laenisian, and not because the colour of his skin was a daily reminder that he was different. He often wondered how that former life would have unfolded if the Golians hadn't wrenched him away from his family and homeland, but it was a pointless exercise. He'd come to accept that his trials had been the path Janus had chosen for him, and every footstep he'd taken had drawn him that much closer to the welcoming arms of the Overgod. It was this newest challenge, however—which Janus in his infinite wisdom had chosen to test him with—that troubled him more than any iron manacles ever could. Looking out over the multitude of rooftops, streets, and bridges, he committed every detail to memory while fighting off the disturbing sensation that he was looking at his beloved city for the last time—and perhaps he was. It was a possibility he couldn't ignore. The journey ahead wouldn't be easy in his condition, and even if he made it to his destination, there was no guarantee that he could be helped. It was a curious sensation—that of coming to terms with one's mortality, and how fleeting life could be. Not a pleasant subject, he concluded.

The mere thought of his ailment brought on a sudden need to cough, but the priest managed to suppress the urge by regulating his breathing and dispelling his anxiety in the way that Brother Paul had taught him. The herbal concoction that the other cleric had taught him to brew and that he'd had this morning was likely beginning to wear off, and he'd have to make some more this evening when they stopped. The moment passed, and he turned reluctantly forward with a sigh. He'd delayed long enough. Spurring the horse forward, he nodded to the guards at the gate and then passed through the cavernous tunnel of the gatehouse and out of the city, Emilio and the wagon following closely behind. Once on the road and away from the stone walls surrounding the capital, the remainder of the day passed uneventfully, the pair winding their way north through the rolling countryside. At first, they passed through several small villages and farmsteads, all part of the vital network that supplied the great city and its citizens with the resources they needed. Though it was winter in Rohne, it meant little here as the weather was mild enough this far south that many crop varieties still thrived. Unlike in most places beyond the northern mountainous isthmus that connected Rohne to the continental mainland, fresh fruits and vegetables were always readily available here.

With the sun dipping low in the west now, they left the cultivated farm fields behind, and the countryside took on a more pastoral character, where cattle lazily grazed or dozed in large meadows, broken up here and there by a fence or copses of olive trees. The further they got from the city, the more the already sparse traffic along the road dwindled, and it had been at least an hour since they'd encountered anyone. On horseback, the trip to Jerothos—the first city on their lengthy route—normally took but a single day's travel, but because they had left later in the day and the wagon was much slower, it would take them three times as long. Brother Owen had continued to ride slightly ahead of the wagon, and thankfully Emilio hadn't made any attempt at unwanted conversation. However, at this rate, it would take nearly a month to reach the Anvalite enclave on the borders of Chemar Forest, and the priest knew that interaction with his companion would be unavoidable sooner rather than later. While he thought of the road in front of him and the distance involved, Owen reflected on the strangeness of the contrast between his personal need for haste and the slowness of their pace. For the time being, he felt confident that it wouldn't be an issue, but he wasn't eager to push his luck. Of course, were it not for the wagon and its contents, all these considerations would be essentially moot.

Like Father Lorimer, he was convinced Dario's remains could provide vital clues that would help Grand Abbess Talia understand what was happening, not only with Flynn, but also with the illness coursing through him. He hadn't wanted to believe it might be true, but it seemed almost certain now that Flynn was indeed the source of whatever was wrong with himself. As he thought about the body of the dead child inside the wagon, he felt a pang of melancholy and regret. In his role as a caregiver, mentor, and teacher—and above all, friend—to the children of the orphanage, he couldn't help but feel that he had failed this boy. Had he made sufficient effort to get to know Dario? To try and help the clearly troubled youth with whatever problems had driven him into the company of bad influences like Carlo? If he'd given Dario the same attention he did to children like Flynn and Elias, might not Dario be alive still? Or was it that the boy simply hadn't wanted his help? If Dario had actively shunned the priest, on whose shoulders lay the burden of responsibility and guilt? The answer was simple, of course—on his. Owen was the adult, and he, along with every other priest in that orphanage, was indirectly responsible for this death. Not Dario. Not Flynn. Maybe some just couldn't be saved in the end, but that didn't mean they weren't worth the effort.

Lost in his thoughts and lulled by the monotony of the road, the cleric didn't notice that the hour had grown so late. It was only when Emilio called to him that he realized it was time for them to stop for the day and make camp. After selecting a fairly sheltered patch of level ground just off the road near some trees, the two men unloaded what they needed from the wagon and laid out their bedrolls a short distance from one another. Brother Owen watched in silence while his companion tended to the horses first and then proceeded to gather some stones to build a crude fire pit. Nodding his thanks after the flames had reached a suitable height, the cleric poured some water into a small kettle he'd brought along and hooked it onto a small iron frame to dangle over the fire. While he waited for the water to boil, he measured a generous pinch of powdered herbs from a small pouch into a tin cup, just as Brother Paul had instructed. When the water began to steam, he filled the cup and allowed the concoction to steep for a minute before drinking. It was bitter, and the hot liquid burned his throat, but the near-miraculous relief he felt immediately was well worth the effort of what had become a daily ritual for him. The rheum and phlegm that had been steadily building up throughout the day in his sinuses and throat cleared up almost instantly, and his breath eased from a steady rasp to a barely perceptible and manageable wheeze, easing the strain on his lungs.

Watching the priest from across the fire where he sat, Emilio rummaged through his pack and lifted something out that was filled with liquid and made a slight sloshing sound as it moved. Popping the stopper at one end, he lifted the spout to his lips and gulped noisily from the wineskin. His eyes never left the priest, and when the other man finally took note of what he was doing, he lowered the container to wipe his mouth with one sleeve and then grinned as he proffered the wineskin to Brother Owen.

"Care to spice up yer tea a little, Brother?"

"No, thank you."

Emilio shrugged and took another pull, smacking his lips after he was done. "Yer sure? This is the good stuff," he shook the wineskin as if to emphasize his point. "Noxos Moon Red, come all the way from Gol." The priest was caught off-guard by this, though he was careful not to show it. He didn't know a lot about wine, but enough to know that if it was imported from Gol, it was sure to be quite expensive—Noxos Moon Red even more so. How was a man of such obviously modest means like Emilio able to afford such a luxury?

"I don't like wine, much less anything that comes from Gol," Brother Owen said, unable to contain his irritation. What was it about this man that set his teeth on edge so easily?

"A'right, a'right... just tryin' to be friendly and share, s'all. And here I thought ya church-types loved makin' wine down in 'dem cellars of yers."

"Your information is out of date by a few hundred years," Owen replied. Thinking of the cellars that he'd visited that very morning to see Flynn, the priest recalled how strangely potent the smell of wine had been down there, and here he was now, talking about that very subject with this man. Was it just coincidence, or was there something else here that eluded him? Before he could think on it more, Emilio continued talking.

"Don't like 'dem Golians, eh? Why's that? Can't say I blame ya—surly bastards, the whole lot of 'em," he laughed at his own words, undeterred by his failure to elicit a similar reaction from the priest. "So, what's the matter with ya anyway, that ya need to go all the way up to Chemar?"

"Were you paid to ask impertinent questions the whole way, or just escort me to my destination?" Owen asked, levelling a hard stare at Emilio.

The other man's smile faded, and his expression became inscrutable, the flicker of the campfire reflecting in the dark orbs of his eyes as they met the priest's own. At length, he took one final swig of the ruby red liquid, stoppered the wineskin, and put it down on the ground next to where he sat. "There's no call to be so curt with me," Emilio said, the earlier humour gone from his voice, replaced by clear resentment. "I may not be a learned man and such, and I've my share of vices that would make ya blush, but I do what I can to make an honest livin' and feed my family—was only tryin' to make conversation."

The words and shift in tone had an immediate effect on Brother Owen. While some would consider such a quality a weakness, he'd always felt that his great capacity for compassion was one of his greatest strengths. Of course, being humble in equal measure meant that he didn't think of himself in those terms, but it had helped him become a tremendous asset for the Janusians, given the nature of the work required at the orphanage. So, it was with a deep sense of personal shame that he reminded himself of the need for tolerance and acceptance of the flaws of others and berated himself for prematurely passing judgement on this man based on his physical appearance and weakness for drink.

"Forgive me," he said with some effort, "I've not quite been myself in recent days. I'm not well, as I'm sure you've already noticed, but I don't wish to discuss that any further." Seeing Emilio frown, he added, "It's not that I think you incapable of understanding, it's that I'm still having difficulty coming to terms with what's happening to me and therefore talking about it just seems to make it worse. Does that make sense?" To the cleric's relief, Emilio nodded in understanding. "How much were you told, anyway?"

"No details, really. Yer secret, whatever it is, is safe. I know my way around horses, and I've travelled this land from one end to the other so... yeah, escortin' a priest and a corpse in a wagon up north seemed like a simple enough job," Emilio explained with a shrug. "I've got a reputation for bein' discreet," he said with a wink and a grin.

"I assume Father Lorimer was the one that hired you?"

"Father who? That yer boss? Nah, t'was that lad at the gate this mornin' what sought me out in the city and hired me. I suppose the coin must've come from your boss, but I didn't meet no Father Lorimer."

This troubled Brother Owen somewhat. It was abundantly clear—for reasons known only to the man—that Father Lorimer placed a great deal of trust in Carlo, but what disturbed the priest in this particular case was that his superior hadn't even deigned to handle this detail in person. Given the recent increase in animosity between him and the Initiate, he was beginning to understand why a man like

Emilio had been hired for this rather than someone a little less...unsavory? Well, a substantial advance payment would certainly explain how Emilio had purchased the expensive wine.

"Is Moon Red your favourite wine then?"

"This?" he held up the wineskin and looked at it as if seeing it for the first time, then gave off a chortle of amusement. "Nah, I can't afford this stuff on a good day, not even with what the lad paid me. Not if I wanna feed my seven kids. Nope, he gave me this as a bonus for takin' the job. Got it from 'dem cellars at the church, he said."

Brother Owen nodded slowly, again pondering whether there was any significance to any of this, and he briefly wondered if Father Lorimer was aware Carlo had given away some of his expensive wine. Come to think of it, he was surprised there was any wine down there at all. Either Father Lorimer spared no expense when he entertained, or he had a few private vices of his own. Ultimately, he decided that the details didn't matter; what did matter was that Carlo had had a personal hand in hiring this man, and given his mistrust of the former, his earlier misgivings about Emilio were now compounded. He wasn't sure what, if anything, the Initiate was up to, but he made a note to keep a watchful eye on his travelling companion.

"I see. Well, I've only one request to make of you for the duration of our journey, and it's a fairly simple one: keep your distance from me. It's nothing personal, believe me; it's for your own health and safety," he said at last, realizing he'd been silent for some time.

Emilio gave him a quizzical look, then shrugged his compliance with the request. "Sure thin', Brother."

Brother Owen felt relief again. Having a valid excuse for establishing a personal boundary between the two men would hopefully disguise the fact that he also didn't fully trust Emilio and why the man was travelling with him. Despite his suspicions, he felt better for having engaged his companion in conversation. Emilio seemed the talkative type, and such folk often tended to let slip something out that they shouldn't. "Your accent is faint, but not unfamiliar to me. Are you from Lundia?"

"Aye, that I am," Emilio admitted, though he seemed unusually subdued in his reply.

"My apologies, I didn't mean to bring up any uncomfortable memories." Brother Owen held up one hand, thinking he had correctly interpreted the flash of pain in the man's eyes. He took a sip of his tea and watched the other intently. Despite himself, he was suddenly curious about Emilio's past.

Emilio silently stoked the embers of the fire with one stick, then put it down and took up the wineskin again. After taking a long pull, he continued to stare at the flames. "Me mum fled to Rohne when me and me brother were still small lads. There'd been a long spell of bad weather and me parents' crops were destroyed and the animals died. The farm was just gone one day. We were in shock... most farmers lost everythin'. Some took to banditry and worse, but Mum and Da got arrested for poachin' on royal land outside Novot. Do ye know what the punishment for poachin' is in Lundia, Brother?"

He didn't know, and given Emilio's dark demeanour, he couldn't imagine it was a crime that was taken lightly, so he shook his head.

"The sentence is hangin'. The men swin' first, and the soldiers force the children to watch as a lesson to discourage lawlessness. So, we watched as our Da kicked and choked out his last breath at the end of a rope because he dared to try and find food for his lads. Mum would have followed him the next day had she not given her body to the guards to buy her escape that night. She took us in hand and fled to the coast where she stole a fishin' boat and had us in the water by daybreak. 'Tis over a hundred and fifty miles across the Strach from Novot to Rohnian shores, but Valsemar of the Deep took pity on us, and we made it somehow."

"That's just horrible," Owen said, remembering the time he'd given himself unto the mercy of the sea in a desperate bid to escape a life of servitude, but at least he'd been a young man in the prime of his life, healthy and strong. He could only imagine how terrified a mother with two small children in her care would have felt in a tiny boat, attempting to cross such a vast distance. Yet, Like Emilio's mother, the priest understood that a watery grave would have been preferable to the alternative.

"Aye, t'was," Emilio recalled the ordeal with a faraway stare into the flames. "By mid-mornin', the tide had begun to flow east and out of the gulf and was pullin' us toward the Storm Sea. She barely managed to work the sail, but it didn't matter in the end—bloody thin' was half-rotted through and fell apart when the wind picked up too much. Mum rowed all day and night until she could row no more, and then she continued to row anyway. To this day, I'm not sure how we survived, but we made landfall on a deserted beach north of the Vranik range. From there we walked, half-starved to death with feet raw and bloodied, until we stumbled upon Alkavar by pure chance. My brother still lives in that city to this day, but I moved on long ago."

"And your mother...?"

"She hun' on long enough to see us become able to take care of ourselves, and then she took her own life," Emilio said casually with a shrug while taking another swig of wine.

"Janus, be merciful! Why? After all that she went through to save you," Owen exclaimed in shock. He never did understand how some people could despair enough to give up like that. Life was such a precious gift, and even in his darkest days as a slave, the despondency that he'd felt only fueled his desire to escape even more and live as a free man once again.

Emilio shrugged. "Well, there's the rub, Brother. The memories of what she'd seen and done—our home lost, Da hangin' from a rope, being ravished by a bunch of men to gain our freedom, fightin' against exhaustion and the sea to escape—t'was too much for one heart to bear. She was never the same, and the nightmares never let her be. She's better off now, wherever she is."

"I'm sorry," the priest said softly, unable to find appropriate words that would offer any comfort after hearing such an awful tale. Much as the Janusians tried to do their part to make the world a better place by easing the lives of those around them through their work, it was sadly still a place filled with all-too-similar tales of injustice and tragedy like that of Emilio's family. He never deluded himself into thinking such things didn't happen—his own early life being a painful reminder of that—but he never let that stop him from trying to make a difference in any way he could.

"Nah, don't be," Emilio shrugged again. "I've had nearly fifty years to think on this, and I know she did what any good mum would do. I'm here because of that, and we couldn't have asked any more from her. I only wish I'd been strong enough to do more with the life she gave me."

"We all have our sins to bear, Emilio," Brother Owen said, smiling and feeling his empathy growing for this man. Self-reflection was always an encouraging trait and a sign that an individual was not beyond turning their life around. "You said you have a family you want to feed, and here you are working toward that worthy goal. If your vice is enjoying wine a little too much, I think Janus can overlook that in the grand scheme of things."

"Hahahaha," Emilio laughed at this, clearly amused by the clergyman's well-meaning attempt to let him know he shouldn't be so hard on himself. "Family? I don't have no family. Did I say I did? Brother, I sincerely hope that when I stand before yer god and he's ready to pass judgment on me for me sins, that he can overlook a lot more than just wine," he grinned through yellow, crooked teeth. "Have ye any idea how many times I've seen the inside of a dungeon cell?"

Brother Owen's smile faded. "No, and it doesn't matter. Your past is what it is and that cannot be changed, but what you choose to do with your future is all that matters, isn't it?" The light of the flames glinted on the shining steel surface of the dagger as it appeared out of nowhere and into Emilio's hand. It had to have been hidden somewhere inside the man's sleeve, but the movement had been too quick and expertly done for the priest to detect. He looked at the weapon apprehensively and then lifted his gaze to look at Emilio in uncertain silence.

"Ye see, Brother, that's where yer wrong," Emilio remarked, his eyes never leaving those of the priest as he flicked the blade through the air between his hands, passing it from one to the other with practiced ease. "The past is who we are, and who we are is what cannot be changed. The future's nothin' more than the next day that we have to live with that knowledge."

The cleric sat perfectly still, not daring to move a muscle except those required to speak. He was quite certain now that he'd badly misjudged who and what Emilio was, and his earlier misgivings came rushing back in a flood. "That's one perspective, yes," he said, doing his best to not show fear and keep his voice steady. "Not really so different from mine, but even so, we must not forget the one thing we all have in common when faced with that next day."

"And what would that be, Brother?"

"Choice."

CHAPTER 23

THE FORM LAY MOTIONLESS on the cold, hard tiles of the temple floor, eyes staring sightlessly at the vaulted ceiling, limbs contorted in a final spasm of agony. No visible hint of life stirred within the body of the fallen Minotaur, yet somehow the consciousness that was Vurax retained sufficient awareness to not only register this fact, but to also observe it from a perspective that was not its own.

'What is this?' he heard his own thought as if spoken aloud, the words echoing inside a boundless void before dissipating like a whisper in the wind. A swirling haze of red smoke partially and briefly obscured the body on the floor, and he felt a surge of unreasoning panic at losing sight of that final link to what had been his physical existence. If this was indeed death, he was not prepared to let go. He tried to somehow will himself to move closer, but found that no movement was possible. He'd felt helpless before—whether when he'd been shackled so heavily by his former masters that he could not move, or from wounds received that had left him so incapacitated that he could not rise again—but this was very different. This was a disembodied existence that left him terrified and filled with utter impotence. The sheer perplexity of it all made him want to shout in fear and rage, but there was an empty inevitability growing inside of him that prevented what he knew would be an ultimately futile protest.

'So ready to give up, are you? I expected more of a fight,' the familiar voice made itself heard, not from any one particular point of origin in this formless realm, but from all around, as if it encompassed all that was left of him.

Always before had he spurned the unwelcome presence—with its insidious whisperings and entreaties—but now, everything had changed. All his life he had preferred to be left alone, content to not have to rely on others for anything, including company. Yet, in that instant, when faced with the terrifying prospect of eternal solitude in this dark emptiness, he clung to that old presence like a drowning man to an errant piece of floating driftwood.

'Am I dead?' he asked, desperately needing some confirmation of the only conclusion he'd been able to draw so far, while simultaneously holding onto the impossible hope that this was somehow a dream or inexplicable hallucination.

'Do you want to be? You can't deny it's been something you've wished for on many an occasion, has it not?'

Not a yes or a no, then. How was he so foolish as to expect that just this once, the presence would ever give him a straight answer to anything? The smoke passed and he saw his body once again, the sad image so wretched in its finality that had he a physical heart still, it would have wrenched with grief for himself. He tried to get a better sense of his surroundings, such as they were, and managed to make out the vague outline of a gigantic golden body, complete with arms, legs, and a head that would not obey any of his commands to move. He remembered the horned statue—a gaudy and ornate representation of the god of the Minotaurs—standing within the walls of the temple in which he'd collapsed. Was he inside the statue then, somehow looking out through its inanimate eyes?

'Are you mourning for yourself? Oh Vurax, how truly pathetic you've become,' the voice mocked. 'I don't make mistakes, so don't let this be the first time I'll ever have to admit that I was wrong about something. What happened to the defiant warrior who laughed in the face of death?'

'I didn't expect that it would come in such a pointless fashion,' he admitted sullenly. 'This is no way for anyone to die.'

'No way for anyone to die? How arrogant have mortals become, to think that they can dictate the terms of what constitutes a good death—in fact, I can't think of a more laughable notion than your constant and irrepressible need to ascribe some form of meaning to that which simply "is".'

He hated this circular talk. Always had. If this thing had a point to make, it never quite seemed to get there, and this time, despite the circumstances, was proving no different. Still, he found himself loathing the thought of being alone even more, bereft of all purpose and meaning as he felt now. What did he have to do that was more important than to listen to its philosophical ramblings? And did he even have a choice? Unsurprisingly, his thoughts were not private. What was surprising was that when the voice spoke again, it was with words that finally made some sense to him.

'You're not dead, Vurax. You seek meaning? Well, here it is—I'm not done with you. Do not bristle like you always do and claim that you are no pawn, for indeed you are not. Such an ugly word—not so unlike slave, don't you think? Rather, think of yourself as an instrument of fate, carefully chosen from among countless others to play a part in something that must, for now, remain concealed from you. But that purpose is something that can't be fulfilled if you continue to stubbornly deny me. Do you know who I am?'

Not dead? The revelation left him just as stunned as if he'd received a confirmation to the contrary. What then was all this? A fevered dream? Some strange property of that cloying incense smoke that had transported him into some deep, nether level of his subconscious? If so, what was all this talk about fate and purpose? Was this his own mind's feeble attempt to come to terms with his newfound freedom and his inability to decide what to do with his life now that he finally had one again?

'Stop thinking about yourself for a damn minute and focus on my question!' the voice roared, impatience fraying at its edges in a way he'd never felt before. Was that fear that Vurax sensed? Was it possible that it could feel that?

'Yes,' he responded at last.

'Who am I?'

'Nothing but a figment of my imagination—a voice that I created inside of me during my darkest moments of despair and solitude so I would have someone to talk to.'

'Wrong. You heard me long before that, even if you ignored me. Then, in captivity, you called to me and found that I had never left you. You used my name then, so speak it again now. Admit that I exist once and for all and become truly free at last. Say it, and claim your destiny, Vurax.'

His only answer was silence.

'Say it!'

'No.'

There was a prolonged quiet, and Vurax thought himself truly alone now. Had he finally banished it? He wasn't convinced, but if it was true that he was not dead, he needed to somehow return to his body, or it would have been a hollow victory.

'You saw with your own eyes, what happened to those Minotaur legionnaires at the fort, and still, you do not believe.'

He heaved a mental sigh. It was not gone after all.

'You heard the Elf's tale of what befell his people, and still, you do not believe.'

'There must be another explanation,' he replied after his own stony silence.

'No, there is only your obstinate refusal to accept the truth.'

'The truth? And what is that truth? That whenever I give into what you say, everyone around me ends up butchered? Is that your truth? Because if it is, then I want no part of it. I never did—I was too weak to accept it before, but no more, do you hear me?'

It was so faint at first that he thought he was only imagining it, but then it grew louder and more insistent, becoming impossible to ignore—a chant that rose from somewhere within the empty void all around him. Within it were words he'd heard before but had always scorned. It was a prayer.

'I hear you, Vurax, but I hear something else as well. Do you?'

He nodded, the physical gesture non-existent in his current incorporeal state, but a reluctant affirmative, nonetheless.

'Not so far from us, a priest is beseeching to be granted the power to save a life. Do you know whose life it is?'

'Kael' he whispered, remembering the name and the one to whom it belonged like they were already part of a very faded and distant memory.

'What meaning will his death have if you do nothing to prevent it?'

'I don't understand.'

'I think that you do. I can heed that prayer and save his life. Or I can ignore it and let him die. Will that be proof enough to you that I am indeed real? The decision is yours, of course, but know this—if you ask me to save him, you cannot deny me ever again. Do not take long; his last remaining breaths are fewer than you think.'

It was not a fair request, and they both knew it. The cost to him—and he did not fool himself into thinking that there wouldn't be one—remained unvoiced, but the alternative meant he would fail his friend, just as he had failed his parents and brother. No amount of pride was worth another life, so if a purpose was what he'd been searching for all along, perhaps it was time to stop denying it and embrace the inevitable. Whatever the sacrifice was that would be asked of him one day, he would face it with courage and honour, but above all, the firm knowledge that it had not been in vain.

'You are Zarvon, the Horned One, creator of all Golians in his own image' he recited the words he'd been made to memorize as a child. 'Save my friend, and I am yours.' There was none of the familiar contempt or anger in those words; only a calm, almost numb acceptance.

There was no gloating cry of victory or even an acknowledgment of his capitulation other than the sound of the prayer fading to silence. Had he waited too long to agree, or would Kael's disembodied spirit soon join him in this disorienting purgatory where he found himself? All-encompassing quietness was all that greeted him.

Sensation returned slowly with a blink of dry eyes and the moistening of a mouth that felt as parched as the dusty steppes of Sarmakan. The arched beams of the temple's ceiling focused slowly into view, and Vurax lifted himself from the floor, his entire body stiff and aching as if he'd been lying in the same position for far too long. Rubbing at sore muscles and fighting through the headache that pounded within his skull, he looked warily at the statue of the god, standing there as it always had—a cold and unfeeling icon that filled him with dread, confusion, and deep resentment. What had he done? Even as the question formed, he could swear there was a slight smirking quality to the golden bull's carved lips that hadn't been there previously. Before he could decide whether his imagination was playing tricks on him after the surreal experience he'd just gone through, he heard the door open behind him.

"There you are! Come quickly, Kael is awake." It was Larios.

Vurax closed his eyes and sighed deeply.

'I'm not ungrateful, but as soon as I do whatever it is that you want me to do, our bargain is finished, my debt repaid,' he called out within his mind. *There was no reply, however, and that troubled him more than any unctuous words he might have heard back.*

Back at Larios' farmhouse that morning, Kael sat on a chair out on the porch, enjoying the crisp morning air and birdsong while musing about his peaceful surroundings. The last thing the centurion remembered was the violent battle on the mountain path, yet here he was now—a few days later and over a hundred miles away—freshly healed from a ghastly wound and sipping contentedly on a warm mug of mulled spiced apple cider. He'd been in many a tight scrape before but how he'd managed to somehow escape this one with his life promised to be an interesting tale indeed, and one that he couldn't wait to hear. His companion had promised to fill in the gaps in his memory before they got underway but before that, Vurax had muttered about something important he needed to discuss with the old Minotaur, and so the two of them were having a private conversation inside the homestead. Kael had to admit he was burning with curiosity, but his growing respect and friendship for Vurax prevented him from even thinking about trying to eavesdrop. Leaning back on the chair, he took another sip of the fragrant drink, savouring the bold flavour and admiring the pastoral view while he waited.

Sitting across the small table from each other, Vurax stared silently at the floor between his feet, Larios' words still echoing in the air of the room, with the weight of the revelation bearing down on his shoulders like the yoke he'd been forced to wear for many years. The retired legionnaire had just finished relating to him who his father had been before traveling to the countryside around Vurgas to settle into a life of quiet anonymity, and Vurax was having a difficult time reconciling what he'd heard about Zerik Baurus with the gentle, unassuming bull he'd known since birth. Just as confounding was the fact that Larios was clearly holding back some key details, specifically about why exactly the former Supreme Legate of all of Gol's legions had given up an illustrious career and all the benefits and recognition that went along with it to become a simple village blacksmith. It was almost as hard to accept as the knowledge that the life of someone like that could end in the obscure ignominy and squalor of a slaver's camp in a remote land, abandoned and forgotten by an empire he'd spent the better part of his life serving.

"If he wanted to put the past behind him, why not change his name?" Vurax asked, trying to make some sense out of it all.

"Because it wasn't really a secret that he'd come here. I think he knew better than to try and completely hide his identity and how difficult that would prove, and with time, people start to forget or even care about certain things. I recognized him immediately because I couldn't call myself a legionnaire and not know Zerik Baurus by sight, let alone by reputation. I can still recall with perfect clarity the day I first saw him. He'd come to Vurgas when he was still Supreme Legate to inspect the Tenth, and he personally signed my discharge papers when I retired. It's a moment I'll never forget, being face-to-face with one's personal hero. As for those folks in the sleepy hamlet he eventually chose to call home, he was merely the welcome addition of someone who knew how to shoe a horse or hammer a dent out of a metal bucket. It's a simple life we live out here in the countryside, Vurax, where peace, quiet, and privacy are the things one most cherishes. I know the appeal, because when I finally left the legion and was allocated some land for my years of service, this is where I chose to spend my modest soldier's pension and make a life for myself and my family. I think that's just what he was looking for as well, and I'm glad he got to experience that for thirty-four years before the tragedy that befell him."

"Yet, you won't tell me why he did it," Vurax looked at Larios, desperate to know more so that he could understand. "Why is that? Should I ask Kael? He's a soldier too. Surely, he would know."

"Yes, most likely he does, as would many others you could ask, but it is not a story that will bring you happiness, Vurax. You have your freedom again, and a chance to start over. Why saddle yourself with the burdens of the past and things that you can't change? Besides, I vowed to Zerik that I would respect his wishes, and I won't go back on that, not even for you. Not all knowledge is beneficial," Larios gently warned. The old veteran ached with empathy for Zerik's son, but he truly believed in his heart that it would be better this way. "You have to ask yourself, if your father didn't tell you, doesn't that say that he didn't think it was important that you know?"

Vurax considered this. There was logic to what Larios was saying, even if his mind still refused to put the matter aside. He thought briefly of turning his question inward and asking the presence lurking there, but he wasn't confident he would get an answer that wasn't riddled with more questions, so he dismissed the idea. He clearly wasn't going to get more out of Larios, and his esteem for the veteran and what he'd done for him this past night wouldn't allow him to force the issue. Should he indeed ask Kael? He needed to think on it more. For now, it was time to say goodbye and get underway. Despite his own personal issues, he hadn't forgotten everything else that was happening, and that getting Treeweaver to Golan was becoming more urgent with each passing day. With a nod of acceptance, Vurax placed his hand over Larios' in a gesture of silent gratitude for what the old bull had shared with him, and then got up and walked to the door.

"You're sure you're feeling well enough to travel?" Vurax asked Kael, eyeing the centurion as if he still couldn't quite come to terms that this was the same person who, only a few hours ago, had been at death's door. The shattered leg was whole once more, the gruesome leg wound gone as if it had never been, and without so much as a limp in the Golian's stride to mark its passing. Gone too were all the other debilitating effects of the infection that had very nearly ended the soldier's life, and Turanis Kael of the Eighth Legion stood before him as hale and hearty as the day the two had met.

"For the last time, Vurax, yes," his friend said with a sincere smile. "I don't think I've ever felt better in my life."

"Alright then, but you might wish you'd passed on to your deserved rest in the grave when you see how we're going to be travelling to Golan," Vurax quipped.

Kael laughed, thinking that nothing could be worse than what he'd just been through, but something in the other's voice told him he was only half jesting. Not one to let his spirits be dampened by Vurax's now-familiar morose remarks, he turned to Larios standing at the doorway a couple of steps away and gave the old veteran an honourable salute. "Thank you for all you've done for me, Principales Larios. Were you still in the service, I'd gladly commend you for a promotion."

Larios smiled and returned the gesture, thumping his fist to his heart. "Those days are long behind me, centurion, and I but did my duty, for in helping to save a fellow soldier's life, I continue to serve my empire in any way I still can."

Kael nodded, and shouldered the pack of provisions Larios had kindly pre-pared for them. "We are humbled by your generosity." He clasped forearms with the old bull in friendship and respect. "Whenever you're ready," he turned to Vurax.

"Go on, I'll catch up shortly," Vurax motioned toward the nearby woods where Treeweaver and Windrider awaited them. Once the centurion was out of earshot, he turned to Larios. "I'm not very good at this so I'll keep it short. What you did for us, for me…a complete stranger at your door in the middle of the night, I—".

Larios held up one hand to forestall whatever Vurax was going to say next and shook his head. "But you're not a stranger, are you? We've established that, so no more needs to be said. Consider it a last favour to a great Golian soldier I once knew and admired. Someone who became a good friend and deserved a better fate than the one the gods saw fit to dispense."

Vurax nodded pensively. "Yes, about my father—the way you spoke of him and knew him from a time before I was even born. Are you positively certain there isn't more that you can tell me?" he made one last attempt, already knowing what he would hear but unable to keep himself from trying despite his resolve a minute ago not to ask again. He simply needed to know.

Larios shook his head. "I told you already—of that I will say no more. There are reasons why he put that part of his life behind him and came here to start anew, and it's not my place or right to tell you what they were," Larios said.

"Then whose place is it?"

"You're going to Golan, are you not? You'll find your answers there before long, I suspect." The old legionnaire took no pleasure in being circumspect like this, but he would honour his vow to Zerik Baurus.

Vurax looked into Larios' eyes, searching vainly there for more clues to this mystery. Finding none, he did not press him further, and this time, it would be final. The old timer had done more than enough to earn his gratitude, and along with that came an unspoken deference for his decision over whatever secret he chose to hold onto. If the answer was out there somewhere, then he would find it. He gave Larios a resolute clasp of his forearm in farewell, and then departed in silence. His heart was heavy with the knowledge that he'd not told the old bull about the fate of the soldiers of the Tenth, but then he couldn't be sure if his sons had been among the fallen. Larios would receive the news in due time anyway, and he fervently hoped it would not be tragic in nature. An impulse overtook him, and he stopped to turn and face the veteran—standing silently in front of his modest farmhouse to watch him go—and gave him a soldier's salute. Larios smiled and saluted back, keeping his fist over his heart until the two departing Golians were lost in the distance.

During the walk through the grassy meadow on their way back to the woods, Vurax took the opportunity to fill Kael in on everything that had happened since the centurion had lost consciousness. He'd waited until now because there were things in his account that he did not feel necessary burdening Larios with, but that he needed to prepare Kael for before they met up with the Elves and their gryphons. For his part, the centurion did his best to keep an open mind about the more fantastical elements of the tale. Had he not been witness to similarly strange events during his campaign in Ur, he might have been more skeptical of Vurax's story. Indeed, it was a testament to how much he'd come to trust his new friend that he was willing to accept that there were Elves helping them. Not only that, but the other had managed to convince him not to contact the Tenth Legion command in Vurgas and give a full report on the loss of the mountain fort to a giants' attack led by a Titan. Had Kael done so, Vurax contended that they could be delayed indefinitely for questioning, and that it was vital that they continue on to Golan with all haste so that Treeweaver could complete his mission. He did not, of course, make any mention of what had happened to him at the fort or the temple.

"You realize I'll probably be court-martialed for dereliction of duty over this?" Kael remarked dejectedly.

"I don't understand much about military laws, but yes, most likely," Vurax replied. Cursing himself for his bluntness, he quickly added, "Look, you don't have to come with us. If you give us enough of a head start, you can still go back and report to your commanders. I'm not enlisted, so I'm not your responsibility. You can make up whatever story you want about how we became separated—if they even care about a lone former slave being transported back to Gol," he offered. He wanted Kael to stay, but he also didn't want to see the soldier's career come to a dishonourable end because of him.

Kael looked at him sideways as they walked. He couldn't deny that he'd thought about taking the very course of action that Vurax was proposing, but he'd dismissed it almost immediately. Ever since he'd subdued the valiant Golian on the field of battle as the other had fought bravely to the last to avenge himself upon his former masters, he'd felt his fate inexplicably bound to Vurax's. Saving each other's lives was becoming a habit, and his honour demanded that he remain at his friend's side through thick and thin. Vurax had done no less for him when he could have simply abandoned Kael in the mountains to die.

"And let a country bumpkin like you blunder around the imperial capital without someone to keep him out of trouble? Right. You'd never come within a mile of the emperor," he laughed.

"Oh, and you will? You never told me you were that fancy and important," Vurax grinned from ear to ear, relieved that Kael wouldn't stand for being left behind.

"I'm not. I told you I was born and raised in the ass-end of nowhere, and I wasn't lying. However, being a veteran of the Fourth and the Urian campaign, I do know one or two people in higher circles. Besides, you forget I'm carrying a missive from Tribune Jalx with details on your captivity and liberation to present before the senate. I'm confident I can get your Elf princeling an audience with the emperor, at least before the lot of you get thrown into a dungeon as lunatics and spies."

Vurax guffawed at that. "I see. So, it's a race to who gets arrested first then—me for telling crazy stories or you for deserting?"

Kael made a mock show of being offended. "What? This isn't desertion! I prefer to call it a 'sensitive diplomatic mission'. I'm supposed to get you to Golan, and that's exactly what I'm doing."

Vurax regarded his friend with fondness. "Thank you. Your help and company are most welcome."

"Hey," Kael protested, "don't go soft on me now. It could seriously damage my opinion of you," he warned with a wink. The other laughed again and clapped him amiably on the shoulder as the pair of them entered the woods in search of their Elven companions.

⚬

Soaring high above the ground, the two gryphons and their four riders sped southward over the wide expanse of the Golian Empire. With hundreds of miles to cover before reaching the capital on the distant southern coast of the Minotaur realm, the days-long journey took them over the remainder of the rugged Northern Province first, and then onward above the vast tracts of rolling plains that dominated the Central Province. Kael, seated firmly behind Windstrider, carefully kept them on a course that would help them avoid being spotted from the ground by staying clear of any towns and villages below. Burdened as they were, the gryphons couldn't fly as high as they normally could, but it was still enough to allow them to remain largely unnoticed by anyone in the empty lands over which they flew. Over shorter distances, flying at night would have been a better choice, but for such a long trek, they needed the daylight to maintain their bearings and guide themselves by geographical features of Gol that Kael could recognize. Keeping the gryphons fed was another matter, however, and the centurion had to grit his teeth and do his best to ignore the occasional unfortunate grazing cow or two, whose devoured carcasses some farmers would mysteriously find in the morning long after they'd departed.

On the third day of their journey, Kael bid them alter their flight path somewhat and angle southeastward as they left the Central Province and approached the Heartlands. The most densely inhabited region of the nation, the Heartlands were aptly named for being the fertile breadbasket that supported the other Golian provinces with its vast agricultural output, feeding a population of millions throughout the empire. With the stunningly colourful patchwork tapestry of endless farmlands, orchards, crop fields, and pastures looming on the southern horizon, it was a prudent move on their part to detour toward the more sparsely settled Eastern Province to avoid detection, even if the delay would cost them an additional day. Turning toward the east, Vurax glimpsed what he thought was just a hint of darkness in the sky at the uttermost edge of the horizon and imagined that it might be the fires that were consuming the homeland of the Syldar. He was about to ask Treeweaver, then thought better of it and kept his silence.

It was late afternoon now, and they were looking for a suitable place to land and make camp when Vurax spotted a wondrous sight to their left. Shimmering as it caught the low light of the setting sun, a vast body of water glittered and sparkled with shades of blue and gold like a gigantic mirror in the distance, stretching from north to south for as far as he could see, and with no discernible sign of a shoreline on the far side.

"Is that the sea?" he asked in awe, and pointed with his newly healed arm at the same time, getting Treeweaver's attention.

The Elf smiled. "No, that's Lake Dal. It sits at the midway point of the mighty Talban River, which is born in the Border Peaks and flows all the way down to empty into the Storm Sea—right outside the walls of Golan, in fact. We're too far away to see it from here, but beyond Lake Dal lie the mountains we call the Wedge, and behind them, my homeland of Syldar." When he mentioned this last, his voice choked with emotion at the fresh memory of recent events in the nation of the Syldarin. He'd been so preoccupied with helping Vurax of late that he tried not to dwell too much on that for now, but not a day passed when he didn't think of his sister, Nimiris, and wondered how she was faring as the new leader of their people. Perhaps there would be some news when they reached the Minotaur capital. Perhaps not.

Guiding the gryphons down toward a ridge of low hills along the lakeshore, the Elves landed the weary creatures so that their passengers could make camp for the night. Though he would never grow accustomed to flying, Vurax had lost some of his fear and apprehension, even if his body continued to complain over spending hours on the backside of a gryphon. He rubbed futilely at the stiffness in his sore backside and looked at Kael in envy, noting not for the first time how much better the other Golian was handling all this. Not only had the centurion made fast friends with the two Syldar in spite of Vurax's earlier fears that Kael would be unwilling to cooperate with supposed enemies of the empire, but he also appeared not overly bothered by the experience of flight nearly as much as Vurax was.

"How do you do it?" Vurax muttered, sitting down with a grunt on a rock in front of their small campfire. He stretched his arms with a wide yawn and looked up at the canvas of bright stars shining in the blanket of velvety darkness of the night sky. They had made camp at the summit of a tall hill crowned with a small copse of trees, giving them a decent amount of cover and a good vantage point from which to keep an eye on the surrounding terrain and lakeshore.

"Do what?" Kael asked without taking his eyes off the meal he was preparing for everyone—a small chunk of dark bread and a slice of cheese, all from Larios' farm, and some lake trout that Windstrider had caught an hour ago. The skin on the pair of large fish sizzled and popped as they hung over the flames on a makeshift spit, releasing an aroma that made Vurax's mouth water.

"Act as if you haven't spent the whole day sitting on the back of those confounded creatures," Vurax groaned, trying unsuccessfully to find a better position. After shifting for a bit, he gave up on the rock and simply sat on the ground.

"Oh, that," Kael laughed teasingly. "Well, though the Eighth is comprised mainly of infantry units, once you rise to the rank of optio or higher, legion officers receive training on horseback riding and fighting. Nothing quite as showy as what those fancy boys from the Sixth and Seventh in the Western Province can do, but I learned enough to allow my muscles to relax when on the back of a moving animal for an extended period. Certainly, enough not to end up a sorry sight like you."

"These aren't horses, Kael," Vurax glared at him crossly, knowing fully well when the other was making fun of his wretchedness.

"Close enough in many ways, and if you're referring to the flying part... well, I think it's glorious," Kael admitted, irritating Vurax even further.

"Well, good for you," the other Golian harrumphed, lying back on the grass with his hands under his head. "How much longer?"

"For what? The fish, or until we reach Golan?"

"Both."

"A couple of minutes ought to do it, and about six or seven more days, I should think." He looked at Treeweaver, who sat just at the edge of the firelight staring in silent thought at the flames. The Elf nodded without looking up.

"Good grief," Vurax groaned again. "I don't think I'm going to make it."

"If you'd rather walk..." Kael suggested. "You know, for someone who spent years in irons and sleeping on hard ground, you seem awfully bothered by a bit of back pain all of a sudden," the centurion remarked, continuing his good-natured teasing. "Only a few short weeks of freedom and you're already going soft."

"Yeah, and here I thought I'd left all of that misery behind," Vurax complained some more.

This time, even Treeweaver smiled. "What will you do when you get to Golan, Vurax?"

The Minotaur pondered the question, his dark eyes searching the stars above as if an answer somehow hidden there would suddenly reveal itself. Truth was, he had no idea. He suspected whatever Zarvon wanted him to do would become apparent soon enough, but for now, he hoped it wouldn't interfere with his promise to help Treeweaver and his people.

"I don't know. Stand at your side when you speak to the emperor, I suppose. After that, who can say?" he replied noncommittally.

"Will you return home to Vurgas?" the Elf asked.

"No," Vurax said without hesitation. There was nothing left for him in his former home but painful memories. "Like I said, I don't know."

Treeweaver took that as a clear sign that the Minotaur wasn't willing to converse any further about this, so he let the matter drop. He himself was quite unsure of what the future would bring, as so much of what he would do next hinged on what the Golian government would decide to do with the news he was going to deliver to them. For now, he couldn't visualize any outcome that wouldn't lead him back to his people as soon as possible, with or without help. If news of the attack on the legion fort arrived before they did, it might just make his task of convincing the emperor a little easier. For now, even Kael did not know what had happened back in Syldar as he'd asked Vurax to keep that in confidence.

"Strange, isn't it, that neither you nor I can return home again? The reasons may be different, but the result is the same—we have both been cast adrift into the world by circumstances beyond our control," the Syldar mused.

"The difference is that you have a purpose still; a duty to fulfill to your people. Me? I don't know what the hell I'm doing," Vurax muttered.

"You've already said it—you're helping me. My purpose is yours now, and I'm grateful for your presence at my side."

"Dinner is ready," Kael interrupted, portioning the fish into small wooden bowls—skilfully shaped like one half of a walnut shell—that Treeweaver had pulled out of his pack, and passing them along with the cheese and bread. Their fare so far had consisted mainly of cured ham and dried strips of beef that Larios had provided, but with that running low now, they would have to rely more on hunting and fishing for the remainder of their journey. For the Elves, less accustomed than the two Golians to a steady diet of animal meat, the fish was a welcome change.

Vurax sat up eagerly and took his dish, savouring the first few mouthfuls of flavourful pink trout meat with a contented sigh. He took a pull from his water canteen and then broke off a piece of bread to mop up some of the juices gathering in the bowl. "This is good," he nodded in thanks to Kael.

"It's alright; not my best effort. Missing something—olive oil, I think. Wish I had some salt too," the centurion mourned.

"All quiet; nothing's out there for a good long distance. I've let Brisa and Asa on their own to hunt for a while," Windstrider announced, walking out from the lengthening shadows around the camp and into the glow of the fire. "You Golians put too much salt into everything. Here, try this. I found some growing nearby." He handed Kael a small bunch of green-leafed herbs and took a bowl for himself before sitting down with them. The Minotaur sniffed at the offering suspiciously, then tore off a few leaves from the stems, spread them over his fish, and took a tentative bite.

"Tastes like soap," the centurion said, making a face that could best be described as unimpressed. "What do you call this?"

"Cilantro," Windstrider said, pulling his long dark hair back to tie it in a utilitarian fashion so he could eat.

"Cilan—what?" Kael protested, picking a small leafy bit from between his teeth. "No, thanks. The only green thing that should go on food is oregano. That, and lots of salt."

"On meat, perhaps," Windstrider conceded, "but on fish? You don't know what you're missing."

"I just tasted it, and I'm not missing anything. You Syldar are a strange people."

"Well, I happen to like it," Vurax commented. He licked his fingers and passed his bowl back to Kael for another helping. When he thought back on what he'd had to survive on for years, a meal like this was a repast fit for the emperor's own table. He looked around the campfire at his three companions and took a long pause to appreciate the feeling of camaraderie among them, along with the serenity of the setting. Here, far removed from everything and everyone, the world was a quiet and peaceful place where he could enjoy his freedom and rest his weary soul. He fixed that sensation in his heart, committing the experience to his memory as he listened to his friends teasing each other good-naturedly. He allowed all his senses to absorb that instant in time—their faces by the firelight; the taste of the seasoned fish; the aroma of wood smoke; the trilling of crickets in the night; the moons and stars shining overhead. He hadn't felt Zarvon's presence since that night at the temple, but he knew the god wasn't far. For the brief respite he'd been given, Vurax gave his silent thanks.

"Treeweaver, give us a song, would you?" Windstrider prompted, putting down his empty bowl.

"I'm not sure if our Golian friends have an ear for Elven singing," Treeweaver laughed.

"That's because they've never heard any," the other Elf shrugged. "What do you say?"

"Can't be worse than your soapy herbs," Kael jibed. "Let's hear it."

In response, Windstrider reached into a satchel lying at his feet where he sat and pulled out a set of reed pipes. Putting the delicate wind instrument to his lips, he began to play, the haunting sound filling the air with a melody that evoked feelings of melancholy and longing for something that had been lost. After the first few notes, Treeweaver lifted his clear voice in song, seamlessly joining the music in a steady tenor:

Far beyond the mists of ancient time,
The Guardian gazed on something sublime,
Long had he sat and pondered in solitude,
Yet now his heart ached with bliss and gratitude.

Alone no more, with the fruits of his labour,
A celebration of his love, a moment to savour,
Three ëler and three nëler for the world to see,
Forever united under the shade of his great tree.

Then he stood, and sang to them by name,
Telemn first, he that was born of flame,
Lina came next, who loved the beauty of life,
Twin souls bonded as husband and wife.

On the wind destined, to soar and fly,
Avalen looked up, gaze as blue as the sky,
Nuamek watched, with adoration and glee,
Her love and loyalty like the depths of the sea.

From the earth to the trees, and all life in between,
Syld of the forests, tended to all that was green,
Uwan the dark, last to receive the Guardian's breath,
Complete now was the cycle of birth and death.

The sound of laughter and song filled the air,
While their wandering feet took them here and there,
This was Erliandol-es-kanar, the beginning of the Elves,
A tale of joy, sorrow, and the truth of ourselves.

The last words of the melody lingered in the air for an ephemeral instant before fading into the night, and with them, the haunting sound of the pipes. Both Treeweaver and Windstrider closed their eyes and remained perfectly still, deep in some kind of reverie. Kael glanced questioningly at Vurax, but the other could only shrug in response. Neither one was willing to break the silence, but as it wore on, Vurax cleared his throat awkwardly, prompting the return of the Syldar from wherever their memory had transported them.

"That was...uh...lovely," the Golian gave what he thought would be an appropriate compliment, both unsure of the significance of what he'd just heard, and not having much of an ear for music. An eternity of involuntarily listening to Sarmakanite drums and droning tribal chants hadn't exactly broadened his horizons in the art.

"Thank you," Treeweaver acknowledged the tribute. "Not something that's easy to translate, especially to a tongue as harsh-sounding as yours is to us, but I trust the essence of what it conveys transcends language."

"Indeed," Vurax nodded. "It seemed like the tale of the birth of your people, but if so, why was I filled with sadness listening to it? And there was a word at the end that you did not translate. It sounded a lot like the name for your god, but what does it mean?"

"*Erliandol-es-kanar*—Dawn Rise. Yes, it is the story of our beginning, or rather the beginning of the beginning, if that makes sense. Those are only the opening verses."

"Why not sing the rest?"

Treeweaver chuckled at this. "Because as much as I would enjoy having you hear it, we don't have several days to spare."

"Several days...?" Vurax shook his head, bewildered by the idea of a song that went on for that long.

"We Elves are introspective by nature, and when you have a history that stretches back to the beginning of the world with lifespans to match, well... we spend a lot of that time remembering. This may be a difficult concept for you to grasp, as we often have difficulty explaining it, but we have the ability to *live* in the past simultaneously with the present by sharing in the collective memory of our people as it passes from one individual to another. The tale that I sang of just now is as present in our memory as this very instant with you and me here," the Syldar explained. "The sadness that you experienced comes from the subsequent loss of innocence and the tragedies that befell our six ancestors and our peoples since that first day."

To live in all the moments of one's life at the same time? It was nearly impossible to grasp the concept, if he understood correctly what Treeweaver had said, and the more he tried to, the more he was glad he couldn't do such a thing. For as long as he might live, Vurax didn't think he would ever be able to forget all the painful things he'd been forced to endure, yet to be able to recall and experience every one of them as if they were happening over and over again was a horrifying thought. He'd rather leave the past where it belonged.

"Peoples? Not people?" the Golian picked up on the difference and re-marked on it.

"After a long period of wandering to every corner of Akar, we Elves grew apart, separating ourselves into five tribes, each going their own way during what we call the Sundering. We are the Syldar, the descendants of Syld, and you've heard me speak of our kin, the Nuamekar, descendants of Nuamek. The others are the Linaar, Telemnar, and Avalenar."

"Five? I thought there were six Elves in your story," Kael interjected.

"There were. The sixth tribe is the one we all return to and are reunited with after we leave this world," Treeweaver said solemnly. The centurion nodded in understanding. The concept was not so different from the spiritual belief of the Minotaurs, whereupon the honoured departed rejoined their ancestors in Zarvon's gloried halls.

"This shared memory of yours—does it allow you to *see* what's happening with your sister and your people right now?" Vurax asked, thinking that whatever new information they had that they could impart to the emperor and the senate might be helpful in making their case.

Treeweaver gave him a sad smile. "No, it doesn't work like that. We need to be in physical contact with each other and undergo a process we call the 'transference' before our memories can be shared."

"And with the death of K'orontïrthon, I fear that our ability to do this will begin to fade. The Father Tree was the living receptacle of our entire people's memory, so there's no telling how that will impact us moving forward," Windstrider revealed. This drew a sharp look from Treeweaver, but it was already too late.

"What's this?" Kael asked, frowning.

"You may as well tell him," Vurax jumped in. "Kael owes you his life as much as I do, but he's about to risk everything by vouching for you before the emperor, and he's doing so on my word alone. I think he deserves to know why you're doing this."

Kael looked from one face to the other, feeling more than a little irritated at the existence of this secret that had been kept from him. Of course, he knew there had to be a reason of grave importance for a Syldar prince—an enemy of the empire for all intents and purposes—to seek an audience with the leader of his people, but he'd done his best to brush that off as something that had been decided he didn't need to know the details of. As someone intimately familiar with the military chain of command and the importance of secrecy at times, he'd been willing so far to trust Vurax's judgement in this. Not because Vurax was his superior, but because he was his friend. Just as he had done with him, Vurax and Treeweaver had forged a strong bond, one where the Elf had managed to convince the Minotaur to help with a task that could end badly for all those involved. Yet, as the days passed and Kael grew more accustomed to and strangely fond of the company of these two individuals, he was nevertheless growing increasingly resentful that a crucial piece of information was being deliberately kept from him.

"Yes, I would very much like to know why you would willingly deliver yourself into the hands of a people with whom you have warred against in the past," Kael asserted, crossing his arms, and puffing out his broad chest.

"Interesting choice of words, given that our 'warring', as you put it, was merely a response to the unprovoked invasion of our homeland by your people," Treeweaver observed, then held up one hand in a placating gesture when he saw Kael bristle at the accusation. "But that is in the past now, and the one responsible for that decision is no longer in power, thankfully, or I would not be attempting this. Vurax is right, though, and I'm not oblivious to what the consequences of aiding us might be for you. Listen then, to the tragic tale of what has befallen my people and what brings me to plead before your emperor like a humble beggar." He said this with no resentment in his voice that Kael could detect, only a grim acceptance of circumstance. So strong was the conviction in the Elf's tone that the centurion was immediately mollified, giving Treeweaver a nod to proceed.

While Treeweaver repeated his story of the devastation of Syldar and near destruction of its people by the Titan and his army of giant humanoids, Vurax paid close attention to Kael's face and body language as the other Golian listened attentively. Though there were certainly times in the telling when Kael evinced surprise and momentary incredulity, specifically around the more fantastical elements of the story, these reactions were mostly tempered by a quiet and calculating demeanour throughout that told Vurax that Kael was viewing the event through the analytical eye of a soldier who'd seen more than his share of battle and dying. When it was over, Kael sat silently in thought for some time, looking into the dancing light of the campfire as if imagining the colossal flames that engulfed the forests and capital of the Syldar kingdom.

"Smoke from fires on that scale will surely have been seen by citizens of the Eastern Province by now, even with mountains in the way. It would not surprise me to find out that those in Golan will have already been informed that something is amiss beyond our eastern border," Kael ruminated. "This will be beneficial in corroborating elements of your story, that's for certain." He did not bother offering condolences or needless platitudes to the two Elves and stuck instead to what was practical. He could tell that both Treeweaver and Windstrider were seasoned warriors, and dwelling on their loss would not help the living. It was how he managed to continue serving the legion after so many years of losing friends.

"And the rest?" Treeweaver asked.

Kael did not need to ask what the Syldar was referring to. "A creature of that size, commanding a vast army of giants—it doesn't exactly invoke a picture of stealth and subtlety. Now that they have attacked Golian Legion fortifications, there are certain to be survivors that can, in due time, confirm what you saw. Not only that, but the devastation that this force is leaving in its wake will be impossible to ignore or explain away. A giants' attack on a patrol is one thing; the destruction of an entire legion fort is another altogether. As for your theory on what this Titan might be or what it wants—well, I've seen some strange things in Ur that made me question my sanity at times, but rather than add my uninformed conjecture here, I'll leave that part of your story to more learned minds than mine," Kael said, delivering what he felt was an honest assessment of the situation and making no attempt at self-deprecation.

Treeweaver nodded. "I think you give yourself too little credit, centurion, but I am grateful for your willingness to not only listen to us but to believe in what we say."

"I do so because I can't think of any other logical reason why you would be doing this. I only hope that our leaders see it in the same way. Military officers like me, we're practical creatures and we know how to deal with knowable elements once the facts are presented. Politicians, on the other hand, don't always do what you or I think should be obvious. From what I've heard of Logris Blackhorn, he seems to be a decent, reasonable, and intelligent bull. It's the senate that worries me." Kael showed his teeth and spat on the ground.

"Is the rule of your emperor not absolute?" Windstrider ventured.

Kael smiled wryly at this. "No. For most of our history, that used to be the case, but as stubborn and resistant to change as we can be, eventually some realized that allowing a single individual to hold that much power invariably leads to a lot of problems. Once in a while though, an emperor comes along that has his own notions and tries to change things back to the old ways. That conflict with your people we just spoke of, for example, that was just the most recent event that senators will point out to justify their own existence. This isn't to say that things are perfect—far from it—but it does tend to keep some of the worst impulses and decisions in check."

Vurax laughed. "He may be a soldier and used to following orders, but you'll find that Kael here is quite progressive in his views," he joked teasingly but fondly. "I don't think we would be friends otherwise, to be honest."

"It seems that as much as you have preconceived notions about the Syldar, the same holds true for how we think of Golians," Windstrider observed. "I guess we're lucky to find ourselves in the company of two Minotaurs that are as open-minded as you two. Let us hope we find more of that at your emperor's court."

"Lucky or fated?" Treeweaver asked meaningfully.

Vurax tilted his head and dipped one horn toward the Elf, knowing which of the two he was implying. "I suppose that depends on which of those you are most likely to believe in. Me? I don't place much stock in either. What I do believe is that I'm tired, my back still hurts like hell, and the prospect of some sleep sounds very appealing right about now. Can we all agree on that?"

"Aye, I think we can," Kael said. "I'll take the first watch."

The Elf scout nodded, and then the four of them prepared to bed down for the night and get some rest before another day of flying. Kael moved away from the firelight so that his eyes could better observe the approach up the hill from the lakeshore below and found himself a good vantage point atop a large boulder. Standing watch took him back to his earliest days in the legion as a fresh munifex recruit on sentry duty, and while many found the activity fraught with anxiety and the anticipation of spotting the enemy, Kael saw it as a tranquil time when he could be alone with his thoughts. He was still trying to make sense of Vurax's story about his encounter with the Elves and the ramifications of what he and Treeweaver had witnessed during the attack on the fort. He thought back to the morning before departing on their journey, when Tribune Jalx and his Kal-dkar had met with him alone in the command tent. During that brief meeting, it was made clear that not only was it the centurion's task to take Vurax to Golan, but that the former slave was to be watched carefully, and that anything unusual about his behaviour should be noted, committed to memory, and reported on later. Nothing too unusual about any of that, Kael had thought, except for the vague impression he'd had when leaving the tent of the disturbing sensation of spidery fingers lightly brushing against his mind. Strange that he would think of that now, but the memory made him feel that he had missed witnessing something very important due to being unconscious after the giants' ambush.

At least an hour had passed, the centurion marking the passage of time by the position of the moonlight's reflection on the calm surface of Lake Dal. He heard the footsteps behind him but did not turn, recognizing Vurax's heavy gait. "It's not your turn yet. Besides, I thought you wanted some sleep."

"My body does, but my mind disagrees," Vurax said. The Golian stopped next to the large, wind-worn rock Kael was sitting on but remained standing. "Something's been plaguing my thoughts since we left Vurgas and I need to ask you something."

"I've noticed. Not that it's unusual for you to be quiet and somewhat distant at times—we've been on the road together long enough for me to accept that as part of who you are—but yes, since the farm, I can tell something's changed," Kael observed. When Vurax didn't say anything, he continued. "So, what's your question?"

Vurax stared at the wide expanse of the red-tinged lake waters in the distance, flared his wide nostrils, and inhaled deeply of the night air before speaking. He'd been trying to work up his courage to approach Kael about this ever since his conversation with Larios, and tonight he'd decided he couldn't put it off any longer. In a few more days they would be in Golan, and he needed to prepare himself for what to expect before that happened. He knew no one in the capital and he trusted Kael, so rather than hear it from the mouth of a stranger, he would ask his friend.

"What can you tell me about Zerik Baurus?"

Kael looked at Vurax, confusion plainly written on his face. He'd had no idea what the other was going to ask him, but of the many things he could think of that Vurax would be curious about, this wasn't one of them.

"Zerik Baurus? Now there's a name steeped in controversy and mystery," Kael mused. "Why do you want to know about him, of all people?"

"Never mind that right now, explain what you just said. What do you mean by 'controversy' and 'mystery'?"

"Yes, I do suppose there's not much use for talk of such things in a small, quiet farming community like the one where you grew up. Not so different from where I'm from, to be honest. You don't know how fortunate you are in that regard—the machinations of politicians sometimes can be enough to make your stomach churn," Kael said casually, only realizing too late what he'd just implied when he caught Vurax's dark look. "Ah shit, I'm sorry. I know there was nothing fortunate about what happened to you and your family. That's not what I meant—"

"Don't worry about it," Vurax cut him off, recognizing that the comment, though insensitive, had been unintended. "Just tell me who he was."

Kael nodded, swallowing dryly and cursing inward at himself for his carelessness. "Alright... but you must understand, these events took place just a year before I was born. Most of what I heard and learned didn't come until much later, after my military draft began. From how the older veterans and officers spoke about him, Zerik Baurus was the greatest Supreme Legate the empire's ever had in recent history, and some would even claim, of all time. To hear it told, only the current commander of the legions even comes close to enjoying the popularity among the rank and file of the army that Baurus once did—that is until the unfortunate series of events that got him exiled."

"And what would those be?" Vurax asked, both eager and hesitant to learn more.

Kael shrugged and continued. "There are varying accounts as to exactly how it happened, and many doubt whether it even did, but it's said Zerik Baurus murdered Emperor Xar Murias on the battlefield during the war with the Syldar over five decades ago."

For a long time after Kael's words had faded into the night, the sounds of the breeze rustling the leaves of nearby trees and crickets trilling their nocturnal rituals were all that could be heard. The centurion waited patiently for Vurax to say something, hoping to glean any hint as to why any of this was important to his friend, but the long period of silence was beginning to concern him. Vurax only stared off into the distance without looking at him, as perfectly still as the rock upon which the centurion sat. This was clearly important in some way, and Kael didn't want to disturb him until he was ready to reveal why. Or not, whatever the case may be.

"Why did he do it?" Vurax asked at length, his voice sounding hoarse with repressed emotion.

"Ooof," Kael blew out his breath. "Now that's a question best left for scholars and historians to debate, but the official explanation given to the people at the time was that Baurus sought the throne for himself by assassinating Murias the Mad. Wouldn't be the first time in our past that something like that happened, but it's been long since that sort of act was permissible in our society due to laws that were enacted to discourage ascending to the throne in such a violent fashion. For his alleged crime, Zerik Baurus was stripped of rank and exiled with nothing to his name but his dishonour."

"You said 'official' explanation—what was said unofficially?" Vurax asked.

"Well, for many, especially among the soldiers of the legion—who could never accept that Baurus would do such a thing—the prevailing rumour was that a small group of politicians, led by an up-and-coming senator by the name of Kalor Sarnius, somehow convinced him to commit the deed so that they could put someone on the throne who would be more easily controllable than Xar Murias. Whether that's true or not, I suspect only a very few know for certain, but Sarnius was made Primus Senator shortly thereafter, so you can draw your own conclusions. What's a fact is that if Baurus had been truly guilty, the penalty for his crime should have been death, and that would've gotten ugly very fast, but instead, he was exiled to some backwater village up near Vurgas, a place called..." Kael fell silent when it all suddenly fell into place in his mind.

Eighteen years ago, he'd been far to the south and still serving in the Fourth on the day that Vurax's home village was attacked, but after he'd transferred to the Eighth, he recalled reading the reports on the constant danger of Sarmakanite raids near the northern frontier, and of seeing the names of the places that had been ransacked, with villagers killed or taken. They'd only gotten bolder and more frequent since, which is what had prompted the emperor to finally send an entire legion north of the mountains and into Sarmakan to put an end to the depredations. One small village's name in particular had caught his attention back then, but he couldn't remember why at the time. He recalled it with stark clarity now—Keros, the place where it was said Zerik Baurus had gone to live out his days in exile.

"Well damn," Kael whispered. "Was he...?"

"My father," Vurax replied without hesitation, "a traitor and a murderer." The words were uttered with such deflation that Kael could almost imagine Vurax somehow shrinking in stature before his eyes. To most Golians, honour was everything, and to learn something like that about your sire would be devastating to one's pride.

"That's a matter of perspective," Kael countered, looking for a way to somehow find something positive in this. "Xar Murias was a terrible emperor by all accounts, so what happened seemed almost inevitable. Both you and I have killed many people for reasons we can justify to ourselves. Are we murderers as well? I don't think you can make that judgment until you know what truly happened on that day, and why."

Vurax looked up at the stars, their light caught and reflected in the dark pools of his eyes. No answers to be found up there, and none that came from inside of him either, for that other voice remained silent too. He drew his lips into a grim line and nodded. Without further word, he returned to the camp, any hope of sleep now even more futile than before.

CHAPTER 24

"He dead?"

"Dunno. Let's find out." The hard kick to his side jolted Darken awake, though just barely. He felt something give inside of him, and if his ribs hadn't been broken before, they surely were now. The young thief collapsed onto the ground next to the wall he'd been slumped against, letting out a low moan in the process.

"Guess that answers that."

Darken heard the voice this time and cracked his eye open to look up blearily, but all he could see was an undefined shadow standing over him. He didn't need to see well to know who it was though, for there was no mistaking that irritating voice and the detestable individual to whom it belonged.

"Fuck you, Gregor," he spat weakly, the metallic taste of blood in his mouth. So, he wasn't dead then, was the obvious conclusion he arrived at, but he had a feeling he would soon wish he was. Just his luck, that of all the people in Arlingtown to find him, it had to be his personal nemesis.

"Would you listen to this asshole?" Gregor laughed in disbelief.

A fist came down this time, striking Darken's head so hard that it bounced off the street cobbles. A pair of hands then took hold of him, roughly shoving him back into a sitting position. He couldn't feel his limbs, which was probably just as well. The less he could feel of whatever Gregor intended to do with him, the better. His head slouched for a bit, and then he managed to muster the effort to look up at his tormentor and give him a bloody, mocking smile.

"My six-year-old brothers hit harder than that, you useless sack of shit," Darken chuckled.

"You've got some stones on you, Darken. I don't know what you've been up to tonight, but you look like hell, and you know what? It ain't nothin' compared to what I'm gonna do to you," Gregor threatened in a low voice, his hot and rank breath close enough for Darken to feel.

"Do your worst, fuck-face." He expected the other teen to do just that, and that's why he was pushing him. If he could make Gregor mad enough, the end might come more swiftly. The bully's face was coming into focus slowly, hateful as ever, but it wasn't the last thing he wanted to see before he left this world. He looked past the other boy to the strip of sky visible between buildings and saw that it was almost dawn. Then he closed his eye and prepared himself.

"Hey Will," Gregor called to his partner. "Watcha' think we should take first?"

"It don't matter, Greg, just make it fast. It's almost light out and folks will be about soon," Will observed nervously.

"No! I'm gonna make this little bastard suffer, just like he done to me! So, what'll it be? He's already lost an eye, looks like. Take the other one? Or maybe an ear? He owes me one of those," Gregor growled, holding his knife close to Darken's face in anticipation.

"Here's a better idea—take your little butter knife and shove it up your ass while you decide, uh? Poke your brain while it's in there, 'cuz there's definitely nothing inside your head," Darken taunted without bothering to open his eye and look at Gregor. There, that should do it. He waited for the blow, but all he got was a few tense seconds of loud, rapid breathing and fuming for his effort.

"You think you're funny, huh? That you're so much better than me? That my knife is a toy? How about I go in on you with one of your fancy blades then? Think they might do a better job? Let's find out. Will, come here."

"Gregor, I think—" Will started to say.

"Get the fuck over here, right now! No one asked you to think!" Gregor yelled shrilly at him. Visibly cowed, Will complied. "Here, I'll hold the bastard tight in case he's faking, and you grab one of his daggers. Make yourself useful—do it!"

Darken felt himself being lifted from the ground as Gregor pinned both his arms behind his back, but when the street tough realized that Darken's legs weren't supporting his weight, he propped him back up against the wall in a half-sitting position. "This fucker's really done for. Hurry up—I wanna get me some payback before he's gone altogether."

"Which one?" Will hesitated, looking from one dagger to the other.

"The fuck does it matter?" Gregor shot back before looking at the choices. His gaze caught sight of the pommel of Garick's dagger with its gleaming black stone and his eyes lit up with greed. "That one—the one with the fancy stone on the pommel. That'll fetch a decent pile of coin for sure... or maybe I'll just keep it for myself."

"No! Keep your grubby fucking paws off that," Darken grunted, opening his eye once more to fix Gregor with a dangerous glare. For what it was worth, he could see much more clearly now.

"Mean something to you, does it? Good, just makes it all the sweeter. Will, take the fucking dagger," Gregor ordered.

The stout lad took a step closer and reached for the dagger's hilt. Ignoring the flare of fresh pain in his side, Darken tried to break free of Gregor's hold but his limbs remained unresponsive. He was too weak, and Gregor was too strong. Will flinched at the feeble attempt knowing that, even in his current state, Darken was not to be underestimated. A few bruising run-ins in the past had driven that lesson home long ago, but Darken's struggle was brief, and the moment passed. Will grabbed Garick's dagger and pulled it free from the sheath that had formerly held Darken's own lost weapon. The second the blade came into view, its reflective ebony surface flared suddenly and brilliantly with red light so bright that Gregor and Darken had to avert their eyes. Still holding the dagger in front of him, Will staggered back and threw his freed hand up to shield his eyes. None of them saw the glowing rune that appeared on the blade first and then flew with blinding speed at the stunned bully.

Gregor and Darken heard a brief, strangled sound right before something heavy collapsed to the ground. When they opened their eyes to look, Will was lying on the street, his body still twitching while blood, thick with brain matter, slowly oozed out of his ears to spill onto the cobblestones. Blood flowed steadily from his open mouth as well, frozen open in a soundless scream, but most horribly of all, where Will's eyes should have been, there were only two scorched and ragged holes from which issued twin wisps of smoke. Still gripped in his lifeless hand was Garick's blade, dark once more.

"What in all the hells...?" Gregor managed to say once he'd recovered from his shock. There was an awful smell of charred flesh in the air, and he retched at the sight of the body. Revulsion and confusion soon turned to anger once more, and the bully tried to shut out the awful image by focusing solely on his helpless victim. "What did you do to him? Answer me! What did you do?" Gregor shouted, eyes bulging in his face as he gripped the front of Darken's leather armour with both hands and slammed him against the wall. When the air rushed from his lungs, the other boy—barely hanging onto consciousness—could only grunt in pain he'd thought himself beyond feeling.

"I...don't...know..." Darken tried to say, but the words came out unintelligibly.

"What?" But this time Gregor didn't wait for an answer, having lost whatever tenuous grasp he'd had on patience and reason.

Darken felt himself slide back down to the ground after Gregor let go of him. What followed was the first of a series of punches and kicks that began to rain down upon his already battered body. In the dim recesses of his mind, he tried to understand how or why he was still conscious, but figured it had to be because the gods had decided to have a good laugh at his expense while he was being punished for the transgressions of the past night. After a while, each individual blow that fell slowly faded into a single, endless marathon of agony, which is why he almost didn't notice when it finally stopped. It took him a bit to gather that either Gregor had finished with him, or that he'd finally slipped through into the realm of death. Bemused, he realized that both of those things could be true at the same time. Yet there was an incessant dull roar in his ears, and he thought it a very cruel joke that he could still feel this much pain in the afterlife. What was the point of that? He decided to peer out at what kind of hellscape awaited him and managed to barely crack open his one good eye before it had time to swell shut altogether.

His disappointment couldn't be greater when he saw that he was still on the street of his hometown. There was Will's body, lying a few feet away to one side, but there was also something else now between him and the corpse of the unfortunate oaf. It wasn't long before he realized that it was another prone figure—Gregor. The young hooligan lay unmoving on his side, eyes open and vacantly staring right at him, mouth open in a slack expression of shock that was almost comical. It took Darken a confused moment while he tried to figure out what strange game the other boy was playing with him now. Then he noticed the blood slowly pooling under Gregor's head. It was only after—as if the world only saw fit to reveal one slow detail at a time to his dulled senses—that he saw the figure standing over Gregor's form, a sturdy, short-hafted and broad-headed hammer gripped tightly in one hand. He tried to say something but could scarcely recognize the blood-choked croak as his own voice. He mustered enough energy somehow to point feebly at the fallen dagger nearby.

"Uncle..." he moaned feebly and then tried to reach for the blade, but the effort proved too much. Before he finally slipped away into a dreamless realm, he tried to look up at the figure standing over him and saw a beautiful face smiling down radiantly, enveloped in a halo of bright light. He whispered her name, just before his consciousness slipped away at last.

"Ellianna."

⚫

"What were you thinking bringing this kid here? Are you daft, man?" a gruff voice sputtered.

"What was I supposed to do? Leave him on that street to die?" was the incredulous reply.

"Yes! That's exactly what you should have done. This is none of our business, Caeden, and nothing good will come from sticking our noses in whatever this is. You mark my words!" There was a long pause, and then,"Why are you looking at me like that? You know I'm not wrong."

"Throughout the many years of friendship we've shared, I've known you to be many things, but cruel and uncaring? That's not the Thurgod Splintershield that I know. Fine, I don't think he'll survive being moved again, but I'll take him elsewhere, though I don't know where."

"Don't you dare try to appeal to my compassion, you hear? I already have one human child to take care of, and now you show up at my door with this...this...this mess!" the Dwarf gestured angrily at the object of his fury.

"Take care of? We're talking about saving the lad's life here, not adopting him, for Rhudkar's sake. What's the matter with you, anyway? Here, at least help me clean up these wounds before it's too late, then I'll get him out of your hair."

"Great, just great," Thurgod continued to mutter gruffly as they set about doing what they could.

"Did you send Ellianna to fetch a healer like I asked?"

"Yes, dammit! I suppose we'd best keep the boy here until they get back then. Be a damn stupid sight if I had to chase you halfway across town to find you again."

"Ellianna...?" The word was barely audible, but there was no mistaking the fact that it came from the battered body that lay on a blanket on the floor of Thurgod's barn. The two men stopped what they were doing, staring down in shock before looking at each other in disbelief.

"Oh my—he's actually awake?" said the Dwarf's companion. "That's a good sign, I think. We should try to keep him that way until help arrives."

"Did he just say 'Ellianna'?" Thurgod asked, dumbstruck.

"That's what I heard too. Like I told you before, he uttered her name before he lost consciousness in the alley. Now do you believe me? That's why I brought him here. I didn't know what else to do." He shifted his attention to the gravely injured boy. "There lad, try not to move too much. You're going to be okay." Caeden tried to make the young man comfortable by bunching up some hay under the blanket to form a crude pillow. Careful as he was, there was hardly a place left on the boy's body that he could touch without eliciting a moan of pain.

Thurgod dipped the rag in his hand into the bucket of cold water at his side, wrung out some of the blood, then dabbed at the boy's shoulder wound. After bringing him inside, they had removed the crude bandage, and the Dwarf had gingerly pried the damaged leather apart carefully to peer underneath. What he saw there filled him with apprehension. Whatever had caused that cut, it had left the flesh around the wound with an ominous-looking greenish black colour. Pus oozed from the gash, and the fetid odour it gave off had made him gag, and he'd smelled some pretty vile stuff in his day. Judging from the boy's overall condition, he was reminded of a violent past among his people before the quiet life he had today, and though there were clear indications the boy had been in an armed clash, most of his wounds were the result of a severe beating, not weapons. Not that it mattered. Despite his angry bluster, he felt a pang of pity for the lad.

"This is pointless, Caeden. I've seen bigger men die from far less. I wouldn't give a bent copper for his chances," Thurgod sighed.

"Don't say that! He can hear you, you know?" Caeden retorted, angrily.

"No need... to lie," the boy croaked. "I know... I'm dying."

"Hush now, save your strength. Help is on the way," Caeden tried to soothe him, squeezing a few drops of water onto lips that were cracked and swollen. The boy's face was a horrible mess, with the blood-soaked cloth wrapped around the ruined eye; the angry red and purplish swollen mass that held the other eye shut; the cut and bruised cheeks, and the nose that had been smashed beyond recognition. When he'd packed his prized work tools into his satchel bag just before dawn that day and walked out his door to head for another routine day of work as a smith, Caeden Smithson had never imagined what he would encounter just a few steps from his humble home. The sight of the dead boy was certainly horrific, but he'd barely paused to consider the body on the ground, focusing instead on the two figures struggling against one another. To call it a fair fight would have been laughable—more like one was beating the other to death without any kind of real opposition. He recognized the aggressor immediately—a local street ruffian with a real nasty reputation by the name of Gregor and just the type of gutter rat that he constantly told his own children to stay away from. He didn't recognize the other boy, but he reminded him so much of his eldest son that before he realized what he was doing, he reacted out of pure instinct and reached for the forging hammer in his bag.

It was over quickly, and after Caeden had overcome the shocked realization of what he'd just done, he had to set aside personal considerations and follow through on trying to save this kid. He didn't bother to check whether Gregor was still alive. Cruel and vicious scum like him didn't deserve his pity. Come to think of it, he had no idea whether the life he was saving was any more deserving than Gregor's. That said, the lad had been so far gone that he was unable to defend himself, and Caeden's moral code couldn't abide abandoning a helpless individual in a situation like that. Whether it was the right thing to do or not, it was too late for that now. His mind racing over what to do next, he quickly discarded the thought of calling the town guard. Whether he had killed Gregor or not was irrelevant—he had violently struck down another citizen of the town, and while there was a chance he might be able to reason with a guardsman over the circumstances and explanation for his act, it would end very differently if a Justicer got involved. He couldn't take the lad into his house either and risk involving his family in this. His door was just around the corner from where this had all taken place, and it would be one of the first to be knocked on for questioning once the bodies were discovered. In fact, he couldn't think of anywhere he could go where there wouldn't be difficult questions to answer, and the lad certainly wasn't in a condition to give him any clues.

He was nearly in a panic when the boy called out a name he recognized, giving him the answer he desperately sought. From there, it was a simple and quick matter to grab the strange dagger the kid had pointed to before passing out and run to fetch his two-wheel cart to load the unconscious lad onto, covering him up with a tarp to keep him out of sight. He made good time in taking a route to the Field Gate that did not involve going through the central plaza or the marketplace, allowing him to avoid anyone else who might already be up at this early hour. When he arrived at the city gate that led to the farmsteads south of Arlingtown, the sun was already peeking over the eastern walls of the settlement. He smiled and nodded at a couple of farmers wheeling their goods in for sale at their market stalls and tried to act as casual as possible when he passed the two guards at the gate. He knew these two well, and it was not unusual for them to see the farrier going out once, sometimes even twice a week to repair someone's farm tools or shoe a horse. They waved him through without so much as a word, and Caeden breathed a sigh of relief when he was far from the walls and hurriedly making his way down a lane away from the main road and toward his friend Thurgod's farm in Greenbury.

He was both troubled and curious as to what connection there could be between this boy and Ellianna. The girl was practically like family to him and had called him 'Uncle Caed' ever since Thurgod had taken her into his own care all those years ago. Yet even when she played with his own boisterous children, she'd always been a shy, quiet, and introspective child, and had continued to be so into her teenage years—definitely not the type of personality that made friends easily or placed her trust in just anyone. Whoever this boy was, he most certainly did not look like someone who worked the fields, so how did the two even know each other? What he feared most, however, was what the usually irascible Dwarf's reaction would be. It was bad enough he was going to show up at his friend's door first thing in the morning with a surprise like this, let alone having to explain why he'd even decided to come there in the first place. Well, he was about to find out because he'd come too far to turn back now, and time was not on the boy's side.

Predictably, Thurgod's pleasure at seeing Caeden had rapidly turned to anger and disbelief when the smith told him why he was there. It was all the man could do to convince the Dwarf to allow him to at least put the boy in the barn, since Thurgod categorically refused to bring him into his cottage. Things only got worse when he told Thurgod that the boy had spoken Ellianna's name, nearly sending the overly protective old Dwarf into a fit of apoplectic rage. There had to be a mistake, he claimed—Caeden had either misheard, or there had to be someone else called Ellianna in town. It got even worse when Caeden had the temerity to suggest that Thurgod go fetch his granddaughter and have her clear up the mystery. Absolutely not, the Dwarf had shouted, though he did finally—after much arguing—agree to wake the girl and send her into town for help, with instructions to be as discreet as possible. He had refused to let the girl into the barn, so Caeden had to believe Thurgod hadn't given her too many details. The smith accepted that small victory, but that didn't mean he was going to give up on finding out what was going on here.

"Keep talking to me, but don't move," he said, trying to sound confidently calm while he tried to gauge how much time had passed since Ellianna had left—an hour at most? "What's your name?"

With one eye shut and the other one gone, it was hard to tell if the boy was still conscious and capable of replying, but though his breathing was shallow, Caeden could tell he was still hanging on—if only just barely.

"Darken," the boy managed to say.

"Hello, Darken. My name is Caeden, and this is Thurgod. I know you can't see us right now, but that's unimportant. What's important is that you know that you're safe and that you tell us who you are and where you live so that we can contact anyone who might be concerned that you are, uh, missing."

"What you should be asking him is what he was doing that he ended up like this, that's what," Thurgod said crossly.

Caeden gave the Dwarf an exasperated look. "Would you give it a rest? If you're not going to be helpful, then wait outside."

"It's my barn! I'll stay if I want to," Thurgod protested. "Besides, I know a thing or two about tending to wounds." The Dwarf thought back to a time in his past when he could have taken matters into his own hands in a situation like this, but he'd chosen to walk away from all that and never look back. He cursed inwardly for even thinking of those times, however briefly, but even with a life fading fast before his eyes, he couldn't bring himself to break the angry oath he'd made the day his brother died in his arms.

"Stay then but stop making matters worse with your big mouth. As for your vaunted healing skills, this isn't a chicken or a cow, you know?"

"That's not what I was referring to," Thurgod growled back. "And what would you know anyway? It's not like the kid is made of iron that you can bang the dents out of him over an anvil."

"Could you two please...stop arguing?" Darken asked, lifting one arm weakly to get their attention. Embarrassed, both men glanced sheepishly at each other and nodded in silent agreement. "Thank you," the boy said, sounding genuinely grateful that the shouting had stopped. He was struggling mightily to stay awake, and it had taken all the energy he had just to move his arm.

"Darken, lad... not to state the obvious, but I have to ask—are you in some kind of trouble? *We* want to help you, but *we* need to know what's going on," Caeden asked, placing emphasis on the 'we' and frowning meaningfully at Thurgod. The Dwarf rolled his eyes but wisely bit back any retort. He wouldn't openly admit it, but he was curious as well. More importantly, if this was indeed a friend of his granddaughter's and he refused to help the boy, he'd never hear the end of it from Ellianna.

"The less you know...the better. Please... if you just let me rest a bit, I'll be no trouble at all and go on my way."

"Well, that sounds ominous," Thurgod groused. "Listen, kid, the only place you're going is straight to the grave unless you stop speaking nonsense and hang on until someone gets here that can fix you up, ya hear?" Darken's head moved a little and the Dwarf took that as a nod. "Good. Caeden, a word with you, if I may?" Unable to do much more for the boy, the smith followed the Dwarf over to the barn doors and out of Darken's earshot.

"Thurgod, I know what you're going to say and—"

"We need to report this," the Dwarf hissed, trying to keep his naturally booming voice down. "The boy was right about one thing—if we don't know what this is about, the Justicers may overlook our involvement as two concerned citizens simply trying to do the right thing. I mean, look at him! You don't just throw on black leather armour and carry two daggers around if all you're planning to do is take an evening stroll. That boy was up to no good, and it went badly in a horrible way." His words had a visibly deflating effect on his friend, and he tried to strike a more conciliatory tone. "Look, I know you well Caeden, you're a kind soul and you want to help save a young life. I'm willing to do what we can to achieve that, but we can't keep this a secret, or it makes us accomplices to whatever he was doing, you understand? So, here's what we're gonna do—you stay here with him and make sure he stays awake, and I'll head into town and bring the guards here to handle this. I know Thomas and Marian at the Field Gate well; they'll be discreet about it." He looked deep into his friend's eyes, confident that Caeden would hear the reason in his words. The smith was irritatingly idealistic sometimes, but he was also practical and dependable. When the human said nothing, the Dwarf nodded, clapped him reassuringly on one shoulder, and turned to leave.

"Thurgod, wait," Caeden called out when his friend began to swing the barn doors open. The Dwarf stopped but did not turn around, waiting. "You can't bring the guards here."

"Why not?"

"Because in order to save this boy's life, I may have killed someone else." There, he'd said it. He never should have kept that from his friend in the first place, but the knowledge that he'd done so was weighing more heavily on his conscience than the act of violence itself.

"You did what?" Thurgod still had his back to him, and his voice was surprisingly low and even, something Caeden rarely experienced.

"I had no choice—it all happened so fast that there simply wasn't enough time to think it through." The Dwarf finally turned around to level his hazel eyes at Caeden, his heavy brow knotted and gnarled like a thundercloud. For the first time in the twenty-seven years since he'd called Thurgod a friend, the smith was unsure what would happen next.

"There are good choices, and there are bad choices, but if there's one thing I've learned from life is that there are *always* choices. Which one does your gut tell you that you made, Caeden?"

"The right choice," the smith said, staring evenly back at the Dwarf.

"Then that's good enough for me," Thurgod pronounced, and walked past Caeden to go back and sit next to where Darken lay, the discussion over.

<hr>

The Anvalite priest clicked his tongue in mingled sadness and frustration while he carefully examined Darken's wounds. The boy's upper garments had been removed, revealing the severe bruising around his broken ribs, but more worryingly, the dark and festering wound on his shoulder where the throwing knife had struck him. A crust of dried blood and pus had formed a disgusting clot that sealed the cut but gave it an ugly appearance that gave the cleric cause for grave concern. Then there was the lad's right eye—or rather what was left of it. An angry red slash from brow to cheek traced the path of the blade, leaving only ruin in its wake when it had sliced straight through the eye. There was much work to be done here, so after that visual assessment, the man set about his work. From a kneeling position on the floor beside Darken, he placed both of his hands on the lad's chest, bowed his head, and closed his eyes. His lips moved slowly, and he began to pray in a low, soft voice.

Some distance away, where they'd been asked to stand so as not to impede the priest's work, Thurgod, Caeden, and Ellianna stood in a small cluster, looking on anxiously at what was happening. Ellianna's forehead was creased with concern, and she wrung her hands constantly while she waited. Once she'd gotten over the shock of recognizing who it was that lay dying in their barn, all questions had been set aside for now—making sure that her new friend lived was the only thing that mattered. Similarly, Caeden stood next to her, one hand on her shoulder, his stubbly face no less apprehensive than hers. For his part, the Dwarf stood a step or two behind them, his twisted features a thunderhead of barely repressed irritation. While he'd made his peace with his friend's decision for the time being, another matter was causing him no small amount of consternation. Before he could let it eat away at him any further, he tugged at his granddaughter's sleeve, nodding meaningfully toward the far corner of the barn when she looked at him. The two walked over, leaving Caeden alone.

"What is it, Grandpa?"

Thurgod crossed his arms and stared at the wall, as if taking a sudden interest in the farming implements that hung there. Ellianna knew the old Dwarf better than he knew himself and understood immediately from his posture that while he was clearly angry, he was taking the time to choose his words carefully. She always reminded herself that, whatever came out of his mouth when he was mad at something, it was always spoken out of love and concern, not recrimination and spite. She also knew exactly what this was about, and she had dreaded it ever since she was old enough to understand that at some point, her life would have to move from out of his shadow and beyond it. She just never imagined that the day would come under such drastic circumstances. When the Dwarf continued to seemingly ignore her, she turned her head to look back at Darken and the priest, and the Dwarf finally took the cue to speak.

"I asked you to bring a healer, not a damned Anvalite!" he grumbled, trying to keep his voice low.

"An Anvalite *is* a healer, Grandpa. The best that we can hope for, in fact," she replied evenly, turning back to look into his eyes.

"You know what I mean. We can't afford a priest—not with the kind of injuries that boy has," he threw his arms up in exasperation to emphasize his point.

"It's precisely because of how badly hurt he is that a priest is his only hope, yet that's what you're concerned about? Coin?" she couldn't hide her disappointment. If there was one person who could make the ornery and opinionated Dwarf feel shame and embarrassment, it was his granddaughter. Normally she felt guilt and regret immediately after, but not this time. Thurgod, his face flushed with heat, avoided her stare and looked at the wall again. "You can withhold my spending coin for a whole year then if it makes you feel better, but that's not really what this is about, is it?"

"No, it's not," he muttered, pulling at his long beard to smooth it—another mannerism Ellianna was intimately familiar with, and one which she knew indicated nervousness and discomfort. She felt a pang of warm affection and wanted nothing more than to hug the one person she would do anything for, but decided to spare the Dwarf any further embarrassment, especially in the presence of others. Before he could say anything further though, she decided to pre-empt him by explaining herself first.

"Grandpa, it's not what you think. Such... things could not be further from my thoughts and likely will stay that way for a good long while. There's something else that's very important to me that's consuming my attention right now, and that's what I wish to concentrate on—not boys. Darken is just a friend—a new friend, yes, but just a friend." She tried to sound as reassuring as possible, safe in the knowledge that what she'd said was the absolute truth. Thurgod had a remarkable ability to see right through her whenever she'd tried to be less than forthcoming with him in the past, leaving her convinced that she must be a terrible liar. Right now, he was looking at her with that expression that he always used when he was searching for something hidden, but when he finally huffed and nodded, she knew she had passed the test.

"Alright, alright, no more talk of that then," he said gruffly. "If you say that's how it is then I trust you. Still, that doesn't allay my concern for your questionable choice of friends." He raised one finger to stop her when she began to say something and called her by her proper name, which was always a sure indication of how serious he was. "Ellianna, listen to me for a moment because I have experience with these things, and instincts don't fail me when it comes to this. Something dark and dangerous hovers over that boy, you hear? Taking a few lumps in a street fight is one thing, but what's happened to him goes well beyond that by several degrees. I daresay your friend Darken is in heaps of trouble beyond the obvious, and now that an Anvalite knows he's here, I think we'll be finding out very soon just how much."

Ellianna considered what Thurgod had said, and she found herself unable to disagree. On the day that they first met, she'd understood right away that Darken lived an unconventional and dangerous life. The way he'd spoken to those bullies and the insults they'd traded left no doubt in her mind that her friend came from a very different world than hers. "You're not wrong, Grandpa. What I never told you though, is that when I met him—on my birthday after I left you at the market—he came to my assistance and saved me from some street thugs that were harassing me. At best they would have robbed me, at worst..." she left the thought unfinished. She didn't like to think about how vulnerable, helpless, and frightened she'd felt back then, but if she was going to convince the Dwarf that her trust in Darken was not misplaced, it would be by appealing to his fierce protectiveness of her.

Thurgod's eyes widened, and the skin on his cheeks grew flushed again, this time with rage. "Why did you never tell me this? And where were you anyway that this came to happen?" the Dwarf sputtered.

"I didn't tell you because I knew this would be exactly how you'd react, and then you'd tear off in search of those boys to do something bad to them. As for where I was... well, I got lost in town on my way to the temple of Anval and took a wrong turn into a bad neighbourhood." She hadn't wanted to get into explaining that part yet, but there was no help for it now.

"The temple of Anval? What—" Thurgod was interrupted by the sound of the priest's prayer growing louder as it reached its climax. They both heard a gasp from Caeden and hurried to his side when a bright golden light began to fill the barn's interior, its source unmistakable. Hands still upon Darken, the *etherus* flowed from the physical conduit that was the priest and entered the battered body in a wave of healing energy that began to repair any injury that it found. The man's eyes were still closed, his mouth whispering words that were now inaudible even as they continued to beseech his patron for this miracle. Ellianna and Caeden watched in awe; Thurgod with suspicion, as the golden glow suffused Darken's form. The boy's laboured breathing eased when the ugly bruising on his sides slowly vanished, and the broken ribs mended under the soothing power of Anval. The wound on his shoulder was cleansed while the flesh pulled itself over the cut to close it, and the process continued throughout his body, with every last small scrape, bruise, cut, and swelling erased as if it had never been. The lone exception came when the magic reached Darken's ruined face. Slowly, his features were restored to what they had once been—smashed nose made whole again, broken cheekbones fused back into shape, left eye relieved of the swollen mass that had sealed it shut—but when it came to where his right eye had been, an angry red scar remained behind to mar the skin. As for the lost orb itself, though it appeared made whole again, the eye was now completely milky white.

The miracle finished, the light faded away and the cleric's shoulders slumped visibly, the man clearly spent from the effort. He continued to kneel there for a while longer, gathering his strength while he re-examined his patient, and then, seemingly satisfied with the result of what he'd done, he pulled a blanket that the Dwarf handed him up to the boy's chin, stood up, and turned to face the other occupants of the barn.

"He is sleeping now and will likely do so for a day or two," the priest said, smoothing the front of his white robes and picking out a few bits of straw from the garment. "This is a necessary part of the healing process, so please do not wake him if you do not need to. The worst is over now, and his natural youth and vigor should help do the rest. Unfortunately, I cannot do anything for his eye—had he been tended to sooner, perhaps, but there are limits to what even we can do. That aside, there remains one reason for concern. There is a poison coursing through his body that is beyond my power to purge completely. I have never experienced anything like it, and thus I am unsure as to what it might do to him over time. While he sleeps, the magic that heals him will hold its effects at bay, but once he wakes... well, I can't be certain. Perhaps if you tell me how he came by his injuries, I can determine how to best deal with this?"

Ellianna, Thurgod, and Caeden all exchanged looks of uncertainty and unease with one another, each of them knowing that none of them had the full answer to that question. The silence grew long and awkward until Caeden, who had brought Darken in, felt compelled to speak.

"We don't exactly know, truth be told," the smith said, nervously shuffling his feet. Something about the holy man's tranquil face and knowing eyes made him feel exposed. He was keenly aware of what he'd had to do to save Darken, and here, in the presence of one whose entire religious beliefs were centered on helping the sick and injured and preserving the sanctity of life, he felt as if he had committed the most grievous of sins. Did the priest have some divine ability to see into his soul? If yes, then he would surely glean the guilt and fear that had taken deep root there. When he heard the Dwarf clear his throat, he didn't miss the prompt for what it was. "I found him like this in an alley near my home," he continued. It was not a lie, but it was not the entire truth, either.

"Very well, but why was he not brought to us immediately?"

"I...uh...I'm a man of very modest means, and the boy... well, I don't even know who he is. I didn't think either one of us would be able to afford your services." Another half-truth.

The priest frowned. "While compensation for what we do is certainly appreciated, the lack thereof would be a grossly inhumane reason to deny someone assistance," he said, clearly disapproving of Caeden's reasoning. Then he shrugged his shoulders in resigned acceptance and seemed to let the matter drop. "It doesn't matter now. The girl had the wisdom to seek our help, and the boy's life has been saved as a result. You need not fear the circumstances under which he came to find himself in this situation, however questionable those may be. Such things are of no concern to Anval or his servants—I merely asked so that I may better understand the nature of his ailment." Everyone seemed visibly relieved by this pronouncement, a fact the priest did not fail to note. As he'd said, however, other than saving a life, all other considerations were irrelevant to him.

"Deacon Ulik, would Lady Morhain be able to help?" Ellianna blurted out hopefully.

The priest arched his eyebrows at this and then ran a hand through his thinning brown hair. "Lady Morhain?" He hadn't considered asking his superior, but then one did not simply bother Jana Morhain with trivial matters. Not that a life was trivial, but the priest was confident the boy was well out of any imminent danger, and as a prominent member of Arlingford's ruling family, the lady had other duties and responsibilities that went beyond those of the church. "You know Lady Morhain?" The man was highly skeptical of this given the girl's obvious status as a peasant, so the answer she gave took him by surprise.

"Yes, I do. She's been mentoring me for the last couple of days, providing me with guidance and advice. In fact, I'm supposed to see her again this afternoon. I could go back with you and ask her personally." While the priest considered her request in silence, she shot a sidelong glance at Thurgod, her eyes pleading silently for the Dwarf to remain quiet when it was painfully clear he was having a great deal of difficulty managing just that. This wasn't at all how she'd imagined she would be broaching the topic of her new rapport with the priestess to her grandfather, but timing, it seemed, was not something one often had control over. She glared at her grandfather in irritation when Thurgod appeared about to open his mouth, only for the Dwarf to grunt in annoyance when Caeden grabbed one of his arms from behind in warning. The look Thurgod shot her left no doubt in her mind that there would be a reckoning later, but for now, he was going to let her have it her way.

As if on cue, the priest finished his musing and assented. "Very well, though I'm skeptical that she will consent to come here," he said, giving the barn a critical eye.

"Leave that to me," Ellianna said confidently, but deep down she hoped for Darken's sake that she was right. Deacon Ulik shrugged, checked on the boy one more time, and then departed with Ellianna in tow.

CHAPTER 25

THE OLDEST BOYS OF the Janusian orphanage formed a single file down the middle aisle of the refectory hall and, one by one, approached the headmaster's table where each teenager paused briefly to stand before the Kal-dkar. The woman's elbows and hands rested on the polished wooden surface where several gleaming platinum discs—each one bearing a ten-pointed red star on its face—were arrayed in front of her in no discernible pattern. The mage had her eyes closed the entire time, yet she seemed to know whenever someone stopped in front of her, a hand lifting to dismissively wave on each newcomer almost as soon as he'd walked up. The line included all of those who had become Initiates in the last year, and Carlo was among them, having joined the line last after leaving Flynn sitting by himself at a table near the back of the hall.

All the other children watched the Test intently, but none more so than Elias, whose eyes darted quickly between what was happening at the head table, and his friend Flynn. The other boy hadn't said a word to anyone since his surprise appearance, and the murmur that his and Carlo's arrival had set off had quickly died to a hush when Father Lorimer called for the Test to begin. He desperately wanted to walk over to greet Flynn, but the glower on Carlo's face the entire time was impossible to ignore. 'Stay away', his expression said loudly and clearly, without the need for words. Even after the Initiate got up to walk to the back of the line, Elias didn't dare to sneak over to Flynn. The hall was quiet and still now, and though everyone present was paying attention to the Test, anyone leaving their seat would be immediately noticed. He had no choice but to remain where he was and wait for an opportunity to present itself later.

The line dwindled quickly, each boy resuming his seat in turn after being summarily dismissed by Alyssa Dumar. Rather than disappointment, the expression on every face was one of relief, likely owing to the mystery surrounding the fate of those rare few that were chosen—an enigma that was wrapped in the fantastical tales conjured up by the fertile imaginations of children. Before long, Carlo's turn came, and Elias found himself holding his breath. Remembering Eric's earlier comment, he couldn't deny he wouldn't be overly upset if the Initiate was selected. He watched in anticipation as the young man approached the table and he paid particular attention to Father Lorimer's expression, knowing how tightly knit the headmaster and the Initiate were. The priest was stone-faced, but his gaze did flick upwards to briefly meet the teenager's blue eyes. Elias could only see Carlo's back from where he sat, but it didn't matter—like the others before him, the mage's hand had come up, but this time it was to signal to the Initiate to remain in place. Her dark eyes opened to take in the boy's impassive face.

"Choose," the single word uttered loudly enough to reach every ear in the hall.

With difficulty, Elias quickly glanced in Flynn's direction, curious to see his friend's reaction. Like everyone else, Flynn's attention was fixed on what was happening at the head table. His face, however, betrayed no emotion other than silent expectation as he leaned forward slightly, waiting to see what would happen. Elias looked back to Carlo, not daring to miss this.

The black-robed youth stared at the discs on the table before him. There were ten in total, each one identical to the next in every discernible way to a casual observer. But this situation was anything but casual. The discs were similar in appearance to the tokens used during the draw at the beginning of Yule, except that these were metal instead of wood, with the ten-pointed star representing Galion the Magus, God of Magic and patron of the Kal-dkar. Carlo slowly lifted one hand, but just before he made his choice, he looked to Alyssa's left and stared straight into the eyes of Father Lorimer for a split second. Then, with his index finger, the Initiate touched one of the tokens and left the digit resting upon the metal, his selection made. Alyssa Dumar's eyes had never left Carlo's face, not even when he had selected the disc, but once he'd done so, she shook her head once and waved him off. The Initiate moved away from the table to walk to his seat next to Flynn. As usual, his face betrayed no emotion whatsoever.

"Damn it!" Elias heard Eric whisper next to him.

Just like that, the Test was over, the palpable tension ebbing out of the room like an ocean tide. Father Lorimer made ready to rise and address the hall but stopped mid-motion when Alyssa Dumar placed one hand on his arm and stopped him. He looked questioningly at his sibling but when she said nothing, he remained seated and waited. The Kal-dkar sat up and walked with purpose to the table where Elias and his friends sat. Every boy's eyes grew huge as the woman passed by them, no one daring to say a word though several mouths were open in astonishment. Nothing like this had ever happened during any of the Tests administered by old Bartholomew in previous years. Elias watched in shock while the mage walked straight in his direction, but he didn't dare to turn when he heard the footsteps stop right behind him. He sat perfectly still and looked straight ahead, trying to do nothing more than breathe, unable to believe this was happening. A moment later, there was an audible gasp of surprise and a shudder from the bench to his right. He chanced a sideways glance and saw the Kal-dkar's hand resting on Georgie's thin shoulder. The small lad's pale eyes were wide with astonishment, and he turned his head to look straight at Elias. So much had happened in so little time that he'd forgotten about the startling comment Georgie had made earlier about something the mage had apparently told him from across the room without actually having spoken to him. At least not in any way that anyone had heard.

The first emotion that went through Elias was sheer relief. While he would often daydream about being chosen by the Test one day and taken away from this place to a life of magic and mystery, he decided today that the prospect wasn't as appealing as he'd once imagined. There was something very unsettling about this Kal-dkar that filled him with unease and fear. Maybe the feeling was completely unwarranted, but the truth deep down was that he could not face the idea of being separated from his friends. The second emotion that followed immediately was shame. He was glad that the mage hadn't come for him as he'd initially feared, but it also made him feel that his reprieve came at the expense of obvious distress for one of his friends. He knew it was irrational to think that he could be in any way responsible for this, but he felt ashamed nonetheless as he swallowed dryly and shrugged his shoulders in confusion at Georgie. The other boy looked away from him and up at Alyssa's face, then got up to follow her when she walked away, his slender frame trembling with each step he took.

"Can you believe this?" Elias heard Eric whispering again. No, he couldn't, and along with that disbelief was a terrifying fear and certainty that he'd just regained a friend with Flynn's return, only to lose another. Just when he thought this couldn't get any worse, he watched as the Kal-dkar walked up to the table where Flynn and Carlo sat together, stopped, and motioned for the former to rise and follow her as well.

"No way..." was all Eric could manage, which was two words more than Elias.

Apparently, Father Lorimer agreed. The headmaster rose swiftly from his seat to glare imperiously at the mage. "Absolutely not! You go too far. These two boys are not of age yet." This set off a murmur of agreement from the other priests present in the room, all of whom had held their silence until now. Tradition and procedure were one thing, the Test being something they had no choice but to tolerate, but this was highly irregular. That the headmaster and Kal-dkar were siblings only made the situation all the more awkward. For her part, Alyssa paid her brother no heed and motioned for the two boys to stand before the head table while she resumed her seat.

"Did you not hear me?" the headmaster of the orphanage thundered, causing the startled clerics to grow silent again. It was rare to witness the senior priest lose his temper, especially in front of all the children.

Alyssa did not look at him, focusing instead on the faces of the two young men in front of her. Georgie remained pale and wide-eyed, shaking like a frightened rabbit looking for a hole in the ground to bolt into, yet paralyzed by the stare of the wolf that slowly stalks it. For his part, Flynn appeared unafraid, almost defiant. Or was it resignation the mage saw there? Alyssa could sense the boy had gone through something traumatic recently, and the roiling waves of *etherus* that emanated from him with raw force as a result were impossible to ignore. She would have to have a long conversation with her brother after this.

"Yes, I heard you just fine, Revered Father. Need I remind you of my royal authority over you in these matters? Or would you care to discuss that personally with the king today? He'll be on his way shortly, so I can easily arrange that, if you wish?" she left the suggestion hanging, forcing the senior priest to decide the next move. For a brief instant when his anger made it difficult to think clearly, he nearly told the arrogant Kal-dkar to do just that. As far back as he could remember to them being children growing up in the Dumar household, everything had always turned into a competition between him and his twin sister. At first it had been little more than a game that they both enjoyed, laughing and teasing each other good-naturedly in the end, no matter who won. As they grew older, however, the competition had only turned fiercer, each one seeking to outdo the other in ways that became increasingly more complex and daring. Unfortunately, it also led to a growing fissure of resentment that had culminated on the day King Aldrik's Kal-dkar had taken her away at the age of fifteen. The smug look she'd given him then was like a final declaration of victory that he refused to accept.

Lorimer Dumar's subsequent climb through the ranks of Corazan's Janusian clergy was driven not only by his own innate ambition but fueled also by an illogical and unreasonable need to assuage his wounded pride and attain a position higher than his sister's. With the illustrious title of Archbishop now within his reach at last, it was the sudden reminder of how quickly all that hard work could be jeopardized that made him step back from making a rash decision he'd regret later. Alyssa had always excelled at goading and manipulating him to sabotage himself from achieving success by playing with his emotions, and she had nearly succeeded again. But he was no longer the short-tempered youth he'd once been, and the stakes for which he played now were much greater than his sister—for all her vaunted intelligence and skill—could possibly dream of. If she took Flynn away, everything could be ruined.

"That won't be necessary," he said curtly, with a tone that Alyssa knew all too well and served as a formal warning to her that this was far from over.

In her position as the court's most eminent mage, and along with all the training instilled upon her by her Kal-dkar peers, there was a seriousness and no-nonsense attitude that was integral to Alyssa's craft. It's not that practitioners of magic were expected to hold themselves above human emotions, but there was a level of responsibility that came with the awesome power they wielded that required a higher degree of control than most people could ever attain. It took years of focus and training to achieve that detachment, and not all were completely successful. Alyssa Dumar was not one to gloat, and were this anyone but her own brother, there would not have been a barely perceptible curl to one corner of her lip in reaction to his words. She allowed herself that small indulgence, however, knowing it would only infuriate him further, and the sharp exhalation of breath that she heard from him confirmed that she had scored another hit. Good. She knew how to deal with him and would do so later. For now, there were more important matters before her.

"You first," she said to Georgie. "Choose."

The small boy had been completely oblivious to the exchange between mage and headmaster, his focus solely on what was about to happen. He flinched visibly when the mage ordered him to proceed, and he raised a trembling hand to hover uncertainly over the discs. Never in his wildest dreams had he imagined that he would be standing here before the king's Kal-dkar, about to be tested a full year before he was due. Shy and unassuming all his short life, Georgie had never thought of himself as special in any way, nor had he even suspected that he might have a connection to the mysterious *etherus*. He certainly had a curiosity on the subject that was greater than most, and had devoured every book on the topic of magic—or at least those few at the orphanage that he was allowed to read—but from what little he had gleaned, he had not developed any of the signs that were normally attributed to someone who was attuned to Akar's arcane weave. In time, and with practice, he hoped to be able to channel a small portion of it like all Janusian priests could, but the thought of being a mage was beyond his capacity to imagine, and imagination was not something he lacked. All that had changed when he'd felt the strange sensation inside of his mind earlier when the Kal-dkar took her seat at the head table.

It had been like a form of mental itch at first, not unlike when you're trying to recall something that you know, yet it remains stubbornly and tantalizingly just out of reach. Whatever it was, it was as if it kept trying to get his attention, growing so insistent that he could no longer ignore it as the odd and passing sensation that he tried to dismiss it as at first. He tried to figure out a way to seek it out and acknowledge it, but he didn't know where to begin or what exactly it was that he was looking for. It was only when Elias had remarked upon the Kal-dkar's physical resemblance to Father Lorimer that the itch suddenly crystalized into a clear voice in his head that called out to him. No—not to him specifically, he realized, but to anyone in the hall that had the ability to hear it. As if a beacon had suddenly shone a light into the dark recesses of his mind and illuminated a room that he never knew existed, the voice focused on his last thought.

'We look alike because your headmaster is my twin brother.'

He'd been curious about the Kal-dkar after seeing her at mass earlier in the day, and he'd been trying hard not to stare at her ever since she'd walked in the refectory. When he heard her voice in his subconscious though, that was when he realized that she was staring right back at him. He couldn't help himself and blurted out to his friends what she'd said in answer to their question, but before he could explain any further, Flynn had arrived. That seemed like an eternity ago. Now he stood before Alyssa Dumar and the table, but it felt more like he was at the edge of a yawning chasm, about to take the plunge into a frightening unknown that would irrevocably alter who he was. He tried to still his trembling to no avail. To fail the Test simply meant one's life would go on as it always had before, with no consequences whatsoever. Once tested, there would be no further attempts in the following years. It took that clarity of thought for him to understand that it was not success in the Test that he feared, but failure. He remembered Martino, whom they'd never seen again. He didn't want to lose Elias, Eric, or Flynn—though with the latter standing beside him, he wasn't so sure—but he had to measure that against the thrill of excitement at the prospect of a new life away from the orphanage. That exhilaration beat back the nervousness until it was gone, and he looked down in surprise, his hand no longer trembling and now steady with confidence.

He closed his eyes, took a deep breath to still his racing thoughts, and then opened them again to look at the discs in a new way. Very faintly at first, but growing progressively brighter, Georgie saw the glowing filaments of golden magical energy as they drifted through the air, connecting and enveloping each one of the metallic objects that bore the symbol of the god of magic. This must be the *etherus* he'd read so much about, he marvelled. He tried to look for a pattern, but the tendrils of light appeared to move at random, flowing to and from the discs in a graceful but lazy dance. He intuited that the Test had something to do with choosing the correct disc, but which one was that? It was clear that they were all enchanted in some fashion, but what made one of them more special than the others? He could feel the Kal-dkar's eyes on him, and the unspoken message in that unseen stare was that his time was nearly up. The pressure became almost too much to bear, and he saw his hand twitch once, a clear sign his nerves were reasserting themselves. No, he told himself. He wouldn't fail. He couldn't fail.

He focused more deeply on what he was seeing, blocking out everything else around him from his consciousness—the mage; the headmaster; Flynn; the refectory hall and the orphans and priests present; even the table itself. Only the discs existed. And then there it was. As the pulses of energy briefly caressed each disc before moving on to the next, the ruby-red star of Galion carved into the platinum circumference of each object flashed ever so briefly with a faint red glow, then dimmed and went out as the *etherus* flowed past, only to light up again as soon as it returned a second later. But on one of the discs, the light of the star lingered—even if only very slightly—for just a split second longer, while the other nine winked rapidly in and out. It was almost too fast to detect, but he saw it clearly now, and so he did not hesitate. With eager confidence, he placed one finger assertively over his choice. As soon as he touched the metal, the hall, along with everyone and everything within it, returned from the void to which his awareness had consigned it. The magical energies dissipated as if they had never been, the discs dark and inert as they had always appeared. He looked straight into the dark brown orbs of the Kal-dkar's eyes to see there the confirmation he sought. There was only the barest hint of a smile on her thin lips, but she nodded in approval.

"Pass. Return to your seat, I will come for you tomorrow."

Georgie walked away, shaken by the experience but feeling as if he was floating on air. When he reached his table and sat down, the smile of incredulity he wore on his small face fell, however, for his friends weren't exactly beaming with pride at his accomplishment. Elias was valiantly trying to smile, but he couldn't hide the mingled confusion and concern in his expression. On the other hand, Eric's deep scowl made Georgie feel like the other boy was looking at him as if he was a complete stranger. The excitement he'd experienced just moments before became tinged with uncertainty, but when he felt Elias's comforting hand on his shoulder, he bravely lifted his head to observe Flynn's turn. Perhaps he wouldn't be going on this journey alone.

At the head table, Alyssa Dumar casually waved both of her hands over the discs in a circular motion without physically touching them. The objects moved as if propelled by an unseen force, shuffling and sliding around the table's surface, flipping over one another with a speed that made it impossible to keep track of the one that Georgie had chosen. When they finally came to a stop, their position was just as random as before.

"Choose."

Flynn didn't move. The last time he'd been asked to select a token with the symbol of a god graven upon it, his life had been fundamentally changed in a way that he didn't like. Yet here he was a mere three weeks later and being asked to do it again. He experienced that odd sensation one feels when they are certain they are reliving a past experience, except in this case there was no doubt in his mind that he'd done this before. He couldn't explain precisely why, but he hadn't felt surprised when the Kal-dkar had come for him. Ever since his accident, events surrounding him had taken such a surreal direction at every opportunity that he didn't even question why he stood before the mage right now. He'd calmly watched as Georgie underwent the Test, but he'd been more interested in observing the reactions of the woman and the man seated in front of him.

In the past couple of weeks, Father Lorimer had gone from being a remote figure at the orphanage to someone he'd seen nearly every day since leaving the hospital. While the man had done his best to explain to Flynn that his isolation was for his own good, he had no illusions as to the real reason after the final conversation with Brother Owen. He was a danger to others, and though the headmaster was making an admirable effort to hide it, Flynn knew that if he somehow passed the Test, the ramifications of leaving the orphanage now would present an extremely undesirable development for the priest—a deduction that only made Flynn even more determined to succeed. At this point, and with Brother Owen gone, he felt no desire to stay. As for the mage, he couldn't really form an opinion because he didn't know her, other than the fact that she gave away nothing. No; that wasn't entirely true. He hadn't missed the exchange between the two adults, where she had clearly established her dominance over the priest. Father Lorimer hadn't necessarily mistreated him, but he mistrusted the man and his motives, and to witness someone vex him in such a fashion pleased him in a perverse way. Moments ago, he'd had half a mind to just select a disc at random and purposefully fail the Test. Now, he'd decided to make a genuine attempt at passing it.

As he'd seen Carlo and Georgie do, Flynn put out one hand and held it over the discs, fingers splayed. The Kal-dkar took note of the black leather glove he wore and arched one eyebrow but said nothing. The young man closed his blue eyes and then opened them again. He didn't know what he would see, or whether he would even see anything at all—in fact, he half expected that there wouldn't be much beyond the odd sensation of premonition that he'd felt when he placed his hand in the token bag. This was much different. He had no way of knowing what Georgie had experienced, but while he too saw the glowing threads of *etherus* flowing between the discs, the energy was not the soothing, golden colour his friend had perceived, but rather a viscous, inky black that pulsed rhythmically with muted intensity, like a heartbeat. While he watched, the magic filaments flowed over the discs, filling the grooves of each ruby star like dark oil, and completely obscuring the rich red colour of the stone until it turned to mirror-like obsidian. Something didn't feel right, and Flynn knew almost immediately that he was the one causing this, a fact that was confirmed when he noticed the sinister-looking coils of energy around the discs were flowing from his very hand.

Beneath the leather, the scar left by Gaurkur's token turned from an omnipresent itch to a flare of white-hot pain.

He gasped in shock and withdrew his hand, closing it into a fist before tucking it under his left arm. The pain disappeared immediately. On the table, the discs appeared unchanged and unaffected by what he'd seen. Unable to contain his shame and disappointment, he fought back tears and walked away from the table abruptly, unwilling to look at either the man or woman who watched him go in perturbed silence. Alyssa frowned, uncertain of what she'd just witnessed, and tried to keep her reaction as neutral as humanly possible against the strange wave of magical energy she'd just felt. During the Test, she could not see what each subject perceived with their own senses; only which of the boys present was sufficiently attuned to the *etherus* to merit being tested, and of course, which of the ten discs was the one touched by Galion himself. She would have staked her life on the fact that Flynn would pass, so strong was his connection to the weave, but his reaction was unlike anything she'd ever experienced. She needed to know more, and one look at the expression of relief and satisfaction on her brother's face told her exactly where she would find the answers she sought.

"It has not been a dull day, Lorimer," the Kal-dkar said, rising from her seat. She gathered the discs and placed them in a small dark blue velvet pouch that hung from her belt. "I'll not be staying for lunch and will leave for the convent now. Once the king is finished here and your duties for the day are complete, I'd like to have a word or two with you in private, Revered Father—perhaps this evening?" She placed deliberate emphasis on his title as if to mock him. "No need to rush home, I can let myself in." Without waiting for a reply, she drew her hood over her head and left the refectory hall through the main doors that led to the courtyard. Broodingly watching her back as she departed, Father Lorimer was already mentally going over how the conversation with his sister would unfold, and what he would say. Around him, priests and children alike felt the tension ebb out of the room in the wake of the mage's exit, and the usual noise of excited chatter from the boys soon filled the large space once more. When the signal came from the head table for the kitchen staff to begin serving lunch, it was all Eric could do to contain his excitement.

"My favourite part. Thought we'd never get there," the big kid said with a wide grin. He elbowed Elias playfully in the ribs, but the other boy was feeling anything but joyful.

"Cut it out, Eric, you oaf," Elias growled in irritation. "Something important just happened, but as usual, you've only got food on the brain and therefore nothing else matters, right?"

Eric's smile fell, and his pudgy face took on an expression of hurt. "Sorry, I was just—"

"Hungry. Yes, I know. You're always hungry. Well, tomorrow you can have Georgie's share since he won't be here any longer." Elias felt his whole world turning upside down. Things were happening too quickly, and none of it made any sense to him. It was a lot of change to accept all at once in a world that had been fairly static for years, and now he was feeling lost and adrift, not knowing what new and unwelcome surprise tomorrow might bring.

"Is that right? Well, next time Peter is about to punch your face in, I'll just keep on walking by then," Eric made an ugly face and crossed his arms, making a point of looking away.

"Next time Peter picks on me—if there is a next time—I'll deal with him myself, thank you very much," Elias retorted angrily, his voice rising so much that the other boys sitting across the table paused in their own conversation to stare at him in silence.

"Shhhhh... guys, please, don't fight," Georgie pleaded. "I don't want this to be how I spend my last day with my friends." His voice sounded so small and forlorn that Elias' anger dissipated immediately, and he nearly burst into tears right there and then. He'd been trying not to think about the fact that he most likely would never see his friend again, but it was a sobering truth that he couldn't escape, no matter how much he wanted to hide from it. Seeing Flynn again helped, of course, but it seemed fairly obvious that something was different about him as well, and that things would never go back to being the same way as before. He really wished that he could talk to someone who would truly listen and help him calm down, like Brother Owen, but he hadn't seen the priest for days. Was it possible he was still ill? He couldn't think of any other reason why the devout cleric would miss the Yule mass and the king's visit. He needed to find out what was going on with him and with Flynn as well, but for the time being, Georgie was absolutely right—his friend deserved better than this.

"I'm so sorry, Georgie. It's a lot to take in all at once. I don't want you to go and it's upsetting me," Elias said, "never mind what you must be going through right now, not knowing what's going to happen." He cringed inwardly at his own words even as he voiced them, knowing they weren't the reassurance he'd hoped to give. Feeling awkward, he turned his head to look at Eric, who'd been listening while pretending not to, and was now looking at them both with watery eyes. "I'm sorry, Eric, I didn't mean what I said." In response, the heavy-set boy sniffled, then pulled a handkerchief from his pocket and blew his nose loudly and moistly into it.

"Ewww, gross," Elias and Georgie said in unison, eliciting a renewed grin from Eric. All three of them laughed with relief, enjoying their camaraderie, and forgetting for a time that tomorrow would be a very different day. Then their table was called, and the boys grabbed their plates and ran off to line up to get their lunch.

Across the room, Flynn's gaze longingly followed his friends, having watched them from afar since returning to his table, and wanting very badly to be sitting with them and sharing in whatever it was that had made them laugh. He was alone for now, Carlo having left momentarily to get their food after instructing him to stay put, but he wasn't feeling hungry whatsoever. In fact, he felt miserable, frightened, and alone. Whatever it was that he'd just experienced during the Test left him filled with anxiety and dread, and all of Brother Owen's words of reassurance hadn't prepared him for yet another shock like this. The pain he'd felt was indescribable; its intensity matched only by the similar occurrence when he'd drawn the token from the bag a few weeks ago. He flexed the fingers of his gloved hand, overcome with an intense hatred for the scarred appendage. He had an irrational, brief, and very vivid image of himself cutting his hand off to be rid of the problem in the most dramatic way possible, but he knew he'd never have the courage to do something so extreme.

He pushed the ghastly vision out of his mind, and tried to think instead about the Kal-dkar's Test. He'd never seen the *etherus* before, and never really imagined that he would. Always in his fantasies and daydreams about what he would do when he was old enough, there were only valiant warriors with shining swords, and dastardly villains or terrible monsters to slay—just like Avakan, the hero in his favourite book. As such, he'd never considered the very unlikely possibility of becoming a mage. He knew almost nothing about what they did and how they did it, and it always seemed to him that magic was kind of a way to cheat around doing things the normal way—except when the priests used it to heal the sick, of course. What little on the subject he had learned in class, though, told him that in those few in whom the *etherus* did manifest itself, it almost never happened until they were a little bit older than he was. Was the mark on his hand somehow responsible for the Kal-dkar's decision to give him the Test? Had she seen or sensed something different about him? Maybe, and maybe not, but in the moment, he figured that if he somehow passed, it might be his one and only chance to leave Father Lorimer's cellar room behind, and perhaps even the orphanage altogether. For that reason alone, he had wanted to succeed, but alas, it seemed the cruel gods had other plans for him. He didn't need the mage's expression of surprise to tell him that the outcome of the Test had not been the one either had hoped for.

Before he could muse on this development any further, Carlo returned to the table with lunch. The Initiate placed the plate in front of him, but Flynn had no interest in the food, morosely pushing the potatoes around the boiled piece of codfish.

"Eat," Carlo said, taking a bite of his own meal.

"I'm not hungry," Flynn replied sullenly.

"Suit yourself."

Flynn cast a sidelong glance at the Initiate. Carlo consumed his own food, but while he did, his watchful gaze never stopped observing what was going on in the refectory. He particularly noticed that the teenage Initiate often looked at the head table, where Father Lorimer sat. The headmaster paid them no heed as he enjoyed his own meal while engrossed in conversation with Father Julius, a visiting priest from the Janusian church in Brakir, a city up the coast. For lack of anything better to do, Flynn stared at the assemblage of clerics that had joined Father Lorimer at the table after the Kal-dkar's departure. Only one seat near the far end of the table was empty—the chair normally occupied by Brother Owen. It had only been an hour or so since he'd said goodbye to his friend, but already he felt his absence very keenly. With Brother Edward gone as well, there was no one left at that table that he felt even remotely close to, although he'd always gotten along rather well with the young and affable Brother Paul.

Thinking of Brother Owen, he cast his mind back to the day he'd first met the priest. It was a memory that always brought up mixed emotions. While he'd made the acquaintance of someone who'd come close to filling the void in his heart left by the death of his father—along with all the comfort that presence brought—he also remembered it as the day he'd said goodbye to his brothers and the house he'd been born in. He wondered how Joshua and the others were doing, and whether he would ever see them again. With his thoughts lingering on the last few days he'd spent with his siblings, he came across another memory, one buried deep in his subconscious. As he looked again at the faces of the priests while they ate, he frowned and wondered why he'd never thought of this before. Not once since he'd arrived at the orphanage had he ever seen the priest that had come to their house on the day before his father had passed away. How strange, he remarked to himself. Was he perhaps one of the clerics that was not attached to the orphanage and whose duties lay solely within the cathedral itself, like Fathers Anthony and Oliver? No, he was sure he had met them all as well.

"Carlo?"

"Yes?"

"How long have you been here?"

"Long enough. Why?"

Flynn looked at the Initiate with a calculating expression. He could scarcely stand the hateful sight of the older boy, and he would never forget or forgive him for his part in the events that resulted in Dario's death, not to mention the Initiate's tacit complicity in the constant bullying of other kids, like his friend Elias. Still, since it seemed he was stuck with this unwanted personal guardian for the time being, it wouldn't hurt to take advantage of the situation and use one's own enemy as a resource, something he'd learned from one of his favourite tales in *The Legend of Starfall.* There were times when an opponent could be worth more alive than dead.

"You must know every priest very well then," he implied casually.

Carlo's dark eyebrows knotted together, and his blue eyes narrowed. Suspicious by nature, he could sense immediately that Flynn was up to something but decided to play along until he discovered what that was. "You could say that, yes."

Flynn nodded and then looked back at the head table. "In the weeks after my mother died, our father fell sick as well. My brother Joshua came all the way here to ask for a Janusian priest to attend, and the very next day, one did."

"And what of it?"

Flynn prided himself in having a very good memory, so he described the priest he'd seen in every detail as if the man were standing before him now. The description matched none of the clerics present in the room, but Flynn did not mention that, waiting to see if Carlo would make the connection.

"Gold-trimmed robes, you said?" Carlo looked more intently at Flynn, trying to read the other boy's expression and body language for any hint of deceit.

"Yes. I remember that most clearly of all. Isn't that strange? I've never seen a priest in robes like those before. Do you know who he was?"

"Doesn't sound like anyone I know—maybe you're remembering him wrong? As for the robes, I think you should stop reading those stupid stories of yours and concentrate more on your studies. If you did, you'd know no one within the church hierarchy is permitted to wear gold trim because there is no such rank."

Carlo's condescendingly superior tone grated on Flynn's pride. He knew he was a good student—Brothers Owen and Edward had often told him as much. So what if he couldn't recall one small, stupid detail about clerical robes and ranks? Still, he made a mental note to look up the subject, though he'd be damned if he would ever acknowledge that to Carlo. He didn't think he was going to get anything more out of the Initiate, so he let the matter drop. He also didn't feel the older boy was lying about not knowing who the priest was, which only deepened the mystery. He regretted not asking Brother Owen while he'd had the chance, but he hadn't thought of it until now. Surely someone else around here would know? The headmaster would for sure, but Flynn had neither the desire nor the courage to ask Father Lorimer questions that would draw further attention to him. His plan for now was to be as compliant as possible, do exactly as he was told, and hopefully be allowed to return to the company of the other boys as a reward for his good behaviour. Concluding that eating his food might be a good start toward that goal, he took a bite of the fish.

The plates were cleared just in time for the king's arrival, and the boys of the orphanage and clerics alike stood up when Aldrik Ormandos, Lion of Rohne, entered the refectory, his pace respectfully slow and measured so that the elderly Archbishop Marcos walking at his side could keep up. Following closely behind the pair walked Princess Gabriela and Chamberlain Wyl. As one, the leaders of Rohne's secular and spiritual states approached the head table to greet the headmaster and the priesthood assembled there, all of whom bowed deeply in a show of respect. That done, the two men turned to face the gathered children, the king waiting while the archbishop performed his benediction. When the children concluded the ritual by raising their voices in unison to chant "The Light of Janus be with you," King Aldrik raised both of his arms, and then lowered them slowly with a smile.

"Greetings children. Please everyone, be seated," he began. As one, the boys sat back down while one of the clerics brought forth a cushioned chair for the archbishop to sit upon. The clerics took their seats as well but the king, his daughter, and the chamberlain, remained standing.

"On this last day of Yule, I come to you here, not merely as part of a long-standing tradition that stretches back to the days of my ancestors, but to fulfill my duty as a symbolic father to every last boy and girl of Rohne. Here, cradled within the arms of Castle Hill and our glorious city of Corazan, and under the care of the devoted Brothers and Sisters of Holy Janus, you stand protected as the precious treasure that you are—the future men and women of this great kingdom. The tragic absence of your parents should not—and does not—lessen your importance to me in any way, and you should never hold yourselves to be inferior to any other child in the land because of it. One day, Janus willing, each and every one of you will become an important and vital part of what makes us the envy of our neighbours. Here, every life is precious, and I stand before you now as I always have since I was your age, to remind you that you will never be forgotten. I ask only that you be good, study hard, and always show the respect that is due to these pious men that dedicate their lives to your care and education. Listen to them, so that you may gain the helpful knowledge and wisdom that they will impart to you, and you will have the tools you need to become an invaluable citizen of the realm, no matter which path you choose."

The boys, disciplined and quiet, listened to this great and formidable figure of a man whose very voice commanded attention, even if most of them had heard this exact same speech several times before. One boy, however, scarcely listened to the king, intent as he was in staring at the princess, all the while trying his hardest to appear as if that wasn't exactly what he was doing. Elias felt his heart racing, positively mesmerized by Princess Gabriela's captivating beauty. He didn't even react when Eric drove one heel into his shin to try to get him to pay attention. He just couldn't understand why he wasn't able to take his eyes off her, and quite frankly, he didn't care. This was what he'd been waiting for all day since seeing her earlier at mass, and now that she was here, he didn't want it to end. He was already dreading the moment when she would leave, and he wasn't sure how he would manage to survive an entire year before seeing her again. His despair was interrupted when he heard the king speak her name, prompting him to begin paying full attention to what Aldrik was saying.

"—introduce to you my daughter, Princess Gabriela. As your future queen, this annual visit will one day become her solemn duty, among many others. To that end, she is here today to observe and gain an understanding of the functions and daily life at the orphanage and convent, as well as meet all of you and share some words of her own. My daughter." King Aldrik took a step back, giving the princess the floor.

Gabriela Ormandos stepped forward, but nothing about her stiff posture and stony expression revealed anything of her thoughts. She acknowledged her father's introduction with the barest hint of a smile that lacked any warmth and then faced the gathered youths. A brief, awkward silence followed as her eyes roamed from face to face, as if seeing the orphans for the first time since she'd walked in. Nearly all of them looked down rather than meet her gaze, as was the custom with royalty unless being addressed directly. When she noticed one who did not avert his eyes and stared back at her, she recognized the look on his enraptured face immediately. It was one she had seen countless times before on the faces of the young noblemen of the court, many of whom vied constantly and tirelessly for her attention and affection. Her father, if he had his way, would eventually see her married off to one of those feckless, fawning men, but she did not for one minute believe in the sincerity of their honeyed words. She knew that they saw her as nothing more than a path to the crown, and the aggrandizement of their own family name and fortune. Yet, while their admiration was one of convenience and opportunity, it would be illogical to think that this hopeless orphan boy's unabashed awe of her presence was anything but genuine. For the first time in many years, Gabriela felt a little bit of warmth return to her heart.

"I know what you must be thinking," she began, her clear voice not unlike her father's in how it elicited immediate attention from a listener. "How can this mere girl—born into a life of privilege and wealth, and given everything she could ever want or need—not be anything but an arrogant, vain, selfish, and prideful creature that couldn't possibly imagine what it must be like to be one of you? What words can a princess—one that lives in a castle that looms daily over your very heads like a reminder of how close to the heavens she is and how low to the earth you are—utter that will not sound hollow and meaningless to you? And even if you weren't thinking of those things just now, have I not just painfully reminded you of having had those thoughts before?" Gabriela paused, looking out over the multitude of heads, not one face daring to look at her, not even that boy she'd noticed before. Behind her, she could hear her father heaving a sigh of resignation. He shouldn't be surprised, and she knew he wouldn't be. He knew what to expect from his daughter, and he'd brought her here, nevertheless.

"Look at me," she said, not as a command, but as a plea. Regardless of the difference between the two, the youths of the orphanage raised their faces to do as she asked. "Don't you see? All that separates me from you is nothing more than an accident of birth—a product of random chance that only the gods see fit to understand. What I'm trying to say by this is that it could just as easily be one of you up here speaking, just as I could be down there among you, listening. Before you think that I don't understand how you feel or what you've gone through, know that I too lost a parent when I was very young. Granted, some of you lost both your mother and father, or worse—have parents that still live, yet gave you up for reasons that you don't understand and very likely will never forgive—but know that I understand the pain of loss, and of living with a void in your heart that can never be filled again. It's that experience that shapes and defines who we are as individuals, not the artificial trappings of social hierarchy. I am not better than you, but I am sincerely humbled by your strength and perseverance that allows you to carry on every day, so that despite the hand you have been given by fate, you can still go on to become those future men and women that my father alluded to—the ones that will go on to make this kingdom the best that it can be—not because you were born with the world in your hand, but because you worked hard to put it there yourself."

The children listened attentively for the most part—the small ones unsure of what the young woman was going on about and wondering when it would be time to go outside and play, and the older ones skeptical and suspicious of why a princess was trying to compare her life to theirs. It's not that many of them didn't grasp what she was saying, it was more a case of not understanding what the point was. She was royalty, and they were low-born orphans, and that was the harsh truth that no amount of pretty words could change. That was the conclusion Flynn had reached as he listened to Princess Gabriela, wondering what, if anything, all this was leading up to. Observant as always, he didn't miss the obvious signs of tension between daughter and father, mainly evident in the king's body language that revealed subtle signs of impatience and annoyance, but he wasn't sure what to make of it. Flynn had seen King Aldrik twice from afar before—when he was little and his father had taken him and his brothers to Corazan's annual summer fair, and again four years ago when a parade had been held to commemorate the fortieth anniversary of his rule. He knew next to nothing about the princess other than the fact that she existed, and to his mind it was only Aldrik that mattered anyway—the brave hero who had avenged the death of his father and ended the giants' threat to the kingdom once and for all by the strength of his sword arm.

When his own father had carved him his treasured wooden knight figurine, Flynn had asked Samuel if the knight was supposed to be someone in particular. When he was told that it could be anyone he imagined it to be, Flynn had decided that it should be the king because there was no one more important or brave in the kingdom than him. Sitting here today, so close to this living legend that he'd idolized all his life, the boy found himself wishing fervently that this annoying, ungrateful girl would shut up, and that the king would talk more about how Flynn could one day become a hero of Rohne like him. Had he bothered to listen more closely, he would have understood that both king and princess were essentially saying the same thing, only in a different way. She'd just said something about 'working hard', and Flynn scoffed inwardly. He looked at her and shook his head slightly, seeing only a pampered and spoiled individual that had never worked a hard day in her whole life. His parents had worked hard. The Brothers of the orphanage worked hard. A high-born girl in a fancy dress and wearing expensive jewellery? Ha! He seriously doubted there was so much as a single granule of grime under one of her long fingernails.

"—which is why I have asked my father and His Eminence permission to begin a new tradition, on this, the Yule eve of the New Year. When spring arrives, we shall—together—welcome the season of renewal and new beginnings with a field trip to the city, organized between the castle and the church, to take you outside of these gloomy walls and see, hear, and feel what awaits you out there one day when you are old enough to determine your own fate. Not everything about life can be learned from a book, and if our goal is that you all grow up to be good citizens of this great kingdom, then it is important that you be given the opportunity to experience that reality for yourselves. What do you say to that?" Gabriela finished talking, her heart racing with uncertainty. She had felt confident when she walked into the refectory, bolstered by the hard-fought-for acceptance days before of her proposal to both the king and Archbishop Marcos. Less than an hour earlier, she had delivered the very same speech to the girls at the convent on the other side of the hill, and the response had been exactly what she'd hoped for—the young women were thrilled by her visit and the prospect of visiting the city every year. Here, among the boys, the sound of her words dissipated in the air and awkward silence followed. She silently questioned whether her plan was just too much of a change for them to accept, especially coming from her and not her father, a figure of male authority. It was a risk she'd been willing to take.

A low murmur of decidedly agitated voices began at her back, confirming her suspicion that the archbishop had not yet advised his priests of her idea. That's fine; she decided—let the old man and the headmaster sort that out between them. If she won the approval of the boys, whatever objections to the idea the conservative priests could mount would be irrelevant. Her father had not been easy to convince either. Aldrik was a staunch traditionalist and wary of what he called his daughter's 'forward' ideas, but despite his protestations, there was little he wouldn't give her if the act helped to bring them a little closer. Gabriela wasn't ashamed to take advantage of that—even if she still loved him dearly deep down. She wasn't sure she would ever forgive him for essentially abdicating his presence in her life as a father after her mother had died. When she needed him most, he'd become too wrapped up in his own misery and grief to remember that he had a six-year-old daughter who was in pain as well. Had it not been for Beran Wyl and his wife, Marion, Gabriela would have grown up alone and without anything resembling the warm love of a parent. Now that she was old enough to marry and Aldrik felt old age creeping up on him, her father suddenly and conveniently remembered that he had a daughter. Well, she was going to make sure she never let him forget that fact from this day on. She understood now what that kind of leverage meant, and she intended to use it.

Behind her, Archbishop Marcos cleared his throat meaningfully, a signal that prompted Father Lorimer to silence the mutterings of the other priests. Gabriela was grateful for the gesture and wanted to thank the head of Corazan's church for his support but refrained so as not to break decorum. Growing up, she'd always liked the old priest, who unfailingly and patiently took the time to answer her many questions and sate her insatiable curiosity. Throughout his tenure as archbishop, Marcos had been a strong advocate for the care and protection of the children in the orphanage and had made several important reforms to how it operated since ascending to his position many years ago. Now that he was close to announcing his retirement, she wanted to make sure that same level of zeal and concern was maintained in his absence, and she intended to be the one that made that happen. The relationship between the crown and the church had not always been as harmonious as it was today, and the archbishop's most likely replacement—or so it was rumoured at court—was not someone she knew very well. The Dumars were a well-established and wealthy family going back to the earliest days of the kingdom, and while she had never spoken with Father Lorimer, she was well acquainted with his sister, the kings' new Kal-dkar advisor, Alyssa. If the headmaster was anything like his cold and aloof sibling, the princess was wary of what the future may hold for these children. When she became queen one day, she had the uneasy feeling that her relationship with the future archbishop would be vastly different than the one her father and Marcos enjoyed today.

The clerics now silent, Gabriela's attention turned back once more to the faces of the two hundred or so orphans that continued to look silently at her. The fear that perhaps she had made a mistake in her overestimation of how receptive to this idea the boys would be took root, and she fought hard to keep her disappointment from her face. Her mind raced, trying to come up with some further words that would excite and convince them, but because she had not anticipated any need for them, she hadn't prepared any. She felt lost, alone, and afraid, just as she had for most of her life, and the weight of all those eyes staring silently at her made all her earlier self-confidence evaporate completely. She thought she was as strong as she'd claimed they were, but perhaps she was nothing but a fraud.

"I..." she began to speak, uncertain of what she would say, but glad at least for having found her voice again. Before she could say anything more, a single boy stood up and began to clap his hands, slowly at first, but gradually increasing the tempo while grinning eagerly. He was alone initially, but then one by one, others joined him, until the entire refectory was filled with the sound of cheers and enthusiasm from all the gathered children. Overcome with emotion, it was all she could do to hold back tears of gratitude at this measure of acceptance that she craved so much. Her eyes met those of the boy who had come to her rescue—the same one she had caught staring at her earlier—and she smiled and nodded in thanks for his support.

"Thank you," she stammered at first, then steadied her voice. "Minister Wyl and Father Lorimer will work out the details, but in just a few short months, I will see you again for our first visit to the city." She then stepped back and ceded the floor to her father once again.

"It warms my heart to see you all so enthusiastic about my daughter's idea. While I admit to it being an unconventional one, it is plain to see that it is something that you all heartily embrace and therefore I would not dare to stand in the way of such joy and anticipation. With His Eminence's blessing, I hereby decree that the orphanage's first annual field trip is now official. And with that, the time has come for us to leave you. I wish you all a merry last day of Yule, and may your next year be filled with happiness and good health." With a smiling flourish and a bow that thrilled the children, the king and his entourage paid their respects to Archbishop Marcos and then exited the refectory to make their way to the carriage that awaited by the cathedral's main gates to take them back to the castle.

"You can sit down now, you dummy," Eric muttered to Elias. "People are starting to stare at you."

Elias, still looking at the door through which the royal party had just exited, scarcely heard his friend's voice. The princess had looked at him—at him! Of course, it had taken every ounce of courage to stand up and applaud her magnificent plan, but as no one else seemed willing to acknowledge the poor young lady, he'd resolved that it would be his solemn duty to come to her rescue, and he'd been more than amply rewarded for it. Not only that, but he would also get another chance to see her again soon without having to wait an entire year for another glimpse of that wonderful smile. This day was turning out to be the best day of his life ever.

"Sit down!" Eric repeated, more forcefully this time. "Now you're just making a complete fool out of yourself, and Carlo is staring at you."

Hearing the Initiate's name brought him crashing down from the cloud he'd been floating on. He risked a glance at Carlo's table and saw that indeed the older teenager was giving him a very unfriendly stare. Elias' eyes shifted nervously to Flynn, and his spirits were lifted once again when his friend gave him a quick wink. Not wanting to press his luck, he heeded Eric's advice and sat down. The big lad gave him a disgusted look and rolled his eyes.

"What's your problem?" Elias asked, feeling his earlier irritation returning. Mostly he was just upset that Gabriela was gone, and he was bothered by the prospect of the interminable wait until spring arrived.

"You are," Eric grumbled. "You're acting like a complete idiot, and if you don't quit it, you're gonna get in trouble. It's not enough that Carlo and Peter already have it in for you, now you're drawing attention from everyone else, including the Brothers?" He glanced nervously at the head table, but the priests had all returned to busily talking amongst themselves, no doubt concerning everything they'd just heard.

Narrowing his eyes in suspicion, Elias scowled at Eric. "You're just jealous," he said firmly.

"Jealous? Me? Of what?" Eric sputtered in disbelief.

"Of me! Of the fact that the princess smiled at me and not you."

"Hmmpff," Eric crossed his arms and looked away. "As if I give a crap about your stupid princess and her ridiculous idea," he pronounced.

"Stupid, is it? Fine, then when the time comes, you can stay here. Maybe that's your plan anyway—sneak into the pantry while everyone is gone and eat all the damn food," Elias accused. It was only a jest meant to mock his friend, but when Eric looked at him, he saw a glint in the other's eyes that told him the other boy was actually intrigued and excited by the possibility. It was all he could do to stop his eyes from rolling so far back into his head that they disappeared altogether. "You're impossible, you know that?" He couldn't hold it any longer and burst into laughter, causing Eric's face to split into a big grin.

Next to them, Georgie smiled at his friends. The small boy was feeling somewhat sad that he wouldn't be there to accompany his friends on this first expedition into the city in the coming year, but that was balanced by the thrill and the mystery of what lay ahead for him. Yet there was something else that was bothering him—something which the royal speeches had only provided a temporary distraction from. With his newly awakened awareness, he'd seen the sinister energy swirling around Flynn when the other had stepped up to take the Test, as well as the resulting flare of dark *etherus* when his friend had pulled back his hand. He had no idea what any of it meant, of course, but he wanted to ask the Kal-dkar at the earliest opportunity. She must've seen it too, he thought, but whether she would deign to give a novice like him any answer at all—well, that remained to be seen. He would just have to bide his time and enjoy his final day with Elias and Eric, but it was to Flynn that his pale blue gaze was drawn now, and he couldn't shake the uneasy feeling that his friend was in some kind of danger.

CHAPTER 26

Over the next four days they followed the course of the Talban, a thick ribbon of blue winding its way south by southwest as it cut through the fertile reaches of the empire. Keeping the Heartlands firmly to their right, they winged their way toward the wide river delta, the hazy line that marked the distant coastline becoming more and more defined with each passing hour. Beyond it, a dark blue mantle stretched to the horizon, merging with the clouded sky at the edge of sight—the Storm Sea. As impressed as he had been by the sight of Lake Dal, Vurax was stunned by the impossible magnitude of the ocean. Strangely, the vast, featureless expanse reminded him of the flat steppes of Sarmakan where one could stand in place, turn slowly to face in every direction, and not see so much as a single hill or lone tree to break the absolute uniformity of the landscape. There was an incomprehensible scale to it that weighed upon the senses, invoking a feeling in oneself as that of being nothing more than a speck of dust when compared to the immensity of the world. Rather than think of it as monotonous, Vurax appreciated the stark openness as an outward expression of the long years he yearned for freedom—no barriers or walls, no obstacles or constraints, nothing at all to stop him from walking—or sailing, in this case—into endlessness.

Lost in his pleasant daydream while gazing at the beauty of the sea and the feelings of longing that the sight stirred inside his soul, he nearly missed Treeweaver's slight shift as he pointed to something on their right. It was late afternoon, and with the sun low in the west, the Minotaur had to squint to see what the Elf was trying to show him. It took him a moment or two, and then he saw it—there, at the point where the river met the sea, the colour of the land shifted from undulating plains and rolling hills of grassy green to a huge stretch of tiny white shapes that covered everything like a gigantic field of stone pebbles along the shore. He'd seen some of the other cities of the empire from afar during their journey south—Vurgas, Murtaur, Horan—but nothing could prepare him for the stunning size of Golan, the sprawling capital of Gol. Coaxing Brisa to gain more altitude, Treeweaver guided them in a long circle high above the city for a single pass so that his passenger could take in the magnificent view. Behind them, carrying Windstrider and Kael, Asa beat its wings to rise and keep up.

"Won't we be seen?" Vurax shouted to make sure the Elf could hear him, even if the latter's ear was mere inches from his mouth. The closer they drew to the coast, the more the wind currents picked up, carrying with them the distinct salty tang of the ocean and the distant cries of seabirds. The two gryphons gamely navigated the sudden gusts of air, banking, and gliding as needed while staying as level as possible for their riders' benefit. While the Golian's confidence in flying had grown considerably over the past week, the sharp adjustments needed to navigate the coastal breezes were starting to make his stomach more than a little queasy.

"We can't stay this high for very long, but don't worry—to anyone looking up, we're nothing more than a pair of tiny dark dots against the sky. Besides, I doubt you'll ever get another chance to see the city from this perspective, so why not?" Treeweaver called back.

Vurax grinned in response, feeling his heart soar with exhilaration at the sight unfolding slowly below. His fear and discomfort quelled for the time being, he gave in to the thrill of the sensation and revelled in yet another rare instant of happiness and wonder in his life. He felt truly free as he took in the glorious vista of the azure sea, windswept cliffs, rocky beaches, and the imperial city of Golan, with its maze-like multitude of houses, streets, plazas, domes, towers, and other buildings in a variety of shapes and sizes. Spread over a series of low hills that hugged the coastline, the metropolis was surrounded by a long line of white walls that shielded it from both land and sea. At the water's edge, protected by lengthy, fortified breakwaters that enclosed a great deep-water bay, was the mile-long harbour. The waterfront thronged at one end with dozens of docked merchant vessels, while dozens more rested at anchor offshore. Hundreds of smaller vessels plied the clear waters between the docks and the ships, all part of a cycle of vibrant activity. On the other end of the harbour were neatly ordered rows upon rows of ships that sat beyond a tall seawall and a series of towers that rose out of the water. Vurax could only surmise he was looking at the naval base for the famed and mighty Golian fleet.

Among the multitude of wondrous sights below that vied for Vurax's attention, there was one particular marvel of architecture that was simply impossible to ignore, and he felt his eyes irresistibly drawn toward it. On a large hill situated at the north end of the city and far from the harbour was what he could only assume was the enormous and sprawling imperial palace, surrounded by several equally impressive but smaller buildings that performed the various administrative functions required to run an entire empire, including the senate chambers. The entire government district and palace were contained within a set of walls of its own, effectively creating a city within a city. Looking at the grandiose spectacle of Golan as a whole, he felt a surge of pride in this monumental achievement of his people, but it was immediately tempered by the knowledge that everything that he saw on the ground had also been built on the backs of countless slaves throughout the centuries. After losing so much of his life to captivity and forced servitude in Sarmakan, he could never again view the practice of slavery in the same offhand way as nearly all other Minotaurs did.

The dark thought passed when the sea swung into view again and he shook it off. Vurax realized they must be beginning their descent because Treeweaver had allowed Windstrider to take the lead. He could see Kael giving the Elf instructions on where to direct the gryphons, and though they had discussed earlier what their plan would be upon arrival, he was still apprehensive about bringing these flying beasts so close to the capital. Following the centurion's counsel, they would fly down the coast for a good distance, land on a deserted and secluded stretch of beach, and then walk up to the coastal road that would eventually lead them to the western gates of the city. Rather than enter the capital itself though, they would walk north until they reached the fortified enclave that housed the legendary First Legion, where Kael intended to report to the military commanders there, deliver his report, and present the missive from Tribune Jalx. As for explaining the presence of the two Elves, that would take some convincing, but Kael was confident that he would be able to persuade the right people of the legitimacy of Treeweaver's identity and the Syldar prince's urgent reason for coming here. Or so they all very fervently hoped.

A short time later, Vurax and Kael stood atop a dune, the former's attention wholly consumed by the ebb and flow of the waves washing upon the shore before being drawn back into the endless expanse of blue, while the latter watched the two Elves bid farewell to the gryphons. The great beasts lowered their feathered heads, nuzzling Treeweaver and Windstrider affectionately with mighty beaks that could rend the flesh from a horse in seconds. With a piercing screech that startled a multitude of seagulls from their perches on the nearby cliffs into flight, Brisa and Asa reared up on their leonine legs and ran down the beach for a short distance before rising upward into the air on powerful wings. The two Syldar watched them go, waving briefly when the gryphons wheeled over them once in a last goodbye before fading from view as they flew eastward.

"Magnificent, aren't they?" Kael said with admiration, watching their former mounts depart.

Distracted by the sight of the sea since they'd landed, it took Vurax some time to reply. "What's that? Oh, yes... and let's not forget terrifying also. I'll be glad if I never have to ride one again in my life. Now if you want to talk magnificence, how about this?" he said, throwing his arms wide as if to encompass the entire ocean in a single embrace.

"My friend, you forget I grew up next to the sea—seeing, smelling, and hearing it every day. As you might imagine, I've had enough to last me a lifetime," the centurion remarked. Kael's jocularity did not match the wary glance he gave his friend, however. Ever since the revelation about Zerik Baurus' past, he'd been waiting for Vurax to say something more, or at the very least, give some kind of indication of how he was dealing with the shock and weight of it all. Yet the former slave hadn't said a word about it and carried on as if the conversation hadn't even taken place. Given the difficulty of the task before them, the fact that Vurax was quite obviously bottling this up and not choosing to deal with it was a fact that concerned the centurion greatly. Still, there was nothing he could do about it until his friend was ready to open himself up to him.

Vurax gave Kael a sidelong glance, trying to ascertain if his friend was being serious. He couldn't imagine a more glorious, soothing sight than this, and he felt almost seductively drawn toward it. "What's it called—the place where you were born?"

"Balis," Kael replied, "a small fishing village in New Gol. It's near Axos, a slightly larger fishing village—wouldn't even appear on most maps if not for the fact that it's on the road leading to Land's End Keep at the southern tip of the Saurian Wall." Seeing no hint of recognition in Vurax's face at hearing any of those names, the soldier chuckled. "See? I told you."

"We're ready to move out," Treeweaver said, walking up the sandy incline to join the two Golians. In his hands, he carried a wrapped bundle containing his and Windstrider's weapons, including their bows. Kael accepted the arms and busied himself securing them to the pack Larios had given him before leaving Vurgas. All of them had agreed that they would stand a far better chance of not being asked a host of inopportune questions if the two Elves weren't walking about wearing weapons. Without them, any casual observer would simply assume them to be slaves and wouldn't give them a second glance.

Vurax looked morosely at the seaside cliffs behind them. "We couldn't have just landed up there?"

"Too close to the road," Kael muttered, fastening one last strap. "The terrain gets flatter closer to the city, so we'll ascend there. Let's get going."

The four of them walked along the beach for about an hour before turning inland where the cliffs gradually faded into a low series of windswept, grass-covered dunes. Picking one of several gently sloping inclines, the small group of travellers made their way to the main coastal thoroughfare that led to one of the many gates lining Golan's tall white walls. This close to the capital of the Golian Empire, the road was busy, with all manner of wagons, carts, riders, and people on foot making their way to and from Golan to any number of the smaller communities that dotted the land in this stretch of the Imperial Province. No one paid much attention to them as they joined the stream of traffic heading east, which suited them perfectly. Trying not to stare overly long at anything or anyone, Vurax took in the varied mix of Golian citizens and merchants going about their daily business, and the omnipresent train of slaves that followed them along everywhere, performing various duties that ranged from driving their masters' wheeled conveyances, to physically carrying their personal belongings on foot. They were nearly all human, though he did catch the odd glimpse of a Dwarf or Elf in the crowd at times. Every time he saw one of Treeweaver's people, he glanced surreptitiously at the two Elves walking beside him, but neither one betrayed any emotion on their passive faces. He wondered what they were thinking and was suitably impressed by their self-control.

The massive walls of Golan loomed ahead, with the road leading straight to an imposing and fortified gatehouse flanked by two tall towers that stood guard over a pair of enormous gates. Beyond those tall doors was a long and wide tunnel through which a multitude of people, vehicles, and animals entered and exited the capital. As Kael had explained during their walk, there were six gates in total around the city, but only three of them were as large and busy as the one they were approaching now, which was called the Storm Gate. Their destination was the Victory Gate near the north side of the city, and following one of the outer roads encircling the walls would be much faster than going in. When they arrived at the crossroads, they turned left and headed through one of the many smaller towns and villages that had grown outside and around the city over the course of time. For all its fortified might, Golan had never been attacked by an enemy since its founding long ago, but as a warlike people by nature, the Minotaurs had taken no chances with protecting the beating heart of their empire.

Vurax gaped and stared at the myriad of strange and new sights all around him, with Kael remarking that they weren't even inside the city proper yet. The former slave had always thought his native Vurgas to be a big city, but then he'd never had much to compare it to. If the size of Golan from the air hadn't been enough to impress its immense size upon him, walking around a good portion of the city from the outside was certainly driving the point home. For their part, Treeweaver and Windstrider did their best to appear unperturbed by the crowds and multitude of buildings all around them. Judging by what little they had described of their homeland, this environment was about as alien to them as it could get, yet despite the discomfort Vurax was sure they must be feeling, they maintained that expressionless air about them that continued to amaze and impress him.

It took almost another hour to reach their destination and the number of citizens about had decreased considerably. Victory Gate was so named for its sole use and purpose as the starting point into the city proper for military parades, held to celebrate successful major campaigns in the field, or to commemorate the great victories of Gol's storied past of war and conquest. Commonly closed to civilian traffic, the gate linked Golan to the extensive armed encampment and headquarters of the First Legion. In honour of the first hero of the Minotaur people and the leader of the slave army that led the revolt against their masters, Victory Gate was flanked by a pair of colossal stone statues of Ravenus the Liberator, each one holding a mighty four-bladed axe high in an upraised arm, the weapons crossing each other over the apex of the gate. Behind the twin statues and adorning the gatehouse towers were long red banners displaying the same axe in gold thread—the symbol of the First Legion—and a giant laurel wreath made of beaten gold was mounted above the gates. Below it, a stone plaque bore engraved words in the Minotaur tongue:

Through these hallowed gates
Pass only those who have fought and bled
For Empire
For Victory
Your sacrifice is forever honoured

"Wait here," Kael told the others before he moved off to approach the guard post at the base of the gatehouse. Two legionnaires, holding shields and long, heavy spears, strode out to meet the centurion. After the ordeal in the Border Peaks, there wasn't much left of the centurion's uniform that was recognizable to a casual observer—the damaged cuirass and leg greaves had been left behind, as had the red cloak and helm—but one ornate shoulder pauldron denoting his rank remained, as did his arm greaves and sword. His salute was returned by the two soldiers, and the three Minotaurs paused to talk amongst themselves just out of hearing range—at least for Vurax.

"He's given them his name and rank and is requesting to speak with one of the tribunes in charge of the First Legion. He claims to bring very urgent news from the north," Treeweaver reported in a low voice.

Watching as Kael pulled out Tribune Jalx's missive for one of the legionnaires to inspect, Vurax raised one eyebrow without looking at the Elf. "You can hear what they're saying from here? You Syldar are full of surprises."

"You mean your big, floppy Minotaur ears are just for show?" Windstrider teased, causing Vurax to chuckle.

"Very funny, but at least the points of our horns are more useful than the points on your ears," the Golian shot back a jibe of his own.

"Sure, if you don't mind not being able to slip a single article of clothing over your head without poking holes into everything," Windstrider replied, scoring another hit.

"Quiet, you two—he's coming back," Treeweaver motioned for silence.

The centurion's face broke into a grin, silently confirming to them that he'd succeeded in his objective. From there, a pair of guards led them up the road away from the city and in the direction of the First Legion's headquarters. When they arrived, the Elves and Vurax were asked to remain behind in a guardhouse to wait while Kael was taken deeper inside the camp to meet with one of the tribunes. When he returned an hour later, it was at the head of an armed escort of legionnaires. With Treeweaver's identity now revealed, Kael explained, the four of them were to be taken directly to the palace, where the Syldar prince would then wait and see if he would be granted an audience with the emperor—provided the request was approved by the Golian ruler's body of advisors. Kael tried to apologize for the burdensome process ahead, but Treeweaver waved it aside by acknowledging that he understood how unusual the circumstances were. Privately though, he just hoped the Golians wouldn't take too long to make their decision. With each day that passed without news of his sister and people, he grew more and more concerned.

Because they were not permitted to pass through Victory Gate, their escorts took them around the city to the northeast where they entered by means of the Imperial Gate. Like the one they just left, this gate too was closed to regular city traffic and normally reserved for the private use of government officials, foreign dignitaries, and the emperor himself. Smaller, but no less impressive in its craftsmanship and significance, the Imperial Gate was heavily and opulently adorned with the regal heraldic crest of Gol—the profile of Ravenus with a crown above his head—meant to convey the empire's long and storied tradition of power and strength. To impress that proud history upon those travelling through, the paved road leading up to the tall, gilded gates was lined on both sides with life-sized marble statues on tall pedestals of all the past emperors of Gol, starting with Ravenus the Liberator in the position closest to the gate. Followed directly across from him by his son, Arivaxos the Bold, the long line of rulers continued down the road to end with the newest statue, that of Logris Blackhorn IV, the current emperor. It was an unapologetic display of wealth and might, and though both Treeweaver and Windstrider remained as stoic as ever while the group walked down the road, Vurax couldn't help but gape wide-eyed at everything.

Even for Turanis Kael, who had been to Golan more than once before, the unexpected privilege and awe of entering the city through the Imperial Gate was not lost on him. He was still somewhat surprised that the tribune he'd spoken to had not questioned him overly long or raised any obstacles to his request, but then he also got the distinct impression that news had already reached the capital that something of great concern was happening in Syldar. The presence of two emissaries of the Elven people at this junction in time was not something the legion officer was likely willing to dismiss as coincidental and lacking urgency, so here they were. At the gates, the legionnaires accompanying them departed, trading escort duty with another quartet of Golian soldiers that awaited them at the gate. Their royal purple cloaks marked them as members of the Imperial Praetorian Guard, the elite soldiers tasked with the protection of the palace and its grounds, as well as the personal safety of the emperor. The exchange made, the small group entered Golan at last, and from there, time seemed to pass in a barely remembered blur of faces, sights, and places.

The Imperial Gate led directly to the walled-off imperial compound, a small city in its own right, and the four of them were each given a room in the guest wing of the massive palace itself, something that Kael had never expected but saw as a very encouraging sign. While they were being shown to their lodgings, the minor official in charge of overseeing their needs politely informed them that they would be brought before the emperor the following afternoon, so when dinner was brought to them that evening, the four of them gathered in Treeweaver's room to discuss what they would say. It was agreed that after an introduction and report from Kael, Vurax would follow with a detailed account of the incident in the Border Peaks. Afterward, the Syldar prince would relate his personal tale, corroborated where possible, and vouched for by Vurax and Kael. The audience would then conclude with Treeweaver's appeal to the emperor for help with the plight of the Syldar people. All agreed on the simple, straightforward plan, and each returned to their rooms for a well-earned night of sleep in a comfortable bed for the first time in a long while.

Last to leave, Vurax turned to regard Treeweaver. "Don't you find all of this a little strange?"

"What do you mean?" the Elf asked.

"Over fifty years ago, my people and yours were relentlessly spilling each other's blood in a vicious war. Now, you're here in this room, in the palace at the heart of the empire, being treated like an honoured guest before seeing the emperor himself. You don't find the least bit of oddness in any of that?"

"Emperor Blackhorn is not Emperor Murias, and for us to have a future, those of us in the present must do what we can to move on from the past. Am I surprised by the civility I've been accorded thus far? Yes—impressed even. It gives me hope where I had very little to begin with, but I take nothing for granted until the Syldar are given leave to cross your lands. For now, I'm just grateful to have an opportunity to at least try to convince your leader."

Vurax nodded. He was trying hard to share in Treeweaver's optimism, but something deep inside prevented him from having the same kind of faith in his own people that the Elf was willing to extend to them. For his friend's sake, he hoped to be proven wrong tomorrow.

"Sleep well," was all he said before closing the door, leaving Treeweaver alone to ponder the uncertain future.

⋯⋯◆⋯⋯

The ostentatious golden throne, carved in the likeness of a sitting Ravenus, Liberator of the Minotaur race, dwarfed everything in the grandiose audience chamber. The statue-like seat of the horned emperor towered above the wide floor below as if to enforce the complete authority and grandiose majesty of the one that sat in the august chair. That person, Logris Blackhorn IV, was a broad-shouldered giant of a Golian, his long, upward curving horns dark like obsidian, and the jet-black hair on his body peppered with silver, marking the onset of a venerable age for the Minotaur Emperor. Born Canrus Logris, he was given the royal title of Blackhorn IV upon his ascension to the throne, owing not to any familial relation to the previous three emperors that bore that name, but rather to the rare physical quality he shared with his predecessors. Clad in his resplendent regalia of office and flanked by a cadre of advisors on the steps of the dais below him, the ruler of the Golian Empire motioned for his guests to approach the throne and speak.

Dressed in the new uniform he'd been given that morning, Turanis Kael, centurion of the Eighth Legion, bowed deeply before dropping to one knee on the tiled floor that was polished to a mirror sheen. Eyes fixed on the emperor's sandaled feet in a gesture of respect, he delivered a summary of his mission as given to him by Tribune Jalx and related the circumstances that had seen the veteran legionnaire come into the company of Vurax and the two Syldar. Those present listened in silence, but it was upon the sovereign of Gol that Vurax focused his sole attention. He had no preconceived notions about Blackhorn other than what little he'd been told during their journey south, so he tried to maintain an open mind, observe, and make up his own judgment about this bull upon whose whim rested the fate of more lives than he could conceive of. Owing to the many years of harsh deprivation and abuse under the lash, he had no great love for authority and blind obedience, but he was willing to set aside his personal distaste for this grand theatre of obsequiousness for the sake of Treeweaver.

An elbow rested upon one knee as the emperor leaned forward to rest his chin upon a hand replete with bejeweled rings. Despite his age, Blackhorn's dark eyes were bright and alert, and his thoughtful and attentive expression left no doubt in Vurax's mind that the emperor was listening carefully to every word. That level of attention was not mirrored by the crowd of officials and politicians arrayed around the throne, nearly all of whom could barely conceal their bored dismissiveness and open distaste for the presence of the two Elves before them. One notable exception was a bull that stood closest to the throne on Blackhorn's right side. He appeared to rival the emperor in advanced age, and his slightly bent posture—coupled with a naturally short stature—made for an unusually small member of their race. Unlike the others in the chamber, who wore finely woven white robes trimmed with red, identifying them as members of the Golian Senate, the trim on this one individual's vestment was uniquely black. Vurax had no idea who this was, but whereas the emperor appeared absorbed with what Kael was saying and devoted his full attention to the centurion, this other bull listened while simultaneously studying each of the four of them in turn with narrow, calculating eyes. More than once Vurax caught the other Golian staring at him with a look so intense and filled with cunning that he found it impossible to not look away, as if the other could uncover any secret he held inside simply by meeting that shrewd, penetrating gaze.

Disturbed by the unsettling feeling, Vurax failed to notice the audience chamber had gone silent, and when he looked at Kael, the other had already stepped back to stand beside him to make a none-too-subtle gesture with his head that the emperor was waiting for him to speak. He cursed under his breath at allowing himself to be rattled by the way the other bull had been scrutinizing him, causing him to miss his cue. He expelled the air from his lungs in a bid to calm his nerves, not understanding how he could feel no fear when facing down a vicious giant in battle, but now found himself filled with nervous anxiety at being made to speak in a room full of haughty and contemptuous politicians. He steeled himself and stepped forward to speak, his bow awkward and stiff, and though he'd initially resisted the notion that he would be required to kneel, he gritted his teeth and went down to one knee. In an intentional break with ceremony, he looked Blackhorn straight in the eyes and made up his mind in that instant over a decision he'd been wrestling with for days.

"My name is Zerik Vurax of Keros, son of Zerik Baurus, oh Great and Mighty Emperor," he stated proudly and without hesitation.

Last night, he'd asked Kael to introduce him simply as Vurax, a freed slave, and today the centurion had honoured his request. It hadn't felt right to saddle his friend with the burden of making that revelation, so he'd decided to take that responsibility upon himself and reclaim his family name, along with whatever else that might bring. Mainly though, he was hoping to provoke one specific reaction, and he was instantly rewarded—not by the gasps of surprise that rippled throughout the chamber, but by the crack in the stony expression on the bull's face standing next to the emperor. The Minotaur's eyes widened considerably before focusing immediately once more to study him with renewed interest. It was a very quick lapse, but Vurax had been watching for it, and his suspicions about the robed bull's identity deepened.

The fact that he now had the chamber's undivided attention didn't come as much of a surprise to him given what he'd learned about his father, but what did catch him off-guard was the undisguised warmth of the smile the emperor was now giving him. He hadn't expected that, and it made him instantly curious about the nature of the past relationship between Blackhorn and his father, and whether the two of them had been rivals, friends, or both. His tentative estimation of the emperor's character went up another notch when Blackhorn made a lifting motion with one hand.

"Rise to your feet, Zerik Vurax. Someone so recently freed from bondage and degradation should not be expected to humble himself with such pointless and servile flattery. Stand before me, tall and proud, and tell me your tale," Blackhorn directed him, his voice resonant and deep, each word delivered slowly and deliberately, leaving no doubt as to their meaning. The command drew another reaction of murmured consternation from those assembled in the chamber, which included a stern look of disapproval from the short Golian at the emperor's right hand. He seemed as if he was about to say something, then thought better of it when Vurax stood up, dipped his horns forward in acknowledgment, and began to relate his story. The former slave made sure to leave out no detail, no matter how humiliating, so that these soft and arrogant nobles could begin to appreciate what he and his family had gone through.

Body and voice shaking with pent-up ire, Vurax described the indignities and torture his mother had endured before her death, the failed slave revolt that saw his father brutally executed for his role in leading it, the vicious and merciless pit fights between slaves that claimed his brother, and the depths of despair that drove him to nearly take his own life as a last and desperate bid for freedom. He told of his participation in the battle between the Sarmakanites and the Eighth Legion cohorts, and his agreement to Tribune Jalx's request that Kael escort him to Golan so that he could personally express his gratitude to the emperor for his freedom. He did not attempt to conceal the cynicism in his tone when he spoke this last, as if to dare any of the politicians present to contradict his belief that it was their inept leadership and neglect that left places like his home of Keros vulnerable to such raids. The tribune had admitted as much by outright telling him that the legion had only marched north of the mountains because the pampered citizens of Golan, living in their comfortable and safe homes, had been deprived too long of the labour and sweat of those toiling away day and night in a remote province far from them.

To his credit—and owing to his promise to Treeweaver that he would not jeopardize his friend's chances of securing help with a vindictive diatribe—Vurax managed to remain in control of his emotions and refrained from directly accusing the emperor and his senate of inaction and responsibility in these events. Yet the words he left unspoken were just as loud as those that echoed throughout the large audience chamber, and a great number of those listening had dropped any pretense of politeness and were regarding him now with naked hostility. Sensing that he had perhaps pushed them too far, Vurax reeled himself in and changed topics by plunging into his account of the attack on the mountain pass, the rescue by the Elves that had saved his and Kael's life, and the destruction of the Tenth Legion's fortified encampment. With the memory of what he saw still vivid in his mind, he related every last fantastical element except his own strange reaction to the presence of the Titan. He saw no advantage in revealing something like that to a room full of strangers when he himself couldn't quite comprehend it either, despite Treeweaver's theory seemingly proving itself to be true.

The conviction and bluntness of his description of what he'd witnessed had the desired effect. The tenor of the chamber changed palpably from contempt to concern, and then to fear. There were also a few clear signs of skepticism, however, the most obvious of which came from the Golian senator at the emperor's side, who several times during Vurax's story leaned in close to speak in a low voice that only Blackhorn could hear. He felt a nearly irresistible urge to climb the steps to the throne and strike the smug look from the politician's face. He almost attributed the violent impulse to the presence lurking inside of him, but whether that was the real source or not, he had to admit that at least in this case, he was in full agreement with it. Not giving in, he shot the senator a meaningful sneer and concluded his story by once more stressing the importance of Treeweaver's role in bringing him here today, and the strength of his belief in vouching for what the Syldarin prince had to say. Before he could step back and cede the floor to the Elf, however, the emperor addressed him.

"Thank you for your honest words. In a city where oftentimes much is said and little is meant, it is refreshing to hear such a raw expression of emotion, freed from social restraint. We could all do with some sincere self-reflection at times, and your emperor appreciates your unapologetic candor. The significance of your horn shrouds is all the more poignant to me now. No words of mine can restore your family to you, nor can they erase the hardship you endured, but you have my condolences and sorrow nonetheless—your father was a good friend to me, and the empire is a lesser place without his valour and humility. There is much anger and resentment in you, which is understandable, but I also sense within you the seeds of honour and temperance that will see you carry on the name of Zerik with pride. We will speak more on this in the coming days." He dismissed Vurax with a nod and then motioned Treeweaver forward.

Vurax wasn't sure what to expect after his show of defiance, but nothing had prepared him for this. He was left confused and disarmed by Blackhorn's conciliatory words and was only too glad that his time to speak was over because he wouldn't have known how to respond. Without thinking, he silently bowed to the emperor and barely took note of Treeweaver's presence when the Elf walked past him.

The prince of the Syldar stood before the emperor of Gol and bowed gracefully from the waist down. As a member of the ruling family of a neighbouring realm—even if one that the Minotaurs had attempted to subjugate through war in the past—Treeweaver was not expected to kneel, and thus he did not. The greetings and formalities quickly dispensed with; the Elf declared his intent to ask the Golian Empire for help, and proceeded to describe the current plight of his people by giving a detailed account of the final days of the Syldar Kingdom. His dispassionate and monotone delivery was a stark counterpoint to the heartfelt passion of Vurax's account. This was a deliberate choice on Treeweaver's part, and it was done not because he didn't feel the pain and anguish of having to relive everything again while he recounted the tragic event, but because he wanted the Golian ruler and his politicians to hear what he had to say as plainly as possible, unfettered by the burden of personal sorrow. Facts—no matter how shocking—not feelings, were what the Minotaurs needed to hear if they were to be moved to action. He only hoped that he could convince them of the truth of his words, and he knew most of that would depend on how much they were willing to believe in Vurax's tale, not his.

When he finished speaking, not a single whisper could be heard throughout the entire throne room. Emperor Blackhorn was looking at him with what Treeweaver had learned to interpret on a Golian's facial features as intense but inscrutable pensiveness. The expressions on the other assembled Minotaurs could best be described as a mixture of suspicion, skepticism, and outright mistrust. Until now, he had not wanted to consider what he would do if he failed here, but the longer he waited for someone to speak, the more he began to come to terms with the conclusion that this endeavour may have well been a costly waste of time. He had one last thing that he could try, and there was no better time for it than now. The Elf loosened the strings on a small leather pouch secured to his belt and reached inside for something. The unexpected action prompted the watchful Praetorian guards arrayed around the chamber to grip the hilts of their swords, ready for anything, but froze and waited as one when the emperor lifted his hand.

"The blood that has been spilled between our two peoples cannot be washed away with mere words, this much I concede. Yet this is not the time to allow old grievances to stand in the way of reason and compassion. Not when the fate of what is left of the Syldar hangs in the balance. I appeal to the unshakeable and mighty pillars of Golian strength and honour to join me in setting aside the past, and I beg that you grant us safe passage through your land so that we have a chance at survival. What has happened in the Border Peaks and in Syldar cannot be ignored, and it would be dangerous to do so. Powerful and unknowable forces are at work here, and it is not only the Elves that they threaten. We have already fought our war against this enemy and lost. Show us mercy, and you have my word that we will be of no further concern to you so that you may fully focus on this threat in the north. As a token of my sincerity and in the spirit of reconciliation between our nations, I return this to you and your empire," Treeweaver said, proffering the object that rested in the palm of his hand to the emperor.

A murmur of curiosity and anticipation flowed through the room as those present sought a glimpse of what the Elf was holding, including Vurax and Kael. No mention of this had been made the entire time they had travelled together with Treeweaver, and both Golians exchanged a look of confusion. Standing silently beside them and staring straight ahead, Windstrider provided them with no clue as to what this was about. Prompted by Blackhorn, one of the Praetorians warily approached the Elf, took the object from his hand, and conveyed it to the waiting emperor. The venerable bull on the throne took the gift, examined it carefully, and then held it up for all to see—a golden chain from which dangled a medallion set with a large, glittering red stone. The whispers in the chamber turned to loud gasps of astonishment.

The eyes of the Golian senator standing next to the throne, wide with surprise just before, were narrowed now with calculating distrust.

"The Eye of Ravenus—where did you get this?" the politician demanded.

The significance of the medallion or its name meant nothing to Vurax, but the reaction of the other Minotaurs at hearing it spoken aloud was more than enough to convince him that something of great import was happening here. He glanced at Kael and saw that the centurion stood stock still with his mouth agape, face frozen with wonder. He was curious to hear what Treeweaver would say, and if the answer would explain why he hadn't told them about any of this.

"I took it from the body of Xar Murias as he lay dead upon the battlefield. I was there at Tharkan Crossing on that fateful day, and I witnessed the act that ended the pointless conflict between Syldar and Gol. May its return to you by my hand be a symbolic gesture representing a new beginning between us," Treeweaver declared. The response he got was less than kind.

"You cannot offer back what was never yours, Elf! You admit to robbing the corpse of our emperor, and now you have the gall to stand here before us and try to leverage a heinous act to get what you want?" the Golian senator was practically seething with outrage.

A number of responses flashed through Treeweaver's mind, none of them conducive to advancing his cause. He'd seen Emperor Murias struck down by his own general, followed by the order for the Golian cohorts to fall back. The death of Murias had turned the tide of the battle, and in the ensuing chaos, the Minotaurs had given no thought or consideration to their fallen ruler during their retreat other than the obvious impact on their morale. He doubted they'd even made any attempt to return to the battlefield to retrieve his body. The Elf was perceptive enough to detect the false indignation of political theatre on display here, and though Blackhorn was the one Golian present he ultimately needed to convince, he was also aware of the senate's powerful influence.

"Respectfully, Senator, I would think someone in your position would appreciate the value of timing and utilizing any advantage at one's disposal when it comes to negotiation. This object was, to all intents and purposes, a spoil of war, and an abandoned one at that. I'm sure you can understand that until now, there was no practical way to return this to you given the complete lack of diplomatic channels between our peoples. I don't claim to have powers of precognition, but I admit it was fortuitous that I held onto this heirloom of yours for all these years, and if any of you here today profess to be Golians of faith, perhaps you will see this as the workings of providence. Whatever your belief, I humbly return this to its rightful owner, Emperor Blackhorn, and leave you with my request to deliberate upon," the Syldar responded. He then bowed once more and waited for the emperor's response.

"A *spoil* of war? Your insolence is matched only by your arrogance," the senator sputtered in anger, pointing an accusatory finger at Treeweaver. "How dare—"

"That's quite enough, Senator Sarnius," Emperor Blackhorn interrupted, holding up one hand. "Prince Treeweaver is right—we shouldn't allow old grievances to distract us from these disturbing and eerily similar accounts that we've just heard, and the return of the Eye of Ravenus at this time is a portent we cannot ignore."

The emperor's next words became mere background noise after that, barely audible to Vurax's ears as he focused all his attention on the bull next to the emperor. So, this was Primus Senator Kalor Sarnius, as he'd suspected all along, the politician responsible for his father's disgraceful exile. The sudden image of his hands around the politician's neck, slowly squeezing the life out of him, was so vivid that he almost took a step forward to make a reality out of that vision. Only the combination of the sharp warning from somewhere inside of him—and the questioning look that Treeweaver gave him over the shoulder when he let out a low grunt of anger—was all that stopped him from making a grave mistake. Even so, he almost brushed all of that aside, the burning need for revenge threatening to consume him completely. With every ounce of strength that he had, he wrested back control of his emotions by promising himself that there would be a reckoning at a more appropriate time and place.

Next to him, Kael had tensed as well, the same realization dawning upon him after hearing the emperor address the senator by name and witnessing his friend's adverse reaction. He'd seen what Vurax could do when lost to rage, and he didn't think there were enough Praetorian guards in the room to stop him quickly enough. Not by a long measure. Thankfully, nothing happened, and neither the emperor nor the senator ever noticed that anything had been dangerously amiss, however briefly. Good thing too, as the emperor appeared ready to render a decision. A last sidelong glance at Vurax's expression and bearing reassured him that the former slave had talked himself down from doing anything rash, and so the centurion went back to listening to what Blackhorn and Sarnius were saying.

"—are duly noted, Senator. Nevertheless, it is my decree that the senate be convened as soon as possible so we can put this matter to a vote. I also want word sent to the Supreme Legate that I'd like a full report verifying what's happening in the north, as well as in Syldar. I find it very troubling that I should be receiving news of such disquieting developments from a civilian and a foreigner rather than my own officials," Blackhorn said, his voice even and measured as always. "No offense meant, Your Highness," he added, smiling at Treeweaver.

"None taken, Your Imperial Majesty," the Elf nodded politely in return.

"My Emperor," Sarnius began, "this is highly irregular. Should we not discuss the matter further—in private—before summoning the senate? Surely—" the senator stopped mid-sentence when Blackhorn locked eyes with him. There was no reproach in that silent look, but something passed between the two older Golians that caused the politician to go silent, bow, and take a step back from the side of the throne. After the awkward moment had passed, the emperor continued.

"Legatus Drukus," he called, prompting a Golian in gold and red silk robes to step forward from a small group to the emperor's left. "See to it that my commands are carried out immediately. In the meantime, I would like to learn more about the grandson of Queen Baliela and the son of Zerik Baurus in a less formal setting than this. You shall remain here in the palace as my guests for now, and we will speak again at dinner tomorrow." When he was done speaking, Blackhorn rapped the knuckles of one hand on the arm of the throne, signalling that the audience was over.

"Why didn't he tell us?" Vurax wondered aloud, pacing the length of his room.

"I don't know," Kael responded with a shrug while helping himself to some grapes from the fruit bowl on the table between them. "What reason would he have had to? Doesn't really change anything, does it?"

Vurax had thought about that already, and the centurion was right—it wouldn't have changed anything—but it still bothered him that Treeweaver had kept something from him. In the short time they had known each other, he'd come to trust the Elf unreservedly, but when Treeweaver had presented the Eye of Ravenus to the emperor, he'd experienced a quick and irrational feeling of betrayal. "Do you suppose he knew?"

"Knew what?" the centurion didn't look at him, busily selecting the perfect red apple out of several candidates in the bowl.

"That the Golian general that he saw strike down Xar Murias was my father," he growled as if it should be obvious what he was driving at.

Kael took a loud bite out of the apple and chewed contentedly. "Vurax, you're becoming paranoid, you know that? Until just a few nights ago you yourself didn't know who your father really was and what he'd done, so how could Treeweaver have possibly known?" When the other cast him a dubious look, he sighed and put the apple down. "Look, I know this whole thing with Zerik Baurus can't be easy to deal with, not with everything else you've already been through, but sometimes a coincidence is just that. If anything, you should be happy that Treeweaver was there that day, and that he brought the Eye back to Gol. Did you feel the reaction in the chamber when he pulled it out? If he was hoping to make an impact, he succeeded admirably. I daresay it helped sway the emperor's decision, even if Sarnius tried his best to undermine that."

Sarnius. Infinitely more so than the Syldar's action in the throne room, the mere mention of the senator's name filled him with intense irritation. He wasn't sure yet what he wanted to say or do, or when he would have an opportunity to see the Primus again, but he promised himself that he wouldn't leave Golan until he'd wrung an explanation out of Sarnius—with his own hands if need be. Right now, he needed to calm down and focus on one annoyance at a time.

"What exactly is the Eye of Ravenus, anyway?" he snapped the question out, pushing Sarnius' smug face out of his mind.

"You honestly don't know? It's basic history, Vurax," Kael frowned, genuinely surprised.

The comment touched a nerve, and Vurax forced himself to bite back a caustic retort. In truth, he was ashamed of the fact that he could barely read, let alone know details about events of the past. While he and his family had lived relatively comfortably and didn't lack the necessities, his early years in the rustic community of Keros had been mostly devoted to helping his father with his work and his mother with her chores. With the benefit of hindsight now shedding some light on his father's reclusive personality and their relative isolation from Golian society, he was beginning to understand why he and his brother had not been sent to school in Vurgas. It was only when he was old enough to think about the approaching time of the military draft that he became self-conscious about his inability to read and write, and what the other soldiers would think of him. Without Baurus' knowledge, Varina began to teach her sons how to read, but before the lessons got very far, their lives were changed forever when their village was raided.

"Why don't you remind me, Kael?" he said through gritted teeth.

The centurion frowned at his friend. Vurax was definitely in a difficult mood tonight, but he decided to ignore his tone and let it pass. "Long, long ago, sometime before Ravenus led the slave uprising that freed our people from the shackles of the giants' hegemony that once covered this land, he was caught trying to steal food for his friends. As punishment and a warning, should he ever try something like that again, the storytellers say that a brutish cyclops overseer, always jealous of those that had two eyes, took a glowing hot iron to Ravenus' right eye and seared it in front of the other slaves to set an example. They say that Ravenus never even flinched once while it was happening because his hatred for his masters burned even hotter than that metal did. Still, the loss of one eye dealt a crippling blow to his pride and left him unable to feel confident enough to wield a weapon effectively because of the injury. To be a worthwhile warrior, one needs to be able to make full use of all of their senses, and the impairment to his sight dashed his plans to be at the forefront of the rebellion he'd been planning for years. Yet he was the one whom destiny had chosen to lift his people from centuries of servitude and to inspire him and rekindle his courage and fire once more, Zarvon came to him one dark night."

Despite being absorbed by the story, Vurax couldn't help but give a low snort of derision at the mention of the Minotaur god. He shouldn't be surprised that the meddlesome deity had played some part in this, but since the Golians had succeeded in freeing themselves, he allowed that the interference could be positive at times. He half expected some gloating comment to echo in his mind, but there was nothing. If Kael heard his reaction, the soldier gave no indication and continued his tale.

"The tale goes that the god stood before Ravenus and opened his left hand, revealing a shining red gem resting on his palm. He then said to him 'More than restore your vision, this will guide your arm to cut down your foes unerringly, for it contains part of my very essence. With it and through it, you shall strike fear into their hearts even as your weapon rends their flesh from their bones.' Ravenus was filled with awe and took the gem, placing it into the ruined eye socket on his face, and lo—he was able to see fully again. But then he looked at the god again and said, 'I am eternally grateful for this gift, mighty Zarvon, but I have no weapon with which to dispense my vengeance.' To this, the god waved his right hand and a wondrous axe with four sharp blades appeared before Ravenus. The slave gripped the huge weapon with both hands, marvelling at its perfect balance and craftsmanship. 'Let this be the instrument of your rage. Now doubt yourself no more and do what you were born to do—free our people,' Zarvon said, and then vanished as if he'd never been.

"On that very same night, word of Ravenus' rekindled spirit flew like a wild spark around the camp, igniting the fires of rebellion in the hearts of all slaves. At first light of the sun, with his sight fully returned and axe in hand, he led our people to victory over the ancient masters, carving a bloody and merciless path through them. It took many years of fighting, but the unstoppable wave of Ravenus' liberation eventually reached every corner of the old empire, and when it was over, the giants were no more, their power broken, the last few driven to hide in the dark holes of remote mountains. Ravenus the Liberator claimed his place as our first new emperor, with the Eye becoming a symbol of his vision for the building of the Golian Empire, while the Axe represented the strength and power necessary to rule and keep it free. After Ravenus died of old age, his son took the Eye and set it upon a golden chain that he wore to honour his sire. From that day onward, the Eye and the Axe have passed down through the centuries to every emperor, the most prized heirlooms of our glorious past."

The story ended and Vurax nodded his thanks to Kael for his telling of the tale. He knew of Ravenus, of course, and his pivotal role in Minotaur history, but not the precise details about the Eye and the Axe, or how exactly the legendary Golian had come into their possession. To him, they had always just been mundane items that had taken on mythical proportions to suit the more fantastical elements of the old tale. He could better understand now the significance of Treeweaver's gesture earlier, and the importance of the Eye being returned to the Golian people. A strange fate indeed that had seen to it that the Syldar prince had been present on the day the Eye was lost. Yet when he thought of that, there was one detail that bothered him.

"Why in hell did Murias take the Eye into battle? It was an awfully stupid risk and look what happened," Vurax growled with a shake of his horned head.

Kael could only shrug. "Who can really say? Perhaps all the stories about his insanity and arrogance were true. Maybe he thought the mystic powers of the Eye would confer victory upon him against the Elves? It was his right as emperor to wear the thing, after all."

"Wouldn't the Axe have been a better choice?" Vurax mused.

"You would think, except since the early days of the empire—and for some reason that the church decided upon long ago—the Axe's function has become ceremonial only. I hear it's kept in a vault somewhere and they only dust it off for coronations or some such."

"Seems like a waste of a fine weapon," the former slave snorted.

"Agreed, but I don't pretend to understand how priests think. Maybe it was a compromise between the church and the state that the two holy relics be evenly controlled by both? I don't know, but what I do know is that I'm exhausted, and you should be too. I think I'm going to turn in. Goodnight." He grabbed another apple from the bowl and headed for the door.

"Stop stealing my fruit. Didn't they put any in your room?" Vurax groused.

"Yeah, just mangoes though—I bloody hate mangoes."

"What are mangoes?"

Kael laughed out loud. "Enough questions for one night. See you in the morning, Vurax," and then he was gone.

CHAPTER 27

Lady Jana Morhain set her satchel down on the straw-covered barn floor and leaned over to peer closely at the sleeping form of the boy, her immaculate appearance and clean attire as incongruous as it could be given her surroundings. The smith, Caeden, stood off to one side, humbly staring at the ground in awe of the holy woman's presence, not daring to look directly at her. Next to him, Thurgod was decidedly less reverential in his posture, standing there with brawny arms crossed in front of his barrel chest, and a scowl set deep within the depths of his yellow beard. He stared at the cleric's back with narrowed eyes, but had made a pact with himself to hold back any caustic remarks out of respect for his granddaughter's heartfelt effort in helping save Darken. He wasn't yet convinced they weren't making a mistake in getting involved, but he would bide his time and be ready to remind everyone that he'd been right all along. Ellianna stood next to Lady Jana, her eyes darting back and forth between the woman and Darken, trying to be patient even as she silently willed the priestess to do something.

Though she had only known the noblewoman for two days, there was something palpably different about Jana today. She had refused to even speak to Deacon Ulik at first, and it wasn't until the man revealed that he was there in the company of Ellianna on a matter of some urgency that she let the young woman into her private office to listen intently and in silence to her earnest request. Minutes later, the two women were walking alone through the town in the direction of the Field Gate. Since leaving the temple, Jana hadn't spoken more than two words to Ellianna, the expression on her normally serene face distracted and troubled just before she drew the cowl of her robe over her head to conceal her identity as they walked. Had something gone wrong with her brother's birthday celebration last night to alter her demeanour so, or did it have something to do with the unusual number of guardsmen that she saw this morning? Ellianna had noted their increased presence earlier when she'd come alone to seek help from the temple, but there seemed to be even more guards on the streets now, and the look on the faces of the few citizens whose path they crossed was one of fear and apprehension. Something was definitely wrong, and it didn't take much for her to suspect that Darken was involved somehow.

Whatever had been preoccupying Lady Jana's thoughts today appeared to have been set aside for now, but the way she was staring silently at Darken's face with an unreadable look on her own was beginning to give Ellianna real cause to believe that perhaps she'd made a mistake in bringing the priestess here. She was having a great deal of difficulty not saying something but valiantly fought down the impulse to do so and continued to wait patiently. When she thought she could stand it no longer, Jana spoke at last, much to the girl's relief.

"Which one of you found him?" Jana asked, without turning around. Her tone was level and betrayed no hint of emotion. Again, a complete contrast to the previous two days, Ellianna thought.

Behind her, Caeden glanced nervously at Thurgod, but the Dwarf's only response was a slight shrug of his shoulders followed by a curt nod.

"That would be me, my lady... uhm, Caeden Smithson, at your service," he managed to reply.

"Caeden Smithson," she repeated the name slowly and in a way that made the man feel as if she was committing it to memory. In his fearful imagination, he could already hear his name on the lips of Justicers as they kicked down the door to his house to arrest him. "Tell me exactly what happened. Leave no detail out."

The smith paled visibly and swallowed dryly. He looked at his friend again, but Thurgod did not meet his eyes. Instead, the Dwarf's gaze was fixed on Ellianna, who waited expectantly. He sighed, knowing that for better or for worse, the only choice he had was to tell the truth as he knew it. So, he did, relating his tale from the time he'd stepped out onto the street that morning, right up to when he'd arrived at Thurgod's door. The entire time that he spoke, Jana's stare remained focused on Darken's face—even through Caeden's gruesome account of how he'd struck down the boy's assailant. It was Ellianna who couldn't keep the astonishment from her face, bringing her hands up to cover her mouth in shock as she listened to her uncle's horrific description, not only of how Darken had come by many of his wounds, but how the kind, gentle man she knew and loved had killed another person—and done so seemingly without hesitation. These past few days had opened her eyes to some ugly truths about the world, and she was quickly realizing how unprepared she was for most of it. Her gaze darted to Thurgod's face, searching there for some reaction that would tell her she wasn't alone in feeling this way, but the pained look on his face before averting his eyes only confirmed to Ellianna that he already knew the full details of Caeden's story.

"Where is the dagger you mentioned?" Jana asked, cutting through the tension that hung heavily in the air.

"Over there, with the rest of what he was wearing," Caeden pointed to the bloody heap of leather and cloth left piled in a corner after the priest had tended to the boy earlier.

The priestess walked over to the area the smith had indicated, the hem of her long white robes covered in grime from the barn's earthen floor. A pair of mottled dairy cows in nearby stalls gave her a wary look as she passed, but the woman paid the animals no heed. Her mind still reeling from what she'd just learned, Ellianna followed Lady Jana almost without thinking, compelled by an inexplicable need to observe everything that the woman did. Ignoring the presence behind her, Jana stopped and then stretched one arm out to hold a hand, fingers spread, over Darken's belongings. She closed her eyes, and her mouth formed words that Ellianna could not hear. The result was immediate—a flash of red light pulsed strongly but briefly from somewhere under the black leather and then was gone. Jana's eyes shot open, the pupils so dilated that her clear blue eyes appeared nearly black before shrinking quickly back to normal. A small gasp escaped her lips, and she turned to face Ellianna. Was that fear the girl saw in the woman's eyes?

"Wait outside," the cleric said without preamble. Ellianna blinked in confusion and parted her lips as if to say something but stopped herself when Jana's delicate eyebrows came together in a disapproving frown. "All of you. Out, now!" The woman's tone invited no argument, and she received none. In a group, Dwarf, man, and girl walked out of the barn and shut the doors behind them, leaving Jana alone inside with Darken.

All three stood outside, an uncomfortable silence between them like a yawning chasm. Ellianna looked at the ground, partially lost in her thoughts as she tried to make sense of Jana's cold and distant behaviour, but also to avoid looking at her uncle. For his part, Caeden began to pace and glance anxiously toward the distant city walls, wondering how soon after the noblewoman left here there would be guards marching down that very road to come and take him away. Even the Dwarf, normally so vocal about anything and everything, could only stare wordlessly for several minutes at the barn doors in confusion.

"Well, what do you suppose that was all about?" Thurgod remarked at last to no one in particular, tugging pensively at his beard. "This isn't what I expected at all."

"Nor I," Ellianna confessed. "While I admit I've only known Lady Jana for two days, she feels like a completely different person this morning." There were hints of resentment, hurt, and confusion in her voice that Thurgod did not miss.

"Two days? Ah, lass, you can know a person for years and yet they still find ways to surprise you out of the blue," he sighed. Ellianna looked at him sharply, wondering if that was a comment directed at her over the things she'd kept from him of late, or if it was a reflection of her own reaction to hearing about what

Caeden had done. If there was a deeper meaning in his words, the Dwarf didn't elaborate further and continued to look at the closed doors. "That business with the dagger and the weird glow—what do you make of that?"

"I'm not sure, but I hope she'll tell us. Something about it is clearly important, but why are you asking me?" Ellianna said with a frown.

"Oh, I don't know... maybe because you have two new friends that you never saw fit to tell me about?" he grumbled acidly. "Can you blame me for wondering what else you might know?" In truth, he'd recognized immediately what the priestess had done, but he wasn't about to complicate things by revealing that. His words about truly knowing someone ran deeper and closer to home than she could guess.

"Can we talk about this some other time?" she shot back crossly.

The Dwarf muttered something unintelligible under his breath. "Fine," he acquiesced with obvious reluctance. "Do you at least remember seeing it before?"

"Seeing what?"

"The dagger!"

Setting her growing irritation aside, she thought about the question—maybe this really was important—but then shook her head. "I can't be sure. I did see him holding two daggers when he scared off those two other boys, but I don't know that one of them was that specific dagger. I couldn't even see it under the armour just now, anyway. What I do know is that Uncle Caed's description of Darken's attackers sounded an awful lot like those two—Gregor and Will, I think their names were."

Caeden made a strangled noise, and both Thurgod and Ellianna turned to look at him. The tall man was leaning against the barn wall, his face buried in one hand, shoulders shaking as he began to sob. Learning the name of the boy he'd killed had clearly hit him hard, and his back slid slowly down the wall until he fell to a sitting position on the ground, arms resting on his knees, head bowed with chin touching his chest while he cried. The sight nearly broke Ellianna's heart—she had never seen her uncle this emotional and vulnerable, and the sight made her feel helpless and want to do what she could to comfort him. It was plain to see the man was haunted by the knowledge of what he'd done, and Ellianna forgave him immediately. Gregor and Will had been awful people, but did they deserve their fate? It was not for her to say, but Darken's life had been saved in the balance, and she needed to acknowledge to herself how grateful she was to Caeden for that. She took a step toward the smith, but Thurgod grabbed her arm and held her back.

"Give him a few moments alone. Taking a life..." the Dwarf paused, his lips drawing a grim line beneath his beard, "...it changes a person fundamentally. He needs to grieve for what he's done. It's when the act no longer bothers you—that's when you know you've lost yourself for good."

Ellianna looked from Caeden to her grandfather, feeling as if she was staring at a complete stranger. She had to remind herself that the Dwarf had seen close to two and a half centuries of life before she'd even been born. Lady Jana's words about a time when her grandpa would finally be ready to talk about his past echoed in her mind, but she somehow couldn't quite bring herself to believe that he would ever be ready. She didn't know why she felt that way, but she did.

"Come inside, I'll make you some breakfast," Thurgod said, walking toward their cottage.

"I'm not hungry," she mumbled.

"That's your heart talking," the Dwarf called back. "Your body will be disagreeing with you in an hour or so. Come on."

"But what about when Lady Jana comes out?" she replied, but Thurgod had already disappeared into the house. She took two steps to follow but then stopped and turned around. Kneeling in front of Caeden, she put one hand gently on his shoulder. The man flinched at the touch but did not look up. "Uncle, are you alright?"

Caeden sniffled and then wiped his eyes on one sleeve of his utilitarian tunic. He nodded once, staring straight ahead with a haunted look in his eyes. "Go on, Lil. When she comes out, I'll let her know you've gone inside to wait."

"Are you sure?"

Another nod. She sighed, leaned forward to tenderly kiss the man's forehead, and did as he asked.

⸻⸻◆⸻⸻

Ellianna moved the piece of dark bread around the plate with her fork, meticulously coating it in the remaining bit of egg yolk. The task finished, she brought the laden utensil to her mouth and chewed slowly and with satisfaction plain upon her young face, savouring that final mouthful of food that was the product of their everyday work at the farm. Washing it down with a cup of fresh milk from their cows, she sat back contentedly, ruefully admitting to herself that she had been hungry, indeed. Across from her, Thurgod ate the last slice of fried ham on his plate, took a deep pull from his ale tankard, and smiled fondly back at her. The two had eaten in companionable silence, each lost in their thoughts and speculation over what would happen in the next few hours. While the Dwarf imagined that the noblewoman would be on her way soon and the boy would become someone else's problem very shortly thereafter, he worried about Caeden's role in all this. In his head, he was already composing the speech that he would deliver before the Justicer Magistrate in defense of his friend's character and actions. As for Ellianna, her vision of the immediate future was far less certain. Once Darken was safely out of danger, she planned to get some straight answers out of Lady Jana concerning the meaning of her dream.

"She's been in there an awful long time, Grandpa," Ellianna commented in concern. She glanced at the two empty plates they'd set at the table just in case. "Should we go and check on them?"

The Dwarf was about to say something in return when the door to the cottage opened. Sunlight spilled onto the small eating area in the centre of the home's modest interior, both heads turning to look at the silhouette of the tall figure that stood framed in the doorway.

"May I come in?" Lady Jana Morhain asked.

"Yes, of course. My house is yours," the Dwarf said, getting up and pulling another chair away from the table as an invitation for the woman to sit. Jana lifted her robes slightly to step over the threshold and took a seat on the proffered chair. The priestess looked at Ellianna, and for the first time today, the girl saw a twinkle of her old self in those blue eyes, making her feel immediately better about what the woman was going to say.

"Would you care for a plateful of the best breakfast within a hundred miles of Arlingtown?" Thurgod boasted proudly. "My granddaughter won't eat any meat—she loves the darn critters too much—but there's plenty of ham left, and I can make a fresh batch of eggs in no time. Everything I use is fresh, including the dill."

Jana smiled at the Dwarf for the first time since she'd laid eyes on him. "I confess the aroma makes your offer an incredibly tempting one, but I must decline. We have urgent matters to discuss and I'm afraid there's little time to waste," she said regretfully.

"I'll have none of that," Thurgod declared. "This won't take any time at all, and I can hear just fine from the kitchen." Before the priestess could protest, he walked through the archway that led to the cooking area at the back of the cottage and busied himself at the iron stove. Ellianna merely shrugged when Jana looked back at her and then offered the woman something to drink.

"Water is fine, thank you." Once she had her cup in front of her, she took a sip, brushed back a stray lock of raven hair from her face, and answered the question that she could see burning in Ellianna's eyes. "The boy will be fine. It was not an easy task, but by the grace of Anval, I was able to cleanse his body of the vile poison inside of him. Deacon Ulik was right to be concerned, and now that it's been dealt with, he should make a full recovery. I had to wake him because I needed to speak with him, and your uncle Caeden is watching over him right now." Jana took another sip of water, and Ellianna took the opportunity to speak.

"Did he tell you what happened?"

Jana put the cup down, pausing to listen to the sounds coming from the kitchen, and then reached across the table to place a hand over Ellianna's. "Yes, he did, but not voluntarily."

Something about the way the woman said that sent a chill through Ellianna's spine. She brusquely jerked her hand back from Jana's touch. "What do you mean?"

With a sigh, Jana withdrew her own hand slowly. She hadn't exaggerated when she'd said there wasn't much time, so she decided to get straight to the heart of the matter. "Ellianna, last night, during my brother's celebration, I became aware that something that I went to great lengths to safeguard was stolen. This object has tremendous significance in ways that I do not have the time to explain to you right now, but I have reason to believe that its theft at this particular point in time is no mere coincidence. More importantly, four lives were lost in Arlingtown this past night, one of them a relative of mine."

The background clatter from the kitchen had ceased but Ellianna's focus didn't permit her to register anything else beyond Jana's words. "What does any of that have to do with Darken? Surely, you're not suggesting he had anything to do with it, are you? I mean, there was that awful business in the alley, and... and Uncle Caed, but..." she stopped, unable to say anymore, eyes beginning to brim with unbidden tears. Was everyone in her life on course to surprise her in some heartrendingly disappointing fashion today? Since having met Darken, she'd spent less than an hour in total in his company, but in that brief time, she'd felt the beginning of a strong and lasting bond. Yet now, in recalling what her grandfather had said about not ever truly knowing someone you always thought you did, she realized that she was nothing but a trusting, naïve fool.

"Ellianna," Jana felt nothing but compassion for the girl, but she saw no choice but to continue. "I'm convinced your friend did not murder anyone last night, but he was very much involved in the events that led to those deaths. Even as we speak, the Justicers and my brother's men are combing the town for someone that fits his description. It won't be long before their search spreads beyond the walls."

"I don't understand," Ellianna said. "You just finished saying he didn't kill anyone. Why are they looking for him?"

"Because the wife of one of the victims saw Darken strike down her husband, a member of my own family. Darken is the killer that everyone is looking for, and in Anika Khelen, they have a very credible eyewitness to the deed. Your friend will hang if he is caught," she bluntly made the pronouncement, not because it gave her any pleasure, but so that Ellianna would hold no illusions as to what his fate would be.

"This doesn't make any sense," Ellianna shook her head, utterly confused. "Is he the killer or not?"

"No, he is not. Darken was not forthcoming with the truth owing to the fact he was protecting someone very dear to him, but this is more important than he realizes. It goes far beyond him, so I was left with no choice and was forced to use the *etherus* to fully understand what happened. I had to know who took what was stolen, and why. In the process, I learned a few more things."

"Are you saying the boy was framed?" Thurgod rumbled as he placed a plate of warm ham and eggs in front of the priestess and then walked around the table to place one arm protectively around his granddaughter's shoulder.

"Yes, the enchantment I wove compelled the boy to reveal only the truth to me, or at least insofar as he perceived it with his own eyes—the real killer somehow wore his face, as Anika's described it. He wasn't present when this happened, but he did speak of the killer's ability to perfectly alter her likeness. It doesn't change the fact that, even if his role was an unwitting one, he was part of a very serious crime last night," Jana explained, her eyes shifting back and forth between the Dwarf and the girl. The plate of food sat before her, ignored. "Those other two boys in the alley were not a part of it in any way other than running across him after he'd already made his escape. Seems he had some history with them, and it ended badly for all parties."

Thurgod puffed his cheeks and then blew his breath out with a loud whoosh. "There's nothing for it then, unless the Justicers see fit to believe what you're saying. I reckon your word carries a fair bit of weight but even so, the followers of Valoria aren't known for leniency. I'm sorry, Lil." The Dwarf squeezed his granddaughter's shoulders in sympathy for what she must be feeling.

"He won't be going back to Arlingtown. He's told me he has family in Briarglen, so that's where he's going to be off to as soon as he can," the priestess stated.

It took Thurgod and Ellianna a very long moment to fully grasp what Jana had just said. The girl's green eyes were suddenly bright and filled with impossible hope, simultaneously joyous and incredulous. The Dwarf's reaction, however, was markedly different. His brow furrowed and his eyes narrowed with suspicion.

"Why would you deceive your own brother and betray the law of his land?" the Dwarf asked, going straight to the point. The practical Dwarf wasn't overly fond of mysteries, and right now, he felt he was staring down his nose at a very big one—and he didn't like it one bit.

"Because what's at stake here is much greater than any of that—Edmund is my brother, yes, and I would do anything for him, but I also serve a higher calling than men and their earthly laws. That boy is our only chance to get back what was taken, and he can't do it if he's rotting in a dungeon cell or feeding the crows while hanging from a gibbet."

Such was the tone of conviction in her words that if she was lying, she was either damned good at it, or she fully believed what she was saying. Again, neither option was particularly reassuring to Thurgod, nor was he shy about making that known. "What makes this kid so special? Why not simply set the Justicers on the trail of whatever you say was stolen? Beggin' your pardon, my lady, but your story is not making much sense to my old ears."

Jana's response was to rise from her seat to her full height and stare down imperiously at the Dwarf across the table from her. "Ellianna told me you were a skeptic, so I'll not bother wasting what little precious time we have left explaining certain things to you," she began.

"Bloody convenient," Thurgod muttered under his breath. Standing behind Ellianna as he did, she paled visibly at the insult and looked quickly at Lady Jana to see if she'd heard. The woman's patience was clearly reaching its limit, and she did not relish the thought of a heated argument between the highborn priestess and her quick-tempered grandfather. She already had the benefit of having both a much more open mind than the Dwarf and being accepting of the fact that Jana knew things that were well beyond her own understanding and limited experience. Beyond that, the very notion that the cleric was offering a glimmer of hope in saving Darken from a horrible fate was enough to override any other concern she might share with the Dwarf.

"Grandpa, please calm down and listen to what Lady Jana has to say," she pleaded, looking up at him.

"Oh, I'm plenty calm," the Dwarf reassured her in a tone she knew all too well as a sign of trouble. "I don't know what the lady here has been filling your head with, but it's not going to work on this Dwarf. I've seen the best that blind faith has to offer, and the lies that people tell themselves to justify the things they do. So, tell me, Lady Jana, why should I trust anything you're saying?"

Jana's normally pale white skin flushed with colour as blood rose to her cheeks. The Dwarf was provoking her, that much any simpleton could see, but even so, the woman was finding it difficult to remain in control and not respond in kind. She nearly did so, but she had to remind herself that playing into his hands would accomplish nothing but drag her into a fruitless fight. Her breathing became measured once more, and she allowed the serenity of Anval to restore peace to her thoughts.

"I don't need to convince you of anything, nor is it my task to restore what you clearly forsook long ago," she said, giving him a penetrating stare that caused him to look away from her abruptly, something Ellianna had never seen Thurgod do. "Your granddaughter, to whom I know you do listen, will do that for me," Jana declared. "Ellianna," she looked at the girl sitting there with her mouth partially open in disbelief, "do you remember the last thing that we talked about yesterday?" When Ellianna nodded, she pressed on. "Good. Know then that the boy in that barn right now is one such as you—someone whose destiny lies beyond the petty arguments of peasant farmers and high priestesses alike. You and he must leave here at once and take your first steps on a journey that was laid out long before either of you were born. I told you where you need to go, and the events of this past night have shown me that the time to do so is now. I had hoped for more time to prepare you better, but the portents cannot be ignored. Your dream has stopped repeating, Ellianna, and its message must be heeded."

"How do you know that Darken is like me?" Ellianna asked. The flood of information was threatening to overwhelm her, so she clung to the one thing that could help her stay afloat in a sea of uncertainty—the knowledge that she wouldn't be doing this alone.

"The dagger that belonged to his uncle—it was used to dispel the wards I put in place to protect what was stolen, and only the power of a god can undo that of another. It is a mighty but dangerous weapon, and it has chosen Darken to be the instrument of the will behind the one whose power created the blade. I can't say more, other than that you should avoid touching it for any reason. Your uncle Caeden was very fortunate in that regard."

"Hold on just a damn minute," Thurgod interjected, waving his arms about. "Has everyone taken leave of their senses here? No one's going to Briarglen, or anywhere for that matter, and what dream are you talking about?"

Jana didn't respond, staring meaningfully at Ellianna instead. The girl knew it was a cue for her to talk but she didn't want to. The last couple of days had been a whirlwind of revelations that, while difficult to accept at face value, she'd at least felt she would have the luxury of having some time to begin to sort things out before deciding what to do. Apparently, she'd been very naïve about that as well. Still, Jana was right—her grandfather had basically declared he wouldn't believe anything the priestess would say from now on, which is why she'd left the task of convincing him up to her. The conclusion she inevitably came to was that she had no choice. Despite not understanding most of what she'd been told, she trusted Jana in a way she couldn't explain, and she needed to make the Dwarf understand that somehow.

"Grandpa, I know I have a lot to explain, but if Lady Jana says we don't have much time, then I believe her. Darken is in real danger, and whether he took part in a theft last night or not, he's not guilty of murder. We can't just let them take him. I won't allow it. I'm asking you to please do what you've done every day since you took me in—trust in me. Let me accompany him as far as Briarglen so that he can at least be safe. After that, I need to figure some things out about myself and my past that the lady said are very important somehow. This is important to me, and I know it's a lot to take in so suddenly—believe me, I know—but I also know in my heart that I must do this." It felt lame, incomplete, and unconvincing even to her own ears, but it was the best she could muster right now even as she fought down her own doubts about all this. She was afraid that if she thought about it too much, she would end up talking herself out of it. She waited for Thurgod to say something, her apprehension growing with every second that he sat there, staring at her in silence with an inscrutable expression on his craggy face.

"Please say something," she pleaded.

"You'd leave the safety and relative comfort of the life I've given you on the word of a complete stranger, and all to help some boy you've only just met? A wanted criminal, no less?" the Dwarf said at last. He didn't sound angry, only confused, and genuinely hurt. "Where did I fail you?"

"Grandpa..." she began softly, hurting as much as he was, "you're not hearing me. This isn't just about him. I'm only finding out now that he's a part of this as well, but ultimately this is about me—about finding myself and my place in this world. Can you accept that? It doesn't have to invalidate everything that you mean to me. Nothing will ever take that away."

"Lil, you have no idea of what the world outside that door can be like," he said, pointing at the cottage door for emphasis. "What you've just heard about that kid being involved in—the horrific things Caeden experienced today—that's only a small taste of what I've tried to protect you from, and now you want to run out headlong into it all? It's dangerous out there, and people are only a small part of that. One day I'll explain to you how I know this," he said, making a heartfelt attempt to dissuade her from making a grave mistake.

"If you had trusted me with that knowledge before today, perhaps I would understand your point better, but sheltering me even more is not what I need right now. I don't need your permission to go, but I'd feel much better if I had it, nonetheless."

"You just don't understand—" he began.

"No, I don't, and I never will if I stay here. Please, Grandpa, let me do this."

"*Out of the question!*" he thundered suddenly, causing Ellianna to flinch and Jana to frown. "You don't know what you're asking, but I do. I've devoted the last decade of my life caring for you, and now you're willing to throw all that away, and for what—a half-arsed story about 'important' things, 'destiny', and a 'message'? Could this be any vaguer? What insane gibberish! But why am I not surprised, considering the source," he railed in anger, glaring his fury at Lady Jana.

It took her a moment to get over the shock of his outburst, but Ellianna had had enough and stood up to face Thurgod. "If that's your answer, then so be it, but you don't get to make this decision for me. All you have to do is decide whether you can make peace with my choice." She walked away with determination in her steps and passed through a doorway on the wall opposite the kitchen. Beyond was the small addition to the cottage that Thurgod had built years ago to serve as the girl's own bedroom, and Ellianna purposefully left the door open so that the Dwarf could see her angrily stuffing clothes into a sack. Thurgod watched her, visibly fuming at this flagrant display of disobedience, and then wheeled on Jana to point a shaking finger at her.

"I won't let her go. This is your fault. Get out of my house!" he snarled, voice low with menace.

Utterly unfazed by his angry demeanour, Lady Jana stared hard at him. "You can't stop her, and if you persist in trying, you will destroy all the good that you have done for her so far. Are you willing to risk that? To forsake the relationship you have with her? Sometimes change—no matter how hard we run from it—is inevitable. If you truly care about her and wish to help, don't stand in her way. Not now."

Thurgod's jaw worked reflexively as if he was biting back words before uttering them. His strong and callused hands balled into fists and relaxed several times, and his squat and stocky frame shook with barely repressed emotion while he matched her stare with an intensity that rivalled her own. But the noblewoman had said what she needed to say, and there was nothing more to be gained by antagonizing the Dwarf further. She broke eye contact and turned away, yet doing so in a manner that should leave no doubt in his mind that this wasn't a victory for him, so much as letting him know that she had no more time for him. Jana stepped outside the cottage and closed the door behind her, leaving Thurgod alone with his troubled thoughts.

When Ellianna emerged from her room at last, she couldn't hide her surprise at seeing the main room empty, with no sign of either Lady Jana or her grandfather. She had heard their raised voices after she'd walked away, of course, but she was no longer listening at that point. The plate of eggs and ham sat there on the table, cold and untouched. She put down the bag of clothes she'd hastily packed and called out.

"Grandpa?"

There was no response other than a loud thud that came from the direction of Thurgod's room, so she walked over and peered cautiously through the partially open door. The Dwarf stood near the foot of his bed with his back to her. On the floor in front of him sat a large ironbound chest that she'd not seen him open for years. The lid was closed, but something metallic resting on top of it caught the sunlight coming through the window and she frowned when she saw what it was—a chainmail shirt, also called a haubergeon due to its shortened sleeves. Leaning against the container was a large, double-headed war hammer with a short haft and leather-wrapped grip. While she watched, the Dwarf—wearing some kind of padded undervest she'd never seen before—slipped his arms into the chain armour to let it slide over his head and shoulders and down to cover his torso and waist.

"A little tighter than I remember," he grumbled to himself.

"What are you doing?" Ellianna called from the doorway.

"What does it look like?" he shot back without turning. After shifting the weight of the metal rings around for a bit until it felt just right, Thurgod picked up a broad leather belt from the bed and cinched it around his waist. When that was done, he lifted the hammer from the floor and slipped the haft into a metal loop on the belt, securing the weapon. Turning around to face Ellianna, he held his arms out to his sides as if to give her a better view of how he looked. "Well, what do you think?" he prompted when she only continued to stare wordlessly.

"I'd be better able to answer your question if you answered mine first—what are you doing?"

His response was to take a few short steps to one wall and look up to regard something that hung there. The object of his attention was a round shield made of pine wood, its outer surface covered with leather and reinforced by a metal rim. A centre boss crafted from burnished steel depicted the stylized face of a Dwarf whose expression was frozen in a bellow of rage, and an intricate design had been carefully stitched into the surface of the leather, radiating out from the boss. The shield's surface was so worn and faded however, that whatever it once depicted was now impossible to make out. More notably, the upper half of the shield had been neatly split, with the blow breaking through the metal rim and cleaving wood and leather nearly all the way down to the boss. Slowly and with reverence, Thurgod reached up and removed the shield from its wall mount. Ellianna noticed that her grandfather's hands shook slightly while he held the shield and ran one finger down the cracked wood.

"Do you know how long this has hung on this wall?" he asked, his normally loud voice barely above a whisper.

Ellianna pondered the question. It had been made clear that time was pressing, but before she left, she wanted to be absolutely certain she would do everything possible to part with her grandfather on good terms. She had a pretty good idea of what he was up to, but rather than voice her objection like she wanted, she sensed that this was very important to him, and if there was one thing he had taught her, it was to be respectful. She turned her attention to the shield, knowing full well that she knew next to nothing about it. Like almost everything else about Thurgod's past life, it was shrouded in mystery and silence. She'd gathered only that it was of great importance to him, and that the never-repaired damage was somehow tied to the last name the Dwarf went by—Splintershield. It had hung there ever since she'd first laid eyes on it when he'd taken her in all those years ago, and she couldn't recall ever seeing him holding it—that is until now.

"No, Grandpa," she answered.

"One hundred and eighty-three years," he said. "Nearly two centuries. Can you believe that? Since the day I built this cottage with my own two hands, I've patched and repaired entire parts of that wall at least five times. Yet that shield has been there that whole time. The last time I used it—the day it was nearly split in twain, and I along with it..." he paused there, his voice becoming hoarse with emotion, and then continued after clearing his throat. "I lost everything that day—everything except my miserable life. That shield was last raised in defence of my family, and I failed them. You're all that I have now, and I won't fail a second time. I can't." He carefully checked the leather strap attached to the back of the shield, making sure the leather was still supple and functional after decades of loving care. Satisfied, he slung the shield over his back, its weight and presence as comforting and reassuring as that of an old and trusted friend. "I never bothered to fix it," he continued. "I left it this way as a reminder of what happens when you become overconfident and careless. This crack mirrors the one in my heart. Since I began to care for you, the wound inside of me has finally begun to heal. I think the time for me to repay my debt to you for that kindness has come at last."

"Grandpa..." she began, her eyes brimming with tears. She could see how difficult this was for him—how much it took for him to open up to her even just this little. Something had happened to the Dwarf, something so horrible that no one should ever have to endure it. It was plain to see just how much guilt he carried inside, and the heavy toll it had taken on him to carry such a burden for so long. She had always suspected it had something to do with his two brothers that he mentioned very rarely and always with clear reticence, but she'd never imagined that he held himself responsible for whatever fate had befallen them. She stepped forward to embrace him tightly, heedless of all the armour and gear he'd strapped around himself. She'd been fighting hard to hold back the terrifying thought of the enormity of what she was about to do—leave the safety and comfort of the half of her life that she could recall with clarity, to strike off into the unknown to reclaim the half she couldn't. To understand that her grandfather meant to come with her and would protect her as he always had washed over her like a flood of relief. She cried and laughed at the same time. When they finally pulled apart, the Dwarf hurriedly ran one brawny forearm across his eyes in a futile and obvious attempt to hide his own tears.

"Now then, let's get you suitably dressed for travel, and the contents of that bag into a proper rucksack. I've got one around here somewhere. Oh, and we're going to need something to eat while on the road, so when you're done, come help me in the pantry. If that lad's coming with us, at his age, I can imagine he must eat like a mountain lion," Thurgod grumbled, sounding more like his old self already. Ellianna watched him go with pride in her smile and love in her eyes and then began to follow his instructions with a renewed sense of hope. Maybe everything would turn out okay after all.

CHAPTER 28

Alyssa Dumar brushed back a tress of dark hair before bending down slightly to examine the collection of bottles inside the cabinet. The dark wooden cupboard, with its ornately decorated glass doors, appeared to be very well stocked. She'd never known her brother to be a habitual imbiber of spirits or wine, so she speculated these must be reserved for guests. Well, she may have gained entry into his home through her own means, but she considered herself a guest, regardless. Let Lorimer argue semantics with her if he wished. Peering closer at the offerings on hand, she opened the cabinet and pulled out a dark green bottle with a red label that had caught her eye.

"Noxos Moon Red. Your guests have expensive tastes, brother," she commented to herself, arching a thin eyebrow. Holding the bottle in one hand, she smiled mischievously and pointed at the stopper with a slender finger tipped by a long black nail. The cork made a soft popping sound and then floated in front of her, held by an invisible force, while at another gesture from that same digit, a crystal glass lifted into the air from a nearby silver tray and drifted casually over to where the mage stood. She poured herself a generous portion, took the glass into her own hand, and inhaled deeply of the rich aroma of the finest grapes Gol had to offer. Sighing in pleasure, she closed her eyes before bringing the vessel to her lips to sip deeply of the ruby-red nectar. The wine was still swirling down her throat when she heard the front door open. She had purposefully left it unlocked after undoing the mechanism with her magic and she hadn't bothered to relock it so that Lorimer would know she was already inside waiting for him. There were footsteps in the hallway, but no biting remark to greet her.

Alyssa turned to face not one man, but two boys, both staring intently at her. She immediately recognized both from earlier in the day, and the fact that they were here didn't surprise her—they were the very reason she had come to speak with her brother. The taller, older one, dressed in the black robe of an Initiate, didn't trouble himself to hide the suspicion and hostility in his eyes, while the younger one behind him couldn't appear more curious at her presence here if he tried. She stared right back at them, not saying anything.

"What are you doing here?" the one called Carlo challenged, sounding surer of himself than she would have expected. This one's got stones, she thought to herself, but then again, he'd proven as much already by deliberately failing the Test right in front of her.

"Whatever I want, child," Alyssa spoke that last with an undertone that should leave no doubt in his mind as to who was really in charge here. There was a smug confidence to this Initiate that she did not care for, and she was rewarded by the effect her undisguised condescension had through the display of twisting emotions playing out across his face. She arched an eyebrow again, inviting him to provide a retort, but to his credit, the Initiate wisely held his tongue. She took another sip of the wine with a bored look, considered the brief exchange over, and dismissively turned her back on both young men. When she heard no movement after a long pause, she directed the empty glass and wine bottle down onto the table with a languid motion of her finger.

"Are you still here?" she asked pointedly, turning her head slightly so that only her shapely nose and chin were visible through the profile of her hood. The question, with its undertone of patience worn thin, had the desired effect. The two young men walked in silence across the room and through the passageway that led to the kitchen area, the one called Flynn in the lead, with Carlo following closely and warily behind. Before the latter disappeared, his voice drifted back to her.

"Don't touch anything else."

Alyssa couldn't help but smile at that. She knew something of arrogant stubbornness herself, and if this lad was her brother's close protégé, she could well understand where he was getting that quality from. Because she'd grown up being a contrarian to Lorimer's overbearing personality, she immediately disregarded Carlo's warning by walking over to a bookshelf, casually perusing the titles on the book spines, then pulling one down. It wasn't so much that the book was of particular interest to her, but more because she felt like touching something to purposefully irritate the haughty Initiate. She even made a mental note to herself not to put the book back in its place as she sat down on a comfortably padded reading chair to settle in and wait for her brother. As she'd already guessed, she didn't have to sit there for very long before Lorimer returned home. She knew her brother as well as she knew herself, and the thought that his sister was in his home without him watching her every move ensured that he would conclude his duties and obligations for the king's visit as quickly as possible, before rushing back to his house to deal with her inopportune visit.

"I see you've made yourself right at home, sister," he said, not bothering to hide his irritation while he hung his cloak in the vestibule by the front door.

Alyssa looked up from the book to meet his glare from across the room with an impudent smile that she knew would annoy him even more. "The service here leaves a lot to be desired, so I was forced to help myself to some refreshments and a way to pass the time. Hope you don't mind. Care for a glass? This is really good," she remarked casually while pointing at the wine. The bottle lifted into the air and half-filled her glass, which she then caused to float over to her waiting hand. She left the container hovering expectantly over a second, empty glass and arched one eyebrow at him.

"You know I don't drink," he snapped, striding authoritatively across the room to take a seat across from the mage. "And this isn't the castle, where you have servants waiting on you hand and foot. You want something here; you do it yourself. Didn't I tell you not to use magic in my home before?"

She ignored his tirade and left him fuming there while she sipped her wine, then put the glass down with her hand. "Yes, you did, and I continue to not understand why."

"Because it is a rare gift and one to be used sparingly and only when absolutely necessary, not to perform cheap tricks and mundane tasks, like pouring yourself a glass of wine. It's disrespectful. I've told you all this before, so why do you insist on making me repeat myself every time?"

"Disrespectful? To whom? To you, or your precious Janus? You do understand my magic comes from a god as well, just not yours, right? And unlike Janus, Galion is not stingy with his 'gift', as you call it. I see it as more of a birthright, to be honest," she retorted dismissively, just as she'd done every other time they got onto this subject. The Kal-dkar predicted what he would say next, and she wasn't disappointed.

"Ah yes, your 'birthright'. Self-entitlement sounds about right for someone that was just born into something, rather than someone that has had to work hard for what they have their entire life. It's that same 'birthright', and the carelessness of your heathen god in bestowing it liberally and irresponsibly in the past that led to the deaths of millions of people, or have you conveniently forgotten that?" he lectured, crossing his arms and leaning back in his chair.

"How can I when you never cease to remind me? I see you like to maintain the subject fresh in your own mind from time to time as well," she said, putting the book down with the cover facing Lorimer so that her brother could see the title. It read 'Sanguis Sorceris', which translated roughly from old Avamori to 'Blood of the Sorcerer'.

He looked at the book then back at the face that so closely resembled his own, only without the lines and creases of a life lived wearing a perpetual frown. "Illuminating, isn't it?" he replied with a sneer.

"Oh, drop the act, Lorimer," she snapped, fed up with his sanctimonious and tiresome superiority. "You're one to lecture me on birthright. Don't think that I don't know how liberally you've spent our family's fortune and influence to ensure that the archbishopric of Rohne falls into your lap when the time comes. We both know very well it's not your love of children and your 'hard work', as you put it, on their behalf that's going to earn you that coveted office." Alyssa knew she'd hit a raw nerve when her brother drew himself up stiffly in his chair and gave her one of the coldest, silent stares she'd ever experienced from him. She didn't believe that he was surprised that she was aware of his machinations, but more that he was preparing himself to draw the line at any hint of interference from her in his personal affairs.

"Why are you here, Alyssa? It's been a very long day, so please make your point and then leave," he said.

"You know very well why I'm here," she said, leaning back in her chair. She rested her elbows on the velvet-cushioned armrests and steepled her fingers in front of her. The body language was meant to convey the fact that she was quite comfortable where she was, and that she did not intend to leave until she was satisfied with his answers. In a ritual performed countless times in their lives, her brother mirrored her, indicating he was just as ready as she was to dig his heels in. "Let's start with that Initiate you dote on so much," she began. When Lorimer stiffened visibly, she knew she was on the right track. "You knew he would pass the Test, yet you told him to choose the wrong token. I want to know why."

"I did?" he asked innocently. He knew he wasn't fooling her whatsoever, yet the part of him that perversely enjoyed sparring with his sister reacted instinctively, like muscle memory, and he decided right then and there that he had an opportunity here to glean some information from her in return. He just had to ensure it was a fair trade and that he would only give as much as he received, if not less.

"Yes, you did. I didn't have to take my eyes off the lad to know that he looked to you for direction when the time came to make his choice, nor that the outcome had already been predetermined between the two of you."

"What makes you think he didn't just fail on his own?"

She gave him an incredulous look. "You don't honestly expect me to believe that, do you? However thoroughly you both planned this, he hesitated long enough for me to see that he knew very well which one of those tokens was the correct one."

"Maybe you're just mistaken," he said, dismissing her claim. "I've seen plenty of children hesitate and second-guess themselves during your stupid Test. That he glanced in my direction then was just pure coincidence, nothing more. I am the headmaster of this orphanage, after all, so it's perfectly natural that he looks to me for guidance."

Alyssa sighed. This was going to be more difficult than she'd anticipated, which only made her even more determined to get to the bottom of it. "Yes, guidance that you discussed in advance. I didn't need the tokens to know there were only three boys in that hall that can channel the *etherus* beyond the meagre teachings you priests dole out like breadcrumbs, Lorimer, so you can stop protesting your innocence in all this. It took but one glance from me when I walked in to find all three of them. Now, the real question is, did you already know this about your Initiate, or did the two of you simply prepare for the possibility that he might only discover his ability today?"

The headmaster sat in silence for a few moments, pondering how best to answer the question. He didn't have to, of course. Alyssa didn't have the authority to compel him—only two people in the entire realm did, and she wasn't one of them—but he also knew that when she seized a lead, trying to dissuade her from pursuing it would be tantamount to attempting to steal a bone from a starving dog. "Your skills have grown," he conceded. He tallied a point for himself in his mind by having her reveal a little more about the extent of her magically enhanced perception. He understood enough about magecraft from his studies to know that the powers and spells wielded by Galion's disciples were as varied as the shape of every tree in a vast forest and as numerous as the grains of sand on an ocean beach. While these often increased with age, only the most powerful among them—the Kal-dkar—could perform feats that dwarfed the capabilities of most other mages. To say this made them extremely dangerous opponents was a gross understatement. Fortunately, he wasn't without his own resources on that subject.

Eyes closed, Lorimer's lips moved almost imperceptibly while he voiced a silent prayer to his patron. The rush of mystical energy that suffused his being drowned out the sound of his sister's laughter, but he didn't care. He opened his eyes to find her grinning at him, every one of her perfect, white teeth on display as if to emphasize her amusement.

"If that's truly your fear, don't you think you should have done that before you walked in that door?" Alyssa's dark orbs glittered with genuine mirth as she regarded his stern face.

"I did," he replied confidently. "It's just that much stronger now."

The mage brought her fingers to her mouth to stop herself from laughing again. Whatever sibling love had once existed between them had long since faded to nothingness, an unfortunate casualty of their lifelong bitter rivalry and warring ambitions. Even so, she wasn't incapable of feeling a twinge of half-remembered affection for her twin brother. "Lorimer, I'm flattered by your precaution, but I'm not a sorceress. That kind of telepathic manipulation is forbidden. You know very well what happened to those that engaged in such practices," she tapped one fingernail on the cover of the book resting on the table between them.

"Forgive me if I don't sound reassured," the priest scoffed. "I've heard tell that some among the Elves and Minotaurs still practice that forbidden art."

"The Elves and Minotaurs didn't enslave the minds of their own kind to wage a horrifying and futile war against their own peoples, turning them into Husks in the process. Galion was more than just in his punishment. If you believe me in nothing else, believe this—if I tried to force you to do something against your will, I would be signing my own death warrant."

"Barbaric," he sneered, "all of it, and yet you question why I would protect a child from joining your ranks? When I become archbishop, this abominable practice will stop, I swear to you."

"Don't be such a hypocrite, Lorimer," Alyssa snapped back. "Your religion is no less cruel in its treatment of those that violate its own sacrosanct rules, so don't you dare lecture me on our methods because yours are just as harsh. Besides, archbishop or not, you know damn well you can't just abolish the Test. Need I remind you that's an inviolate decree that comes down from the Imperium, and one to which the Holy Patriarch of Avamor himself consented to long ago?"

"The Imperium hasn't had any authority over this realm for centuries, or need I remind you as well?" he challenged.

"Be that as it may, the law is older than Rohne itself, unless you plan to take that up with the leader of your church. If you become archbishop, you'll certainly get a voice at the table or are you planning to take your aspirations even further than I thought?" she stopped herself there, realizing for the first time that she may have underestimated her brother. He decided not to answer, leaving her to chew on her doubts for a minute or two. The resultant sigh of exasperation from Alyssa was always a good sign he'd gotten well and truly under her skin. If this played out the way it always did, next she would appeal to his reason. He wasn't disappointed.

"Stop being a stubborn ass for just once in your life and consider what could happen if those destined to wield the *etherus* were left to fend for themselves—untrained, unsupervised, and unsupported. Do you truly think that's a good idea? Do you really see no value in what we do? They can't all become priests, Lorimer. And what about the ones that aren't here under your roof for you to guide and protect? Are we to ignore and abandon them as well?"

The headmaster listened patiently. Alyssa wasn't wrong, of course. Mages had no place in the church, and due to there being fewer and fewer born each generation with that talent, most realms on Akar had enacted laws to cultivate and protect their development. The Test was one such measure, a method by which senior practitioners could find those rare instances of fledgling power and provide careful nurturing and mentorship. His gaze drifted to the table, the book and the history contained within its pages an abject reminder that things hadn't always been this way. Though the Great Sorcerous War had been fought more than a thousand years ago, the repercussions of its cataclysmic conclusion were still felt to this day. For his own reasons though, he didn't want his sister to get her clutches into either Carlo or Flynn. As if summoned by that very thought, the sound of footsteps in the hallway heralded the return of the Initiate, who stopped at the entrance to the room. He was alone.

"Everything is as it should be," Carlo said cryptically.

"Thank you, you may retire for the evening," Father Lorimer replied. In response, the Initiate walked across the room in the direction of the front door without looking at either of the adults, and left the house. Watching him go in silence, Alyssa tapped one finger pensively on her lower lip.

Lorimer didn't miss the gesture. "What?"

"Just thinking about the way that lad carries himself—the way he talks, and his mannerisms. Is he...?" she didn't finish the question, letting it hang in the air with all the weight of its implication. She got an icy stare in return.

"I'm not even going to dignify that with an answer."

Alyssa decided to let the matter drop. She knew how far she could push her brother, and that line had been reached. She didn't actually care whether or not Carlo was her nephew, though if he were, it would go a long way toward helping her understand the connection between these two. However, setting aside the fact that Janusian priests swore an oath of celibacy, she really couldn't picture her brother going through the bother and effort to sire a child—unless of course, it furthered his own ends somehow. More likely than not, the youth had simply taken to mimicking his superior after following him around all his life and doing his bidding.

"Alright then," she moved on. "I don't know what you're grooming him for, but I'll leave you to it. I just hope you know what you're doing. The ones we most often place our faith and trust in usually prove to be those who disappoint us most greatly in the end. Be wary, my brother."

"Speaking from experience, Alyssa? It must be a sad thing to live in paranoia," he jibed.

"Hardly, but even a small dose of caution can pay off in ways we can never anticipate. Keep both eyes on that one," she warned. "Now, I want to talk to you about the other boy—the one called Flynn."

Lorimer heaved a deep sigh. "Must we? It's getting late, and I wasn't jesting when I said I've had a long day. Don't you have anything better to do than to harass me with inopportune questions?"

"Yes, we must. This isn't about personal interest, though I am admittedly curious, but you know very well that I'm here as an extension of my duties—not only to my Order but also to the king. Who is that boy, and why is he being kept here, isolated from the rest? I know it has something to do with the recent incident, so I'd counsel you now to be forthcoming with me in this matter. That child is practically overflowing with *etherus*, but the feeling of...*wrongness* about it is unlike anything I've ever felt before."

The headmaster tried his best not to betray any emotion, and though his expression remained impassive, he couldn't keep from paling visibly at her words. When he saw his sister's eyes narrow, he knew he'd given himself away. "What 'incident' are you referring to?" he said through clenched teeth, dropping any pretense of being unfazed by her questions.

"The one that resulted in the death of one of your charges. *That* incident."

"Are you spying on me?" he snarled, not bothering to hide the anger in his voice.

"You mean like your own informants in the castle that report to you about the goings on at court? No, nothing like that, and you needn't turn the orphanage upside down looking for disloyal clerics—magic has more benefits than you give it credit for," she said, opening the game up a bit more by offering him a morsel of information in return for the one she'd already taken without his knowledge.

"It can't be all that great if you're asking me for details. What exactly do you know, and who have you told?" Lorimer recovered quickly, jockeying for the advantage once more.

"No one—what do you take me for?" she retorted, offended that he would think her that careless. "I know only that you didn't waste time in disposing of the body, but beyond the obvious way in which news of this tragedy would impact the orphanage and the archbishop, I'm left wondering what else you're hiding, and why," Alyssa questioned, glancing meaningfully at the passageway she'd seen Flynn disappear through earlier. She didn't miss her brother's quick and furtive glance in the same direction and decided to try a different approach. It was a long shot, but she needed to get through to him. "Lorimer, whatever this is, please—let me help you." She surprised herself at her earnestness, and the genuine tone of appeal in her words did not go unnoticed. The headmaster looked up sharply at the Kal-dkar, eyes narrowed with suspicion, to stare at the face that had once been so familiar to him but had come to belong to a stranger in recent years.

"Why do you care, Alyssa? Are you really that desperate for more children to teach magic to?" he asked, genuinely curious. "When we were young, you often spoke of having your own—of raising a family. I haven't forgotten the yearning in your voice when you spoke of it. Is this some twisted way of making up for the fact that that became impossible?"

That stung, the barb digging deep to penetrate the one place in her heart that she kept carefully guarded from everyone else. Yet she recognized that Lorimer's intention here was not to reopen that old wound—even if he had done so regardless—but to force her to confront that truth about herself and draw an honest answer out of her. An important part of a Kal-dkar's conditioning involved methodically stripping away the layers of emotion that bound an apprentice to his or her family, replacing them with an unbreakable devotion to the Order. In the case of the contentious relationship she shared with Lorimer, that hadn't been difficult. Even less so with her parents, now long deceased. But the reality of never being able to have a family of her own was a deep pain that no amount of training and meditation had managed to scour away.

"It's as close as I am permitted to come to that, Lorimer," she admitted with a whisper, struggling to keep the hurt from her voice, "but it's only part of it. Regret is not a luxury someone in my position can afford." She closed her eyes, and took a long breath to collect herself, angry and embarrassed that she'd allowed him to expose her vulnerability. Her carefully constructed façade of confidence and control crumbled momentarily, revealing not an emotionless and calculating Kal-dkar, but a human being like any other. Yet, when she felt his hand hesitatingly touch hers, she realized that the door that Lorimer had opened could be crossed in the opposite direction. She didn't withdraw her hand and looked straight into eyes that were a mirror to her own. "I have accepted the fate that life chose for me and am proud of what I've accomplished for myself, no matter the personal sacrifices that took. Things are as they were meant to be. Beyond that, you know I have a sworn duty to protect the king and this realm. If this child poses a threat in any way, I must stop him. Help me understand what's going on, Lor, so that I don't make the wrong choice by mistake. Please."

She hadn't called him by that name in a long, long time, and he knew manipulation when he heard it, especially when it came from his sister. All he heard now was sincerity.

"I wish I could be certain, Aly..." he began, swallowing dryly. Then his gaze became unfocused as his mind regressed through time to take hold of a memory that never strayed far from his thoughts, no matter how much he wished at times that wasn't the case. "He spoke to me, you know? I heard His voice, and I knew that it wasn't a dream. I can still hear the words as if He'd just uttered them, and they haunt me to this day," Lorimer recounted.

"He? Who are you talking about? Who spoke to you?" Alyssa asked gently but insistently. She understood immediately this was very important, but she had to be careful not to do anything that would cause her brother to mistrust her again and withhold anything that might be a critical piece of information. His reply left her briefly stunned.

"Janus."

"Are you sure, Lor?" she continued after regaining her composure, squeezing his hand to reassure herself as much as her brother.

"Yes, there was no mistaking it," the headmaster asserted, looking at his sister once more. What she glimpsed in his eyes filled her with a nameless dread. It was only a feeling, something that defied logical explanation, but the raw fear that emanated from him to wash over her convinced Alyssa that Lorimer was telling the truth.

"When did this happen?"

"Thirteen years ago," he replied without hesitation.

"And what did he say?"

The headmaster recoiled and withdrew his hand abruptly as if stung, physically breaking the fragile bond that had been so tentatively and painstakingly reforged between the two siblings. "I can't tell you that!"

Alyssa cursed under her breath. She had pushed him too far and needed to get him back before it was too late. Her next words were chosen quickly but with great care. "I'm sorry, Lor. This is deeply personal, I understand that. Tell me only what you want to...or can."

The headmaster stared at the mage, his natural mistrust of her battling with his desperate need to share what he knew with someone else. He'd been keeping this secret for a very long time now, and the weight of what he knew had turned what was an already reserved man into someone that was unapologetically aloof, preferring no one's company but his own. Even among the Brothers of the orphanage, he couldn't think of a single one that he could call a friend. The only one he'd even come close to taking into his confidence on this was Brother Owen, but he'd quickly realized the cleric had a big blind spot when it came to Flynn, and that made him a liability. That, and his too pure of a soul. He did not regret sending the man away, hopefully for good—when the time came that he needed to do with the child what he must, E'on Abdalla would be one less obstacle in his way. As for Alyssa, the headmaster realized with a sudden flash of insight that the Kal-dkar could be of far more use to him than the hindrance he'd always viewed her as. He too chose his next words carefully.

"I put the token in the bag, Alyssa."

"Token? What token?"

"The same one I've been using for years, waiting for the day he would come. It's how he was supposed to reveal himself... and it worked. All this time—all those children—and now I know which one."

"Did he—no, don't tell me that," she stopped herself, lest her direct question make him pull back again. Besides, she felt confident she could eventually reason out why he'd received this knowledge. "It's very clear that the boy is special in a way that frightens you, Lorimer—and if it frightens you, then it frightens me. I could sense as much when he stood before me, and now you've confirmed that. I can't be sure why, but I'm certain you will tell me when you're ready. In the meantime, you can't expect me to simply ignore what little I've learned today. What can I do, brother? Are you confident that what you're doing now is sufficient to accomplish whatever it is that you know is in store for this boy?"

"Can you peer into the future and tell me that?" he asked, only half jokingly.

"I'm not a chronomancer, Lor. The last of them were hunted down and slain long ago by the sorcerers," again she tapped the book on the table with one fingernail to remind him. "Perhaps it was for the best," the Kal-dkar said pensively, "knowledge of what lies ahead can often prove more dangerous than ignorance."

"This silly field trip the princess has planned—you have to stop it," he brusquely stated, catching her off-guard.

"What? Why?"

"Because under no circumstances must that boy be allowed out into the city, do you understand?" Lorimer replied vehemently.

"No, I don't understand. That's the whole reason for this conversation in the first place," she tried to control her exasperation. "Look, you've already sequestered him away from all the other boys. Why not simply keep him here when the time comes?"

"If only it were that simple. Marcos dotes on these children—Gabriela most of all. I can picture perfectly just how simple it was for her to convince him of this, but what matters here is that he would do anything for that girl, and that includes making absolutely certain that every single child on record, both here and at the convent, will be taking part in this."

"If he's still the archbishop by spring, that is," she reminded him.

"I can't discount that possibility. I thought he would make the announcement today, but he didn't," Lorimer leaned back in his chair, covering his face with one hand in a futile attempt to hide the frustration he felt.

"The princess is very strong-willed," Alyssa said, thinking of how much the girl reminded her of herself at the same age. To be fair, not much had changed since those days. "I'll do what I can, but know that if she's already managed to convince both her father and the archbishop to do what she wants, then you'd best start thinking of another way to keep Flynn here."

Lorimer looked at his sister through a gap in his fingers and heaved a sigh. His gaze then drifted to the bottle of wine she'd opened a while back. "I think maybe I'll have some of that after all."

CHAPTER 29

THE SENSATION WAS THAT of an odd tingling at first, like a gentle breeze that softly stirred the hair covering Vurax's body. When that feeling became more forceful and insistent, causing his skin to crawl as if something cold and clammy had made contact with it, he shivered in his sleep and attempted to brush the impression away by turning restlessly in bed. In the world of dreams where his subconscious now walked, he was lost in a dense, cold fog—one so thick that he had completely lost his bearings, and wandered endlessly in a hazy and featureless realm, never arriving anywhere. He could not remember how he'd gotten into this predicament—where he'd been or where he was going—and within the eerie silence of his thoughts, not even his own footfalls could be heard. Frustration rising, he stopped once more to look around, noticing for the first time that the fog was now so thick that he could scarcely see his own hands and feet. As sinuous tendrils of mist coiled about his body, he swatted frantically at them, but the fog defied his increasingly desperate efforts. When the white wisps coiled almost sensuously around his neck and began to choke the breath from his lungs by insinuating themselves into his mouth and nostrils, he gasped for air so violently that he startled himself awake at last.

Vurax opened his eyes and sat up abruptly in bed, taking in a breath of air to steady himself. The sensation of asphyxiation had felt all too real, and after what had happened inside the temple in Vurgas, he was left feeling particularly disturbed by this unwanted reminder of that harrowing experience. He shivered and rubbed his arms reflexively, wanting to rid himself of the revoltingly slimy sensation of that fog on his skin, when he realized that he still felt cold. Expelling the breath that he'd taken in, he watched it form in front of his face as a small white cloud—a virtual impossibility during late summer in Golan. Just that evening at dinner he had remarked how the heat in southern Gol reminded him of Sarmakan. No, something was not right here, a conclusion that was reinforced when a movement out of the corner of his eye caught his immediate attention. There, in the darkness at the far end of his chamber, a soft, pulsating light outlined the crack between the floor and the closed door to his room. While he watched in confusion, a glowing mist slowly crept in under the thin opening, rising briefly as if exploring the new space it found itself in before settling languidly back down, blanketing the floor of the room as it moved.

"What in blazes...?" Vurax cursed under his breath, ears twitching to pick up any sound from outside the room while he stared in disbelief at the strange phenomenon. When he heard nothing, he threw off the covers abruptly and climbed out of bed. The floor felt like ice on his bare feet, sending another shiver down his spine. Dressing himself quickly while keeping a wary eye on the slowly advancing mist, he instinctively went to grab for his battle axe, then snorted with irritation when he remembered that his weapon had been taken away when they'd arrived at the palace. Adjusting one last strap on his breastplate, he fought down the lump of dread that was forming in his throat. The fear of things that he could not explain had become an all-too common sensation in his life recently, and he didn't have to be convinced that whatever was happening outside of that door was clearly unnatural in origin. Thankfully, the odd mist didn't seem to be rising any higher than knee height, so as reluctant as he was to allow it to touch him, he saw no other choice if he wanted to leave the windowless room he'd been assigned. At least he wouldn't have to risk breathing it in for now. He wasn't sure why he'd had that thought, but his instincts were telling him that it wouldn't be a good idea. Giving his brother's horn rings at his chest a reassuring pat, he took a cautious step, then another, then waded into the fog-like substance filling the room, every sense alert for danger.

As soon as he touched the chilling mist, it reacted to his presence immediately like it had a sentience of its own. Coils of luminous fog entwined themselves about his form, winding and rising quickly as they reached for his face even while he twisted violently to avoid letting it envelop him. Just like in his dream, the vapour resisted his attempts to disperse it, stubbornly clinging to the Golian and twisting to seek out his face with sinister purpose. The touch of the mist on his hair and skin felt repulsive and unnerving—viscous and oily without being wet. He held his breath as long as he could while quickening his pace to reach the door. He didn't know what he'd find on the other side, but he would gain nothing by remaining inside the bedchamber. He closed one hand about the handle and pulled—only to find the door stuck fast. Puzzlement warred with annoyance as he tried again, more forcefully this time, but the confusion soon gave way to a distinct feeling of panic when the door refused to yield to him. He knew the door had been left unlocked, or at least it had been that way before he'd gone to sleep.

He pounded on the barrier with both fists, then bashed it violently with his shoulder, all to no avail. The wooden door may as well have been made of solid stone. His exertions to keep the mist at bay and to escape the room soon exhausted the supply of air he had left in his burning lungs. The desperate Minotaur fought to the last to not take in a fog-filled breath, but his body's instinctive need for life-sustaining air quickly overrode his willpower. Remembering his dream, he steeled himself for what would come next and opened his mouth with a ragged gasp so that he could breathe, his body slumping against the door. Pulsing like a slow, steady heartbeat, the glowing mist rushed down his throat, causing him to gag and retch in revulsion. There was no pain, but rather a numbness as the cold spread throughout his body, probing, and then...nothing. His chest heaved while he took short, measured breaths, but the mist slowly withdrew, seemingly no longer interested in him, and returning to cover the floor with its cold caress. He had no idea what had just happened, but one thing he could be certain of was the distasteful and lingering sensation of that thick, viscid chill violating his very essence as it penetrated deep within his body. Unable to contain himself any longer, he expelled the contents of his last meal, taking a small measure of perverse satisfaction when the mist pulled away from the warm vomit that pooled on the floor.

Using the wall for support, Vurax pushed himself up, taking a pause to fight down the last vestiges of queasiness that he felt. That done, he took one last look about the room, noting that the entire floor area was now fully engulfed by the mist, and then turned his attention to the door once more. He put his hand on the handle and this time the door swung open inexplicably and effortlessly. The Golian's eyes widened in surprise at what he saw beyond, the expression followed by a string of curses muttered under his breath. Without further delay, he stepped through the threshold and out into the hallway. The long passage was dark, even though it too was blanketed by the glowing fog in either direction as far as he could see. Despite the bright luminescence within it, the mist didn't actually appear to provide any illumination. He also noted that the oil lamps, spaced at regular intervals along the walls, were all out. An eerie silence hung like a shroud over everything. He wasn't sure if it was still nighttime outside or if the sun was shining on a new day—in here, it felt as if the entire imperial palace of Golan had been cast into an uncanny and surreal nether realm of shadows.

The doorway immediately across the hall from his yawned open into darkness, the cold mist flowing lazily through the opening in the same fashion as it had into his own room. They were in the guest wing of the palace, and he knew his companions were all lodged nearby. Without hesitation, he crossed the passage and entered the other chamber, the one belonging to Windstrider. A quick scan revealed no sign of the Syldar Elf within, though the bed covers were disturbed. Unlike his own room, however, this one faced one of the palace's inner courtyards, and Vurax's eyes went immediately to the open window on the far wall. It was dark outside as well, confirming his suspicion that it was still night, but as he stepped up to the opening so he could peer out, he stumbled into something concealed by the mist. Looking down, he saw the dark shape on the floor before him and bent down to see what it was. Musing again on the strange fact that the glowing fog did not illuminate its surroundings, he probed slowly about with his hands, quickly realizing that the object was a body. The skin felt rigid and cold to his touch, like an ice block, and when he lifted the prone figure from the mist so that he could see its features, his heart sank when he stared into Windstrider's lifeless eyes. The Elf's skin had turned incredibly pale, and his lips were almost completely white. More horrifying than that, a bloodless gash across the Syldar's throat gaped up at the Minotaur like a ghastly grin, the ragged tips of flesh a light shade of blue. The body's posture and position told him that the elf had likely met his grisly fate while trying to reach the window—or trying to prevent something from coming through it.

He hadn't had nearly enough time to claim that he knew Windstrider well, but the soft-spoken, witty Elf had seemed like a brother to Treeweaver, and he felt a lump form in his throat at the tragic sight of the body. This loss would be hard to bear on top of everything else that the Syldar prince had already endured in recent times. Thinking of him and Kael, Vurax was filled with a renewed sense of urgency and fear. There would be time to mourn later, so he lowered the body gently back down to the floor and cautiously looked out the window. The night was clear, and the stars shone uncaringly in the firmament above like they always did, while Temeros and one of her smaller sisters, Ilios, cast down their pale glow in conjunction. Outside, however, the palace grounds were completely covered in the same pulsating fog that had made its way inside the sprawling palace building. Movement on the far side of the courtyard caught his attention where a dark shape moved between the stone columns of an arcaded passage. He was about to call out to it for help when the figure stopped abruptly and turned toward him. The shadows that shrouded the indistinct form were pierced by twin pinpoints of blue light at the height where eyes should have been, and Vurax felt a sharp spike of cold run down his spine when they flashed with penetrating intensity and that soulless stare met his own gaze. Hissing in shock, he withdrew hastily from the window opening.

'What was that thing?' his thoughts raced. He tried to process what he'd just seen and questioned whether his eyes were playing tricks on him, now fully convinced that the situation was far, far grimmer than he had thought upon waking. As if the presence of a strange mist here in the most secure place in the heart of Golan wasn't worrisome enough, now he had to contend with the revelation that some form of supernatural killer was lurking about, searching for more prey. 'Where in blazes were the guards?' he wondered not for the first time since he'd left his room. If he hadn't been certain before, he now felt it was imperative that he find a weapon, and fast. Moving toward the door so as to not be seen from the window, he left the room and turned left toward Treeweaver's room. He found the door closed but it opened easily when he turned the handle. Swallowing dryly and preparing himself for what he might find, he entered the room with caution, eyes darting about as he searched the dark space within for signs of danger.

Just like the previous two chambers, the mist covered the floor here as well, and just as in Windstrider's room, the window was open. Taking care to not make himself visible to anyone outside this time, Vurax crept along one wall and approached the bed, seeing that not only was it empty, it also didn't look like it had been slept in at all. Puzzled but still fearful of the worst, he looked about for a body partially concealed by the low-lying fog, but after a bit of searching, he came away satisfied that he was alone. Perhaps his friend still lived, but if so, where had he gone? He fought down the urge to peer out the window and see if the strange creature with the blue eyes was still out there but decided against it. Urgency pulled at him again and he hastened across the hall to the door to Kael's room, finding it closed as well. To his great relief, this one also opened effortlessly. Located on the same side of the building as Vurax's own chamber, Kael's room was similarly windowless, but even in what would normally be considered pitch-black conditions despite the glowing mist's presence, his ability to see fairly well in the dark allowed him to discern the outline of the centurion's form lying on the bed. Whether Kael still lived was another matter, a fact Vurax was fearful to ascertain. Exhaling a puff of misty breath with a shiver, he brushed his reluctance aside and walked up to the bed.

Kael was lying on one side with his back to him and thus he couldn't tell if the other Minotaur was breathing or not. He put his hand on one shoulder and immediately closed his eyes with a sigh of relief when he felt not deathly cold but warmth instead. "Kael?" he called out softly, attempting to shake the soldier awake. When the sleeping Minotaur didn't react, Vurax shook him again, more insistently this time. Again, there was no reaction. "Kael! Wake up, damn it," he raised his voice, but Kael remained unresponsive. Having had enough, he turned the centurion over and placed two fingers under the lower jaw to check for a pulse. He found one, albeit very faint, and the other Golian still drew breath even if shallowly. Frowning, he pulled back one of Kael's eyelids, only to find the orb completely rolled up in its socket. He had no time to do anything else when he felt the already cool air in the room drop suddenly and sharply to a bone-chilling level that made all his hair stand up on end. Other than a low, sibilant whisper, there was no other change in the environment that any of his physical senses could detect, but his warrior's instincts told him unequivocally that there was a presence behind him where none had been before. Before he could dwell on that warning any further, he dove abruptly to one side, narrowly avoiding the attack that followed a split second later. Tumbling through the mist-covered floor, he jumped back to his feet in one smooth motion to face his would-be killer in a defensive crouch. He had no idea what he expected to see, but nothing—not even that distant glimpse from the window—could have prepared him for the horror that stood before him.

The first thing Vurax noticed was that the entirety of the strange creature's form was partially transparent, and he was startled to see the outline of the room behind its horrible form. The spectral apparition reared up as tall as a Golian, its entire upper body resting on a series of thick coils that tapered down to end in a twitching tail. There was no mistaking the creature's resemblance to a snake, covered as it was in iridescent scales of pale blue and icy white all the way through to its horribly inhuman visage. Its wide jaws opened partially to reveal long, curved fangs, through which a forked tongue flicked out, tasting the air before it. Two small holes glistened wetly where a nose should have been, and above it all stood narrow reptilian eyes that shone with a bright, sapphire glow. Like the deadly cobra, a wide hood flared out from behind its head, but the similarity to a serpent came to a shocking turn at the pair of articulated arms that protruded from the creature's decidedly human-like torso. Rippling with sinuous muscles and tendons, the scaled appendages ended in elongated hands with thin fingers, each tipped by slender but deadly-looking claws. One of these hands gripped the ornate hilt of a long, curved blade, its cruelly serrated edge glowing with the same blue colour as the creature's eyes while it steamed in the room's air. With a slow, deliberate motion, the intruder pulled the strange weapon back from the space where Vurax had just been and hissed at him. The combination of the insidious sound and hypnotic side-to-side motion of the creature's swaying body mesmerized the Golian and caused him to momentarily lower his guard in confusion.

Seizing the opportunity, the monstrosity lunged forward in a blur of motion too fast for the dazed Golian to react and sank its fangs into the Minotaur's shoulder. Vurax screamed in pain, not so much from the sensation of the long points piercing flesh and muscle, but from the shock of numbing cold that instantly penetrated his body, quickly radiating outward and deeper from the entry wound. Despite its ethereal appearance, the monster felt solid and real enough, shuddering while it pumped chilling venom into him, its surprising weight bearing the Golian down to one knee. Vurax's body temperature dropped so abruptly that every part of him felt leaden and devoid of feeling within seconds. The urge to close his eyes and sink into sleep threatened to overwhelm him but he knew that if he did so, he would never wake again. He tried to will his arms to move and throw off the creature, but the paralyzed limbs would not respond. It didn't matter in the end. Satisfied that its foe had been effectively neutralized, the beast released him, letting the Golian's body slump to the floor like a puppet with its strings cut. Strange eyes flashed bright sapphire as it regarded its victim dispassionately, then the beast turned to the bed and Kael's unconscious figure. Lying on his side, Vurax helplessly followed the monster's movements with his eyes when he felt the familiar presence within him stir awake, even as his consciousness nearly faded altogether.

'You can save yourself and your friend,' he heard the familiar whisper in the back of his mind.

The fact that he could now put a name to the manifestation made him trust it no more than before. He knew what accepting the offer would cost him, but the price of ignoring the help would be much higher—and final. Without hesitation, he cast aside the fragile barrier that kept his individuality separate from the divine power he had somehow inherited, and allowed it to take over.

The resulting rush of energy raced through Vurax's veins with the speed of uncontrolled wildfire, burning away the chill that had completely immobilized him while slowly draining his life away. Invigorated with sudden power, the Minotaur exploded into action, jumping up from the floor to grab the monster's wrist with his left hand in one motion and effectively stopping the downward swing that surely would have ended Kael's life. Hissing with surprise and anger, the serpentine creature twisted and spun to face its assailant with impossible speed, jaws wide, and fangs dripping with pale blue ichor. Eyes of frosty azure glared with hatred—their intensity matched only by the crimson fury of the Golian's own triumphant scowl—just before the Minotaur's hammer-like right fist landed squarely between them. The mighty blow stunned Vurax's otherworldly opponent, forcing it to drop its weapon. However, the reprieve was short-lived, and the creature recovered quickly, dodging the next blow in a blur of movement, then darting in low to sink its teeth anew into the Minotaur's exposed ribs. Glowing orbs of blue widened in shock and pain, and the creature jerked its head back with a loud hiss almost immediately, smoke rising from its scorched fangs. The blazing heat now smoldering through Vurax's blood was clearly more than the monster's bone-freezing cold could withstand, and when the monster withdrew abruptly, the Golian did not squander the opportunity.

The wraith-like monster thrashed in tortured pain, thick tail lashing defensively back and forth in front of it to ward off the unexpected intensity and menace of this foe. The creature's overconfidence in thinking it had quickly dispatched just another wretched Golian was proving to be its downfall. The torment it suffered was like needles of white-hot agony that shot through from its burned mouth and all the way to its brain, setting aflame everything in between. The powerful tail slapped hard into the charging Minotaur but failed to stop him.

Neither did the sharp claws that raked across its adversary's face just before the pair of horns impaled it through the chest and drove it backwards with irresistible force into a wall. Frenzied, it continued to claw desperately at the Golian, savaging his back with deep, bloody furrows, but Vurax did not feel anything except the all-consuming rage that inflamed every muscle and nerve inside of him. Roaring with fury, he continued to press the full weight of his body into pinning the monster's translucent body to the unyielding wall, driving deeper until the tips of his horns met stone. Then he began to rain powerful blows with his fists against the creature's flanks, rewarded by the sickening sound of bones cracking under the relentless attack.

The creature had long since ceased its death struggles before the Minotaur finally stopped his furious assault. He pulled his head back and snorted in ire at the corpse as it slid off his horns to slump in a nerveless mass to the mist-covered floor. While he watched, the creature's body began to fade slowly from view until it was gone altogether as if it had never existed. Apprehensively, he kicked out with his foot but felt nothing there. He did notice for the first time, however, that the mist was reacting differently to him now—it shrank and pulled away, seemingly repelled by his presence. Snorting in amusement at this unexpected development, he walked back to Kael's bed and marvelled at the level of control that he felt. Never before had he been able to allow the blood rage to overtake him while simultaneously and consciously directing his actions in a manner other than to kill whatever stood in his path. The wrath still burned inside him, barely kept in check, but an understanding had been reached on that night back in Vurgas, and its effects were now being felt, leaving him filled with exultation. Heeding the inner voice's whispers, he slowly blew his warm breath upon the centurion's face, creating a small cloud of hot air that chased away the cold's unnatural grip on his friend. The reaction was almost instant—Kael's chest rose and fell with renewed vigor and his eyes snapped open to stare at his friend's face looming over him.

"Vurax?" the Golian soldier blinked in surprise and lifted himself up onto his elbows. "What are you doing in my room and what's happened to your face? I was having the strangest dream, and..." he paused when he shivered and noticed the mist covering the entire floor of the room.

"It wasn't a dream," Vurax mused, "at least not a normal one. Do you feel alright otherwise?"

"You mean other than the fact that it's freezing in here and there's a creepy, glowing mist all over my room? Sure, I feel great," Kael quipped with annoyance.

"It's much worse than that. The palace has been breached by an assassin, possibly more. Windstrider's dead, Treeweaver is missing, and there's no sign of anyone else. I tried to wake you, but nothing seemed to work—something to do with this mist, I'm guessing. That's when some...*thing*...showed up and attacked me. We fought but I managed to kill it," Vurax related, keeping a wary eye on the chamber's open door.

Kael's jaw worked wordlessly as the veteran soldier's mind tried to process what he'd just heard. He sat up fully in bed, his mind instantly alert. "An assassin? Here?"

Vurax didn't respond, but instead bent down to pick something up from the floor. In his hands, he held the creature's strange blade, holding it out so that Kael could see it clearly. The look of shock and recognition on the other's face was more than enough to confirm Vurax's suspicions.

"You've seen one of these before, haven't you?" he asked.

"Yes," Kael swallowed before continuing. "Not as elaborate or well-made as that one, but yes, I've seen the like," he confirmed, staring fixedly at the weapon. "Vurax, that's an Urian blade."

Vurax nodded pensively. "I thought so, and this one was glowing until I killed its owner. You know, from the time this whole thing began, there was a ring of familiarity to it all, just like in that story you told me—the mists, the whispering hiss, the serpent-like creature with blue-green scales—Kael, it had to be a Saurian, and there was one in this room. It murdered Windstrider, and would have done the same to us both had I not slain it by—" he stopped himself, but not before the crimson heat in his eyes flared within the shadows of the room. He glanced quickly at Kael, but the centurion was already getting up and hadn't noticed the brief flash. The veteran shivered again when his feet touched the floor, but the mist did not rise up to touch him, still kept at bay by Vurax's presence. Moving to the bench where he had placed his armour, he began to dress himself while looking around.

"Where's the body?" Kael asked at last.

"That's just it—there isn't one."

Kael paused in the middle of tightening a buckle. "What do you mean, there isn't one? I thought you said you killed the assassin!"

"I did, I'm certain of it, but then—hey, don't give me that look like I'm imagining things. These are real enough," he pointed to the pale puncture wounds on his shoulder and side, as well as the bloody gashes on his face and back. "Kael, I swear to you, the body just disappeared in front of me. There was something odd about it too—transparent-like, as if it wasn't entirely here to begin with—and it was cold...so blood-freezing cold." Then he remembered something else and frowned. "I thought you said Ur was an unbearably hot and humid place?"

"It is," Kael stared at him, "but out of all the things that don't make any sense right now, hot or cold are the least of my concern. Vurax, the very heart of our empire has been infiltrated by the enemy. Do you have any idea what this means?"

Vurax conceded that he didn't, but they weren't going to find out by standing in the room while more of those things could be lurking about out there. When Kael cursed at the lack of a weapon, Vurax proffered the serrated Urian blade to him, but the centurion gave the weapon a sidelong glance, snorted, and shook his head. Shrugging, Vurax decided to hold onto it—it wasn't an axe, but it would have to do. Together, the two Golians left the bedchamber, carefully checking the hallway for signs of anyone, friendly or otherwise. Finding only more eerie mists and silence, they took the passage that led back in the direction of the central hub of the palace, hoping to somehow find the armoury where their weapons had been stored. When they passed Treeweaver's room, Vurax peered inside again, but the bedchamber remained unoccupied. When he moved away, he noticed that Kael had lagged and stood outside Windstrider's door, staring intently at something beyond the threshold. In alarm, Vurax watched as the mists slowly began to rise and twist around the unsuspecting centurion's legs, glowing tendrils questing upward.

"Kael!" Vurax hissed in warning. "Stay close to me, damn it," he called out, moving back toward the startled Minotaur. He reached his friend in three steps, and when he did, the mists shrank back and away from him. Though the burning blood rage inside him had simmered down to fitful embers, he maintained his connection to it, waiting to draw upon its power at a moment's notice. The centurion blinked in confusion as if seeing Vurax for the first time, and frowned at his friend's strong reaction.

"I was passing the door, glanced in, and saw the open window. I can't be sure, but I think I saw something move on the far side of the courtyard. There was a blue light, and then it was gone. Vurax, it looked like eyes," Kael looked at him, uncertainty and dread in his voice.

Had the former slave not seen the same thing and experienced those same feelings this night, he would have questioned the veteran soldier's bravery and sanity. As it were, he merely nodded and pulled him away from the opening. "I know—I saw the same thing earlier. There's definitely more than one then. Let's keep moving."

Kael nodded and followed, but not before one last glance at Windstrider's room. He felt a pang of sorrow for their fallen friend, but there would be time for mourning later. Or at least he hoped so. "What do you make of this fog? Why does it pull away from you and not me?"

Vurax knew the reason, but this wasn't the time for complicated explanations. "Maybe I smell strongly." It was a nervous attempt at levity and when it failed to elicit so much as a smile from either of them, Vurax shrugged. "I don't know. There must be some kind of magic in the mists that makes you fall asleep and prevents you from waking up no matter what—the perfect tool for an assassin.

I guess I woke up before it could get to me, and now it won't come near me for some reason. Let's count ourselves lucky that it doesn't." He didn't have to look at Kael to tell that the other wasn't entirely satisfied with this explanation, but like him, the centurion wisely decided that this was something that could wait. Staying alive was more important right now. The pair continued onward until they reached a junction in the hallway. The mists were everywhere, but nothing else moved other than the two of them. Moving slowly and with caution, it wasn't long before they found the first Golian body slumped against one wall, the pale puncture wounds near the neck revealing the manner in which the unfortunate bull had met his death.

"Praetorian guard," Kael muttered, indicating the purple cloak and imperial crest on the breastplate. "Poor bastard never even had a chance to draw his weapon," he observed as he pulled the leaf-bladed gladius from its scabbard, testing its heft. Searching around in the mist, he lifted a round steel shield from the floor and strapped it to one forearm, then nodded for them to continue onward. The further they explored down the wing that housed the living quarters of the palace, the more bodies they found. Guards, functionaries, servants, and slaves—Golians and humans alike, all slain in one gruesome fashion or another—paralyzed by venom and ultimately drained of the warmth of life. Whether eviscerated by wickedly sharp claws, or throats torn open by vicious blades—as was the case for those still in their beds—there was hardly any evidence of a struggle from nearly every individual they found. As they made these horrific discoveries, there was also no sign of the enemy and the two Golians began to despair of finding anyone else alive.

"Kael, do you think they may have attacked the city as well?" Vurax asked, stepping over yet another cold corpse in the corridor they were in.

The centurion gave him a look that revealed he'd already considered that possibility. "One problem at a time," was all he said, keeping an eye behind them while Vurax moved up to cautiously look around the corners of the next hallway junction. They were nearing their destination at last but given the sheer size of the palace and their deliberately slow pace, it felt like they'd been walking for hours. Not that either Minotaur felt that was a bad thing, as the arrival of dawn could perhaps bring some hope of dispelling this nightmare and driving away the horrors that could be lurking in every shadow. Every window they passed, however, only confirmed that daylight was still far away. The next passage they came to widened considerably, eventually opening into a wide and cavernous circular chamber that continued past two upper floors, rising to a grandiose domed ceiling painted with frescoes depicting the military victories of past emperors. Several stairways around the large rotunda rose to connect to the floors above, and a multitude of other passageways led off in different directions from where they stood. Here too—like everywhere else—the mists flowed over the floor and stairs like a cold blanket of death.

"Which way?" Vurax asked, unable to recall the exact direction they'd come from just the day before. Kael moved up to look, but he was having trouble getting his bearings as well. He'd never been here before, and the entire palace was like a small city unto itself, the multiple buildings, courtyards, and gardens covering an entire square mile, all connected by inner passages or outdoor paths, not to mention the sections of the complex that ran below ground. He was about to give it his best guess when they heard a struggle from somewhere above them, followed by a shout. So much time had passed since they'd heard anything but the sound of each other's voices that it took both of them a second to react—which was all that was needed for the body to crash to the ground a few mere paces in front of them.

"Fuck!" Vurax cursed, jumping back in surprise and anger. The broken form lying on the tiled misty marble floor belonged to a Minotaur, the horned head twisted at an unnatural angle but leaving the unfortunate's face mercifully covered by the purple cloak that was even now darkening with blood. Another shout echoed down to them, cut short by a grunt of pain. Due to the ceiling's overhang, they couldn't see what was happening above, so with a quick nod of understanding, both Vurax and Kael raced for the nearest stairway, blades at the ready. Taking the broad steps three at a time, the two Golians reached the second level of the chamber to find a scene of chaos unfolding.

A lone Praetorian guard fought valiantly to hold back two of the snake-like creatures, his movements growing more sluggish with each passing second. Vurax didn't need to see a wound to know what was happening to him. Around the struggling Golian, the forms of three more Praetorians lay on the floor in an unmoving heap, weapons and shields barely visible through the mist where they lay scattered across the tiled floor. Vurax and Kael ran to help the guard, but he was already doomed. Too weak to lift his shield in his own defense, the Praetorian stumbled to one knee, allowing one of the glowing blue blades to dart in and nearly decapitate the unfortunate Minotaur with one vicious blow. Their cruel weapons steaming in the cold air, the pair of Urian assassins turned and hissed in unison at their new opponents, fangs dripping with milky blue venom in anticipation of new prey.

"Get down!" came the shout from the shadows somewhere off to their left.

Every muscle pounding with adrenaline, Vurax and Kael reacted with pure instinct, speed, and experience gained from their respective years of combat in the legion and fighting pits of Sarmakan. Both Golians dropped to the ground at the exact same time that a figure in black robes stepped out from the darkness created by the void under the stairs leading up to the third floor. Its head and face were covered by a deep cowl, but the curving horns that jutted to either side were unmistakably Golian. A slender hand covered in white hair lifted from a wide sleeve, fingers spread wide, and the two prone Golians felt rather than saw the vortex of swirling energy that blasted outward and passed over them to crash into the two Urians. The invisible force picked up the two creatures as if they were weightless, spun heads over thrashing tails through the air, and sent both over the stone balustrade overlooking the floor below.

Not wasting any time, the two Golians jumped back to their feet. While Kael went to check to see if any of the downed Praetorians still lived, Vurax looked down onto the lower level, trying to find any sign of the creatures. He didn't see anything, but he couldn't be sure yet what that meant. The body of the Urian he'd fought had vanished when the creature died, and he wasn't convinced the fall had been sufficient to vanquish both new monsters. Every sense alert, he turned his attention to the stairs going down, prepared for any threat that might come from that direction. The Minotaur waited tensely but nothing happened. He heard talking behind him but remained focused on the slow-moving mist flowing along the stairway, watching intently as if the glowing substance could provide any clue to the enemy's whereabouts. His patience was rewarded when he perceived a disturbance in the fog, like a boat cutting swiftly through water. He barely had time to raise his weapon before there was a flash of blue eyes and the creature appeared suddenly before him, its own blade slicing downward toward his neck.

The two weapons clashed against one another and before the Urian could recover, Vurax swung hard with his free arm, delivering a ringing blow to the side of the monster's head. The Urian hissed and spat, glaring its hatred at its opponent, and lashing out with a clawed hand to rake at the Minotaur's face. Vurax winced in pain and recoiled from the creature's icy touch, taking a step backward. Hearing a commotion nearby, he risked a quick glance to the side and spotted the second Urian advancing on Kael and the robed Golian. Anger and urgency burned within him, and he surrendered control to the rage. Before the Urian could swing its weapon again, the Golian launched himself forward with a wordless snarl, tackling the snake-like body around the midsection, and toppling the creature backward with his momentum. Were it not for the fires of fury that boiled his blood, he felt as if he would have frozen solid from coming into full contact with the monster, but just as it did back in his room, the heat drove back the chill, protecting him like a full suit of armour. Unable to see the drop behind them clearly, however, the driving force of the attack sent both combatants over the top step and tumbling down the stairs in a flailing tangle of limbs.

"Use fire!" Vurax shouted before he vanished from sight.

Close by and alerted by the sudden appearance of one of the Urians at the top of the stairs, Kael looked frantically about for the second creature that he'd glimpsed right before it had faded from view. There was another stairway leading down not far from his position, but the constant motion of the shifting mists made it difficult for him to look everywhere at once for something that could apparently vanish from sight at will. Give him a solid, flesh and blood opponent on the field of battle, and the veteran centurion felt more than confident in his ability to prevail. Here, in this mist-filled world and transported backward through the years to his time spent in Ur, he felt a rising panic at reliving a nightmare that still haunted him to this day. There was no time for this, he told himself, barely maintaining control of his dread.

"Soldier, to your right," the robed figure called out behind him, the voice distinctly female.

Reacting instinctively, Kael thrust his gladius in the direction indicated and was rewarded when Golian steel connected with Urian flesh, the surprised creature becoming partially visible as the sword pierced its scaly side. Kael looked at the monster, finally able to put a face to the unseen horror that had plagued his sleep for countless nights. The Urian's breath was putrid, the foul exhalation smelling like rotting meat and washing over him when the creature spat in pain, massive jaws opened wide as it hissed. Droplets of freezing venom sprayed outward, turning the hair that covered the Minotaur's body into miniature icicles. Leaning into the attack, Kael screamed in mingled fear and anger, twisting the blade as he did so. For every friend he had lost and every soldier under his command that had been taken into that sinister, dark jungle to never be seen again, he drove the creature backward with all the strength of his pent-up guilt and rage, shouting curses as he went. But Kael's blind stab had not struck anything vital, and the resilient creature was far from finished.

A clawed hand shot down to clutch the Golian's wrist, grasping the hilt of the gladius, while the Urian's other arm delivered a vicious cut to its opponent's flank with its own blade. Kael's victorious shout turned to a howl of pain, the flesh from hand to elbow turning bluish white from the Urian's vise-like grip, while the slashing wound to his side burned briefly with freezing cold, then became numb so abruptly that he felt his strength drain from him almost instantly. His attack effectively stopped, Kael's legs buckled, and he fell to the misty floor, his weapon arm still held up by the Urian that was raising its sword again for the killing stroke. He thought he'd heard Vurax shouting something about fire, and his mind tried to summon the recollection of warmth, trying to push past how cold he felt. Would it be this cold when he was dead? He hoped not, remembering how much he enjoyed the warm sun when he was a child playing by the seashore near his home village of Balis. The memory was pleasant, and he felt sleepy, wanting to lose himself in it. He closed his eyes and waited for that warmth to envelop him.

The heat washed over him like a soothing balm, chasing away the nagging chill and bringing a contented smile to his lips. He must've fallen asleep by the water and a blustery breeze from the sea had cooled him down, leaving him shivering where he lay. But now the comforting sun had returned to drive off the cold and the bad dreams. His mother must be worried, he thought. Perhaps it was time to go home. Smiling, young Turanis Kael opened his eyes, shielding them from the bright glare overhead with one hand.

A rushing stream of angry, orange-red flames flowed like a river from the outstretched white-haired hands of the Golian Kal-dkar, roaring and crackling with furious intensity as they passed over the prone centurion to wash over the Urian assassin. The creature was instantly immolated by the inferno, the searing heat the very antithesis of the ice flowing through the veins of its translucent body. The painful hissing died down to a tormented gurgle, then its struggles ceased altogether as the incinerated remains of the Urian collapsed to the floor, the mist recoiling back from the blackened and smoking pile of ash. Kael tried to shake off the numbness he felt, rising sluggishly to his feet. He couldn't see Vurax, and when he turned to the Golian War-mage to give her a nod of thanks for saving his life, he watched in confusion as she leaned against a wall unsteadily and slowly sank to the floor. It was then he noticed that the fog was beginning to rise around him again, even while it appeared to leave the Kal-dkar alone. Without a second thought, he shook off the last vestiges of lethargy and rushed to her side, catching her before she collapsed altogether. To his relief, the mists did not follow, and he wondered silently where the hell Vurax had gotten to. While he pondered what to do next, he inspected the cut to his side, but luckily the blade had been deflected by a rib and the wound only looked worse than it was.

"Are you hurt? I don't see any blood," he asked of the bova he was supporting. He felt uncomfortable coming into physical contact with the arcane practitioner, knowing they tended to be particular about such things, but he had no alternative but to overcome his reluctance.

"Not in a manner that you'd understand," she replied, pulling the hood back to reveal her face to him.

He did not think he knew her—the Kal-dkar of Gol were notoriously private and seldom revealed their faces in public, oftentimes wearing stylized metallic masks under their cowls—but something about her voice sounded oddly familiar. "You'd be surprised. I've fought alongside members of your order before. Is it your...?" he paused, leaving the question unfinished.

"Yes," she nodded weakly, locking pale blue eyes with his, "my *etherus* is spent. If more of those things appear, I am defenseless."

Kael cursed under his breath. The vast majority of Golians would not have known what the War-mage was referring to, but his rank and years in the military had afforded him a rudimentary and necessary understanding of the mystical bond between the Kal-dkar and the source of their magic—a mysterious energy they called the *etherus*. Once depleted, the user would need considerable time to rest in order to restore their connection to that power—time they did not have. That she had allowed herself to reach this dangerously vulnerable state told him she had likely fought several more battles this night than just the one he and Vurax had stumbled upon.

"Milady," he bowed his head respectfully, "my humble life is yours. I owe you no less." The Kal-dkar did not acknowledge his pledge in any way, nor did he expect her to. In a race where haughty pride was a commonplace characteristic among its members, the War-mages of Gol took that trait to another level, serving only at the emperor's pleasure, and even then, doing so only when it served their own enigmatic aims. Though she was utterly defenseless in his hands, the centurion nevertheless accepted his low-born station and embraced his duty. "Can you stand? We need to find my companion." He didn't hear any sounds from below and was growing increasingly worried about Vurax.

"No," the War-mage refused sharply. "We cannot leave my charge. I order you to remain here and protect him."

"Your charge?" Kael looked around, stunned by this new revelation, yet seeing only the dead Praetorians nearby. "Forgive my confusion, but what in Zarvon's name are you talking about?"

When she didn't reply, he turned to look at her, seeing that her eyes had closed, and her head was slumped forward. "Hey, hey, hey, stay with me." Once again, he felt that discomfort when touching her but saw no other choice. Lifting her chin, he shook one shoulder gently but insistently. To his relief, her eyes fluttered open and she stared at him as if seeing him for the first time before recognition came back to them.

"What is it?" she sounded more than a little irritated at being roused. Her weakened body demanded that she rest, and the need to do so was becoming harder and harder to resist.

"You mentioned your 'charge'—whom are you referring to?"

Her only response was to nod feebly in the direction of the staircase from under which she'd emerged earlier. It was only a few paces away, but moving swiftly while he fought through the pain in his side, he risked the fog to explore around the corner and peered into the deep shadows that lay there. His breath caught when he saw the prone Golian lying hidden in the narrow space, his unconscious form nearly completely covered by the mist.

"Tribune Jalx," he marveled, stunned yet again. There was no mistaking the uniform and familiar features of his commanding officer from the Eighth Legion. Acting with haste, he grabbed the other unceremoniously by the ankles and pulled him back to where the Kal-dkar rested before the fog could envelop him. Thankfully, and despite her weakened condition, the glowing substance continued to avoid the War-mage, creating a small clear island on the floor where the three Golians could find temporary refuge. Despite his best attempts, Kael couldn't seem to rouse Jalx, and the centurion remembered the unnatural sleep he himself had fallen under before Vurax found him. He could only conclude that the tribune had fallen victim to the effect of the mists.

"Shit," he cursed and gave up on trying to wake the officer in exasperation, "now what do we do?"

———◆———

The voice that lived somewhere inside of Vurax shouted incessantly for him to get up. He tried to ignore it at first, thinking that it was nothing more than yet another strange dream, but the voice wouldn't let him go so easily. He did the only thing he could to silence it by opening his eyes. The Golian lay on the tiled floor at the bottom of the stairs, the Urian sword still held in one hand, the upper half of the blade snapped off where he'd driven it with all his might through the chest of the creature he'd been battling when they fell. The strange metal had gone cleanly through the monster and broken when it hit the floor beneath it. There was no sign of the Urian, of course, and that was the confirmation he needed that he'd finished off the creature this time. Then he remembered there'd been another. With a groan, he lifted his bruised body from the floor and climbed back up the stairs, the broken weapon held before him at the ready.

"Kael!" he shouted once he got to the top, looking about for his friend through the mists that still covered everything.

"Over here," came the reply. Walking to where he'd heard the voice, he found the centurion seated with his back to the wall near another set of stairs. A second Golian was slumped beside him, while a third lay on the floor nearby. He noticed Kael holding his side and frowned.

"Just a flesh wound," he dismissed the unspoken question with a wave of his hand, "and probably a cracked rib...or two," he added with a wry grin. "I'll be fine."

Vurax nodded, knowing his friend had survived much worse. "Who are these two?"

"A Kal-dkar who slew the other Urian and saved my life while doing so, and...Tribune Jalx."

"Jalx? What in blazes is he doing here? I thought the Eighth was still in Sarmakan." Vurax's frown deepened while he looked around for any sign of more Urians. They may have survived the attack, but the danger was far from gone.

"They should be. I don't understand it either. Maybe he's come back to the capital to deliver his report on the northern campaign? Typically, the Eighth's legate would do that, but it's not unusual for such a duty to be delegated to one of his subordinates," Kael offered by way of explanation, though he didn't sound convinced. "Doesn't do much to explain how he could possibly have gotten here so quickly though."

"Well, whatever the reason, it doesn't matter right now as we've got bigger problems on our hands. I assume they're alive or you would have told me otherwise by now," Vurax observed.

"Yes—the tribune seems unwounded, but he's fallen under whatever it is that these mists do to people. As for the War-mage... it's hard to explain as I barely understand it myself, but she won't be going anywhere soon."

Something stirred in Vurax's memory, and he gave the bova a sharp look. "Hold on, is this the same Kal-dkar that was in Jalx's tent with us that day we first met?"

"That's it," Kael remarked, his memory jolted by Vurax's question. "I knew her voice sounded strangely familiar."

Upon having his suspicion confirmed, Vurax took one step forward toward the War-mage, broken blade in one hand, the other clenched into a fist. Seeing the murderous red glint in the other's eyes, Kael threw one arm protectively across the unconscious bova. "Hey! What do you think you're doing?"

"You were standing a few steps away when it happened but back in Sarmakan, that bitch went poking around inside my head. Be grateful that you never have cause to find out what that feels like," Vurax spat through gritted teeth.

Kael rose from the floor to draw his eyes level with Vurax's, his gaze no less intense than his friend's. "What is wrong with you? Think carefully on what you do next, Vurax," he warned. "Beyond the fact that I wouldn't be here if it weren't for her, she is the tribune's adjunct—he who's directly responsible for your freedom, or have you forgotten that? What do you think your life will be worth when he wakes up to find out you've killed her, never mind that you will be guilty of murdering another Golian in the emperor's own home?"

"*If* he wakes up," Vurax answered evenly through his teeth. "You wouldn't be here either if it weren't for me, or have *you* forgotten that?"

The barb struck home, and Kael could not mask the hurt in his eyes. It was difficult enough for a decorated soldier such as him to acknowledge that his life was indebted to not just one, but two individuals, yet to have that thrown in his face like an accusation now was a blow to his pride more painful than any physical wound he'd ever received. The centurion accepted that Vurax's bluntness was a part of who he was, and it was a refreshing quality at times, but his incredible lack of tact continued to push away anyone who tried to get too close. Despite that, Kael had to acknowledge that though Vurax all too easily allowed emotion and violence to control his actions, his friend was right in this instance. Still, aside from the fact that he wouldn't allow himself to contemplate cold-blooded murder as a form of justice; he also felt a strange compulsion to protect this Kal-dkar at all costs. The sensation was fleeting, and it fled his awareness before he could identify clearly what its source was, leaving him uncertain of his own reasoning. He tried to pull on the thread of whatever it was that was hiding in his subconscious but could no longer find a trace of it, and the more he tried, the more he forgot what it was he was looking for until he simply stopped in confusion.

Focusing his thoughts once more, he realized he'd been staring at the unconscious mage. He lifted his gaze back to look at Vurax, ignored the other's aggressive posture, and stared directly into his eyes again, searching within those red-tinged orbs for any hint of his friend that he could latch onto and reason with. He'd seen Vurax like this before, when they'd first met on the field of battle, and if not for the multitude of fatal wounds that covered the former slave's body that day, the centurion was certain that the blow that had finally brought the raging Minotaur down would not have been effective in the least. Standing face to face with him now, Kael knew that he would be no physical match for Vurax, which is why his only chance was to try to reach through the barely restrained fury he now faced and appeal to the bull lost somewhere inside. He fought through the swirling crimson maelstrom of hatred and extended a hand to a drowning friend, pleading for him to take it before he was lost forever beneath the waves.

"Don't do this, Vurax, please..." Kael whispered, desperate to break the seemingly impenetrable wall before him. Vurax's contorted expression did not change, and while Kael felt that perhaps it was merely wishful thinking, he nevertheless imagined as the seconds slipped by that he could feel the internal struggle for control that his friend was waging.

"You don't...understand..." Vurax snarled at last through bared teeth, the words coming through slowly and with great effort, the balled fists squeezing so hard that blood dripped from where his nails cut into the palms of his hands. He fought mightily to silence the primal instinct inside of him, wracked by doubt and regret over being naive enough to think that the voice would honour the bargain they had struck that night back in the temple. What a fool he'd been, he cursed himself. Now his friend would pay the ultimate price for his own hubris. Yet, even as that realization struck him with all the weight of the guilt and shame he knew would follow his next action, he felt the fires suddenly recede and a measure of control return. The glow in his eyes dimmed, and his muscles relaxed visibly, the tension slowly ebbing from him.

Kael heaved a sigh of relief and reached out to support Vurax, who seemed suddenly unsteady on his feet. "You had me worried for a moment there, big guy," the centurion said with a grin from ear to ear.

Vurax squeezed the other's arm reassuringly and simply nodded wordlessly in acknowledgment of Kael's presence. The look he gave the centurion now was completely free of taint and held only gratitude for the other's unflagging friendship. "Thanks for being the conscience I seemingly lack at times," he grinned sheepishly. Then more seriously, "I would have gone straight through you, Kael...and then her," he stated calmly as he glanced at the Kal-dkar, chilled by the realization of what he'd been about to do. "It shames me to know that even in death, you would forgive me," he whispered.

"Yeah, I would," Kael replied without a second thought. "The emperor, on the other hand, might have taken a dim view of your actions in—"

"The emperor won't be sharing his views any time soon—he's dead," the voice stated, interrupting Kael and Vurax. They hadn't heard anyone approach and their heads snapped in the newcomer's direction, instantly recognizing Treeweaver as he stood at the top of the nearby stairs, bow held in one hand, an arrow ready at the string. The Elf managed a weak smile through the awful bruise that swelled one eye shut and the bloody gash on his face that marred his normally flawless skin. Then he collapsed to the floor in front of them. Vurax moved instinctively toward the Elf, fearful of the mists and their effect, only to notice for the first time that they were completely gone.

CHAPTER 30

Lady Jana waited patiently outside after leaving the house, raising an eyebrow in silence when she eventually saw Thurgod following Ellianna out, dressed as if he was about to face down an entire army. The Dwarf's fierce hazel eyes locked with Jana's pale blue ones, his bearded face twisting into a deep scowl of defiance, to which she responded with a knowing half-smile. That was about as much of an apology as she was going to get and she knew it, but she could be gracious in victory. She inclined her head ever-so-slightly to him when he walked past, eliciting a grudging nod of acknowledgment in return. There was an understanding between them now, and the thought was a reassuring one for Ellianna's sake.

A short distance away by the barn doors, Caeden and Darken waited, the latter looking visibly healthier than he'd had earlier that morning, though he still appeared a bit unsteady on his feet. From the waist down he still wore the black leather pants and greaves that Garick had given to him, but the upper body portion of the armour that protected his abdomen, torso, and arms lay on the ground next to him. His undershirt, torn and bloodied, was gone, and only a horse blanket covered his shoulders. His youthful face, marred by its new scar and milky eye, broke into an open grin at the sight of Ellianna. She returned the sentiment with her eyes, keenly aware that Thurgod was watching her like a hawk. Deacon Ulik's words about the boy needing more rest to fully recover came back to her, but the need to leave as soon as possible had overridden the wisdom of that course of action. Giving the human youth a critical look while walking up, Thurgod made a small adjustment to the shield and heavy pack on his back.

"It's good to see you standing, lad, but you look like you'll fall over again if so much as a fly lands on you. Pity," he remarked with a heavy sigh, "guess I'll be the one carrying this pack for most of our journey."

"*Our* journey?" Darken sounded confused, looking from Ellianna to Lady Jana and back to Thurgod. "You're coming with us?"

"You can safely bet your scrawny behind on that astute observation, young man. You didn't think I'd let my granddaughter go running off into the wilderness all alone with only a wanted miscreant like you for company—or did ya?" the Dwarf groused.

Despite himself, Darken felt the flush of heat rise to his cheeks. "Beggin' your pardon, sir, but I didn't exactly plan to be going anywhere myself. I'm ever so sorry I dragged Ellianna into this, but I'm grateful for your kindness in taking me in. As soon as we get to Briarglen, I won't be a burden to you anymore," Darken fumbled the apology, flustered with embarrassment, and wounded pride. He didn't like to be in anyone's debt, and Thurgod was cut from a very different mould than his friend Caeden, who had saved Darken's life. In speaking with the farrier and thanking him, he'd been overwhelmed by the man's humility and compassion in claiming to have only done the right thing. With the Dwarf, however, he foresaw a very difficult hill to climb ahead of him. He'd seen Thurgod around town enough times to know what the result of getting on his bad side would lead to, and his next words only served to confirm Darken's thoughts and need for caution.

"Never mind all that," Thurgod dismissed him with a wave of one large hand. "What's done is done, and the sooner we get this over with so we can all return to our lives, the better. I'm coming with you, and that's that. Besides, you've only got one good eye now, but I've got two—one each to keep on the both of you." He fixed his gaze meaningfully on Darken's face, and the youth gave him a curt nod that implied he understood the double meaning behind that statement. "Good. Alright then, we'll need to get you some new clothes to wear, preferably something that doesn't draw as much attention as whatever this is," he said, critically eyeing the black leather armour. "If you'd been wearing something made out of dependable, sturdy metal, you wouldn't have ended up like you did."

"It was a gift from my uncle, and it's coming with me," Darken bristled defensively at the comment. "But yes, I do need a new shirt," he agreed begrudgingly.

Thurgod had already turned away, however. "Any last words of wisdom before we head off on this confounded venture of yours, my lady?" he shot the barb at the priestess who stood patiently waiting nearby.

The woman displayed that selfsame wisdom by pointedly ignoring the Dwarf's tiresome needling and addressed Ellianna instead. "There is little more that I can tell you, other than to exercise great caution and to keep an open mind about what you may find. Darken is not the only one here with family in Briarglen, so when you arrive, seek out someone by the name of Stryk Aukren. Tell him that I sent you, and that you're looking for the whereabouts of Dawnhollow. He will understand and should be able to help you. Do not speak of this to anyone else, no matter how friendly or harmless they may seem to you. I will do what I can to delay any pursuit my brother may mount, but I can't promise how long that will last so do not tarry overlong on the road."

"And what of my brothers?" Darken spoke up. "You promised you'd see to them until my parents return."

"Yes, and I will fulfill that promise. I'll send someone to speak to the family where they are staying and ensure they remain safe and well-looked after. Once your uncle's identity is uncovered, any place and anyone with links to him will be watched very closely, and you must accept that when your parents arrive back in Arlingtown, they'll be facing some very difficult news and questions, but I will do my best to let them know that you are safe without alerting the Justicers to where you've gone."

"But if they question them, won't they find out that I have relatives in Briarglen and possibly look for me there?" he argued. The truth of it was that fear of his father's wrath overrode any concern of being caught by Arlingford's enforcers of the law. If it came to that, he felt he might prefer the relative safety of a dungeon cell over facing his father for everything that had happened.

"Leave that to me, but if I feel that you are no longer safe where you are, I will send word as quickly as I can. Your path lies alongside Ellianna's, so when she leaves Briarglen, I counsel you to go with her."

Thurgod let out his breath in explosive fashion. "This just keeps getting better and better," he complained with an exasperated sigh. "Looks like I need to make some arrangements for a longer absence than I thought. After I lock up, we'll stop by Oswald and Mary's home on the way out of Greenbury." When Jana looked at him questioningly, he added, "They're farmers that worked for me in the past. Good people that I would trust with my life. Their son and daughter have been farmhands here for the last two seasons, and Janik is just about this here lad's age and size, so we can get him some clothes there. They'll look after things and feed the animals while we're gone, and they won't say a word to any damn Justicer who comes knocking; you can count on that. We'll be back with plenty of time to tend to the fields, I've no doubt of that," he stated confidently.

The priestess looked at Ellianna and the girl nodded reassuringly. "Then it's settled," Jana declared before turning to the smith. "Caeden Smithson, your part ends here. Secrecy and discretion are key, so carry on to the other communities around Arlingtown today as if you are going about your normal work. Do not return to town through the Field Gate if that is not your usual route, understood?"

"Yes, my lady," Caeden replied with a mixture of relief for himself, but also anxiety over the thought of people he cared about going off into a situation where he would be unable to help any further. There was a small and rebelliously bold part of him that impulsively made him want to go with them, but there was just absolutely no way that would be practical—not with a wife and several children at home who depended on him. Whatever thoughts of adventure the dependable smith might have once entertained in his life, that particular thought had long since faded into nothing more than a quaint fantasy. "I'll drop by and check on Oswald as often as I can. Help them out with anything they need," he promised, stepping forward to clasp a rugged hand around Thurgod's thick forearm. The Dwarf heartily returned the gesture with his own grip, nodding up at his friend in silent gratitude. Caeden then gave Ellianna a tight hug. "You take care of yourself, you hear, Lil?" After she nodded, he waved to Darken and trundled off with his cart and tools.

"The world needs more men like that one," Thurgod mused, watching his friend go.

"Indeed," Jana agreed. "It is high time I left as well. I'm sure my absence has been noticed by now, but I left Deacon Ulik with instructions to tell anyone looking for me that I was not to be disturbed. Let's hope no one's been too insistent. I don't suppose you can avail yourself of horses for this journey? Briarglen is a three-day ride away, but it will take twice as long if you walk."

"A fair argument, but horses are expensive and I'm but a peasant farmer, as my lady pointed out. I've but one that pulls my plow, and she's not fit to ride anyway," the Dwarf lamented.

The priestess considered his words, then reached into the small shoulder satchel she had brought with her, drawing forth a small pouch that jingled when held. "There's a stable on the road west just outside of Arville. Do you know of it?" When the Dwarf nodded, she tossed him the pouch, which he deftly caught with one hand. "There's enough in that to get you what you need. Go in alone; keep these two out of sight. I bid you a safe journey." Jana walked up to Ellianna and held the girl's hands in hers, then leaned in close, her voice low. "When you reach your destination, keep an open mind. Whatever you tell yourself that you will find, it will not be what you expect."

"You keep saying that. What *will* I find?" Ellianna asked apprehensively. Not for the first time, she wished Jana would just speak plainly, but she knew it was futile even before the woman answered.

"Your purpose," Jana whispered. She squeezed Ellianna's hands tightly and smiled, but the girl looked forlorn and downcast at the prospect of parting. "Be strong, I know you can do this. One last thing that you must not forget," she glanced at Darken to make sure the young man was out of earshot. "Your new friend has a purpose of his own, one which I am not permitted to see. For the foreseeable future, you are clearly meant to walk together, but there may come a time when your paths will diverge. If that happens, do not fight against it, do you understand?"

She didn't, but she nodded anyway. She smiled bravely and released Jana's hands before the tears she felt coming could betray her again. If she was going to be strong, she needed to start now. "Will I see you again?"

"I think so," Jana winked, and then took her leave, walking in the direction of the city without turning back. Ellianna stared at the woman as she wound her way down the path away from the farm until Jana was out of sight when she passed beyond the trees of a small orchard. She could scarcely believe how upside down her life had turned since a mere two days ago, nor could she ignore the absolute certainty that she felt in her heart that things would only get much stranger from here. Shaking the frightful thought away, she glanced at Darken, who stood some distance away looking at her pensively. If she thought her life had taken an abrupt turn, she couldn't even imagine how much worse it was for him. Before long, she would have to make a point of asking how he was coping with all this, especially the death of his uncle. For now, he seemed altogether too calm, and that worried her.

"Alright, the house is locked up, and it's time to go. Are you ready, Lil?" Thurgod asked, joining her where she stood.

"No," she said in a small voice, but started walking anyway.

⸻⬦⸻

Baron Edmund Taffen, the second of his name after his grandfather, stood with his hands clasped behind his back while he looked up at the large painting that hung from the wall in his younger sister's private office. In the portrait, he looked much as he did now, right down to his long hair and beard, but a careful observer would note the deeper lines on his careworn face, and the dark circles under the grey eyes. One such person was Jana Morhain, who walked into the room even now, and walked silently to sit behind her desk, her eyes never leaving her brother. The man continued to look at the painting and ignored her entrance, though whether it was purposefully or because of distractedness, she could not be sure. What she did know was that Edmund's mood could be unpredictable, and his presence here in the temple was unusual, to say the least. A secular man to the core, Edmund had never had much time or inclination for religion, which meant this was a personal visit.

"Good morning, brother," Jana broke the silence. She closed the book that she'd been reading earlier in the day and carefully placed it inside one of the desk's drawers.

Edmund kept his back to her. "How do they do that, do you suppose?" he asked in his deep, low voice. The Baron of Arlingford had a measured and deliberate way of speaking that those who did not know him often mistook for a slowness of the mind. It invariably resulted in people underestimating Edmund, much to their eventual chagrin.

"How does who do what?" Jana asked, trying to sound as casual as possible. A man of sparse conversation, Edmund often took his time getting to the heart of the subject, but there was meaning and purpose behind every word he spoke on his way there, and Jana had learned long ago to listen carefully for clues.

"Artists," he replied. "Take this portrait, for example—the people depicted in it *look* like you and me, frozen in a point in time that has faded into memory, but are they still us? Or are they strangers from the past, peering back from the other side?" He paused, but she knew he wasn't waiting for an answer. "It's a window into a time that we can't return to no matter how much we may desire it. Alfred and Robert are no longer with us, yet there they stand, as if the tragedy that took them from us had never taken place. When I look at this painting, I try to think of myself and who I was in that moment, when those two men beside me were alive, but this image—and what I feel in my heart now—are two things that can never be reconciled again."

There was a wistful melancholy to his voice and manner that told Jana that this wasn't really about Alfred or Robert, but Gwendolyn instead. After his young wife's death several years ago, Edmund had never forgiven himself for his inadvertent role in the boating accident that took her life in such an untimely fashion. Haunted by the event and overwrought with pain, Edmund rose from bed one day and destroyed every existing portrait of Gwendolyn and anything else that represented her in a futile effort to assuage his guilt. The memory of her face had become too much to bear, and when that act of despair failed to change anything, Edmund had come very close to taking his own life. It was only the sudden and fateful news of his sister's pregnancy that brought him back from the brink.

"The portrait helps me reconnect with the joy that I felt when Mika was born, that's all. That Alfred and Robert are gone, sad as that may be, does not alter my remembrance of that experience. Death is an unavoidable part of life, and when Kalut summons us to his side, even Anval must bow to fate," she replied. It was a delicate subject as always, one she was wary of engaging in with Edmund given the memories it dredged up for him, but he'd brought up the subject, and she was not one to shy from stating her opinion. Even after all this time, she still clung to the hope that her brother would one day emerge from the dark room where he'd placed his grieving soul and emerge back into light and happiness once more.

"Ah yes, faith... how I sometimes envy the comfort that it brings you at times like this, dear sister." Edmund turned slowly and looked intently at her face. There was something hard in his eyes that she did not like, but she smiled pleasantly, nevertheless. "It's 'afternoon', by the way," he remarked.

"I'm sorry?" she asked, nonplussed.

"When you walked in, you said 'good morning'. It's well past midday."

"I must've lost track of time."

"That's not like you. What consumed your attention so? I hear tell you were seen in Greenbury today. That's very unusual."

"I was tending to a patient, if you must know."

He arched both of his bushy eyebrows, making a show of surprise. "A patient? You're the High Priestess of Anval in all of Arlingford. Don't you have others to perform such menial tasks for you?"

"Saving a life is never menial, Edmund. There was a boy—a farm-hand—that suffered a grievous injury while working at daybreak. I sent Deacon Ulik to see to him, but the matter proved more dire than we'd anticipated so he requested my help. I'm happy to say the boy will make a full recovery," she said, never once taking her eyes off his. She knew that Edmund was parsing through her words, searching for any sign of deception. A line creased his forehead, and he pursed his lips in thought.

"You're right, of course, a life is never trivial. Four of them were lost last night, in fact, including that of one of our own family," he stated, eerily echoing her own words to Ellianna earlier.

"I'm keenly aware of that. I'm on my way to see Anika and her children as soon as I'm done speaking with you, but I fail to see how any of that has anything to do with what I was doing today," she shot back, unable to keep the rising irritation from her voice.

"I'm simply curious as to whether you heard or saw anything unusual during your travels through town today—anything that can aid in the in-vestigation, perhaps?"

"No, nothing. Well, not unless you count all the Justicers out on the streets. Have they discovered anything?" She did her best to quell her annoy-ance, keenly aware that any further agitation on her part would only serve to make her brother suspicious.

"Yes, as a matter of fact. The identity of the dead man in Giordy's house is one Garick Valhik, a small-time scoundrel and gambler well known to some of my men. The killer, however—the one that got away—is his nephew, apparently. Goes by the name of Darken, I was told," he said, almost too casually for her liking when speaking about such a serious matter. It was becoming abundantly clear that Edmund knew more than he was letting on, but whether it had anything to do with her involvement, she couldn't be sure yet. She returned his stare with a blank expression. If he was waiting for a flicker of recognition at the mention of the name, she gave him none.

"Good, then I'm sure Lord Justice Kalder has the matter well in hand and this criminal will be caught in no time," Jana said. "If there's nothing more I can do for you, Edmund, I really need to get on with my day. As you said, more time has already gotten away from me than I thought."

Edmund looked at her through narrow eyes, stroked his beard with one hand, and nodded his assent, his questions over. He turned to leave, his boots making a loud sound on the polished floor tiles. When he got to the door, he stopped. "There's one last thing," he said without turning. "Last night, during the celebration, it was you that knew something was wrong and had me send the Justicers to the Khelen's home, but you still haven't told me how you knew."

She stared at his back. "The Claw of Rauvir was stolen. I thought you knew that already."

"I do. It doesn't answer my question."

"The ward that protected it was mine. I placed it there after Braydon gifted the Claw to Giordy and Anika on their wedding day."

"A divine ward? I see. In that case, I think it follows that this is no ordinary thief that we're after, but one with the ability to somehow steal one of the most well-protected objects in the Shining Crescent."

"And?"

"And that means your knowledge of how this could be done is far greater than Lord Justice Kalder's, which makes you a far better candidate to catch this thief, don't you think? I'd like for you to meet with her by tomorrow and get this investigation under way. She's already been told to expect you."

Stunned by this pronouncement, she was unable to reply before he opened the door and left, his echoing footsteps fading down the hallway. What was her brother trying to do, and how much did he know? He wasn't one to play games, and the safety of the citizens under his protection was his one paramount concern, so nothing unusual there. On the surface, the conversation they'd just had was well in line with that, so why was she filled with unease after his departure? Was he placing her in charge of solving this crime as some kind of loyalty test? The thought made her bristle inwardly with not only resentment and irritation, but also frustration over knowing she couldn't simply tell Edmund the truth. She knew her brother better than anyone else alive, and men like him were unyielding when it came to challenging their perception and conviction over matters concerning their judgment and the enforcement of the law.

It was critical to note that he hadn't given her an express order but more of an implied suggestion for her to follow, but it made no difference—she knew exactly what he expected of her, and now she had to contend with the awkward position he'd placed her in. Not only that, if she found her brother difficult to deal with at times, he was a complete joy compared to the dour and humourless Lord Kalder, and the thought of assisting an investigation under the woman's lead was beyond even her considerable limits of patience and tolerance. She leaned back in her chair, steepled her fingers against her lips, and was trying to figure a way out of this mess when it suddenly dawned on her that her brother had given her a gift in disguise. During her walk back, she'd already been trying to formulate a plan to throw the Justicers off Ellianna's and Darken's scent long enough for them to get far enough from Arlingtown, but now that she was directly involved in the search for the killer, she was in the perfect position to directly influence and even stymie the efforts altogether. Yes, this might just work, she smiled to herself, but she would need to be extra careful. Before she could allow any of that to begin to occupy her time though, she had some important reading to finish—research that had been interrupted by Ellianna that morning, and again by Edmund just minutes ago.

She opened the drawer and pulled out the same book she'd put away earlier. It was more of an archive than a book, to be precise, and it contained detailed information on a series of events that had taken place long ago. Opening the page to where she'd left off, she ran one finger down to the entry with a date nearly three centuries past. Next to the number was the word 'Dawnhollow', but she skipped most of the account that followed, having confirmed all the details already that morning. The words on the page had been written by a predecessor of hers, the head of the Arlingtown church in those bygone days. The name of the man was not important, only the decisions he'd had to make, and the account of his observations and reasoning for his actions. Given what she'd read, she couldn't say she would have done any differently, even if she felt her heart would have broken, just as this man's had if his words were a fair indication of his emotional state at the time.

She scanned further down, looking for what she sought—the one particular family name among others that she'd read long ago when studying the history of the barony and this most tragic of footnotes. Her memory hadn't played tricks on her, though she found that a part of herself still held onto the slim hope that perhaps it had. There it was, right at the top of the list, owing to the fact that the individual to whom it belonged was noted by the priest as being the first to show signs of the lethal sickness that had struck down every inhabitant of Dawnhollow, without exception.

Artem Delaris, adult male – deceased
- Ranel Delaris, adult female, wife – deceased
- Ellianna Delaris, young female, daughter – deceased

'Without exception,' Jana mouthed the words silently. Despite the warmth of the high sun outside, she felt a shiver run down her spine and pulled the sides of her robe tighter around her body. For the first time since meeting Ellianna, she hoped she hadn't made a mistake in sending the girl to Dawnhollow, but she had a lot of questions, and she was certain now that they would only be found there.

CHAPTER 31

THE HOURS AND MINUTES passed without any awareness of the inexorable progress of time other than the realization that, for Flynn, sleep simply wouldn't come. It was the last night of the year, but it felt just like any other when he lay awake in bed staring at the ceiling of his room. Between the Test, the princess's announcement, and the presence of the mage upstairs, the events of that day had done plenty to overstimulate his mind to the point that allowing himself to simply drift off seemed like a very remote possibility just then. Worse, the more he tried to make any sense out of it all, the more frustrated he grew, which in turn led to even more restlessness. As if in response to his dark mood, his hand itched horribly, but he resisted the urge to scratch at it, almost as if by doing so, he was denying the hated limb the attention it craved. He knew he was being silly, but he didn't care. He shifted in bed to make himself more comfortable and pondered whether he should read something to distract himself. *The Legend of Starfall* was safely tucked into a hole he'd cut into the back of his mattress, but his eyes drifted on impulse to the dimly lit small pile of books on the table in the middle of the room. It was then that he noticed something very odd by the glow of the lamp he'd left on.

The door to his room was almost at the edge of the light, but something didn't seem right about it. When he finally figured out what was different, he thought for sure the shadows must be playing tricks on him, because it looked for all the world like the door was slightly ajar. He sat up immediately, excitement and fear sending a chill down his spine. In the days since this room had become his home to all intents and purposes, the routine each evening had always been the same. Father Lorimer would spend some time with him before supper to make sure he was continuing to recover from his ordeal, check up on his readings, and then he would leave just before Carlo arrived with his meal. The Initiate never failed to lock the door after he left, and Flynn wouldn't see either of them until the next morning, when he was allowed to eat breakfast with both of them upstairs and then got to spend a little time outside in the back garden under Carlo's watchful eye. But tonight, he had an unexplainable feeling that something very unusual was going on.

Never taking his eyes off the door—as if by doing so he would find it closed when he looked again—Flynn pulled his clothes on and slipped into his shoes. When he stood up, he stopped before taking a step. Why had he gotten dressed, he thought to himself. What exactly was he planning on doing? He was suddenly reminded of the night when he'd snuck out of the dormitory to go down to the crypt beneath the cathedral. He'd felt strangely drawn to the place, almost like a form of subconscious compulsion had driven him to do something foolish and potentially dangerous, and here he was now, experiencing the same thing. Except this time, he wasn't sure what his destination would be other than he wanted to be out of his room at any cost. Maybe he could use the broken window in the dormitory to go pay his friends a visit in the middle of the night. He would dearly love to be able to say goodbye to Georgie before the lad was taken away in the morning to begin his training. Yes, he resolved, that's what he would do. He took his first step and then stopped again, hesitating. What if it was a test of some kind? What if Father Lorimer was waiting on the other side to scold him about the errors of his ways, or worse, a trap set up by Carlo to teach him a harsh lesson?

'Flynn'

All the colour drained from his face, and he felt his knees grow weak when he heard that familiar spectral voice whispering his name like a mournful sigh. The faint sound had barely dissipated in the air when the door very slowly opened all the way into the room, the faint light from the table lamp spilling out to reveal nothing and no one in the shadows that beckoned beyond. At the same time, he felt a tangible brush of icy air caress his face, gently disturbing a few strands of hair on his head on its way past him. The strength of the breeze—if that's what it was—would hardly have been sufficient to push the door open, but the biggest question on his mind was where had it come from? He was underground, and there were no doors to the outside in the depths of the cellar. He felt far less certain now that this was a good idea, and he did not relish the thought of repeating the experience he'd had down in the crypt, whatever that had been. In the weeks since that had happened, he'd tried to think of a way of both uncovering the mystery of Brother Edward's past, and of exploring the old tower to satisfy his curiosity about Father Mateo. However, with the arrival of Yule and everything else that had occurred since, he hadn't had any time to pursue either one of those plans. Yet now that he'd heard that voice, he wondered if he wasn't being given an opportunity to do so.

'Flynn', the darkness beyond the open door called insistently to him.

Flynn had no recollection of how he'd gotten to the threshold of the room, but it seems he'd found the courage to somehow place one foot in front of the other to find himself before the doorway. He glanced back into the room and at the lamp sitting on the table, but decided against going back to retrieve it. He didn't know what unknown horrors from beyond the grave awaited him in the dark, but it was the real fear of those that were living that he could be sure of. If he brought the light with him, it would easily give him away to Father Lorimer or Carlo if they were about, and he simply couldn't risk that. Taking a deep breath to summon more of that courage that had gotten him this far, he stepped outside the room and closed the door behind him, plunging his surroundings into impenetrable gloom. With its collection of alcoves, wooden racks, and ancient casks, the confines of the large cellar were almost labyrinthine, so he waited for his eyes to adjust to the darkness before proceeding. He'd travelled this path enough times to know the location of the pillars that supported the low ceiling above, so he reached out tentatively to find the first one to his left, and then carefully measured his steps to find the next one, and so on until he reached the stairway. Thankfully, nothing living or otherwise impeded his progress, a fact that filled him with relief and renewed confidence.

Looking up the short flight of steps to the closed door at the top, Flynn could make out a sliver of light coming through underneath. Someone was still up at this late hour then, and not for the first time, he reconsidered what he was doing. It wasn't too late to go back, crawl in under his blanket, and pretend this was all just a very weird dream. The thought wasn't even complete when he felt his foot on the first step, followed by the next. There was that disturbing sensation again, as if something—or someone—was guiding his steps, but he paid it no heed. Keeping one hand on the wall to help prevent a noisy misstep, he slowly and silently crept his way up to the doorway and paused to listen. Though very faint, he could hear voices, but through the thick wood, it was difficult to ascertain how distant they might be. The only way to find out was to try and open the door, so he placed one hand on the handle and quietly asked Janus that it not be locked. He didn't miss the irony of asking the God of Light for a little help while he sulked in the shadows, but perhaps others of his divine siblings were also looking out for him that night because the handle turned without resistance. Carefully, he opened the door a crack to have a better listen.

He could make out a man and a woman's voice engaged in conversation, though they were too far away for him to make out what was being said. He was certain one of the voices was Father Lorimer, and the other must surely belong to the king's Kal-dkar. She was still here then? It didn't matter, he thought. What was important was that there be no one present in the kitchen as he slowly opened the door further to take a careful look around. As he'd hoped, the room was brightly lit but empty. Without further hesitation and not wishing to tempt his luck by waiting needlessly, he pushed the door open a bit more—just enough to slide his body through. Keeping low to the tiled floor, he slunk his way down one side of a long table and continued to the back door that led to the yard behind the house. All the while, he kept one wary eye on the open archway that connected the kitchen to the rest of the house. He also kept his ears open to try and detect any change in the voices, or more specifically, any indication that they might have stopped altogether, but the conversation continued, uninterrupted, and so did he.

His good fortune held out when he found that the back door was unlocked as well. Safely tucked in behind the walls of the orphanage as they were, Flynn supposed there wasn't much call to keep doors locked around here, unless it was his room of course, or the dormitory itself to prevent wayward children from wandering out in the middle of the night. How quickly and easily adults forgot how resourceful children could be, he chuckled inwardly. Bolstered by that thought and his success so far, he snuck outside and quietly closed the door behind him. The evening air was unusually chill tonight and he instantly regretted not putting something a little thicker on. He wasn't about to go back though, so he dashed across the carefully tended grass and trimmed hedges that adorned the private garden behind the headmaster's house and made for the small gate. He looked around first to make sure no one was out and about on the orphanage grounds, and when he didn't see anyone, he slipped out, pausing to relish his victorious freedom.

The feeling of elation was short-lived when he realized he had no clear destination in mind. He'd been so concerned with getting out that he hadn't really given any thought as to how to accomplish what he'd told himself he was going to do. Sneaking into the dormitory carried a high risk of being caught by the Initiate doing his rounds, and he needed to avoid that at all costs. Maybe he'd still get a chance to say goodbye to Georgie in the morning if he asked nicely and Father Lorimer was feeling kind, he wondered. Setting that idea aside for now, he recalled his thoughts before he'd left his room, but he hadn't the faintest notion of how to pursue either of those other threads. Going back to the crypt didn't make sense, and other than trying to somehow get into Brother Edward's old cell to search for clues about the priest's life, he didn't know where to begin with that. He'd always meant to ask Brother Owen for help in that endeavour, but that avenue was closed off to him now. That left the tower, but returning to his earlier musing about locked doors, he was suddenly reminded that the tower was locked up as well, and that was one barrier he couldn't hope to get through so easily without a key—a key that was no doubt located somewhere in the house he'd just left. He nearly despaired then, cursing himself for foolishly coming out here without any kind of a concrete plan. What the hell was he thinking, and just how far did he think he could push this nonsense before he got caught and made things worse for himself than they already were?

'Flynn'

Colder than the night air, he felt the glacial breeze pass over and through him again, and the direction it flowed from was unmistakable—its jagged shape outlined clearly in the soft moonlight of Temeros, the ruined tower rose like a contorted claw, torturously reaching to the heavens.

Something was waiting for him inside—he could feel it with every fibre of his being. Brother Owen's warning aside, and despite his firm belief that Elias hadn't lied to him about his ordeal inside the ruin, the compulsion he'd felt since his arrival at the orphanage to explore the place had grown stronger than his fear of what he might find. He couldn't be sure that the apparition he'd seen in the crypt was real, but if it was, and it had wanted to harm him, surely it would have done so at the time, no? He half expected a whispered answer to come drifting in the air, but when it didn't, he decided there was only one way to answer this mystery once and for all. A small yet loud part of his consciousness yelled at him to turn back, but he doggedly ignored it, shoving it somewhere deep down inside his head until he could no longer hear its desperate warnings. Reaching the tower door, he placed his gloved hand on it with a strange sense of confidence. Unsurprisingly, he found it unlocked as well, further dispelling any remaining notions of coincidence he might have had. His path was clear, and it no longer mattered to him whether something had guided his steps here, or whether he'd come of his own accord—at this point, the two possibilities had simply merged to provide the one result he desired. Dismissing one last, lingering hesitation, he pushed the old iron door open and stepped inside.

The ground floor of the old tower was faintly illuminated here and there by Temeros, whose pale glow shone down through the broken rafters and cracked stone above Flynn's head, casting an eerie, reddish sheen over everything it touched. Motes of dust drifted lazily in the air, passing in and out of the soft beams of moonlight, before settling on whatever they encountered, including him. He glanced around at what had once been a large, circular chamber, though a large portion of it was now inaccessible due to being choked with rubble and debris from the upper floors. A crumbling staircase wound up one wall to his right, several of the stone steps missing before ending at a landing that led to what remained of the floor of the chamber above. He counted at least one more level beyond that before he could catch a glimpse of the very top of the structure open to the night sky, yet it was to the centre of the area he was in that his attention was drawn.

There, a huge, twisted frame of rusted iron protruded through the shattered tilework of the chamber floor, the broken gears and bent levers hinting at the strange object's mechanical nature. Trapped inside that metal prison and partially sunk into the cellar below was a long, tapered brass cylinder that leaned at an angle where it had fallen from its original perch at the top of the tower. When it crashed to the bottom, the enormous mechanism and its housing had torn a path of destruction through the structure before reaching its final resting place. Though he'd never seen anything like it before, Flynn knew instantly what this was.

"Father Mateo's telescope," he whispered in awe.

He couldn't fathom the level of skill and knowledge necessary to craft such a device, but from what he'd read in his textbooks about the intriguing study of the skies, he couldn't help but feel a pang of regret and dismay that a tool so wondrous as this had been simply left here in ruin to rust and decay until the end of time. He wondered if perhaps it was simply too damaged to repair, or worse, no one cared enough to try? He walked up and reached through the bent supporting frame to run the fingers of his undamaged hand down the telescope's surface. The polished yellow metal felt smooth and cool to the touch, and he briefly closed his eyes, trying to imagine what the last person to use this instrument had seen before he died. Everything was dark while he tried to summon up some fanciful vision from the depths of his imagination, and then a white flash of blinding light washed over his mind's eye with such violent intensity that he gasped and staggered back in surprise. A chunk of masonry debris on the floor hit the back of his heel and he lost his balance, turning the stumble into a fall. He got a small scrape on his hand from a sharp piece of flagstone tile for his misfortune, but mostly he was just dazed and left blinking furiously from the aftereffect of that light.

'Flynn'

The boy froze when he heard the whisper again, certain that its source was nearby. As if to confirm the uncanny sensation, he felt that cold draft of air again, this time from his left. He looked in that direction, and he saw there—barely visible in a pool of darkness cast by the shadow of the telescope—the outline of a trapdoor in the floor. That had to be the way down to the cellar, he reasoned. The place where Peter and Dario had thrown Elias. He tried not to dwell on the irony of willingly going into a place where his friend had suffered a frightening, traumatic experience, but he felt he was very close to getting some kind of an answer. He only wished he knew what the question was. Not bothering to stand up, he crawled the short distance to the trapdoor on hands and knees, placed his hands around the large metal pull-ring, and lifted. The ironbound wood of the trapdoor showed the ravages of time, but he managed to open it without too much effort, wincing when the old hinges groaned in protest. Well, it's not as if whatever awaited him below didn't already know he was here, he mused. He brought his face down to the opening to peer into the blackness below and was greeted by the dank odour of mildew and decay. He could barely make out the top step of the old ladder that Elias had mentioned, and it looked decrepit indeed, but if it had held his friend's weight just a few short years ago, he was willing to risk and see if it would hold his.

Flynn's instinct proved correct, and slowly and carefully testing each step as he went, he made it down to the bottom. Almost no moonlight reached this far, thus he couldn't see a thing, but confident he'd retained his bearings, he turned and walked cautiously in the direction of where the bottom portion of the fallen telescope would be, holding his hands out in front of him so that he wouldn't walk headlong into it. Seconds later, he was rewarded by the feel of solid metal ahead, so he stopped and turned to face the silent gloom, waiting for something to happen. He knew that he should be terrified by all accounts, but strangely, he wasn't. He didn't know why he lacked fear, only that somehow, he knew he was meant to be here, and perhaps that was the only reason he needed. He continued to wait, listening intently to the silence all around him for any clue as to what to do, but heard nothing but the sound of his own breathing. So dark and still was the world around him that he wondered for an instant if all of this wasn't just happening inside of his own mind. What if he was simply asleep back in his bed in Father Lorimer's house, having the strangest, most vivid dream ever?

"I'm here," he called into the void, hoping that the sound of his voice would either elicit a response of some sort, or cause him to wake up if he was indeed dreaming.

The temperature of the already cool air in the cellar dropped sharply and noticeably, and he braced himself for what might happen next. The terror in Elias' voice as he'd told him his story and shown him the mark on his shoulder came rushing back to him in a flood of anxiety and fear, forcefully chasing away the eerie calm he'd felt earlier. When a dim spot of light appeared and a spectral form began to take shape just a few paces away from him, he felt his knees grow weak, and his entire body began to shake uncontrollably. Transfixed and unable to make his feet move, he watched the apparition coalesce slowly into the world of the living with a mixture of fascination and dread. The ghostly entity was identical in every way to the one he'd seen in the tomb below the cathedral, right down to the soft glow of bluish luminescence that emanated from the sleeves and hood. Fighting to regain his courage, he forced his mouth to work.

"Father Mateo?" he managed to gasp.

'Flynn' came the now-familiar reply, carried in the air as if from a hundred different directions all at once. Even in the presence of the spectre, the voice sounded hollow and slightly distorted, as if it had travelled an incredible distance before reaching his ears. He took the response as an acknowledgment to his question, confirming his suspicion that this was indeed the spirit of the astronomer priest

that had perished in this very tower nearly a century ago. When the ghost of Father Mateo didn't move or say anything else, he took a deep breath to calm his nerves and braved another query.

"What is it you want from me?" he asked, phrasing the words in what he hoped sounded like a plea, not a demand.

Though the air was perfectly still within the confines of the tower's basement, the spectre's frayed robes whipped about as if perpetually caught in a gust of otherworldly wind. In a repeat of the previous time Flynn had witnessed the ghost manifest itself, the figure raised one arm, a translucent finger pointing directly at him like an accusation. Puzzled, he frowned and tried to decipher the meaning of the gesture, only to come to the sudden realization that it wasn't him the phantom was indicating, but what was behind him. At least that's what his intuition told him. Testing his theory, he turned slightly to brush the telescope's surface with his fingers, bracing himself for another disturbing flash like before. Nothing happened.

"This? Is this why I'm here?" He was gratified to see the shrouded head nod in acquiescence, but wondered if there was a way that they could communicate better. The spirit seemed capable of uttering his name in some fashion, so why not say more? "Is there a way that you can tell me or show me what you want?"

Convinced now that the ghost of the priest meant him no harm, he remained nevertheless conscious of the passage of time, and that dawn could very well come before he was back in his bed. Though he had hoped for a reaction, he was still startled when the phantom drifted toward him, closing the short distance between them in the blink of an eye. He flinched fearfully and steeled himself for the icy touch of the spectre's hands on his flesh, but instead, Father Mateo stopped a mere handsbreadth away from him and pointed at the ground near the base of the telescope. Recovering from his fright, Flynn looked down to where the stone floor was bathed in the pale azure light pulsing softly from the spirit. The ancient tiles were cracked and heaved from the tremendous impact of the telescope and mixed with the shattered pieces of stonework was a large pile of what he took to be dust at first. Not understanding what he was being shown, he looked back at Father Mateo and shrugged in confusion. The spectre responded by hovering lower and pointing more forcefully at the dust.

Flynn frowned again and pursed his lips, thinking he was missing something obvious. He tried to recollect everything he'd heard about Father Mateo, the tower, and the night when the priest had died. The vision of the flash of blinding light he'd experienced earlier, coupled with Brother Owen's voice describing how the priest's body had never been found—those had to be the clues he needed to solve this mystery.

"Is that...you?" he asked, hesitantly.

The ghostly head under the hood nodded in confirmation. Because Flynn couldn't think of anything else to do, he instinctively reached down with his hand and scooped up a handful of what he now knew to be ashes. If he'd been expecting something to happen, he was disappointed when nothing did, but this time he knew what he'd done wrong without having to look back at the spectre. Swallowing hard, he reluctantly removed the glove from his other hand, the hated skull-like mark on his flesh catching the ethereal light of the phantom in a sinister way that sent a shiver down his spine. Then he poured the ashes of what had once been Father Mateo's body onto the scar and closed his hand into a fist, ready for anything.

'*At last.*' It was Father Mateo's voice again. This time it sounded a little clearer and much closer but tinged with a distinct echo of human emotion that evinced genuine relief.

"Why did you bring me here?" Flynn asked, curiosity and excitement returning with full force. He couldn't wait for a chance to tell his friends that he'd spoken with an actual ghost.

'*The impulse to come here was your own. I merely did what I could to facilitate that desire,*' the spirit of Father Mateo uttered, the words fading in and out as if caught in the same wind that buffeted the ghost's ethereal form.

"If you say so... but I still don't understand why—why have you picked *me* to speak to? Is there something you want me to do?" he was full of questions and had to stop himself there. He didn't know how long the spirit would remain tangible, and he wanted to find out as much as he could before it departed like before. He waited expectantly, deeply unsure of what he would hear.

'*I wish to make a bargain with you, Flynn. I offer you knowledge in exchange for a chance at the eternal rest I have long been denied,*' the ghost declared. '*Do you agree to this? Know that if you do, your soul will be bound to your promise. Break it, and your fate will be as mine.*'

Flynn was taken aback by this, even though he sensed no threat or menace in the spirit's words. It was a mere statement of fact, and the risk was being laid out for him in advance. Before he could make such a momentous decision, however, he needed to know a little more. He dearly wished he could ask Brother Owen for advice first, then laughed inwardly when he pictured the absurdity of that imaginary conversation. He didn't need his sensible friend to be present to know what he would hear from him.

"What sort of knowledge? What could you possibly want me to know that I'd chance ending up like you if I fail in your task?" Flynn asked, trying to press his one advantage. It was clear the spirit needed his help with something, and it had waited nearly a hundred years for this very occasion. Perhaps it had tried before, like the time when Elias had encountered the ghost, but there was some strange fate at work here that had brought him before the spirit this night, and he wanted to know why. That was the burgeoning adult inside of him talking. Then there was the teenage boy part of him that marvelled briefly at the prospect of becoming a roaming phantom, able to go places and see things without anyone knowing, but the exciting thought was fleeting. There was a palpable sadness and melancholic longing that permeated his being whilst in the presence of the ghost, and this did not seem like an existence—if it could be called that—that he should envy. If anything, it felt like an awful curse.

'My request of you is this—bring my remains to the tomb where I was meant to lay, so that I may find peace and fully cross into the Beyond. For that simple act of kindness and mercy, I will show you what I saw in the last moments of my life,' Father Mateo's spectre implored.

"You mean when you looked through this? Before the lightning struck?" Flynn asked, gesturing to the telescope. The apparition merely nodded in reply. "I don't understand. Why is that important?"

'Much will be made clear once you see with your own eyes. I cannot influence the crucial decision I foresee you will one day have to make, other than to prepare you with the truth now.'

Flynn sighed in exasperation. The spirit was being deliberately vague for reasons he couldn't unravel, and this whole idea was making him uncomfortable. What was being asked of him did not seem difficult—he'd stood before Father Mateo's tomb once before, so he felt confident in his ability to retrace his steps and return there—provided he could get out of his room unnoticed again, but one problem at a time. So, what then was holding him back? Why did he have the ominous feeling that if he agreed, he would be setting his foot down upon a road from which he would never be able to step out of again? What future decision of his could be so important to merit something like this extraordinarily strange and disturbing encounter? He could have sworn he hadn't spoken those questions out loud, but the spirit answered them anyway.

'Twice now you have been marked by the gods. When you feel the third and final brush of their touch, you will know that your destiny is upon you. This is not something you can avoid, Flynn, no matter how hard you try. The choice before you is whether you wish to learn the truth that has been kept from us all, or whether you allow ignorance's shroud to veil your eyes until the end.'

Truth. There was that word again. What was this frustratingly cryptic apparition on about? And marked twice? By the gods? Trembling, Flynn looked at the hand clutching Father Mateo's ashes then lifted it in front of the spectre's shrouded face.

"You're saying *they* did this? Twice? But why? And when was the first time?" The fear he'd felt before in being in the presence of a restless soul from beyond the grave had been replaced by a nameless dread vastly more profound, and infinitely more frightening. He wished fervently and hopelessly that he'd remained in bed this night and just ignored the open door and his thrice-cursed impulse to go poking his nose into places and things where he shouldn't. In his mind, he could hear Brother Owen's admonishing voice telling him so.

'At the time of your birth, and though you cannot see that mark, it is plainly visible to my sight. As to why? They have placed a special task upon you—one the effects of which are only just now beginning to be felt. What you are is what they have made you,' was the enigmatic explanation.

"What I am?" he whispered to himself. This time, there was no response from the ghost.

Though he'd heard the words, their meaning and portent were far beyond his capacity to comprehend. He was a thirteen-year-old orphan boy, with simple dreams and modest aspirations of one day leaving this place, having a family once again, and maybe, just maybe, becoming a knight in the service of the king. Perhaps acceding to the spirit's request would help clear things up somewhat? Whatever this 'truth' was that it spoke of, he'd reached the point in his mind now where he was becoming numb and oddly indifferent to the weight of these stunning revelations. What did he have to lose by agreeing? Certainly not his sanity, as that seemed to have fled as far away as possible when this surreal conversation had begun. Or maybe there was still a chance he would wake up in his bed and have a good laugh at the utterly ridiculous meanderings of his subconscious.

"Show me."

As if it had expected no other answer, the spectre reached with one translucent hand to grasp Flynn's own. The boy tensed and flinched, anticipating the freezing cold touch of the grave upon his flesh, but there was only a mild discomfort that he found surprisingly tolerable. The ghostly grip did not feel altogether solid, but rather like a gentle yet insistent pressure that guided his hand unmistakably toward the telescope. Careful not to let go of the ashes, he touched the instrument's metallic surface and closed his eyes, ready for anything.

The vision was blurry and unfocused at first, not unlike what one experiences sometimes when slowly opening their eyes in the morning to shake off the last vestiges of a deep sleep. All that he could perceive at first was that he was looking at something that was a pale crimson in colour, though not uniformly so. Here and there, he could detect slight variations in the colour—dark patches and irregular lines that reminded him of wrinkles and stains on a piece of fabric. A twist of a dial, a push on a lever, and the image became sharper and nitid, everything within the circular confines of his viewing field popping into view with a clarity that he found both startling in its intensity, and astonishing in its detail. Tall mountains! Deep valleys! Endless plains! It was a world not unlike his own in many respects—as he'd hoped to prove—but also one where there was no sign of life that he could discern. Devoid of any forests, rivers, lakes, or oceans, the red landscape was barren and empty.

The newly installed and marvellous etherus-infused lens, representing the culmination of his painstaking research, was showing him the surface of Temeros in a way that he'd never thought possible to witness, but his disappointment at finding it so desolate in appearance was difficult to accept. There had to be something there, he told himself again, or the purpose of his life's work would all be for nothing. At the turn of a crank, the image began to move slowly to one side in what became an increasingly fruitless search for proof that his long-held belief was correct. Instead, what he found shook him down to the very foundations of his soul. What he took at first to be yet another deep crevasse, quickly grew in width and depth so great that he could not see the far side, or where it began and stopped. It was when he saw the first pinpoints of light twinkling in what he mistook for the dark depths of that vast canyon that he realized with a jolt that they were stars. But how was this possible?

His hand pulled frantically on the lever, a lump of anxiety and confusion forming in his throat. The image became blurry once more as everything shrank in size until the very outer edges of Temeros came into view. The dial turned, and the focus returned, bringing with it the most incredible and unexpected thing he had ever seen. The largest of Akar's three moons—the one called the Dragon's Eye of Temeros in honour of the mythical beast after which it was named—was no longer whole. Instead of the perfect globe that he should be seeing, the giant red jewel of the night sky was shattered in twain, its two cracked halves separated by a floating belt of slowly tumbling rubble that filled the starlit void between them. His mind struggled to comprehend what he was seeing because it simply made absolutely no sense. First, what he needed to confirm was whether he'd somehow missed the fact that he'd gone quite insane. To that end, he did the only thing he could think of and tore himself away from the telescope's viewing apparatus to stare upward with his naked eye. There, through the glass dome that formed the roof of the tower's observatory, Temeros floated in the sky as it always had since the dawn of time, when the first Elves, Dwarves, and men to walk Akar had lifted their eyes up in wonder and awe at the majesty of its nocturnal presence and everlasting light.

A single, perfect orb. Whole and unmarred.

Had he made an error of some kind in his work? Was the lens he'd laboured so long to craft and perfect defective in some way? Worse—had he misinterpreted the strange and prophetic dream he'd received all those years ago—the one that had turned his eyes forever upward in search of answers? Or perhaps this was exactly what he was supposed to see? He looked through the telescope again and saw the same thing he'd witnessed just now. Akar's largest moon was—to put it in the simplest terms he could conceive—broken. What incredible force or power could have caused such a thing, and when had it happened, were the next questions that immediately *sprang to mind, but there was more. Why was this hidden from mortal eyes? Was this the work of the gods?*

The thought of the divine immortals reminded him of his original purpose here tonight. The image of the ball of fire streaking across the red, unfamiliar horizon had been seared into his memory since the time he'd been a young man, fresh from having taken his first vows of service to the glory of Janus. He was convinced that the strange landscape had been Temeros, and what he could finally see of the crimson moon's surface confirmed that he'd been right in his initial guess. He just needed to find the point of impact of that mysterious object, and after that... well, he simply didn't know what the discovery would mean, only that he desperately wanted to understand why he'd dreamt about it. Whether that event was tied to whatever had smashed the Dragon's Eye would be something he could investigate later.

It took a lot of time before he found what he sought—hours perhaps—and the task was made more difficult by the thick clouds that began to move in from the ocean to the south of the city. He spared a quick thought about how strange that was, given that all his careful calculations had pointed to a perfectly clear evening for him to test the lens at last. No matter. It was an inconvenience to be sure, given his vision of the moon was completely obscured for minutes at a time by the fast-moving clouds, but his persistence and impatience wouldn't allow him to give up his search and wait for a better night. What he prayed to the Lifegiver for was that it didn't start to rain. If water drops fell on the exterior lens, the resulting refraction effect would make it impossible for him to continue until everything dried off. Thankfully, no rain came, but the clear patches were quickly becoming more infrequent when his efforts finally paid off.

Lying near a ridge of low hills leading to one of the more impressive mountain ranges on the moon's surface, he nearly dismissed the dark line as a shadow, but when he increased the range on the telescope to its maximum magnification, he quickly realized his mistake. The terrain had been disturbed in a manner which did not appear natural—like a long scar cutting across the ground in a perfectly straight line. He followed it eastward for quite some distance to where the dark gouge abruptly ceased to exist, but there was nothing else of note at that end. Deducing that must be the starting point, he excitedly turned the crank to make the instrument move in the opposite direction. He had no way of telling if the geological features that he could see on Temeros were analogous to those of Akar in size, but if they were similar, judging by the circumference of the nearby hills, whatever had left that wound on the terrain was of considerable dimensions. He thought again about that ball of fire, flying at an impossible speed over the horizon before vanishing from sight, and the eerie glow that brightened the night sky an instant later in the wake of its passing. This had to be it!

He made a rough calculation while the telescope moved, using the current magnification factor and the number of degrees the instrument had swivelled to estimate the total length of that blackened cut to be roughly two miles in length. The ground to either side of it had been heaved aside violently, and though he could not peer any closer, he thought he could see what looked like a collection of small objects scattered along the full distance of the scar. Were they merely rocks...or debris of some kind? Fingers trembling with barely contained excitement, he nudged the instrument to the far western end of this strange phenomenon to come upon its endpoint at last. His jaw went slack with amazement. There was something there, its incredible and fiery journey having come to a final resting place at the base of a tall peak. Had the mountain not been there to act as an insurmountable obstacle in its path, who knows how much farther it could have travelled.

'It', he thought to himself. What was 'it'?

Even with all the pieces of itself that it had left behind during its dramatic arrival on the surface of Temeros, the object appeared to be quite large, or so he guessed. Its colour was silvery-white and slightly reflective, like metal, though it seemed a sizeable portion of it was buried under the crimson soil. Its shape—or what was left of it—was vaguely triangular, or at least from the angle he was viewing it from. His curiosity had reached a fever pitch. What was he looking at? Had the object's crash been the cause of the cataclysm that had cracked the moon? No, it just didn't seem possible given its small mass relative to the vast size of the celestial body where it had gone down. Was this the doing of the gods then? By Janus! Were those lights he just saw blink momentarily along one side of the object's surface? This was it. It had to be. He was right. There was life on Temeros, and it had come from...elsewhere! But where? Simultaneous with that awestruck revelation, a particularly dark and ominous cloud interposed itself between the moon and the skies above the tower, completely blocking his view. He'd been so wrapped up in his discovery that he hadn't even noticed the wind had picked up to a tremendous strength. He could hear its howl now, whistling with fierce intensity while it rushed over the city of Corazan.

At first, he thought his imagination was playing tricks on him, but he heard it clearly and unmistakably—there was a voice in that wind.

"You see too much, Mateo."

"Who said that? What is it that I see?" He shouted forcefully into the wind, but his words were ripped away as soon as they left his mouth. The voice heard him, nevertheless.

"That which mortal eyes were never meant to behold."

A jagged bolt of lightning crackled downward from the black clouds with blinding intensity, striking the roof of the tower with purposeful fury and lethal force. The discharge of raw energy sizzled along the telescope's surface, accompanied by a deafening boom that split the air like a giant pounding on a huge war drum.

The precious lens exploded into a thousand shards, but there was no time to lament the loss of the irreplaceable artifact—Mateo's world detonated in a flash of white light and a mercifully brief burst of searing hot pain, followed immediately by the peaceful darkness of oblivion.

Flynn opened his eyes with a shudder and gulped raggedly to get a breath of air, feeling as if some force had taken hold of him and was trying to drag him down into an abyss of nothingness. He stomped his feet to reassure himself of the floor beneath them, and he was grateful for the sudden solidity of the world around him, though the darkness did not go away. He pulled his trembling hand away from the telescope and it was only then that he realized that Father Mateo's ghostly form was no longer in the cellar with him—or at least not in a way that he could detect with his senses. Ignoring the spirit's absence for now, his thoughts turned to what he'd just experienced. The spectre had spoken of seeing the truth, but he was left only with more questions in his mind, and that dazzling after-image in his eyes.

"What did all of that mean?" he whispered into the gloom.

The telltale drop in temperature heralded the spirit's brief return from the netherworld where it had been consigned, though this time it did not manifest itself physically.

'It means that perhaps those whom we call gods are not what we've been taught to believe,' came the disembodied reply.

"What are they then?"

'Travellers.'

"Travellers? Travellers from where?"

'From another place, Flynn—a world beyond the stars.'

ABOUT THE AUTHOR

RAFAEL CANOA WAS BORN and raised in Setúbal, Portugal, and immigrated to Vancouver, Canada, with his family during his early teens. He resides in Vancouver to this day.

From an early age, he developed a fertile imagination and a fascination for anything to do with fantasy and science fiction. The pivotal moment in his lifelong dedication to this form of literature came when he discovered a copy of *The Hobbit* by J.R.R. Tolkien, left forgotten under a desk in his tenth grade English class. From there, it was a quick journey to *The Lord of the Rings* and everything that lay beyond. As an avid gamemaster and player of several tabletop role playing games for decades now, he found a natural progression in writing a novel series about those imaginary worlds.

When he's in the real world, Rafael has studied the English language academically and has recently begun to explore the field of copy editing and writing. Grounding his life is a long and colourful tenure in the realm of bartending, enjoying his books, video games, collectibles, and traveling with his wife as often as possible.

Bloodlines is Rafael's first novel and the opening volume in the *Children of a Forgotten Star* series. Book II is coming soon.

THE END?

Not if you want to dive into more of Crystal Lake Publishing's Tales from the Darkest Depths!

Check out our amazing website and online store or download our latest catalog here.

We always have great new projects and content on the website to dive into, as well as a newsletter, behind the scenes options, social media platforms, our own dark fiction shared-world series and our very own webstore. Our webstore even has categories specifically for KU books, non-fiction, anthologies, and of course more novels and novellas.

Readers...

Thank you for reading *Bloodlines*. We hope you enjoyed this novel. If you have a moment, please review *Bloodlines* at the store where you bought it.

Help other readers by telling them why you enjoyed this book. No need to write an in-depth discussion. Even a single sentence will be greatly appreciated. Reviews go a long way to helping a book sell, and is great for an author's career. It'll also help us to continue publishing quality books.

Thank you again for taking the time to journey with Crystal Lake Publishing.

You will find links to all our social media platforms on our Linktree page.
https://linktr.ee/CrystalLakePublishing

Follow us on Amazon:

MISSION STATEMENT

Since its founding in August 2012, Crystal Lake has quickly become one of the world's leading publishers of Dark Fiction and Horror books. In 2023, Crystal Lake officially transitioned into an entertainment company, joining several other divisions, genres, and imprints, including Torrid Waters, Crystal Lake Comics, Crystal Lake Games, Crystal Lake Kids, and many more.

While we strive to present only the highest quality fiction and entertainment, we also endeavour to support authors along their writing journey. We offer our time and experience in non-fiction projects, as well as author mentoring and services, at competitive prices.

With several Bram Stoker Award wins and many other wins and nominations (including the HWA's Specialty Press Award), Crystal Lake Publishing puts integrity, honor, and respect at the forefront of our publishing operations.

We strive for each book and outreach program we spearhead to not only entertain and touch or comment on issues that affect our readers, but also to strengthen and support the Dark Fiction field and its authors.

Not only do we find and publish authors we believe are destined for greatness, but we strive to work with men and women who endeavour to be decent human beings who care more for others than themselves, while still being hard working, driven, and passionate artists and storytellers.

Crystal Lake Publishing is and will always be a beacon of what passion and dedication, combined with overwhelming teamwork and respect, can accomplish. We endeavour to know each and every one of our readers, while building personal relationships with our authors, reviewers, bloggers, podcasters, bookstores, and libraries.

We will be as trustworthy, forthright, and transparent as any business can be, while also keeping most of the headaches away from our authors, since it's our job to solve the problems so they can stay in a creative mind. Which of course also means paying our authors.

We do not just publish books, we present to you worlds within your world, doors within your mind, from talented authors who sacrifice so much for a moment of your time.

There are some amazing small presses out there, and through collaboration and open forums we will continue to support other presses in the goal of helping authors and showing the world what quality small presses are capable of accomplishing. No one wins when a small press goes down, so we will always be there to support hardworking, legitimate presses and their authors. We don't see Crystal

Lake as the best press out there, but we will always strive to be the best, strive to be the most interactive and grateful, and even blessed press around. No matter what happens over time, we will also take our mission very seriously while appreciating where we are and enjoying the journey.

What do we offer our authors that they can't do for themselves through self-publishing?

We are big supporters of self-publishing (especially hybrid publishing), if done with care, patience, and planning. However, not every author has the time or inclination to do market research, advertise, and set up book launch strategies. Although a lot of authors are successful in doing it all, strong small presses will always be there for the authors who just want to do what they do best: write.

What we offer is experience, industry knowledge, contacts and trust built up over years. And due to our strong brand and trusting fanbase, every Crystal Lake Publishing book comes with weight of respect. In time our fans begin to trust our judgment and will try a new author purely based on our support of said author.

With each launch we strive to fine-tune our approach, learn from our mistakes, and increase our reach. We continue to assure our authors that we're here for them and that we'll carry the weight of the launch and dealing with third parties while they focus on their strengths—be it writing, interviews, blogs, signings, etc.

We also offer several mentoring packages to authors that include knowledge and skills they can use in both traditional and self-publishing endeavours.

We look forward to launching many new careers.

This is what we believe in. What we stand for. This will be our legacy.

Welcome to Crystal Lake Publishing—Where Stories Come Alive!